Hedley turned Victorina until she stood facing the gate and raised her clothes. In confusion she hid her face in her hands as Hedley's fingers stole beneath her skirts to explore her hidden treasures. Her sweet skin was firm and warm to the touch.

On a sudden impulse he pulled off his cap, threw it to the damp ground and knelt on it to prevent his tweed breeches from acquiring grass stains. He lifted high Victorina's clothes – and then, what delights were revealed to him as he parted her pretty drawers to expose her tender flesh!

'I trust myself to you, body and soul,' Victorina exclaimed in a tearful voice. 'Be gentle with me, Hedley, I implore you!'

'Your honour is safe with me,' he replied as he bent forward to kiss the snowy cheeks of her virgin bottom and unfastened his breeches . . .

The Mysteries of Women

Anonymous

HEADLINE DELTA

This omnibus edition first published in 1994
by HEADLINE BOOK PUBLISHING

A HEADLINE DELTA paperback

10 9 8 7 6 5 4 3 2 1

ISBN 0 7472 4401 4

Printed and bound in Great Britain by
HarperCollins Manufacturing, Glasgow

HEADLINE BOOK PUBLISHING
A division of Hodder Headline PLC
338 Euston Road
London NW1 3BH

CONTENTS

The Pleasures of Women

The Secrets of Women

The Delights of Women

The Pleasures of Women

PUBLISHER'S NOTE

There is no author's name on the title-page of the surviving copies of 'The Pleasures of Women' and no date, which is normal for most Victorian erotic literature. The only indication given of the book's origin is the initials 'A.Mck.H.' without any sign of whether this refers to author, printer or publisher.

Most fortunately, the novel is listed in Henry Spencer Ashbee's monumental catalogue of his collection of erotica. As is well known, this summarises plots and records Ashbee's views of the merits of chosen books, and is for this reason our best guide to Victorian underground literature.

Ashbee had this to say of 'The Pleasures of Women':

'This tale has some pretensions, being not a mere tissue of amatory adventures, but aiming at a delineation of character. It is by no means badly written, and is from the pen of one acquainted with the art of composition, although the author's name must for the present be withheld.

'It is a very natural and powerfully written tale, which describes the progression of an idle young man along the ways of infamy, laying his lustful hand on every female who crosses his path, sparing none, not even the most innocent.

'The scenes depicted are doubtless from the author's own experience, and are remarkable for lasciviousness. Be that as it may, it is a pleasant and readable book, which may be taken to present a characteristic picture of the manners of a certain class of people.'

The writer's anonymity was preserved in Ashbee's catalogue, but elsewhere in his papers is to be found the name of a friend and fellow-collector, Alexander McKendrie Hammond, undoubtedly the author of 'The Pleasures of Women'. This A.McK.H. was a Scot, born in Perth, but educated and resident in England. He was a barrister of the Middle Temple and, like Mr Gladstone, took an interest in the welfare of fallen girls.

Several works of fiction are known by the same hand, and all of them deal with what Hammond's friend Ashbee called 'scenes of remarkable lasciviousness'. It is hoped to republish them all.

CHAPTER 1
A Weekend Out of Town

In the year 1876 Mr Hedley Gillingham was twenty-three years of age and the fortunate recipient of a quarterly allowance from his father sufficient to make it possible for him to maintain his own modest establishment in London and pursue a life of leisure. On a Friday in June of that year, having been invited to pass the weekend with the family of his fiancée, he took a train from Waterloo Station.

It was a mid-morning service, departing at 10.02, and the train was almost empty. Hedley had a first-class compartment to himself and made the most of it. He stretched out his long legs, lit a cigarette and immersed himself in *The Times*, but he found little there to interest him. There was a lengthy report of the Prime Minister's speech to Parliament on the dire effect if there were to be a declaration of war by the Czar of Russia on Turkey, but Hedley found politics unreasonably tedious and he subsided into a comfortable half-sleep, his hat tipped forward over his face.

A long and delicious reverie about his fiancée, Miss Victorina Hapgood, occupied his drowsing thoughts. He had been engaged to be married to her for almost three months and they intended to marry in the Spring of the following year. Miss Hapgood was eighteen years old and her loveliness was stunning. She was of middle height and most excitingly full of figure, with long ash-brown hair set in ringlets, clear hazel eyes, and a full red mouth that invited kisses.

Needless to say, it was not until they were officially engaged that Hedley had been allowed to kiss her, for she was a well brought-up and modest young lady. Nor had there ever been many occasions when he was alone with her, her mother being a woman of principle, but the old proverb warns that 'love laughs at locksmiths' and Mrs Hapgood would have been well advised to have borne it in mind. Hedley felt a strong and passionate love for his fiancee and was by nature impatient of all restraint.

Mrs Hapgood would have been shocked and dismayed to learn that Hedley had taken advantage of every opportunity that served to familiarise himself with the personal charms of her beautiful daughter. At unsupervised moments he had kissed Victorina full on the lips and, not satisfied with that, he had slipped his tongue into her mouth. When he was certain that there would be no interruptions for the next five minutes, he had dared to put his hands on her full breasts, outside her clothes, and feel them with relish.

There had been, on his visit last weekend to stay with the Hapgood family, a delirious moment when he had been passing by the door of Victorina's room on his way down for an early turn round the garden before breakfast. On a sudden impulse, he had thrown open the door and gone in, to discover the charming girl in only her short chemise, standing before the wash-stand and splashing warm water over her face. In three strides he was across the room and held her tightly to him, her startled face turned up to his, as he crushed his mouth on hers.

Nor was that the total profit he snatched from this happy but unforeseen chance – despite Victorina's maidenly blushes he ran his hands over the full cheeks of her bottom, delighting in the feel of her soft flesh through the thin cotton of her chemise. She pulled her mouth away from his and her lips opened to reprove him for his unmannerly familiarity, when he brought a hand up under her chemise and clasped her warm and furry pussy. Her words remained unspoken, her hazel eyes opened wide in shock and horror, and she almost swooned in Hedley's arms.

With a final parting kiss and an impassioned murmur of 'I love you, my dearest Victorina,' he released the trembling girl and left her room quickly. His promenade in the garden was abandoned – Mr John Thomas was so stiffly rampant that Hedley was compelled to return to his own room and relieve his unruly friend's nervous tension by hand, before he was in a fit condition to go down for breakfast.

A vivid memory of how Victorina's warm little muff had felt in the palm of his hand had remained with him all the week in London, and he fully intended to find opportunities this weekend to repeat the delightful experience with his beloved. Thoughts of this, and the anticipation of pleasures to come, made the time pass very quickly as the train puffed south-west along the line of the river Thames. It stopped at a station or two, but it was only when Hedley heard a porter on the platform call out 'Wimbledon' that he heard someone getting into the compartment with him.

He paid no attention, being so deeply sunk into his sensual day-dream that he was more than half asleep.

Carriage doors were slammed, a whistle blew, the train
rattled on again, and after a minute or two Hedley heard
a loud and unmistakable gasp of surprise. He opened his
eyes drowsily and saw, sitting across from him, a lady
attired in deepest black, a widow to judge from her long-
sleeved and high-necked dress and the veil that concealed her face.

She was buxom of figure, Hedley noted, being a young
man who never failed to notice these characteristics, her
age not easy to guess, her face being concealed, but
thirty or so, he opined and in her prime. Seeking the
reason for the gasp of surprise that had roused him from
his reverie, he glanced down and saw that the discarded
newspaper had slipped from his lap to the floor and that
his day-dreaming of feeling Victorina's virginal *Miss* had
stiffened Mr John Thomas, as was to be expected. That
gentleman's ample length and girth were plainly outlined
through the thin grey material of the trouser leg down
which he was trapped.

The black veil made it virtually impossible to see in
which direction the lady's eyes were now staring, but she
had not turned her head away in horror. To Hedley's
mind there was no question about it – the widow lady
was transfixed by the sight of his stiff rudder. The
problem he wrestled with was: what, if anything, should
he do to relieve her embarrassment? Long experience
warned Hedley that in this condition Mr John Thomas
was intractable, however unsuitable the occasion and
time. Hence the necessity of returning to his bedroom
after feeling Victorina, before descending to the kippers
and eggs and bacon.

If he sat up and turned his hard-on friend up alongside
his belly, that would be less obvious, but it required him
to use his hand and to see a strange man touch himself

4

would no doubt offend the lady greatly. He could stand up and lower the window a little, putting his back to her for the few seconds required for the adjustment, but she would surely complain about the draught and dirty smoke blowing in if he opened a window.

Hedley was certain that his cheeks were blushing – not from shame, for he had been a stranger to that emotion all his life, but from a feeling of social clumsiness as how to proceed. This unfamiliar awkwardness made matters worse – Mr John Thomas took it in his head to twitch strongly under his cloth concealment, and it seemed to Hedley that another suppressed gasp escaped the lady's lips. Since the situation couldn't be cured, it must be endured, he thought, and closed his eyes again and continued his imitation of being fast alseep.

Now that his attention had been drawn to his somberly clad travelling-companion, he surveyed her surreptitiously under lowered eye-lids. Inside her mourning dress, he saw with great interest, there lurked a pair of heavy breasts – a good deal more than a handful each for a lively man. In fact, his survey attested that she was very well-made, the widow opposite, well-fed and well-rounded.

If her black dress were removed, there would appear a pair of white shoulders, Hedley concluded, white because the skin of her neck was white and firm. Below those shoulders a man would come across two breasts as round and polished as marble, displaying the lovely contrast of milk-white skin and crimson buds. Hedley's almost-closed eyes gazed lower, to the inviting soft swell of her belly. Under her close-fitting black satin, it was very handsomely shaped – it would be like a cushion for a man to lie on. Such a woman should be well and often rogered.

What shape and size was her tufted mount? he wondered. His explorations of the companionship of women in London had taught him that they were very variously shaped in this department. Cunnies ranged from the large and protruding with pouting lips, to the flat and inconspicuously split. Some were covered with a profuse growth of curly hair, some were almost bare, graced only with a few wisps. Hedley loved them all, as every man of sense did, whether shaggy as a bear or nude as an egg, though he had his preferences.

It occurred to him, now it was too late, that he could have solved the social problem simply enough by picking up his *Times* from the carriage floor and, under the pretence of reading it, spread it over his lap. Now that he had embarked upon this scheme of being totally unaware of anything untoward happening, he decided to continue with it and trust that she left the train before he did.

Mr John Thomas put an wickedly inconvenient thought into his mind – suppose that the lady intended to travel further, and remained seated when he was forced to rise to his feet and pass close by her to leave the train? In that event, Master John would pass within two feet of her veiled face, and it was a racing certainly that he would take the opportunity to bound inside his hiding-place to draw her attention!

It was therefore with mingled relief and disappoint-ment that Hedley watched her rise to her feet when the train stopped at Surbiton. He maintained his pose of being asleep, when to his utter amazement, she stretched out her arm and pressed her gloved hand over his throbbing bulge, giving it a momentary squeeze, before leaving the compartment hurriedly and slamming the door behind her.

The engine whistled and the train jerked forward, as

Hedley sat up in astonishment, to peer out of the window at the lady's black-clad back vanishing past the ticket-collector. *Damn it all*, he thought, she wasn't the least bit embarrassed! What a fool I am – what a chance I missed there! I could have had a feel of her to help pass the journey!

The Hapgood family lived in that desirable portion of Surrey known as Burwood Park, and the station for it was Walton-upon-Thames. Hedley got out of the train and waited while a porter got his bags down from the rack and trundled them on his barrow to the ticket-barrier. Outside the station, the Hapgood's groom was waiting with a smart little pony-trap they used for station work. The groom's name was Tom, a well-set man of forty or so, neatly dressed in a brown bowler hat, chequered jacket, whip-cord breeches and polished riding-boots. He tipped his hat to Hedley and stacked his luggage behind the seat.

The groom was one of two outdoor servants at The Larches, as the Hapgood home was named, the other being the gardener, Ben. The four indoor servants were all female, as strict propriety required, Mrs Hapgood's husband having died ten or twelve years previously. Tom climbed up beside Hedley, made a clicking sound with his tongue, and the horse trotted obediently off. From the station it was a pleasant twenty minute drive along tree-lined roads to their destination.

The Larches was a large and comfortable family home set well back from the road in extensive grounds, with the nearest neighbour a quarter of a mile away. The pony-cart turned along a gravelled drive leading through the trees from which the house took its name, and halted before the front porch. Mrs Hapgood herself came out to greet Hedley, a well-fleshed woman with large breasts, fast approaching forty but still very handsome. Hedley shook her hand warmly, not yet having progressed to the status of kissing her cheek, and she welcomed him cordially.

In the hall Victorina was waiting, restraining her eagerness to see her fiance with commendable modesty. At the sight of her Hedley's heart bounded – she seemed to him so calmly beautiful and so graceful, her light brunette hair descending in soft ringlets well below her shoulders, her eyes shining with delight as he pressed both her hands gently into his. She wore a high-necked white blouse with a cameo brooch at the throat, the folds of thin muslin perfectly moulding her prominent bosom.

Below the fringed hem of her full skirt there peeped out the toe of a little grey-buttoned shoe, and Hedley sighed as his imagination supplied a vision of the full calf above the foot in that shoe, of the shapely leg concealed within Victorina's skirt and petticoats, of her ivory-white thighs and of the warm and maiden *motte* that lay between those thighs. To think that he had clasped it, if only for a moment, a week ago!

When the greetings were completed and Hedley's bags carried upstairs by a maid, he retired to the room assigned to him to wash his hands and face and change his clothes before lunch. It was a pleasant room, overlooking the greenhouse at the side of the house, with a comfortable bed and matching furnishings in dark polished oak. The maid unpacked his luggage and put his clothes away in the wardrobe and chest of drawers, except an outfit suitable for informal country wear.

As soon as she had left the room, Hedley took off his elegant grey suit and threw himself on the high bed in his shirt, to rest for half an hour from the fatigue of his journey from town. Lying comfortably on his back, he held his ivory-backed hand-mirror above his face and studied his reflection with pride and pleasure. What the glass showed him was a long and handsome face, narrowing down from the cheek-bones to a pointed chin, chestnut-brown hair worn long, and parted in the middle, so that soft wings curved over his brow, to his ears.

In bodily form he was a tall and willowy young man, pleasing to the ladies, as he knew well. The most recent proof of that had been the widow on the train from London – if only the journey had been a longer one, there would have been time to explore how far she would allow him to go with her! All the way, was Hedley's expert guess, and never having had a woman on a railway train, it would have been an experience to treasure.

On a whim he pulled up his shirt to his belly-button and used the looking-glass to examine Mr John Thomas, who lay in uncustomary slackness.

'Little does the lady in widow's weeds know what a treat she has missed,' Hedley said aloud, addressing his remark to the limp shaft between his thighs. 'I am perfectly certain that you would have brought sunshine into her life – and I think she was of the same mind, for she could not resist touching you as she left the train.'

Mr John Thomas was flattered at having this interest taken in him and slowly reared up from his sleep, stretching himself mightily, until he stood eight inches tall and as straight as a Grenadier on parade.

'My goodness, you *are* in a state!' said Hedley, taking his preening friend in hand. 'But I must insist that you preserve your strength in case an opportunity arises to make advances to my darling Victorina. Only consider the shame if she were to express an interest in you – not

9

at all likely, I know – but let us suppose that by some miracle she did, and that you were too tired to raise your head, because you had squandered all your resources in a handkerchief! Such a dreadful catastrophe doesn't bear even thinking about!'

What did bear thinking about, and at some length, was the prospect, however unlikely it might be – that Miss Victorina might swoon dead away when they were alone together and fall on to the drawing-room couch. Instead of attempting to revive her by chafing her hands and patting her cheeks, Hedley knew that he would raise her skirts and spread her legs far apart, to bare her little muff and finger it – and press hot kisses to the sweet and virginal lips it covered!

Mr John Thomas relished that prospect and, in his usual head-strong way, jumped for joy and planted into Hedley's mind the question of what he would do next. Would he plunge him, Mr John Thomas, into the delicious part of Victorina he had kissed in so intimate a manner? Heaven knows what the outcome of this conversation might have been, if the gong that summoned the family to luncheon had not sounded through the house.

Hedley sprang from the bed and dressed himself hurriedly in the clothes laid out for him by the maid, cramming his reluctant companion into brown tweed knee-breeches. Knitted green knee-length stockings, sturdy walking shoes and a Norfolk jacket transformed the gentleman about town into the perfect country squire, and Hedley raced downstairs to drink a glass of sherry wine with Mrs Hapgood and Victorina before they went into the dining-room.

The other sister, Adelaide, was considered too young for intoxicants and had to content herself with a glass of still lemonade. She was a pretty child, eighteen months younger than Hedley's fiancee, but with the same clear complexion and eyes, and at sixteen she already gave every promise of growing up to be as considerable a beauty as her sister. Hedley shook hands with her politely, and she giggled a little in a very girlish manner.

The meals at The Larches were always substantial and good, for Mrs Hapgood had a treasure of a cook. Luncheon started with a thick beef soup, very nourishing and sustaining, followed by slices of turbot cooked lightly in white wine. Then came the main course – a whole saddle of mutton with roasted potatoes and sweet turnips. As the only gentleman present, Hedley was requested to carve, a skill that he had developed early in his life of leisure. Afterwards there was peach syllabub, the fruit grown in the greenhouse before the window of Hedley's bedroom, and then cheese – a half Stilton to cut from.

After coffee in the drawing-room, Mrs Hapgood announced that she intended to withdraw to her room for an hour's rest before tea-time. Hedley ventured to suggest to Victorina that they should take a short stroll in the gardens and she went upstairs for a jacket and hat. They left the house by the main entrance, Hedley picking up a stout ash walking-stick from the hall-stand on the way, and walked round to the more extensive flower gardens at the back.

During the late morning a light shower of rain had fallen, and now that the sun was out again the lawns glistened bright green and the colours of the flowerbeds were enhanced. Walking side by side and only a little distance apart, Hedley and his beloved strolled past the lily pond and on through the displays of pinks and azaleas and tea roses, to the massed hollyhocks and rhododendrons beneath the thick back hedge. An arch was cut in it to lead into the kitchen garden, where Ben grew all the vegetables the family ate.

At the back of the kitchen garden an old and ivy-grown brick wall marked the boundary, and a wicket gate gave access into a paddock behind the house. Hedley was searching for a private place, where he could kiss Victorina in secret, and perhaps even pursue his exploration of her charming person further, if she would let him. The prospect of clasping her little muff in his palm once more sent the blood racing through his veins.

Unruly Mr John Thomas was tucked safely up against Hedley's belly, out of sight, though by no means out of mind. Urged on by his keen desire, Hedley opened the wicket and stood aside while Victorina passed through. Once on the other side of the high wall, screened from prying eyes in the house, he drew her arm through his and led her slowly along a path barely discernible in the grass, talking to her all the while in loving terms, and she was pleased to listen to his courtship.

Soon the wall and the house were left behind, and they came to a quick-set hedge dividing the paddock from a meadow beyond, where they halted at a five-barred gate under a great oak tree. Hedley hung his borrowed walking-stick over the top bar of the gate to free both hands, and without further ado, clasped his fiancee by the waist, while in poetic language, he told her of the depth and strength of his love for her.

Very boldly, as if of right, he pulled off her grey kid-skin glove and stroked her little white hand. He raised it to his lips, to press kisses of homage and devotion on the soft palm and then on each finger-tip in turn. He assured Victorina with all fervour that his love was eternal and unchanging, and he allowed himself the familiarity of touching the tip of his tongue to the palm of her hand, drawing a gasp from her.

With what raptures these words of love of his were received, for she loved him as sincerely as he loved her! Hedley gazed in delight at her half-closed eyes, her fluttering eye-lashes, and the rapid palpitations of her bosom under her clothes. At once he took advantage of her charming confusion to steal a kiss from those full red lips.

Victorina's face blushed a delicate pink, but she did not rebuff him. He touched his lips to hers once more, his eyes open to admire her beauty, and when he observed that she was becoming almost as animated as he was himself, he pressed his advantage further by repeating his kisses with growing fervour, until she was breathless and trembling against him, her eyes closed in tender rapture.

'My darling,' he murmured, 'my darling girl . . .'

Becoming bold to the point of madness, he undid the buttons of the tight-waisted green velvet jacket she had put on for their stroll, and ran his hand feverishly over her full bosom, pressing the tender flesh through the thin material of her blouse. At his touch she gasped loudly and her face turned as pale as a sheet.

'Hedley – what are you doing?' she exclaimed in alarm.

'I am so head over heels in love with you that when I am near you my senses desert me completely,' he said passionately, while he enjoyed a good feel of her bubbies, 'I cannot sleep at night for thinking of you. I lie awake through the long dark hours, your name on my lips, and every fibre of my being aches to crush you in my arms.'

His declaration was a little overdone, as is the way

13

with young men in love. It was true that he had on several occasions experienced sensual dreams concerning Victorina, delightful dreams in which his sleeping mind had taken remarkable liberties with her person. On occasion he had even woken to find himself in the throes of a gushing emission, and on other occasions he had required a few minutes of five-finger exercises before he had appeased his raging desires sufficient to fall asleep again.

To claim that he endured sleeplessness on her behalf was mere fiction, not that Miss Hapgood was to know that. Nor could she even guess, innocent and inexperienced as she was in the ways of men, that in the concealment of Hedley's trousers, Mr John Thomas was twitching.

'I know it is hard for you to exercise a proper restraint, my dear,' she said, bashfulness causing her face to blush most prettily as Hedley unpinned her brooch and then slowly unbuttoned her blouse from neck to waist, and delved down into her loose chemise to fondle her bare breasts, 'but you must be patient until we are man and wife.'

'Yes, my sweet, it is hard,' he answered her, 'it is very hard indeed, harder than you could ever imagine,' and he placed her hand on the long bulge in his trousers.

Victorina's face turned crimson to the roots of her hair when she realised what it was that she was touching.

'Hedley, no!' she cried, and would have pulled her hand away, but he held it there by force, gripping her wrist cruelly and rubbing her palm over his jerking shaft.

'Do not be afraid of it, dearest Victorina,' he said. 'When you and I are married this dear possession of mine will become the most important thing in your life. Far from wishing to take your hand away, you will beg me by night and by day to allow you to stroke it to stiffness, so that it may satisfy you.'

At that, she stared at him speechless, her mouth opening and closing like a goldfish in its glass bowl. She was a maiden standing at the top of a long and slippery slope down into sensuality and licentiousness, and she struggled to preserve her honour, as her conscience insisted. Yet she loved Hedley and wished with all her heart to make him happy, and this warm sentiment made her unsure how to rescue her virtue from the wiles of temptation.

The devil was in Hedley that day and he was lost to all sense of decency or reason. He stooped to slip a hand under her clothes, and carried it lightly but very quickly up the length of her leg, until it was between her closed thighs.

'Stop!' she cried in a voice that trembled and faded. 'You must stop these gross familiarities! What can you be thinking of, to take advantage of me in this way? You will ruin me!'

How very often in the past had Hedley cause, as he had now, to call down blessings on whoever it may have been who first invented female drawers, those twin legs of dainty material, slit up the front and back and joined together only at the waist by a string tied in a neat bow! They furnished the wearer with a sense of modesty, in that her private parts were covered, and permitted the exercise of her natural functions without removing them, merely by pulling them aside.

By the same token, their friendly design made it possible for a lady's devoted admirer to gain access to her innermost secrets by inserting a hand through the open slit of her drawers. If the truth were told, Hedley's hand had investigated many a pair of drawers in London, and he was no stranger to the practicalities of rogering a woman against a wall, his rod doing its duty through the long slit in her underclothes.

'Ruin you, my darling? Never!' he declared hotly, to soothe his fiancee's fears, while his hand roamed freely. 'Gladly would I lay down my life before I allowed any harm to come to you! Trust me, my dearest Victorina, trust in me!'

In spite of the nervous contractions of her thighs, he opened her drawers and touched her silky curls, and at once Mr John Thomas leaped in triumph against her hand. He clasped her mound and then his forefinger parted the warm lips gently and searched out her secret nub. She leaned heavily against him, half-fainting, and he smothered her plaintive little protests with luscious kisses, thrusting the velvet tip of his tongue into her mouth.

'Oh, oh, Hedley, my dearest . . . what are you doing to me?' she sighed, and her legs trembled in spasmodic contractions.

Hedley's own sensations, as he continued to finger her, were so intensely powerful, and his fleshy shaft was throbbing so strongly, that he was certain he would spend in his trousers at any moment. His disengaged arm clasped Victorina round the waist, holding her tightly to him, trapping his pulsing shaft against her leg, while his busy fingers in her cunny felt a gentle moisture appear.

The thought uppermost in his mind at this tremendous moment was to find somewhere to lie down with Victorina, so that his play could continue in comfort and at a leisurely pace. But wherever he looked, the grass was wet and unsuitable for his purpose. But as the saying has it, 'needs must when the devil drives' – and that is much the same thing as the other old saying that a standing shaft knows no conscience. He turned Victorina until she stood facing the gate and raised her clothes behind to feel her bottom with both his hands.

In confusion she hid her face in her hands on the top bar of the gate as Hedley's hands rifled the treasures of her snowy bottom, so firm and warm to the touch. On a sudden impulse he pulled off his tweed cap, threw it to the damp ground and knelt on it, to preserve his tweed beeches from acquiring the grass stains that would betray what he had been about. He lifted high Victorina's clothes – and then, what delights were revealed to his gaze! Mr John Thomas bounded like a tethered greyhound straining at its leash, as Hedley parted her pretty drawers to expose her tender flesh!

He forced her feet widely apart with his free hand, until her thighs opened to let him see the lips of her plump and pouting cunny, deliciously feathered with light brunette curls. The blood pounded in his temples so strongly as he bent forward and kissed her bottom and licked between the round cheeks that he thought he would faint with sheer delight. That lovely bottom, that virginal slit – it was all his!

He stood up again and arranged Victorina so that she was bending over, her arms resting on the gate, and brought Mr John Thomas to the ready, pressing the swollen head just slightly between the lips of her cunny. A long shudder passed through her at the touch and in great discomposure she turned her head to stare pink-faced over her shoulder at Hedley.

'I trust myself to you, body and soul,' she exclaimed in a tearful voice, 'be gentle with me, Hedley, I implore you . . .'

'You darling, you love me as as I love you!' he replied. 'Your honour is safe with me, Victorina!'

He had placed one hand under her belly to hold her still, whilst with the other he kept Mr John Thomas straight to the mark. Then, after a deep breath, he pushed forward vigorously, and the head entered about an inch. Victorina trembled like a trapped bird held in a poacher's rough hand, and uttered a little cry of dismay, but Hedley at once gave a ruthless push and the deed was done. She shrieked, and he and Mr John Thomas together had taken full and throbbing possession of her inmost charms.

Hedley felt her tight sheath of flesh contracting on his shaft in the most delicious manner. He gave an easy thrust or two and worked very gently, though his desire was so strong as to require all of his abilities to restrain himself. Not that it proved possible to hold himself back for long – for Mr John Thomas unleashed very soon took charge of events and went about his business at a fast clip. Victorina shook under his thrusts and Hedley gave a long cry as the spasms of a copious spend convulsed him.

He leaned trembling against her dear back, his breathing returning by stages to normal, while his limbs relaxed in the rapturous lethargy of satisfied love. The same unbelievable thought kept running through his head, over and over again:

'I've had her – I've truly had my dearest Vickie! I've fetched off up her darling pussy!'

CHAPTER 2
An Unfinished Game of Croquet

Mrs Hapgood was a staunch supporter of the Church of England and a loyal organiser of her parish charities for the poor and unfortunate. On Saturday afternoon she and Victorina set off together in the carriage, on some matter concerning local young women who had fallen and were, in consequence, distressed and in need of the necessities of life.

Little Adelaide and Hedley went outdoors to play a game of croquet on the lawn and before long he was winning very easily.

'It's not fair,' she said with a pout, 'you're bigger than me and can hit the balls harder.'

'The question is not how hard, but how true you strike,' he answered, his mind occupied with the game he wanted to play with Victorina, not the game of croquet with her sister. 'If you fail to strike true, you run off at an angle and miss the hoop completely.'

'Show me what you mean,' she said.

Hedley stood close behind her and reached round to place his hands over hers on the mallet shaft.

'It's very simple,' he said, 'keep your eye on the ball

and swing the mallet easily and straight, aiming at the hoop . . .'

Adelaide leaned forward, swinging the mallet to and fro in little movements that did not touch the wooden ball, asking if he meant like that. His hands on hers guided her swing, and he became suddenly aware that her posture was pressing her bottom tightly against his thighs. Not only that, but he also became aware that this gentle and sustained pressure was having a very definite effect on him, an effect which, though utterly reprehensible, was extremely pleasant.

The truth was that Adelaide was no longer the half-grown schoolgirl her appearance suggested. Under her mother's strict interpretation of growing up, she would be dressed in the short clothes of childhood and wear her long hair in braided pigtails until her eighteenth birthday, which was a year and a half off yet. Nevertheless, to Hedley's exeperienced eye, the white-stockinged legs visibly below Adelaide's knee-length gingham dress, and the gentle swell of the breasts beneath its bodice, told a tale of almost-ripe young womanhood.

Under the law, Adelaide had been of an age to marry for some time, not that her protective mother would contemplate any such application from a young man for her hand, even if any had offered. In London, that metropolis of lost innocence and debauched virtue, Hedley could not help but see the many girls of Adelaide's age, and even younger, who paraded all afternoon and evening in the precincts of the Haymarket, that well-known centre of dissipation, to offer the freedom of their young bodies to any man with five shillings to spend.

Be that as it may, Adelaide was a well-brought-up daughter of a well-to-do family, not an unfortunate street-girl, and in all decency Hedley ought not to be entertaining thoughts about her which he would not dare divulge to her mother. The fact remained, that Adelaide was wriggling her bottom deliberately against him, and his body was responding in the natural way to her provocation.

On oath Hedley would have been compelled to admit that, in this matter of Adelaide, he was not entirely blameless. At first it had been mere playfulness, presenting his cheek to her for a girlish kiss when he gave her a cachou or a piece of treacle toffee – insignificant little exchanges of touch. After he had engaged himself to marry her sister, Adelaide had accepted him as one of the family, and had begun to seek out the loving little touches and caresses as often as she was able.

At first he was amused by her girlish high spirits, but soon she was plaguing him beyond bearing when he visited the house. On one occasion when he was sitting in the morning-room alone, reading the newspaper, and she had thrown her arms about his neck gleefully, he decided to administer a short corrective shock to her forwardness, and bring her back to a proper sense of what was fitting. With this commendable purpose in mind, he dropped *The Morning Post* and reached round her tiny waist, put his hands up her short dress and felt her warm bottom.

What he anticipated would happen was that she would blush scarlet at the touch of his hands on so private a part of her body, and jump away from him like a scalded cat, her lesson learned. To his very great astonishment, nothing of the sort took place. On the contrary, Adelaide giggled loudly and kissed his cheek, her delicious little bottom wriggling against the palms of his hands in a suggestive manner.

He knew he should desist at once, but Hedley was weak and utterly without moral fibre in anything that concerned sensual pleasures. Instead of removing his hands from Adelaide's young person, he opened her short drawers at the back and gave the little cheeks of her bottom a good feel. She stood there by his chair and let him have his way, giggling all the time, and in the heat of his folly he went so far as to slip a hand in between her slender young thighs and touch her slit.

It was only when a footstep was heard at the door, that Adelaide sprang away from him and crossed the room silently to stare out of the window. Milly, one of the parlour-maids came in to attend to some trivial domestic task, and Hedley quickly raised his newspaper to hide his flushed face and his bulging trousers. If Adelaide had not been present, he would not have hesitated to take hold of the parlour-maid and thrust a hand up her clothes, female servants being fair game.

After a good feel of her, and if the omens were auspicious, he might very well have gone so far as to pin Milly against the mantelpiece and slip Mr John Thomas into her commodity for a quick 'poke', as it was known among the young men of Hedley's acquaintance. Half a crown in her hand after the deed would keep Milly sweet and uncomplaining.

On the other hand, if Adelaide had not been there to play her tricks, he would not be in the condition of stiffness responsible for bringing into consideration the question of rogering so very plain a girl as Milly. While she was still busy about her task, he stood up with care and left the room, to prevent any resumption of Adelaide's attentions towards him, fearing that if he lost control of himself, the outcome might be blameworthy in the extreme.

All that his hasty retreat accomplished was to postpone the renewal of her interest in him. He was soon made aware that, under a pretence of innocent childishness, Adelaide's pleasure was by fleeting touch or gesture to give him a hard stand, with no heed to where they were or what were the circumstances. Not even the pretence of others deterred her from playing her sly game with Hedley's nerves, to his enormous embarrassment.

Even a scene of idyllic domestic tranquillity had been once disturbed in an alarming manner – on an evening when the whole family were sitting together in the drawing-room after dinnner. Mrs Hapgood was engrossed in her petit-point, and Victorina sat with an elbow resting on the arm of her chair to support her cheek on her little hand, as she listened to Hedley reading aloud from a novel by a well-loved author, Mr Trollope.

Under the guise of being a mere child and exempt from the dictates of etiquette, Adelaide flung herself down at Hedley's feet to listen to his reading, her elbows on the cushions of the sofa where he sat, staring at his handsome face. In this position her actions were shielded from observation by her mother and her sister, and before Hedley was even halfway down the page, her hand had crept up his thigh and was stroking him to stiffness.

Hedley was very fearful that his voice would quaver under Adelaide's secret titillation and draw attention to his plight, for which he would be held responsible. That said, he admitted to himself that it was extraordinarily pleasant to be rubbed through the woollen material of his trousers by so pretty a young lady and he did not put a stop to the game by crossing his legs tightly until the heavy throbbing warned him that the climax was not very far off.

There had been an occasion when Adelaide's boldness and his own reluctance to bring it to a halt almost led to disaster. He had developed a head cold during his stay one weekend and had stayed in bed all Saturday morning to coddle it. Adelaide came into his room with yellow tulips from the garden and arranged them in a vase on the dressing-table. Instead of leaving him to doze, she seated herself on his bed and dived a hand under the bed clothes, tugged up his nightshirt and seized his slack rod in her warm little hand!

Keeping his voice low, Hedley begged her to be more careful, the house being full of people, family and servants, and the possibility of interruption very great. Her reply was to toss up her short dress and completely expose her drawers, while her clutching hand excited him rapidly to a hardness that was wholly inappropriate, in view of the disparities between him and her, and his trusted position in the household.

For all his worthy intentions, the plain fact was that she wanted to feel him and he was too weak to refuse her – and before long he no longer wished to refuse her, he wanted to be felt. She juggled with him under the bed clothes, grinning all the while, and he lay on his back with his legs apart. He was well advanced along the path to ultimate delight when the door opened and Mrs Hapgood entered the room, bearing a silver tray on which stood a glass of hot milk and rum for his cold.

It was much like the occasion a week or two before, when the parlour-maid had interrupted, while he was feeling Adelaide's bottom, except that this time there was no warning footstep. Hedley's heart was in his mouth, and the only saving grace was that, balancing the tray, Mrs Hapgood was compelled to stand sideways to the door to close it, before she turned to look towards

24

the invalid. In that breathing space, Adelaide's hand was withdrawn with the speed of a striking snake, and she was standing two steps away from the bed, taking her leave after bringing him flowers to cheer his sick room.

For Hedley there was no such easy escape. Mrs Hapgood noted his flushed face and trembling body and concluded that his cold was getting worse, perhaps spreading down from his nose to his chest, and to ascertain by how much his temperature had risen, she placed a soft hand on his fevered brow. The attitude of her body while she bent over him brought her full breasts close to his face, only a layer or two of thin material hiding those luscious globes from his bulging eyes.

She supported him with an arm around his shoulders while he sat up and drank off his hot milk and rum, and in this position his head was cradled on her bosom and his breathing was so constricted by his emotions that it cost him an enormous effort to swallow the healing potion. His rebellious shaft was at full stretch, and only the thickness of the bed clothes that covered him kept his shameful secret from his solicitous hostess.

'How you shake!' she exclaimed, her tone kindness itself. 'The fever is worse than I thought – you must stay in bed until it breaks. Lie down and sleep, Hedley, and let Nature's healing hand do its work!'

It was a hand other than Nature's that Hedley was desperate to have alleviate his suffering, but he gave Mrs Hapgood a wan smile as she tucked the bed clothes tightly about his neck and smoothed his brow with tender fingers. She drew the curtains to dim the room, and no sooner was she out the door than Hedley had his nightshirt up to his belly-button and, with a brisk hand, satisfied the urgent needs of his throbbing part.

All of this had led up to the moment when Hedley

stood on the croquet lawn, his arms around Adelaide to guide her stroke, while her bottom squirmed against him and he rubbed himself gently against the soft little cheeks under her gingham dress. She looked over her shoulder at him with a pink face, then without taking aim, swung her mallet and drove her ball straight through the next hoop.

He released her and she stared up at the sky, commented that it had clouded over and might even rain, and suggested that the match be abandoned and they go indoors. Hedley was stiff inside his white flannels and he turned his back to the house, in case any of the servants were looking out, while he slipped his life-long friend up under his tightly-buttoned First Eleven striped blazer for concealment during the walk to the house.

In the morning-room he sat on the wide window seat, while little Adelaide stood before him and stared at his trousers.

'I know its name,' said she pertly.

'Do you, then? What is it?'

'I'll whisper in your ear,' she offered, and without waiting for an answer, she pushed his knees apart and stood between his thighs. She put her arms round his neck and her warm breath tickled his ear as she passed on the secret she knew.

'Its name is Harry Horn,' she whispered.

'Who told you that?' Hedley asked, laughing a little.

'Never mind who told me – it's true, isn't it?'

'Yes,' said he in all solemnity, 'he answers to Harry Horn.'

Adelaide stood upright between his thighs and held up her clothes around her waist to show him her white drawers. Fresh from his triumph with Victorina the day before, and hot-blooded for more pleasure with females,

Hedley untied the string of her drawers and let them fall round her knees, while he gazed at her bare and slender thighs. He ran his hands over the softly rounded curves of her bottom, while she stood smiling at him, her brown eyes shining.

The hair was far from fully grown on her delicious little mound, which had the merest covering of down, leaving her sweet young slit almost bare. The lips pouted forward, and Hedley put a hand between her thighs and stroked her gently, making her shiver with delight. He pressed with a gentle finger-tip between those rosy lips until he found her little love-knot.

Such precociousness in a girl of sixteen was not natural, he was sure – someone had initiated Miss Adelaide into the pleasure of being touched on the privities, and of touching another person's. Who that might be he had no thought, and when he asked her again, she giggled and threw herself upon the window seat beside him. She bent over his lap and had his trousers gaping open in an instant and took Harry Horn between her palms. She closed both hands about the shaft so that only his purple head stood out, the little eye open, as if about to offer a tribute.

'Does that feel nice?' she asked, as bold as any woman of the streets, young or old.

'Yes, very nice,' Hedley replied, and his thick shaft pulsed in her hands and gave every indication that he was enjoying the sensations of being felt and would like her to continue.

She bent over him further, to plant a tiny moist kiss on the throbbing head of Master Harry Horn, and then from kissing she took to licking, as if she held a toffee-apple on a stick. The delicious touch of her lips soon inflamed Hedley beyond all restraint and when she took him into her mouth, and tongued him busily, he became swiftly heated to the utmost and was almost spending when he jerked Harry Horn out of her grasp.

'Stop, stop,' he cried. 'Addie, my darling girl, I shall do something I shall regret in a moment, I know I shall!'

'Are you afraid the cream will come shooting out?' she asked with a look far too knowing for a young lady of her years.

Hedley drew in deep breaths to calm himself before replying that he was only just in time to prevent it and then, with a chuckle, he lifted her light form in his arms and sat her across his lap. With the tip of his middle finger he tickled the soft lips of her bare cunny until her bottom was squirming about on his lap, then he parted them with the most delicate touch and advanced a little into her, to find her tiny button.

Adelaide squealed in delight as she threw her arms round his neck and showered tiny kisses on his forehead and face. Young though she was, her desire was very real and demanded to be appeased.

In a frenzy of doubt and ambiguous motives, Hedley asked himself what he was doing – what possessed him that he could think of defiling this sweet young girl! Why was he doing it? The answer he supplied to his own question was that Adelaide had commenced the intimacies and had amply proved that she was by no means an innocent young girl. There was no doubt in his mind that she had been interfered with – her hot breath was on his cheek and she was panting as he caressed her bud with a delicate finger-tip.

'Oh Hedley!' she exclaimed. 'You are very good at it!' and almost at once quick little tremors passed through her slight body and she writhed against him as she came off.

'How do you know I'm good at it unless someone else has done it to you before?' he whispered gently, but her only answer was 'That is none of your concern, Hedley.'

When she had recovered, she insisted on reciprocating his kind compliments to her, and climbed off his lap to kneel on the floor between his legs. She opened his trousers further, so as to bare every portion of what grew between his thighs, and reached in to bring out his hairy knick-knacks and roll them between her fingers.

Scarce able to breathe for sensation, Hedley watched her bow her slender neck and bring her mouth to the tip of Harry Horn. She started at the purple head and ran her tongue all the way down the shaft and back up again to the top – and after a few passes Master Harry glistened with moisture from head to root, especially the head, which swelled to an ever larger and more impressive size.

Hedley's face was burning and he was astonished beyond words by the forbidden knowledge this sweet young girl possessed, whoever her teacher had been.

'Addie – you know what will happen if you keep on doing that to me,' he said, and she removed her tongue from him long enough to smile and say, 'I want to see how much I can make come out of this big fat thing of yours.'

Then, suiting the action to the word, she resumed her most agreeable attentions, until Hedley's nerves were strained to the utmost pitch of luxurious excitment, and Harry Horn was jutting out before him like the bowsprit of a sailing-ship. Seeing his condition, Adelaide took hold of his stiffness in her grasp and passed her little hand rapidly up and down the thick shaft, sucking the head fully into her mouth, to apply the tip of her tongue to it.

'I'm going to fetch off!' he exclaimed, and immediately she pulled him out of her mouth.

'I want to see you do it!' she cried.

She held his twitching length tightly in her fist while she flicked her wet tongue quickly up and down the tiny groove under the almost bursting head.

'Oh, oh!' Hedley cried out in a strained voice, and heaved his backside up and down to assist her. With a few more motions of her hand she had brought him right to the point of emission – when she uttered a gasp of surprise and jumped up and away from him! At that desperate moment he heard the sound of wheels on the gravel drive and, startled almost witless, turned his head to see the carriage bearing his fiancee and his future mother-in-law approaching the house at a spanking trot.

Adelaide snatched up her fallen drawers and held them tight to her belly under her clothes, while she turned and fled from the room. Frantic that he would be discovered in a state of exposure he could never hope to explain, Hedley crammed away poor frustrated Harry Horn and, with fingers that trembled, he struggled to do up his buttons. Even then, when all was secure, the bulge was so pronounced that it was out of the question to allow anyone to see him in that condition.

He leaped to his feet and strode across the room, to pass through the hall before Victorina and Mrs Hapgood had time to descend from the carriage and enter the house. Uppermost in his mind was the consideration that it was vitally urgent to attain the seclusion of his own room quickly – every step he took was torment, for Harry Horn's skin had rolled back of itself and bared his throbbing head, so that the movements of walking rubbed it against his shirt.

Hedley took the stairs at a run and was on the half-landing before he heard below the door open and voices in the hall. He was safe – or almost so – and panting loudly with the effort, he took the turn and dashed up the remainder of the stairs, out of sight at last from the hall below. He had reckoned without the effect of the heavy friction of his clothes on swollen and sensitive Master Horn. For that almost apoplectic gentleman this unwanted rubbing was too much – he jumped ominously against Hedley's belly and then, unbidden, gushed out his hot essence in forceful gouts.

At this most sudden and unexpected release of his tensions Hedley's legs buckled beneath him. He sank to his knees on the wooden stairs, doubled over and pressing both hands against his throbbing shaft, which was hurling defiant jets up inside his shirt. When he could breath again, the comic aspect of his mishap struck him, and he burst into laughter.

The instrument was, one said, a Stradivarius, encased in
light amber and breathily carved walnut, and with
gleaming white ivory keys. Victoria seated herself on
the long stool and glanced through the sheet music on
the rack, looking for something suitable, and worthy of
the occasion. Fledley took up his station beside her,
standing with a straight back, and one hand thrust into
the breast of his buttoned evening-jacket—a hieratic
stance that testified to his many virtues.

CHAPTER 3
A Duet on a Sunday Evening

After a good trencherman's dinner on Sunday evening of thick and spicy mulligatawny soup, Dover sole, and a haunch of roast Angus beef, black treacle pudding, and best Cheddar cheese, Hedley and the family Hapgood assembled in the drawing-room to drink coffee. He was of a mind to protect himself from Adelaide's dangerous attentions by suggesting to his fiancee that they should entertain her Mama by singing a duet together.

He had a light and pleasing tenor voice and was often asked to sing after dinner. Victorina was a very proficient player of the pianoforte and had also enjoyed the benefits of singing lessons. Mrs Hapgood at once declared that Hedley's suggestion was an excellent one, and Adelaide clapped her hands eagerly.

The instrument was first-rate, a Broadwood, cased in lightly polished and ornately carved walnut, and with gleaming white ivory keys. Victorina seated herself on the long stool and glanced through the sheet music on the rack, looking for something suitable and worthy of the occasion. Hedley took up his station beside her, standing with a straight back, and one hand thrust into the breast of his buttoned evening-jacket, a Napoleonic stance that testified to his manly virtues.

At length Victorina struck a chord to signify that she was ready and Hedley glanced down to see what piece of music she had chosen. How beautiful was her hair in the soft yellow glow of the gas light! He smiled in approval and, as her fingers played skilfully over the keyboard, his voice was joined with her soft soprano in the words of a popular and romantic ballard:

> *'Pale hands I loved,*
> *Beside the Shalimar,*
> *Pale hands, pink-tipped,*
> *Like lotus-buds that float*
> *On Shalimar in summer . . .'*

As they raised their melodious lament, Hedley gazed down at Victorina's lily-white hands moving so deftly on the key-board and wished with all his heart that those lovely fingers were playing with Master Harry Horn, who was standing to attention. When the song ended, Victorina cast so tender a glance up at Hedley that his knees trembled at the strength of his adoration for her. Greatly daring, she chose another ballad and played the introduction, her face still turned up to Hedley, her eyes shining with love and devotion, as together they sang:

> *Speak to me of love . . .*
> *And say what I'm longing to hear . . .*
> *Tender words of love . . .'*

Mrs Hapgood listened with the gleam of a tear in her eye, no doubt remembering the days when her late husband had courted her with similar words and music. There was no opportunity for little Adelaide to make mischief, for at Hedley's gentle but firm insistence one ballad followed another, until Mrs Hapgood announced that it was her younger daughter's bed-time.

Adelaide wished them goodnight individually, with a kiss on the cheek for each, including Hedley and, her mother and sister being unsighted by their relative positions, the minx bestowed a light and quick touch on the front of his trousers, before leaving the room. In her absence, the others settled at the card table for a game or two of three-handed whist. At ten the parlour-maid brought in tea and cold meat sandwiches by way of supper, to stave off any pangs of hunger during the night, and by ten-thirty the household had retired to bed.

After he had turned out the gas light and got into his bed, Hedley found it impossible to sleep, for his thoughts were full of images of his beloved Victorina. Whilst he had been standing at the piano beside her, joining his voice with her dear voice and turning the pages of the score for her, he had been afforded a glorious view down the front of her white evening-gown. The vista of her snowy globes had inflamed his active imagination, and the glad memory of his conquest on Friday burned in his mind and straightened the back of Mr Harry Horn.

Hedley told himself that, until his dying day, he would cherish the recollection of Victorina leaning on the gate while he raised her clothes behind and presented his stiff peg to the soft lips of her cunny. The darling girl had stared over her shoulder, her beautiful face flushed a charming rose-pink, and she had begged him to be gentle. It was an unreasonable request in such delicate circumstances, when a man's needs must be cruel to be kind.

There was a barrier to be penetrated, and with one ruthless push Hedley had demolished it and was lodged in her tight and maiden cunny. A minute of two of thrusting and his essence was gushing into her, making her his own for ever. When he withdrew at last from her trembling body, there was a little smear of scarlet to attest to the virginity he had taken. He wiped it from himself and from between her thighs with his handkerchief, a handkerchief that had become for him a treasured memento.

'She let me do it to her, my beloved Vickie,' he thought as he lay sleepless. 'How sublime was that spend in her dear little cunny – so much more superb than a routine fetching off up the slits of the women I am acquainted with in London. What would I give to have my darling girl here with me in bed!'

Everyone knows the truth of the saying that if wishes came true, then beggars would ride on horseback. It was a ride that Hedley pined for, though not on horseback, and wishing would not bring it about. It was undeniable that Fortune favoured the bold, he reminded himself, for it was boldness that had secured bliss for him on Friday, and might do so again.

He got up and drew on his long dressing-gown over his nightshirt. On bare feet, he crept out of his own room and along the dark passage towards the door behind which lay his beloved. It was a perilous journey through the ornamental chests, Chinese vase-stands, Siamese screens carved of ebony wood, stuffed and mounted birds of prey under glass domes, arrangements of tall, feathery elephant grass in jardinieres, and other tasteful decorations along the passage. The only light was that of the moon through a window at the end, and by this fitful beam Hedley ran the gauntlet towards the prize he sought.

At the door to Mrs Hapgood's room he paused to press an ear against the wood, and was heartened by the sound of a gentle snoring. He moved on cautiously, and halted again to listen at Adelaide's door, where he heard nothing at all. On he went, and almost came to grief when he struck his shin against the sharp corner of a brass-bound sea-chest and in his anguish exclaimed loudly 'Damn it to hell!' before he could prevent himself.

He stood still, waiting, excuses running through his mind if he had roused anyone. He settled on an attack of indigestion as the most credible excuse, and intended to claim that he was on his way to the kitchen to look for bicarbonate of soda, and had missed his way in the dark, the stairs being in the opposite direction from the one he was taking. None of this subterfuge proved to be necessary – five minutes passed and there was no sound of anyone stirring, and so Hedley took courage and walked slowly on, until his hand found the knob of Victorina's door.

The moonlight in her room was strong enough to let him see, while he crossed to her bed, that she lay on her side, facing him, and she was not asleep. She sat up with a stifled cry, and for Hedley it was the work of a moment to sink to his knees at her bedside and press an impassioned kiss to her soft mouth.

'This is so very wrong, my darling,' she murmured in the faintest of voices, when his lips released hers, 'I allowed you to lead me astray once – I beg you not to try me again.'

He made no answer, but put his hands on her shoulders and pressed her gently backward among the pillows, his face close to hers. Again his hot tongue parted her lips and plunged fully into her mouth in a long searching caress, while his groping fingers found the buttons of her high-necked nightgown and undid them. He kissed her breathless while his hand entered the thin folds of her night attire and took possession of her satiny globes.

'Hedley, ah Hedley . . . no more or I am lost,' she sighed, as soon as his tongue was withdrawn, but he had already parted her thin gown to take the darling tips of her breasts in his mouth.

He wanted to look at her body, knowing it must be beautiful, but he dare not strike a match to put on the gas light. With a sweep of his arm he threw the bed clothes to the foot of the bed and lifted up her nightgown to her chin, and stared at her in the silvery moonlight. Her legs were well-rounded and shapely, her full orbs rose lusciously upwards, tipped with firm buds, her belly was round and gently swelling, without the trace of a bulge.

With a little exclamation of outraged modesty, she tried to cover the most interesting portions of her body with her hands, but Hedley forestalled her by seizing her wrists and pinning her arms on the pillows above her head, to reveal the luxuriant hair under her armpits. But all this was as nothing to the centre of bliss from which he could not keep his eyes – the dark triangle of fleece which shaded her plump little mound.

There was not enough light to ascertain the true colour of that delightful tuft, although he guessed it to be much the same shade as her ash-brown hair. Then, unable to tolerate his stare at her nakedness any longer, she twisted in his grip and turned away, until her back was to him and he saw her bottom, two plump and dimpled cheeks that he could not resist kissing.

He put his arms about her and turned her toward him,

then kissed her again and felt her bosom, and it seemed to him that her two breasts were thrusting up into his hands. The buds were hard as coral, but tender to his touch. His hot palms held each breast as in a cup, clasping and softly kneading. His wet tongue left her sighing mouth and licked about each breast in turn, passing from the one to the other, sucking at them in a delicate gluttony.

A moment more and he drew her nightgown up over her head, so that she lay before him in her fresh young nakedness. His hand softly separated her legs, he uttered a sob of purest joy as he fingered the silky hair of her motte.

'Hedley, no more,' she pleaded, her little hands clutching at the lapels of his dressing-gown in supplication. 'There will be no mystery left on our wedding night, no secret to share, if you insist on ransacking everything now!'

'I love you more than life itself!' Hedley gasped. 'Do not ask me to wait any longer – as much use to expect that a tidal wave can be stemmed with a word!'

He threw himself on the bed beside her, and covered her body with fiery kisses. The tip of his middle finger pressed subtly between her legs, forcing her tight petals softly apart, insinuating itself between them, touching the secret bud of her body, making it swell and throb with sensation. Soon his head bent lower, his lips pressed upon that yearning bud, and then the delicate thrust of his tongue opened her close petals wider and forced itself in.

'Ah, my dearest Hedley!' she gasped, clasping her hands over her own breasts and flinging her legs apart.

Hedley's attentions to her ceased just long enough for him to rip off his dressing-gown and nightshirt, and he knelt naked beside her. He caught one of her wrists and pressed into her palm the strong and quivering shaft that rose from between his thights. Her fingers closed round it uncertainly.

'You have taken many liberties with me,' she murmured, half swooning with the emotions that raced through her, 'but the thought of touching you has never entered my head, never!'

'Then you shall begin now, my dear,' said he, 'hold me in your soft little hand and feel my strength!'

'I am afraid of it,' she sighed, 'it will destroy me!'

'Not a bit of it!' said he, 'this dearest part of me loves you with a passion you cannot yet imagine.'

'Has it a name?' she asked. 'Or am I to think of it only as Little Hedley?'

'*Little* anything at all would be a most inappropriate name,' he replied, and with a rapid decision he raised Mr John Thomas to the peerage in gratitude for past favours received, telling Victorina that the staunch and trusted friend she held in her palm was named Lord Dickie.

At first she handled his manly charm somewhat nervously but after a while she became familiar with the impressive length and thickness he had to offer.

'Lord Dickie presents his compliments and trusts that you will honour his devotion to your person with a kiss,' said Hedley, and thrilled to the gasp of horror Victorina uttered.

When he first committed himself to this adventure, there had been some doubt and confusion in his mind as to what he might hope for – on their stroll he had been fortunate in catching her off guard and had taken full advantage of her. In her own bed, with all the household within earshot, her resistance to his advances might very well be stronger. It had been possible, he was sure, that she could have sent him away with only a chaste kiss on the cheek for his pains.

He had been luckier than he had any right to hope – within ten minutes of entering her room, he had felt her bubbies, seen her naked body, kissed her bottom and fingered her darling slit – there was every chance that she would let him go all the way with her now, if he persevered.

'Lord Dickie is waiting for your kiss, my dearest,' said he.

Victorina gasped again in maidenly outrage and then pressed a quick kiss halfway along Lord Dickie's shaft, setting that gentleman bounding and nodding.

'A very cousinly kiss!' exclaimed Hedley. 'I believe that you and he are on closer terms than that – kiss him fully, my dear, kiss him with loving affection.'

With becoming timidity and many a hesitation, she touched her soft lips to Lord Dickie's smooth head, and was encouraged by Hedley's loving words to do so again and again – and when at last she understood the full meaning that his words conveyed, she blushed dark red and opened her mouth to caress the hot and swollen nobleman with her tongue.

'That's the way of it!' cried Hedley, and it was not long before Lord Dickie thrust forward between her lips, making her gasp. Having no conscience to hamper his desires, the stiff peer would surely have continued in this pleasant little game until the climax overtook him, but Hedley loved his fiancee too much to risk offending her by a course of action her innocence and modesty would find impossible to comprehend.

He pulled Lord Dickie out of her mouth, pushed her down on her back with some urgency, and pressed her knees apart. She stared open-mouthed in the moonlight, her eyes fixed as if mesmerised by the long and pale-skinned rod displayed before her. In a moment, Hedley's bare belly was on hers, his hands grasping at her bubbies while Lord Dickie was forcing open her secret gates, to plunge into her depths. She moaned a little to be pierced so implacably, for though she was a maiden no more, her cunny was still tight.

Hedley's mouth fastened on hers and his hands slid under her bottom to grip her soft cheeks fiercely, while he tupped with short strokes. Her dear belly rose up bravely to meet his push, and he suppressed a cry of delight when he felt the source of bliss within him overflow and send a flood surging along his shaft. At once, he pulled out of Victorina's slit and shot his essence in thick gushes along her satiny skin, right up past her belly-button, as high as her bubbies.

He had entertained no such scruples when he ended her maidenhood under the oak tree two days before. On that occasion she and he were upright, and it was an article of faith among Hedley's friends that a woman will take no harm from being rogered while standing up. If she were lying on her back when she received the vital fluid, that was another and entirely different matter, calling for the precautions he had observed by withdrawing in the very nick of time.

When Lord Dickie had lost his aristocratic stiffness, Hedley lay beside Victorina and wiped her belly dry with the tail of his own nightshirt. He took her in his arms and murmured to her of his love for a long time – long enough, if the truth were told, for His Lordship to regain his interest in the beautiful girl against whose naked thigh he was pressed.

'Come to the window, my dearest,' Hedley suggested, 'come to the window with me and stand with me for a moment or two in the glorious moonlight – this night is one which we shall remember for all our lives together!'

Suitably encouraged, she stood with him at the window, his arm about her waist, while they gazed out at the velvet black starry sky and a three-quarters full yellow moon. He had not been able to persuade her to stand naked, as he was, her sense of decorum insisting that she donned her long nightgown before going anywhere near a window, even in the middle of the night and half a mile away from the nearest neighbour.

Hedley threw open the casement windows, and together they breathed in the cool midnight air. They heard the cry of a night bird skimming across the top of the larches, and saw a flicker under a tree, where the white scut of a rabbit's tail showed for a moment, as it went about its nocturnal affairs. How peaceful was the scene, how idyllic! Hedley had tasted bliss that night between his fiancee's thighs and had every expectation of doing so again before returning to his own bed.

Above all else, he was desirous of repeating his triumphant deed at the five-barred gate, when his darling had bent over to allow him to penetrate her from the rear and shoot his essence up her cunny, without anxiety or afterthought. It was fully his intention to arrange her in that position once more and give himself the deep pleasure of coming off inside her.

Happily for his plans, Victorina's nightgown was a summer garment of the thinnest cotton, with bows of pink ribbon at the neck, where it was buttoned, and at the wrists, where the full sleeves were gathered in. It scarcely impeded Hedley at all as he reached behind his darling girl to give her bottom a good feel, and then, turning sideways to her, to give her breasts a very thorough feel, until their tips were hard and prominent through the thin cotton material.

'Oh, my dear one, if only I had the words to tell you how much I love you!' he exclaimed, and slipped behind her, to rub hard-on Lord Dickie in the cleft between her soft cheeks, while his hands played feverishly over her bubbies.

'And I you!' she replied in a soft and tender voice, and urged by his hands on her hips, she bent over to put her folded arms on the windowsill. All lay in shadow, and Hedley could discern nothing of the plump and pouting cunny between her open legs. His hand told him that its adornment of light curls was as wet as the lips of her slit and his heart beat furiously at the thought that he would be inside his beloved in an instant.

He stood close to her bottom, raised her nightgown and with a careful hand brought Lord Dickie to the mark and pushed him slowly in. He felt Victorina tremble as she accepted the full length and girth of her noble playmate and then, without turning her head to look at him, she asked a question.

'Hedley, dearest – how often do husbands do this to their wives? Do you know?'

'Very often,' he replied judiciously, letting Lord Dickie have his way and slide easily in and out, 'why do you ask?'

'I know so little of these private matters,' she said. 'It is sheer ignorance on my part, but I have no idea whether the marital act is performed once a month or once a day. Indeed, how could I have any knowledge of these things, since they cannot be spoken of?'

'You may speak of these matters to me at any time you please, and I shall endeavour to enlighten you,' Hedley sighed, his hands up her loose nightgown to play with her bubbies while he rogered away slowly and with relish.

'You are underestimating the interest taken by healthy young persons in the act of love,' he continued slowly. 'When you and I are married, my dear, you will find that we shall do it together twice every night, and once or more often during the day, according to the demands of domestic duties and of social intercourse with friends.'

'So very often?' she cried in astonishment, her bottom pushing back in time with his thrust. 'With all my heart I hope that I am strong enough to sustain your ardour, my dearest – I would rather die than disappoint you!'

Hedley's heart soared with love and admiration at these words, but he was beyond speaking in reply. Lord Dickie bounded inside his warm lodging and began to spout long jets of thick essence, shaking Hedley with rapture. There was no call for any precaution, Victorina being on her feet, and he gripped her soft bubbies and dragged her ever closer to him, while he spent fiercely inside her.

CHAPTER 4
An Introduction on a Railway Train

On the morning of the Friday following his night of rapture in Victorina's room, Hedley again caught the 10.02 train from Waterloo Station to spend the weekend with the Hapgoods. He was anticipating a pleasant stay, reasonably sure now that his darling would not deny herself to him, and his intent was to visit her room in secrecy every night of his stay.

Through the purlieus of Battersea the railway line ran along behind streets of terraced houses, the bottoms of their gardens fenced off from the permanent way, which here was elevated on an embankment. Through the window of his compartment Hedley gazed down into a row of gardens, in many of which washing was hanging to dry. He was fascinated by those washing-lines which exhibited female drawers to flutter in the breeze.

He amused himself by letting his fancy roam freely over the question of what shape and texture of female derriere filled those drawers, and he stared at the upstairs windows of the houses. What was taking place in those back bedrooms? he asked himself, and he answered his own question with speculations that even at Friday mid-morning the owners of those drawers hanging on the line were being soundly rogered.

As if to support his theorising, a net curtain stirred at a distant window and sent him into fervid imaginings of a naked and neglected young wife standing there, longing for a strong man to come to her, and fingering her cunny to alleviate her lonely distress. Needless to say, with thoughts of this kind running through his head, Lord Dickie was soon as stiff as a poker and when the train drew alongside the platform at Wimbledon, Hedley dropped the window and put his head out, in the forlorn hope that the widow who had displayed a passing interest in him might be waiting there.

To his surprise and delight, there she stood – sombrely attired in the same black dress and hat, with a veil over her face. As the train came to a clanking halt, with a whistle of escaping steam from the engine, Hedley leaned further out of the window to raise his hat to the widow and bow slightly. Her head turned in his direction and she stood as if uncertain for a few moments.

To hasten her decision, Hedley swung open the door and stepped down on to the platform, holding it open in invitation. Had he been an ordinary-looking man, the widow might well have declined to share a closed compartment with him alone, but that day he looked exceptionally spruce and well-to-do in a suit of dove-grey, with a satin bow tie and a pink carnation in his buttonhole. He raised his tall hat to her yet again and nodded politely towards the open carriage door.

'All aboard!' a porter called out, and the widow hurried along the platform and got into Hedley's compartment. He leaped in after her with joy in his heart, the porter slammed the door shut and the train moved forward jerkily.

The veiled widow had taken a seat with her back to the

engine. With great elan, Hedley sat down beside her, raised his hat again and introduced himself, staring without restraint at the bodice of her black dress, where her proud breasts swelled it out in a way that did his heart good to see. She seemed not in the least put out by this very direct approach, but responded by telling him that she was Mrs Lottie Mayhew.

'Am I correct in thinking that you caught this train last Friday,' Hedley asked with a pleasant smile, parting his thighs on the seat, to afford her a view of the stiff shaft that was outlined by his close-fitting trousers.

'That's right,' she agreed. 'I've been catching this train on Tuesdays and Fridays for weeks past. I recall now seeing you were on it last Friday, asleep in a corner by the window. You wore a dark suit that day and a rosebud buttonhole.'

She spoke cheerfully, but in a South London accent which Hedley found rather common.

'I was half-asleep,' he conceded, and feeling very sure of himself now that he had enticed her into his compartment and she had told him her name, he continued:

'Allow me to introduce a friend of mine who is an admirer of yours and wishes to express his sentiments in person.'

'Who might that be?' she asked.

He reached for her gloved hand and placed it over the hard rod in his trousers.

'I have the pleasure to present a dear and close friend of mine, Mr Stevie Stiff,' he said.

Lottie chuckled behind her veil and stared down into his lap without the least sign of being disconcerted.

'If he's as much the dandy as you are, then I'm pleased to meet him,' she said.

49

'We share the same tastes, he and I,' Hedley assured her.

'Then I must shake hands with him,' and she leaned over Hedley in a most familiar way, while with short but nimble fingers she unbuttoned his trousers and waistcoat. He leaned back against the seat comfortably, stretched out his legs and spread them, watching Lottie open his trousers gaping wide and hitch up his shirt. She took out his long hard rod, clasped it in her palm and shook it solemnly.

'How do you do, Mr Stevie Stiff,' she said, weighing him in her hand. 'What a big strong fellow you are!'

The introduction effected, to Hedley's dismay she started to put him away again, and Mr Stiff was so taken aback that he leaped furiously in her hand.

'He refuses to be dismissed so summarily,' Hedley explained with a smile.

'Oh, does he? He's the headstrong sort, is he?'

Hedley said nothing – she had her answer when his manly charm jerked angrily in her hand.

'Headstrong is right!' she exclaimed. 'If you ask me, he's cocksure, this Mr Stevie Stiff. He's the bullying sort, who abuses his strength by imposing on weak women. Well, he's met his match this time.'

Slowly she removed the black cloth glove from her right hand and flicked Mr Stevie Stiff with it.

'I know his sort,' she said earnestly, 'there's only one way to deal with them. They have to be taken down a peg or two.'

'You are very strict,' sighed Hedley, his hat pushed forward over his eyes by the seat-back against which he was lolling.

'It's the only way,' Lottie declared. 'I'll take the starch

right out of this rude friend of yours and he'll give us no more trouble, mark my words.'

Without as much as a by-your-leave, she started to rub up and down firmly, her gloved left hand groping in Hedley's trousers to get hold of his knick-knacks. That young gentleman was in the Seventh Heaven – never in his life had he had so interesting a journey on a railway train. Matters were going very well when the train began to brake and Lottie's attentions slackened.

'Don't stop, I beg you!' cried Hedley.

'You and your friend will have to be patient a while,' Lottie answered, 'unless you want the people on the platform to see him being dealt with as he deserves.'

While she spoke she tucked Mr Stevie Stiff under Hedley's shirt and buttoned his long jacket, to conceal all that she had left his trousers undone.

'No one must come in!' Hedley gasped.

As the train ran into the station and stopped, Lottie stood up and lowered the window, to discourage anyone from entering. Meanwhile, Hedley sat very still, breathing lightly and keeping his legs well apart, mindful that any unwary movement might precipitate the climax, as on the occasion when he ran upstairs after playing with little Adelaide. In his condition of overstretched nerves, it seemed like hours before the train moved on again.

Lottie resumed her seat beside him, opened his jacket and laid hold of his quivering shaft again.

'He's trembling with fear, your friend Mr Stevie Stiff,' she said. 'Did he think he'd been sent to bed in the dark without his supper, the wretch?'

Her short fingers moved faster on him, displaying an expert ease that sent such thrills through Hedley that he sighed aloud and his stretched-out legs twitched uncontrollably.

'It's as I thought,' Lottie observed, 'he's cocksure enough when he finds a young girl he can browbeat, but he hasn't the courage to stand up long when he comes across a woman of spirit and sense. He'll burst into tears in a minute, I'll be bound!'

'Shall he apologise to you?' asked Hedley, his voice faint.

'I'll make sure he does,' said Lottie. 'He's had about all he can take – we'll have tears of remorse from him now!'

Hedley cried out and his legs jerked spasmodically as his essence came gushing up and out, spraying her hand with creamy white spurts.

'That's it!' said she, flicking his shaft very fast, 'I knew all along it would end like this – Mr Stevie Stiff will be Mr Stevie Slack by the time I'm done with him!'

After Hedley had finished and been made decent again, his buttons all fastened and his dangler soft in his trousers, he sat up straight and gently turned up Lottie's veil. She was no beauty, but she had a pleasant and wholesome face and an expression of permanent good nature. Now that he could see her properly, Hedley put her age at under thirty, though not by much. A conversation was opened, each on easy terms with the other, and when the train pulled into Surbiton station and she told Hedley that this was her stop, he asked if he might escort her home.

She agreed without demur, and waited for him while he had his bags taken to the Left Luggage Office for safe keeping and despatched a message by telegraph to The Larches, to say that he was unavoidably detained and would arrive later in the day. Then with a good heart and a clear conscience he accompanied Lottie to her home, a modest but neat terraced house in red brick and stucco.

'Do you live here alone?' Hedley asked curiously.

'I did for a month or two after my husband passed away,' she answered, leading him into the front parlour, 'but for the last twelve month I've let two rooms upstairs to a respectable young married couple.'

Seeing the doubtful expression that crossed his face, she smiled and told him that they both had jobs and were out of the house all day. She invited him to be seated, and took off her wide-brimmed black hat with the veil, to reveal that her hair was a bright ginger in colour. She declared that she was parched for a cup of tea and went off to the kitchen, leaving Hedley to inspect the treasures of her parlour, when he would have preferred to examine the treasures of her body.

There was a row of porcelain figures along the mantelpiece and a large mirror in a mahogany frame on the wall over it. The prize exhibit was a large hand-tinted photograph in an oval silver frame, showing Lottie ten years younger, and a young man Hedley took to be her deceased husband. She was shown sitting primly on a chair with her knees tight together and her hands folded in her lap. The man, who wore a heavy black moustache, stood beside her, one hand on her shoulder in the pride of ownership, and a smirk on his face.

In five minutes Lottie came back with a tray loaded with a large floral pattern teapot, milk, sugar, cups, saucers, spoons, tea-strainer, slop bowl, sugar spoon and Heaven knows what else. Hedley's appetite had returned, though not for tea, and his state of excitement knew no bounds. Nevertheless, he was compelled by politeness to sit on the sofa facing Lottie, who was out of harm's reach, and drink a cup of tea with her.

When she rose to refill their cups from the teapot standing on the tray on the sideboard, Hedley decided that enough was enough. It was not tea he had come here for. He slid forward off the sofa on to his knees and threw his arms round Lottie's thighs, his fingers sinking into her fleshy bottom.

'Be careful!' she cried. 'You'll have me over!'

'I mean to,' he assured her.

He lifted her black dress and her petticoats, wondering for just a moment whether her mourning extended as far as black underclothes, but they proved to be white enough, and the only touch of severity was the black ribbons with which her drawers were pulled close below her knees. Hedley gazed in delight upon a pair of strong thighs inside the thin cotton, and without hesitation he pulled open the slit of her drawers and caught sight of a fine tangled fleece of ginger-coloured hair.

With a shrug of her shoulders to indicate that resistance was pointless, Lottie put the empty teacups out of the way on the mantelpiece, while Hedley lifted her skirts higher and kissed her thighs. He pressed his face to them and breathed in the scent of garden lavender, with which her underclothes were perfumed. His busy hand pulled loose the string of her drawers and he dragged them down her legs to bare her belly and lick her belly-button, but her stays robbed him of this delight.

'Wait just a minute,' said she, glancing at the large window and the lace-net curtain that shielded her privacy from the sight of inquisitive passers-by, 'I've never been had here in the parlour before.'

'Then it's high time you were,' he replied.

He released his grip on her bottom long enough for her to strip down to chemise and stockings, the annoying stays flung aside on the carpet with her other clothes. At once Hedley sat her on the sofa, and threw himself on his knees between her open legs to examine her ginger-haired cunny. When he had seen all he wanted, he lifted her legs and set her stockinged feet on the edge of the sofa, beside her bottom, forcing her knees up and apart.

'My – we're going to play a game of Attitudes, I see,' said Lottie, a broad smile on her face.

Hedley inserted two fingers into her thick-lipped slit and played there until she was satisfactorily wet.

'Is Mr Stevie Stiff in a fit condition to do his duty – or have I ruined his chances for the day?' she asked.

'My friend is in the ideal conditon for what lies before him,' Hedley announced with pride and confidence.

He pulled open his trouser buttons and firmly took in hand his dearest friend. Lottie let her head fall back on the sofa and stared up at the ceiling in an ecstasy of anticipation, while Hedley put Mr Stevie Stiff's hot and throbbing head to her ginger commodity and pressed forward. Lottie was capacious, and the easiest of pushes took him all the way in, so that his belly was against hers, and he rogered her fiercely.

'Oh yes, he's cocksure again,' said Lottie in a knowing tone of voice, 'but he won't last long, the way he's going at it – he'll soon spend his two-pennorth and be done for.'

Hedley pulled her loose chemise up to her chin to bare her big soft bubbies. They were starting to sag, but they were white-skinned still, with plump buds set in red-brown circles as big as Hedley's palm, and they were a fine double handful to grasp and knead. All too soon, a lightning-flash of ecstasy ripped through his body, making him cry out loudly as his essence spurted into her.

'Don't you dare stop now!' Lottie exclaimed shrilly when she felt his sap shooting. 'Keep going!'

Hedley was well-disposed towards her, even though

he had spent copiously, and he kept his hard thrusting going until the climax came for her and she moaned and shuddered against him, her plump belly quaking with delight.

When they had recovered a little from the lethargy of love satisfied, they sat side by side, Lottie in only her chemise and stockings and Hedley fully dressed, while they refreshed themselves with another cup of tea and talked. Although he had no interest in the topic, Hedley knew she would think him not very polite if he failed to ask how her husband had passed away at so early an age. Her reply astounded him.

'My poor Alfie was carried off by pneumonia,' she said, her voice suitably hushed for so solemn a subject. 'He fell in the water and wore his wet clothes for hours, though I begged and prayed him not to. Next day he had a bad cold on the chest and was in bed, and in three days he had such a fever I ran for the doctor. But there was nothing he could do, and inside a week my poor Alfie was gone.'

She wiped a token tear from her cheek with the hem of her chemise, giving Hedley an attractive view of her domed belly with its deeply inset button, and her big soft breasts.

'How very tragic – you have my deepest sympathies,' he said, slipping a hand between her warm thighs as if to comfort her in her loss. 'Did he fall into the Thames?'

'No, it was the sea,' she replied. 'We were down at Brighton for the day. He was under-manager at the Gas Light and Coke Company, and it was the Works Outing. We went to the Minstrel Show at the end of the pier, and in the interval we took a turn round outside the theatre to get a breath of air – it had been stifling hot all day, you see. Alfie had been drinking porter since we got there and he was merry – in fact, he suddenly wanted his matrimonials behind the theatre. Well, I've never been one to say no to that, so I put my back against the wall and picked up my skirts for him.'

'As a good wife should,' Hedley commented in full approval, 'but how did he come to fall in the sea?'

'The trouble was that he'd had a few too many and he couldn't get it properly hard-on – a regular case of Brewer's Droop, if ever I saw one! He tried and tried, and I tried for him, but it was like trying to thread a darning-needle with mending wool. Then he burst out laughing and went staggering backwards fom me, hit the railing and tipped over with his boots up in the air and vanished off the end of the pier! There I stood dumbfounded – holding my clothes up and showing everything I've got! And then I heard a splash and Alfie shout out for help!'

'Good God!' Hedley exclaimed, struggling not to laugh at this ridiculous story. 'Could he swim?'

'Not a stroke! But some boatmen pulled him out and landed him on the beach, and he seemed none the worse for it – in fact he couldn't stop laughing. I wanted him to get out of his wet clothes, but he wouldn't hear of it and it was midnight before we got home on the excursion train. By then he had taken a chill, though neither of us knew it. And a week later, he had passed away from it.'

'I've never heard a more extraordinary story,' said Hedley, his belly aching from suppressing his mirth.

'Nor I,' said Lottie, cheering up now that her tale was told and decently appreciated. 'Well, that's life – Alfie died for love, you might say, although I never got that last seeing-to.'

'You've made up for it since, though,' Hedley suggested, his fingers stroking slowly between her closed thighs, feeling the wiry tuft of hair that covered her privities.

'Do you blame me?'

'Lord, no! I'm greatly in favour of having it as often as you can get it, and with anyone that takes your fancy.'

'You would be, being a man, and young, and good-looking, and well-off, and unmarried, if I'm right,' said Lottie, 'but for a woman it's not so easy. If you don't take care all the time to hide what you're about, you'll lose your name and be thought a whore. I'll tell you something, Mr Hedley Gillingham, you're the first man I've ever brought here to my own home.'

'I am honoured,' said he, 'and I shall endeavour to return the compliment in the best way I can.'

He stood up and undressed completely, knowing that women found his body attractive. Lottie watched him from where she sat, her mouth open a little and her red tongue moistening her lips when she slid a hand up and down the inside of his naked thigh, the rasp of her nails on his skin making him to sigh.

'Mr Stevie Stiff is living up to his name again,' she said, and fingered him so thoroughly that he jumped in her hand like a Jack-in-the-Box. Hedley put his hands on her shoulders and turned her to lie full length along the sofa, then leaned over her and jerked up her chemise to uncover her lolling bubbies. He felt them and kissed them until she was breathing rapidly, then opened her with two fingers and dabbled lightly in her slippery moisture.

'Do me!' Lottie murmured, her eyes rolling up in her head, but Hedley continued to feast his eyes on her ginger curls, and the wet lips of her cunny. He went down on his knees by her to bite it gently, and feel her plump flesh between his teeth.

'Oh, my! You've left it too late now!' Lottie groaned. 'I'm coming off!'

Hedley slid his fingers into her and opened her wide, baring the little bud of her delights, and with a rapid touch threw her into rapturous convulsions. When the delightful shuddering slowed, he gave her no respite – in a moment he was on top of her, lying between her wide-open thighs, his hot belly on hers. With a fierce jerk of his loins he rammed Mr Stevie Stiff right up her, until his brown curls mingled with her ginger curls.

'You'll kill me!' she moaned when he began to slide in and out with magisterial strength and deliberation. 'I can't!'

She was mistaken about that, and for the next five minutes Hedley demonstrated to her that she was capable of more than she knew. She writhed under him, returning thrust for thrust, heaving her belly up to meet him, and when he reached the short sharp strokes, she shrieked and started to fetch off. Her transports were long, loud and frantic, and came to a totally exhausted halt only after Hedley had inundated her slit with spurting floods of desire and had no more to give.

The time being after midday, and the sweet exertions of love having brought on the pangs of hunger, Lottie invited Hedley to stay for a bite to eat. When they were dressed again, she laid the table in her back-kitchen and offered him cold ham and brawn, with bottled beer. It was very different from the sort of lunch he had missed at The Larches, but he fell to with as sharp an appetite as Lottie's.

While they were eating he enquired casually how it came about that she took the train from Wimbledon back to Surbiton twice a week. He was surprised to see Lottie's round face turn pink, but in a few moments she had recovered her habitual poise and looked at him across the table with a conspiratorial smile. She explained that she stayed overnight with her married sister and caught the train back the next morning.

Thinking nothing of it, Hedley asked if Lottie's sister was unwell, to require these regular visits. He was informed that sister Annie was seven months in the family way with her sixth child and, like Lottie, as strong as a dray-horse.

'Look,' said Lottie, seeing his faintly puzzled expression, 'I might as well be straight with you, seeing what good friends we've become already. Annie's husband is a regular stickler for his matrimonials four times a week, and has been since the day they were wed. By the time she's six months gone, it's too uncomfortable for her to oblige him, and so I pop over to Wimbledon for two nights a week to take her place.'

'Your sister lets you sleep with her husband?' cried Hedley. 'I've never heard anything like it! What sort of man is he, to make these demands on her – and on you?'

'Bertie is a very proper sort of man,' said Lottie. 'He's headmaster of a school, and very well-spoken.'

'Is he any good in between the sheets?' Hedley enquired.

'Not as good as you, if that's what you mean,' she answered. 'He's a bit too brisk and businesslike for my choice, but I've no reason to complain – he has me twice every time I stay there, and rolls me round his bed like a big doll.'

'You lie with him in the marriage-bed?' Hedley asked, still unable to take in what Lottie was telling him.

'That's right. With five children in the house there's no spare rooms,' said Lottie. 'Annie sleeps downstairs on the couch when I'm there, and brings a cup of tea up to us first thing in the morning, to get Bertie up and off to his school in time.'

'She comes into the room and sees you lying in bed with her husband?'

'You sound surprised – but why shouldn't she? He's a man of very strong passions. He has to have his oats four times a week and if I don't oblige, he'll be off with some other woman – and where would that leave Annie? As things are, we keep it in the family, and each of us gets something out of it.'

'All that poking and he never gets you in the family way?' Hedley asked.

'My poor Alfie never could either, though he certainly tried hard enough! And Bertie puts Annie in the family way regular as clockwork every year, but never once me in all the years I've been going there. So there must be something wrong with me,' she said with a sigh.

'You went there to take your sister's place in bed when your husband was alive?' Hedley exclaimed. 'Didn't he mind?'

'Alfie was Bertie's brother,' Lottie explained, 'he was only doing him a favour by lending me to him when Annie couldn't give Bertie his rights.'

'Tell me more,' said Hedley, his voice sounding strained as emotions built up in him, 'how are matters arranged precisely between the three of you when you go there?'

'By seven the children have been put to bed,' said Lottie, looking at him curiously, 'we sit and talk for an hour or two, and about half past nine Annie makes us a cup of cocoa. While she goes upstairs to undress, I make up a bed for her on the couch. She comes down in her nightdress and Bertie and I kiss her goodnight and go up to the bedroom.'

'And then?' Hedley demanded, his face dark with passion.

'Bertie puts the light out and we undress and get into bed together. He's strange about that – it all has to be in the dark and he makes sure the curtains are tight drawn.'

'He's never seen you naked?'

'Not so much as my knee,' Lottie answered with a laugh, 'and he'll never let me touch his you-know-what, hard or soft. Annie's never had a feel of it either, she told me. But once Bertie gets his hand between my legs, he brings me off a couple of times in short order, to make me properly wet before he jumps on top – and then he's like a bolting horse!'

Hedley sat silent, staring at her across the table with his mouth hanging open. Although he had come off several times in the past hour or two and was completely drained of all sexual desire, or so he thought, Lottie's matter-of-fact story of the unusual relationships in her family had excited his curiosity wonderfully. Images ran through his mind of plump Lottie on her back naked on a feather-bed, her legs wide apart for Albert to ram up her ginger-haired cunny.

'Are you all right?' she asked as he pushed his chair back and rose from the table, his eyes shining.

Neither of them had dressed fully for lunch – Hedley was in his shirt and trousers. He pulled Lottie to her feet and close to him, then pressed her hand against his trousers, where his staff stood like a bar of iron.

'So that's it!' said Lottie, undoing his buttons and slipping her hand inside. He leaned against her as if his legs would collapse, supporting his weight with his hands on her shoulders. She had Mr Stevie Stiff right out of his trousers, but he was covered by Hedley's shirt, and she could not feel him bare.

'I thought I'd settled his hash for today,' said Lottie with a chuckle. 'What brought this on?'

'I've got to have you!' Hedley gasped. 'Rest your backside on the table-top!'

'You remind me of my poor Alfie!' she replied, with a peal of laughter. 'Mind you don't fall over backwards into the sea.'

To make herself decent while they had lunch together, she had put on only her chemise and black dress – and while Hedley scrabbled at his shirt-flap to free his throbbing shaft, she hoisted the dress up round her waist, revealing that she wore no petticoats or drawers. With a grin on her face, she spread her feet well apart and leaned her bottom on the table, to show her bright ginger tuft between white thighs. Hedley gave a gasp of relief and jammed Mr Stiff straight up her and rogered away stupendously, until he came off in a flurry of hot spurts and trembling limbs.

'Lovely!' exclaimed Lottie. 'It felt like I was being raped that time – it really did! Come into the bedroom and strip while I tell you naughty tales about how Bertie had me off last night, till you feel like doing me again.'

...after a night of deep and restful slumber, Martin Arriva
Still found himself refreshed enough to unfold a vivid
dream — Hedley's unconscious brain, he believed that

CHAPTER 5
A Lesson on the Pianoforte

It was late in the afternoon before Hedley took his leave of Lottie Mayhew and made his way back to the station, to reclaim his luggage and await the next train to Walton-upon-Thames. He completed his journey to Burwood Park in time to change for dinner, and to allay the anxieties of the ladies of the house. After the delivery of his telegraph message that morning they had feared that he had met with some unfortunate mishap, but he invented suitable excuses and soon all was smiles again.

After dinner they sat in the drawing-room together for a game of Mah-Jong, and Hedley could hardly suppress his yawns. His delightful exertions with Lottie had sapped his strength for the time being and he was pleased when Mrs Hapgood suggested an early night for them all, in view of the event planned for the next day. By ten Hedley was in his nightshirt and in bed fast asleep. There was no creeping through a silent house to Victorina's room that night!

Satiated though he was by Lottie's divine lubricity, after a night of deep and restful slumber, Master Stevie Stiff found himself refreshed enough to unfold a vivid dream in Hedley's unconscious brain. He believed that he was on the platform of a railway station again, seated on a green-painted bench beside Lottie Mayhew in her widow's mourning black. His hand was up her clothes between her legs, to feel something soft and warm.

A vastly long express came rolling through the station without stopping, the beat of the pistons and grinding of the wheels deafening. Lottie was shouting to make herself heard over the noise, that they should have been on that train, and Hedley shouted back that it didn't matter because there would be another in a few minutes. He thought she replied that she couldn't come off on a station platform, only on a train.

When Hedley woke up, he was unable to remember anything of what happened next in his dream, but he guessed that it must have been pleasant because Mr Stevie Stiff was living up to his name. The tap on the door that had awakened him was the maid bringing his morning cup of tea and biscuit, a long-established custom in the Hapgood household. Hedley wriggled against the pillows, to get his back against the bed-head, and half sit up.

Milly set his cup of tea, with a sweet biscuit resting in the saucer, on the night-table beside him, and as usual, wished him a good morning and announced that it was eight o'clock. She was a plain woman in her middle thirties but, even so, Hedley was casting about in his mind for some excuse to detain her at his bedside for a little longer.

While she went to the window to draw back the half-closed curtains, he enquired about the weather. She informed him that the sun was out and all the signs were that it was going to be a beautiful day.

'You're right, Milly, it's quite hot already – I feel it here,' said Hedley, and he threw back the bed clothes.

The maid turned from the window and, seeing him lying fully uncovered in his nightshirt, her eyes alighted immediately on the prominence where Master Stiff twitched strongly under the thin linen. The faintest of pinks for a moment touched her cheeks and Hedley gave her an encouraging smile while he pulled up his nightshirt to reveal his condition openly. Milly put her hands on her hips and stared down at his rod, hard as a broom handle, and under her gaze it nodded up and down.

Milly's bubbies looked to be flattish underneath her dress and long white apron, but that was of little consequence, for all that Hedley wanted from her was the use of her cunny for a minute or two. He gestured with his hand, inviting her to lie down on the bed beside him, whereupon he would have her clothes up to her belly-button in a second and be between her legs. He expected no very great ecstasy from the proposed coupling, only a welcome relief from his present hard-on state.

There was some curiosity in his mind as to what the maid's response would be when he pushed his rod up her and rogered her hard and fast – would she blush and simper? Would she grin and hump her backside up to meet his poking? Would she come off? If she did, it was to be hoped that she did it quietly and in as lady-like manner as she could manage, not in the same noisy and unchecked way that Lottie Mayhew had, for it would never do for suggestive whimpering and crying to be heard by the occupants of the other upstairs rooms.

To his disappointment, nothing of the sort took place – Milly looked away from where Mr Stevie was straining with hope, and looked Hedley in the eye.

'Get along with you, Mr Gillingham,' she said, 'I've

got my work to do – I've no time for your nonsense.'

'Hold him in your hand, then,' said he, trying to rescue something from the wreckage of his plans, 'only for a minute – that's all it will take, Milly!'

'Hold him in your own hand,' she retorted, and as she swept out of the room without another glance at his pride, she informed Hedley that cook was well advanced with breakfast and he should not linger too long in bed.

Hedley held his dissatisfied friend in his left hand for luck while he drank his morning tea, telling him silently that the loss was Milly's, for she had been offered the opportunity to start her day in style by accommodating so fine and strong a fellow – but she lacked the sense to take advantage of what was thus made available to her.

Mr Stiff throbbed in Hedley's hand and refused to be calmed quite so easily – he insisted that what Milly had meant by her parting advice was that a firm stroking by Hedley would resolve his problem in a couple of minutes, and give pleasure to them both. Certainly not, Hedley replied silently, denying the impudent plea – after breakfast I intend to take my dearest Victorina for a walk to a certain five-barred gate – do you suppose that I will let you squander your resources in the palm of my hand when in an hour you will be inside my darling?

The moment that his tea was finished, Hedley rose from bed and doused Mr Stevie Stiff in plenty of cold water, to dash his hopes. Twenty minutes later, shaved and dressed, Hedley was seated in the breakfast-room, taking in sustenance for a busy day, in the form of kedgeree, a pair of grilled pork chops, half a dozen rashers of well-cured bacon, two or three fried eggs, and plenty of toast and best butter.

The ladies joined him at various stages of breakfast, Mrs Hapgood first, then Adelaide, and Victorina the last. At once the conversation was of that evening's grand party, to which Victorina and Hedley were invited. The occasion was the engagement to be married of a dear friend of Victorina's – a girl of her own age, Georgina Playfair, whose family resided at nearby Weybridge. The invitations were for eight o'clock, which made it necessary to bring forward dinner by an hour at The Larches, a change in domestic routine which created confusion in the kitchen.

As is the way in households where females reign supreme and unchecked, the nervous atmosphere continued to develop after breakfast, culminating in a sudden decision by Victorina that her long white evening-gloves were too old to wear to so important a social function as her dearest friend's betrothal party. By eleven o'clock, Tom had the carriage at the door and Victorina and Mrs Hapgood set off to buy a pair of new gloves.

Hedley was far too sensible a person to become involved in ladies' shopping expeditions. Greatly displeased that there was to be no stroll that morning to the gate with Victorina and a session of delightful love-making on the grass, he took a turn round the gardens to quieten his nerves. When he returned to the house he heard little Adelaide at her pianoforte practice. By dint of application she was already a player of some accomplishment, and it was with pleasure that Hedley heard her performance of Mr Balfe's ever-popular ballad, 'I Dreamt That I Dwelt in Marble Halls.'

There was a pause at the end of it, then Hedley heard her begin to play the opening bars of 'A Londonderry Air' and went into the drawing-room to congratulate her on her playing. She thanked him for his compliment and invited him to share the piano stool with her and turn the pages of the sheet music. Carelessly, he complied with her suggestion, for although he recalled with grave misgivings that she had tempted him into fingering her the last time they were alone together, the fact was that he was still aroused from his failed attempt on the parlour-maid.

If only dear Victorina had not gone chasing off with her Mama to purchase gloves! If only she had stayed and gone with him for a walk in the sunshine! What bliss would have awaited them both in some quiet corner of the meadow beyond the gate! But it was useless to cry over spilt milk. He sat down beside Adelaide, and instead of resuming her playing, she enquired:

'Would you care to feel my pussy, Hedley?'

'How do you come to know that word?' he asked, his brows knitted in surprise. 'Who has told it to you?'

'Why should I give my secrets away for nothing?' she replied pertly. 'Fair exchange is no robbery – tell me a secret of yours and I will answer your question.'

'But I have no secrets of that sort!' he exclaimed.

'Everybody in the world has secrets,' she said with a slow smile. 'Have you forgotten how I let you feel me last weekend, when we sat on the window seat? And I had Harry Horn out and stroked him for you. Only Mama came home and interrupted us before there was time to make him shoot off.'

To hear these words and expressions in the mouth of so young and innocent-seeming a girl was extraordinary, thought Hedley.

'No, I hadn't forgotten,' he said, 'but that's a secret you and I share, and which we must always keep from other people, especially your Mama.'

'I know that,' she said with a dismissive shrug, 'but you have secrets I don't know. Tell me one of them, and I'll tell you one of mine.'

'What, for example?' he asked, reluctant to become enmeshed in an exchange of confidences with the girl.

'You feel Vickie's pussy, I suppose,' she astonished him by saying, 'so why not mine? You did last week.'

'Adelaide! How can you say such a thing about your sister! If anyone overheard so gross an accusation of immorality, her reputation would be destroyed and her life ruined!'

'There's nobody to hear what we're saying,' she answered, unabashed, 'so you can tell the truth – how often do you feel Vickie's pussy? Do you let her play with Harry Horn?'

'Can I trust you?' he asked. 'If I answer your question, will you tell me who taught you these words?'

'I swear on the Bible,' said Adelaide.

'Then yes, in absolute and total confidence, I admit that I have had a feel of your sister's pussy. But if you ever tell that to a living soul, I shall deny it and say you made it up. Now it's your turn to confess to me.'

'Was it nice?' she asked, ignoring his suggestion that she should reciprocate by telling all. 'Did Harry Horn stand up?'

She took his hand and conveyed it under her short dress and up between her girlish thighs.

'You may put your fingers in my drawers, Hedley,' she said, with all the aplomb of a woman of the world twice her age.

Hedley opened her drawers to touch her flesh, and she spread open her thighs to let his fingers touch the merest trace of soft fluff between them. The little lips were soft and warm to his fingertips and she closed her eyes when, very gently, he tickled the tiny button concealed within them. She honoured her promise to him by explaining

71

that she had been taught the words she knew for male and female privities by Tom the groom.

'Great Heaven!' Hedley exclaimed, scandalised to learn that a servant had debauched this pure and unsuspecting daugher of a fine old family. 'Tell me what the blackguard did to you!'

Nothing loth, Adelaide explained that she had been fingered many a time by the groom, in the hay-loft above the stables. In reply to Hedley's demand to hear how this inopportune and most unhealthy relationship began, she giggled and squeezed her slim thighs together on his hand, and reached into his lap to flip open his buttons and feel inside under his shirt to take hold of his twitching rod.

'It was one Sunday evening before dinner, when I went back to the stables to give the horses an apple, after we'd come back from Church,' she said. 'Tom said he'd got some carrots in the hay-loft and the horses would like them, and he'd show me where he'd put them. I climbed up the steps to the loft, and he came up behind me, and – you know how very steep those steps are – well, I think my floot slipped, because suddenly Tom caught me in his arms to stop me from falling. He pressed himself against my back and hugged me so hard I could hardly breathe.'

'That was no accident!' Hedley declared in high dudgeon, his finger tickling her moist little bud. 'The vile fellow took advantage of you deliberately! What happened then?'

'I hardly know what happened,' she said, her unseen hand stroking slowly up and down Hedley's thick shaft inside his trousers. 'It was so exciting! I was half lying down on the steps, with Tom tight behind me, and somehow it felt as if he were on top of me. His arms were round my waist and he got his hand up my dress and touched me between the legs – and it felt so strange that I didn't know what to do.'

'The man's a degenerate and a criminal!' Hedley cried. 'He should be horse-whipped and flung into gaol for life!'

'You're jealous,' said Adelaide, 'Tom's my dear friend and I like him a lot. I'm not going to tell you any more if you get so upset about it and threaten nasty things.'

'I won't say another word,' Hedley promised. 'Do go on.'

'Well . . . if you promise . . . lying there up the steps I felt a most peculiar sensation, as if my tum-tum had turned suddenly inside out. It was strange and very nice at the same time, and I'd never felt anything like it before. Tom helped me up the rest of the steps to the loft after that, and we sat on a bale of hay and I asked him about it. I was sure he knew, because he made it happen, and he told me that I'd fetched off.'

Hedley was about to call the groom a ruffian and worse, but remembered his promise and bit back the words.

'After that Tom opened his trousers and showed me Harry Horn and told me his name and I was very excited to see what it was like,' she went on, 'a lovely big pink rod standing straight up. He told me that men have this rod and sometimes it's limp and small and dangles inside their trousers, but it swells up and stretches itself out when they see a girl they want to play with. Just like yours is now, Hedley.'

'I cannot deny it,' he said softly, thrills of pleasure rippling through him from her fingering.

'I asked Tom if men could fetch off the way I had when he'd stroked my pussy on the steps, and he showed me how to stroke Harry Horn up and down – and he went red in the face and white creamy liquid came shooting out of him . . .'

During her exposition of these arousing events, Adelaide had eased Hedley's shaft out of his open trousers unnoticed, and her little hand played along its swollen girth, caressing it and wheedling it to respond to her advances. Hedley was unaware of his surroundings, drowning in lascivious sensation.

'Yours is longer and fatter than Tom's,' she advised him, 'but he is stronger than you because he works all day, and so I think you will shoot less than he does.'

Her words were the final push that flung Hedley over the brink of sanity and civilised behaviour into the delirium of the senses. His loins jerked, and a sudden emission of the essence of virile love spattered the ivory keys of the piano, making Adelaide giggle to see it.

'There – that's more than I thought!' she said. 'Do you let Vickie play with Harry Horn and fetch him off?'

'Equal exchange, secret for secret,' he responded languidly when he was calmer, 'I told you one of mine, you told me one of yours. If you want to hear another, you must tell me one.'

She sat thoughtful for a moment or two, staring at the wet and softening shaft between her fingers.

'I'll tell you something else that Tom told me,' she said, 'but you have to promise never to repeat it to a soul.'

'Very well, I promise,' said he, curious to learn what other information the groom had passed on to Adelaide.

She glanced round the drawing-room, as if fearful of being overheard relating forbidden knowledge, then leaned closer and put her mouth against his ear.

'Tom says that men and women can make each other fetch off together if the gentleman puts Harry Horn inside the lady's pussy. But I don't really believe him. What do you think?'

'Why do you think he might be mistaken?'

'Well, look at the size of your Harry Horn, and look at the size of my pussy. It would never go in.'

'You and Tom never tried this experiment?' Hedley asked, almost holding his breath in relief that Adelaide was still maiden, technically speaking, and that vile as the groom was, he had spared her the final infamy of defloration by his vulgar lower-class tool.

She shook her pretty head and said she went to the stables most days to have her pussy played with, and to fetch off Tom, but he had never tried to put his shaft inside her, for the obvious reason that it would split her wide open.

'Where do you believe that new babies come from, Adelaide?' Hedley asked.

'Everybody knows that,' she replied immediately. 'The doctor brings them in his little black bag when married ladies are ready for them. But what does that have to do with it?'

'Nothing at all,' he answered, determined not to let himself be trapped into supplanting Mrs Hapgood as the enlightener of her younger daughter's ignorance of the mechanics of sexual intercourse and human reproduction. To subvert her mind from the dangerous topic, he tickled her little bud, smiling to see how her thighs slid wider apart on the piano stool and her eyes shone with wild excitement.

'I'm fetching off, Hedley!' she sighed. 'Oh, that's nice!'

Whether she attained the climax or not, Hedley could not be certain, but she jumped up from the long stool and turned to fling a leg over his thighs and sit herself astride his lap.

'You didn't answer my question,' she accused him. 'Tell me what you think – I want to know.'

'I've forgotten the question now,' he said. 'What was it?'

'Do you think Tom was right about gentlemen putting Harry Horn into ladies' pussies? Have you ever heard of this?'

Hedley experienced a pang of queasy doubt in his stomach and knew himself to be on very dangerous ground. He played for time to think, smiling at Adelaide's pink-flushed and pretty face.

'Well?' she demanded, scenting his hesitation and guessing that there was a secret here to be told – and most unwilling to be fobbed off. To avoid her burning stare of interrogation, he glanced down into his lap, and saw that she had tucked her short dress right up round her slender waist and pulled open the slit of her drawers.

'I have heard tell of this,' said he with reluctance, 'but I don't think we should discuss it.'

'Why ever not, Hedley?' she cried. 'You owe me a secret.'

'Because it concerns adults,' he temporised.

The attempt to bar all further consideration of the topic was a mistake, as Hedley quickly realised, for it confirmed her suspicion that here lay a mystery of great interest, and fired her to pursue her quest for it. Hedley stared down open-mouthed to see her fingers stretching open her almost bare little slit, and a moment later she had somehow managed to get the swollen purple head of Mr Harry Horn inside.

'No – we mustn't do that!' he gasped.

His fingers were roaming ineffectually over her slender thighs, in a half-hearted attempt to put a stop to

Adelaide's games. Undeterred, she pushed slowly forward against him, and he observed how his shaft stretched her virginal little cunny to twice or three times its normal size.

'Stop there, while it still feels nice,' he implored her. 'Any more and it will hurt you!'

The urgency of his words, and his expression of mingled anxiety and pleasure, had its effect on her. She ceased to edge closer, and no more of his eight-inch length than the head was swallowed up. Not that her madcap experiment was at an end – for she placed her small hands on his shoulders and leaned forward to kiss his mouth, while she twitched against him.

Her hot kiss and the movements of her loins were equally inexpert – but together they set Hedley's blood racing faster in his veins. The thought that by seizing her waist and jerking his shaft a dozen times he could deflower and roger this pretty girl was too much for him. He felt the sap starting to race up his rod, and in another second it would fill her slit in a delirium of sensation! He dragged it out of her in the very nick of time, and with a long gasping moan of heavenly enjoyment, he gushed his copious flood against her belly.

'No, not yet!' Adelaide cried, and he realised that she fully expected to be carried up to the climax, and was afraid that it was all over before she had reached her goal.

Hedley put his hand between her legs, and a finger between the wet lips of her dilated split, to rub her little bud until she shuddered and bit his lips, and then sank limply against his chest. He looked at her, pulling her wet drawers open, to see in utter astonishment the traces of what she had enticed him to do – the white sap trickling down her flat little belly to her almost hairless motte.

'Adelaide, my dearest girl,' he whispered in her ear, 'you must go to your room and wipe yourself dry at once.'

She giggled and kissed him, and retorted that he must wipe the piano keys, or Victorina would make an embarrassing discovery next time she played.

CHAPTER 6
A Most Candid Confession

On their late return to The Larches from Georgina's engagement party, Victorina was very fatigued. The dancing, the excitement of being in company, a glass or two of champagne – and above all the ecstatic sensations to which Hedley had subjected her in the carriage during the journey home – all had combined to exhaust her. Although it was well after midnight, Mrs Hapgood was sitting up, awaiting their return, the servants being in bed long ago.

She was in the drawing-room, and laid out on the sideboard was a large tray of sandwiches, covered over with a fine linen cloth, in the event that the young people were in urgent need of nourishment before retiring. Victorina kissed her Mama goodnight, saying that it had been a most marvellous evening, and went upstairs. Hedley was feeling distinctly peckish after his exertions and announced he would stay down for long enough to eat a sandwich or two.

'Then I shall stay and keep you company, Hedley,' said Mrs Hapgood, 'for there are several serious matters that I wish to discuss with you.'

Hedley threw himself onto a sofa while Mrs Hapgood brought the plate of sandwiches to him, before going to the dining-room to fetch a heavy silver tray with a siphon and a decanter and glasses.

'A little brandy,' said she, pouring a stiff one for him.

It may well be that her motives were innocent in this, but it may also be that she had observed that Hedley was a good halfway along the road to intoxication from the considerable quantities of champagne he had imbibed during the evening. He drank off the brandy very thoughtlessly while he was eating a ham sandwhich, and made no demur when Mrs Hapgood refilled his glass from the decanter.

For twenty minutes or so she asked questions about the party and whether Hedley had enjoyed himself. She enquired who was there among the guests, what music was played, how many times had he danced with Victorina, what other young gentlemen had partnered her in dances . . . all of the conversation was pointless and so dull that Hedley emptied several more glasses of brandy without thinking what he was doing.

Eventually, when Mrs Hapgood observed that she had made him drunk beyond redemption, she turned her questioning to the real topic of her interest. She approached it with great delicacy and good form, as befitted a lady of her position, but by slow stages it was borne in on Hedley that she was enquiring about his ability to be a vigorous husband to her daughter.

'You may make your mind easy on that score,' he answered, trying to speak without slurring his words. 'Everything is in good order and I am healthy and hot-natured.'

'I believed the same of my late husband,' said she, 'but in the event he proved to be a sad disappointment.'

Hedley stared at his future mother-in-law owlishly, trying to take in what she was saying.

'Am I to understand,' he began, then forgot what form of polite words he had intended to use, 'that the late Mr Hapgood was not . . . did not . . . was unable . . . could not provide you with your full marital rights? I mean, surely he must have, for the living testimony is your two beautiful daughters . . .'

'Mr Hapgood did not deny me the proper rights of a wife,' she replied primly, 'but never more than once a fortnight. More than that he believed to be injurious to the health.'

'Good Lord!' said Hedley. 'Once a fortnight! My word!'

Mrs Hapgood leaned forward in her chair and poured more pale golden brandy into his glass.

'You surely understand that I wish to reassure myself that my dear daughter Victorina will be spared the frustrations that were my fate in marriage,' she said. 'How often would you think right and proper, when Victorina is your wife?'

'Every night,' said he, grinning at her, 'twice.'

'Hedley – coarse jests and foolish boasting are wholly inappropriate when we are talking of a matter as serious as this. What you have said makes me think that you are without experience of the intimacies of life, for not even a Frenchman would expect to achieve that rate of frequency. I greatly fear that you are as unsullied as my dear daughter. Tell me frankly, and I will not hold it against you, have you ever had relations with a woman?'

'Lots of times,' he answered, made reckless by the brandy.

'This conversation is extremely distasteful to me, as I am sure you understand,' she said, 'but I must ask you to set my mind at rest – what sort of women?'

'Not whores,' he said quickly, 'I have never been with one of those for money.'

'Do not dare utter that word in my presence?' she cried.

'My deepest apologies,' he muttered, grinning foolishly.

'I ask you again, what sort of women – married women?' she demanded. 'Must I accept that you have committed adultery?'

'Why, yes, to be sure,' he answered, much puzzled by her attitude, 'many a time. But a lot of the girls I know in London are not married, so the question of adultery and coveting another man's wife doesn't arise.'

'You are providing me with very unwelcome evidence of loose living, Hedley! I never dreamed it of you!'

'A chap has to sow his wild oats,' said he stoutly. 'You had an unusual experience with Mr Hapgood – take it from me that most men are hot-blooded, and unless they can release their nervous tensions regularly, their health suffers.'

'You are twenty-three now, Hedley – at what age did you first embark on this career of licentiousness?'

If Hedley had been sober he would never have considered giving an answer to a question of that sort, and by the same token, Mrs Hapgood would never have dared to ask it. Sober he was not – the plentiful supply of brandy had done its work, and Hedley was drunk enough to enjoy relating to her his earliest encounter with sexual pleasures.

'I was sixteen at the time,' he said with a broad smile.

'Heavens!' cried Mrs Hapgood. 'A mere boy! How is it even possible that at so tender an age you could take an interest in matters of this kind?'

'Bit of an accident, really,' he mumbled with a grin. 'You know my mother died when I was born, and my father left all of my early upbringing to nurse-maids

and female servants. One day, because of some mis-
demeanour, the maid who was then looking after me
gave me a spanking – this was a fairly frequent
occurrence, for I was never a dutiful child. But on this
day, when she unbuttoned my trousers and took them
down to beat me, suddenly my male part was stiff – and I
was so ashamed that I could feel my face burning red.'

'Merciful heaven!' exclaimed Mrs Hapgood. 'What
scenes of iniquity – I am appalled, Hedley!'

'Mabel, that was her name,' he went on cheerfully,
unaware of the distress he was causing his hostess, 'she
said nothing and seemed not to notice the reason for my
shame. She sat down on a kitchen chair and took me
across her knees, and while she was smacking my bare
bottom, to my astonishment her other arm slid under my
waist and she took hold of my affair. Oh yes, she had
noticed my stiffness and she was taking advantage of it!
She tugged at it in a curious and way, and as you may
imagine, it did not take her long to achieve what she
aimed at. A most powerful sensation seized me, the like
of which I had not known before – in short, I had an
emission for the first time, and sprayed my virgin essence
on her apron.'

'Monstrous!' Mrs Hapgood moaned. 'Not another
word!'

Her intimate and unusual enquiries into Hedley's
abilities to promote her daughter's marital bliss had
revealed more than she could ever have expected. Her
clasped hands trembled in her lap and she was blushing a
fierce red but Hedley was too drunk to heed her words
and happily continued with the account of his sentimental education.

'After that first time, this fascinating new game
became a daily occurrence,' said he, 'but without the

spanking, for I had fallen so in love with Mabel then that I behaved well, to please her. The frolic she devised was to seat herself and have me stand between her legs, and she would pull her clothes up to her waist and open her drawers to show me how she differed from me. In this position she would play with my stiff dickie until I shot my boyish offering over her brunette fur. This game continued throughout my holidays from public school.'

Mrs Hapgood had recovered enough of her composure of mind to give his story her critical attention, and she recognised that as proof of his ability to honour a wife's privileges there was a fatal flaw of weakness in it. She resumed her questioning, to satisfy herself that her daughter would be in proper hands.

'Your disgraceful story merely serves to convince me that in the hands of a depraved female you are capable up to a certain point,' said she. 'Nevertheless, what you have described is far from the intimacies of the marriage-bed. I must ask you to tell me if you have ever had correct relations with a woman.'

'You mean lying on her back with her legs open?' he asked, somewhat puzzled by her disbelieving tone. 'Hundreds, if not thousands – who bothers to keep count? I started before I left public school and kept going right up until I fell in love with Victorina and asked her to marry me.'

In his intoxicated state, Hedley thought himself to be very cunning to slip in the lie about stopping poking when he began to be seriously attracted to Victorina. Mrs Hapgood appeared not to notice his assumed virtue.

'I am truly appalled by your dissolute relevations!' she exclaimed, pressing a hand to her plump and heaving bosom as if to calm its palpitation. 'One hears of unspeakable acts taking place amongst the unfortunate in the slums of the East End of London – whole families living and sleeping in one room, young girls depraved by their fathers and brothers, married woman sharing a bed with their growing sons, girl children becoming mothers! These people are little better than wild animals who know no better – but you are the only son of a gentleman of means and family! How is it possible that your early life has been so utterly tainted with vice?'

In her condition of agitation, she recharged his glass with brandy, although he had already disposed of more than enough to loosen his tongue.

'Ah, yes, my respected Papa,' he said, 'he's the one to blame, you know. His business is in the importation of essential oils – rose, bergamot, lavender, and the like – and he travels extensively about the countries of Europe to purchase from those who supply him. I saw little of him before I was sent away to school, and not much more when I went home on holidays. The summer I turned seventeen he was away about his affairs in the Balkans and he arranged for me to spend the school holidays with his unmarried sister. She has a small income of her own and lives simply, though comfortably, with just one servant, in a pretty villa at Potters Bar.'

'Spare me any further details,' said Mrs Hapgood in dismay, 'You betrayed your aunt's trust by seducing her maid while her back was turned!'

Not a bit of it!' exclaimed Hedley with an idiotic grin on his face. 'Aunt Maude seduced me.'

Mrs Hapgood stared at him wild-eyed, unable to believe her own ears. Her mouth hung open and her face was pale. Hedley, slumped down on the sofa, rambled on.

'I'd always thought of her as my maiden aunt,' said he, 'but the events of my stay with her that summer changed my view – Maude was no maiden. It began after lunch one day, when we sat talking in her sitting-room, side by side on a sofa. For a long time I didn't twig what she was about, but she had set out to deliberately put my high-strung nervous system on edge. She brushed gently against my shoulder and thigh, and soon she had aroused me to a condition of great excitement. My peg was stiff in my trouser leg, I can tell you!'

'How old was your Aunt?' Mrs Hapgood asked faintly.

'She's a year or two older than my Papa – she would be forty-three or forty-four when this happened.'

'But what sort of woman can she be!' Mrs Hapgood exclaimed incredulously, 'to seduce a boy of seventeen?'

'A fine big well-fleshed woman,' said Hedley in a tone of warm approval, 'not unlike you, if I may say so, though I think she dyes her hair because it is always jet-black, without even a single grey hair to be seen.'

'What happened between you and this wicked person?' Mrs Hapgood asked in an expiring voice. 'I shudder to think what you are going to tell me, but I feel that as Victorina's mother it is my duty to know the worst.'

'Aunt Maude turned a little towards me and drew me to her bosom,' Hedley explained obligingly, 'while her fingers crept across my thigh and into the buttons of my trousers. I could hardly believe my luck when I felt her pulling them open, one by one, until she could get hold of my hard-on.'

In the commotion that reigned in her mind, Mrs Hapgood failed to notice that Heldey's intoxication had reached a point where he had applied a most vulgar description to his male part – or if she did notice it, she let it pass unchecked.

'I've always been a forward sort of fellow,' he said with tipsy cheeriness, 'and so I returned the compliment by reaching under Aunt Maude's clothes, and straight up between her legs to the source of delight. That was one of the most memorable moments of my life – to feel under my fingers her curly hair and warm flesh – it was bliss beyond my imagination. It was impossible to control myself any longer – I was gasping for breath and I spouted a jet of hot essence into the hand that was caressing me.'

Mrs Hapgood's face was a study in turmoil, as her insulted modesty warred with her natural curiosity. When she spoke, it was with difficulty, for her breathing had become irregular.

'This is merely a repetition of what happened to you at the hands of the maid-servant,' she said. 'You have yet to convince me that you have any experience of the correct union of male and female.'

'I'm coming to that,' Hedley answered. 'I beg you not to rush my happy childhood memories! Maude gave me a few minutes to recover and then showed me how to pull up her dress and her petticoats to expose her stockings and drawers. She herself opened the slit of her drawers and showed me her brown-haired split. To be truthful, I knew what a cunny looked like from my games with Mabel, but I'd never touched one before, not even Mabel's, for she never allowed that.'

The expression 'cunny' brought a gasp from Mrs Hapgood's lips. She stared at Heldey in a most accusing way and solemnly declaimed:

'A man may not marry his father's sister – those are the very words set down in the Book of Common Prayer you use every Sunday in church. That being so, it follows that a man may not uncover the nakedness of his father's sister. You have sinned, Hedley, grievously and un-pardonably.'

'I expect you're right,' he said, giving not the least sign that he understood the gravity of her words, 'even though Aunt Maude uncovered her own nakedness to show me. I thought it was the nicest thing I'd ever seen, especially when she lay down on the sofa and helped me lie on top of her. She took hold of my peg, which was stiff as a poker again, and guided it to her opening – the instant I felt it touching warm flesh, with one push I was up her – up a woman for the first time in my life!'

All that he had drunk was fast rendering Hedley unconscious – he was slumped so far down on the sofa that he was almost on his back, his legs sticking out across the carpet. His eyes were nine-tenths closed and his voice was so low and wavering that Mrs Hapgood could hardly make out his maunderings.

'What did you say?' she asked. 'I didn't hear that.'

'Maude was crying out *Give it to me, my darling boy*,' Hedley went on, ignoring the request to repeat himself, '*Give me your sweet virgin sap* – or something like that, and she was squirming about underneath me and I was rogering her like a good 'un! In about thirty seconds flat I shot off in her like a fire brigade hose-pipe, and Maudie kept on kissing me and saying, *I've made a man of you, Hedley*.'

His story ended, he lasped into silence and fell asleep, and Mrs Hapgood stared at him for some time, her mind in a complete turmoil at what she had heard, and her hands clutching at the padded arms of her chair. Eventually she roused him and helped him slowly up the stairs to his room, being reluctant to fetch a servant to assist her and so allow him be seen in a condition of drunkenness.

With an arm about his waist to support him and to guide his faltering steps, she got him into his room, his head lolling on her shoulder and most of his weight on her. He was blissfully unaware of where he was and what was going on about him, but his eyes opened for a while when he found himself sitting on the side of his bed. In the soft glow of the gas light turned half-down, Mrs Hapgood was helping him off with his cravat.

He had no knowledge of her undressing him completely, but he was shaken awake by a hand on his shoulder to find himself flat on his back on the bed, his trousers off and Mrs Hapgood asking for an explanation of the wet stain on his underwear.

'Must have fetched off,' he mumbled, unable to remember.

'I know that!' she said, shaking him again to keep him awake. 'But when – and in what circumstances? I dare not let myself think that you would stoop so low as to take advantage of my daughter's affections and tamper with her honour!'

'Certainly not!' said he, his voice slurred and thick. 'My darling little fiancee is as pure as the driven snow!'

'Then how did this shameful emission come about? I insist that you tell me! After what you have told me of yourself, I am in fear of how very close my innocent daughter has come to being dishonoured!'

'Her virtue is as safe in my hands as if it were in the Bank of England,' he said vaguely, not at all sure what he meant, but believing that it sounded well.

'Do you give me your word as a gentleman?' she demanded.

'You have my word. Damned peculiar though – to fetch off and not be able to remember when,' he mumbled, his mind so fuddled that he had no concept of

89

what he was saying, 'did you handle me downstairs?'

'Hedley!' she cried, outraged by so atrociously insulting a suggestion, but her indignation went unheard, for Hedley had fallen asleep.

When he woke up again, he found himself lying on top of the bed with his legs apart, his frilly evening shirt up round his chest, and Mrs Hapgood lying beside him. The light was still burning and she gave the appearance of examining Mr John Thomas closely, for she had him in the palm of her hand, with her face within a hand-span of him. She also appeared to have removed most of her clothing, down to her chemise and drawers. Hedley stared uncomprehendingly for a while and then dozed off again.

He knew that he was dreaming when he found himself lying on top of Mrs Hapgood, her chemise pulled up to display her broad and plump white belly, her legs widely parted and her drawers open to show a handsome bush of dark hair. She was pushing her belly up at him, and though his mind could not grasp her words, there could be no doubt that she was urging him to roger her – and waking or sleeping, Hedley had never in his life refused.

At the first push his rod failed to go in. He knew that the direction was the right one, for he was holding her slit open with thumb and forefinger, but something was amiss – and it did not take long to discern what it was. Dismay overtook Hedley's confused mind, for there below him lay a woman offering him her ready commodity, and for the first time in his life his peg had failed him. Try as he might, it would not rise to the occasion.

Mrs Hapgood felt down his belly and took his limp affair in her hand, to shake it briskly and chafe it between her fingers, hoping to arouse its interest. All was without avail, for it remained obstinately limp and small. 'It is the brandy,' she said in tones of great disappointment, and with those words in his mind, Hedley fell asleep once again.

The next time he awoke, it was to acute thrills of pleasure, and he found Mrs Hapgood on top of him. How she had managed it, he neither knew or cared. The yellow gas light revealed that she was now stark naked, and she was seated astride his belly. Her big breasts had become slack with the years, and without the support of her corset, they hung down weightily. Hedley put out his hand to reach for them, but she took his wrists and held his arms pinioned to the pillows.

With a drunken giggle, Hedley raised his head and tried to suck her long dangling bubbies. For a while he couldn't catch either of them in his mouth, though he tried hard enough, going first for one and then for the other, as if he were bobbing for crab apples on Allhallows Eve. Finally he managed to get hold of one between his lips, for all the world like a baby sucking, while Mrs Hapgood rode him in stately rhythm.

Through the haziness of his intoxication, Hedley could feel how her cunny gripped and milked him, with a determination and skill he had never before experienced.

'You are . . .' he said in approval, releasing her right breast from his eager mouth, and then forgot what he had intended, and was compelled to fall silent.

'What am I?' she asked, rising up and down on his belly as if she sat a trotting horse. 'What am I, Hedley – as shameless as you. Am I as debauched as you are? Am I given over to vice and depravity, as you have confessed tonight that you are?'

'You are . . .' he tried again, and was again defeated.

'Do I disgust you?' she demanded. 'Am I too old and

ungainly to please a handsome young man about town like you? I'm still younger than your Aunt when she first had you. But perhaps you would prefer me to cease what I am doing and go to my own room – is that what you want? You only have to say!'

'No, no!' gasped he, horrified at the mere thought that his pleasure might be abruptly terminated. 'Keep on doing it – it is very agreeable and I beg you not to stop!'

'Then what am I?' she asked again. 'How were you about to describe me? As a whore?'

'You are a surprise packet,' he said, jerking up his loins to meet her downward thrust. 'A lovely warm snug horn-gripping surprise packet! Give me your bubbie!'

Mrs Hapgood leaned forward to pin his wrists tight to the pillows so that he was powerless to use his hands on her, while she dangled the tip of a long soft breast above his open mouth. He sucked at it greedily, while her cunny milked him with such artistry that in another minute or two she brought him off.

The spasms were delicious and he could not hold back his cry of ecstasy – a most violent shuddering overcame him and her together as his hot fluid bounded up his thick shaft of flesh. At once Mrs Hapgood flung her heavy body forward over him, her hot mouth on his mouth to silence his cries, while he shook as if in a high fever, and gushed into her wet cunny.

CHAPTER 7
A Sunday Afternoon Walk

On Sunday morning, when Milly awoke Hedley with the usual cup of tea and biscuit, he had no desire to pull up his nightshirt and expose his shaft to her – for he sat up slowly with a pale face, the vilest of headaches, and a queasy stomach. The maid took pity on him and went for a Seidlitz powder for his biliousness, stirred it in a glass of water, and held his head while he drank down the effervescent mixture. He lay down again for a while, with closed eyes, waiting for his wretchedness to settle a little.

The events of the night before were completely blurred in his mind. He had a shadowy recollection of standing in the dark and licking Georgina Playfair's big white breasts, and he felt a certain trepidation that he might have disgraced himself at her engagement party. He thought he had had a feel of Victorina on the way home, and he further thought he might have rogered her in the carriage, but it was impossible to be sure.

There was the vaguest memory of being offered a sandwich by Mrs Hapgood and talking to her alone. It seemed that there was something she had wanted to know – that much had stuck in his mind – but no hint of what it was lingered in his recollection now. There was a peculiar area of blankness – he had no memory whatsoever of getting to his room and undressing for bed. He thought he'd had strange dreams in the night – about Auntie Maude, perhaps, but he couldn't be sure.

Hedley had been drunk plenty of times before and had woken up the next day to foggy memories, but never on so extensive a scale. This was the rummest go he'd ever had, but it all would come back eventually, if his past experience was anything to go on. In half an hour he felt strong enough to rise from his bed and shave, nicking himself twice, and then dress.

He was the last down to breakfast and took his seat with no appetite. He asked for coffee instead of tea, and after several cups was well enough to eat two or three scrambled eggs with a slice of dry toast. The ladies rallied him a little, though in perfect good nature, on his crapulousness, and as soon as he could escape from the table, he went for a turn around the garden to clear his head.

At half past the hour of ten, in their Sunday finery, Hedley and the Hapgoods set off together in the carriage for church. Beside him on the carriage seat, facing rearwards, sat dearest Victorina, delicious in a jade green dress and braided jacket to match, cut artfully to throw into prominence her full and swelling bosom, and to show to good advantage the slenderness of her darling waist. On her head was perched a hat with a long and curling ostrich feather that was very eye-catching.

Adelaide sat beside her mother, with her prayer book in her gloved hands and eyes cast down – the very picture of young-girl purity in a white dress with a pink sash and bow, and a straw boater hat on her head. Hedley himself was attired in a most elegant suit of clerical grey, which somewhat accentuated the pallor of his face caused by last night's drinking bout. He wore a new black silk top-hat, and had a rosebud buttonhole, picked for him in the garden that morning by Victorina.

Mrs Hapgood, seated opposite Hedley, their knees almost touching in the confines of the carriage, was extremely regal in steel-grey satin trimmed with velvet black ribbons, but to him it seemed that her manner was cooler than ordinary, and he became anxious that he had in some way unwittingly offended her the previous evening. He spoke to her with all the friendliness he could muster, but her curt replies let him understand that she was in no mood for conversation.

Heldey had always enjoyed Morning Service on Sundays, and at St Cuthbert's there was ample opportunity for sturdy hymn-singing. His headache had abated and he joined in 'All Things Bright and Beautiful' with a will, gazing with adoration at Victorina's lovely face as he sang the words. She blushed a pretty pink and rewarded him with a delightful little smile. Hedley's heart beat faster and, remembering he was to take her for a walk that afternoon, the seemingly lifeless Lord Dickie twitched faintly.

The only tedious part of Divine Service, for Hedley, was the sermon. The Reverend Quintin Gutteridge mounted the pulpit in his freshly-laundered white and violet vestments, his gold-rimmed spectacles gleaming with goodwill and piety, to announce that his text was taken from the Book of Zechariah: 'Thus speaketh the Lord of Hosts, saying, Behold the man whose name is THE BRANCH; and he shall grow up out of his place, and he shall build the temple of the Lord.'

The pew was hard to sit upon, and Hedley became very swiftly bored while the Vicar droned on to expound his obscure text. He let his thoughts drift to less exalted considerations and into his mind came a memory that caused him to suppress a gasp. He had suddenly remembered what it was he had dreamed in the night – and it was astonishing! In his mind's eye was a vision of Mrs Hapgood stark naked, sitting astride his belly, with great slack bubbies dangling over his face!

If the Reverend Gutteridge had glanced down from the pulpit at Hedley, he would have congratulated himself that his sermon was giving food for thought to one member of his congregation, for a look of profound concentration had spread over Hedley's face while he was exploring the memory of his dream further. He thought that he'd tried to get hold of her long bubbies for a good feel, but she held his wrists and pinned his arms to the pillows while she rode him.

What a perfectly marvellous dream, thought Hedley; it went to show what the imagination could run to, when inspired by brandy and champagne. He'd dreamed that he'd got the end of one of her dangling bubbies in his mouth and had a good suck at it. She had a fat belly and a big bush of dark brown hair – he remembered well now – and he fetched off in her cunny. It had been a 'wet dream', as the vulgar phrase had it, and he must have soaked his nightshirt!

It was odd that he hadn't woken up at the moment of emission, as he always had before, but he had been very tipsy last night, no doubt of that. It was odder still that he'd dreamed of rogering Mrs Hapgood, rather than Victorina, or even Adelaide, but the mind was a surprise packet of the unexpected when it was opened. That expression jolted his memory again, and he looked along the pew, past Victorina, to her mother, who was gazing up at the preaching Vicar with an expression of incomprehension on her face.

Hedley's breath was checked in his throat by a disconcerting possibility that presented itself – *had it been a dream*? In the past, after evenings of drinking with his friends, he had often experienced very vivid dreams. That apart, the memory of lying naked on his back and being rogered by Mrs Hapgood was now so real in his mind that he hardly knew what to believe. He glanced along the pew at her again, studying the weight of her bosom under her steel-grey dress and assessing it against the recollection of his dream.

There was a coherence about this perplexing memory that very often failed in dreams. At the climax, she had not vanished into thin air and left him to spurt his essence into his nightclothes – he had a very clear vision of naked Mrs Hapgood flinging herself down on him to stop his mouth with her own while he shot up her. On the other hand, he had not the least memory of her dismounting afterwards and going away.

Moreover, in the dream he had been as stark naked as she was – but he had woken up this morning in his nightshirt. I must know the truth of it! he exclaimed to himself silenty. Had he truly committed this astounding deed? Had he really come off up Vickie's Mama in the dead of night – or was his imagination guilty of a fearful insult to that respected lady? Surely it was a dream – but he felt that he would go mad with uncertainty unless he got to the bottom of it!

Torment his mind how he might, there was no way Hedley could come at the truth of it. The Vicar's sermon went unheard as more and more confusing pictures of Mrs Hapgood's naked person were unfurled in his mind – some of them extemely stirring in their effect on him. By half past twelve Morning Service was ended, and the little family embarked for home and luncheon. The carriage was uncomfortably crowded on the homeward journey, for the Reverend Quintin Gutteridge travelled with them.

He and Mrs Hapgood were friends of many years standing. He was a gentleman of fifty, or thereabouts, a widower, somewhat plump, amiable of disposition, well-regarded by the well-to-do members of his flock, and by the deserving poor of the parish. He was invited to lunch at The Larches on one Sunday in four, and on this particular day he shared the forward-facing seat of the crriage with Mrs Hapgood, whilst Adelaide squeezed herself between Victorina and Hedley.

For Hedley the drive was a nightmare – Adelaide wriggled her body against him and rubbed her thigh against his to inflame his passions. She seized upon every excuse to lean across him and point out through the window some trivial feature of the passing landscape – each time her slender body screened the movements of her hand and she felt in Hedley's lap and gave Mr Harry Horn a good squeeze. Long before Tom turned the matched pair into the drive, Hedley had difficulty in concealing his inconvenient stiffness.

At luncheon Adelaide was seated corner-wise from Hedley and she proceeded to throw him into near panic by rubbing Mr Harry Horn under the table with her foot. She unbuttoned one of her shoes and put her stockinged foot up between his knees, pressing hard against his trouser buttons and with her nimble toes massaging what she could feel under the cloth. Hedley was terrified that this very indecent play would be discovered – and in the presence of a clergyman!

He clamped his thighs together to discourage the sly minx, but with an angelic expression on her pretty face she pressed her stockinged foot hard between his legs and refused to be budged. Hedley sat tight against the table, the damask cloth covering what was going on, and did his best to participate in the general conversation, whilst Adelaide's busy little foot was nearly making him spend.

At three the Vicar took his leave, Mrs Hapgood retired to her room for her usual afternoon rest, and Hedley was at last at liberty to take his fiancee for the long-awaited walk. The queasiness with which he had been afflicted in the morning was gone and he led her gently through the wicket gate into the paddock, then to the five-barred gate of hallowed memory. Here, he observed, a charming pink blush touched Victorina's cheeks, for this was the sacred spot on which Lord Dickie had pierced her maiden slit for the first time.

They went on across the meadow, towards a spinney that stood on a slight rise, well away from the footpath. At Hedley's suggestion they rested, seating themselves on the grass in the shade of the trees, and after they had satisfied themselves that they were alone and unobserved, he put his arms about her and kissed her. Emboldened by the warmth with which Victorina returned his kiss, he removed with gentle care her hat with the curling ostrich feathers and drew her to the ground, so that they lay face to face in the sweet-smelling grass.

He told her how much he loved her, and kissed her again. She opened her mouth a little to inhale his passionate breath, then touched his lips with the tip of her tongue, but timidly, as if frightened by her own forwardness. His hug made her bolder, and she slipped her tongue into his mouth, and after a while, she thrust it in and out, almost as if she were enticing him to perform a similar action on her lovely body. His hand crept up her petticoats until it lay between her thighs.

'Oh, I shall swoon Hedley!' she whispered, her legs locked together to prevent any further advance. 'I am not strong enough to bear these emotions, my dearest! Do you truly love me – tell me how matters stand – my life depends on it!'

'How can you doubt me for an instant, after all we have been to each other?' he sighed.

'Perhaps we have been too much to each other,' she replied. 'I have been told that there are men who deceive those who love them, and take advantage of their trust, by professing eternal devotion, when all that they are after is a cheap thrill.'

'A cheap thrill! Good Lord – who has been speaking to you in such vulgar terms?' Hedley asked, most displeased to have his bout of rogering brought to a standstill before it had even begun. 'Was it your Mama?'

'No, if you must know, it was Georgina. She was telling me how very properly Miles behaves towards her at all times. He has kissed her on the lips only once – when she accepted his proposal of marriage. I asked her if she knew whether every gentleman behaves so towards his betrothed, and she told me she had heard that some did not, though she was quite certain that you behaved as correctly as Miles. I blushed at her words and would have hidden my face if I had been able. I am sure that she guessed my secret shame.'

In the privacy of his thoughts Hedley damned Georgina for a mischief-maker. He was convinced she had set these doubts in Victorina's mind because he had stirred up her emotions by his talk of love, and by licking her bare white bubbies. Heaven alone knew what she might have said to Victorina if Hedley had gone so far as to feel her cunny in the dark conservatory! He determined to have his own back on Miss Georgina – and at the very first opportunity – by removing her troublesome virginity.

'There was no need to be put out by her words,' he assured Victorina. 'It is very likely that she was not telling you the truth. You must not believe all you hear.'

'But Georgina would never tell an untruth – most especially not to me!' exclaimed Victorina. 'We have been friends since we were children! She is the soul of honour!'

'As are you, my lovely innocent girl,' said he. 'But only consider this – you would never tell an untruth to her. Yet you feel under no obligation, for all your long friendship, to tell her of the private joys between you and me. With good reason, for these are the deep and solemn secrets of love, and too precious to divulge.'

'But are you suggesting that she has allowed Miles to take liberties with her?' she asked, a puzzled look on her face.

'I take leave to doubt this assertion of hers that Miles has enjoyed no more than one brief kiss,' Hedley answered.

'But he would never dare go as far as you have,' she said with a blush and a little stammer of bashfulness, 'not Miles!'

'No one else knows what takes place between two people who love each other and are to be married,' he told her. 'Whatever your friend may tell you, I do not sincerely believe that she will stand a maiden at the altar on the day of her wedding.'

To dispel the confusion and doubt he saw on Victorina's face, he vowed that he loved her beyond reason and life itself, and with that, before she could ask any more inconvenient questions he drew her tongue into his mouth and sucked it. He took his hand from between her thighs to unbutton his trousers, and taking hold of her dainty hand he put it into the gap, and under his shirt. Her fingers tightened on Lord Dickie and her bosom rose and fell swiftly in her braided green jacket.

Her beautiful face was a fiery red, and when Hedley put his hand under her petticoats again, her thighs fell loosely away from each other. She uttered a little sob of pleasure mingled with shame while she let his fingers advance until he touched the silky curls that covered her slit. 'My darling girl,' he sighed, and he tickled the soft and warm lips that lay under his sensitive fingers. All this was delightful and Hedley was in no hurry to spoil his pleasure by ending it too soon.

After five or ten minutes of delicious handling of each other, he pulled up her skirts, his tongue in her mouth, and rolled over to lie between her parted legs. He tucked his shirt up to bare his belly, and lifted the front of her green dress well up and turned it back upon her, then the same with her petticoats, to expose her grey silk stockings. Lastly he turned up her chemise to uncover her pretty drawers, and untied the string, leaving her sweet dimpled belly as bare as his own.

He stared in ecstasy at her beautiful thighs, gleaming white, then at the brown silky hair of her bush and the pouting lips of her cunny. Lord Dickie jumped so hard in Victorina's hand that Hedley thought he was about to spend. He leaned over his beloved to press his hot mouth to her slit for a moment, before he got between her legs and supported himself on one arm while he brought the head of Lord Dickie to the right spot and pressed in slowly.

'Oh, Hedley,' cried she, 'you are so masterful!'

With a long thrust he was deep within her, and her tender flesh clasped and sucked at his peg. He let her feel his full weight on her body, and treated her to a bout of hard rogering. He was breathing quickly, panting almost, as he worked on her, causing thrilling tremors to shake her from head to foot. All too soon he felt himself about to spend and pulled out of her warm slit, letting his essence rush out in thick jets on her quivering belly. Her body stiffened in ecstatic spasms, she uttered a tiny shriek and collapsed fainting beneath him.

Hedley eased himself off Victorina, who lay limp and only partly-conscious, pulled down her petticoats with a gentle hand and did up his trouser-buttons. In a few moments Victorina was sitting up, her clothes perfectly arranged again and her hat on her head. Hedley raised her to her feet and she allowed him to lead her further into the spinney, to where they could sit behind a tall tree, well hid from any who might pass in the meadow. He unbuttoned her jacket and the bodice of her green dress, and pulled down her chemise so that he could get at her bubbies and kiss and suck them. She denied him nothing, apparently satisfied that his passion went beyond the mere desire for a 'cheap thrill'.

When they lay down to consummate their rapture, she told him that she was somewhat wearied from the overwhelming force of the emotions he had made her experience the first time. Hedley assured her that he knew how to be gentle, and turned her on her side, facing away from him. He raised her clothes over her bottom and put his hand in through the rearward slit of her drawers, his heart pounding like a hammer on an anvil at the remembrance of how he had enjoyed her the first time, standing at the gate.

With his fingers he first opened the soft lips of her cunny and ripped open his trousers and took hold of Lord Dickie, revelling in the feel of the thickness and strength in his palm. He brought the swollen head up to the curly-haired lips between Victorina's thighs and pushed in.

At the feel of his manly shaft piercing her, Victorina began to shiver, and then she sobbed a little in helpless pleasure. When Hedley felt his shaft drenched with her delicious moisture, he thrust deeper into her, and gripped her tightly by the hips. A few bold strokes, and the whole of his shaft was in her, his belly pressed against her soft bottom – and he rode in and out easily, not wishing to tire her further.

'Oh, my dearest,' she cried, soon enough, 'I feel again the emotions that cause me alarm and delight at the same time.'

'Rid yourself of any lingering alarm,' he replied, 'here is only delight, my darling girl!'

'Yes!' cried she. 'If this is a cheap thrill, then so be it – I wish it could be prolonged forever!'

Hedley plunged faster, knowing she was now ready for it now, his arms round her to grasp her uncovered bubbies. Behind his closed eye-lids there had formed unbidden an image of Mrs Hapgood's long white bubbies dangling above his face, just out of reach of his hungry mouth.

'Oh, oh, oh!' sighed Hedley, quite powerless to banish the perverse picture from his mind.

As his frenzy mounted, the obsession gripped him tighter and he was hardly aware that his shaft was probing his fiancee's wet cunny with ruthless strength. He was half mad with passion and he stabbed ever more fiercely, shaking Victorina's frail body with his powerful thrusts, until at last the floodgates were opened and his tide of desire gushed into her.

She gasped out his name as if she were dying, and it

was too late to pull out of her now, even if he had the will – he would make her stand upright as soon as he had finished spending, to drain his vital fluid out of her! Such was his intention, but the muscles of Victorina's belly had contracted to grip his shaft and suck the last drop from him greedily. Only then did she give a long sigh and fall senseless against him.

CHAPTER 8
A Bone Is Picked

After the strenuous delights of his Sunday afternoon walk with Victorina across the meadows, Hedley rested on his bed for an hour or two before it was time to begin dressing for dinner. It had been an afternoon to remember, and he was in hope that the bliss it had brought him might be repeated later that evening, when the household was in bed and asleep. The contemplation of creeping silently into his beloved's room and playing with her in her own bed was so exciting that Johnny Jump-Up, true to his name despite his recent exertions in the spinney, rose to his full height.

The slight tinge of doubt that existed in Hedley's mind was whether Victorina would be recovered enough by bed-time to sustain his renewed advances. How many times could a tender young female come off in one day? That was the question to which he had no clear answer. Some ladies of his acquaintance in London had proved themselves capable of sustaining the climax half a dozen times before fatigue overtook them and slackened their naked limbs in restoring sleep.

Lottie Mayhew at Surbiton was not a lady, of course, not in any sense, and it had taken no less than ten repetitions of the sensual crisis to fell her – so worthy a partner for a romp had she shown herself to be! That aside, it had to be recognised that dearest Vickie was a sensitive young lady of eighteen, only just initiated into the joys of love. The sensations she experienced were so overwhelming that she was left half-swooning in delight each time that Hedley had rogered her.

To rehearse in his mind the joys of the afternoon occupied Hedley's attentions pleasurably for the longest time. He held Johnny Jump-Up in his hand in a comradely fashion, pleased that he had enjoyed his exercise that day. He was still pondering whether his lovely fiancee would be strong enough to lie on her back that night and take his throbbing shaft into her delicious young body, when a glance at his pocket-watch on the night-table suggested that he ought to start dressing for dinner.

He rose languidly from his bed and crossed the room, wearing only his shirt, to stand before the open window and breath in the golden evening sunshine and listen to the late trilling of birds. He gazed out in harmony of spirit, over the colourful flowerbeds, where a few striped bees still hummed drowsily in a last foray before they returned to their hive for the night.

He was deep in contemplation of the tranquil pleasures of the garden when there sounded a light tap at his door and, thinking that it was the maid bringing towels or popping in to turn down the bed, he did not trouble to call out. The door swung open, to admit Mrs Hapgood. She wore an oyster-grey evening-gown with a trim of jet beads round the neckline, but the stateliness of her appearance was overshadowed by the frowning ill-humour to be descried on her face.

Hedley felt himself blush to be caught half-dressed by his future mother-in-law, and stammered out hasty apologies, but she was in high dudgeon and hardly aware of his attire, much less put out by his lack of it. She instructed him sternly to sit down and listen, there being an urgent matter to be settled in private – a matter that would not wait. So saying, she took an arm-chair by the window, her back straight as a Grenadier's.

The situation in which he found himself was without parallel in Hedley's experience. Somewhat at a loss, he sat down on the side of his bed, tucked his shirt round his thighs as best he might, folded his arms and looked at his hostess in trepidation as he waited for her to broach the subject in her mind.

'Time is short,' she said, 'tomorrow you return to town and there will be no opportunity before you leave to speak to you.'

'I am at your service,' said he, wondering what on earth was in her mind to enter a gentleman's room in this way. It was of necessity a matter of the gravest import – with a sinking heart he concluded that she had found out somehow that he had rogered her daughter that very afternoon.

'I will not beat about the bush,' she began, giving all the nervous signs of one steeling herself to perform an unpleasant duty, 'last evening when you brought my daughter home from her friend's party, I made certain enquiries of you. As Victorina's mother I have the right and the duty to satisfy myself that she will be in good hands when she is a married woman.'

'I understand that,' said Hedley, greatly relieved that the delicious, though illicit, events of the afternoon seemed not to be the cause of Mrs Hapgood's ire, 'but I've been completely open with you about my prospects. My father promises to double my yearly allowance when I marry, and I am his only child and his sole heir – all this you know.'

'Your financial affairs are not in question,' Mrs Hapgood informed him in a tone of resentment. 'What is of the greatest concern to me is your moral character. On that I fear that I am far from being satisfied. Last evening you confessed such dreadful things to me that I am assailed by the gravest of doubts at the prospect of entrusting my dear child to you.'

Hedley stared at her open-mouthed.

'To be truthful,' he said with reluctance, 'I can't recall much of what I told you – I was slightly tipsy at the time. But I cannot believe that there was anything very discreditable.'

'You were in your cups,' she agreed coldly. 'You used low and vile words in my hearing – I was shocked beyond belief.'

'I say! Did I really?' Hedley exclaimed in dismay. 'What on earth did I blurt out?'

Mrs Hapgood transfixed him with a steely glare and snorted like a fractious horse.

'You can hardly expect me to soil my lips with words that would bring the blush of shame to the cheek of the lowest of the low,' she said.

'Did I swear and blaspheme?' Hedley asked, his spirits at a very low ebb, faced with this evidence of lack of moral fibre.

'At least I was spared that,' Mrs Hapgood breathed, turning her eyes upwards towards Heaven in thankfulness. 'You disgraced yourself irreparably by making use of obscene expressions to refer to certain portions of the female anatomy and to the marital act. I find it impossible to understand how a well-bred young gentleman can be aware of such gutter expressions.'

It was in Hedley's mind to make enquiry how a well-bred lady in her middle years could recognise and understand such words, but he thought it better not to enrage her further.

'That was awfully impolite of me,' he said, ignorant as to which particular words he could have used in a conversation of which he had no memory, 'I beg you will pardon me.'

Mrs Hapgood swept aside his apology with a flick of her hand and continued her accusations against him:

'Using expressions that would foul the lips of the lowest wretch in the vilest pot-house, you volunteered the information that you had been abused by a maid-servant when you were a boy – physically misused! Do you deny it?'

'Good Lord, did I tell you that?' exclaimed Hedley. 'I must have been blind drunk – I never before mentioned it to a soul. But it's pitching it a bit strong to call it being abused – it was no more than a game. Nevertheless, I trust that you will accept my humblest apologies for assaulting your modesty with a tale not fit for a lady's ears.'

'Then you do not deny it?' she said in an outraged tone.

'Deny that it happened? That would be pointless now,' said he, 'but I have a right to your pity and forgiveness, for I was a naive youth and did not know what Mabel was doing to me.'

'A single lapse I would forgive, if not understand,' replied Mrs Hapgood, 'but by your own account it became a daily habit – or have you forgotten you told me of standing in the closest proximity to the evil girl while she exposed herself to you and debauched you by hand over her person? You had the bare-faced effrontery to describe this scene of vice as *a frolic* – and to me, the mother of your intended bride! What have you to say for yourself now, sir?'

'I've been a fool,' said he.

His meaning was that he had been a fool to tell Mrs Hapgood of his childhood escapades, but she understood his words in the sense that he was reproaching himself for youthful folly.

'Yes, you have been a fool, and more than a fool, Hedley,' she said, her mouth pursed ominously. 'Your foolishness sank to the depths of viciousness worthy of Sodom and Gomorrah before they were destroyed by fire, when you uncovered the nakedness of your father's sister.'

'Good God!' cried he. 'Did I tell you about Aunt Maude? I must have been paralytic-drunk to divulge so much!'

'Yes, you told me about your abominable Aunt,' Mrs Hapgood confirmed, 'although I found it incredible to hear of such low, degenerate and unnatural passion in so young a man. You told me in an almost boastful fashion how that wicked woman bared her person in broad daylight and taught you immorality far beyond your years! You did a very wrong thing, Hedley – so very wrong indeed that the human mind can scarcely encompass the enormity of it. For all your life you are tainted by it.'

'Oh, surely not!' he said, aware that it would be fatal to smile at the exaggeration. 'I mean, having Auntie might look a bit rum to an outsider, and I won't pretend that the clergy would approve, but I was only a lad at the time.'

'Vice is ever quick to excuse itself,' Mrs Hapgood said sententiously. 'But the plain truth is that you are a moral leper. Take heed for your immortal soul, Hedley – tell me honestly now, was it that once only, or did you return again to your folly?'

'I cannot tell a lie,' said he, thinking to himself that he might as well be hung for a sheep as a lamb, 'after that first time, we had a little frolic on her sofa every afternoon. At night she let me sleep naked in her bed with her, and I have no need to tell you what jolly antics that led to, night after night. I was sorry when the hols were over and I had to go back to school.'

There was a lengthy silence, during which Mrs Hapgood stared at him, her plump face white as a sheet and her mouth hanging half-open. When she recovered her composure she spoke a tone more indicative of sorrow than anger.

'All this is very horrid for the mother of young girls to hear, Hedley, but I am an understanding person and I see all too well that you were led astray by those older and more experienced than yourself, the maid-servant and this reprobate relation of yours. But I would be failing abysmally in my responsibilities if I did not point out that these highly unfortunate early experiences do not inspire confidence for the present or the future. Even if we can put all this behind us, can you with hand on heart assure me that my innocent daughter has come to no moral harm at your hands?'

'Moral harm? What do you mean?'

'You have committed acts that no decent man should or ever would,' she explained. 'There is serious danger that Victorina had been degraded by close contact with you. Have you had the temerity to touch her – I must know!'

'You may set your mind at rest,' he lied stoutly. 'Dearest Vickie is an angel of virtue and purity – I would lay down my life before harming one hair on her head!'

'Thank God for that!' Mrs Hapgood cried fervently. 'I could not sleep a wink last night for the hideous terror that haunted me after listening to your foul confessions! The night was made terrible for me by visions of my sweet girl being sullied by your unclean hands!'

Hedley struggled with himself to suppress unworthy thoughts that rose into his mind at these words – happy memories of his hands eagerly 'sullying' Victorina's soft young breasts and of fingering her plump-lipped cunny. His present position, vis-a-vis her irate mother, was precarious, yet in spite of that, Johnny Jump-Up stirred underneath his shirt. Hedley smoothed the the cotton down his legs and as far over his knees as it would go, to cover his thighs from Mrs Hapgood's glare.

'Sleep easily tonight,' he said, trying to calm her fears, 'your darling girl is a clean-cut gem and I treasure her – she is in safe hands with me. No least breath of scandal shall ever besmirch her honour – she will stand beside me at the altar a virginal lily of purity, and after we are married I expect that married love will cause her to blossom like a rose in summer.'

'Do you regard yourself as an expert on married love?' Mrs Hapgood asked coldly. 'My understanding is that your experience of it has been with other men's wives.'

'My word – whatever gave you that idea?'

'You gave it to me. You stand condemned by your own words last evening, when you confessed to adultery on more than one occasion, and with more than one partner. After such a career of vice, how can you in all honesty imagine that you could ever be a suitable husband for my daughter?'

'My credentials for marrying Victorina are that I love her,' he answered pugnaciously. 'As for the rest, young men sow their wild oats and there is no point denying the fact, whether you approve of it or not.'

'Your so-called credentials are inadequate,' said she in

a cutting tone. 'I cannot for one moment consider letting my girl marry a lascivious degenerate such as you have admitted yourself to be. The engagement is at an end. I shall inform Victorina of that decision after dinner.'

Thus cast off, Hedley had no more to lose and became daring to the point of recklessness.

'Before we part,' he said, his demeanour calm, 'there is one question I would ask you. I hope you will do me the courtesy of giving me an answer to it.'

'Ask your question – it will make no difference,' said she, her voice determined, as she started to rise from her chair.

'Perhaps not, but it will preserve my sanity, which I find under threat from an uncertainty that fogs my thoughts. Tell me plainly now, if you will – was it only a wild and whirling dream brought on by over-indulgence in brandy, or did you roger me last night, here on this bed?'

The shock of his words brought a loud gasp of indignation from Mrs Hapgood's lips, and she fell back weakly into her chair, her cheeks a flaming red.

'What do you mean?' she cried. 'How dare you say such vile things! How dare you! You shall leave my house at once!'

'You made me as drunk as a Lord last evening,' said Hedley, ever more certain of his ground, 'and it seemed to me that I woke up in the night in this room and on this bed – to find you on top of me. The candle was still lit, so I could see that you were stark naked – you sat across my belly with your legs wide, and I saw your big brown bush. I tried to get a hold on your bubbies, but you pinned my arms to the pillow.'

'Monstrous lies!' Mrs Hapgood gasped out, her hands at her mouth in horror. 'You must be mad to say such things!'

'I fear I shall become so unless I get to the bottom of this mystery,' said he. 'You spiked yourself on my shaft and I tried for the longest time to catch the end of a bubbie in my mouth – and when I did get hold of one to suck, you bounced up and down on me like a jockey bringing in the Derby winner.'

Mrs Hapgood's mouth was opening and closing soundlessly, like a goldfish in a lily pond. White-faced and wild-eyed, she stared at Hedley, who stood up and strode across the carpet to her. He stood with hands on hips and confronted her boldly, Johnny Jump-Up as stiff as a rod under his shirt.

'Now – answer me!' he ordered her. 'Was it a dream?'

She said nothing, for the powerful nature of the emotions he had inflicted on her had robbed her temporarily of the ability to speak. Actions speak louder than words, and what she did was more eloquent than any declaration she could have made – she put her hand slowly and uncertainly under Hedley's shirt – and grasped the object whose simple amusements she had condemned so roundly not five minutes before.

Hedley stared down at her with a sense of vindication, whilst she lifted his shirt and pressed her mouth to his shaft in a long wet kiss that sent shivers of pleasurable sensation all through his body. He could see down the front of her grey dress, with its embroidery of jet beads, to where her large white bubbies were pushed upwards by her corset. He remembered how slackly they had dangled over his mouth when she had him on his back – and at the thought Johnny jumped against her mouth.

She kissed him again, then fell to rubbing his shaft while she held his shirt high with her other hand and licked his bare belly. Hedley's hands were at her bosom, to fumble at the neckline of her dress, in the hope of reaching and feeling a wealth of soft flesh.

'Ah, would you, sir!' she exclaimed, and she redoubled her manipulation of his rock-hard shaft. 'Who gave you permission to touch me? I cannot be held responsible for your lewd dreams – you are a base fellow, a deplorable scoundrel!'

'I confess that I am,' said he with a smile, 'but I know the truth now – it was no dream! You made me drunk and then you helped me upstairs and undressed me – a slight memory is coming back to me now.'

'This is the merest fantasy of an over-heated mind,' said she, her tongue licking round his belly-button.

'It may be so,' he replied, 'but the fantasy was yours, not mine, and you transformed it into reality in this very room. I was as helpless as a child and you stripped me naked – I lay flat on my back on the bed and you sat astride me and had me!'

'Not for a moment will I concede that anything out of the ordinary happened last night, apart from your drunkenness,' she countered. 'But if – and I say *if*, mark you – *if* there were conducted certain *experiments*, then they were in the nature of a discreet investigation.'

By then Hedley had both hands down inside her dress and was kneading her big lax bubbies with a great deal of pleasure.

'What was being investigated?' he asked curiously.

'Your masculine ability to make my daughter happy by the regular provision of her marital rights,' Mrs Hapgood replied, her face a handsome shade of full red from her emotions.

'Was the outcome of the experiment judged satisfactory?' he asked.

'Only in part,' she answered evasively. 'The intoxicants

you had consumed somewhat retarded the results, which might best be described as inconclusive.'

'Small wonder you had no wink of sleep last night,' Hedley cried, 'but it was not concern for your daughter's well-being that kept you awake and made you fatigued – it was a concern to pleasure your cunny on me!'

'That coarse word again!' Mrs Hapgood exclaimed. 'I shall swoon away if I hear it once more! Say it again, I beg you!'

'Cunny? But what do you call the love-parts between your legs, if not that?'

'No word exists for it that can be used without a sense of shame in polite conversation,' she said faintly.

'Are we having a polite conversation?' he asked, spasms of sensation shaking him as her attentions to Johnny Jump-Up began to have a decisive effect.

She made no answer, and none was needed, for Hedley was gripping her bubbies tightly to maintain his balance, as his legs started to tremble and he felt the crisis coming on. At once Mrs Hapgood released his throbbing shaft and landed a stinging slap on his bare bottom.

'I know what you want to do,' she said with the laugh of one who has turned the tables, 'but I've no intention of letting you! The gong will sound for dinner directly.'

She took his wrists and pulled his hands away from her fat breasts and out of her dress. Hedley stood dumbfounded while she rose from her chair and turned away from him to the door. In the state to which she had raised him, what could he do but satisfy his bursting rod in any way that presented itself to him? On bare feet and with his shaking shaft in his hand, he bounded across the room in hot pursuit.

He overtook her at the very moment that her hand

was on the doorknob, and he swooped down and up again, to seize the hem of her dress and drag her skirts and petticoats up as high as her hips, to reveal her bottom in white cambric drawers.

'Hedley – no more now!' she exclaimed.

'Oh!' he sighed, 'I am too hot to wait any longer – I must shoot into you now! Spread your legs for me!'

'There is no time for nonsense like that,' she said briskly, turning the doorknob in her hand to take her leave.

It was too late for such admonitions. Hedley's stiff shaft was leaping wildly in his clasping hand and so delirious was he with sensation that he did not hear her words – not that he would have paid any heed to them if he had. He panted with lewd desire while he thrust Johnny Jump-Up bare-headed into the rearward slit of Mrs Hapgood's drawers, and then, with a few furious strokes of his hand, he caused himself to spend in a raging flood up the bare and fleshy cheeks of her rump.

In her urgency to leave, she had already opened the bedroom door a crack – assailed now from behind, she pushed it quickly shut and leaned heavily on it, while his warm essence foamed against her soft flesh. The dinner gong sounded at the exact moment that Hedley's last squirt pulsed out between her cheeks, and she heaved a long sigh.

'You have soaked my drawers through, you wicked boy!' said she in a voice that was almost a purr of pleasure. 'I must go and change them before dinner!'

'Put me out of my misery,' said he, keeping her pressed to the door so that she could not escape.

'You've done that with your own hand,' she replied, making her plump bottom wriggle against him, 'what more can I do?'

'I mean tell me you have forgiven my youthful indiscretions and that I am restored fully to your esteem. Vow to me that my engagement to marry Vickie has regained your approval.'

'I have reconsidered my decision to break it off, which was over-hasty, perhaps,' said she, 'but in the circumstances I feel that a longer period of probation is necessary, in which I may assure myself that you have reformed your character. You must accept an engagement of two years, reckoning from now, as a test of the sincerity of your devotion to my daughter.'

'One year,' he bargained, sliding his softening shaft along the wet crease of her rump. 'Longer than that I cannot wait.'

'Eighteen months,' she countered, trying to look at him over her shoulder, a calculating smile on her face.

'Agreed,' said he at once.

He could guess well enough what was in her mind in enforcing the delay, and he had not the least objection to rogering her, as well as his darling girl, on his visits to The Larches. He must keep well clear of Adelaide, for her youthful eagerness and lack of good sense presented a serious risk of discovery. The bargain struck, Mrs Hapgood turned with her back to the door, to put her plump hands on his shoulders and kiss him on the mouth. Her skirts and petticoats were still bunched round her waist and she murmured against his cheek:

'Put your hand between my legs and bring me off quickly, dearest Hedley, for you have me left high and dry and I cannot sit at table in this condition.'

CHAPTER 9
A Jolly Bunch Of Chums Together

In London, it was Hedley's pleasant custom to dine once a week at the Cafe Royal in Regent Street with a particular group of men friends. They gave themselves the name of 'The Becky Sharp Club' as an act of jovial homage to the lively young heroine of Mr Thackery's novel, who rogered her way round fashionable London. There were eight members in all, but not all found it convenient to be present every week. On the Tuesday after his return from The Larches and his escapade with Mrs Hapgood, Hedley found only three others assembled in the restaurant.

A most handsome meal was consumed, washed down with plenty of excellent wine. They started with an avocado and egg mousse, then smoked mackerel made piquant with lemon mayonnaise, to be followed by chicken a la Kieff, somewhat a speciality of the chef de cuisine, and rounded off with orange and brandy sorbet. The talk was that of close friends, tales and jokes and noisy laughter, the four men enjoying themselves greatly.

In a more serious moment an enquiry was made as to whether a date had yet been set for the nuptials of

Hedley and the lovely Miss Hapgood, since it went without saying that all members of 'The Becky Sharp Club' would be invited to attend. The question embarrassed Hedley, for he did not want to confess that the wedding had been deferred for another eighteen months.

To admit that much would surely have led to more enquiries as to the reason for the delay. Even with his closest friends, it was out of the question to reveal that it was because he had rogered his fiancee's mother, or was it more precise to say that she had got him under her thumb, by making him drunk and extracting his darkest secrets, before rogering him? He turned the query aside by assuring his friends that they would learn the date in good time to be present, and the talk moved on.

As always after a dinner of the club, when good food and wine and brandy made tongues wag, the topic of conversation was women – and the members' success with them. It was a tradition, established from the time of the first dinner, that each man must regale the others with a faithful account of his best achievement with a female since the last meeting. The member judged to have told the liveliest tale had his dinner free, the bill being shared between the others.

The order of speaking was determined by the toss of a coin, and the chums settled with Havana cigars and port and brandy to hear the Hon. Randolph Joynes, whom chance had chosen to speak first. He was a tall, thin gentleman of twenty-four, fair-haired and extremely elegant of manner and stylish of dress. He spoke with a slight drawl that amused his friends when his words were, as so often, of bawdy events.

'As you well know,' he began, smiling briefly round the table, 'it is my habit, when the letch is upon me, to take a hansom cab to the East End, and stroll about the dirty streets of Spitalfields or Shoreditch, to view life at its rawest, and to pick up a willing young whore for a shilling or two. Last Sunday evening, after dining with my revered Mama at her house, I felt a great need of a whore's commodity and hastened to my usual haunts.

'In a dismal public house in Brick Street I came across one who took my fancy – a woman of twenty or thereabouts – with yellow-dyed hair and a slyly insolent expression that was a direct challenge to me. I engaged her in conversation and bought her a glass or two of execrable gin, and saw that she would suit me well. Her pimp hastened to my side to settle the business.

'He was a low fellow in a brown bowler hat pushed back to show a quiff of greasy hair on his forehead. He touched his forelock to me and called me a "toff" – I was in full fig, having dined with Mama – tails, white tie, silk top-hat and silver-knobbed cane. Seven shillings and sixpence changed hands – he would have taken half that, but I wanted full service and no complaining after.

'The fellow gave me a strange look, knowing I intended to do more with his doxy than lie on her belly, but greed overcame any lingering scruples he may have entertained, and he ordered her to take me to her lodging and follow my wishes to the smallest particular, or otherwise he would have the skin off her "arse", as he quaintly put it.'

'Are you not afraid of being struck unconscious and robbed when you walk in the crime-ridden alleys and streets of the East End?' Hedley interrupted. 'Or of being stabbed to death by some wretch who envies what you have?'

'Not in the least,' said Randolph. 'Moral superiority is its own protection – the most vicious of curs shrinks back from a gentleman. To resume then if I may, Nelly, for that was her name, conducted me to her hovel in an adjacent alley. She had a room of about twelve feet square, furnished with a bed, a table and two chairs, on one of which I placed myself, while I instructed her to remove all her clothing, while I watched her.

'Her garb was of the cheapest, as you can well imagine – a black straw bonnet, a shawl and a brown linsey dress much bedraggled at the hem from the dirt of the streets. When that came off I saw that she wore two petticoats of flannel, sadly stained, black-ribbed wool stockings and mid-calf boots, never cleaned since they first were purchased, and with many a missing button. Now we were down to her chemise and drawers, at which she paused and looked at me enquiringly.

'These people wash very little and rarely remove all their clothing, even when they roger each other, and in consequence Nelly was not certain that I intended her to be stark naked. I leaned back at my ease in the chair and commanded her to continue – she obeyed with such reluctance that I was convinced this was the first time she had been completely undressed for years – perhaps not since she was a baby in arms.'

'My word, Randolph!' exclaimed Hedley. 'The strange things you know! What kind of bubbies had she – big or small?'

The other men chuckled at his eagerness and then pressed the narrator to answer his question.

'Not very large,' he said judiciously, 'and lying slackly on her chest, for all her youth. Her belly was good – round and plumpish, with a deep-sunk button, and her bush was a shade of light brown, not at all like the artificial yellow of her head. She stood to pose for me in the gas light, and I must confess to becoming hard-on at the sight of her pale flesh. She thought I had come to her fusty den to have her on her back, of course, but I told her to get down on her hands and knees, with her bare bottom towards me.

'Evidently the threat of her pimp to thrash her carried much weight, for she did exactly what I required of her and went down, though with an odd look on her face. I sat there in my finery, white gloves on my hands and top-hat on my head, and contemplated her white backside sticking out towards me, and her curly-haired split, to my heart's content. She kept on glancing at me over her naked shoulder, the pert expression of the public house changed now for one of puzzlement, and at last she summoned the courage to ask if I intended to do her like that – doggie-style, she called it.'

'Ah, Randolph, my old buck – what a dance you lead these poor whores you pick up in the slums!' said Digby Wilton-Gooch. 'I know what I would have done to her in your place, if her bare backside had been beckoning to me!'

'Yes, Digby, all here are acquainted with your jolly little ways with the women,' replied Randolph. 'But to continue – after staring at her rear view until my shaft was wobbling like a metronome, I got down behind her for a closer look at her big hairy slit. I peeled my gloves off and spread it apart, and then I couldn't resist rubbing inside with my fingers until I had made it slippery.

'By then the wench was shaking and moaning and crying out, her belly heaving and her bubbies flopping – she wanted to be done and had the impudence to ask me! Naturally, I refused copulation with a creature of the streets, and jumped astride her back as if she were a two-year-old mare. I pulled her hair loose from its pins and found it quite long enough to use as a bearing-rein to keep her head up while she carried me round the room, I clamped my knees into her sides and tucked my feet up behind to grip her, and set her moving with a smart cut or two with my stick across her flanks.'

Hedley refilled his glass with port and passed on the bottle with hands that trembled from the emotion stirred in him by the story. He vowed silently to emulate Randolph at the earliest chance that arose and experience for himself the feel of riding a bare-back woman.

'I kept my mare ambling round the cracked linoleum until she collapsed under me,' said Randolph, 'whereupon I sat down on the chair again with my legs spread and prodded Nelly's behind with my foot until she stirred. I had her crawl to me on hands and knees, and told her to undo my buttons and get out my hard-on shaft. The sly creature fingered me over-eagerly, as if she would be rid of my company by bringing me off in her hand, but a word from me stopped that.

'On my command she bent her neck and took me into her mouth. I am exceptionally well endowed in this respect, and she could contain no more than half of my massive rod before I felt the unhooded purple head touch the back of her throat. I told her I hoped she appreciated the considerable honour bestowed on her in being allowed to suck a gentleman's rod. Her hairy slit, I was pleased to inform her, was too common a lodging-house for a gentleman of my quality to rest in, even for the short time it took to spend.

'She wished to make some retort – some insolence or other, I suppose – but I gagged her by seizing the dyed hair above her ears to hold her fast while I slid my shaft in fast rhythmic thrusts between her lips. Her eyes rolled up to stare at me in helpless pleading, but seeing me implacable, she submitted to my will and tongued me until the sensations were beyond compare delicious. As I neared the climax I cried *Suck hard, Nelly, you flea-bitten little strumpet!* and my juice squirted into her mouth and I slumped in a trembling and writhing heap.'

Randolph fell silent, and the others stared at him, mouths open and their minds inflamed by his narrative.

'That concludes my contribution to the entertainment,' he said with a smile. 'I hope it will pay for my dinner.'

Warm congratulations were showered upon him, while Digby Wilton-Gooch shook his hand and declared his escapade to be a capital wheeze. Then the faces around the table turned to gaze at Hedley, who had drawn second place in the batting order. He was in a quandary – although he had passed a weekend rogering his fiancee, her little sister and her mama, since the club last dined together, it was out of the question to dishonour the Hapgood name by hinting at his antics in that quarter.

His chums knew that he had been down to The Larches for the weekend with his fiancee's family, and from that he was able to draw sudden inspiration – he related how he had been woken early in the morning by a maid-servant bringing him tea, and found that Mr Stevie Stiff was in a rampant condition. He told how he had thrown aside the bed clothes and pulled up his nightshirt to explose his throbbing shaft.

To speak the truth, that was the end of the affair, for at the sight of Mr Stiff, Milly had blushed pink and walked out of the room. Invention came to Hedley's aid, and he boldly lied his way through an account of how Milly had been so impressed by his display that she had got on to the bed with him to take Master Stevie in her hand and massage him, all the time asking if that's how he liked it.

'I truly believe she had grown up on a farm,' said Hedley, 'and was expert in milking the dairy cows, for the clasp of her hand and the way she stripped my shaft up and down caused it to stand like a flag-mast! I let her continue for some minutes, and when I couldn't stand any more I dragged her down on her back and had her dress up to finger her cunny, which I had not before examined in all the times I have stayed with the family.

'I got on top of her and stuck Master Stevie up her – he was so hard that it was almost painful, and I was rogering away briskly when she cried out – *Poke me, sir, poke me senseless!* You can imagine the state I was in at that moment! She shrieked and fetched off before I did, but I kept on plugging and before her tremors had stopped, I spent in her.'

'Good man!' exclaimed Randolph. 'Female servants are there to do the master's bidding – your conduct towards this Milly was very gentlemanly and correct! A topping tale, Hedley!'

'There is more,' said he with brazen untruth. 'Needless to say I followed up my advantage by going to her room that night when the household was asleep. But I'll not bore you with that, for it was simple rogering all night long, of the kind we are all familiar with. I gave her half a sovereign on leaving and she begged me to come to her room whenever I am staying with the family. I am sure that John here has a more unusual story to tell than mine, and I willingly yield the floor to him.'

John Delamere, seated on Hedley's right, was the fourth son of a Bishop, but in no way Church-minded. He was a shortish, plump, smiling young man of twenty-two, with dark smooth hair and a heavily drooping moustache. He drank more than was good for him, but none of his friends thought the worse of him for that.

'I'll tell you how I spent Saturday afternoon,' he said with a broad grin. 'While you chaps were in the country for your boring weekends with friends and relatives, I took myself off to visit Mrs Lilian Baxter of Church Terrace, Chelsea.'

The mention of this well-known brothel that catered for the gentry brought a smile to the faces around the table – John's idiosyncrasies were a source of much amusement to his friends.

'I paid my respects to Mrs Baxter and asked for the services of Bella,' said he. 'She's a splendid piece of female flesh, this Bella – a stoutly-built and raven-haired woman of thirty, dark-eyed and taller than me, with bubbies big enough to drown between . . . ah, bliss! Dressed in only her chemise and drawers, she led me into the chastisement-room and with her own dear hands removed my jacket and waistcoat, before strapping my wrists to the top bar of the flogging-frame that stood in the centre of the room.

'When she strapped my ankles, dragging my legs roughly apart, I was the prey of such Heavenly sensation that the Reverend Ramrod in my trousers stood up hard and strong. Held fast in the strong leather straps, I was helpless to free myself, or to protect myself, had I wanted to. I felt Bella's hands round me, opening my trousers and letting them down, and pulling my under-clothes down to my knees . . .

'This closeness of her hands to my tonsured friend had the expected effect – he nodded his head in wildest enthusiasm, but Bella handled him roughly and with words of contempt – yet even her disdainful touch was exciting beyond words. She tucked my shirt-tail up behind and stood back and I turned my head to feast my eyes on her! How my heart leaped to see her cold and stern face with its dark sombre brows above those deep eyes so filled with contempt for my plight . . . her full figure with soft fleshy curves filling out her thin muslin chemise! I could not speak for the love and desire I felt for her at that moment.'

John's story tailed off as he became lost in contemplation of the wonder of that remembered moment. His chums grinned at each other, and while Randolph poured brandy into a glass and pressed it into John's hand, Digby shook him by the shoulder to draw his attention.

'Dear old fellow – don't keep it to yourself!' said Digby. 'We are waiting on your every word.'

'Ah, if you could have heard her voice then!' cried John, after a long swallow of brandy. 'It was low-pitched and vibrant and when she said, *I despise you, you miserable fool!* there was a coldness in it that gripped my heart and squeezed it until I uttered gasps of delight. *You have put yourself in my power,* she said, *and now you shall feel the bitterness of my contempt for your weakness.* So saying, she strode to a rack on the wall where are kept the instruments of punishment and caressing each with her hand, she mused aloud, *Shall it be the birch today – or the cat-of-nine-tails – or the slave-whip – or the cane – or the leather strap? Which will best answer my purpose?*'

Under the table, Hedley's shaft stood as stiff as a broom handle and was shaking against his hot belly. For the hundredth time he reflected on how very exciting were the lives of his friends, and how dull his own seemed to him in comparison. Eyes ablaze, he stared at John, wondering what came next.

'I pleaded with her,' said John. '*Not the cane*, I implored her, and being naturally perverse, as I well knew, it was the school-room cane she drew forth from the rack. *Kiss the rod!* she cried, drawing the length of pliable cane harshly across my mouth. Then she threw back her arm and struck me across the backside with it and I winced and cried out in pain, for it cut into my flesh like a knife.

'*Whine, you cur, whine!* she exclaimed, and thrashed at my shrinking flesh with heartless force. Soon I was crying out continuously under her blows and begging her to stop. *You will get no mercy from me*, said she and as she continued to thrash my behind, the cruel pain changed to a sensation of pleasant warmth, then of blazing heat diffused right through my loins and belly, until it located itself in my leaping shaft.

'Then in a strong voice I cried out ecstatically:

> *O garment not golden but gilded,*
> *O garden where all men may dwell,*
> *O tower not of ivory, but builded*
> *By hands that reach heaven from hell;*
> *O mystical rose of the mire,*
> *O house not of gold but of gain,*
> *O house of unquenchable fire,*
> *Our Lady of Pain!'*

'Poetry!' Hedley exclaimed. 'Is it Lord Tennyson?'

'Do you not recognise Mr Swinburne's sublime and deathless lines?' asked John, his countenance shining with glorious memories and with the copious quantities of liquor he had drunk. 'No more interruptions, I entreat you! To tell of my sojourn in Paradise is to relive it, in all its splendour!'

'Yes, shut up, Hedley,' said Randolph. 'We've heard of your adventure – now we are hearing of John's.

Continue, old top – if this young idiot says another word I shall brain him with the brandy bottle.'

'Picture me – if you can – hanging there in my bonds,' said John, 'my backside bare and criss-crossed with the red weals of my caning, my shaft grown huge and bounding with every slash across my torn cheeks!

'My head was turned to one side to stare in rapture at Bella, at the swinging of her heavy breasts under her chemise each time she brought her arm swiftly down to hit me, at the tuft of jet-black hair that showed in her armpit when her muscular arm went up and back for the next stroke, at the rivulets of sweat running down her broad face, at the dark patch where her chemise was stuck to her belly with the perspiration of her great efforts!

'In my tortured body and mind, and in my innermost soul, the sensations grew intolerably strong, and at last there came the moment when I shrieked and gushed out my sap in long spurts that arched through the air and splashed on the carpet a yard or more from my bound feet – my tribute to wonderful Bella! I hung in my cruel bonds, totally spent and my body racked with agony – but my mind was aflame with golden glory, and with my fainting breath I whispered a blessing on my fair tormentor:

> *I have passed from the outermost portal*
> *To the shrine where a sin is a prayer;*
> *What care though the service be mortal?*
> *O our Lady of Torture, what care?*
> *All thine the last wine that I pour is,*
> *The last in the chalice we drain,*
> *O fierce and luxuriant Dolores,*
> *Our Lady of Pain.'*

Hedley was sorely tempted to speak in praise of John's tale, but having been threatened with sudden concussion if he dared to interrupt, he held his peace. There was a breathless silence when John finished speaking, the minds of his friends in thrall to the strange enchantment of his words – as if by some sorcery he had carried them into that private room in Chelsea and made them prisoners there. He broke the spell by giggling drunkenly and calling to the waiter to bring another bottle of brandy.

'Damn fine tale,' said Randolph, 'though if it had been me visiting Mrs Baxter, I would have wanted the roles reversed – I would much enjoy laying a cane across the fat posterior of this Bella of yours.'

Then looking at Digby Wilton-Gooch, he suggested that he would have to go some if he expected to beat John to the prize of a free dinner. Obviously he regarded John's contribution as superior to his own tale of tyrannising a young East End whore, and had dismissed Hedley's false account of rogering a skivvy as too everyday an occurrence for serious consideration.

'I'll do my best,' said Digby with a laugh, 'but I'm a very straightforward sort of chap and can't compete with the poetic rhapsody of a cane across John's backside.'

Digby was a strong and athletic gentleman of twenty-six, handsome in a way women liked, with curly dark hair and sideboards, and heavy eyebrows that met above his nose.

'I popped round to see Lady Amberson at her house in Cadogan Square this afternoon,' he began. 'She's by way of being a sort of distant kinswoman of mine, as you may know. Before Amberson wed her she was a Billington-Smythe – the Gloucestershire branch of the family – and my Pater was a cousin of Frederick Billington-Smythe of the Shropshire branch. But to come to the point, she and His Lordship have been out of town for some weeks, he being laid up in the ancestral home with a nasty go of the gout.'

While Digby was talking, Hedley, John and Randolph exchanged questioning looks. They knew Lady Amberson to be neither very young nor very goodlooking, and wondered what attraction she held for her strapping young distant cousin. He observed their doubtful glances and correctly interpreted them. He threw back his head to laugh and then, to settle their uncertainties, explained that she was a devotee of 'Greek Love'.

'A footman showed me up,' he resumed, 'not into the drawing-room but into the Pink Parlour, which is Augusta's own private little retreat when she wants solitude. She shook hands and said how glad she was to see me, the day being slow and dreary, with worse promised for the evening, when she and His Lordship were bidden to a dinner party given by the Duke and Duchess of Fawley for the Prime Minister.

'She went on to inform me sadly that, since coming up from the country, nothing entertaining had happened, and she felt forlorn and empty. *I have the very thing for you!* I cried, and pressed her hand against my constant travelling companion. *Yes, I remember that monster of yours very well*, cried she, *help me out of this skirt!*

'She was wearing a white silk blouse with a frilly front and a long black skirt – in a trice I was on my knees by her side to find the placket and unfasten it, so that it fell to the floor and she stepped out of it. Below the blouse there was revealed the lower part of her pretty lace-trimmed chemise, and I raised that with an eager hand to confirm the truth of Augusta's proud boast that she had never in her life worn drawers, believing them vulgar.

'She bent forward from the waist, displaying for me her rump, full and round, white and soft – and with her long fingers she stroked cheeks as comfortable as a pair of pillows. And then – what a sight for sore eyes! – her fingers slowly parted those magnificent cheeks! Believe me, Roger the Lodger was leaping about in my trousers as if he had contracted St Vitus Dance! *I haven't been touched for ages!* complained Augusta, *kiss my backside, darling boy.*

'Down on my knees in homage, my mind in a whirl of delight, I kissed her aristocratic rump – you fellows who haven't seen it can have no conception of its beauty – not flabby nor sagging, as with many a lady of thirty-nine summers, but round, robust and fleshy, most generous in its proportions! With the wet tip of my tongue I touched the secret knot of puckered muscle concealed between the cheeks she was parting so widely for me.

'I well knew what Augusta wanted of me, and when her little cries of bliss told me that she was ready, I stood up and tore open my buttons! Out sprang Master Horn, trembling in his eagerness, like a thoroughbred race-horse before the Off! Augusta bent over and rested her hands on the stuffed back of a chair, and I put my hands on her hips and pressed Master Horn's head into the knot I had made wet with my tongue.

'Ah, the joy of that instant, when I was mounted on her big round rump and my shaft was sunk up Augusta's bung-hole! It held me close, although there was nothing virginal about it, for its constant use over the years had trained it well to stretch to a size that comfortably accommodated my throbbing shaft. Her hand was under her chemise, fingering her cunny, while I tupped her from the rear. *Harder!* she cried. *Plumb me to the depths of my being – split me wide open!*

'We approached the climax together in perfect harmony of body and mind, like a rider and his mount coming up to a tall hedge. My arms were round Augusta's waist and my fingers sank deep into the flesh of her big soft belly to hold her steady – I reached up under her chemise and caught hold of the fat bubbies dangling there, and almost wrenched them off in the fury of my poking.

'She cried out in rapture, and thumped herself back against my belly and thighs – at the very moment I shot my essence into her hot and clinging bowels! The thrill was stupendous and I thought I would never stop spending! Words fail me to convey the tremendous satisfaction of those divine moments, the throb in my hugely swollen shaft, the incredible release and joy of fetching off into that noble white bottom of hers!'

CHAPTER 10
A Rare Opportunity For Comparisons

After 'The Becky Sharp Club' dinner was over, Hedley took his leave of his friends outside the Cafe Royal, shaking hands all round, while they stood on the pavement and waited for a four-wheeler. The other three were off together on an expedition to Mrs Tookey's in Tottenham Court Road, where there were fresh young whores to be made use of. John Delamere had agreed on condition that one could be found who could consent to take his trousers down and spank him severely, cost what it may.

Randolph Joynes had retorted he didn't doubt that Mrs Tookey herself would undertake to chastise him severely, for a couple of guineas. The chums knew Hedley would not join in their adventure, for he was ever disinclined to pay cash for what his good looks got him for nothing. He said his cheery goodnights and, it being a fine summer evening, he decided to return on foot to his lodgings, for he had set his heart on poking his landlady.

He strolled the length of Regent Street, smiling and fending off the whores who pressed forward to offer their services, and he recalled with amusement the anguish with which John Delamere had greeted Digby Wilton-Gooch's jolly tale of knot-holing Lady Amberson. At the voting for whose story had entertained the company the best, all voices had been for John's poetic tale of having his backside thrashed by fat Bella.

Over a last glass, Hedley had taken the opportunity to ask Digby whether, given a free choice, his preference was for the front entrance or the back door.

'Down between my legs lies the very shaft which only two or three hours ago was six inches up the rearward passage of a Peeress of the Realm,' Digby replied with a merry chuckle. 'For me it's the Greek style every time. It's unsurpassed for sheer pleasure, my dear chap – the front door is for married men desirious of heirs.'

Hedley had confessed that never in his life had he rogered a woman in that manner, at which both Digby and Randolph laughed heartily. Not so John, who nodded his head in solemn approval of Hedley's innocence of such matters, and gave it as his firm belief that Digby's habit was a monstrous and blasphemous abuse of the divine flesh of womanhood.

Hedley's rooms were in Great Portland Street, where he had the first floor up of a well-kept and well-furnished house. He let himself in at the street door with his latch-key and then, instead of making his way upstairs to his own bed, he tapped lightly at the door leading to the landlady's quarters. There was a long wait with no response, and he tapped again, thinking that Mrs Potter must be asleep, when he heard a key turn in the lock and the door opened.

That she had retired for the night and that his summons had brought her from her bed was obvious from the flowered woollen dressing-gown she had put on, buttoned close to her neck and descending to her ankles, with carpet slippers showing beneath. Her dark brown hair was unpinned, and lay over her shoulders and down her back. She stared uncertainly at Hedley at first, and then smiled at him knowingly.

'Dined very well, have you, Mr Gillingham?' she asked, her tone redolent of familiarity. 'You've got the look about you of a gentleman who has looked on the wine when it is red.'

'And the champagne too,' said he, 'and the brandy, though neither was red. I've walked all the way from the bottom end of Regent Street, Florrie, and I'm worn out. I don't think I can get up the stairs until I've rested my legs for a minute.'

Mrs Florence Potter was a woman of thirty or so, a tall and lean woman, who had been deserted some years before by Mr Potter. He had disappeared one Friday evening in the direction of South London with a seventeen-year-old shop-girl, leaving his wronged wife with two small children to bring up. She had taken to Hedley as soon as he became her first floor tenant, and he had persuaded her a time or two to let him have her.

'You can come in and sit down for a minute till you feel strong enough to climb the staircase,' she said with a wink, 'but keep your voice down and don't trip over anything in the dark, because my cherubs are asleep in the back room.'

'I won't wake the little darlings,' Hedley promised, smiling at her in the way he knew would make her feel weak at the knees and moist between the legs. She stood aside to let him in, and as she closed the door again she exclaimed in mock alarm for her virtue:

'Whatever am I thinking of! You can't come in here at this hour – with me in my nightclothes and no drawers on!'

'Good Lord!' cried Hedley with a grin. 'Is this true?'

With his belly against hers, he pressed her backwards close to the wall and held her there while he opened her dressing-gown from top to bottom and got his knees between hers, to force her legs apart.

'You're not to take advantage of a poor defenceless woman!' she said with a giggle. 'It's shameful, what you're doing!'

Hedley reached down to get his fingers under the hem of her long cotton night-dress, and slid them up between her thighs to clasp her hairy warm motte in the palm of his hand.

'My word, yes,' he agreed, 'you've no drawers on, Florrie my dear – I hold your bare cunny in my hand!'

'You're a beast,' she murmured, her hand rubbing at his long shaft through his trouers, 'you think that's all I'm here for – a slit for you to twiddle when the mood takes you. What I want never enters your head, does it?'

'But I know exactly what you want,' he replied, his middle finger playing inside her moistness, 'and you're getting it.'

She leaned back against the wall, her legs spread and her eyes closed, enjoying the luxurious feel he gave her.

'That's enough,' she whispered at last, 'you've got me all wet and sticky – let's go and sit down.'

'You were already wet and sticky when I started,' said he with a chuckle. 'You were lying in bed bringing yourself off when you heard me at the door.'

'I'll thank you not to cast aspersions,' she retorted most humorously. 'I was in the sleep of the just when you knocked.'

'Then you had finished fetching off and were dozing,' said he, for having felt her slit he was sure of his ground.

'That's for me to know and you to guess,' she said

140

pertly, and tugged at his wrist. 'Let's go where we can sit down and I'll polish you off in style.'

Hedley let her remove his hand from her hairy slit and went after her into her sitting-room. The gas light was off, but the curtains were open and there was more than enough light from the street lamps outside for what the pair of them had in mind. He took off his black silk topper and Florrie slid his opera-cloak from his shoulders, folded it with house-wifely care and laid it over a chair.

'You're a proper swell in your evening fig,' said she, her palm pressed for a moment to his face in a gesture of affection he found over-familiar towards him in a woman of her station in life. The fact that he rogered her from time to time did not imply a friendship between them, after all, but he enjoyed to be flattered, and for the sake of that he forgave her.

'Been out with your posh friends for a bite to eat?' she asked, her hand sliding up and down his trousers where his hard rod distended the cloth. 'How is it you come back here to me for a poke instead of having one of those fine ladies you take out to the theatre? Won't they open their legs for you? Does a hand up their clothes make them ticklish? Or is it just that you don't fancy any of them?'

'I've had my hand in all their drawers,' Hedley answered with a grin, 'and I've had them on their backs with their legs wide open. And I'll let you in on a secret – not one of them is half as good a poke as you are, Florrie.'

On the sofa they sat, and whilst they were chatting, he had her dressing-gown right off, and her nightgown up around her lean waist. Her thighs slid apart to encourage the advance of his fingers, their mouths joined in a wet kiss, and they fell silent, she in the voluptuous enjoyment

141

of having her cunny fingered, he in the feeling of it.

'Let's have your trousers undone and see what you've got,' said she, unbuttoning him swiftly.

'I've brought an old acquaintance of yours whom you'll be pleased to see again,' Hedley told her.

'Why, it's One-Eyed Jack!' she said, taking out his shaft and dandling it between her fingers.

By stages she coaxed him into her bedroom, where a candle still burned. She helped him out of his clothes expertly, and he lay on the thick down-stuffed counterpane in only his starch-fronted evening shirt, the front turned up to bare the shaft that stood up from his belly like a flagstaff. She lay beside him, her nightgown bundled up round her waist, and handled him whilst he fluttered his fingers in her wet slit.

'I must do it, Florrie!' cried he in another minute or two.

At once she rolled onto her back and spread her legs wide. Hedley pulled his shirt up to his chest and laid his bare belly on hers, One-Eyed Jack found the way easily enough into her ready cunny, and they lay mouth to mouth, sucking each other's hot breath. Hedley's hands gripped the thin cheeks of her rump and she jerked her belly up to meet his poking.

'Not so fast!' gasped she. 'Slow down or it will be over in a few seconds!'

'First a fast poke – then I'll do you all night slowly!' he cried, his belly beating a fast tattoo on hers that stirred sensations in her that swept away her desire to prolong the bout. Her fingers clawed over his flesh from his naked rump up under his shirt to his shoulderblades and with rapid jabs he spent convulsively, and she cried out as she too reached the climax of passion.

While they rested, side by side, her hand inside his

shirt to stroke his chest with gentle finger-tips, she enquired about his fiancee in Burwood Park and the wedding arrangements. His reply was evasive, as it could not be otherwise, but Florrie had the shrewdness to detect that he was hiding an inconvenient truth from her and framed her questions slyly to draw him out.

'It's mortal hard for a hot-natured young gentleman like you to be head over heels in love with a beautiful young lady, and she with you, and then be barred from giving free rein to the passion you feel for her,' said she.

'An impossible position,' sighed Hedley.

'I've had the pleasure of seeing Miss Hapgood,' Florrie went on, 'when she's come here with her mother to take tea with you, after they've been shopping in town. Without the word of a lie, she's the loveliest young lady I've seen for many a year. That picture of her that stands on your mantelpiece upstairs doesn't do her justice.'

'Yes,' sighed Hedley, 'she is the most beautiful girl in the world and I love her beyond all sense and reason.'

'Life is strange,' said Florrie sympathetically. 'Fate has been good to you and you have found and wooed the young lady you most want to take in your arms and make love to – yet society and convention join together to say that she's the one you mustn't lay a finger on till you're man and wife.'

'But I can dream!' said he, a salacious tone to his voice.

'And I know you dream about her often,' said Florrie with an impudent giggle, 'because I see the white stains on the front of your nightshirts when I put them in the wash.'

'Dear Florrie – you understand my predicament so well,' said Hedley with a sigh. 'The consolation you give me at times like these is very precious to me.'

Florrie's hand had glided slowly down from his chest to his warm belly, and from there to One-Eyed Jack, who lay peacefully between his thighs. With a gentle finger-tip she tickled the soft shaft and head, causing Hedley to sigh in languid delight.

'It's hard to judge what a fully-clothed person's body looks like when stripped bare,' said she, greatly daring, 'but my guess is that Miss Hapgood has a full and firm white bosom, and a more graspable behind than mine.'

She heard Hedley's gasp of surprise at her words and thought she had gone too far in speaking thus of the lady whom he would marry, but his next words showed that he had taken no offence. In the lulling half-dark of the quiet bedroom, little tremors of bliss spreading through his belly from her slow manipulation of his shaft, Hedley had forgotten he was associating with a social inferior and let his tongue run away with him.

'Can you keep a great secret, Florrie?' he whispered, 'My love for Miss Hapgood is so all-embracing and soul-shaking that I *have* dared to do the forbidden deed! I have touched her!'

Florrie's hand was moving with gentle stealth on his growing shaft, as if she would draw out his confidences with his sap.

'Ah, I can't say I'm very surprised that a hot-blooded and loving gentleman like yourself finds it hard to resist the temptation of being alone with your beautiful fiancee,' she said, her voice full of warm understanding. 'How far did she let you go – have you had a feel of her bare bosom?'

'I have,' he murmured, 'and her breasts are divinely full and firm – satiny globes as white as alabaster, with points as pink and delicate as rosebuds.'

'Did you suck them?' Florrie whispered in his ear.

'Yes,' said he, a little boastful now that he had embarked on this exposure of private concerns. 'And I've gone further – I've felt her snowy bottom, so smooth and firm to the touch!'

'You've had her clothes up and your hand in her drawers!' exclaimed Florrie in mock astonishment.

'My hand has rested between her thighs and I have fingered her warm and silky-tufted mound,' he answered proudly.

'Oh, what a naughty boy you've been!' cried Florrie, and squeezed his rock-hard shaft in her clenched hand. 'You ought to have your backside properly tanned for what you've done to that sweet young lady! Yet what delights you have tasted! The mention of it has got me hot and bothered again! You'll have to do me to calm me down!'

He too was ready again, for she had made sure of that with her stroking and tickling and pressing and tugging, but not for what Florrie was expecting, for the devil was in him. He laid her on her back, hitched up his crumpled evening-shirt, and his throbbing shaft in his hand, he knelt straddling her belly.

'Make a cunny of your bubbies, Florrie!' he cried.

He lay over her, his legs gripping round her waist and his shaft on her bosom. She squeezed her slack bubbies round it and held it fast in the soft flesh whilst he began to tup.

'I'll wager you've not done this to Miss Hapgood,' said she in a low and lecherous voice. 'She'd never let you!'

'Oh, Florrie!' he sighed. 'What a good sort you are!'

In the flickering candle-light she stared at the crimson head that was sliding between her white-skinned bubbies and she wriggled her bottom in a vain attempt to rub her wet motte against him to obtain satisfaction. But his thighs were holding her too tightly, and with his body in the way she could not reach her slit with her own hands.

While Hedley rogered her bubbies, his head was filled with whirling comparisons – would he ever be able to teach his dear Vickie to welcome his sexual approaches with the open-hearted love of being done that Florrie displayed? When Vickie was his wife, she would obey him implicitly, and if the urge took him to make use of her beautiful bubbies as he was using Florrie's, she would comply – but would she enjoy it? Or lie dutifully on her back, waiting for him to fetch off and leave her alone?

True, she had let him have her from behind, standing in the dark at the bedroom window – but would she show enthusiasm if he wanted her sitting on the kitchen table with her legs apart, like Lottie? An even more lickerishly exciting question went through Hedley's mind – would darling Vickie sit naked over his belly and roger *him* while he sucked at her bubbies – as her mother had done?

'Oh!' he moaned suddenly, the images in his mind making him speed up his stroke. 'Look, Florrie – I'm coming off!'

An instant later the little eye in his shaft opened wide and out flew jets of creamy essence, to fall in a copious shower on Florrie's face and neck. She let him finish, and when One-Eyed Jack's last pearly tear hung quivering, she rolled Hedley off her, to lie on his back heaving contented sighs. The hem of her nightgown served to dry off her wet cheeks and chin, then she took hold of Hedley's shaft.

It was fast losing its hardness, but it was still big and she knew that with the proper treatment it would stand

146

up once more. She dragged his shirt well up out of the way and stroked the half-hard shaft with deft fingers until it began to grow longer, when she took it in her mouth. Hedley surrendered in lascivious abandon, and in only a few moments his shaft was as hard and stiff as it had been when he had plunged it between her bubbies and spent there. Florrie was confident of success now and she licked One-Eyed Jack's head with her hot tongue.

'You're driving me wild again,' Hedley cried out in delight, 'I want to shoot off – I must have you, Florrie!'

She laughed and said, 'You're stiff enough for it – where do you want to poke me this time?'

'Let me feel you,' said he, putting a hand between her lean thighs to touch the wet lips of her cunny.

She turned on her back, her legs spread wide apart for him, and was silent in her voluptuous enjoyment as he fingered and twiddled her open cleft. After a while he heaved himself up and over, to kneel between her legs, and Florrie pulled her nightgown over her head, discarding it on the floor, to let him see her stark naked.

Uttering long and continuous sighs, Hedley gazed down at the temple of pleasure, observing with an eager eye the short, thick, crisp, yet silky dark-brown hair that partly covered her motte, growing down by the sides and leaving the thin lips free. In the rapture to which she had aroused him he bent his neck and licked and sucked those wet pink lips, until she cried *That will do! I don't want to come off so! Poke me!* and she jerked her cunny back from his mouth.

Hedley knelt upright for a moment to rip the shirt from his back, then stretched her thighs roughly apart, and in the next second his peg was buried deep in her. Now she had her wish – he rode vigorously up and down

147

on her belly, whilst their naked bodies and limbs were entwined in the fascinating movements of poking. What joy – what Heaven – but alas, how evanescent! In no more than a minute, with tongues joined, he shed his seed into her clinging tunnel!

He felt her cunny tighten to grip One-Eyed Jack as he spent and her juices ran slippery and warm, for Florrie was coming off as strongly as he did inside her – and she was enjoying it even more, being a woman voluptuous to her marrow.

'Fill my belly full!' she exclaimed, and her back arched off the bed to thrust her loins hard against him and drive him in her to the hilt.

She was a prudent woman who considered two children enough to care for and wanted no more, and so when they had recovered their powers of locomotion, she got up to wash herself at the wash-stand under the window. Hedley chuckled to see her put herself to this trouble, but she had less faith than he in the beneficial effects of standing erect and jumping up and down a few times after she had been thoroughly rogered. When she had dried herself on the towel, she returned naked to the bedside.

'Let me have you again,' Hedley murmured, smiling up at her from where he lay at his ease. She laughed and told him that he couldn't do it again so soon, but when he moved his clasping hand away from his shaft, she saw that it was nearly full size. She got on the bed, laid hold of it, passed one thigh over him so that his fingers could reach her slit, and so they lay for a while, handling each other. When she was sure she had him in a right frame of mind, she renewed her questioning.

'You said you'd had a feel between Miss Hapgood's legs,' she began, 'then you can answer me something I've wondered about more than once — does a well-bred young lady like her go wet and slippy down there when she's interfered with?'

'Why yes,' said he. 'I played with her delicious mound, and the hair on it is like silk! The lips are so perfectly formed, so delicious to feel, that I thought I would spend at once in my trousers, the first time I ever touched her!'

'You have a warm nature,' Florrie murmured in approval, 'but you haven't given me a proper answer — did she become wet from your feeling?'

'Her heavenly little cunny became slippery with so sweet a juice that I wanted to thrust my shaft right up it,' he said.

'But you did no such thing, of course,' Florrie led him on. 'No one knows better than me how passionate you can be, but I'm sure you didn't allow a gentle tampering with her privates to get out of hand. You held back and behaved like the gentleman I know you are — you respected the young lady's virginity.'

'I've been a worse boy than you know,' he whispered, almost fetching off to the slow rhythm of Florrie's fingers playing up and down his trembling shaft.

'You don't mean to say . . . ?' she murmured in pretended shock. 'Are you telling me that you took advantage of Miss Hapgood — that you've had it up her?'

'Oh, Florrie,' he sighed, his voice faint as if he were at the point of expiring. 'Please try to understand, dear, dear, Florrie, my passions got out of hand — she is so lovely and my desire is so very strong! When I felt her sweet moisture on my fingers, it was impossible to hold back any longer — I pushed my shaft into her maiden slit!'

'You took her maidenhead!' exclaimed Florrie. 'Oh, you have been naughty, my lad! At least I hope you had the sense to pull out before it was too late.'

'The sensations felt too beautiful to spoil by withdrawing,' he admitted, 'I fetched off in her!'

'Oh my!' said Florrie. 'You've made me so hot with your tale that I've got to have *you*!'

With no more ado, she threw a leg over his belly and slid herself on top of him, her slack little bubbies pressed flat on his chest. It was the work of a moment to steer One-Eyed Jack up her open and slippery cunny, to make their bodies one again. Hedley was content to lie still and let her have her way with him, and he was rewarded with a poke that lasted longer and was more intense in its mental pleasure and more complete in its physical enjoyment than when he had done her.

For a quarter of an hour she gave herself up to a delicious squirming on his belly, her cunny holding his shaft, hardening it further with little nippings and tuggings, before she let him spend in a tidal wave of delight. Nor was she in any hurry to dismount after she too had attained the climax, but lay on him, with his softening shaft inside her comfortable body, in the somnolence of voluptuous fatigue. He was completely without defences when she resumed her enquiries about Miss Victorina Hapgood.

'Was it just the one time you had her?' she wanted to know, 'Or have you done her a lot?'

'A few times,' he murmured contentedly. 'I crept into her room at night and had her on her back in her own bed.'

'Lord – I knew you were a bold one, but to poke a girl in bed at night under the nose of her family – I'm blessed if that doesn't take the biscuit!' said Florrie. 'There's something else you can tell me that's puzzled me often – do genteel young ladies like Miss Hapgood come off when they're rogered? Or do they lie quiet and still and let you make use of their slit until you're finished? My husband used to say that real ladies don't know anything about coming off – only common women like me, he said, who can never get enough of it.'

The question caused Hedley to consider carefully. He thought back to the hour they'd passed in mutual solace in the spinney behind The Larches. On the first time he had her that afternoon he had pulled out and spent on her beautiful white belly. Later on, when he had her for the second time under the trees, he had been carried away by matchless sensations and gushed his sap clear up her cunny – but had *she* come off either time?

In the carriage returning from Georgina Playfair's party, dear little Vickie had been very keen to have her slit felt – she had of her own accord straddled his thighs to let him put Lord Dickie up her. She had given every indication of enjoying all that he did to her, and of wanting him to keep on doing it. She had almost swooned against his chest with the force of her thrills – but had she come off?

'Well?' said Florrie. 'Are you going to tell me or not?'

'I'm hanged if I know if she did or not,' he said finally.

Florrie shook her head in disapproval of his ignorance of the female sexual spasm.

'If you want my advice,' said she, 'you'll start making sure that the young lady comes off properly every time you have it up her, or after a time she'll find poking tedious and without point, and her legs will stay closed when you most fancy her.'

With that pearl of wisdom delivered, she slid off him and went to wash herself again. She put on her nightgown and went to fetch a bottle of gin from her sitting-room, declaring that a drop of it would perk him up for his climb upstairs to his own bed. Hedley realised that he was being dismissed politely, although he was not yet ready to leave.

His evening shirt was torn beyond repair, and he sat naked and cross-legged on the bed, much like a South Sea Islander, to drink a glass of gin-and-water with Florrie. He was well aware that he had said quite the wrong thing in reply to her question as to whether genteel young ladies achieved the bodily climax in love-making. His honest reply had been mistaken for indifference and he had forfeited a measure of Florrie's goodwill towards him.

He made a special effort to win back her esteem, and in the time they were chatting they drank half the bottle of gin between them. Florrie was eventually won over by his renewed attentions to her so that, after much urging, she gratified him by lifting her nightgown up to her armpits and standing beside the bed, in the glow of the candle-light, for his inspection. He pleased her by telling her how exciting he found her body.

He praised the warm feelability of her soft little bubbies, the exquisitely nervous line of her slender thighs, and he told her how very horn-raising was the contrast between her white belly and her dark brown bush. She sat down again on the side of the bed, near to him, and her hands crossed with his as she reached for his growing shaft and he felt up between her thighs under her nightgown.

In the calm silence of shared voluptuous thoughts, fingers played with shaft and slit, once more arousing the strongest and most thrilling sensations the human frame can sustain, At last, aroused beyond all restraint, Hedley slid off the bed and was on his knees at her feet. He pushed her nightgown higher, to reveal her bush and belly, and pressed his lips to the warm inside of her thighs.

'I want to kiss your slit,' he murmured.

'I won't let you!' said she, nearly but not quite won over to her former high opinion of him.

He pressed his face between her thighs and rubbed his nose in the curls of her motte, and soon enough she fell back on the bed. Her thin legs opened like a pair of nutcrackers and she rested them upon his bare shoulders while he clasped the small taut cheeks of her bottom. Now his hot mouth had full freedom to seek her newly-washed slit and lick it with delight.

'Leave off, you beast,' she sighed at first, her small hands clenched into fists that beat the bed, then she submitted and Hedley heard her sigh *Oh, yes, you beastly man, you* . . . He felt a gentle and tremulous motion in her belly, then her thighs came slowly together to trap his head between them. He tongued her rapidly, savouring her wetness, until she opened wide her thighs again – a long sigh escaped her and she came off with intense pleasure.

One-Eyed Jack was stiff as a rod of iron, and Hedley stood up and put his belly on Florrie's trembling belly. He dragged her nightgown up her body, to bare her hard-pointed bubbies and suck at them thirstily.

'No, don't – not again!' she moaned, and covered her curly-haired motte with her hands.

Hedley seized her wrists and pulled her hands away from the slit he was dying to enter, and saw how open and wet were the lips. He plunged his shaft into it, and found that the moisture he had drawn from her with his tongue gave a sensation of smooth wet velvet clinging to him. He thrust and thrust, mad for her, driving One-Eyed Jack deep into her belly, until he could penetrate no further. Soon he felt Florrie's cunny grip him, and she cried out impudently *Do me, you beast – do me hard – I* know how to come off, even if your young lady doesn't!' and in another moment, all was done and he had spent profusely inside her.

CHAPTER 11
A Shadow Over Conjugal Bliss

On Friday morning it was Hedley's intention to catch the 10.02 from Waterloo and meet Lottie Mayhew when she boarded it down the line. He looked forward to a most enjoyable afternoon of rogering her to a standstill, before continuing his journey to Walton-upon-Thames for another weekend with the Hapgoods. Matters turned out otherwise, for in the post that morning he received a letter from an old flame of his.

Miss Honorine Castle begged him to call upon her that very afternoon, and her missive breathed so notable a sense of total sincerity and urgency that Hedley was impressed. What the matter could be, he had not the least idea – he had been her ardent lover for a twelve-month, but three months had elapsed since their last meeting, and in that time both he and she had become engaged to be married.

Miss Honorine Castle was an actress, who had played small roles in Shakespearean comedies for some years before achieving a measure of public renown in a revival of the stage version of Mrs Henry Wood's greatly-admired 'East Lynne'. Hedley well knew there was no point in calling on her before three, for she did not rise until midday at the earliest, and never left the house before it was time to go to the theatre.

He was aware that she had been resting between theatrical engagements for a considerable period, but he was quite sure that her manner of life would not have changed. Accordingly, he despatched a message by telegraph to Mrs Hapgood, to say that family business delayed him in London, but that he would arrive at The Larches that evening.

At half past the hour of three, elegantly attired in a pale grey suit, Hedley presented himself at Miss Castle's apartment in Regent's Park and was shown upstairs by a lady's-maid he had not seen there before. Honorine was in her boudoir, sitting on a brocade chaise-longue and sipping a cup of chocolate. It was too early in the day for her to think of dressing, and she wore a wrap of pale blue satin and slippers of embroidered silk.

As with many another actress, Honorine's true age was not to be discovered. Hedley was aware that she was older than he, but beyond that he had never given much thought to the matter. She wore her hair short, in tight curls, and its colour was the jet black of youth, but to kiss her was to observe close up that under her face-powder there was a network of fine lines below her black eyes.

Nevertheless, as Hedley had good reason to know, her small and white-skinned breasts were perfectly round, with no sign of sagging, and her thighs were firm and smooth. Indeed, as he stood over her to take her hand and kiss her, he noted that her wrap was tied so negligently at the waist that the upper half of those voluptuous bubbies was exposed to his view. The sight pleased him greatly, and compensated for the inconvenience of postponing his journey to be with his darling Victorina.

They greeted each other with the warmth of good friends and former lovers, though with a certain touch of restraint now that each was promised elsewhere. His lips grazed her cheek lightly and her fingers gave his hand the tiniest of squeezes before relinquishing it, for she was impatient to launch into the business for which she had summoned Hedley to her side.

'How fine you look, dear Hedley,' she said. 'Did you have that suit made to court Miss Hapgood in? No matter – you have read in the newspapers the announcement that I am to be married to Sir Norris Wyndham-Norris . . .'

She paused to give him time to proffer his congratulations and his fervent wishes for her happiness. She nodded in polite acknowledgement and then continued with what she had brought him to her apartment to convey.

'Thank you for your kind wishes, darling Hedley,' cried she, 'but there is a great difficulty – and it relates not only to my future but also to yours with Miss Hapgood.'

'What do you mean?' he asked, frowning at the merest threat to the well-being of his betrothed.

'Hedley – hear me out in full,' said Honorine. 'Your memory is surely as vivid as mine of those dear days – not so very long ago – when we loved each other with a deep and passionate love. How well I remember them, those halcyon days – you were at the stage-door every evening, to carry me off to dinner and then to make love to me the whole night.'

'Ah – days of wild and unrepeatable joy,' Hedley replied in a noncommittal tone of voice.

'And those those madly romantic letters you wrote to me,' she went on, 'letters that burned like fire on the

157

page, that breathed a breathtaking passion like a perfume that drugs the senses and throws the reader into a daze of bliss . . .'

Hedley nodded and smiled and said nothing. Honorine reached down beside her and from behind a pink silk cushion she brought out an envelope and from it took a many-paged letter.

'Honorine – what is the purpose of this?' he asked.

'We shall come to that all too soon, I fear,' she replied. 'First let me refresh your memory, so that the full weight of the threat that hangs over our heads will be apparent to you.'

'Threat? What threat – tell me at once!' he cried, but she shook her head and began to read from the letter:

'Last night, Honorine, my dearest dear, after we quit the party at Romano's and drove in great haste to your apartment, I in my desperate eagerness to have you quite unable to wait until we arrived, but needs must clasp you to my chest in the hansom cab and thrust my hand down your bosom to feel your darling bubbies . . . we were no sooner up the stairs and in your boudoir than with feverish hands I stripped you until there was not a stitch on your divine ivory body except your stockings . . .'

'I say – did I write that?' Hedley exclaimed, his suspicion in abeyance at the thought of his own cleverness. 'It's very good, isn't it – it brings that night back vividly!'

Honorine paid no attention to his comments but read a snatch from the next page:

'Your soft white hand opened my trousers and took hold of my manly shaft, and gently drew back his hood, so that I felt your warm breath on him, and then the touch of your velvety tongue . . . I was dying for you, Honorine, dying and only you could save me then . . . ah, that

moment of divine joy when I laid you on your back on the couch and split you with my rod of iron . . .'

Hedley was smiling foolishly as he listened, and his hand lay on the bulge in his trousers, which was growing longer.

'Oh, that ecstatic moment,' Honorine read on, 'when our lips were joined in a long and luscious kiss and I spent in you! My emission was so soul-dissolving that together we cried out in delight – our paean of joy so loud and strong that your maid Ida came running up the stairs in a fright and saw us in the midst of our bliss . . . she stood in the doorway with one hand to her mouth and a bewildered expression on her face, then she blushed scarlet and turned and fled . . .'*

'What a lark that was!' said Hedley, grinning broadly.

'One that is liable to have tragic consequences,' Honorine told him. 'What do you suppose would happen if by any mischance your compromising letters fell into the hands of Sir Norris or Miss Hapgood?'

'But that's out of the question,' cried Hedley, 'for surely they are kept under lock and key in your writing-desk – and the time has come for you to consign them to the flames. Come, let me help you burn them now.'

Honorine handed him the letter from which she had read a few lines, with the comment that he could burn it whenever he pleased, but there were many others, as he very well knew.

'And we will burn them also,' he said. 'Where are they?'

'That is where our difficulty lies. A fortnight ago I had occasion to dismiss the servant who interrupted our joys – she had become insolent over her wages, which were somewhat in arrears, owing to an oversight on the part of my bankers. She waited until I was out and ransacked the apartment, and took your letters and some other personal property of mine that must not fall into the wrong hands.'

Her blue satin had fallen away from her legs, uncovering her delicious round knees and her thighs as high as the gartered tops of her grey silk stockings.

'Lord – it's blackmail!' exclaimed Hedley, staring in fascination at her exposed thighs and hoping to see more if she moved again. 'We must call in Scotland Yard at once!'

'Don't be a fool,' said Honorine calmly. 'She's a sly little bitch and you can be sure that if she's arrested, the letters will be in the post to your fiancee and mine. We have no choice but to pay her what she asks for their return.'

'How much?' he cried out in anguish.

'The wicked girl left me this one letter with a scribble of her own on the back of it to say that the other letters will be returned on payment of the sum of £1,000. Half from you and half from me is the slut's impudent suggestion, and she refuses to take a penny less. But there is a further and insoluble problem, my dear – I do not have the money to give.'

'Nor should you be intimidated in this vile way,' said he gallantly. 'The responsibility is mine alone – I wrote the letters. I shall pay the whole sum – my Papa is good for it.'

'Oh, my darling boy!' cried Honorine, her bosom heaving in emotion so profound that her white bubbies almost popped out. 'You have rescued my honour and my impending marriage – I shall be in your debt forever! I shall write today to the wretched girl at the address she has given in Clerkenwell, and open the negotiations for the return of the letters. And I humbly beg your forgiveness for allowing them to be stolen in this way.'

'No, it is I who should be asking your pardon,' he said, 'for if I had not indulged myself in writing those letters we would be under no shadow of jeopardy now.'

He dropped to his knees before her, and looking to her first for permission, he took in his hand one of her dainty little feet. It was clad in a slipper of soft glove-leather, which was embroidered with red and gold stitching, and he bowed his head to press a humble kiss of remorse on it. In doing so he must have raised it a trifle higher than he thought, or perhaps Honorine moved her legs, for the satin wrap slipped from her thighs and he saw that she wore no drawers. Above her crimson-gartered stockings, her naked thighs were revealed, round and smooth, almost up to the paradise of love itself.

'You are forgiven with all my heart, Hedley,' said she with a winsome smile, 'for I loved you with an equal passion, and your letters were a delight to read when I lay in bed late in the mornings and knew that I must wait until evening before you would be at my side again.'

As if to prove the truth of her words, her long legs opened just enough to give him a glimpse of the curls that covered her motte, and they were as jet-black as the curls on her head. She saw his gaze was fixed on her most intimate part, and she smiled and accused him tenderly of tricking her by raising her foot into letting him catch sight of a secret reserved for Sir Norris Wyndham-Norris alone.

'Ah, if things had been otherwise,' she continued, making no move to replace her wrap and hide her black-haired delight from his eyes, 'if our Fates had been differently arranged, and you, my darling boy, were as rich as Croesus, then I believe that you and I would now be living in married bliss, and Sir Norris and Miss Hapgood could look elsewhere. But it will be too many years before you come into your inheritance, and the cruel years will not let me wait. You will always be very close to my heart, Hedley, and I shall miss the strength of that virile young shaft of yours.'

At once Hedley ripped open his trousers to let the object of her praise jut out for her to see – hard as steel, and thick and long enough to make her sigh. Her dainty slippered foot pressed against its length, and the expression on his face advised her of the depth of his feelings at that moment. She told him to unbutton his waistcoat and put his hands behind his back and look at her.

'*Sir Percy Pokingham,*' said she softly, using the nickname they had bestowed upon Hedley's shaft in the time of their intimacy. 'Sir Percy Pokingham, Knight of the Bath and Grand Commander of the Order of the Muff, General Officer Commanding, Master of the Hunt, and a most tireless rider to hounds!'

So saying, she untied the belt of her wrap and let it fall open, presenting to Hedley's eager gaze the sight of the most delightful bubbies imaginable, firm and round, the skin milk-white and tipped with crimson berries. He stared in speechless delight, and his very soul was yearning for the privilege of feeling those matchless globes, while with a curious smile on her face Honorine rubbed the soft sole of her slipper along Sir Percy's quivering length.

'Your shiny black pussy is beautiful beyond words,' Hedley murmured, lost in sensations of blissful transport.

'Do you know Mr Harcourt's celebrated verses?' she asked, her thighs opening a trifle further to indulge him.

'Proud Nature, which is everywhere the same
Imparts to lustful man a burning flame,
In Greenland's ice or Equatorial fire
All men alike indulge their hot desire;

All men alike feel passion's fleshly heat,
And all alike hard-on their climax greet,
So that wherever in this world you go,
Still you will find the same voluptuous glow;

Hot rapture throbs through every purple vein.
And dies to spurt, and its enjoyment gain;
Amongst the dark, the brown, the red, the fair,
Woman unclothed is Empress everywhere.'

'Oh, yes, yes, yes . . .' Hedley sighed, almost ready to greet the climax himself under the friction of her dainty foot.

'Sometimes when I recite those lines I change a word or two at the end,' she said with a slow and lascivious smile, 'so—

Amongst the curls so black or brown or fair,
Cunny when stripped is Empress everywhere.'

Hedley's overstretched nerves could stand no more, and with a long moan of bliss, he spent in a shower that drenched her little foot and splashed up her stockinged leg almost to her knee. Before he had finished spurting, he flung himself bodily forward between her thighs, forcing them to open widely and let him have full sight of her swelling Mount of Venus – with its fleece of thick black curly hair that grew some way up her flat white

163

belly and for an inch or two down the insides of her long thighs.

Under his ardent onslaught Honorine fell back in her chair and in a trice his tongue was between the pouting lips of her pussy and licking at her enlarged nub. The touch galvanised her and she shrieked with delight: *Oh, you will make me do it!*

In another minute her feet left the floor and her legs waved in the air in a flurry of uncontrolled action as she attained the supreme point and fainted into ecstasy. Her fervour raised Hedley to the highest possible state of excitement – he flung his jacket to the carpet, wrenched up his shirt, threw her legs over his shoulders and plunged his swollen peg into her slit.

'Hedley – there is no one like you!' she sighed.

She was coming down from the peak of fetching off, her legs trembling and her breath fluttering in her open red mouth, but Hedley seized her round bubbies in his hands, whether she would or no, and rolled them briskly while he thrust up her slippery pussy with admirable strength. Miss Pussy very soon recovered her keen relish for being rogered, and he could feel the warm pulsations on his dilated shaft.

He became so aroused that, almost before he was ready, he gushed a stream of his essence into her, and she squealed as if expiring. They were both of them exhausted for a time by the climax, and they remained joined together for some minutes, to the prolongation of the after-glow of delight.

'Oh, Honorine, what a pearl amongst women you are,' Hedley sighed, kissing her cheeks and eyes, 'how divinely lascivious is your nature, how matchless your power to give the supreme pleasure a man can know!'

'We've had some blissfully happy times together, you

and I,' said she. 'Sit at my feet, dearest boy, and rest your head on my lap for a moment or two, while we remember our past joys together, for we may never have a chance to do so again.'

She raised her feet from the floor and stretched herself on her side on the chaise-longue, her blue wrap arranged discreetly to cover her black-haired motte but to expose her slender white thighs. Hedley sat on the carpet and rested his cheek on her warm thigh, above her stocking-top, staring up at her face with warm and open devotion.

'Dearest Honorine,' said he, 'please tell me if you love the man you have consented to marry.'

'You are impudent, Sir!' she replied, tapping his cheek with her finger-tips. 'I might ask you the same question – do you love Miss Hapgood?'

'With all my heart,' he answered at once.

A little offended by the readiness of his reply, Honorine asked if he had yet discovered whether Miss Hapgood was able to thrill him as she herself could, or did he intend to marry her and find out too late that he had a timid virgin as a bed-mate.

'I'm not entirely a fool,' he said with a smile at her show of peevishness. 'I have made a trial of her capability to be a satisfactory wife.'

'I knew it!' exclaimed Honorine. 'I knew you could never resist deflowering any young girl who fell into your hands – genteel or common. Speak freely, then – does she excite you as I do, Hedley – tell me the truth now!'

'She is just eighteen and her body excites me,' he said, 'for it is very beautiful. But she lacks all your divine experience – she knows nothing. When I show her my shaft she is mesmerised by it and lets me do whatever I choose to her.'

'How did you first have her?' Honorine asked curiously. 'In my youth every young girl of good family was so closely guarded by her mother that not even the most determined ravager of her honour had the least chance of success.'

'I had permission to take her for a walk,' said he, 'and in a field, leaning on a gate, I raised her dress from behind and slipped Sir Percy up her – it was as simple as that. Later that day, when all were asleep, I stole into her room and into bed with her.'

'It is quite clear that Miss Hapgood is as interested as you in the delights of love,' Honorine declared. 'That is unusual in a well brought up girl – perhaps you are lucky, my dear, in finding one who will give you all the pleasure you seek. Does she respond well to being had?'

It was the same question that Florrie Potter had asked him, and the answer to it was still as obscure to Hedley.

'I am endeavouring to find out,' he said frankly. 'Each time I have had my belly on hers and Sir Percy is snug in her warm pussy, her dear little belly rises up bravely to meet my poking – but she gives me no sign that she has achieved the climax. What do you think, Honorine – may she be frigid?'

'Do you continue poking inside her until you spend?'

'No – that would be risky, with her on her back. When I feel the ecstatic throb begin inside me, I pull out of her slit and shoot on her belly. Do you think that makes a difference?'

'No doubt of it,' said she. 'You rob her of her bliss by pulling out of her at the final moment. If you did that to me I would never speak to you again! Poke her to the finish and she'll come off as well as any woman, mark my words.'

'You have reassured me, dear Honorine. Now it is your turn to be open with me – are you not grievously disappointed with Sir Norris when he rogers you? I hardly think a man of fifty can satisfy you – even I have been vanquished by you at times.'

'No woman of sense is disappointed in bed by a gentleman who has £20,000 a year, a town house, a country seat, and a title,' she replied. 'Especially not now when I have found a way of making him rise to the occasion.'

'Tell me,' Hedley pleaded, agog to hear of it.

'There is no great mystery to it,' she said with a laugh, 'Sir Norris was at Eton College during his youth, where he was flogged in the best traditions of that famous scholastic establishment. When I knew this, everything followed. He comes to call and I take him to my bedroom, lock the door and strip to my chemise and drawers, while he sits in a chair and becomes red in the face.

'When I am ready, I take a birch from the cupboard and lead Sir Norris by the hand to the bed. He lies on his face while I pull down his trousers and tuck up his shirt. He has a good plump behind – an excellent target – to which I apply the birch with vigour. After a time, when his bottom is a fiery red, scratched and striped from the birching, he screams for mercy and swears that he loves me.

'Upon my demanding proof, he turns over on the bed to display his short thick rod standing hard from its nest of grey hair. I throw off the few stitches that preserve my decency and jump on to the bed beside him – he is on top of me at once, and I open my thighs and in goes his shaft to the hilt! I throw my legs over his behind and he pokes away at me, with much sighing and puffing, taking so long about it that I come off four or five times before he spends.'

During Honorine's account of bringing the wealthy baronet up to the mark, Hedley had opened her wrap to kiss her belly and her black-curled slit. He saw the invitation in her dark eyes and laid himself on the chaise-longue beside her, his hands on her soft bubbies. Honorine's fingers were grazing along Sir Percy's length with flying touches, and then she sat up and leaned over him, breathing her hot breath on his belly as her lips wandered down it and into his groin.

In heavenly delight though Hedley was, there slipped into his mind, unbidden and unwelcome, the thought that he had only her word that Ida had taken his letters and wanted cash for them. Suppose, came the shocking thought, that dearest Honorine needed cash to pay off embarrassing debts before wedding Sir Norris! The tale could be a fabrication, a plot hatched up between mistress and maid . . .

Perhaps Honorine, very well versed in the ways of gentlemen, had some inkling of what passed through Hedley's mind. She removed any inclination of his to pursue his unworthy train of thought by nuzzling her nose into his curls and pressing with wet lips a kiss to Sir Percy's throbbing flesh. Hedley saw her tongue dart out to flick over the uncovered head – purple and swollen with passion – and tremors of bliss ran up and down his spine.

For an instant she slipped the whole head into her mouth, to let it feel the warmth and wetness, before pushing it out again with her tongue. Waves of delicious sensation rushed through Hedley's body, as with cunning fingers she massaged his long thick shaft, and he knew that in another moment he would fetch off. Honorine knew it almost before he did, and she swallowed Sir Percy complete, sucking him into her mouth to the limit and Hedley writhed in spasms of joy as he spurted.

CHAPTER 12
A Night of many Surprises

After he had enjoyed Miss Honorine Castle to the full, Hedley took her for old time's sake to dinner at Bastiano's, both of them being much in need of refreshment and sustenance after their romp together. They dined well and talked long, and as a result, Hedley arrived at Waterloo Station only in the nick of time to catch the last train to Walton-upon-Thames.

At so late an hour there were few travellers, and he had the luxury of a compartment to himself. He stretched himself at full length along the seat, and with his hat tipped over his eyes he half-dozed as the train rattled along, savouring the feeling of calm lassitude that spread through him in the wake of his delicious frolics with Honorine. Sir Percy Pokingham had been pressed into action beyond the call of duty, and he had acquitted himself manfully.

It soon appeared, however, that Sir Percy had by no means exhausted himself, for into Hedley's drowsy mind he insinuated an odd but interesting thought. Honorine had been disdainful of Hedley's choice, as she expressed it, of a timid virgin as a bed-mate, and she had demanded whether Victorina excited him as greatly as she did. His reply had been equivocal – for although he loved his finacee truly, she had much yet to learn.

Here was an unrivalled opportunity to put it to the test, was the sly suggestion Sir Percy put into Hedley's mind – *hot from Honorine's pussy, plunge into dear Vickie's, and know how they differ and in what degree.* Hedley had consumed a great quantity of champagne at dinner with his former inamorata, and thought Sir Percy's idea a capital one. He would creep silently in Vickie's room and repeat with her all the pleasures he had tasted earlier with Honorine!

So the journey passed pleasantly, until he reached his stop and found that there was no conveyance available to take him to The Larches. He set out to walk, for it was a clear and warm summer night, with the moon well up, and eventually he turned into the drive and kept to the grass, avoiding the gravel. The house lay ahead, in complete darkness, and for the first time a doubt entered his mind as to the advisability of arriving so very late.

It was obvious that everyone was abed, the front door was locked and nothing stirred. To ring the bell and arouse the household was a daunting prospect, and he walked slowly round the house, hoping to find a way in. His diligence was rewarded at length by the sight of a gleam of light between the curtains of the drawing-room. He tried the handle of the french windows, and found he could enter by that way.

The gas light brackets on the walls had been turned down low, transforming the room into a domain of soft and restful shadows. Whilst he stood considering what next to do now that he had surreptitiously entered the house, Hedley saw with some astonishment that Mrs Hapgood sat half-sprawling in a wing chair. Her head lay against the high chair back, her eyes were closed, and she was in a pleasant doze.

She wore a navy blue evening-gown cut straight across the bosom, so that her heavy bubbies were half visible. Hedley's shaft was already at full stretch in his trousers, for he had amused himself during the long walk from the railway station with thoughts of rogering darling Vickie throughout the night. Observing her Mama in innocent slumber brought to his mind the lewd recollection of her visit to his room, on the last time he had been a guest in this house.

Sir Percy, already half-hard, leapt to attention at the fond memory of how he had fetched off to the strokes of Hedley's hand and soaked Mrs Hapgood's drawers right through, while she was trapped face-forward to the bedroom door! He had been thrust bare-headed against the soft flesh of her bottom and had spent there in a foaming flood, whilst the dinner gong sounded through the house!

In his condition of high arousal, the renewed temptation was more than Hedley could resist. He knelt silently at Mrs Hapgood's feet and lifted her plump bubbies out of her dress to suck them in turn. She sighed in her sleep and slid down a little in her chair. He put the tip of his tongue to the russet berries of her breasts and teased them boldly.

He knew then that he must have her, come what may, for his shaft was throbbing painfully in his trousers. With a hand that shook a little, he raised her dress in front until he had a full view of her legs, encased in white silk stockings, and her swelling thighs filling out her white cambric drawers. He felt through the slit in front to touch her handsome bush, then drew aside her chemise and stretched out her legs, placing her feet wide apart, to reveal all.

Still she slept on peacefully and, emboldened by his

mounting desires, Hedley untied the string of her drawers to lay bare her domed belly, so full and heavy that its button was lost to sight in a deep fold. He laid his cheek against that broad expanse of soft flesh as if it were a down-stuffed pillow on a bed, and revelled in the sensations it provoked in him. He pressed wet kisses to it, and licked it slowly and with intense delight, from its deep-set button right down to where the thick brown curls began.

Her pussy fascinated him – he gazed in wonderment whilst he fingered the thick fleshy lips, and told himself that it was into this warm slit that Mr Hapgood had plunged his shaft and gushed the seed into her womb that had grown to be Victorina! Through this same pliable orifice, nine months later, his beloved had come into the light of day!

Hedley licked his fore-finger to wet it, and introduced it gently into the admirable slit before him until he touched the sensual button and tickled it. Mrs Hapgood did not wake up, but behaved as if she were having a voluptuous dream – the tempo of her breathing quickened and her body twitched a little on the chair. As Hedley continued to play gently with her, he saw that her belly had begun to heave in and out, and her uncovered ample bubbies were rising and falling rapidly.

Her pussy had become very wet, and as the divine climax made its approach known, she woke at last. Her brown eyes opened, full of surprise to find herself in so indecent a plight, but the expression turned to pleasure when she came to realise that Hedley had her clothes up to feel her. Her backside slithered forward on the chair, to bring her hairy mound closer to him.

Hedley, nothing loth, pulled open his trouser buttons and let his throbbing shaft leap out. Mrs Hapgood took a firm hold with her left hand, her right displacing his to open the lips of her slit, and in another second she had brought him to the mark between her parted thighs. Two determined thrusts slid Sir Percy into her up to his pompoms, and the chair began to creak beneath his attack, Mrs Hapgood returning jab for jab.

'Oh what bliss, dear Hedley!' she sighed. 'Deeper, deeper, I beg you! Push in deeper!'

'Louisa!' he gasped, daring *in extremis* to address her for the first time by her name. 'Oh, Louisa, dearest – I am so far up you that we have become one! I'm spending in your cunny!'

Her plump round backside wiggled convulsively on the chair and she moaned as she received his hot and gushing admiration.

'Adorable boy!' she exclaimed. 'Give me all of it!'

When they recovered their tranquillity, there were necessary explanations – of the duration of the family affair that had delayed him in London, of her sending her daughters to bed at eleven and sitting up for his arrival, of the strange power of his emotions on finding her asleep in the drawing-room, and his irresistible urge to have her. She wanted him to join her in bed for a repetition of their pleasure, but Hedley claimed to be worn out and insisted on sleeping alone for that night.

They went up the staircase with an arm around each other's waist, and at her bedroom door he kissed her a warm good-night and gave her soft motte a parting squeeze through her dress. He was certain that before the weekend was over Louisa would find occasion to get him alone and lie on her back for him, and the prospect pleased him, though he was hard put to it to say why. That lay in the future – for tonight it was his darling Vickie he wanted.

After an afternoon with Honorine Castle and a quick poke in the drawing-room with Louisa, he found it unusual in himself to still retain the energy to consider poking his fiancee, but the words Honorine had spoken stuck fast in his mind and sustained his interest. He changed to nightshirt and dressing-gown and sat for another fifteen minutes in his room to give Louisa time to go to bed and fall asleep before he went prowling along the passage towards Victorina's room.

He entered slowly, holding his breath when he heard the door creak, and stood in the silvery moonlight listening to gentle breathing from the bed. As his eyes became accustomed to the level of light, the spectacle that met his gaze was astounding – there were two people in Victorina's bed! Hardly able to believe the evidence of his own eyes, he crossed the room with muffled footsteps and stood at the foot of the bed to stare – and saw that Vickie's sister was in bed with her. Both young ladies were asleep, cuddled close in each other's arms.

For some moments Hedley stood in thought, then very gently raised the sheet that covered the beautiful sisters. The sight that greeted him made Sir Percy waggle like a metronome under his nightshirt – the darling girls lay lip to lip and bosom against bosom, their long nightdresses up round their waists, Adelaide's slim thigh between Victorina's, their hands at each other's sources of delight. Hedley gazed in open-mouthed joy at Victorina's curly-haired pussy, half-hidden under Adelaide's girlish fingers, and then at Adelaide's almost bare little slit where Victorina's long slender hand lay.

There was not the slightest doubt what had been enacted in this bed – the darling girls had played with each other's warm privities and caressed each other to

176

the climax – it might be many times – before they had fallen at last into the sleep of satiation. That being so, Hedley reached the conclusion that there was nothing now remaining to hinder his pleasures and at once slipped off his clothing and got into bed with them.

He was on Victorina's side of the bed and she lay turned away from him. He reached over her bare and rounded hip to stroke her soft belly and then eased aside Adelaide's fingers and took possession of his darling girl's moist slit in his own hand. She half-woke, murmuring: *Don't tire me out, Adelaide – I want to get up early in the morning and look my best when my darling Hedley arrives.*

'I am here with you now, my love,' Hedley murmured, 'and you are so lovely that I am almost swooning with emotion.'

His middle finger was between the parted lips of her slit to stroke her sticky little button, and his stiff shaft lay throbbing between the round cheeks of her bottom. She came wide awake at once, as did Adelaide, who took in the scene with a giggle, while Victorina trembled in dismay and embarrassment that both fiance and sister had learned that she permitted each the liberty of her beautiful young body.

Hedley found the position so perversely stimulating that, in spite of the many exertions of the day, he wanted to possess his beloved immediately and roger her to a copious spend. Her dear moisture was on his fingers, and Sir Percy was shaking in his excitement, but Victorina stopped him. She turned over to face him and hid her face against his bare shoulder.

'I am so ashamed,' said she coyly. 'What will you think of me, my dearest! My disappointment when you did not arrive by bedtime was so crushing that I foolishly said yes to Adelaide when she offered to keep me company until I fell asleep.'

'You need feel no embarrassment, my darling girl,' said he, his nose burrowing into her sweet-smelling hair, his lips grazing her soft cheek, and his hand between her thighs to ease her distress, 'I am sure that dear Adelaide was a great comfort to you.'

'We came to bed late, for we expected you and only gave you up at eleven,' she murmured, 'but Adelaide was so very naughty and frolicsome that I hardly knew which way to turn . . . nothing I did would deter her from caressing me and so insatiable was she that I soon went to sleep out of sheer fatigue.'

'She's fibbing,' said Adelaide, with her schoolgirl giggle, 'once I'd felt her pussy and made her fetch off, she wanted to do it again and again – she wore us both out.'

Hedley became so aroused at Adelaide's words that he feared he was about to spend against Victorina's bare bottom. His hand clenched on her warm motte, driving his middle finger deeper into her wetness, so that she trembled and gave a little cry.

'Are you going to put Harry Horn into her pussy?' Adelaide asked, her voice full of eager curiosity.

'Yes, I am,' Hedley exclaimed softly. 'Me feelings for her are so strong that unless I lie on her belly and have her at once, I shall die!'

He threw himself upon Victorina, who protested that he was behaving indecently and with a lack of respect for her honour, in the presence of her sister. She opened her legs slowly, as a sign of her modesty, but wide enough to receive the guest and make him welcome. Hedley gripped the cheeks of her bottom to give himself a firm purchase and tupped her with swift strokes, making the bed shake and creak to his every movement.

'Do you mean to shoot your cream into her pussy?' Adelaide enquired, greatly interested in what was taking place so close to her.

Hedley detached a hand from Victorina's bottom and felt between Adelaide's legs. She had turned over on her side to see her sister rogered, and her nightdress was round her waist. At the touch of Hedley's hand on her thigh she raised her knee, to give him free access to her almost bare-lipped slit. He pressed a gentle finger into it, and soon she was squirming about and trembling passionately.

At the supreme instant when the two lovers were fused most closely together, sighing and shuddering, and Hedley's essence overflowed into Vickie's quivering belly, Adelaide exclaimed in a shrill voice: *I'm fetching off, Hedley!*

'And so am I!' cried Victorina.

Her candid admission aroused Hedley to new heights while he was in the very act of spending, so that his shaft swelled yet thicker and his blissful spasms were prolonged far beyond the ordinary, and his emission was so very abundant that he felt himself lose consciousness for a few moments.

'Vickie – darling girl! You did it with me at last,' he happily murmured, when the power of speech was restored to him.

'Oh, Hedley – what heavenly joy you bestowed upon me then,' Victorina whispered, her lips seeking his in a long kiss.

'Three for the price of one – that's not bad,' Adelaide said by way of irreverent comment. 'Shall we do it again?'

'No more,' Victorina sighed as Hedley withdrew and rolled off her. 'I am completely exhausted by love.'

'We'll see about that,' Adelaide declared.

She threw the covering sheet to the foot of the bed and sat up to seize the hem of Victorina's nightdress and pull it up from her waist to her armpits, exposing her soft belly and her full white breasts. To excite her sister again, she lay her head upon the bosom she had bared and licked the red berries of those delicious bubbies. Hedley watched in delight, holding in his hand a limp Mr Harry Horn and hoping he would revive.

His resources had been stretched to the limit by his frolics with dear Honorine and his quick poke in the drawing-room with Louisa, not half an hour before. In these circumstances, Master Horn had performed valiantly when he found himself sheathed in Victorina's cunny – which had been so very well prepared by Adelaide's fingers! The spirit was willing, thought Hedley, but the flesh was weak – it was unlikely that Harry Horn would stand again that night.

He reckoned without the arousing effect of two pretty young ladies embracing at his side. Under the stimulus of Adelaide's tongue, Victorina's sighs of protest had very soon died away and her bottom was squirming softly on the bed, disturbing Hedley's lethargy. Adelaide hurled herself between her sister's white thighs, where she pressed her mouth to the curly-lipped entry to the temple of all delight, and began a play so pleasant that Victorina's little cries soon made it evident that she was again approaching the climax.

'Oh, Addy – I'm going to do it again,' she sighed.

Hedley was inspired to reverse his position on the bed, head to foot, in order to raise Adelaide's nightdress higher and kiss her delicious bare bottom. Meanwhile, he placed Harry Horn in her hand, and she jiggled him with the expert touch she had been taught by Tom the groom, until his size and stiffness were satisfactory again. Hedley no longer cared how many times he had spent that day – his urgent desire was to do so once more.

He nipped the soft flesh of Adelaide's bottom gently between his teeth, making her body jerk, and he fingered between her parted thighs, rubbing her wet nub lightly. He could feel the sweet perspiration of sexual excitement on her slender young body, and he speeded up his caresses until she cried out in sharp pleasure and came off, bucking and shuddering.

In the selfsame instant, Victorina moaned and writhed under the provocation of Adelaide's tongue lapping between her legs, and the bed shook to the convulsions of her delight. The presence of two beautiful young ladies attaining the sweet climax next to him in bed was more than Hedley's nervous system could tolerate, and he participated in the general ecstasy by shooting his sap into the palm of Adelaide's little hand.

After the three of them together had soared like Daedalus to the very summit of pleasure, their pinions could bear them no longer and they sank back to earth, to lie still in gentle contentment. The experience had been so intoxicating that Victorina fell into a sound sleep, while it took Adelaide and Hedley a good quarter of an hour to recover themselves.

How it had come about he did not know, but Hedley found that he was now lying between his sleeping fiancee and her sister. Adelaide had Mr Harry Horn in her hand, though he was soft and small after his supreme effort.

'I mean to have him in my pussy too,' she whispered giggling in Hedley's ear.

'I fear you must be disappointed tonight, dearest

Adelaide, for he is too fatigued to be of service to you,' said he.

The thought that Adelaide was insatiable had not yet taken root in Hedley's mind, as it was to do so from this night on. She paid not the least attention to his words, but threw herself over his belly and pressed hot kisses on the moist and limp shaft she held. Soon she began licking, as she had done on the day when she and Hedley had played and then abandoned a game of croquet on the lawn, for a different game indoors.

The wet caress of her tongue caused Hedley to sigh wistfully that he had no more to give. To mollify her and satisfy her desires as best he could, he tickled her barely-fledged and yet slippery cunny until her bottom was squirming deliciously. With a delicate touch, he opened the lips and pressed a finger into her, to touch her tiny button. At once she took his shaft right into her mouth, and tongued it swiftly – and after a time, to Hedley's intense surprise, Mr Harry Horn was stiff again.

'Now you can put him in me!' said she, with a giggle.

To favour his depleted strength, Hedley turned her over on her side and lay close up to her back and bottom. Adelaide was trembling and almost speechless with delight as the instant of her first poke came close – she raised her knee, as he showed her, to open her thighs, whereupon Hedley put the head of his newly-stiffened shaft to her wet pussy, gripped her tightly by her slender hips, and told her to take a deep breath.

With the soft little cheeks of her bottom snuggled against his belly, Hedley straightened himself and penetrated her from behind, a position thus far unknown to her. The consideration that he was taking the precious virginity of a sixteen-year-old girl hardened Hedley's long shaft to the firmness of iron, and he thrust upwards into Adelaide's tender little pussy without a thought for her ordeal.

Adelaide cried out once as her maidenhead was torn through, and then fell silent, letting him do as he chose. He brought her hand down between her thighs to the point where he was most intimately united with her, and taught her how to squeeze the root of his shaft while he rocked slowly back and forth in her.

'Hedley – you're actually doing me,' she sighed, her unbound long hair falling over his face as she tossed her head on the pillow. 'Shall you fetch off in my pussy?'

'Oh yes, Addy,' said he softly. 'Tell me how it feels to you now – is it pleasant?'

His hands had crept up under her nightdress to hold and feel her soft little breasts, warm and delicious in his clasp. She answered that it felt divine and he kissed her neck and cheek as he rogered her slowly but insistently. He had done so much that day that it took a long time for his desires to mount towards the peak, yet now that Sir Percy was lodged in another soft pussy, he was certain of what was going to happen.

After ten or fifteen minutes of gentle tupping, Hedley felt the familiar delicious throb in his belly. Without a moment to consider whether he ought to pull out and spend on Adelaide's bottom, he held her close and changed his stroke to fast short digs as the climax came on. Hard-worked Harry Horn bounded in spasms of delight and flicked his last few drops of sap into Adelaide's tight little pussy.

CHAPTER 13
A Turning Of The Tables

On his return to London after a long weekend at Burwood Park, during the course of which he had gratified his fiancee seven times, her sister twice fewer, and their mother four times, Hedley retired to his bed in Great Portland Street after lunch and slept soundly until Tuesday morning. Over breakfast he found awaiting him a note sent round by Honorine, advising him of the address where her dismissed maid, Ida Scroggins, could be interviewed.

It must be confessed that Hedley had taken no steps to call upon his father at his house by Hampstead Heath to ask for the £1,000 Ida had demanded for the safe return of his indiscreet letters. One good reason for this was that Hedley had no confidence at all that Mr Gillingham Senior would oblige him with hard cash for a purpose he would have thought disgraceful. A further and even more compelling reason was that Hedley knew his father to be abroad, with no prospect of an early return.

After breakfast he took time and pains to dress himself in his finest – a dark, almost black, suit of an inspired cut, with crisp white linen and a white carnation for a button-hole – and sallied forth to call upon his bankers, the well-known Messrs. Coutts, in the Strand.

His business there concluded, he lunched excellently well in a chop-house nearby, and drank half a bottle of port with his meal, to fortify himself against the ordeal to come.

He took a hansom cab to Clerkenwell, twenty pounds in gold the total sum he had to bargain with when he met Ida. It was a very long way from £1,000, but Hedley intended to trust to his wits and his looks to make up the difference. His cab dropped him outside a tenement building of dismal aspect, and the gift of a penny to an urchin sitting on the steps gained him the information that the Scroggins household was to be found on the fourth floor.

He climbed the dirty stone stairs, found a door from which paint twenty years old was peeling, and knocked with the knob of his smart walking-cane. He heard voices raised inside, and in a couple of minutes there were shuffling steps behind the door, and it was opened to him by Ida herself. Hedley gazed at her in mild surprise – no longer was she the neat and trim maid he had known in Miss Castle's employ – in only a fortnight she had let herself become a slattern.

She stood before him in a crumpled white blouse that needed washing, and a torn grey skirt, below which her stockinged feet showed without shoes or slippers. Her dark brown hair was not drawn up into a large bun on top of her head, as when she had been in service, but it hung uncombed and untidy about her neck and shoulders. The weather had been very warm of late, it being the month of July, and Hedley caught a distinct aroma of perspiration from Ida's body.

'Took your time getting here,' said she ungraciously. 'I've been expecting you since last Thursday.'

'Good day to you, Ida,' said Hedley, not put out at all,

and he raised his hat politely. 'Matters of importance take time to arrange – may I come in?'

She turned away from the door, and Hedley observed the swing of her bubbies under her loose blouse. He was prepared to wager then that she wore nothing else under it, not even a chemise – and from the wag of her backside as she went ahead of him, she had no petticoats under her skirt. Her sluttishness excited him strangely, and he made a silent vow to have her before he left the building, come what may.

Ida led him into a cramped living-room, where a scratched table and four chairs pushed close round it jostled for space with a worn couch and two wooden armchairs flanking an empty grate. In one of these sat a fat woman of an indeterminate age, in the other a thuggish man of perhaps twenty-five, wearing corduroy trousers and a shirt without collar or tie. Hedley looked at the pair enquiringly, not pleased to have witnesses to the transaction.

'This is my Ma,' said Ida, 'and my brother Len – he's here to see there's no rough stuff.'

Hedley stared briefly at the bruiser, who glared back at him in silence and made no attempt to rise from his chair, although Mrs Scroggins remembered her manners so far as to bob her head and mutter that she was pleased to meet him. Hedley, uninvited, took a seat in the centre of the couch, his ebony stick planted upright between his feet and his gloved hands clasped over the silver knob.

'Have you brought the money?' Ida asked, standing with her hands on the back of a battered dining-chair.

'Do you have the letters here?' he replied.

'Straight swap,' said she, frowning at him, 'Money in one hand, letters in the other, fair hand-over and be on your way.'

'Not so fast, Ida,' Hedley said with an easy smile. 'I must have time to examine the letters properly before I accept them, to be sure that I'm getting what I've come for. And there are points to be agreed between us – of not troubling Miss Castle again, and so on. I think it best we withdraw to another room and settle these matters in private between the two of us.'

Ida looked at her mother – either for support or inspiration – and announced that there wasn't another room to go into. When Hedley asked where she slept at night, she pointed to the couch he sat upon. Brother Len said in a surly voice that he wasn't letting her use his bedroom for her silly jawing and upset his mastiff bitch and her litter in there.

'You can use my room,' said Mrs Scroggins, after her daughter had stared at her for some time, 'only you're not to touch anything or go moving things about – you hear me?'

The room into which Ida conducted Hedley was hot and fusty, the window tight closed and the sun beating on it. Almost all of the space was taken up by a sag-backed double bed, the only other item of furniture an old wardrobe with the door hanging open. There being nowhere else to sit, Hedley took a seat on the side of the bed, and Ida sat beside him without a qualm. He removed his gloves and threw them on the bed with his hat and stick, then took her hand in his.

He talked nicely to her for some time, of nothing very much, but letting her see clearly that he had a strong letch for her. In his mind was the oft-expressed opinion of his chum, the Hon. Randolph Joynes, that it was universally known that young women of the lower classes were always at the disposal of gentlemen, and they understood what a considerable honour was bestowed on them when they were rogered by their betters.

'Go on with you!' said Ida with a sly grin when Hedley put his hand on her knee. 'You won't get round me like that – not when there's the matter of cash to be settled between us.'

'But that's been settled already,' Hedley answered, with a pleasant smile, transferring his hand to her bosom to feel her soft bubbies through her crumpled blouse, 'the amount has been set and I have come here to effect the exchange with you – to take what you have to offer and give you cash in return. I see nothing to be discussed on that score, my dear. I wanted to get you away from the others for a purpose you can well guess.'

'Then hand over the money and you shall have the papers – and then we're at liberty to do other things,' said she.

'I can't wait while I read through all the letters,' Hedley replied. 'That can come later – I must have you now, dear Ida, I am so hot for you!'

While he was talking, he undid the buttons of her blouse, to find as he thought, that once he had opened it, her bubbies were bare. They were of a middle size and not at all badly shaped, though their red tips pointed away from each other, as if they squinted. He felt them soundly, then bowed his head and sucked at the buds until he had made them stand up, and as he did so he became ever more intoxicated by the heady aroma of sweet perspiration that rose from Ida's flesh.

Deciding that discretion was the better part, and that she would sooner arrive at getting the money by giving way to him, Ida let herself fall backwards on the bed, her legs dangling over the side, and with her own hands pulled up her skirt. Her grey linsey stockings were in poor repair, Hedley saw, with runs and snags and a hole in one heel. They were gartered above her knees and she had on no drawers or chemise.

'Come on, then,' she whispered as his hand slid up her bare thigh towards the object of his desires, 'but do me quietly – I don't want them to hear us,' and she nodded towards the door, beyond which her mother and brother sat in morose silence.

Hedley was gazing in delight at her brown-haired motte – he thought it one of the most lascivious he had ever laid eyes on, being full and prominent, as if thrusting forward from between her legs. The fleshy lips pouted well clear of a bush of thick brown hair, as if ready to press a warm kiss to any shaft that came close enough. Hedley's fingers stroked quickly up and down this plaything, then slid inside to find a good-sized button.

'Well?' Ida whispered. 'Are you going to fiddle about with your fingers, or are you going to do me proper?'

By way of answer Hedley opened his trousers and pulled out into sight his hard-on shaft. Ida's wet tongue came out to lick round her mouth when she saw the size of what was displayed, and slid her legs wider apart. In an instant Hedley was over her, his shaft between her thighs and its head butting at the lips of her voluptuous cunny.

Ida insinuated a hand between their bellies to prise open her split for him, and with a long push he sank his length into her. At once she threw her head back, closed her eyes, and bucked her belly up at him in a lively rhythm, muttering to him to *Get on with it!* He needed little urging, for the wretched squalor of the circumstances had aroused him immoderately. He assaulted Ida's belly with short sharp jabs, and within a minute of penetrating her, he spent copiously in her hot cunny.

She pushed him off her body almost before the last drop was delivered, and stood up to give herself a perfunctory wipe with the hem of her skirt. Hedley remained on the bed, half-lying on his side, his legs drawn up and his trousers open, so that his wet and softening shaft hung out in full view.

'There, you've had me,' said Ida, not troubling to do up her blouse, and leaving her bubbies to swing to her movements, 'now we can get on with the business. Get the cash out.'

'Certainly, my dear,' said he, with a boldness that he was far from feeling, 'bring the letters here.'

To his very great surprise she turned up her skirt, and from a pocket sewn to the inside, produced a slim packet of ten or a dozen letters in their envelopes. To encourage her, Hedley felt in his waistcoat pocket for a few gold sovereigns, and counted them out one by one on the bed. He was confident that she was unable to picture how great a sum £1,000 would be in coin of the realm, and he thought he might without too great an effort bamboozle her with the sight of newly-minted gold.

'One . . . two . . . three . . . four . . . five,' he counted, then stopped to chide her gently, 'but surely you mean to put down the letters in return?'

'There's your letters!' said she, casting the entire bundle on to the bed beside the richly gleaming gold coins.

'Did you enjoy reading them, Ida?' he asked with a smile, setting out no more money for the present.

'Oh my, the things you and Miss Castle did to each other!' she sighed, sitting down beside him again on the bed. 'I didn't know where to hide my face for blushing.'

'They set up a pretty tremor or two here, I'll wager,' said Hedley, his hand in her lap to feel her plump pussy through her skirt. 'Who did you find to solace your yearning?'

'Only my own hand, for in Miss Castle's service I was never allowed followers and she hardly ever gave me a day off. I lay in my bed at night, when you were with her, and brought to mind what I'd read in your letters while I pleasured myself to sleep with my fingers.'

'And since then?' he enquired.

'Since I've been staying with Ma I've come to know a drayman who drinks in the Prince Albert. He takes me to his lodgings every night and does me till I'm bow-legged.'

'Lucky girl!' Hedley murmured, bestowing an affectionate squeeze on her cunny. 'There's nothing in the world to match a rogering bout that ends only when both partners drop from blind fatigue. I want to have you again, Ida – is there any way to get rid of your family and cast off restraint – I'll do you bow-legged *and* cross-eyed too, my girl!'

'Give me five shillings and I'll send Len to the grog-shop to get a bottle or two for us,' said she.

'But that will take no more than five minutes! Is there now other way you can think of?'

'With five shillings in his pocket he'll be blind drunk for a week,' said Ida. 'We shan't see him again today, believe me.'

'And your mother – will she go with him?' Hedley asked as he fished in his trouser pocket for two silver half-crowns.'

'Lord, don't trouble your mind about Ma! She had a meat pie and two quarts of ale not half an hour before you came to the door – she'll be fast asleep by now.'

Ida buttoned up her blouse, took the cash and went out of the room. Hedley heard voices mumbling, then footsteps and the slam of a door. Ida returned to report that Len had been sent on his errand and that Ma had nodded off in her chair and could be forgotten about. She threw herself down on the bed and took the five gold sovereigns in her hand, to study closely, as if she had never before seen so admirable a likeness of good Queen Victoria. Hedley seized the opportunity to unbutton her blouse again and handle her soft bubbies.

'Ida, my dear,' he said, feeling her with delight, 'you are a lovely poke and a nice girl, and for that reason I wish to ensure that you get your money and at the same time I want to protect you from becoming involved in a criminal act. Perhaps no one has told you of it, but the penalty is a severe whipping on your bare back by the common hangman, followed up by branding on the breast with a red-hot iron, and transportation in chains to the Australian colonies as a convict field-labourer for the remainder of your natural life.'

Not for one minute did Hedley believe that such penalties were inflicted on apprehended blackmailers, but he was certain that Ida was even more ignorant of the law than he was. She stared at him with an expression of horror on her face.

'For your own protection, Ida,' he continued, assured that he had her entire attention, 'what I suggest to you is this – return these letters to me without payment or duress, and I will give you the money in return for rogering you. By that device, as you can clearly see, you receive the cash and commit no felony, since taking money for spreading your legs involves no law-breaking.'

'This needs a bit of thinking about,' said she, wrinkling her forehead in puzzlement.

She went to the decrepit wardrobe and from it brought

out a gin bottle three-quarters full, explaining that this was Ma's night-time hoard, in case she needed a drop to get her off to sleep. Hedley generously offered to replace it, or pay the cash value thereof. There were no glasses, and so each of them took a turn to drink from the bottle neck. Hedley restricted himself to sips, but Ida treated herself to full-mouthed swigs.

'What you're telling me,' she said after much thought, during which time Hedley amused himself playing with her bare bubbies, 'is that I'm better off, as regards the law, that is, to be whoring, than to take money for these letters?'

'Dear Ida,' Hedley murmured, 'you and I know very well that there is no question of your really turning whore – it is a mere subterfuge to keep you clear of a dangerous charge of extorting money with menaces – a very serious offence. Whoever advised you to risk so dreadful a punishment did not have your true interests at heart.'

'I've been made use of!' Ida exclaimed, and she up-ended the gin bottle and poured the oily liquid down her throat.

'I fear so,' Hedley sighed, most sympathetically. 'What does Miss Castle need the money for – do you know, my dear?'

The liquor was already taking an effect on Ida, and mingled with her sense of grievance, it blinded her to Hedley's bluff.

'She has a son at boarding-school,' said Ida, 'and she's got behindhand with the fees. The boy's about twelve and no one knows who the father is – I'm pretty sure Miss Castle doesn't know herself. She wants to get the boy settled before she marries Sir Norris. You can't blame her for that, only it seems to me now that she's taken advantage of me – I run all the risk!'

'How much is your share of the money to be, Ida?' asked Hedley, stroking the firm tips of her bubbies. 'Half of it?'

'Lord, no! A hundred pounds she promised me, that's all.'

'But how does she mean to ensure that you deliver the money into her hand, and not run off with the whole sum?'

'She's got proof that I lifted a watch from her jewel box,' Ida confessed. 'She said she'd have me taken up as a thief if I didn't help her with her plan to bilk you – and you being so good to me! I'm sorry – truly I am!'

'Think no more of it. Once the letters are in my possesion I will make sure that Miss Castle surrenders whatever proof she may hold over you. Leave it to me.'

To comfort Ida, he turned her on her back and sucked her bubbies very thoroughly. Soon she forgot her troubles and gave all the signs that she was ready to be tupped. In Hedley's mind was the memory of Randolph's tale of rogering a young whore on her hands and knees in the East End, and he told Ida that he wanted her not on her back again, but in doggie-style.

She took another long pull at the gin bottle, set it down on the floor and stripped off blouse and skirt to be naked except for her raggedy stockings. With a grin at Hedley she climbed on to the bed and took up position on her hands and knees.

'I don't mind sticking my arse up in the air for a gent like you,' said she. 'You've got a good John Thomas on you.'

In a trice, Hedley threw off his jacket, flipped open the buttons of his waistcoat and was on the bed behind her. He felt the plump globes of her backside and dabbled with his fingers into her voluptuously pouting split, revelling in the slippery feel of her moisture on his fingers.

'Let me feel you slide up my cunny from behind,' exclaimed Ida, wriggling her bottom about in pleasure.

Hedley pulled his shirt up to his chest and thrust his belly closely to the cheeks of her behind. Mr John Thomas found his way into her without assistance, and Hedley pushed forward till he had filled Ida's cunny full of hot hard gristle. With both hands he reached forward to seize her dangling bubbies and squeeze them, whilst he bounced against her hams.

'Do me as hard as you can,' she sighed, 'I love it!'

At that he put a hand on the nape of her neck and bent her spine forward, until her elbows, forearms and forehead touched the bed and lay on it – and only her backside was raised up for his convenience. Holding her fast in this attitude of complete submission, he rattled away merrily, savouring his descent into squalor to the very full, until at last he squirted his essence into her, with a loud cry of delight.

'Don't stop!' cried she. 'I'm coming off!' and Hedley in his convulsive spending forced her face down into the bed and kept up his attack, while she shrieked and her body shuddered to the spasms of her delight.

They lay down on the bed to rest themselves, neither of them thinking that the session was yet over. Hedley refreshed his energies with a few sips of gin, and Ida kept sucking at the bottle until it was empty. She had entered into a condition of intoxication, all thought of £1,000 wiped from her mind. Hedley let his hand lie over her hairy pussy, trying to remember when he had last seen so naturally voluptuous a specimen as this.

His middle finger lay in her wet slit, she sprawling with

her legs apart, and he tickled her button until she sighed and came off again. Pleased with the result, he did it to her again – and then again – until he had brought her off seven times on the trot. Whether she was yet either bow-legged or cross-eyed, she at least was hopelessly drunk from the gin she had imbibed.

Hedley's share of the bottle had been just sufficient to put him in a mood for unfamiliar experimentation. Now that he had tried for himself the pleasures of the dominant poke described by Randolph Joynes, he was of a mind to repeat the escapade of Digby Wilton-Gooch with Lady Augusta. Ida lay limp and quite unresisting, and she giggled when he turned her over face down and dragged her by her ankles across the width of the bed. He arranged for her to lie half on it, draped over the side, her feet trailing the floor and her naked rump exposed.

Hedley slipped Mr John Thomas for a few moments between the lips of Ida's pouting pussy, to lubricate him for what was to follow, then lay over her back to put Johnny to the puckered knot-hole hidden in the crease of her cheeks. He took a long breath and pushed, and felt his shaft sliding straight into her. She murmured a little beneath him, but was too drunk to be coherent, and whether her muttering indicated disapproval or delight, Hedley could not make out.

He passed his hand under her thigh, to pry open her wet slit and finger her button. *All up*, she muttered woozily, but Hedley could make no sense of the words, nor was he in a mood to try. New and ecstatic sensations flooded through him, although they emanated less perhaps from the physical fact of where he was lodged than from the mental image of the perversity of his act.

The rhythmic thrusts of his shaft and the movement of

his fingers over her button roused Ida to new pleasure, and she began to gasp in time with his strokes. She was writhing under him, the cushions of her bare cheeks against his belly serving to intensify his sensations to a veritable delirium.

'Oh, Ida you lovely slut!' Hedley gasped in a yet hitherto unknown joy. 'I'm going to spend in your knot-hole!'

Whether she understood his words is a question that cannot be answered, but she heaved herself under him and pushed back against his furiouis strokes, before uttering one single shrill cry and collapsing senseless. With a long moan of bliss, Hedley shivered and discharged his essence into her ravished behind, and even as he lay dribbling out his final drops, he heard the door open behind him, and he turned to see Ida's mother stand flabbergasted on the threshold.

'Murderer! What have you gone to our Ida?' she shrieked, seeing her daughter lying face down and still.

Hedley pulled out of Ida, like a cork from a narrow-necked bottle, and stood up with Mr John Thomas in his hand, to dry him on his shirt. Mrs Scroggins eyes flickered unbelievingly from Ida's rump, where a trickle of white sap ran down her leg from her flooded passage, to the girth and length of the shaft between Hedley's fingers, and then back to Ida's behind, while Hedley tucked Mr Thomas away and buttoned his trousers and waistcoat.

'There is no need for alarm,' said he with a friendly smile, 'I was rogering your daughter, with her ready consent, but she has fallen unconscious from an excess of alcohol.'

'My gin!' cried the harridan, catching sight of the empty bottle that had rolled under the bed, at which the grounds of her indignation changed. 'You've drunk all my gin!'

Hedley put on his jacket and hat, picked up his gloves and walking cane, and slipped the bundle of comprising letters into his pocket. He intended to burn them when he reached his own rooms, and then Honorine Castle and Ida could both go hang. The recipient of his perverse passion lay snoring softly through her open mouth, sprawled in an ungainly fashion over the edge of the bed, and as limp as a rag.

Hedley felt underneath her bubbies, squashed against the bed by her sleeping weight, for the five gold sovereigns upon which she had collapsed. Four of them he put back quickly into his wasitcoat pocket. The fifth, which was payment enough in his opinion, for the return of the letters and for the use of her twin commodities, he inserted edge-wise between the wet lips of her brown-haired pussy, and with his fore-finger pushed it well up, to be found when Ida awoke.

Ever the gentleman, he put his hand into his trouser pocket and found a shilling to give to the dumbfounded Mrs Scroggins.

'For you, Madam,' he said, tipping his hat to her.

He manoeuvred himself round her awkward bulk and out into the living-room, as a prelude to his departure.

'Be so good as to buy yourself all the gin you can drink,' said he, 'and give, if you please, my regards to your daughter when she wakes up, and tell that I enjoyed poking her, both fore and aft.'

CHAPTER 14
A Stealthy Entrance By Night

It had been in Hedley's mind ever since the weekend of the party to celebrate the engagement to be married of Mr Reginald Askwith and Miss Georgina Playfair that he owed to himself the pleasure of relieving the beautiful Miss Playfair of the burden of her virginity. She had set doubts in his beloved Victorina's heart of the sincerity of his love, by informing her that there were men who took a vile and deceiving advantage of their betrothed in the pursuit of cheap thrills.

To arrange to be alone with Georgina, or any other engaged young lady, for long enough to have his way was impossible, of course, without recourse to the most elaborate of stratagems. Hedley turned the problem over in his mind for some time before he hit upon a capital wheeze – inspired by what had taken place when he arrived very late at The Larches and found Mrs Hapgood asleep in the drawing-room on her own.

In mid-week, he caught the last train from Waterloo Station and went on past Walton-upon-Thames to Weybridge, the nearest to the Playfair family residence. It was almost midnight when he at last stood outside the house – a large and very imposing edifice in the Gothic Revival style, with turrets and pinnacles and pointed windows. There were no lights to be seen at any window, but to be prudent, Hedley found a garden bench and sat down to wait for another half-hour.

The bench was at the rear of the house, on the edge of the lawn, and Hedley could see the conservatory where he had stirred up Georgina's tender emotions by his talk of love, and by putting his hands down her dress and under her bountiful breasts, to lever them out and kiss and lick their buds. He had pressed her to tell him whether she could have loved him, if events had turned out differently, and she had murmured: *Yes – I could love you, Hedley.*

Sitting at his ease in the starlight, under a plane tree, Hedley recalled that he had been so elated by her admission of secret tender feelings towards him that he was at the point of hoisting up her ball gown to finger her virgin slit a little, when they had been disturbed by the approach of other guests. A spoiled opportunity, thought he, his hand in his trouser pocket to stroke Jolly Roger, who had straightened his back and grown in size at the memory of Georgina's big white bubbies.

A distant church clock struck the quarter and there had been no sound or movement from the house while Hedley had been waiting and watching. He decided he had allowed time enough and that all within were asleep in their beds. He went very quietly to the outbuilding where he knew the gardeners stored their tools and equipment, and there stripped himself stark naked and left his clothes bundled handily in case the alarm was raised and it became necessary to decamp hastily, dressed or not.

He selected from the gardeners' equipment a short ladder and carried it across to the house, keeping well in the shadows in case anyone drew back a curtain to look out, for his pale bare skin would be very visible in the darkness. He counted off the upper windows from the left side of the house, and set the ladder on the grass firmly, with its top end below the second window.

He knew which window was the one he sought, for in seemingly casual talk with Victorina he had ascertained the layout of the Playfair domicile above stairs – his darling having many a time been taken up to her dear friend's room to look at a new dress or some other female frippery. Georgina was the middle of five children, all of whom had rooms that looked over the lawn, their parents sleeping in a much grander room at the front.

The rungs of the ladder were uncomfortable under his bare feet and he hoped, as he climbed silently upwards, that there would be no necessity to descend in a hurry and make a run for it. The casement window was open, to let a little air circulate inside on so warm a night, and in a moment or two Hedley was over the sill and in the room. He tiptoed slowly to the bed, to make sure he was in the correct room, and with relief saw that Georgina lay on the bed asleep.

She had thrown aside the covering sheet and lay on her back, her long blonde hair unbound and cascading over her arm bent under her head. Two buttons had been left undone at the neck of her fine white nightdress, and Hedley had the merest glimpse of the soft white skin just above the division of her bubbies, which swelled globe-like under the thin cloth. The movements of gentle sleep had caused her nightdress to ride up a little, so that her shapely legs were uncovered as high as the knee.

Hedley sat lightly on the side of the bed and contemplated the sleeping young lady's fair form. Jolly Roger stood at full stretch, thrusting upwards from between Hedley's thighs and shaking like a flag-staff whipped about by a strong gale. *Soon, very soon,* Hedley wordlessly addressed his closest friend, *you shall revel your fill in the soft cunny of this dear creature spread so enticingly before us!*

Proceeding with the utmost caution, he took hold of the lace hem of Georgina's nightdress and eased it further up her legs, until he had laid bare her round and tender thighs, almost to the seat of delight itself. What an object of contemplation are the uncovered thighs of a lovely young woman, he thought, and how happy an artist like Sir Lawrence Alma-Tadema who without reproach could have the prettiest of models pose naked for him day after day, with pink-tipped bubbies and dimpled belly and softly-rounded thighs and curly fleece all in plain view – and show his finished painting of her at the Royal Academy!

With fingers that trembled slightly, Hedley eased up another inch or two the hem of Georgina's nightdress, to uncover the join of her thighs – and there, in the romantic dimness of the night, fully exposed to his admiring gaze, lay her virginal pussy, the curls on it so light in colour that he knew they had to be the same light yellow as her hair. Jolly Roger lurched forwards and backwards at the sight, and Hedley needed all his restraint not to throw himself upon the sleeping girl's belly and ravish her at once.

He stretched himself slowly alongside Georgina on the bed, slid his arm carefully round her neck, and turned her face to his. He kissed her mouth with a soft and tender passion as she awoke, to melt away her natural fears. Her eyes opened and she stared uncomprehendingly at Hedley's face so close to her own on the pillow.

'Georgina, dearest Georgina, how I love you, love

you, love you,' he murmured, his repetition intended to penetrate into her mind as she became aware of her circumstances, 'because I love you and you love me I have come to you in a dream, a dream of rapture, a dream of love untrammelled to find its highest and most ecstatic expression.'

'A dream?' she murmured back, her breath warm and sweet on his face. 'Is this a dream? But it seems so real . . .'

'The passion that has brought on your dream is so strong and true that reality has been transcended, my dearest Georgina,' said he, 'only follow your heart, your deepest feelings – let them transport you to realms of bliss before undreamed-of.'

To give her a foretaste of the bliss he proposed, Hedley pulled up her nightdress to bare her big white-skinned bubbies to his hands and lips. It was beyond all description as his mouth flew from soft globe to globe, his tongue climbing each in turn to the tip, his lips seizing each little rosebud in turn to worry at it tenderly, until he heard her joyful sighs.

While he ravished her bosom with his mouth, his hand was between Georgina's soft thighs, forcing them apart to allow his eager hands to roam boldly, higher and higher on the soft flesh of her beautiful thighs, until his fingers touched her silky-haired motte. He raised his head to kiss her mouth whilst his fingers caressed the lips of her warm slit, and the feeling was evidently so very delicious that she opened her thighs wider.

'Oh, Hedley, my dearest dear,' she sighed, 'not even in a dream must you take such liberties . . .'

'In dreams, all things are permitted,' he murmured, his lips grazing her mouth in tiny kisses, 'anything that has ever found its way into your most secret of thoughts and longings – all those delights you dare not name, even to yourself! All this is offered to you now – do not let your natural modesty spoil your bliss, for dreams like this are very rare, and when you wake tomorrow you will be sad if you have held back in any slightest way from the acme of delight.'

Thus admonished, she made no further objection when Hedley's finger went inside her, and moved with infinite delicacy over her button, tending her growing arousal and helping it grow yet stronger and more delightful – until at last the most exquisite thrill passed through her body, and she lay sighing and spent in his arm.

'Hedley, my own boy, I am dying of bliss,' she sighed rather than spoke, 'I am undone with your kisses and touches – I will resist nothing! I am yours to take!'

To his delight and surprise, she thrust her tongue into his mouth and took Jolly Roger in her dainty hand and played with him with such warm affection that it was too much for Hedley's fiery blood, and his hot spending gushed all over her fingers.

'Oh, what a wicked boy to do it so quickly,' she exclaimed. 'You have cheated me of my fill of love.'

'Not so,' Hedley assured her, his hands roving yet about her naked and lovely body as she held onto his wet shaft.

'But you've done it already,' said she regretfully, 'he's not stiff enough to do anything to me now.'

Hedley was privately consumed with wonder how it was that a delicately-reared eighteen-year-old lady like Georgina had achieved sufficient familiarity with the performance of the male organ to know that fetching off was shortly followed by softness and limpness, and that in that condition it was of no practical use to her.

Notwithstanding, he encouraged her to play with Jolly Roger, promising that she would shortly have him stiff again.

In the meanwhile he licked the firm tips of her big soft bubbies and fingered her wet pussy. Jolly Roger was not abashed at the over-eagerness of his first response and very soon stood again hard-on. Hedley was about to mount Georgina's lovely body when a great crashing from below made him catch his breath in apprehension and pause motionless, fearful that he would at any moment be discovered naked in Georgina's bed.

A raucous voice made itself heard coming up the staircase, raised in a drunken and tuneless rendering of Captain Sellon's lament for a clapped-out lover:

> '*The glance of love, the heaving breast*
> *To my bosom so fondly pressed,*
> *The rapturous sigh, the amorous pant,*
> *I shall look for, long for, want*
>
> > *No more!*'

'How strange that my brother Ambrose should disturb my dream with his beastly intoxication,' said Georgina in a small and puzzled voice. 'How can this be?'

Her little hand that had been slipping up and down Hedley's sturdy shaft, to his delectation, slowed and stopped. To divert her attention from a dangerous train of thought that might very easily dispel the fond illusion of being sound asleep and therefore beyond all ordinary daytime restrictions of morality, Hedley applied his fingers to the rosebud set within her cleft and soon had her sighing and squirming with delight.

It was as well he did, for while he pushed Georgina towards the soft abyss of rapture, another voice made itself heard on the landing outside – that of Mr Hereward

Playfair himself, the paterfamilias of the tribe. He rebuked his son for yet again rousing the house with his drunken and obscene maunderings, and castigated him bitterly for spending his evenings carousing in the company of wastrels and bawds.

'Get to bed at once, Sir!' Mr Playfair commanded his son in a voice of thunder, by way of conclusion. 'To bed before I forget myself and strike you down! Tomorrow I shall have words to say to you that you will regret hearing!'

There was the sound of a fall, as Ambrose in his eagerness to be gone tripped over his own feet and measured his length on the landing carpet, followed by his hysterical laughter as he strove to stand up again. There was an accompaniment of loud snorts of indignation from his father, stumbling steps, then a door was opened and slammed. The house fell still and silent again, and in Hedley's arms Georgina came off and lay trembling and spent.

'Oh, dearest Hedley – I see you mean me to die in my dream of passion,' she murmured faintly. 'How I love you – do it to me again, I beg you – let me never wake up!'

Hedley took his hand from between her thighs and found her wrist, to put her hand on his long and thick shaft – hot and nervously twitching, but velvety in her palm. To maintain her at a high level of arousal, his fingers moved gently in her wet little cunny.

'But you can't possibly put this into me!' she gasped. 'It is much too big!'

'In dreams everything is possible,' said he, 'even the impossible – surely you know that.'

'Oh, yes, of course,' she said, her natural alarm soothed by his assertion.

He fingered her for a few minutes more, then spread

her on her back with her legs widely parted, while he kissed her mouth and cheeks, her eyes and her ears, her throat and neck, slowly driving her frantic with desire. He tucked her nighdress well up above her bubbies and knelt between her open legs to look at the beauties of her body while he played with her. Even with so little light in the room to aid his observation, Georgina on her back naked was a superb sight for a man with a shaft like an iron bar between his thighs.

The light-coloured tuft of hair between her thighs was very small and the lips of her slit so closely moulded to each other that they were almost invisible beneath her silken curls. With sighs of near-ecstasy, Hedley stroked her belly, the insides of her soft rounded thighs and up over her curly little bush. Then before she had time to become afraid, he was on her belly and lay between her legs, the unhooded head of his shaft touching the entrance to her cunny.

Here, on the very brink of felicity, he paused. Partly it was to let her become accustomed to the feel of a man's weight on her belly and bubbies, and partly for his own benefit – for he wanted to savour to the very utmost these magical instants before the defloration of a beautiful young maiden. Moments as intensely emotional as this came but infrequently in the space of a man's lifetime – half a dozen times, if he were bold.

Experienced women he could have in plenty, in London and out of it, and 'virgins' could be bought and paid for in the brothels of Kensington and Mayfair, he knew. Good though the poking was with pretty young women, there was no telling how many other shafts had reamed out their cunnies before his dissolved them into panting bliss, claim though they might that never had they been so soundly done.

As for the paid-for virgins, the thought of a transaction for cash was sufficient to deter Hedley from taking an interest in such escapades – and even if the girl's virginity had been guaranteed in writing by a judge and two bishops, he would not have believed it. There was nothing at all in the entire world, Hedley was convinced, that could be compared with the rapture of taking the maidenhead of an innocent young lady.

'Hold me tight,' he said to Georgina, and with one strong push he was inside her, astonished that he had met with little resistance. He began to roger her with slow and easy strokes to spin out the never-to-be-repeated pleasure of having her for the very first time.

'Oh!' said she. 'Then this is what it's like!'

It was a long and delicious joust, and he pleasured her to the full before he reached the short strokes, by which time she was gurgling in delight and pulling him close to her. Finally, when he flooded her cunny with his rapturous torrent, her arms around his neck almost squeezed the breath out of him as she grappled him to her big soft bubbies with all her force, her body convulsing and heaving under him.

'How very wonderful,' said she appreciatively, when the power of articulation returned to her, 'I had no idea of the delight that love unrestrained can bestow on the human frame! Did you know it was like that, my darling?'

'I am lost in wonder myself,' he replied. 'For me too it was the first time I have been privileged to taste the joys of love to the full.'

In truth, he was experiencing a fine feeling of satisfaction and elation at being the first to possess Georgina, and his lie was intended to reassure her that she was still deep in her dream of bliss, for who in real life ever heard of a young man about town who was a virgin? His words had a gratifying effect on Georgina, who clasped Jolly Roger, now limp again, in the warm palm of her hand.

'Oh, Hedley,' she sighed, 'then mine is the first that this dear thing has been into – the warm flood I felt deep within me was the first tribute he has ever poured into a girl? Oh, how truly marvellous this dream is – I wish I could dream it every night of the week!'

Hedley was astounded to hear such thoughts expressed by a young lady, and he concluded that the device of persuading her she was asleep and dreaming had released her deepest and most carefully concealed desires. He would try it again when chance served, since the outcome was so pleasing. Of its efficacy he received more proof before long, when Georgina had managed to tease Jolly Roger back to a state of alertness.

'Can we really do anything we wish, Hedley?' she whispered in his ear.

'In dreams everything is possible,' said he, 'everything the mind can invent and the heart desire.'

'Then I mean to do *you*,' said she.

Before he had got over the shock of hearing that, she had climbed over him to sit astride his belly, with her big white bubbies dangling above him. He put up his hands to feel them, and while he rolled them in his palms Georgina had reached between her thighs to hold Jolly Roger upright and force him up into the warm depths of her cunny.

'Does it insult your manhood, to have me above you?' she asked, her long fingers trailing along his belly.

'How could it?' he murmured. 'This is a dream – I have you and you have me, turn and turn about.'

Georgina rose and fell slowly on him, and the soft folds of her pussy throbbed and contracted on his enraptured shaft – he and she would have spent together very soon, but for her tender precaution in doing him languidly and calling a halt every few minutes to prevent too impatient a response by his pulsating shaft inside her.

After fifteen or twenty rapturous minutes of this play, her own sensations had grown so powerful that they caused her to shudder and sigh. Almost faint with delight, she gasped out to Hedley: *I am gorged with voluptuousness . . . Oh, the feel of your enormous shaft in me! I must have you now, my darling, I must have you! Give it to me hot and strong!* With that she rammed herself rapidly up and down on him, and he moaned in joy to feel his emission gushing into her.

She was content after that to lie cuddled in his arms, her beautiful body satisfied and at peace. Soon she fell asleep, and Hedley too dozed for a while, waking with a start to the realisation that he must be gone before the house was stirring. He looked at the window, and it was still dark outside, from which he drew the conclusion that there was time to enjoy his bedmate's warm body once more before he climbed down the ladder and dressed among the gardener's brooms and spades.

Georgina had turned over as she slept and lay on her side, her large round bottom close into Hedley's lap and her back against his chest. Her legs were bent at the knee and drawn up, he ascertained with his hand, and it was the work of a moment to take hold of hard-on Jolly Roger, and with thumb and finger uncover his head, before guiding him to her slit. A strong but slow push took him up into Georgina's still slippery depths.

Her nightdress was around her neck, for she had fallen

to sleep like that, and there was no bar to his hands stealing up to hold and feel her bubbies, so deliciously big and soft in his grasp, while he was tupping her steadily. In a minute or so she half-woke, pressed herself more closely to him and murmured in gratification, though the gentle words that reached Hedley's ears gave him no reason at all for self-congratulation.

'Darling Reggie – I love it when you do me,' she sighed in a sleepy voice. 'I had such a nice dream, but the real thing is so much nicer.'

At the mention of her fiance's name, the realisation dawned in Hedley's mind that Georgina had long ceased to be a virgin when he had slid Jolly Roger up her so joyfully. It could not be doubted that Reginald Askwith had been having her for ages, and she was well versed in the ways of love, to judge from the words she knew – more experienced than darling Victorina!

The thought that he had deceived himself over her annoyed Hedley and he gripped her bubbies tightly and thrust fiercely into her soft pussy. *Yes, use me hard*, Georgina gasped, almost out of breath and obviously enjoying what he was doing to her. That annoyed him yet more, and he stabbed into her with short fast digs until he felt the first throb of the climax in his belly. Georgina became aware of his condition and thrust her bottom back at him to meet his strokes.

'Oh, be careful, my dearest!' she cried softly. 'Be sure to pull out before you spend – it would be an awfully bad disgrace to be in the family way when I stand at the altar with you!'

'Have no fear,' Hedley exclaimed. 'All will be well!'

With all his strength he pushed his jolting shaft further up her, at the very moment his essence started to pour from him. Georgina gave a tiny cry of surprise and came off in long and rolling convulsions of delight, while Hedley soared high in his triumphant self-esteem at spending in her pussy. If there were any lasting effects – if Georgina's soft belly grew big – then the blame would be laid on Reggie, he gloated to himself.

CHAPTER 15
An Afternoon Social Call

On the first Monday in August Hedley prolonged his weekend stay with the Hapgoods and took Victorina and Adelaide out for a picnic on the banks of the Thames by Hampton Court. He would have preferred it if Adelaide had stayed at home, to give him an opportunity of having Victorina in some pleasantly secluded spot, but Mrs Hapgood made a point of asking him to include her youngest daughter.

Nothing had ever been said by Hedley to either sister, or by them to him, about the romp the three of them had enjoyed with each other in Victorina's bed. It was as if it had never been, and his explanation of this was that both young ladies were so astonished and vexed by their own behaviour that they had convinced themselves that it had been only a dream.

The weather, which had been so fine for weeks past, took a turn for the worse on the morning of the picnic, and when the rugs were spread and an appetising variety of cold meats and other food set out on plates, a sudden shower sent the three of them scurrying for the carriage. They sat for half an hour and lunched on cold roast chicken legs, pressed ox tongue, slices of beef and ham, hard-boiled eggs, and all washed down with a bottle of excellent Hock.

When the food was eaten and the sky gave no sign of clearing yet, they told Tom the groom to take them home. Victorina said that the dismal weather had given her a headache, and went up to her room to rest. Adelaide settled herself in the morning-room with a book, and Hedley was left to his own devices. After a while he decided to make his way stealthily to Victorina's room to see if the headache was a mere ruse – it occurred to him that she might be lying on her bed waiting for him.

He gained the landing and was passing by the closed door of Mrs Hapgood's room when he heard from inside a sound that made him pause to listen further. He heard it again, yet it was too indistinct to confirm his suspicions. He glanced left and right and finding himself to be unobserved, he moved on silent feet to the door and pressed an ear to the panel.

There could be no doubt of it now – in the privacy of her room Mrs Hapgood and another person were conducting a curious conversation, in which the phrases were punctuated by little sighs and exclamations expressing a lively pleasure. In short, Hedley reached the conclusion that she was being rogered, and his brain ran wild with speculation as to who her partner might be. Surely it could not be her pious friend the Reverend Quintin Gutteridge, bestowing a blessing on her brown-haired pussy!

Agog with curiosity, Hedley went down on his knees on the landing carpet to put an eye to the keyhole. He was familiar with the inside of Louisa Hapgood's room, although decency said that he ought not to be, this being forbidden territory, but he had been invited in secretly on his last few stays at The Larches, to give his fiancee's mother a rattling good poke. A large old-fashioned four-poster bed stood by the wall to the left of the windows, and two stuffed chairs and a round table to the right, covered with a crocheted cloth.

On the table stood a teapot and cups on a silver tray, and a large cream sponge cake with several slices cut out of it – but the partakers of these social refreshments had abandoned the chairs and betaken themselves to a setting more convenient for their shameless intentions. Side by side on the edge of the old four-poster sat Mrs Hapgood and her close friend, pretty Mrs Amelia Ballard – and neither lady was fully clothed!

Mrs Ballard was another resident of Burwood Park – indeed, her home was hardly a mile from The Larches. She was married to the well-respected Major Ballard, a man older than herself, who had been retired for some years from active service with the Bengal Rifles. Mrs Ballard was a year or two above thirty, round of face, dark-haired, with a fringe over her forehead. Hedley had met her several times when she had called at The Larches, and had found her to be an agreeable lady, with a better-developed sense of humour than is usual in females.

It was therefore with exceeding interest that he observed that both she and Louisa had removed their dresses, petticoats, stays and other garments, until their modesty had no more than the frail covering of chemise and drawers. Even as he watched, Amelia Ballard lifted her ribbon-trimmed chemise in front, so that Louisa could untie the string of her drawers and pull them down, thus baring her belly and thighs.

At this Hedley flattened his cheek against the door, to bring his eye closer to the keyhole for a better view of the plump and curly-haired cunny that seemed to pop from between Amelia's creamy-white and smooth-skinned thighs. He observed Louisa mumble a few words to her friend, who raised her face to reward her with a kiss, then Louisa ran her fingers up the inside of Amelia's thigh, from her stocking top to the tender skin next to the triangle of dark curls that covered her motte.

Soon she slid her inquisitive forefinger into Amelia's pink slit, and *Oh*, cried Amelia, her belly twitching to the darts of sensation that shot through her.

'Oh, how wonderfully indecent, to watch you feeling me like this, my dearest Louisa!' said Amelia, staring down at the ravishment of her pussy by her friend's fingers.

Her words expressed a sentiment with which Hedley found himself in wholehearted agreement – and Jolly Roger, who was stiff as a broomstick, signified his approval by hard jerks. Louisa was murmuring endearments in Amelia's ear, and all the time her fingers were playing with her at will, stroking and fluttering in her wet curls, then finding her hidden nub and agitating it so cleverly that Amelia sighed and collapsed backwards onto the bed.

By now Hedley's dearest companion had become so swollen and strong that he could be ignored no longer. With a quick glance left and right along the landing to ensure that he was alone, Hedley tugged furiously at his buttons to open them and let his throbbing shaft leap out freely. He glanced down, exhilarated to see it so thick and lively, and clasped its hot length in his hand to comfort its loneliness, while he returned his eye to the keyhole.

He was in time to see Louisa bring a footstool close to the bed and sit on it, with Amelia's legs spread on either side of her, the lips of her dark-curled pussy parted wide to display a little of the deliciously moist pink interior. Louisa used both her thumbs to open Amelia wider, and then tickled inside with her finger-tips. In her mounting excitement she spoke loudly enough for Hedley to make out her words.

'Ah, how your darling cunny throbs at my touch, Amelia,' she exclaimed. 'Before I have finished with it, trust me, I shall make you scream in delight!'

With that, she pulled Amelia's legs wider apart and bent down to bury her face between her thighs. For Hedley it was as if he were in the room himself, his head between those creamy thighs, his wet tongue licking the pink lips of Amelia's cunny in its nest of dark hair. His breathing grew shorter and he was unable to prevent his hand from tightening its grip on Jolly Roger and sliding up and down in his yearning.

'Oh, oh, how quickly I feel it coming on!' cried Amelia.

Louisa was applying her tongue to the manipulation of her friend's open cunny with the skill of long practice, making her body writhe and twist as the emotions within her were building towards a release. Hedley wished that his trembling shaft were the recipient of Louisa's wet caresses, and he tried as best he could, in his condition of near-delirium, to recall if she had taken him into her mouth on the occasion when he was drunk.

Whether she had or not, he determined feverishly to make her pleasure him in that way at the first opportunity that arose. Honorine, dishonourable bitch that she had proved to be, had used her tongue on him to send waves of delicious sensation rushed through his body. She had swallowed Jolly Roger and made him spend in her mouth – Louisa must be persuaded to grant the same favour.

How delicious was the sight of her light-brunette head down between Amelia's milk-white thighs, her red tongue flickering! Amelia was crying out and swooning from the force of the fierce sensations – and then recovering again under the continuous and tingling caresses of Louisa's darting tongue. Her legs kicked on the footstool beside her friend and her prolonged moans of bliss announced the imminent arrival of the supreme moment.

On the other side of the closed bedroom door, the moment had also arrived for Hedley. He was hardly able to breath, although his mouth was hanging wide open, and his body shook fiercely in spasms that racked him from head to toe. His clasped hand flew up and down Jolly Roger, and the voluptuous sensations in his loins grew to an explosion so powerful that he sank back helplessly on his heels and sprayed the door with the creamy evidence of his passion.

Used though he was to extended bouts of rogering with ladies of all kinds, Hedley found that the climax on this occasion was so superior that it was followed by the onset of lassitude both delightful and disabling together. His head seemed full of wild and whirling stars, and a pleasant giddiness gripped him almost as if he were in the early stages of intoxication on the finest champagne – and had there been a looking-glass nearby, he could have observed the foolish grin on his face.

In this condition, Hedley betook himself to his own room, to lie on his bed for a while, Jolly Roger hanging small and limp out of his trousers. Quite soon he dozed, and he dreamed very pleasingly that he was rogering both Louisa Hapgood and Amelia Ballard at the same time – for with the carefree omnipotence of the dreaming mind, he found himself to be provided with *two* shafts, side by side. He wondered if his two spendings would be at the same moment, or one after the other, but before that question resolved itself, he woke up.

He awoke to the joy of Jolly Roger standing hard, and by his watch he had been asleep for almost an hour. He tiptoed back to Louisa's door, but a glance through the keyhole revealed that the ladies had completed their games and gone downstairs. He went along to Victorina's room, to try his luck with her, but that too was empty, and there was nothing for it but to make himself decent and go down to join the ladies of the house and the visitor in tea and cucumber sandwiches.

Later that day, when the visitor had gone and opportunity served to be alone with Louisa for twenty minutes, Hedley spoke to her boldly of what he had been privileged to see. At first she was covered in blushes and embarrassment, but her nature was voluptuous in the extreme – as Hedley had cause to know – and she quickly dispensed with modesty and was persuaded to let him accompany her when she went to call on Mrs Ballard.

He left no doubt in Louisa's mind why he wished to make the visit, and with a gleam in her eye, she undertook to call on Amelia the next morning to acquaint her with the position. She proposed that he should remain at The Larches for the whole of the week and go visiting with her on the next day but one – and by way of a payment for acting the procuress for him, Louisa extracted a promise to come to her that night in her room.

That night, when all were in bed, he slipped silently into Victorina's room, stripped her naked and rogered her soundly – but only once. As soon as he had pulled Jolly Roger out of her, wet and shrinking, he kissed her goodnight and left her to her sweet slumber, while he made his way next to her mother's room. Louisa was awaiting his arrival with such impatience that she had her nightgown up round her middle and had fingered her cunny until it was wet and ready.

After he had poked her twice on her back, Hedley attempted to persuade her to bring him off with her tongue, as she had done to Amelia Ballard, but the suggestion was not received with any enthusiasm. Louisa was not averse to experimentation, and she lay over him and squeezed his shaft between her large slack bubbies, and so brought him off again, to spurt over her neck and chin.

When she realised that his interest was beginning to flag, she had him lie facing her while she held Jolly Roger's head in her slit, and fetched him off slowly by hand against her button, causing herself to reach the climax at the same time. All of this was pleasant enough, but what Hedley truly longed for, she denied him – and eventually she lay on her back for him to mount her again and put her to sleep with a final poke.

Nevertheless, she was as good as her word, and on Wednesday afternoon Hedley accompanied her to 'Brahmaputra' for such was the name of Major and Mrs Ballard's residence. The interior of the house was as exotic as the name, for the door was opened by a dark-complexioned manservant dressed all in white – turban, long tunic and trousers – and the hall seemed filled with hollowed-out elephant's feet, ivory tusks, bamboo tables, brass gongs, mounted tiger's heads, stuffed and rearing cobras and a hundred other trophies of many years spent in India.

'Your mistress is expecting us, Sabhu,' said Louisa to the servant, who pressed his palms together and bowed his head and led them into a parlour at the back of the house, with a view over a large rose garden. Mrs Ballard rose from a settee made of bamboo and gazelle hide, and came forward to the middle of a huge tiger skin that lay on the floor, to greet them. She and Louisa kissed each other on both cheeks – to Hedley she held out a hand and gave him a coolly appraising look.

They took seats and Mrs Ballard rang for tea. It was served by another Indian servant, a woman of pale brown skin who wore a striking saffron-yellow dress to her bare and brass-bangled ankles, and a many-coloured saree draped about her head and upper body. Throughout the taking of tea the conversation was entirely polite and trivial, that of any friends paying a social call. Hedley was beginning to wonder if Louisa had played him false, when Mrs Ballard put down her cup and saucer and looked him in the eye.

'I understand from my friend Louisa that you have insisted on coming here after having the impertinence to spy on us at an inconvenient moment, Mr Gillingham,' said she with a smile on her pretty face. 'Are you completely without shame, Sir?'

'Why, yes,' he replied, returning her smile, 'the truth is I was so taken by your revels together that I have a great wish to join in, my dear Mrs Ballard.'

'Spoken like a man who knows his own mind!' cried she.

With no more ado, she put an arm round the waist of Louisa, who sat next to her on the settee, and hauled her clothes up to her waist. This laid bare an expanse of rounded legs in white stockings and frilly blue drawers containing her full thighs. Louisa squealed a little in sudden surprise, but Amelia held her firmly, while her free hand played across her exposed legs.

'Look at these well-shaped thighs,' she urged, 'You've seen them before, haven't you, you naughty man?'

Hedley watched in utter fascination as Amelia's hand crossed over from one thigh to the other, her fingers running lightly at first over what lay beneath, then returning to linger over the curls concealed by the thin material of Louisa's drawers, searching delicately for the hidden slit. *Ah!* sighed Hedley, his rapture mounting fast, and he slid apart his thighs on his chair, to give Jolly Roger more room in his clothes.

Amelia's right arm lay around Louisa's waist, and it was with her left hand that she caressed her friend in this knowing and insistent manner. She wore a broad gold wedding-ring on her third finger, and this and her other fingers slowly insinuated themselves in the slit of Louisa's drawers. Her eyes were fixed on Hedley's face and her smile grew broader while she opened the slit of the garment a little, to tantalise him with just a glimpse of light-brown curls.

'Louisa has told me everything about you, Hedley,' said she softly. 'I am fully aware that you have many a time uncovered this bush of hers and tampered with her pussy.'

Hedley's breathing became irregular at the sight of Amelia teasing those curls, her fingers twining and toying in them, and as the drawers were pulled ever wider open, he was staring at the pouting lips of Louisa's pussy. So slowly that he could imagine and almost feel the delicious progress upon his own skin, Amelia's fingers slipped between those enticing lips and into Louisa's very depths.

'Oh yes, Amelia, my dearest!' murmured Louisa, her eyes half closed and her hat with its bunch of artificial flowers nodding on her head with her tender agitation.

Hedley stared with open mouth and bulging eyes at Amelia's fingers sliding into Louisa up to the second joint, and then out and then in again. He was scarcely able to breath as those teasing fingers withdrew and then, made slippery with Louisa's evident excitement, eased their way up to that most sensitive of spots at the top of her slit.

Louisa bucked and squealed and rolled her bottom on the settee, but Amelia held her firm. Before Hedley's bemused eyes, the gold wedding-ring on her finger winked in and out of view, glistening with Louisa's moisture, and he leaned forward in hs chair to drink in the entrancing sight, the stiff shaft inside his trousers throbbing like a trapped wild animal struggling to be free.

'Would you like to see her come off?' asked Amelia, fingers sliding rapidly now in Louisa's wet pussy. 'It won't be the first time you've seen her do it, I know that – but I doubt you can make her squeal when she fetches off as I can.'

Hedley saw that Amelia was sliding the slippery gold of her wedding-ring over the protruding pink nub of flesh exposed to view by opening Louisa's slit. Faster and faster she rubbed as Louisa's breath came in short gasps, interspersed with broken words and exclamations:

'Yes . . . faster! Oh, I'm coming off . . . oh, don't stop . . .'

In a flurry of wriggling hips and quivering thighs, Louisa jerked and shuddered, and for long seconds seemed to quite lose control of herself. But for Amelia's firm arm about her waist she would have collapsed on the settee at full length.

'Oh yes, my pretty!' Amelia urged her. 'Do it nicely for me now – your handsome son-in-law-to-be is almost spending inside his trousers to see you come off in my hand!'

As soon as Louisa's spasms had run their course, Hedley rose from his chair and threw himself on the settee between the two ladies, jerked open his trousers with a shaking hand and pulled Amelia on to his lap, his fingers up her clothes to explore her wet cunny. Louisa stared at what he was doing to her friend, her face pink with emotion, and he reached out to put his other hand through the opening of her drawers and stroke her warm belly. At that she moved closer and threw her arms about Amelia's neck and kissed her on the mouth.

Hedley twined his fingers in the hairy thicket between Louisa's legs and she swung her bottom round closer to him and slid her hips up and down in a slow rhythm that rubbed her bud against his fingers. He brought his face close to hers, laying his cheek along her cheek, and pushed the tip of his tongue in between her lips, to touch hers and Amelia's tongues twining together, so that the three of them kissed.

His fingers under Amelia's petticoats were probing ever deeper inside her, tickling her button, exactly as he was also tickling Louisa, and he wondered if he could make them both come off at the same moment. To this worthy end, he devoted his attention to their pussies equally, caressing them in the same tempo, left hand working at Amelia on his lap and his right hand performing the same office for Louisa.

Louisa's tender parts were deliciously sensitive from being brought off once already, and it was she who attained the summit first. Her whole body shuddered and her cunny seemed to tremble against his hand, and she cried out in her spasms. Even before she was finished, Amelia cried out, *Oh, oh – you lovely man –*

I'm there now! and rubbed herself against his fingers with a violent passion as the climax seized her.

Scarcely had her throes subsided than Hedley had thrown her from his lap onto the settee and was down on his knees between Louisa's parted feet. He pulled her forward until she lay very nearly on her back, with her bottom protruding over the edge of the settee, her clothes all up turned, her thighs stretched wide open. He let down his trousers and tucked up his shirt – and drove Mr John Thomas up her hairy wet slit.

Amelia had taken up a position of advantage, seated alongside her friend on the settee, where she had a good view of the action.

'Oh, Louisa,' she gasped faintly, 'I've never seen you poked before! How delicious a sight – his shaft is in you to the hilt, my dearest, and your cunny is like a wet mouth sucking at him . . . you must be nearly coming off again . . .'

Hedley heaved backward and forward in her slit, faster and faster, and leaned right forward above her to drive Jolly Roger into her even deeper, until she had him all up inside her. She moaned and sighed and bounded upward to meet his short, sharp thrusts, and in another moment he spent copiously and filled her belly with his hot flood.

'Now me!' cried Amelia, throwing herself on her back with her legs splayed outward and her clothes up round her middle.

Hedley pulled his hard-swollen and crimson-headed shaft from Louisa's slit and, without even a pause for breath, was between Amelia's parted knees, his hands tugging at the string of her drawers to loose it and pull them down. Louisa came at once to his assistance, her deft fingers opening the moist lips of her friend's haven of love to let him view the delicate pink inside and the firm little nub of her joy.

To Hedley's experienced eye, the inviting entrance seemed somewhat narrower than Louisa's, although as a young married woman she was, it could be presumed, rogered much more often than widowed Louisa. Before the thought could go further, Louisa's hand guided the head of his throbbing shaft to the seat of pleasure and lodged it just within. He felt how closely it gripped him, how velvet-smooth it felt, how wonderful were the sensations it imparted!

Amelia was so aroused that her bottom pushed up to meet his thrust, and Hedley found his shaft embedded as deeply in her as a man could wish or hope. He paused to enjoy the voluptuous pressure of her tightly-clasping sheath, but Louisa would have none of it – she stripped his trousers down to uncover his rump and her fingers were between the naked cheeks, stroking and probing. In another instant a finger-tip was working its way up his knot-hole, until he could restrain his ardour no longer and thrust hard and fast into Amelia.

'Oh, great Heaven!' she cried out. 'Oh, the sensations – dear Hedley, I'm dying!'

Louisa's finger forced its way into Hedley further, sliding in past the second knuckle, and with a cry that was almost a shriek, he felt the floodgates of passion give way within him, and a furious torrent was loosed to race up into the deepest recesses of Amelia's tightly gripping cunny.

CHAPTER 16
A Marital Catastrophe Narrowly Averted

From London Hedley wrote to Mrs Amelia Ballard a confidential letter, which he entrusted to the General Post Office, telling her of his great happiness in meeting her in the presence of Louisa Hapgood, but begging for a private interview. It was in his mind that if he could get Amelia on her own, she might be persuaded to venture further along the stranger byways of love than when her intimate friend Louisa was there.

There was in Amelia Ballard's dark and gleaming eyes a touch of mischief, thought he, that could lead her into unknown romps, if the occasion were right. It might be possible to pursue this possibility among the three of them, but he had some doubts of that, fearing that there was a chance of making Louisa jealous if matters went too far for her. Naturally, he wished heartily to retain Louisa's esteem, not only because she was a good and willing poke, but also for the excellent reason that in due course she would become his mother-in-law.

The reply he received from Amelia two days later – it was more of a note scribbled on lilac writing-paper than a letter – set his pulses racing with delight. In a few words dashed down in haste, she instructed him to present himself at seven that very evening at 'Brahmaputra', and to take precautions that he was not observed approaching the house.

Agog with excitement, Hedley caught an early evening train from Waterloo and found it unpleasantly crowded with employees of City counting-houses making their way home. He concentrated his attention upon an afternoon newspaper he had bought, and no one disturbed him. To give no one at Walton-upon-Thames railway station cause to remember him, he ignored the waiting cabs and struck out on foot, by a circuitous route, for his destination. His eagerness had made him early, and he was compelled to dally for fifteen minutes in the concealment of a tree before he went quickly up the drive to the front door.

The instant he touched the bell, the door flew open – and there stood Amelia's Indian maid in her yellow dress but with a different saree – this one a mingling of mauves and reds. She had clearly been stationed there well in advance, to let him in at once when he arrived, though the door was not visible from the roadway. She greeted him with bowed head and palms pressed together, but saying not a word as she led the way across the trophy-cluttered hall and up the staircase, moving with absolute silence on sandalled feet.

The small room to which she showed him was obviously Amelia's private sitting-room, furnished with a couple of armchairs and a sofa much less foreign and more comfortable of appearance than the Indian artefacts below. Hedley found the lady of the house there waiting for him, wearing a long and loosely-belted dress of palest green, which went well with her dark hair. She first extended her hand to him as if to be shaken, but he seized it and pulled her to him, and rained kisses on her upturned face.

'Dear Hedley,' she said fondly, when he released her mouth from under his own, 'how delightfully impatient you are of the forms of etiquette when you want something, such as me. But do sit down for a moment while I explain a few things at least. I have a decanter of the Major's best Scottish whisky here, and soda to go with it – a drink will enliven us for our frolic.'

Hedley kept his arms around her waist, his hands stroking her belly gently, while she poured two glasses of whisky and splashed in a dash of soda. That done, she released herself and sat in one of the padded armchairs and pointed him to the seat opposite her. Major Ballard, she told Hedley unasked, was in London, attending a meeting of the membership committee of his Club, to blackball some scoundrel he disliked. Afterwards he would, by old custom, get too drunk to return home that night.

Hedley raised his glass in salutation to her and drank. She went on to say that the manservant had the day off and would not be seen before morning, the cook came in by the day only, and the maid, Sushila, was utterly loyal to her mistress. In effect, Hedley and Amelia had the house to themselves for the next twelve hours at least. Having acquainted him with the facts, Amelia raised her glass to her lips and sipped the invigorating pale golden liquor.

Sitting in his chair facing her, Hedley put out his red wet tongue and waggled it at her. Amelia smiled and put her feet up in his lap, where Sir Percy Pokingham was making his presence felt, hitched up her thin green dress and opened wide her legs, until Hedley could see the slit of her drawers between her fine plump thighs. The position of her legs pulled it open a little and through it was visible a fringe of dark-brown hair.

'There is no more beautiful sight in the whole world than a pretty cunny waiting to be poked,' cried Hedley.

'To be poked? Fie, Sir!' said she. 'You were sticking out your tongue at my cunny – I take that to mean you intend to kiss it until you bring me off.'

Before he could reply, she was up out of her chair to throw a long shapely leg over his lap and stand with her dress held round her hips. The sweetly perfumed join of her thighs, still modestly covered by her white drawers, was no more than a handbreadth from Hedley's face and there was no possibility of resistance. He set down his glass and used both hands to untie the bow that held the string of her drawers tightly round her waist, and pulled them down until he had bared her belly and dark bush.

There sat he at his ease in a comfortable chair, while Amelia displayed her lovely secret charms to him – a rounded belly in which the button was sunk deep, and below, a soft-lipped cunny that was almost hid from sight in thick dark-brown curls. All this delighted Hedley, for his peg had been standing long, and its insistent demand to be indulged was like to drive him to distraction unless something was done speedily to release the delicious tension.

Hedley leaned forward and, almost delirious with lust that gripped him, opened Amelia's slit with eager fingers and plunged his tongue into her. *Ah*, sighed she at once and he clasped the bare cheeks of her bottom in his hands to hold her close while he licked and ravished her swollen nub, as he had seen Louisa do to her. Her loins jerked back and forth, and in only moments she gasped *I'm coming off* . . . Hedley gripped her more tightly to support her through the voluptuous climax.

He stared at her with a face scarlet with emotion and eyes that blazed with desire, and she took pity on him. Her white belly shaking still in spasms of delight, she reached down to drag open his trousers and take out a throbbing Sir Percy – and in a trice she had bent her knees and forced him right up her wet cunny. *Oh!* gasped Hedley as up plunged his shaft into that soft clasp, and *Ah!* sighed she as he rogered her quickly.

She lifted her loose green dress and her chemise to her neck to uncover her bubbies for him, and he bowed his head to suck at their swollen tips. His hands were on her milk-white thighs, holding her in a grip of iron as he thrust upwards.

'Yes, push harder!' Amelia moaned, and her wet pussy held Sir Percy in a loving grasp, until that energetic gentleman at last leaped for joy and shot out his sap, while Hedley sank on her breasts, still kissing them in his frenzy of rapture.

When he was done, Amelia uncorked herself and poured more of the Major's whisky for them both, to restore their strength. She curled up on the floor at Hedley's feet, her dress pulled decently down, and her arms resting on his thighs to support herself. Sir Percy lay at rest and fully exposed by Hedley's open trousers, and was an object of fascination to Amelia, whose dark eyes never moved away from him.

While Hedley refreshed himself with long sips of excellent Scotch whisky for what was yet to come, he enquired of Amelia how it had come about that she and Louisa Hapgood had entered together upon Sapphic pleasures, since both of them obviously loved nothing better than to be soundly rogered by a man. She told him that for respectable ladies in their station in life to entertain a male lover was so fraught with danger to their reputation that to satisfy each other was preferable.

'That I understand,' said he with a grin, 'but now you and she share a male lover – me! What do you say to that?'

'What I say is, Sir, that Louisa has an unfair advantage, in that she can have you at will when you stay at The Larches,' cried Amelia, 'whereas great difficulties lie in my path! But now I have you here alone, be warned that I mean to take full advantage of you, Hedley!'

'And I of you,' he replied, 'but tell me how it started with you and Louisa – which of you first seduced the other?'

Amelia explained that it had happened without any very clear intention on the part of either. A friendship had been formed when she and the Major had come home from India and settled in Burwood Park. One afternoon, in this very room, said she, they were talking of husbands and their ways and the intimacies of marriage, when Amelia had mentioned in confidence that Indian women shaved their persons bare and that the Major had insisted that she did so, from the first day of their marriage.

Louisa said she had never heard anything so very indecent, but it was generally believed that Eastern men made strange demands on women. She found it impossible to imagine how a grown woman would look, when reduced by a razor to the nudity of childhood. Amelia explained that in a hot climate there were advantages of being hairless, and after a little more talk of the subject, she asked Louisa if she would like to see.

In her years in India, Amelia had become used to having her secret portion examined by other females, for it was her Indian maid who performed the office of shaving smooth her cunny twice a week. Thinking little of it, she raised her skirt and opened her drawers to let her friend observe the effect of this odd Eastern custom. Louisa, blushing crimson, moved closer and was staring as if mesmerised by what she saw.

'It won't bite you,' said Amelia, with a little laugh at the bemused expression on her friend's face.

As if the words were an invitation, Louisa slowly put out a hand and touched the soft white-skinned split that was exposed to her gaze. Then with a sudden gasp she sank to her knees on the carpet and pulled Amelia's drawers wide open and ran her fingers up the insides of her soft thighs. Amelia stretched out her arm to touch her friend's flushed cheek, and thus caressed, Louisa stroked those bare lips delicately.

British though she was to the core, Amelia made herself no exception to the native-born ladies of Indian harems who, when their natural parts were handled by maidservants to denude them of hair, became aroused by the touch and were then satisfied by the same means – the clever fingers of their maids. Amelia pulled her smooth slit open with two hands, to show Louisa that it had become moist inside.

Seeing her friend's blushes renewed, Amelia began slowly to stroke herself, and Louisa stared enrapt at the fingers moving over an uncovered little nub. Before long she fell in with her wishes, pushed Amelia's hand away and caressed her slippery nub for her. Amelia lay back on her chair at ease, watching through half-closed eyes, until Louisa brought her off in quick spasms. Afterwards she returned the compliment, dabbling neatly in Louisa's hairy pussy, and so it had continued ever since, the two friends obliging each other five or six times a week.

'But your pussy is not shaved now,' exclaimed Hedley, much disappointed. 'What a pity!'

Amelia informed him that the Major had completely changed his tastes since leaving India, and insisted on having her in what he was pleased to call the 'English style'. When Hedley asked with great curiosity what that might be, for he had never heard of it before, she related with blushes that the Major's way now was to order her to bend over, then flip up her petticoats and drag down her drawers, to subject her curly-haired pussy to a prolonged examination, which never failed to stiffen his shaft.

'And then?' asked Hedley, almost breathless with eagerness to know, and Amelia told him that when the Major had played with her in this uncomfortable position to his satisfaction, he then spanked her bare bottom a dozen times or more before he rammed himself into her from behind. Upon which, she added, his business was soon done, for he spent within ten seconds or so of penetrating her.

The manner in which Amelia spoke of her husband left no doubt in Hedley's mind that she disliked and despised him and had no pangs of conscience about betraying him with another – whether woman or man. When he put this to her, she agreed at once, and declared that what she desired most in the entire world was to be poked sensless in the Major's own bed, as an expression of her distaste for him. Ever the gentleman, Hedley rose to his feet, ready to serve her, Sir Percy sticking straight out in front of him, for her account of how she and Louisa played together had stiffened him again.

The marital bedroom was next door to Amelia's small parlour and, in an excess of romantic emotion, Hedley slipped his arms under Amelia and lifted her from her chair. She threw her arms around his neck and pressed kisses to his lips while he carried her through the door and laid her on the marriage-bed – a broad and high-standing arena for love, with elaborate brass rails at head and foot, bedecked with knobs and curlicues – though by Amelia's account it was entirely neglected by her husband in favour of the standing poke.

'Now is the moment for your sweet revenge,' cried Hedley. 'Are you acquainted with the lines of Mr Thomas Campbell?

> *One moment may with bliss repay*
> *Unnumbered hours of pain;*
> *Such was the sob and the mutual throb*
> *Of the Knight embracing Jane,*

– and here is my gallant Knight in the devoted service of your darling Lady Jane – Sir Percy Pokingham himself in the flesh – who will throb in you until you sob with delight!'

'Oh, yes, yes!' Amelia exclaimed, pulling her loose dress up to her middle to reveal dark-haired Lady Jane to her champion.

Off came Hedley's jacket and waistcoat, his tie and shoes, and he threw himself beside Amelia, an arm around her, to draw her face to his and imprint hot kisses on her lips and cheeks. Meanwhile, his other hand took possession of her bosom through her thin dress, and rolled and squeezed her soft bubbies.

'You shall lie naked on your back on the Major's bed and be rogered to within an inch of your life,' cried Hedley.

'Yes – take what is his and use it for your pleasures!'

she replied. 'Do whatever you like with me – all of me! The more you wrong him, the more I will love you for it!'

Hedley raised her dress over her head and threw it off – and then her chemise and drawers, leaving her only in her pale grey stockings. She lay on her back with her legs well parted, while he, on hands and knees, stripped down her stockings slowly and with great delicacy. What lovely legs he now beheld, so rounded and shapely, the skin so smooth and white! He stroked her feet and ankles, calves and knees, with eager hands – and kissed the insides of her thighs until his blood was on fire, his fingers wandering higher and higher on the soft flesh.

'I am yours, all of me,' Amelia sighed rather than spoke, 'whatever your desire may be, darling Hedley, I will not resist – have me how you will, forwards, backwards, or upside down!'

He kissed up the length of her body to her face, whereupon she thrust her tongue into his mouth and handled his shaft and pompoms in a frenzy of impatient desire that proved too much for his fiery blood. While she clasped his quivering shaft, he threw himself over her, seized her head and forced Sir Percy straightway between her lips – it was done in an instant and his essence spurted into her mouth.

When he released her and rolled away, she smiled at him and wiped her mouth with her fingers.

'Ah, if only my husband knew you had done that to me,' said she, 'that would show him the utter contempt in which I hold him! But you, Sir, are a wicked man to come off so fast – and give me no time to enjoy it! I see I must teach you better bed manners – take off your clothes at once and let me have my fill of love.'

Hedley threw everything off and was as naked as she.

He took her in his arms and they rolled on to the bed together, her soft hand grasping Sir Percy and tugging at him, until Hedley tried to mount her lovely body.

'He is only half hard-on – he isn't stiff enough yet to do anything to me,' she sighed, her soft bubbies heaving. 'You spend too often, Hedley – I will say nothing of your beautiful young fiancee, since Louisa tells me you have given her your word that you have never touched her, though I have my own view on that matter – but between Louisa and your female friends in London, how often do you do it – five or six times a week?'

'A dozen times a week at least,' said he, 'and usually more than that, depending on which of my female friends I meet.'

'I know how to make him stiff,' Amelia said, her eyes agleam at his words. 'Sit over my body and lay him in my bosom.'

She wriggled herself more comfortable on her back while Hedley threw a leg across her and sat over her, his limp shaft lying between her white, soft globes. She caressed it with her hand and made her bubbies close upon it, so that he could slide between them.

'You can trust me,' she whispered. 'I promise not to breathe a word to Louisa, even though she is my best friend – you've had this lovely big shaft up Victorina's pussy, haven't you?'

'You are very inquisitive,' said he with a slow smile. 'Your cunny I will satisfy gladly, but not your curiosity.'

'There, now he's fine and stiff,' she said, abandoning the topic for the present, 'do it faster, dear Hedley.'

He was by then as eager again as if he had not spent that day at all, and his shaft was as thick and hard as any woman could wish for. The delicious sight of it as it slid between Amelia's compressed bubbies brought on strong sensations that overcame him until he was almost swooning with rapture, and he emitted a flood of hot desire on to her white skin.

'Oh, my dear Amelia – what a stunner you are!' he gasped as he gushed. 'I could play with you all night!'

'And so you shall,' said she with a smile that showed she meant business, 'all night long, Hedley – I promise you!'

When he drooped over her bespattered bubbies, his passion spent, she slid her hands underneath his thighs to reach her neglected slit and rub it quickly. In moments she attained the climax and writhed between his legs. Side by side they lay in the pleasant lethargy of gratified desire for a while, until their strength returned, and Hedley began to wonder if in Amelia Ballard he had at last met a pretty woman able to match his lustfulness.

'Now, Sir,' said she, seizing the initiative when she felt his shaft standing again in her palm. 'My desire has long been for a St George – which my husband has never allowed me, he holding it unmanly to lie under a female. But you have no such silly qualms, I am certain, and in any case, you have no choice in the matter, so you may lie on your back for me.'

This was quickly done, her soft white belly laid over Hedley's, while she held Sir Percy Pokingham in her hand and brought his head up to the mark. In another moment, with a jerk of her loins, she forced him into the wet depths of her cunny, and its soft and velvet folds squeezed and slid along the noble and enraptured gentleman.

'The Major is a fool,' sighed Hedley. 'All this he might have if he would – but he chooses instead to spank you and poke you standing!'

'All the more left for you,' said Amelia, 'and now, Sir, you have shown me your walk and your trot – I wish to make trial of your gallop. Hup, Sir!'

With that, she bounced up and down on his shaft with frantic vigour, and the brass bedstead creaked and rattled under them, so that it must be heard throughout the house, and Hedley knew he would spend very soon. *Hup, hup, hup*, Amelia encouraged him, as if he were an Arab steed between her thighs and she riding him in the Derby. It could not last – she rammed herself so fast and hard on him that his loins jerked up between her legs and he moaned in rapture to feel his torrent gushing into her hot and clinging cunny.

Amelia came off noisily, heaving up and down on him, then sat still and sagging forward, and he saw the sweet perspiration of love running in drops between her bubbies and down her belly. He took her by the waist and eased her off, to lie on her back beside him, her head on his chest.

'That was superb,' said she. 'You have made it possible for me to fulfil a long-standing ambition and I am more grateful than you know. You may call the next bout when you are ready for it, my dear, but you must let me rest a little first.'

They rested for twenty minutes or so, toying with each other a little to maintain their interest at a high level, and into Hedley's mind came a wicked thought. He told Amelia that he had thought of a means by which she could express to the very full all the scorn she felt for the Major. After hearing that, she was impatient to learn what he had in mind, especially when he added that it was so close to – and yet so distant from – the Major's own brutal way with her.

'I want to do it!' she cried. 'What is it? Tell me!'

Hedley smiled to himself at the inordinate curiosity which often led women into odd predicaments. Judging that Amelia had reached a condition of impatience keen enough to serve his end, he let his hand roam over her bubbies and belly while he told her the story with which Digby Wilton-Gooch had entertained his chums of 'The Becky Sharp Club' at the Cafe Royal.

He recounted how Digby had bared Lady Augusta's aristocratic rump and gone down on his knees to kiss it in homage. He had parted her fleshy cheeks to lick along the crease between them and touch, with the wet tip of his tongue, the hidden knot of puckered muscle there until she cried out in bliss. Then he stood up to rip open his buttons and release his shaft, and Her Ladyship rested her hands on a chair and bent over.

'Oh no!' exclaimed Amelia in an ecstatic whisper. 'He didn't do that to her – not that!'

He did though, Hedley assured her – Digby had sunk his peg into the knot-hole he had wet with his tongue and lain over her back to mount her big round rump. He tupped her hard and fast and together they approached the climax in unison, his arms about her and up under her chemise to feel her bubbies.

'Digby's word for it was *stupendous*,' said Hedley, his hand between Amelia's thighs to caress her wet slit. 'He said that when he fetched off in her bottom the sensations were so very stupendous that they both were crying out in rapture.'

The letch that had taken hold of Hedley was to test whether Digby had been exaggerating the joys of the rearward entry. He had made a trial of it with Ida Scroggins, but she had been drunk and unconscious at the time, and there had been no great or unusual satisfaction in what he did to her – certainly not as Digby had claimed for it. The secret, perhaps, was for the female participant to be fully aware, and as enthusiastic to be back-scuttled as Lady Augusta evidently was.

'I want you to do it to me!' exclaimed Amelia. 'Then when next the Major inflicts himself on me, I shall hold in my mind the memory of you rogering me by another entrance, and deep in my heart I shall be laughing in contempt at his puny effort.'

'I knew you were game for anything,' said Hedley with a grin of encouragement. 'Get up and lean over with your arms on the bed-rail, while I kneel behind you and kiss your bottom.'

No sooner said than it was done – Amelia stood at the foot of the bed, supporting herself by the brass rail with her bubbies dangling over it. Hedley knelt behind her on the carpet, both hands feeling the generously round and fleshy cheeks presented for his admiration. He kissed them wetly, he nipped them with his teeth, and when he asked Amelia to open them and her hands pulled them apart, he breathed hotly into the crease and on to the pouting little knot-hole she had exposed to his fervid gaze.

'Do it!' cried she eagerly. 'I want to feel you inside me, Hedley my dearest – I offer you this undreamed-of virginity!'

Sir Percy Pokingham had risen to his longest, thickest and strongest from his curly brown nest between Hedley's thighs, his purple head nodding to indicate this readiness for anything. Hedley put his hands on Amelia's hips and hauled himself to his feet, his belly pressed to the cheeks she was parting so widely for him. In three seconds more he would be deep into her.

Shudders of delight ran through Hedley's entire body and made his knees weak, whilst Amelia had already begun to sob in the bliss of anticipation, as Sir Percy touched her warm knot-hole and paused before plunging into it – when the sound of carriage wheels outside the house made them start.

'Good God – it's my husband!' Amelia exclaimed. 'I thought he would be drunk and sleep tonight at his Club! Make haste or he will catch us – he has pistols in the house and will kill you to protect his pride! Take your clothes and go down the back stairs!'

She was reaching for her nightgown to cover her nakedness when Hedley pressed a last fond kiss to her lily-white bottom, before seizing up his clothes in his arms and dashing bare foot out of the room. He could hear heavy footsteps coming upstairs as he made for the back of the house and a way down, and it was not until he stood in the dark at the foot of the back stairs that he dare draw breath and dress himself.

Distantly he heard the sound of a hand smacking on soft flesh and guessed that the Major had returned to enjoy his conjugal rights. About a dozen smacks he gave, Amelia had said, before he thrust up her cunny from the rear – and it occurred to Hedley that the Major would find Amelia's slit more than ordinarily wet and slippery tonight when he pushed in. It was to be hoped he was too drunk to enquire why this should be so!

If not, then there would be awkward and ugly questions – and if Amelia flung her infidelity in her husband's face to spite him, there might follow a hue and cry through the house to trap the departing adulterer! Though he was only half-dressed, in his shirt and waistcoast, but as yet without trousers, socks or shoes, Hedley felt about in the dark for the back door and turned the knob – to discover the door locked and no key in evidence!

He was in a state of panic when he heard a rustle close to him in the dark and his nostrils caught a spicy fragrance – and a hand was laid gently on his arm and another over his mouth to silence his exclamation of surprise.

'Do not be afraid, Sahib,' a female voice whispered close to his ear, 'it is Sushila and I am here to help you.'

Hedley nodded his head to indicate that he understood, and the warm hand that lay softly over his mouth was removed.

'You must not try to go yet, Sahib – it is not safe,' the maid-servant said quietly. 'Wait a little until the Major-sahib has tired himself on the Memsahib's body and fallen asleep – then no one will hear you go. I will take you to the kitchen to wait – you can put your clothes on there more easily – but move very quietly, please.'

She guided him by the arm into the kitchen, which too was in pitch darkness, the blinds being drawn down the windows, and they stood silent together. By now the spicy and musky perfume that reached Hedley from the Indian woman was having an effect on him – Sir Percy was standing hard-on under his shirt. This was only to be expected, Hedley thought when he understood what was happening to him, for his desire had been almost at the top peak when he had fled unsatisfied from Amelia's bedroom.

Young female servants were meant to be used by gentlemen – as Randolph Joynes never failed to remind his friends – and Hedley caught Sushila in his arms and began by handling her bosom through her thin dress. She wriggled a little as if to escape, but not with much conviction, and soon Hedley had his other hand under her long dress to explore her nether attractions. Up between her thighs he touched a pussy shaved smooth and bare.

A bolt of excitement flashed through his body like midsummer lightning as he felt her soft warm split, and almost made him spend at once, his legs shaking under him. As if in a dream he heard Sushila complain that her mistress would surely dismiss her and send her back to India in disgrace if ever she heard of the liberty he was taking with her person.

'Your mistress upstairs is being poked by the Major,' said Hedley in reply. 'I heard him smacking her bare backside – by now his shaft is well up her and he is near to spending.'

Sushila gasped at his words and then fell silent, and Hedley laid his middle finger along the slit between the smooth lips of her cunny, and pressed firmly inside to tickle her nub.

In another moment, with no urging from him, she was down on her knees to lift his shirt and suck his throbbing shaft right into her mouth. In the darkness Hedley reached down and found her shoulders with both hands, and used her as to support his trembling legs. What was happening to him unsought was far more exotic than his most sensual dreams, and he knew he was about to fetch off faster than ever before in his life. The feel of Sushila's bare-shaven cunny had almost undone him, and now she demonstrated with ease now to polish him off.

Whilst her mouth worked strongly at his shaft, stimulating it to swell thicker and longer, and her tongue lapped over the unhooded head, her hands crept under his shirt, to stroke and to squeeze the cheeks of his bottom. Hedley gasped in a spasm of rapture when he felt her sharp finger-nails dig deep into his flesh, and then, while he tupped blindly between the lips that engulfed him, she pushed a stiff finger into his knot-hole. A blaze of sensation roared through him like wild fire, making him squeal and he spent copiously in the Indian woman's sucking mouth.

CHAPTER 17
An Astounding Piece of News

On a Tuesday in early September Hedley woke up in his rooms in Great Portland Street feeling pleased with himself, much at his ease with the world, and generally content with life. His weekend at Burwood Park had been gratifying in the extreme – he had passed Friday night in Victorina's bed rogering her with gusto, then on Saturday night, he had gone to her mother's room and there satisfied his lusts on Louisa's well-fleshed body.

On Sunday afternoon, the weather being sunny, he had taken Victorina for a walk as far as the spinney, where he twice had her on her back for his delight. Late on Sunday night he had visited Adelaide's bed, where he had played with her for an hour or more, bringing her off twice by hand and once with the assistance of Mr Harry Horn.

Monday had been a day of rest for Hedley, much needed after his delicious exertions, but now he had woken refreshed and restored and ready again. There was the pleasure of 'The Becky Sharp Club' dinner to look forward to that evening, after which he would roger the handiest female – probably Florrie Potter on his return to Great Portland Street.

On Wednesday Mrs Hapgood and Victorina were to

come to town for a day's shopping, and would take tea with him in his rooms about three in the afternoon. There was mighty little chance of getting Vickie on her own for long enough to slip Lord Dickie up her for a quick poke, but Hedley was fairly sure there would be opportunities when Mrs Hapgood was out of the room to have a friendly feel of Vickie, and similarly, when Vickie was out of the room to give Mrs Hapgood's pussy a brief touch-up.

These pleasantly optimistic thoughts ran through Hedley's mind whilst he made a hearty breakfast of porridge with cream, followed by a pair of kippers. After he had finished eating, he sat in an arm-chair and was running through *The Times* with no great interest, when Mrs Potter came in to clear the table. She had permanent difficulty in keeping a house-maid to look after her tenants, even at a wage as high as £20 a year, and often she was reduced to doing the cooking and housework herself.

She was wearing a plain brown dress, with a starched white long apron over it, and had tucked up her hair under a mobcap while she attended to domestic duties. For all that, her mood was cheery and when she had stacked the plates and dishes on a tray, she left it on the table and stood staring at Hedley with her hands on her hips and a knowing grin on her face.

'I can tell what you're thinking,' she said.

'What am I thinking, Florrie?' he asked, and let his boring newspaper slip idly from his fingers to the carpet.

'About Miss Hapgood,' said she, nodding her head at the large photograph in its silver frame on the mantel-piece.

It was a head and shoulders study of Victorina, taken at a photographic studio in Oxford Street, showing her lovely face in half profile, to the advantage of the classical lines of her features. Hedley had considered more than once whether it might be possible to bribe the photographer to take another for him – of Vickie nude from the waist up – if he could persuade her to pose for it! The thought of a picture of her bare and flawless bubbies at his bedside was wholly delightful.

'Why do you say that?' he asked Mrs Potter.

'Because it shows,' she replied with a grin, and pointed to his lap, 'you can't hide those thoughts, you know.'

Hedley had not yet shaved and dressed for the day – he had breakfasted in his nightshirt and orange silk dressing-gown, bare feet thrust into morocco leather slippers. A glance in the direction of Florrie's finger revealed an impressive bulge that confirmed the stiffness of his shaft.

'I was having some very pleasant thoughts just before you came in,' he admitted with a slow smile.

'Oh, what a beast you are!' cried Florrie, and she took a step nearer and leaned down to squeeze his shaft in her hand. 'It's rock hard! You ought to have your backside properly tanned for having impure thoughts in front of a picture of that sweet young lady!'

Whilst she stood at the side of his chair, gripping his hard shaft between her fingers through his nightclothes, Hedley put down an arm to reach under the hem of her dress and up between her legs, until his hand was in her drawers and he was holding her warm pussy.

'Are delicate thoughts about a beautiful young lady always impure?' he asked. 'Or are they the passion of love?'

'I doubt if there's any difference, where you're concerned,' retorted Florrie. 'You can stop your hanky-panky – I've got my housework to do and no time for that.'

'Ah, but there's always time for a *feel*,' said he in his winning way. 'Think of it like this, dear Florrie – in fifteen or twenty years a time will come when no one wants to feel you – or me, for that matter! So take all that life offers while you can, and never, never turn away a friend's helping hand.'

'The things you say!' she exclaimed, and she moved her feet apart to open her legs for him. 'I dare not think what you would be doing to yourself now if I weren't here – that nightshirt would be up to your belly-button, I'll be bound, and Mrs Fist and her five daughters would be at their work throttling One-Eyed Jack!'

Her arm lay along his shoulders as she leaned over him from his right side, the attitude of her body bringing her bubbies close to his face, with only a layer or two of thin clothing to protect those soft globes from his eager mouth. His breathing grew short as she opened his dressing-gown and pulled up his nightshirt to bare his thighs and belly – and his shaft gave a vigorous bound as it was uncovered to view.

'Lord, how it jumps!' Florrie exclaimed. 'You've gone and put yourself in a worse state than I thought, sitting here and staring at Miss Hapgood's portrait with no good in your mind! If you ask me, you're the one in need of a helping hand!'

So saying, she massaged One-Eyed Jack with cunning and with expectation, but Hedley's ambitions had by then ranged further than Florrie's intentions, and his fingers in her slit teased shrewdly at her wet button, stirring her emotions to outpace his own. She began to gasp and sigh and press her cheek close to his, the passes of her hand quickening in proportion as her sensations grew – but she was no match for Hedley in this game.

'I'm coming off!' she cried. 'I can't help myself!'

As her spasms began and her parted legs shook under her, Hedley seized the back of her neck with his free hand, to pull her over the chair-arm and sprawl face down on him, her belly sideways over his, her hands on the carpet to his left and her uncovered legs thrust out in the air to his right. His hand was down between their bodies, to take hole of One-Eyed Jack and guide him to her cunny, so that he might thrust quickly in.

As events proved, she had provoked his emotions too strongly for his stratagem to be successful – even as he insinuated his jerking shaft into her drawers, the familiar throbbing started in his belly and a moment later he was spending between her fleshy thighs in a raging flood, his hot essence spurting over her curly-haired pussy and not into it. Florrie wriggled and heaved and kicked, but he held her firmly down across his lap until he had finished completely.

'You beast!' she cried when he released her and she at last struggled to her feet, holding her dress up about her waist to protect it from staining. 'You've wet my drawers!'

Hedley burst out laughing – the parallel was so exact with his romp when he held Mrs Hapgood pinned against his bedroom door, and had fetched off over her bottom.

'What's so funny?' Florrie demanded, still uncertain if she should be angry or pleased. 'Why are you laughing at me?'

Hedley assured her that he was laughing out of pure pleasure and not because there was anything the least comic in what they had done together, which he found wholly delicious. Suitably mollified, Florrie wiped between her legs with the end of her white apron, shaking her head over the impetuosity of Hedley's nature. She sat on his knee to wipe One-Eyed Jack dry, and even handled him a little before pulling down Hedley's nightshirt.

He told her with a smile that he knew no better start to a day and she kissed his cheek and expressed a fond hope that she might have the pleasure of his company that evening, after his dinner with his friends. Hedley informed her that he thought it likely he would return in a mood to roger her bow-legged, and with a final pat on his now limp shaft, she departed to change her under-clothes and resume her domestic duties.

Hedley stayed where he was, comfortably seated and enjoying the gentle lethargy that ensues from the climax, his thoughts straying back to darling Victorina, whose photograph gazed down smiling at him from the mantel-piece. Vivid in his memory was an image of the night in her bedroom when they had stood side by side at the window gazing at a big yellow moon set in a black and starry sky.

Ah, the glad memory of persuading dearest Vickie to bend forward with her arms on the sill, while he put his hand under her nightdress to feel the plump and pouting cunny between her legs – still wet from his rogering! He had stood close behind her and bared her bottom – and oh! how she had trembled when he pushed Lord Dickie into her slit!

These fond recollections were so delightful that Hedley was still in his dressing-gown, slumped down in his chair, His Lordship returned to his noble condition of stiffness, at half past eleven o'clock – when the tranquil-lity of his meditations was shattered by a brisk knock on the door of his sitting-room, and Florrie Potter entered in breathless haste.

'Mr Gillingham!' cried she. 'Mrs Hapgood is below asking to see you – and she's in a fearful temper! What am I to do?'

'Good Lord!' said he, starting up from his chair. 'What on earth can she want? I can't receive her like this – you must keep her below, Florrie, while I shave and dress. Offer her a cup of tea or a glass of Madeira to occupy her!'

It was not to be. Louisa Hapgood swept uninvited into the room, her face flushed pink and her eyes afire with rage and shame under the brim of her ostrich-plumed hat. She stared hard at Florrie until the landlady's spirit was crushed and she fled the room, closing the door sharply behind her, then turned her full Gorgon glare upon Hedley, who stood nervously twiddling the sash of his orange dressing-gown.

'I never thought to say this, but you are a low, degraded, filthy, disgusting character!' she trumpeted at him. 'I must speak straight from the shoulder – you are a sexual monster, for you have committed acts that no gentleman ever would!'

'I say!' Hedley protested. 'Steady on! You've been keen enough to get me into your bed at night, and you didn't mind it a bit when I rogered you and Amelia Ballard side by side – why this hullabaloo now? What have I done?'

'What have you done?' she exclaimed in high dudgeon. 'You have sullied and degraded my two lovely daughters, that's what you have done, Sir – and you have put them both in the family way, Victorina and Adelaide!'

'Oh, damnation!' said Hedley, somewhat inadequately. 'And I was so careful with them both!'

'Yes, you may well add blasphemy to the long list of

your crimes!' said Louisa, her voice as unbending as cast iron. 'You lied to me when I asked for your word as a gentleman that you had not touched my darling Victorina – you swore that you would respect her innocence and her virtue.'

'These things happen,' said Hedley, 'and I am only flesh and blood. I fear that my passionate love for Vickie got the better of me. But there's no harm done that cannot be mended – we must bring forward our wedding-day. As for Adelaide, I am sorry for her plight and hasten to offer my deepest apologies to you.'

'Apologies! Do you think that's enough?' Louisa demanded, her face becoming darker yet with fury.

'What else can I say?' cried he. 'The law will not allow me to marry both of your girls – or would you have me turn Muslim and take two wives?'

'You dare to make jokes with me!' she hissed. 'Listen to me, Hedley, there is worse yet. You have shamed *me* besides my daughters – you have put *me* in the family way too.'

'God save us!' he gasped in astonishment. 'Surely not . . . if you will forgive me for speaking frankly, Louisa, I took you to be beyond the age of child-bearing.'

'And so I thought myself,' said she, her face scarlet with shame, 'but we were both mistaken.'

'Are you certain of this?' he asked with a frown.

'Of course I am – a little friend who ought to have visited me has not done so, any more than he has my girls. What more proof could anyone require?'

'When did you find out about them?' Hedley asked curiously.

'At breakfast this morning Victorina broke into tears and confessed to me that she was in the family way and could keep it to herself no longer. Before I could get over my amazement, Adelaide began to weep and admitted to the same condition! I caught the very next train to London to confront you with this appalling news.'

'And your own interesting condition – how long have you been aware of that, if I may enquire?' Hedley asked her.

'I have suspected it for some weeks, but would not face the truth until compelled to do so by my daughters' admissions of unchastity and its shameful reward.'

Hedley sank weakly into his armchair, at a loss for what to say next, or to do. For any man to learn he is to be father to no less than three children by unmarried ladies is more than enough for one morning, especially a morning that had started as happily for Hedley as this one. Fortunately, the practical Louisa had devised a plan of action on the train journey coming up to town, and she took a seat on his red leather chesterfield while she explained it to him.

'Tomorrow you and Victorina will call at the vicarage and notify the Reverend Quintin Gutteridge of your intention to marry before the end of this month,' said she. 'He will publish the banns for the first time on Sunday, and three weeks later you will be married. The shortness of the time will cause great difficulties in making ready, but that we must accept with as good grace as we may. Immediately after the wedding you will take Victorina abroad on honeymoon – I have decided upon Vevey in Switzerland for you, a pleasant resort beside Lake Geneva.'

'I would prefer Paris,' said Hedley, attempting to assert his will to some small extent.

'Out of the question,' Louisa declared firmly, 'as you

will understand if you allow me to continue. Whilst you and your bride are at Vevey, I want you to make enquiries about villas to rent by the lakeside. When you have had a month of honeymoon Adelaide and I will join you, and the four of us will move into the villa you have selected and hire servants. We shall remain there unknown amongst foreigners, until all three children are born in the spring of next year.'

'Excellent so far,' Hedley pronounced, 'your friends and mine may guess what they like, but nothing will be known for certain if we are abroad for so long. But what of our return?'

'An announcement will be inserted in the newspapers to the effect that Mrs Hedley Gillingham has given birth to triplets,' said Louisa. 'You will move into The Larches with us and the children will be brought up as yours and Victorina's.'

The bold simplicity of her plan pleased Hedley, and his ready acceptance of it pleased Louisa. She removed her black coat and hat while he rang the bell for Mrs Potter to bring up tea, and over a cup or two they discussed details and reached agreement. They were of one mind that for a young lady to have triplets was not at all genteel, but the ruse served their purpose better than any other, and they must therefore learn to be reconciled to it.

An hour after Louisa's thunderous entrance into the sitting-room, she and Hedley were the best of friends again. It was agreed that he should return with her that day to Burwood Park, to reassure his dejected fiancee that all was well and his love for her burned as brightly as ever, and that but for occasional trips to town he would remain at The Larches until the wedding – she suggested he might save his money by giving up his rooms, but he persuaded her it was useful to retain a pied-a-terre for the time being.

The guiding factor in his mind was a reluctance to give up the pleasures of poking Florrie until he had to, and of having somewhere to collapse for the night after a drunken spree with his chums. By way of compensation for what he might give up in town was the prospect of being close enough to be able to pay secret and regular calls on dearest Amelia, when the Major was absent from 'Brahmaputra'.

'If you will excuse me, I will shave and dress and take you for a bite of lunch before we catch our train, Louisa,' Hedley drawled lazily as he rose and stretched. It was then that the devil got into him again and with a grin he reminded his future mother-in-law that in the good old days the bearers of bad tidings were tortured or whipped. Louisa stared at him without comprehension, and he enlightened her by saying:

'You have brought me this unwelcome news – and for that you must suffer. I propose to punish you.'

Before there was time for her to ask what he meant, he was on his knees before the chesterfield, reaching for the buttons of her ivory lace blouse. In a trice he had them undone and pulled down her chemise to the top of her corset, at which her breasts seemed to fall out of their secret hiding place into his hands, and he handled their bulky softness. The rosebud on each bubbie stood out firm and long, surrounded by a reddish-brown halo.

'What can you be thinking of?' Louisa gasped, amazement in her voice. 'You think that you have leave to make casual use of my body, after the infamy you have perpetrated – you are a menace to British woman-hood!'

Hedley was fondling her with both hands, greedy for

the feel of her warm flesh. He bowed his head to lick her buds one after the other and before she had time to collect her wits and deny him the use of her bubbies, he smiled up at her and made clear his point of view:

'What am I thinking of, Louisa my dear? I am thinking that when you insisted on many months of engagement between Vickie and me, it was not to allow time to examine my moral character, as you pretended, and assure yourself that the earlier defects were now wiped away – it was to give yourself time to enjoy my services to your pussy. Now that we have learned of the price to be paid for our pleasure together, it does not change the fact that pleasure it was – and still is.'

Louisa blushed but did not deny the truth of his words, only raised a note of prudent doubt:

'But here in your sitting-room in the middle of the day?' she said, her eye-brows raised.

Whether it was the place or the time she found inconvenient, Hedley did not trouble to enquire, but set his lips to her bubbies to tease them, while his hands felt up her legs, under her long navy blue skirt, until he stroked her plump thighs.

'You must stop this at once,' said she. 'Heavens above – if the landlady should come in and see us!'

For all her protestations, it seemed to Hedley that she was resisting only in token, and not in fact. Her brown eyes were downcast as if in modesty, but it was possible that she was staring at the bulge under his orange dressing-gown, and with one hand he untied the sash and let the gown fall open. The fine linen of his nightshirt was pushed out by a shaft as stiff as a tent-pole, and he quickly raised his garment to his waist for Louisa to see Johnny Jump-Up in all his glory. She uttered a stifled gasp and fell silent.

At once Hedley took advantage of her momentary paralysis of mind, and pulled her from the chesterfield and turned her round with her back to him, and pushed her forward again on it, her knees on the carpet, her bubbies on the seat, and her backside to him. She murmured in dismay at the indignity of her position when he raised her skirt and her petticoats, and saw the rotundity of her rump in lace-edged drawers and, emerging from them, her strong legs in their dark stockings.

Johnny Jump-Up lived up to his name and bounded for joy as Hedley opened the rearward slit of Louisa's drawers and beheld the lovely cheeks of her bottom, firm-fleshed and lily-white. Below these beautiful globes, where the twin colums of her thighs met, her fat and hairy cunny seemed almost to wink at him in welcome, and he at once burrowed a couple of fingers into it to encourage it to become moist.

'Oh, Hedley,' she murmured, 'if you must, then be quick – I shall die of shame here on my knees if we are discovered.'

'There is no fear of that,' he comforted her, 'Mrs Potter is not likely to disturb us, you may be sure,' and so saying, he placed his twitching peg against her pussy and pushed, and sank into her with the ease of a knife into a pound of butter. His bare belly was against her backside and he went at her briskly. She complained a little to be so casually used for another's pleasure, but her sensual feeligs defeated her indignation.

'Hedley, you wicked, wicked boy!' she cried, thrusting her bottom back at him to meet his strokes. 'Have you the strength to roger three of us regularly when you live with us?'

'More than enough!' he sighed. 'I shall sleep a night with each of you in turn!'

At that moment he hardly knew what he was saying, so intense were the emotions that possessed him, and he was quite unaware he was making promises that he might be held to later on. Very soon he reached the climax of voluptuousness and flooded her cunny with his spurting essence. She moaned and sighed and her fleshy backside shook, and up under her loosened corset his palms felt her belly become tense as she came off against him.

CHAPTER 18
An Amicable Settlement is Reached

Attired for the country in a green tweed suit and a soft hat with a turn-down brim all round, Hedley escorted Mrs Hapgood to Waterloo Station for a sustaining luncheon in the restaurant of Brown Windsor soup, steak and kidney pie, and chocolate pudding with whipped cream, before they caught the 2.44 train. Few were travelling at that time of the afternoon, and it was possible to find a compartment to themselves, in which to continue their discussion of the arrangements to be made for early celebration of the nuptials.

The weather had continued sunny for a week past, and in the small and closed compartment the air was hot and dusty. The regular puffing of the engine, the rhythmic beat of the wheels on steel rails, and the swaying of the carriage combined, as always, to promote in Hedley a strong sexual arousal. In the gardens of the houses that backed onto the track by Vauxhall and Battersea he noted the chemises and drawers hung out on washing-lines to dry in the sun, and Mr John Thomas stood hard.

Louisa sat in a corner by the window, her breathing slow and her eyes half-shut, as she succumbed to the soporific effects of her luncheon, but Hedley sat alert and fidgety, and turned his attention towards her. The stifling heat in the compartment had caused her to remove her dark coat, and place it, folded neatly, on the luggage-rack above her head, affording Hedley a view of the generous swell of her bubbies in her lace blouse.

With great delicacy, so as not to disturb her tranquillity, he stooped to the floor to slide his hand under her long navy blue skirt and up between her legs, his fingers tracing lightly over her stockings, until he reached her knees. Her eyes opened to stare at him in mild surprise, but her knees moved apart and his hand passed on between her plump thighs and into the slit of her drawers, to touch her hairy pussy.

'Hedley – this is most indecent,' she whispered. 'What can you be thinking of, to run the risk of an intimate gesture in a public place like this?'

'Fortunately for your reputation,' said he, 'no one can come into the compartment between stations to see what I am doing to you under your clothes. Lean back and enjoy it, for I mean to bring you off before we reach the next stop.'

His finger-tip moved deftly over her hidden nub and soon she was writhing in delicious spasms and exclaiming that she would go out of her mind with joy. *Yes, do!* cried Hedley, delighted by the way her body throbbed and her big bosom heaved under her blouse. As her excitement mounted, her thighs were opening and closing on his hand and he thrust three fingers into her wet cunny.

'We are almost at the station' he exclaimed, glancing out of the window. 'You must come off now, Louisa!'

His fingers ravished her until she gave a convulsive jolt, her body became taut and arched away from the back-rest, and she uttered a long loud sigh of rapture as she reached the climax of pleasure. Hedley took his hand from under her clothes and sat away from her, but tremors still shook her when the train, with a squeal of brakes and the hiss of steam ground to a halt at Platform 4 of Clapham Junction station.

Hedley had become so aroused by the smooth wet open feel of Louisa's cunny that his hand was back in her drawers the moment that the train left the station. He pulled off her feathered hat and threw it on the seat opposite, to kiss her cheek while he felt her. Nor could he resist putting her hand between his own legs, to let her feel the stiffness of his shaft.

She tugged at his buttons, to have Mr John Thomas out in the open and bring him off in her hand, but Hedley asked her to leave that for a while, for a great letch was on him to play with her until she could bear no more. She held his shaft through his trousers, squeezing it firmly, whilst she let her pussy be fingered and stroked again, her eyes shut, her knees well apart in her skirt.

'Don't tire me out, I beg you, my dearest boy' she murmured. 'We shall be at Walton soon enough, and I shall be too fatigued to stand upright.'

Hedley ignored her plea and drove on heedlessly, stimulating her with three joined fingers, and in another minute she moaned loudly and her belly shuddered in long spasms as she came off yet again. After that, he let her rest for a while, her head on his shoulder, but he kept his hand up her clothes, even while the train was standing at the platform of Wimbledon Station. No one came into their compartment, although a station porter who was passing with a barrow glanced through the window and had the impertinence to grin at what he saw.

The train rattled onwards again and Louisa had her

breath back – Hedley clasped her motte in his palm and murmured:

'This dear slit of yours . . . this soft channel through which my beloved Vickie entered the world eighteen years ago! How greatly I respect and honour it! And how greatly it arouses me!'

'Then you too feel this faint thrill of incest, Hedley?' she sighed, and when he nodded, she continued, 'I am to be your Mama-in-law soon – what we are doing is forbidden by morality and the strictest laws of religion . . . we have sinned together, Hedley, sinned most fearfully!'

'Yet how delicious a sin it is,' he answered, and his voice shook with emotion as his fingers slid into her slit, 'and how gladly would I repeat this thrill of half-incest with you!'

Through the tweed of his trousers his shaft throbbed wildly in the tight grasp of Louisa's fingers – so wildly that she was certain he was fetching off and instantly succumbed herself, sighing and shuddering under the compelling rub of his hand.

When the train halted at Surbiton, Hedley became anxious in case Lottie Mayhew should be on the platform, though he knew of no reason why she should be, on a Tuesday afternoon. He made an excuse to Louisa about fresh air, let down the window and rose to stand with his head out of it. His hat was off and if Lottie had been there her eye would have been caught by his chestnut-brown hair and his long and handsome face, the cheeks pink from his entrancing games with Louisa.

Happily, the delightfully lubricious Lottie was not among the three or four waiting on the platform, but Hedley thought it sensible to maintain his position to deter any inconsiderate passenger from entering the compartment and spoiling his fun. He had reckoned without Louisa's own sense of fun – while he stood with his head out of the window, she put a hand under his jacket from behind and felt his bottom, fingering between the cheeks and under his pompoms.

When the train moved out of the station, he pulled up the window and turned to face her, Mr John Thomas vibrating inside his trousers like a plucked harp-string. The carriage jerked as the train passed over points, and threw Hedley off his balance, so that he seized with both hands the luggage rack over Louisa's head to prevent himself from falling. Whilst he was suspended there, she ripped open his trousers and flipped out his shaft.

'Now I have you!' cried she.

Mr John Thomas was at the level of her face – with a mutter of incoherent words, she leaned forward to suck him into her mouth and lick him. Hedley uttered a gasp of bliss, reminded of how the Hindu woman at Amelia's house had fetched him off in the dark. Although Louisa's experience was more of tonguing a slit than a shaft, the sensations that rippled through Hedley elevated him into the Seventh Heaven of delight.

His hands clutching at the luggage-rack, he stared down and saw that she had extracted Mr John Thomas and his accoutrements completely from his gaping trousers. The thick shaft stood to a full eight inches, the velvety head unhooded to receive the loving attentions of Louisa's tongue. How it shook between her fingers, how it tried to thrust ever higher, how it tried to swell it self up to an impossible size in its frenzy of lust!'

Louisa's dark brown eyes rolled up to meet his, and in them he could detect the gleam of admiration and curiosity – she was impressed by the strength and vigour of sinful Mr John Thomas. Her tongue lapped over the uncovered head – dilated with strong passion and purple-red, sending ripples of bliss along Hedley's spine. The strong throbbing of his shaft in her fingers advised him that he was almost at the point of spending.

'I'm fetching off, Louisa!' he gasped.

His body was shaking and his whole weight hung from the grip of his hands on the rack above her head. He felt the warmth and wetness of her mouth engulf him as she sucked in the whole head and an instant later he was crying out and shuddering in spasms of joy as he shot off. The ecstasy was so acute that even after he had finished spurting, he hung from the rack staring at Louisa with the fixity of the intoxicated. A drop of his cream trickled down her chin, and he knew he must have her again!

His shaft remained thick, strong and heavy – it was the work of a moment to drop his hands to Louisa's shoulders and fling her sideways on the dusty seat. Her knees were bent and her feet higher than her head, letting her skirts and petticoats slip back to her thighs. Hedley turned them up as high as her bosom with a flick of his hand, and with her own fingers Louisa pulled open the slit of her drawers and offered him her wet-lipped cunny.

Her red-flushed face was turned up towards him, and her eyes glowed in the delight of anticipation. Hedley threw himself on her, between her raised legs, set the hot and throbbing head of Mr John Thomas to her slit and pushed forward. She was, as he well knew, generously sized, and his earlier fingering had made her cunny so very slippery that he seemed to glide all the way into her, until his belly was flat on hers, and he was rogering her forcefully.

'Oh, Hedley – I shall die of happiness,' she exclaimed, and her loins rose to his thrusts.

Hedley had passed beyond the point of hearing and

speaking. A jagged bolt of lightning seemed to flash through him and he cried out fiercely as his essence spurted into her.

'It's too much – I can't bear it! I shall faint!' moaned Louisa, then a dying shriek announced the onset of the climax, and her plump belly shuddered under him.

When they were recovered sufficiently to make themselves decent of appearance again, they leaned on each other in the sweet lassitude of satisfied desire, Louisa's head on Hedley's shoulder, resting until the train reached their destination at Walton-upon-Thames.

At The Larches, Hedley found his darling Victorina pleased and relieved to see him, as was also her sister Adelaide, their mood being a little subdued, as well it might be for two young ladies in their predicament. Mrs Hapgood rang for tea, and the four of them sat in the drawing-room to discuss their plans and make the best of the situation. After the strenuous pleasures she had enjoyed on the train, Louisa had sunk into an amiable and placid contentment, and agreed with all suggestions made.

They talked until dinner time, ate a simple yet hearty meal of Dover sole and roasted duck, rounded off with a goosberry souffle, and resumed the close discussion of their plans for the wedding and the honeymoon, and then the triple accouchement in Switzerland. Hedley had downed a bottle of Hock and almost two of Burgundy with his dinner, and most of a decanter of Port after, and felt himself to be in fine fettle after the delights of the day so far – and ready for more!

When Mrs Hapgood at length announced that it was Adelaide's bed-time, that young lady kissed her mother and sister, then threw her arms round Hedley's neck and said in all seriousness that she forgave him for what he had done to her. Half an hour later, Mrs Hapgood said, her eyelids drooping, that she would retire, for her journey to London and back had fatigued her. As it had, thought Hedley with a grin for he had fingered her off three times in the train before poking her – not to mention the rogering she had before that in his rooms.

It seemed that Mrs Hapgood was of the opinion that Hedley had done his worst to her daughter, and no further harm could come to her, for he and Victorina were left alone together in the drawing-room for the first time ever. He turned the moment to good use by leading her by the hand to the sofa, took her in his arms and pressed his greedy lips to hers. *Hedley, don't*! she murmured into his mouth, trying calmly to free herself from his embrace.

Hedley's hand was down the top of her grey satin evening dress to feel her soft bubbies, and he ran his fingers over their rosebud tips until Victorina shivered and surrendered to him. They exchanged a long and loving kiss, their wet tongues touching between parted lips.

'There is nothing more to fear, dearest girl,' said he. 'In only three weeks you shall be my wife. All the delight we have enjoyed together shall be repeated every night – and in the day as often as we can be alone. Put your hand in my trousers and hold Lord Dickie – he is longing for your touch!'

Somewhat timidly, she placed her hand on the long bulge down his trouser leg, and gasped to feel how hard-on his shaft was standing. She gave His Lordship a gentle rubbing through the cloth that covered him, until he was jerking like a snared bird on a branch. Reassured by Hedley's words that there was nothing to fear, she undid his buttons and slipped her hand under his shirt to take hold of his hot shaft and pull it upright.

Their lips met in long-drawn kisses of purest rapture, while Hedley's hand insinuated itself under the skirts of her dress and felt between her thighs to find the opening of her drawers.

'Oh, how greedy you are for sensation,' she sighed, 'you feel me at every opportunity!' and her legs opened for him.

'My darling girl!' Hedley gasped, in a veritable heaven of bliss as his finger-tips touched her silky curls and the warm flesh of her luscious slit.

He could feel his fingers wet with a delicious moisture, and knew that his beloved was fast becoming as aroused as he was. In his breast his heart leaped for joy and very soon her urgent gasps and the little spasms that shook her advised him that she would shortly come off. His finger-tip played over her nub and she whimpered in helpless delight as she reached the climax of passion and gave herself up to the pleasure of it.

'Hedley – take me up to my room and . . . have me!' she sighed in his ear, when she was able to speak again.

'Yes, yes, my dearest . . . oh, yes,' he answered faintly, and spent in her dainty hand, a torrent that caused her to cry out in astonishment and regret.

'Too late,' she said, sadness in her voice. 'It's done!'

She spoke without full knowledge of her betrothed. The wine was hot in Hedley and his blood was up – he felt ready to roger Vickie all night long.

'Too late? Not so,' said he, buttoning up his trousers over his wet shaft, 'come upstairs with me now.'

He rose from the sofa and pulled her to her feet, out of the drawing-room and up the staircase, an arm about her slender waist to guide her steps. Outside her bedroom door she kissed him lightly on the lips and begged for five minutes alone to prepare herself for bed. Hedley was reluctant to relinquish his hold, but gave way at last. When her door closed on him, he went to his own room, took off all his clothes and put on his dressing-gown.

When the five minutes were up, he tiptoed along the passage, pausing at Mrs Hapgood's door to listen for a moment. Although Victorina's condition was past help, he was sure that Louisa would have strenuous objections to her daughter being rogered again before she became Hedley's wife. He could hear nothing, and through the keyhole he could discern nothing in the dark. Louisa had been seen to so thoroughly that afternoon in the railway carriage that now she slept the sleep of the just.

He moved on with caution to Victorina's room, turned the doorknob soundlessly and went in. The gas light was on at half full, illuminating the room with a soft golden glow, in which his beloved lay in her bed, her face toward the door and her shining ash-brown hair unbound and spread out on the pillow. He sat on the edge of the bed, to stroke her face and gaze at her in silent delight.

Lord Dickie stood at full stretch at the sight of so much female loveliness, and Hedley threw off his dressing-gown to show himself naked and ready. He turned back the bed-clothes, and sighed in admiration at the nightdress Victorina had put on – full-sleeved, with ribbons and buttons at the wrists, the bodice sewn in broderie-anglaise style, and a lace frill round the throat. He leaned over her to kiss her soft mouth, and they mingled their sighs of passion.

A moment later he had her nightdress up round her waist and was lost in speechless awe at the lovely sight she presented. His hand glided over her beautiful white thighs, towards the pink slit set in the light-brown curls, and with gentle fingers he held it open to gaze at the delicate pink tint of the interior. Inspired, he asked if she knew the verse of Mr Austin Steadman-Temple, and when she shook her head in wonder, he recited it for her:

> *'Ah, to behold that lovely split,*
> *Of bliss the very centre;*
> *To feel that sweet and darling slit,*
> *Where he she loves may enter!'*

He heard her long sigh, and threw himself upon her, his mouth seizing greedily on her cunny, his hands under her bare bottom to grasp the cheeks, as if to hold her fast while he licked her pink and secret nub. Victorina sighed again and wriggled under his assault, overwhelmed by her emotions, half-willing and yet half-afraid to abandon herself entirely to delirious sensation. The violence of that sweet conflict within her grew so great that she almost swooned when his agile tongue forced her to come off, whether she would or not.

When she was restored to herself again, she was blushing and hardly able to meet his eyes as he leaned over her and played so sweetly with her full bubbies. Their berries were soon firm under his fingers, and he progressed calmly towards his goal, sliding his hand down her belly to pass it, trembling with joy, over her smooth thighs. He clasped in his palm her curly-haired pussy and smiled with love as he repeated the words: *Here lies the centre of bliss, my dearest Vickie.*

His finger found the way into her pussy and he caressed her hidden nub, slippery from his tonguing, and from her own sweet arousal. On the bed her legs parted slowly, as if of their own will, and Hedley put one knee between hers, and then the other, separating her legs further. He lay down on her beautiful naked body, his weight supported on an elbow, while he felt between her thighs to caress her little nub still.

When he brought the tip of his shaft to her wet cunny and she felt it pressing between the lips, she gasped aloud thrice and shivered beneath him. With little exclamations of love, Hedley lowered his belly to hers and with a slow push sank into her. Oh, the ineffable rapture of that moment! Oh, the divine sensations that ran through him and through the beloved girl under him, as Lord Dickie throbbed in her warm slit.

'Oh, my darling Hedley – it isn't possible again so soon,' Victorina sighed, 'the human organism cannot sustain so strong an emotion repeated so often.'

Hedley was sliding in and out of her with long slow pushes, and in spite of her apprehension, soon she began to writhe and shiver with pleasure. He asked her to raise her knees, and she did as he wished, without knowing why, and then gave a long moan of bliss as he thrust in deeper. All unnecessary modesty was gone now, and she lay beneath him in unabashed delight, urging him on with little cries.

Her knees rose higher, now that she understood the reason to open herself wide for him, her feet left the bed and in great daring she laid her legs over his thighs and crossed her ankles to make him her prisoner. Faster and shorter he dug into her soft slit, until in a wild convulsive jerking he spent in it, shooting a torrent up into her heaving belly. Victorina grasped at his head to pull his mouth to hers, and whispered in a dying voice *Hedley* . . .

Whilst they lay in each other's arms, by degrees recovering their senses, she put her mouth close to his ear and asked him if it would be always like this. He assured her that it would be so – every night – but then remembering that he had no wish to lose the perverse pleasure of rogering her mother, he said that, on second thoughts, he must not impose his own selfish desires on her. Her young and tender body, he said, and the delicacy of her emotions, would be over-strained if he had her *every* night. There would be nights when he let her sleep alone.

In his mind was the memory of dangling that afternoon from a luggage rack, his trousers agape, and fetching off in Louisa's hot mouth. In that act he had enjoyed the keenest sensations that he could ever recall, and he fervently wished them to be repeated. To this end, he set himself to arouse Victorina once more, praising the beauty of her young and well-shaped body, while he handled her until she was trembling with excitement.

He ran his lips and tongue over the warm satin skin of her bubbies and belly, savouring the delicious taste of her, and when he saw she was his to dispose of as he chose, he asked her to kiss the rod that had given her so much pleasure and would give her more. She sat up naked, and he knelt on the bed in the space between her parted legs, whilst she blushed prettily and bowed her head to plant a tiny kiss on the purple head of his stiff-again shaft.

He was playing with her bubbies, speaking to her in a low and loving voice, and soon her trepidation was overcome and she had the confidence to hold the head of his trembling shaft in between her lips and nervously touch her tongue to its velvety skin. *More, more, my dearest girl*! he sighed, and to show her what he meant, he held her head in gentle hands while he thrust into her mouth.

Her eyes were staring up at his face, startled and confused by what was being done. Hedley smiled down at her with tender passion, and slid backwards and forwards slowly for half a minute, then the most blissful convulsions shook his body and he spurted prodigiously into her mouth. He heard her gurgle as she felt the first gush on her tongue, and then she was sucking hard to drain him, her fingers clawing at his bare bottom.

In his arms she fell asleep for a time, and Hedley rested content with the unexpected gratifications the day had brought him. He had been sucked off by two different and exciting women – sucked off twice in one day! Yet before forty minutes had passed, his thoughts were running lewdly on other varieties of sensual enjoyment, and Lord Dickie was stirring from sleepy limpness to stand straight and stiff once more. Hedley kissed Vickie's mouth until she awoke and responded to him.

'Dearest,' said he, caressing her warm belly, 'You have freely given me the precious flower of your maidenhood, yet if you truly love me there is another blossom you will allow me to pluck, to complete the nosegay of our delights.'

'Oh Hedley, you know that you are my only true love,' she replied. 'Everything I have is yours! To ensure your happiness I will do anything you ask of me. What is it that you want?'

'Then turn over,' he said, his voice trembling with love and affection for her willing surrender.

She obeyed him, turning over face down on the pillows, and thereby offering her bare round bottom to his warm licking. After a while he parted her legs widely and lay over her back, to place his hard and quivering shaft in the split between her luscious cheeks.

As he touched the tip of Lord Dickie to her tiny pucked nut, he murmured against her neck:

'Dearest girl, I adore every little bit of you so much that I want to love you all over – to lick you from head to toe, and to spurt my vital fluid into every darling orifice you have!'

He heard her little gasp when he inserted His Lordship's head into her tight little opening, and he pressed forward into her depths, slowly and yet strongly. When she murmured a little he reached under her to play with her cunny, and got a finger inside it to comfort her by touching her button.

'But this is so different from how you have loved me before, Hedley,' she complained softly. 'Are you certain, my darling, that this is right and proper between engaged couples?'

'It is the ultimate intimacy,' he reassured her.

He could feel Lord Dickie beginning to penetrate, opening her more and more, and he exerted a little more pressure to get in further. Victorina gave a cry, muffled by the pillow. When half of his shaft was inside, Hedley began to tup her, but with caution, so as not to cause pain.

'Hedley,' she whispered, 'oh Hedley my dear, how strange the feeling . . . how very irregular, my dearest boy – and yet . . .'

The soft swell of her fleshy cheeks was under Hedley's belly and he was almost beside himself with delicious sensation. He murmured to Victorina that he loved her more than ever woman had been loved before, all the time rogering her backside with slow strokes, to the moment when the nervous spasm took place and his essence flooded her. She shrieked and squirmed under him, and then lay perfectly still and limp.

The excess of her emotions had caused her to swoon away. Hedley uncorked himself and turned her on her back, to chafe her hands and rub her soft belly until she stirred and sighed.

'My darling – forgive me for subjecting you to my desires,' cried he, delighted with the experience and quite sure that he would repeat it on another occasion.

'Hedley – you have had all of me now,' she murmured, her arms about his neck, 'How very glad I am that I can make you happy! Pay no attention to my weakness, I beg you – use me in every way you wish, and I shall find my happiness in serving yours.'

They hugged and kissed until Victorina fell asleep, holding a small and wet Lord Dickie in her hand. When he was sure that he wouldn't wake her, Hedley eased himself from her clasp and left the bed, put the sheet lightly over her and tiptoed out of the room, turning off the gas light as he left. The repeated bliss he had experienced in Vickie's bed, her desire to please him and her readiness to let him have her in all ways he could think of – this had convinced him that married life with her would be an extended orgy.

In the darkness of his own room he threw back the bed-clothes, and there was Adelaide! She was completely naked and had gone to sleep waiting for him, her back and little bottom turned towards him. His exclamation of surprise woke her, and she turned over onto her back to stare up at him with a sleepy grin, the lily-white skin of her bubbies and belly gleaming in the dim light. Hedley grinned back at her, then lay beside her and put his hand between her slender thighs, to feel her soft little slit . . .

The Secrets of Women

PUBLISHER'S NOTE

As is normal for most Victorian erotic literature, the title-page of *The Secrets of Woman* has neither an author's name or a date. The only designation is the initials *A.McK.H.* These are known to be the initials of Alexander McKendrie Hammond, a Scot resident in England, who was described by that greatest collector of erotica, Henry Spencer Ashbee, as 'a barrister in good standing.'

In the catalogue of his collection of underground Victorian classics, Ashbee says this of *The Secrets of Women*:

'The present work is certainly one of the most remarkable upon its subject, viz., physical love and its aberrations between persons bound by close ties of blood. We may fairly assert that this book is the most subversive of morality and unblushingly indecent of any we have read.'

CHAPTER 1
An Investigation Leads to a Curious Discovery

It is commonly accepted and thought commendable that when an author brings a book before the public he ought to write a few words by way of introduction. The present author humbly begs to be excused this unnecessary duty, having nothing at all to say about the characters of his most unusual story other than what is contained within the book itself. The gentle reader is asked to accompany the author to a house situated in Seymour Place, London, where Mr Monty Standish was comfortably lodged. This young gentleman had only recently celebrated the twenty-third anniversary of his birth, and had in fullest measure the spring and zest of youth.

The year was that in which Mr Gladstone promised to abolish the Income Tax and was so wretchedly disbelieved by the public that his party lost the General Election and he was forced to give way as Prime Minister to Mr Disraeli. On an afternoon in May of that year, at about four o'clock, Monty Standish was at home in his rooms in Seymour Place, enjoying a cup of tea and a slice or two of Madeira cake, and reading with much amusement a book he had purchased the day before in Greek Street,

Soho. The book was entitled *Lady Bumslapper's Boarding School for Young Ladies*, and was offered as a true and genuine account of some odd events in a Gloucestershire educational establishment.

True or not, the delightful and Sapphic events of which the book spared no detail had a marked effect on Monty, whose shaft was standing at full stretch within his trousers. Shortly after that his reading was interrupted by a creaking noise from the ceiling above him − a sound which forced itself into his reluctant awareness. He glanced up towards the source of the interruption, wondering what the top-floor tenant could be at. Not that it required more than a moment of Monty's vigorous imagination to supply the answer. He dropped his book and went into the bedroom that adjoined his sitting room, and found that he was standing directly underneath the origin of the creaking.

The sound was unmistakably that of a creaking bedstead, and there was only one human activity known to Monty that caused wooden bedsteads to creak in so regular a rhythm. The top-floor tenant was rogering a visitor on his bed − it could be nothing else! Monty sat on the side of his own bed and stared upwards to the white-papered ceiling above him and pondered how unusual and remarkable it was to be directly beneath a woman laid on her back with her legs parted and a strong shaft plunging into her pussy.

At this point it is expedient to give some small account of the household where this curious scene is placed. At 17 Seymour Place, only a step or two away from Edgware Road and a stroll from the Marble Arch and Oxford Street, stood a typical London house in a long terrace of such houses. The landlady was named Mrs Gifford, and who owned the property only she knew. The basement was given over to kitchen, laundry and other domestic offices; the ground floor was occupied by Mrs Gifford herself, there being no visible evidence that there was, or ever had been, a Mr Gifford.

Nor was one required, for the landlady's mode of life was to let out two floors of the well-furnished house to respectable gentlemen. The first floor up had been occupied for the past seven months by Monty Standish, a young man in sadly reduced circumstances who nevertheless contrived to exist comfortably without work, on an investment left to him by his grandfather. The floor above him was let out to Mr Selwyn Courtney-Stoke, a young gentleman with a position in the Board of Education, who had lived there for about three weeks. On the top floor of the house were the attics, where Mrs Gifford's two servants slept — the cook-general and the skivvy.

There could be not the slightest doubt, therefore, in Monty's mind who was responsible for the creaking over his head. It was Mr Selwyn Courtney-Stoke, rogering away for dear life. Monty's manly shaft had been fully hard before ever he moved into his bedroom to trace the sound overhead — this pleasing stiffness being the direct result of his reading about the unconventional teaching methods at the Boarding School for Young Ladies. After hearing what was taking place in the room above him, his shaft had become so thick and swollen and strong that it could not be neglected for another instant.

Monty slipped his hand under his waistcoat and down the front of his trousers without opening the buttons, and grasped his throbbing shaft to curb its leaping movements, which threatened to squander his resources if allowed to continue unchecked. He sighed in amazement to feel how long and thick his One-Eyed Jack

3

had grown. He sighed again to hear the high-pitched squeak that had first attracted his attention now speeding up into a rapid and sustained groaning of wooden bedstead joints.

This passionate tattoo unambiguously informed the panting and agog listener below that his upstairs neighbour had reached the short strokes! There was a staccato rattle of bed-legs on the floor, and Monty gasped loudly in the realisation that this was the instant when the woman on her back above him was straining her belly upwards to have her pussy filled!

And while Monty had done nothing to provoke the bodily spasm, the crucial moment had also arrived for him. He was hardly able to breath, though his mouth was hanging open, and all his limbs shook fiercely in tremors that racked him from head to toe. His clasped hand gripped One-Eyed Jack tightly to hold him still, but that apoplectic gentleman refused to be restrained. He jumped ominously in Monty's grasp, rubbing his uncovered head quickly against the linen underdrawers that enclosed him.

At this sudden and unexpected sensation, Monty was undone. He ripped wide open his waistcoat and trouser buttons, pulled out his shirt, and let his shaft burst raging out into the light of day. Whilst he stared in alarm and dismay at One-Eyed Jack's shiny and swollen head, he gasped, *Down, Sir, down! I forbid you to . . .* but his command was never completed, for the pent-up desire inside his belly swelled to an uncontrollable explosion. His muscles clenched and he fell over backwards on the bed as, defiant and unbidden, One-Eyed Jack hurled the hot elixir of his passion in a raging flood up his belly, soaking the front of his shirt.

'You beast!' Monty was gasping out to each wet throb of his shaft. 'Stop it, I say! I forbid you to come off,

4

you lustful beast!' but it was to no purpose, for One-Eyed Jack continued until he had fully satisfied himself.

When Monty recovered his senses, the creaking overhead had stopped and all was silence. No doubt Mr Selwyn Courtney-Stoke had withdrawn by now from the friendly pussy that had received his tribute. The lady had surely risen from the bed to attend to whatever precautions she took in order to evade the natural consequences of being poked — intimate ablutions at the wash stand, most probably. The image of a well-rogered pussy being washed was an interesting one, but even more interesting than that was the question of who the lady might be.

In the short time that Selwyn Courtney-Stoke had occupied the floor above, Monty had made his acquaintance in a casual way. They had introduced themselves to each other on the occasion of their first accidental meeting on the stairs. They exchanged a *good morning* and a *good evening* whenever they caught sight of each other, and Monty's inquisitiveness had led him to enquire of Mrs Gifford, and of the skivvy who cleaned his room, what more they knew of the new tenant. It was in this way he learned that Courtney-Stoke had come to London from Berkshire to take up an appointment in the Board of Education.

In person he seemed a somewhat diffident young man, of about five-and-twenty, very neatly dressed and handsome in a rather weak sort of way. He went out in the morning at nine and came back in the afternoon at three-thirty, the hours of work at the Board of Education being far from demanding. Monty knew this because, having no regular employment of his own, he had time to observe the household before he took himself out in mid-morning to meet his friends.

The problem that was now occupying Monty's mind, as he lay on his back in the pleasantly languid aftermath of his involuntary sexual emission was this — how could the general effeteness of the upstairs tenant's deportment be reconciled with the lusty rogering he had just engaged in?

Since Courtney-Stoke had moved into Seymour Place, there had been only one lady Monty had seen visit him — a dark-haired charmer in fashionably expensive clothes. Enquiries to the skivvy as to her identity had produced the information that she was a sister of Mr Courtney-Stoke who dropped in on him for tea when she was in town shopping. Other than her, there had been no female visitors at all upstairs, yet Courtney-Stoke had achieved a sufficient degree of friendship with someone to roger her in broad daylight!

His curiosity raging, Monty sat up and took off his trousers to mop himself dry. When he was presentable again, his clothes properly adjusted and his hair brushed, he moved back into his sitting room and stood by the door to the landing, to listen closely for sounds of movement. Five or six minutes later his diligence was rewarded by footfalls on the stairs, coming down from the floor above. He picked up his hat and waited until he heard footsteps right outside his door, then flung it open and stepped out onto the landing, exactly in time to come face to face with Courtney-Stoke and the dark-haired charmer.

'Good day, Selwyn,' said Monty very pleasantly, and bowing slightly to the lady at the same time.

'Good day to you,' Selwyn replied. 'You haven't met my sister — Mrs Fanshawe. She's in town on a shopping spree. Gwendolen, my dear, allow me to present Mr Monty Standish.'

Monty shook Mrs Fanshawe's gloved little hand and smiled at her in as charming a way as he could. He was sorely puzzled by the position — if Selwyn had rogered this pretty lady, then she very evidently could not be his sister. But if she truly was his sister, then Selwyn had not rogered her. So much was clear. The three of them descended the stairs together, while Selwyn explained that he was escorting Mrs Fanshawe to the railway station to catch her train home. Monty thought her delightful — in her face and form those features which suggested weakness in Selwyn were displayed as a most enchanting femininity, so that Monty was disposed to give some credence to the suggestion that there was a family relationship between the two of them. Perhaps Mrs Fanshawe was Selwyn's cousin, but why then pretend that she was his sister? Here lay a mystery to be unravelled.

Outside the house Selwyn steered Mrs Fanshawe towards where the hansom cabs waited, and Monty bade the two of them goodbye, raised his shiny top hat and walked the other way. He halted as soon as he was round the corner, and let a minute or two pass. When he turned back to the house, Selwyn and his friend were nowhere to be seen, and Monty strode swiftly through the front door and up the stairs, straight past the door to his own rooms and on up another flight to Selwyn's door.

Doors were never locked, for this was not a hotel or a common lodging house. Inside Selwyn's sitting room, Monty paused with his back to the door and looked round. He had been in this room many times before, when Naunton Cox had it, he having become a good friend before his misfortune. The room was almost as it had always been, furnished with comfortable heavy chairs and a settee. Naunton's rack of pipes was gone from the mantelpiece and his collection of walking sticks from the stand by the door. On the wall over the fireplace the new occupant had hung a large framed water colour of a village green with a cow up to its knees in the duck pond and a small church in the distance.

The real difference was that in Naunton's time the room was always redolent of the strong and manly smell of good tobacco — and that was gone completely. There was another and infinitely more interesting fragrance in the air — that of the expensive perfume Mrs Fanshawe was wearing when Monty was introduced. It was hard to put a name to it. Monty thought it might be a kind of patchouli, but it seemed more delicate than that, and it was certainly provoking to a man's fancies, no doubt of it!

He crossed the room with light and rapid step and went into the bedroom. What he had expected to see, he had no clear idea, but the sight of a perfectly made bed came as a surprise. It would have seemed more in keeping for the bed to be rumpled up if pretty Mrs Fanshawe had been vigorously rogered on it twenty minutes before. Yet the blue and yellow counterpane was as flat and smooth as if it had remained totally untouched since it had been made that morning.

Monty was beginning to doubt whether anything of interest had taken place on the bed at all that day — the creaking he heard might have had some other cause. To settle it one way or the other, he took hold of the bed clothes and with a sweep of his arm flung them to the foot of the bed — and there was all the evidence necessary! There on the bottom sheet was a damp patch which he knew from his own experience was caused by a wet pussy dribbling a little when a well-poked woman lay with her legs apart after the conclusion of the act.

There could be no doubt of it, Selwyn had given his

visitor a thorough rogering on this very bed. Therefore she was not his sister and he was lying — but to what purpose? Under the guise of shopping she gave her husband the slip and came to London to be pleasured by Selwyn. That was clear, and enviable too, for the truth was that Monty was much taken by Mrs Fanshawe. He had seen her for only a few minutes and exchanged no words with her other than the courtesies of a formal introduction, yet he had a great and throbbing desire to make use of her pussy.

He sat on the edge of the bed and contemplated the damp patch while giving himself the considerable pleasure of speculation on Gwendolen Fanshawe's pussy. The hair under her bonnet had been of a very dark brown hue that might be particularised as walnut by a man of a romantic trend — and it might well be imagined that the curls between her thighs were of the same rich shade. Monty had also observed during their brief meeting that she was a full-fleshed woman, ample of bosom and of hip — and from that he concluded that the Mount of Venus that so drew his thoughts would be plump and prominent.

Needless to say, these fervid imaginings as to the shape and colouration of Mrs Fanshawe's secret parts were inflammatory in the extreme to a nature so unrestrained as Monty's. Though only fifteen minutes had elapsed since he collapsed in convulsions of ecstasy to the furious spouting of One-Eyed Jack, his blood was again racing hotly through his veins and Jack was standing hard once more and making his presence felt by means of strong and impatient jerking inside Monty's trousers.

'No!' Monty said aloud. 'I refuse absolutely to be tricked yet again into an act of beastly self-pollution!' and while he was making his protest and stating his determination to control his passion, even at that moment he was undoing his buttons and easing out his twitching shaft to ease the unbearable pressure of his clothes on its swollen length.

What unseemliness might have transpired next on the bed with the damp patch if Monty had been left undisturbed can be only a matter for impure conjecture. What happened in fact was that in through the half-open door of Selwyn Courtney-Stoke's bedroom came Minnie Briggs, the sixteen-year-old skivvy, to find Monty seated on the bed and stroking his stiff shaft.

'Lord love us, Mr Standish — whatever are you doing?' asked the girl, an impudent grin on her face.

After the first shock of discovery, Monty's fears were quick to be calmed and he grinned back, for he was on friendly terms with Minnie. Some might have categorised the terms as much more friendly than was proper between a gentleman and a housemaid, for there had been many a time in the past six months when, with nothing else to occupy his attention for half an hour, he had given the girl half-a-crown to stroke his manly shaft while he felt her pussy. Beyond that he had never ventured to go with her, apprehensive of making her belly swell if he did.

'You know very well what I am doing, Minnie,' said he boldly, 'come here and take hold of my shaft and stroke it for me — and you shall have a silver half-crown.'

'You've got no conscience at all, the way you tempt and abuse a poor girl,' Minnie answered, and wiped her hands on her apron as she came across the room to sit beside him and take hold of his shaking length, 'oh my — it's wet and sticky already. You don't need me — you've done something naughty to yourself.'

'Not so,' said Monty, opening his legs, 'something unexpected happened to me, but it hasn't calmed me at all, as you see.'

Whilst Minnie treated his quivering shaft to a brisk stroke that would soon bring him off, Monty put his hand up her loose brown skirt and pushed her knees apart.

'What was it brought on this unexpected *something* that made you wet and sticky?' Minnie asked with a sideways grin at him. 'As if I couldn't guess what you've been up to — you've been reading one of the wicked books you buy — and reading it one-handed, I'll be bound.'

'No, it wasn't that,' Monty said, pushing his finger up into the girl's pussy, 'it was the creaking of this bed — I heard it down in my rooms and I knew that Mr Courtney-Stoke was rogering Mrs Fanshawe. She's very pretty, don't you think?'

'Ah, you want to give her a poke yourself, that's it,' Minnie said slyly, handling Monty's shaft very firmly, 'you're right out of luck there. You'll have to keep on dreaming of her, and fetch off in your hand when you hear the bed creaking.'

'What makes you so certain that Mrs Fanshawe wouldn't look at me?' demanded Monty. 'The ladies like me — why shouldn't I win the same divine reward as Courtney-Stoke has already, if I set myself out to charm her and win her esteem?'

'You've got no chance at all to get in with her,' said Minnie with a firm shake of her head, 'no more than fly to the moon. They're brother and sister and they're red-hot for each other. She's here twice a week to be poked by him.'

'That's ridiculous,' said Monty, his voice hardly more than a faint sigh, so delightful were the tremors that flitted though his belly from the girl's hand manipulating his engorged shaft, 'brothers don't poke their sisters — that would be a monstrous and unnatural act!'

'It must be different where you come from,' said Minnie, her tone filled with disbelief, 'but I was born in Hoxton and every girl in the street got poked by her brother.'

'This unspeakable depravity may be usual in the slums of the East End of London, perhaps,' Monty gasped, 'but Courtney-Stoke and Mrs Fanshawe were born into a family of means and education — how can you suggest for an instant that they would take part in practices so viciously degenerate?'

'You're a nice gentleman, but a bit simple,' was Minnie's impertinent reply, 'people with money aren't made different to us poor people. Mrs Fanshawe's got a hole between her legs just like me, and she likes it filled and her brother's got a shaft he likes to poke with. If you ask me, it's natural enough he's been sticking it up her ever since the day he could get it to stand up straight.'

The girl's words and the image they summoned of Gwendolen on her back with her legs spread apart, for a poke by her brother, was more than Monty could stand. It was a matter of the utmost desperation to get his shaft up a pussy and relieve himself of the letch that burned through his body and mind. The true object of his desires was miles away, but Minnie was at hand, and she was stroking One-Eyed Jack, who stuck so boldly up out of his open trousers.

At once Monty seized on the opportunity by snatching his hand away from the girl's pussy to take her by the hips and turn her to face away from him. Before she had time to protest, he had a hand on the nape of her neck to push her down on the bed, until her knees were on the carpet and her belly lay on the rumpled bed sheet, her backside to him.

'What are you doing?' she demanded, and before he

answered, Monty flipped up her skirt and underskirt to reveal her baggy drawers and her legs in coarse black stockings.

'You, Minnie,' he said, 'I'm going to do you, and afterwards you shall have five shillings.'

One-Eyed Jack twitched in delight when Monty pulled open the rearward slit of Minnie's drawers and beheld the twin cheeks of her bottom. Below, in the join of her thighs, her girlish and sparsely-fledged pussy awaited his pleasure. He pressed two of his fingers into it and rubbed her button, to make it grow wet.

'Oh, Mr Standish,' said she, 'if you're going to poke me, be quick about it before Mr Courtney-Stoke comes back and finds us at it on his bed!'

'Not much fear of that,' Monty assured her, 'he's taking Mrs Fanshawe to the railway station – I heard him say so. You'll be well rogered, my girl, and your pussy as slippy as a buttered bun, before anyone disturbs us.'

With that, he put One-Eyed Jack to Minnie's pussy and pushed. He expected her to be tight and difficult to pierce, but he sank into her with ease – right in, until his belly was flat against her backside, and he went at her briskly.

'You're a wicked gentleman, you are, Mr Standish – poking me on the same bed where Mrs Fanshawe's only this minute been given a pussy-full by her brother!' Minnie cried out as she jerked her hips back at him to meet his strokes.

'And now it's your turn for a pussy-full!' Monty gasped, his voice failing as the passion rose so strongly in him that he was like to faint with sensation.

'You've never wanted to poke me before,' said Minnie, 'though you've made me fetch you off with my hand times enough. Are you going to want to do this to me again?'

'Daily,' he sighed as he rammed away into her wet slit, 'not a morning goes by but I wake up hard-on like an iron bar — from now on I'll have you when you bring the morning tea.'

At that instant he hardly knew what he was saying, so intense were the emotions that held him in their grasp. He had no real intention of making promises to the housemaid that she might seek to hold him to later on. He had untied the bow behind her back that held her long apron, and thrust his hands up inside her loose and ill-fitting clothes, to grasp her bare titties. Faster and faster he plunged into her slippery pussy, a vivid picture of pretty Mrs Gwendolen Fanshawe behind his closed eyes — Gwendolen on her back, on this very bed, undressed down to her chemise and drawers, her creamy thighs wide apart to offer him her hairy slit.

'Oh, oh, oh!' Monty sighed, imagining himself lying with his trousers down round his knees and his shirt turned up to bare himself, his belly on Gwendolen's, whilst One-Eyed Jack thrust deep into her.

As Monty's frenzy mounted, he was unaware that he was ramming against little Minnie's bottom, and ravaging her wet pussy with a ruthless strength that shook her thin body under him. He was lost in his imagined rogering of Gwendolen, and he stabbed ever more fiercely, until at last the floodgates burst open in his belly and his hot tide of desire gushed into her.

Minnie cried out *Oh my*! and the bare cheeks of her backside battered against him. She, too, was in the very throes of coming off, the muscles of her belly contracting to grip his shaft and suck out the last drop of his spurting essence.

CHAPTER 2
Secrets Observed Through a Spyhole

Three days after the stirring events so far related, Monty was awakened at half past eight o'clock, as was his customary way, by a sharp tap at the door of his bedroom. Equally customary for him was the condition in which he awoke, with One-Eyed Jack fully rampant under his nightshirt. Monty was pretty sure that he had been dreaming about Gwendolen Fanshawe, although sadly he was unable to remember the details of what he had dreamed he was doing to that dark-haired charmer.

The knocker at the door who had woken him up was Minnie, the little skivvy bringing his morning cup of tea. She set it down on the night table beside him, and whilst she was at the window to raise the blind and draw back the curtains, he half sat up and wriggled his back against the soft pillows, to make himself comfortable.

'Good morning to you, Minnie,' he said, and he threw back the bedclothes to uncover himself. Minnie turned from the window and, seeing him lying in his nightshirt, her eyes alighted at once on the long bulge where his stiff shaft twitched strongly beneath the thin linen. The faintest of grins touched her mouth and Monty returned an encouraging smile, while he hauled up his nightshirt to his belly button and exposed his condition.

Minnie put her hands on her aproned hips and stared down at One-Eyed Jack, nodding up and down under her gaze, as hard as a brush handle. Although Monty had told the girl, when he poked her on Selwyn Courtney-Stoke's bed, that it was his intention to make daily use of her pussy, he had not done anything of the sort. She was, to his way of thinking, a plain little thing and none too well-washed, if the truth were told, and he had poked her only because she happened to be available at a moment of extreme need.

Other than that, he had no particular use for her, his needs being very thoroughly catered for on a regular basis by a dear friend — Mrs Cecily Massingham, a young widow who lived in St John's Wood. But now that he had awoken this morning in the grip of a strong letch — an aftermath of his dream of beautiful Gwendolen — Monty decided that he would make use of Minnie's pussy for a minute or two.

With his hand he gestured that she should sit down on the bed beside him, and he asked her to pull up her clothes and let him have a feel of her commodity. She sat on the side of the bed, facing him, but to his disappointment, her skirts remained down about her ankles and nothing of her body was shown to him. She handed him his cup of tea, to keep his hands busy, and stared thoughtfully at One-Eyed Jack, who was straining upwards in the hope of being handled by her.

'None of your nonsense, Mr Standish,' she said, 'I've no time in the mornings for all that — I've got my work to do and Mrs Gifford will be after me if she thinks I'm not hard at it.'

'At least hold my shaft in your hand,' Monty

suggested, 'only for a minute, and I'll give you a half-crown. It won't take any longer than that, Minnie, and a kind-hearted girl like you will never leave me in so desperate a plight!'

'Looks to me as if you've been holding it in your own hand,' she retorted. 'Get along with you!'

All the same, she clasped Monty's hot and hard shaft in the palm of her hand and jerked it up and down a time or two.

'That's it,' Monty sighed, his eyes closing in pleasurable anticipation of having his physical tension expertly relieved, but Minnie soon ceased her manipulation of him.

'I'll tell you what, Mr Standish,' said she, grinning at him as his eyes opened in surprise at her failure to continue the manual treatment she had begun, 'as you're so hard-on for Mrs Fanshawe, what would you say to seeing her given a good poking by Mr Courtney-Stoke? You'd have to stay very quiet, but you'd get a good look at her bits and pieces, if that's what you want — and you'd see her pussy being filled. What about it?'

His shaft answered for Monty by jumping in the girl's hand so fiercely that she giggled.

'Cost you ten shillings,' she said. 'Are you on?'

'When?' he asked, hardly able to believe his luck.

'This afternoon. She's coming to see him — I know because he told me when I took his morning tea and he ordered an extra cup and a whole fruit cake for four o'clock.'

'Can you really put me in a position to see what they do?' asked Monty doubtfully.

'I've watched them myself,' said Minnie. 'Is it yes or no? Do you want to see Mrs Fanshawe on her back with her legs open and her pussy wide open for her brother to shove his dolly-whacker up her?'

'Yes!' Monty exclaimed, his own dolly-whacker jerking hotly in the girl's hand. 'But how can this be achieved?'

'Never you mind how,' said Minnie, 'just leave that to me. You'll give me ten shillings for the peepshow, you promise?'

'Willingly! You shall have the cash before you go!'

'I trust a gentleman's word,' Minnie assured him. 'I'll take it this afternoon. Be ready and waiting for me at four o'clock, and I'll be here to lead the way.'

'You're a good girl, Minnie,' Monty exclaimed.

'Yes, I'm a good girl, I am,' she agreed with a grin, 'except when a gentleman pushes money into my hand. Then I'm a bad girl for him, I am. Now what do you want me to do about this hard-on you've been flashing about ever since I brought your tea?'

Monty drank his cooling tea and set the cup out of the way on his night table.

'What would you suggest, Minnie?' he asked her with a grin. 'I wake up every morning of the week and find it in this stiff-necked mood.'

'Stuck up, is it?' said Minnie. 'There's only one way to go then — it'll have to be taken down a peg, to learn it not to be so cocky.'

'I'm sure you're right,' Monty sighed, 'a touch of strictness is the only thing for it in this state. I'm too soft-hearted, that's my trouble — I let it do as it likes.'

'You leave it to me,' she said briskly, 'and I'll soon knock the stuffing out of it. You'll have no more trouble from this hairy monster this morning, I'll see to that.'

With this promise, she started to rub firmly up and down the straining shaft she held, whilst meanwhile, her other hand was groping between Monty's spread thighs

18

to take hold of his soft knick-knacks and roll them in her fingers. Monty lay back at his ease against his pillows, breathing faster and more irregularly as his passions were raised, and mindful that at any moment now he was going to fetch off in a spectacular manner.

'Your dolly-whacker's shaking like a leaf,' Minnie announced, the rapid movement of her fingers sending such thrills through Monty that he gasped aloud and his belly twitched wildly, 'it's had about all it can take, if you ask me, and in a minute it'll come to a sticky end.'

Monty cried out in a frenzy of sensation and his legs jerked spasmodically as his thick white essence came gushing out in long jets like a fountain.

'Lor' love you, Mr Standish — just look at that!' Minnie exclaimed in awe to see how high the spurts flew and the force with which Monty was spraying the front of his nightshirt.'

'Oh, oh, oh!' Monty moaned to his delicious spasms.

'I've never seen anything like it,' said Minnie in admiration as the last creamy drop of sap hung trembling from One-Eyed Jack, 'you won't get another rise out of your diddler for an hour or two after that effort — it'll be on the slack for the rest of the morning, mark my words, Mr Standish.'

She was grossly underestimating Monty's admirable powers of recuperation. He had another nap after she'd wiped his belly dry with a corner of her long apron, and when he eventually got up, at about ten o'clock, he was much refreshed. He dressed and went out for lunch in a chophouse nearby, with a glass or two of porter, to prepare himself for the treat that he had been promised that afternoon. By three he was back in his own rooms, and to pass the time pleasantly he brought out from a drawer of his sideboard the book he had been reading when first he heard the bed creak upstairs that drew his attention to the rogering of Gwendolen Fanshawe by her brother, Selwyn.

Monty settled himself comfortably in his arm-chair and opened *Lady Bumslapper's Boarding School for Young Ladies* at the page where he had left off and proceeded with his investigation of teaching methods in this most unorthodox establishment.

. . . by the order of Her Ladyship, the offending girl was made to lie on the ladder that leaned against the study wall, while the two female servants secured her to it, with her arms and legs well stretched out. Her Ladyship had always preferred the use of the short ladder to the whipping-horse or whipping-post, declaring that the spaces between rungs made it easier to get at the vulnerable parts of the victim.

'Now, Harriet, my dear' said she to Miss Jarndyne, 'you see this wicked girl, Millicent, prepared for her punishment. Take up the instrument of chastisement and show me how briskly you are able to wield it.'

Whips and birches were never made use of in Lady Bumslapper's establishment, for she thought it a monstrous cruel spoiling of female loveliness to break the skin of a white young bottom and draw blood. The weapon with which miscreant young ladies were made to understand the errors of their ways was a whalebone strip, pulled from a worn-out pair of corsets. It was light and flexible and made a great crack across a bottom, stinging most fearfully, but without doing damage.

Miss Harriet inspected the lashings that pinioned Millicent's wrists to the ladder above her head, and her ankles to the rung first off the ground, then crouched underneath her to examine the bonds from below and test with her hand that they would hold firm, however much

20

the victim writhed. The frightened girl stared at her through the rungs of the ladder with a pale face, pleading in a whisper to be pardoned.

Without deigning to reply Miss Harriet ran an immodest hand up under the girl's loose chemise to squeeze her plump titties, and pinched their rosebuds with cruel fingers, hard enough to bring tears to Millicent's innocent eyes.

'Oh, Miss Jarndyne,' said she faintly, 'I must ask you not to touch me on that portion of my person.'

Her tormentor laughed at her and deliberately increased her agony of mind by putting both hands up her chemise, to handle her titties freely. Then, satisfied that she had asserted her authority, she fetched a cushion from the sofa and pushed it between the girl's bare belly and the ladder — not as might be thought to protect her from bruising against the wood, but to force her bottom outwards for the lash.

The servants had pinned Millicent's drawers to the sides, to present her nether cheeks prominently, and had tucked up her chemise under her arms. All was ready, the victim awaited her dread Fate — yet with the cruelty implicit in her nature, Miss Harriet kept her in suspense a while longer. Laughing harshly, she passed a searching hand over the terrified girl's bottom.

'Excellently plump,' said she with relish, 'soft and delicate flesh for the lash! Ah, how I am going to make you sob, Millicent!'

'Have mercy,' the hapless girl pleaded, her face stained with tears, 'forgive me, I beg you, and I will never offend again.'

'It is too late to ask for pardon now,' said Miss Harriet. 'You have bitterly offended Her Ladyship, who is here today to witness your punishment. There will be no *pardon until these young cheeks have blushed under the sting of chastisement. After that, we shall see.'*

Whilst she was adding to her victim's sufferings by her hard words, Miss Harriet's scornful hand roved over her uncovered bottom, and slipped down below the cheeks, to probe shamelessly between the girl's thighs and touch her secret furry place.

'A cut or two here would serve to teach you better manners in future,' said she, and her finger pried into Millicent's lower lips, 'well, I shall think of a use for your girlish plaything when the punishment is completed. I shall make you shriek out a second time while I have you bound to the ladder, though it will be for a different reason.'

'Not that! Spare me, I implore you!' gasped Millicent. 'You may beat me all you will, Miss Jarndyne, but do not outrage my maidenly modesty! Lady Bumslapper — I throw myself on your mercy to save me from violation at the hands of Miss Jarndyne.'

'Tush, girl — hold your tongue and take your punishment ,' Her Ladyship replied. 'As for the rest, it is my earnest intention to give your pussy a good tousling myself, after Miss Harriet has had her fill of it. You'll be carried to your bed senseless from coming off, when I've done with you.'

'By George!' Monty exclaimed, astonished by the methods of discipline in use in female boarding schools. His shaft was standing at full stretch in his trousers, despite the exercise it had undergone that morning at the hands of the skivvy. Soon after four o'clock he heard footsteps go past on the stairs outside his door, and knew that Selwyn had brought his sister to his rooms for tea. In another five minutes he heard more steps and guessed it to be Minnie taking up their tea tray. He put away his book and sat impatiently waiting.

A light tap at his door and in came Minnie, grinning and with a finger pressed to her lips to enjoin silence. Monty nodded to her that he perfectly understood and, when she beckoned to him, he rose from his chair and in complete silence followed her out of his rooms and up the stairs. They went up past Selwyn's door and on to the attic stairs, which Monty had never seen before. They were uncarpeted, narrow and steep, so that as Minnie led the way up, her bottom was not far from Monty's face.

With a merry grin he slid his hand under her skirts and up between her legs, to the slit of her drawers, until he had hold of her pussy. She squealed in surprise when he gripped her, but suppressed her outcry quickly, and went the rest of the way to her room bow-legged, Monty's hand preventing her from closing her legs properly.

Her room under the roof was small and cramped, with a window let into the slates. There was a small iron-framed bed, a chair with a split seat, and a washstand that looked rickety. In a whisper she told Monty to sit on the bed and wait, and make no noise. He did, and watched with great interest as she dragged aside a strip of old brown carpet that lay on the floor, and went down on her hands and knees on the bare boards.

There was, he saw, a short floorboard, and with a teaspoon she produced from her apron pocket Minnie levered it up and put it to the side, out of the way, to reveal thick joists and the ceiling of the room below. At last he understood how he was to be shown the rogering of Gwendolen Fanshawe, and at once he was off the bed and down on hands and knees beside the maid. She turned her head to grin at him, and moved away a little to let him see that there was a small spy-hole in the plaster of the ceiling below. Directly under it lay Selwyn's bed, virginally made up with sheets and checkered counterpane.

It was to be presumed that Selwyn and his visitor were still having tea in the sitting room. The refreshment did not detain them long — in not more than five minutes from the time that Monty first looked through the ceiling, he became aware of the sound of voices in the bedroom beneath him. Very greatly to his disappointment, there was nothing to be seen, for the occupants of the room were out of range of his limited view. He sat back on his heels to rest, and motioned Minnie to keep watch.

Very soon she tugged at his sleeve and pointed downwards with a grin that told him the curtain had risen on the drama he had come to see. He applied his eye to the hole, and to his delight observed Gwendolen on the bed. She had removed whatever stylish gown she had been wearing that day and lay on her back with her pretty chemise turned up high and her rounded legs spread apart to show her lace-trimmed white drawers.

She was so very beautiful that Monty's heart was in his mouth and he could hardly breath for the emotions that had him by the throat. In his trousers his shaft was almost painfully stiff, and it throbbed to little tremors of sensation. Then Selwyn was kneeling beside his sister on the bed, and he had undressed to his shirt, which he had tucked up round his waist, Gwendolen stretched out a dainty hand to grasp her brother's outstanding shaft, and her eyes seemed to glow with a languishing desire.

For truth to tell, Monty was in honesty compelled to admit to himself, Selwyn Courtney-Stoke's shaft was outstanding indeed. At full stretch, it was a good eight inches long, and thick in proportion. Monty had always regarded himself as pleasantly and well-enough endowed, but he had never been able to muster more than six inches, however provocative his partner, however deft her touch, however enchanting the circumstances of the poke. He was, he had to admit, jealous of Selwyn for yet another reason besides his privilege of rogering Gwendolen.

Monty put his head as close to the joist as he could get, to bring his eye closer to the aperture for a better view. He saw Selwyn open the slit of his sister's drawers to reveal the most charming curly-haired pussy Monty could ever recall seeing in his life — a delight of a pussy that pouted out between smooth-skinned white thighs. Gwendolen raised her head from the pillow to murmur a few words in a low voice to her brother, who leaned over and pressed a kiss on the plump lips of the pussy Monty would have killed for.

'Oh, oh, my dearest Selwyn ,' exclaimed Gwendolen, speaking loudly enough this time for the Peeping Tom in the room above to hear her words. Selwyn was staring intently into her glowing eyes while he ran his hands up the insides of her parted legs, from the tops of her white stockings right up to the delicate skin nearest the bush of dark curls that covered her pussy.

'What's he doing to her?' Minnie whispered in Monty's ear. 'He has a plate of mutton sometimes .'

'Plate of mutton? What do you mean?' Monty asked.

By way of answer Minnie stuck out her tongue and made rapid licking movements with it.

'Oh my Lord!' Monty sighed, smitten by the thought of using his tongue on Gwendolen's pussy mutton to bring her off.

'Oh my darling!' Gwendolen exclaimed loudly below, as Selwyn slid his fingers into her pretty pink slit.

'Oh, my darling boy!' she cried out again, and her body was twitching to the darts of sensation that shot through her.

'How I do love to watch myself feel you like this, dearest,' said Selwyn, staring down at his fingers ravishing his sister's wet pussy, 'even though I am keenly aware that what you and I do together is very wrong and unnatural. Ah, if only I had the will to refrain from submitting to your lusts! This fearful moral weakness is a great source of turmoil and anxiety to me.'

It was obvious to Monty up above that the turmoil within her belly that Gwendolen was experiencing owed nothing to a sense of moral weakness and everything to Selwyn's fingers playing in her. She had begun to sigh without pause and to gasp out words of endearment and encouragement to her brother, whose skilful fingers stroked and fluttered in her open pussy, gliding over her hidden button until she uttered a shriek and writhed in convulsive joy on the bed.

To observe the woman of his choicest dreams come off caused Monty's shaft to jerk hard, so that he felt compelled to take hold of it through the material of his trousers and hold it tightly. He was unaware, rapt as he was in his erotic pleasure, that Minnie was crouching close beside him, her cheek pressed against his cheek, so that she too could look through the spyhole with him and observe what went on below.

Well might she huddle against Monty to catch a glimpse of the enthralling drama that was being enacted on the stage of the bed, for the final act had arrived and the denouement was close at hand. Monty caught his breath when he saw Selwyn beside his sister, supporting himself on one elbow, while she spread her stockinged legs wider still. To prepare the way for his entry, Selwyn pulled her dark-curled pussy open with his inquisitive fingers, so displaying the deliciously moist pink interior.

'Oh, how your pussy throbs to my touch,' Selwyn cried

loudly enough for Monty to hear, 'even though I have just made you come off! I promise you will faint in ecstasy before I have done with you!'

He seemed completely reconciled to his moral weakness as he pushed his sister's legs wider apart with his knee and lay over her belly, guiding with his hand the bare and purple head of his impressive shaft between her thighs, to bring it to her open pussy. For Monty it was as if he were in the room himself, his hand between those creamy thighs to feel the pink lips of Gwendolen's pussy, set in its nest of dark hair. His breathing grew shorter and he was unable to prevent his hand from tightening its grip on One-Eyed Jack and sliding up and down in his yearning.

Truth to tell, he was so very far gone that he had forgotten about Minnie's impudent sense of humour. Whilst he knelt with his head down and his bottom up, she reached under his jacket from behind and, through the tight-stretched material over his bottom, ran her fingers briskly up and down between the cheeks and under his knick-knacks. One-Eyed Jack was pleased by what she was doing and he began vibrating in Monty's trousers like a violin string plucked *pizzicato*.

Down below, Selwyn was up his lovely sister to the hilt and plunging hard and fast, eliciting cries of bliss from her.

'Oh, oh, Selwyn — how quickly I feel myself coming on!' she cried, her legs kicking up in quick jerks off the bed while he poked away at her with the appetite of a man who has not had a woman for a day or two.

Under this urgent stimulus, Gwendolen's body writhed and twisted on the bed, the sensations within her gathering towards a luscious climax. Again and again she seemed almost to swoon from the exquisite thrills that coursed through her, and each time she recovered her force and jolted her belly up at him in time with the thrusts of his darting shaft. Her stockinged legs kicked up off the bed, as high as if stretching up towards the hidden observer above, and her prolonged shrieks of bliss told of the arrival of the supreme moment.

Monty moaned softly and shuddered, and under the stimulus of Minnie's fingers rubbing fast and furious between the cheeks of his backside, One-Eyed Jack leaped like an Australian kangaroo and then discharged his frantic lust in Monty's underdrawers. Monty collapsed forward, pressing his cheek painfully against a hard corner of the joist, whilst he squeezed both his hands against the front of his trousers to control his throbbing shaft, which continued to spit its defiance until it was satisfied. When the outpouring stopped and Monty caught his breath, the absurdly comic aspect of what had happened struck him, and he chuckled — till Minnie clapped a hand over his mouth to silence him.

The sudden emission had calmed his nervous system so fully that he got up from the floor and went to lie on Minnie's bed to rest for a while. His drenched shirt-front and underdrawers were clammy and sticky on his belly, and he considered that he had had a good ten shillings' worth. There was to be a bonus, for he had barely dozed off when Minnie shook his arm.

'Come and have a look at this, Mr Standish,' she whispered urgently, 'you'll never guess what they're up to!'

Monty went back to the spyhole at once, and what he saw drew a long sigh of astonished delight from his lips. Down below on the bed, beautiful Gwendolen was stark naked, having taken off her thin chemise and drawers for a most unusual purpose. She had rolled her chemise into a sort of rope, and with it she had bound Selwyn's hands together above his head, and attached them to the bed head by means of her stockings. With her drawers she was gagging him, even as Monty watched, forcing a rolled-up part of the delicate garment into his open mouth and tying the legs firmly together behind his head.

When she had him helpless and silenced, she sat across his thighs and her fingers played with his limp shaft, her desire to again provoke and satisfy the most powerful and thrilling sensations of lust that the human frame can sustain. She pushed Selwyn's shirt higher, to bare his belly and chest, and flicked with her fingernails at the red-brown buds on his hairless chest.

'I'm going to lick your barley-sugar stick,' Monty heard her say to her brother, who shook his head violently and struggled underneath her, as if his perception of moral weakness had returned to trouble his conscience.

Demur as he might, Gwendolen had him in her power, and she pressed her beautiful face between his thighs and rubbed her nose in the curls about his shaft, and soon his wriggling came to a stop and he lay still on the bed. His legs parted like a pair of scissors and Gwendolen knelt between them while she bent over and took his lengthening shaft into her mouth.

'By Jove!' Monty exclaimed, his fervid imagination insisting that it would be superb beyond all human deserving to enjoy the privilege of Gwendolen's tongue licking over the distended head of his shaft! It seemed that she was expert at this work, for in a short space of time she straightened her back and held Selwyn's shaft in her fist — grown to its full eight-inch size and strength.

With no more ado, she threw a leg over his belly and sat on top of him, her round and pretty titties rolling up and down to her movements. In a moment she had guided Selwyn's length into her open and slippery pussy. There was no objection now from Selwyn — he was content to lie under his sister and let her do as she pleased with him. For a quarter of an hour Monty watched her delicious ride on Selwyn's belly, before she let him come off in violent upheavals, which brought on her own climactic satisfaction at once.

In Monty's trousers One-Eyed Jack was hard as a ramrod and raging to have his lusts gratified immediately. Without as much as a by-your-leave Monty seized the girl at his side by her ankles and pulled her knees smartly from under her, so that she collapsed face down on the floorboards. He dragged her clothes halfway up her back and ripped open her drawers to bare the cheeks of her backside, and dabbled with his fingers into her wet pussy, for she too had been greatly affected by what she had watched.

'Put it up me,' Minnie gasped, wriggling her bottom about. Monty jerked open his trouser buttons and pulled his shirt up to his chest and flung himself upon her. Her thin thighs were wide apart when he passed his hands under them, to pry open her wet slit and finger her button.

'Do me,' she gasped, 'do me quick!' and she lifted her loins up from the floor until the velvet purple head of Monty's shaft found the entry to her pussy and he rammed in with fast jerks. Ecstatic sensations flooded through him, whilst the thrusts of his shaft inside her and the rub of his fingers on her button roused Minnie to an intensity of pleasure that made her gasp in time with his strokes. She was writhing under him, the cushions of her bare cheeks against his belly serving to intensify his pleasure to a veritable delirium.

'Oh Minnie, you lovely little slut!' Monty gasped out as he approached his zenith. 'Your pussy's drenching wet!

'Do me hard!' she moaned. 'Fill me full!'

'I'm fetching off, Minnie!' he cried, and his belly thumped against the cheeks of her behind, whilst his plunging shaft gushed hot essence into her. She shuddered beneath him, heaving her backside up to meet his furious strokes and she came off so intensely that she collapsed senseless. Monty lay tranquil on her hot and limp body whilst he recovered from his delightful exertions, feeling his last creamy drops dribble into her.

CHAPTER 3
An Exchange of Confidences

Selwyn Courtney-Stoke had only been a few months in London with his position at the Board of Education and had not yet made any friends of note. He was therefore flattered to be invited to lunch at a decent restaurant by Monty, in furtherance of the plan the latter young gentleman had formed to bring Gwendolen Fanshawe's personal charms within his grasp.

To achieve, without waste of time, the degree of cordiality needed for his purposes, Monty plied his guest with food and drink — most especially drink. The meal started with a meaty beef soup, and continued with goujons of turbot cooked in white wine. Then came the main course — thick slices from a baron of beef, with roasted potatoes, parsnips and sprouts. Afterwards they tucked into cabinet pudding with cream, and finished with generous portions of Stilton. To wash down all this deal of food they drank between them four bottles of claret and two of Sauternes, and then turned to a fine crusty old port with their cheese.

Selwyn ate everything set before him but, as Monty guessed, he was not accustomed to drinking on this heroic scale and was soon in a most receptive state of mind. He listened with great interest when Monty told him how well he had been acquainted with Mr Naunton Cox, the previous occupant of the rooms Selwyn now had, and he asked Monty many questions about him.

'You may find my curiosity in regard to Mr Cox somewhat odd,' said Selwyn, speaking carefully to disguise his intoxication, 'but there is a particular reason for my interest. What it is, I cannot possibly, as a gentleman, reveal, but you may take my word that it is quite extraordinary.'

'Everything to do with dear old Naunton was extraordinary,' Monty replied with a knowing smile. 'His secrets are safe with me — you may tell me your reason.'

Selwyn dropped his voice and leaned across the table top to whisper that, on moving into the rooms vacated by Naunton Cox, he had to his amazement discovered in the bottom of the bedroom wardrobe a pair of female drawers. What did Monty make of that? he enquired.

'Why, only that some lady friend of his went home with a bare backside,' said Monty, with a laugh. 'He entertained ladies in his rooms very frequently and, beyond a shadow of doubt, they all removed their drawers for him.'

'Lord above — he was a ladies' man!' Selwyn exclaimed.

'I am sure that you are a gentleman who may be entrusted with another gentleman's confidences,' said Monty, as he topped up Selwyn's half-full glass. 'I was never present when Naunton's lady friends visited him, but I shall confide to you the secret particulars of a most enthralling outing he took me on — not long before he was compelled to quit London in a devilish hurry and install himself in Paris for the next twelvemonth or so — or until all has blown over and is forgotten.'

'Great Scot!' Selwyn cried 'How on earth did his misfortune come about?'

'That's another story altogether,' said Monty, 'and one which I do not yet feel able to entrust to you. Let me continue with the account of my call with him to the home of Mrs Gladys Lee in Margaret Street, which as I am sure you are aware, runs off Regent Street at the top end, joining it to Cavendish Square.'

'Mrs Lee?' said Selwyn, wrinkling his forehead in thought, 'I am sure I have heard the lady's name mentioned. Is she well-known in society?'

'Only in a certain kind of society,' Monty informed him. 'She is a well-known whoremonger, catering to the gentry. Naunton had the pleasure of her acquaintance for some time past, making use of the facilities of her private establishment whenever the mood came upon him. We lunched together at Romano's one day and sat talking over the brandy until past three in the afternoon, when of a sudden Naunton declared that he had a hard letch for a fresh young girl's commodity. I was in a like condition, for the liquor had brought me on stiff, and when he proposed a call on Mrs Lee and at his expense — I was delighted.'

'It was decent of him to pay,' said Selwyn, 'I can see that you were good friends, indeed. But how fresh can a girl be in a house like that? Surely the incessant pounding of lustful men takes off the bloom of youth?'

'Naunton said something of the same to Mrs Lee when we sat in her parlour and shared a bottle of port wine with her. "That may be," said she, "but I have a charming young girl in the house who is not a day over seventeen and has all the appearance of the dew of tender youth and virginity still upon her. You may make the fullest use of her for three guineas apiece."

35

''Five guineas the pair of us and we'll have her together,'' was Naunton's rejoinder, and Mrs Lee winked at us and said, *Done!* She led us upstairs and tapped on a bedroom door, advising us that Miss Emmy was resting in preparation for a most important visitor that evening, for the Earl of Atherton was expected to call after dinner and regale himself with her youthful charms.'

'Good Heavens,' said Selwyn, 'she mentioned his name to you? But he is a most respectable gentleman, and the newspaper never fails to report in their fullness the stern warnings he utters in the House of Lords — how decent family life is in threat of decay when thoughtless and pleasure-seeking men squander their substance on the pursuit of immorality.'

'Yes, I've read his Lordship on the subject a time or two,' said Monty, a broad grin across his face. 'Yet nevertheless it seems that he is well-known at Mrs Lee's. To resume though, for I have scant interest in the lewd fumblings of ageing noblemen, Mrs Lee left Naunton and me to go on into Miss Emmy's room. Ah, what a beauty she is, that dearest girl! Seventeen, as the old bawd had told us, and with fine golden hair and a skin like cream. She lay on the bed in her chemise and stockings — no stays or drawers, and my heart was pounding at the sight!'

'She wore no drawers?' Selwyn whispered, his pale blue eyes shining. 'Could you see her thighs, Monty?'

'Her thighs,' Monty repeated slowly, 'her soft, lovely bare thighs — yes, I could see them. And much more besides. Her eyes were closed, her shoes off and her stockinged legs spread apart, the knees drawn up. There in full view lay that choicest flower of female beauty, that delicious plaything that nestled between her creamy-white thighs! Oh, the heart-stopping beauty of what I saw then

36

— her curly bush of nut-brown hair and the soft pink lips of her pussy. Her dainty hand lay across her belly and between her legs, her long slender fingers moving slowly to pleasure herself.'

'You mean she was stroking her pussy to fetch herself off?' Selwyn asked breathlessly. 'I can't believe it — never have I seen a girl do that to herself! I don't believe they do.'

Monty noted away in his memory the declaration of disbelief, promising himself to take advantage of Selwyn's innocence when the moment was right, by showing him a woman pleasuring herself with her fingers.

'On hearing our entry into the room,' he continued, smiling to see how tight a hold he had on Selwyn's imagination, 'Miss Emmy's blue eyes opened to gaze at us, and a fond smile spread over her pretty face. Her fingers lingered in her pussy as she bid us bolt the door and come to her. She spread her legs a little more as we approached and my greedy eyes devoured her pussy. The sight of it drew me irresistibly to her, just as if it were a strong magnet and the hard shaft in my trousers a bar of iron to feel its attraction. I could see that Naunton felt the same keen lust, more so perhaps even than I, for he undid his trousers and was rubbing his shaft in his hand as we sat on the bed-edge, on either side of the lovely girl.'

'But . . . was this not embarrassing for you — and for him — to have another man present and observe you in so excited a state of mind and body?' asked Selwyn, his cheeks pale from emotion.

'Why, no,' Monty answered with a laugh, 'a stranger perhaps might be inconvenient, but a friend — neither he nor I gave the other a thought, we were too intent on Miss Emmy's bare pussy. She spoke to us then, and her words sent thrills of delight up my spine.'

'What did she say?' Selwyn whispered. 'Tell me, Monty.'

'She drew open her pussy a little to show us the pink inner lips and her proud little nub standing above the entrance to her depths and she said, *This is what you've come to see, isn't it*? I could hardly speak for the intensity of my emotions, but succeeded in saying that it was very beautiful indeed, and to think that so tender a morsel could give such rapture to a man. Naunton was quite as strongly affected as I was, if not more so, but he retained sufficient control of his voice to request, *May I kiss it, Miss Emmy*?'

From Selwyn there issued a soft moan that brought a smile to Monty's lips.

'She gave him permission in an affectionate murmur,' he went on, 'and Naunton knelt on the bed between her parted legs and put his lips to the soft and yielding pink blossom that was the centre and heart of her female nature. I half-heard the softest of sounds then, between a sigh and a moan, and for the life of me I knew not which of them had uttered it — Naunton or Miss Emmy. I saw his tongue flickering up and down between delicious parted pink lips in the nut-brown little nest and this time it was clearly she who made the sweet sounds of delight I heard.'

Selwyn's face was becoming an ever darker red and his eyes had closed almost completely, as the account continued. Monty noted the signs and congratulated himself that it would not be overly difficult to separate him from Gwendolen, so that he might the better enjoy her himself.

'By now I too had my trousers open and my stiff shaft in my hand,' he said, 'stroking myself a little whilst I watched the pleasuring of Miss Emmy. She was gasping breathless words of instructions to Naunton the whole time — *lick slow, lick fast, slow down, put the tip of your tongue to the left, now over to the right* . . . and all this he most dutifully and carefully obeyed, ravaging her with sensations so divine that she was rolling her backside on the bed and her titties were rising and falling vigorously in her chemise, to her heavy breathing.

'I could see there was only one way of it. Her hips moved in a rapid motion and she shook convulsively from head to foot. A shriek escaped her lips and she came off, rubbing her wet and open pussy against Naunton's fiery red face, I could bear no more — with an exclamation of impatience I pushed him aside and threw myself on Miss Emmy. One hard push took me deep into her hot belly, right to the very hilt, until my curls were entwined with hers.'

'Oh my dear Lord!' Selwyn gasped, his slender body shaking with the force of the emotions that Monty's description aroused in him. 'Oh Monty — I would give anything to have been with you then — anything!'

'There is better yet,' said Monty. 'She was still coming off from Naunton's stimulation, and whilst I plunged hard and fast into her pussy, she continued coming off and coming off. She cried out without stop and tore at me with her fingers, pulled at my hair and bit at my lips and cheeks in the very fury of her passion. It could not last — no human frame was capable of withstanding sensations so immensely overpowering! I felt the fast surge of my sap up One-Eyed Jack, and in great spasms I flooded her pulsating pussy . . .'

'Heavens above!' Selwyn gasped, his eyes staring wildly and his weakly handsome face crimson with emotion at the high point of Monty's story.

'Hardly had I squirted my last drop into her than

Naunton gripped me by the shoulders and dragged me from her. I rolled over on the bed, my wet shaft still jerking spasmodically in the aftermath of spending in her, and lay still in a delightful lethargy to watch Naunton use her pussy for his pleasure. She lay twitching and murmuring, her chemise up to her belly button and her body limp and unresisting. Naunton was on his knees between her open thighs — he seized her under the knees and hoisted her legs up in the air, parted them and hung them over his shoulders, in such a way to raise her backside right off the bed. His fingers were dabbling at her wet pussy, and in an instant I saw him bring his stiff affair up to the mark and drive it into her with a powerful push.'

'But she didn't come off a third time?' Selwyn asked in a gasping whisper, so that Monty wondered if his new friend had perhaps fetched off in his trousers by accident.

'Patience, and all will be revealed,' said Monty with a grin, 'Miss Emmy moaned and shook to his thrusts, and he moaned too, in time with her. Her bare backside swayed and squirmed against Naunton's thighs, and on a whim I pulled her chemise up to her chin, to observe how her bare titties wobbled like jelly to his thrusting. *Suck them!* she moaned, her eyes darting a look of pleading at me. I rolled close to her and set my mouth to the nearest of her pleasure domes, and sucked at its red-brown tip. My new position on the bed put my back toward Naunton, but I heard the rasping of his breath and felt the force of his jabs through Miss Emmy's soft body.

'How he held out so long I cannot tell, but when at last he spent, it was as if a mighty earthquake tore its way through Miss Emmy's belly. She screeched and shook to the spasms of his fetching off, as she had to mine, and then gave a soft sigh and fainted clean away through the intensity of her ecstasy.'

'Monty,' Selwyn whispered in an expiring voice, 'give me your word that you will take me to Mrs Lee's house so that we may share Miss Emmy together, for I shall never be capable of sleep again until I have experienced for myself the ecstasy you have described. Do this for me, and I am in your debt forever!'

'Nothing easier, my dear old fellow,' said Monty, pleased to see that his angling had landed the fish he was after, 'but let us finish the bottle first. I'm glad you accepted my invitation of lunch today — as you can imagine, since poor Naunton fled I've missed having a good chum to roust about with.'

'After what you've told me about him, I can well understand,' said Selwyn, emptying his glass quickly. 'What terrible chain of circumstances brought about his downfall? Do you feel able to confide in me?'

'Well, if I have your word of honour never to repeat what I tell you,' said Monty.

'I swear it, on my honour!' Selwyn exclaimed.

'The Church of England was his undoing,' said Monty. 'He had been to visit an old uncle near Effingham — an uncle from whom he had important expectations, there being no other relatives with any claim on the old fellow's fortune when he finally pops off. All went well, according to Naunton, and after lunch he bade his uncle goodbye and took the next train back to town. It was the middle of the afternoon and a stopping train, with very few on board, and he found him himself travelling with a lady to whom he had been introduced and knew slightly.

'This was the wife of the vicar of the church attended by Naunton's uncle, and the vicar and his wife had been guests at uncle's house for lunch on a couple of occasions when Naunton had been there. Mrs . . . I will not reveal the lady's surname, for that would be the despicable act of a cad and a rotter, but I will refer to her as Louise.

'You must understand, Selwyn, that I have never met Louise and have only Naunton's word for it that, though near on forty, she is still an attractive woman. Fair-haired, he said, with a porcelain complexion and an hour-glass figure. Since you have not met Naunton, you cannot have any inkling of how personable he is and how attractive he can make himself to members of the opposite sex, when he has a mind to avail himself of their dear little facilities. Not even a respectable married woman going on forty, the mother of grown children — and moreover — the wife of a vicar of the Church of England, could long withstand his blandishments.

'As to why he wanted Louise — even he himself was not wholly sure, when I questioned him after disaster had struck. He said that he was bored by the visit to Uncle Harriman, that he was bored by the slow train journey, that he had lunched very well and given uncle's best port wine a thrashing, that nobody else was in the compartment and it seemed a dreadful waste not to take advantage of that — in brief, he had a letch for a woman, and the only one to hand was Louise. He set himself to winning her affections, and such is his charm of person that before long she made no objection when he undid the buttons down her jacket and had a feel of her titties through her blouse.

'They were, said he to me afterwards, nicely swelling titties and when Louise had become accustomed to his hands upon her, he undid her blouse and felt down inside her chemise, above her stays, to get his hands on these bounties of nature in their bare state. She made some little

42

complaint but he closed her mouth with a kiss to spare himself an intended reproach.

'Her silence secured, and she almost swooning from the excess of her conflicting emotions, Naunton treated himself to a good and generous feel of her big soft domes, talking to her all the while in a soothing and comforting manner. When he thought her ready for it, he leaned over and plunged his face between those plump titties, and with both hands pressed her soft flesh to his cheeks.'

'Oh, the bliss of it!' murmured Selwyn, putting the palms of his hands to his cheeks. 'Lord, Monty — this friend of yours is a sheer delight to hear about! I wish I could meet him!'

'No problem there,' Monty replied at once, 'we can pop across to Paris at any time and see what the rogue is up to. I warrant he'll have us rogering a troupe of mademoiselles before we've had time to unpack. Ask for a few days off from the Board of Education and we'll slip across the Channel by the weekend.'

'The weekend,' said Selwyn, suddenly crestfallen, 'no, that won't do, Monty — I have given my word to stay with my sister and her family this weekend next.'

'A pity,' said Monty, eyeing him thoughtfully, 'let me know when you can.'

It was clear to him that Selwyn's sister had the ascendancy of her brother to the point where he could take no independent action of his own, but deferred to her wishes in all. He could not go to Paris to roger a Frenchie or two because Gwendolen wanted him at the weekend to satisfy her — that was about the size of it.

'Well then, to get back to Naunton and Louise on the train to town,' said Monty with a grin. 'We left our hero in process of plunging his face between her bare titties. Louise allowed him to enjoy that pleasure for some time

43

before she announced that matters had gone as far as they were going and commanded him to desist. Far from releasing her, now that she had shown herself to be prepared to submit to him in this — and therefore would submit further, according to all his previous experience with women, Naunton had it in mind to hoist up her skirts and stroke her muff a little.

'Whether Louise could be aroused within the duration of the train journey to so delightful a condition that she would lie along the compartment seat for Naunton to put his shaft up her was not yet clear to him — which was as good a reason as any to make the attempt. So make it he did — he put his hand under her skirt and petticoats and up between her legs. When he got as high as her knees, he told me, her eyes opened so widely that they seemed round in shape, and her obvious surprise caused him to wonder if the vicar had never put his hand up her clothes during the hours of daylight.

'Be that as it may, her knees moved apart and his hand passed on between her thighs and into her drawers, to touch her hairy pussy. He played with it for some time, by his account, teasing it to become slippery with the moisture of excitement, soothing Louise, and raising up her expectations of what further delight might follow. Before anything could ensue, the train slowed and came to a stands till in a station.'

'How very vexing,' Selwyn exclaimed, his fingers drumming on the white tablecloth in his agitation, 'to be interrupted at so precious a moment!'

Monty nodded his agreement and continued his narrative.

'Needless to say, Naunton had the strongest determination to prevent any busybody passenger from entering the compartment and spoiling his game with

Louise — and to this end he let down the window and rose to stand with his head out of it. He spied two or three waiting on the platform, and thought it prudent to stand there with a stern expression on his face to drive away any inconsiderate traveller. At last the train pulled out of station, he closed the window and turned to face Louise again, hot with the letch for her.

'During the halt she had done up her blouse and her jacket, and her fleshy charms were concealed from him. She told him to stay away from her and remain where he was, standing with his back to the window, and make no further attempt on her honour. None but her reverend husband had ever touched her person before today, she informed him, and although Naunton had taken caddish advantage of a moment of weakness on her part, that was the end of it.

'Well, of course, Naunton knew better than to believe a word of this pious rigmarole. Louise needed to be coaxed a little, that was all. She was staring at the bulge in his trousers, for One-Eyed Jack was at full stand and vibrating merrily. He flicked his buttons open and let it leap out like a Jack-in-the-Box, at the level of her face, she sitting and he standing. *But it's so big!* cried she in surprise, from which he deduced that the Reverend was not so generously endowed. *And strong too*, said Naunton, *feel for yourself!*

'Her cheeks fiery red and with incoherent words on her lips, Louise leaned forward to take hold of his monster and feel its strength. He rested his back comfortably on the closed window and stared down to watch her pull out his palpitating item and his hairy accoutrements from his gaping trousers and gaze at all in wonder. In a frenzy of lust his thick shaft stood to its fullest height and shook between her fingers, trying to thrust ever higher and swell itself up to an impossible girth.

'Louise's eyes rolled up to meet his, and he claims that they were shining with admiration and curiosity, and she was visibly impressed by the size and promise of his apparatus. Her hand slid up and down its length, sending continuous little ripples of bliss along Naunton's nerves. Not that his sensations stopped him from wondering how a vicar's wife had learned to pleasure a man's part so expertly that she was fast bringing him to the point of spending.

'*You'll make me fetch off in a minute, Louise*, he gasped and reached down to rip open her jacket and blouse and plunge both hands down her chemise to grasp her titties and squeeze them. She, too, had become highly aroused in handling his parts, and both she and he were so entirely engrossed in sensual delights that neither was aware of the train's rattling pace slackening. Louise bent forward to engulf the purple head of his shaft in her wet mouth, her hand slipping rapidly up and down all the while, and an instant later he cried out and she jerked her head away from him as he came off in joyful spasms.'

'Oh, my Lord,' Selwyn was murmuring, his hands out of sight in his lap beneath the tablecloth.

'There was Naunton, doubled over, One-Eyed Jack spurting in Louise's hand, and her face streaked with the creamy trickles of his spending — and the train had stopped in the station at Clapham Junction. Even then not all was lost, you might think, for Naunton's back was to the window and nobody could get in past him. But horror of horrors — the platform was now on the other side of the train — and the door beyond Louise was opened and a middle aged gentleman handed up into the compartment his wife and three half-grown children.

'There was no possibility of Naunton concealing what he and Louise had been at. The wife fled with shrieks of distress and outraged modesty to fetch the nearest railway official, driving the children before her like frightened sheep. For a moment or two, Naunton confessed to me afterwards, it was in his mind to leap out of the door behind him and make his escape over the tracks, abandoning Louise to her fate. But that would have been the act of a complete bounder, to leave a lady in the lurch.

'But apart from that, it was pointless to run, for Naunton and the indignant gentleman happened to be well acquainted with each other, he being the manager of the branch where Naunton banks. There was nothing for it but to tuck away his wilting mascot and put the best face on things he could. But Mr Bramley, for that is the name of the banking gent, refused to be talked round. Louise was allowed to depart, after a long lecture on vice and depravity, Bramley holding the view that Naunton alone was to blame, and had forced his vile attentions on a married lady travelling alone.

'It took Mrs Bramley so very long to find a porter while her husband held Naunton by the arm on the platform, that as soon as Louise was clear of the station, Naunton broke loose from his captor and ran for it. He came back here, and while he threw a few clothes into a bag, he told me what had happened. He asked me to look after the rest of his things and vanished in a cab to catch the boat train and leave these shores before Bramley had time to find his address at the bank and send a constable round to arrest him.'

'Interfering with a vicar's wife on a train!' said Selwyn, his voice faint with wonder at the prospect. 'I see the truth of your claim that Mr Naunton Cox is an extraordinary person in all respects. Oh, to have the courage to undertake so very exciting an act! I would give anything to be so bold!'

'But my dear fellow, you must not underrate yourself,' said Monty, seeing by the high colour of Selwyn's cheeks and the bright shine in his eyes that the moment was right to risk all, 'to my mind, rogering your own sister calls for more sustained bravery than most men possess, or are ever like to.'

Selwyn's mouth fell open and he stared dumbly over the table at Monty, who calmly poured the last of the port wine into their glasses.

'Come, come, Selwyn,' he said easily, 'no need for that look of surprise. We are men of the world, you and I, and we have no difficulty in understanding these things. Mrs Fanshawe is very beautiful, and you are a lucky dog to have the pleasure of her intimate company. How long has she been yours?'

'Since you have guessed so much,' said Selwyn, 'you may as well know all. It will bring me some relief of mind and heart, I do believe, to tell another of my darkest secret. You are a most understanding friend, Monty, and I am more grateful to you than you can know for not condemning my moral weakness.'

'We all have moral weaknesses,' Monty said generously. 'Mine is an inability to leave a pussy untouched, however inopportune the circumstances. Poor Naunton's was much the same, hence his misfortune on a railway train. How did it first come to pass, this unusual connection between you and your charming sister?'

'Years ago,' Selwyn confessed, eager now to unburden himself of his secret. 'We were brought up near Reading, and since my Father's constrained circumstances made it impossible for him to send me to boarding school, I was a day school boy and grew up therefore in close proximity to Gwendolen. She is two years older than I am, and was a pretty child who has since grown to an attractive woman.'

'A beautiful woman,' Monty corrected him.

'Yes, well . . . how it came about I cannot now remember, but at an age when she and I were neither children nor fully grown-up, I fell into the habit of feeling Gwendolen's titties, under the pretence of examining their size, as each day they grew riper. She, loving her brother, made no objection to this solicitude, and one day, whilst I was engaged in this way, unfamiliar and powerful sensations tore through my unsuspecting body. A hot stickiness made itself apparent in my underwear — what it could be, I did not know, for I was as innocent as a babe of fleshly things even then, at sixteen years of age. You will laugh at me perhaps, but I had fetched off for the first time in my life! My exclamation and shudders had captured the keen interest of my dear sister Gwendolen, who wished to be informed of what had taken place. Since I could not explain, she took it upon herself to open my trousers and investigate — and we together saw the wet evidence of my climax of sensation.'

'Without knowing what it was, even then?' asked Monty.

'Exactly so, but with all the enthusiasm of youth, my wilting shaft quickly stood again when Gwendolen fingered it to see how it worked. I asked her to show me hers, and she lay down on the sofa and lifted her skirt. I opened her drawers and saw she had no long thick part as I had — indeed, for the first time in my life I saw a girl's pussy. It seemed to me to be so delicious a thing that I could not forbear kissing it — and from that I progressed to licking the pretty toy. Soon enough,

Gwendolen cried out in surprise and joy, and shook to the spasms of her own first coming off.'

'I say!' Monty exclaimed. 'What a piece of luck for you!'

'I do not see matters in that light,' responded Selwyn, 'for the events of that day undermined my moral nature so profoundly that I have been a victim of my own sensuality from then up to this very day. When Gwendolen was tranquil again, she sat up on the sofa and I stood in front of her, guiding her hand to my shaft, which soon grew stiff again when she felt it. The devil was in me that day – I asked her to take my shaft in her mouth, and she sucked it until I fetched off again.

'You can well imagine that from that day onwards we repeated the pleasure whenever opportunity served us, sometimes bringing each other off two or three times a day, by hand and mouth, and in this wicked course we continued together for three or four weeks. But then came that fateful day when Nature prompted our ignorance to join the organs of our pleasure, Gwendolen's and mine – in short, blind and fumbling Chance taught us how the deed was done, and we committed the fearful crime of incest with each other! I thrust my shaft into Gwendolen's pussy and we came off together, my sticky fluid spurting into her belly!'

CHAPTER 4
A Two-Step with Mrs Massingham

Twice a week it was Monty's pleasant custom to pay a visit to a dear friend of his, Mrs Cecily Massingham. She was a widow of seven-and-twenty, who lived in St John's Wood in a pleasantly secluded villa. Uncharitable persons might incline towards a harsh description of Mrs Massingham's mode of living, but to do so would serve merely to illustrate their unfeeling ignorance of the facts. She was not the kept woman of a wealthy man, as were so many of the pretty ladies of St John's Wood. No, having been once married, she had vowed and declared never again in all her days to entrust her happiness and well-being to any one man, no matter how well-to-do or good natured.

The truth of it was that Mrs Massingham took up subscriptions from five or six gentlemen who were captivated by her personal charms. Each was allotted his afternoons or evenings, and this prevented the inconvenience of two gentlemen finding themselves calling on her at the same time. Each was aware that there were other admirers, but no questions were asked and no details were forthcoming. In this way, all were kept happy, and the expense to each of the admirers was moderate.

It was to Mrs Massingham's villa that Monty conducted Selwyn the day after their lunch together. Selwyn had wanted to visit Mrs Lee in Margaret Street to avail himself of the delights of Miss Emmy, but he was far too fuddled by drink when they left the restaurant, and Monty was compelled to put him in a hansom cab and take him back to their rooms, to sleep it off. With the aid of Minnie he had removed Selwyn's outer clothing and got him into bed, after which Monty went out again to pay a short visit to Mrs Massingham.

It was not his day to call, and he ran a fearful risk of interrupting some other gentleman busy about his own legitimate affairs with the lady, but it was necessary to give her certain information for the following day — information that concerned Selwyn and how he was to be dealt with.

'Bamboozle him for me, my dear Cecily,' Monty instructed her, 'he has never had but one woman in his life, and that his own sister, and may therefore be judged very nearly a virgin. It is my most urgent necessity to take this sister away from him, with your very able assistance. Nor shall you be the worse off by it, Selwyn shall be enrolled amongst the privileged few who share your affections, for he can well afford it.'

In this curious manner and for these more curious reasons, Selwyn found himself carried to St John's Wood in the afternoon of the very next day, and introduced to the charming Mrs Cecily Massingham. She was in her upstairs sitting room when the maid brought them to her, and she was dressed with exceptional and improper informality in a long silk negligee of pale pink. The pretty ribbon-bows down the front served not to keep it closed about her person, but as adornment, and from beneath its dainty hem peeped out the toes of her little slippers of finest white kid-skin.

The introductions were made, and while Selwyn shook her hand, Cecily rendered her apologies in blushing confusion for her very informal attire. She had been suffering from a cold in the head, she said untruthfully, and this had compelled her to keep her bed. She was now fully recovered, but not yet strong enough to venture out of the house, and Monty had surprised her in *déshabille* by calling unexpected.

There was a great deal more of this, all of which Selwyn took seriously and believed. The upshot of it was that he sat down by Monty on the sofa, as suggested, and joined in the small talk with no suspicion that pretty Mrs Massingham was any other than a lady of virtue and reputation, albeit one with eccentric notions of propriety of dress when receiving gentlemen callers. She had seated herself in an armchair opposite the two men, and during their conversation she unobtrusively allowed her pink wrap to fall open below the knee, while her legs surreptitiously moved a little apart, to stretch the thin silk material across her thighs.

Monty winked secretly at her in approval, and looked at her legs with pleasure. He glanced across at Selwyn, sitting beside him with his back straight and his hands clasped in his lap, to make sure that he too had a proper appreciation of what he was being given a glimpse of. Selwyn's face blushed a faint pink to be caught in the act, as he looked up and caught Monty's eye, but Monty gave him a conspiratorial grin. They both stared at Cecily's legs — she all this time pretending not to be aware of their lustful gaze.

Whilst she engaged in stylish small talk, her negligee

fell open a little further yet and the firm flesh of her rounded thighs could be seen — only for a little way, of course — a gleam of creamy flesh to about midway, let us say, to where her legs joined. Naturally, this was in itself sufficient to set male thoughts racing and speculating on the dark-haired mystery that undoubtedly lay hidden between those beautiful thighs.

'I am so glad that you came to visit me today, Monty,' said Cecily, 'for I have been very dull this past day or two with my head cold. And to invite Mr Courtney-Stoke along to meet me was a friendly thought. I am in your debt, my dear friend.'

Until then, her warm feminine secrets had been protected by the overfold of her negligee, though only just. She changed her position on her armchair slightly, as if to make herself more comfortable, and for an instant the sweet mystery was visible! The dark-curled charms between smooth thighs were shown — if only for the space of a heartbeat — to the staring eyes of her two visitors!

There was not even time to gasp in surprise before she rose from her chair and took a turn slowly about the room, her silk negligee decently in place again, concealing all, right down to her slippered feet. She pulled the thin material closely about herself, displaying her hourglass figure to good advantage — the swelling of her bosom, the smallness of her waist and the fullness of her backside. She strolled about the room as if to stretch her legs a little, and the delightful manner in which the generous cheeks of her bottom rolled under the negligee caused Monty and Selwyn to exchange a glance filled with surmise.

Cecily stood for a moment at the window, seeming to gaze out, though screened from the observation of pedestrians below by the full white lace curtains. She turned on her heel to face her visitors, and uttered a little exclamation of dismay — her left slipper had twisted from her foot! Before either of the men could fling himself gallantly on his knees at her feet, to replace it, she raised her leg crossways before her, the knee crooked, and she bent over to replace the errant slipper. In doing so, the bowed posture seemed to cause the front of her negligee to fall open under the weight of her bosom. Her pair of plump white titties rolled out into plain view, making Monty and Selwyn sigh in the same instant.

With a little cry of embarrassment, Cecily stood upright once more again and swiftly lifted her bare titties back into her evidently inadequate negligee, pulling it close to conceal her soft delights. There was the faintest flicker of a smile on her face as she stared at the two men and saw the long bulges that had appeared in their laps. She apologised most sincerely and humbly to them for the embarrassment she had caused and the offence to their sense of propriety, by allowing her person to become exposed in so very awkward and impolite a manner.

Monty grinned and said nothing, leaving it to Selwyn to give his solemn assurance that no offence had been taken — indeed, the accidental uncovering of so beautiful a lady's charms was, as every visitor to the Royal Academy of Art could explain, a source of the truest aesthetic pleasure. The sublimest of oil paintings by our greatest artists, said he, depicted the nude female form in classical poses, and were generally accepted to be inspirational in their grandeur and style.

Furthermore, Selwyn continued, if the choice were left up to him, far from feeling aggrieved in any way by a brief glimpse of Mrs Massingham's uncovered bosom, the exposing of her truly exquisite bodily form would be not be of so brief duration, but prolonged and enduring

— and far more *complete*, if he might so term it, than blind Chance had allowed!

'You are far too kind, Mr Courtney-Stoke,' Cecily murmured in a thrilling voice. 'So meagre a store of female charm as I have been endowed with by a niggardly Providence can scarcely appeal to a man of taste and distinction like yourself. Dear Monty is pleased to flatter me at times by informing me that I am not outright ugly, but I know very well that his protestations rise from friendship, not from a strict regard for the truth, though they are none the less welcome for that.'

'No, no, no,' Selwyn exclaimed, 'I must forbid you to discount your own charms in this excessively modest way! Monty speaks no more than the plain truth — you are a very fine woman, Mrs Massingham, beautiful of face and divine of form!'

Instead of returning to her armchair, Cecily joined the men on the sofa, placing herself right in the centre of it, between the two of them. They exchanged a glance of secret delight, and gazed downwards, and were rewarded by a most thrilling view of Cecily's smooth white thighs, her negligee having fallen open at her lap once more.

'Forgive what may strike you as excessive familiarity, but I am still a trifle feverish from my head cold. Do you really think me beautiful?' she said to Selwyn, her dark brown eyes gazing soulfully into his.

While the young man so addressed struggled to find words adequate to convey to her his deepest feelings, Monty took Cecily's slim hand in his own, raised it to his lips and kissed the palm.

'Cecily — you are a stunner,' he told her, admiration in his voice. 'I might even go so far as to say that you are the most deliciously provocative woman I am acquainted with.'

'Only *might* say?' she exclaimed. 'Fie, sir — what sort of a compliment to a lady is that? What do you say, Mr Courtney-Stoke — is it only *might* with you ,too?'

'Mrs Massingham — you are wholly adorable,' he babbled. 'May I hope for the inestimable privilege of calling you Cecily?'

'You may do so,' she answered softly, 'for your heartfelt and open devotion has surely earned that right. As for you, Monty, you conceal your true feelings — however unconcerned you may try to appear, the strength of your adoration for me is no less than dear Selwyn's — and the proof is prominently visible.'

With those flattering words, she reached out into both their laps and lightly tapped a long bulge with the forefinger of each hand. At the touch, both the men shivered in delight, and Monty responded by tugging open the bow of her belt and parting her thin silk negligee. His hand slid up Cecily's smooth flesh and cupped the big soft bubbie nearest to him.

There followed an astonished expostulation of *I say, really!* from Selwyn, a pause, and then Cecily took his hand and raised it to her other plump bubbie.

'Oh, Cecily,' Selwyn murmured in an expiring voice, 'this is far beyond my wildest imaginings, to experience such bliss as your tender and agreeable nature now affords me!'

'Imaginings?' she responded. 'What can you possibly mean by that, Selwyn? Am I to believe that you have forgotten yourself far enough to have the unmitigated impertinence to imagine that you might indulge in familiarities with me?'

'No!' he exclaimed in horror that he had offended her.

'Then what?' she demanded. 'I insist on being told what your words meant — explain to me at once how far these *imaginings* of yours have been encouraged to go in your overheated mind.'

While Selwyn was suffering agonies of mind, Monty sat with a grin of pure joy on his face, enjoying the opportunity to watch Cecily use her wiles on an innocent. To encourage and stimulate her efforts, he put his other hand behind her and slid his palm down the thin material that covered her smooth back, until he could feel underneath her. He pressed his fingers between the plump cheeks of her backside, until an exploring fingertip found the tight little knot that nestled between them, and he tickled it through the silk.

'Forgive me, Cecily,' Selwyn was gasping, 'forgive me, I beg you — the truth is that your beauty of face and form is so very arousing that I was unable to control my emotions when you were walking about the room — my degenerate imagination began to suggest to me the most shameful things. I confess freely that I suffer from a moral weakness that has been with me since my youth, but in spite of the reprehensible flaw in my character, I do respect you greatly, you must believe me!'

'Respect me indeed!' Cecily exclaimed in a voice trembling to the lively emotions Monty's stimulation of her rearward opening was causing. 'How can you claim to respect me when you imagined yourself performing shameful acts on my naked and defenceless body? Tell me what it was you thought of doing to me — or I shall request you to leave my home at once!'

'I am a beast — unfit for the company of delicately nurtured ladies — I fully confess it!' Selwyn moaned. 'I throw myself on your mercy and beg humbly for your forgiveness.'

'Confess fully — and I shall not be harsh with you,' Cecily replied. 'I have formed a warm regard for you,

Selwyn, I cannot deny it, but I must have your confidence – and therefore I must have a full knowledge of your moral weakness. What did you want to do to me? Tell me now or leave instantly!'

'You give me no choice,' Selwyn said in a shaking voice. 'To be cast out from your adorable presence and barred from seeing you again would be a fate far worse than death. I shall admit all, bitterly ashamed though I am.'

His agitation of mind was so extreme that he seemed to have lost sight of the fact that his cupped hand clasped Cecily's right bubbie and kneaded it, or that on his thigh lay the warm hand of the brunette beauty who tormented him by demanding to be told thoughts he would have preferred to keep to himself. Nevertheless, the mutual touching of sensitive portions of the body was having an effect upon him, turning his cheeks a bright and feverish red, and putting a quaver into his voice when he made his confession to Cecily.

'It was when you were standing by the window,' he said in a voice so subdued that Cecily leaned towards him to hear him the better. 'There was the unbelievably sublime moment when you leaned over to adjust your slipper, and your heavenly bosom was uncovered . . . I know that in politeness I ought to have averted my eyes from your private person, but I lacked the strength to do so. And while I in my uncontained rudeness gazed in rapture at your personal charms, I suddenly and unaccountably imagined – no, I cannot say it aloud!'

This was the man, Monty was thinking, who had been rogering his own sister on a regular basis. Whilst he did that twice a week without a qualm, he had become tongue-tied and bashful in the presence of Cecily – who was a paid woman. There was only one possible explanation he could think of for this reluctance — Selwyn was so taken by Cecily at first sight that he was halfway to being in love with her, a most satisfactory state of affairs for Monty.

'You must say it to me,' she urged Selwyn. 'Say it, my dear, and you will be relieved of this burden of guilt that weighs on you. Tell your friend Cecily what it was that came into your mind to do to her, when she stood at the window.'

'You give me courage,' he replied. 'I shall be in your debt forever, Cecily. You are so understanding that I shall risk my reputation with you by setting out my moral weakness in full. While you stood there at the window, adjusting your negligee to cover your bosom, I experienced a most tremendous urge to fling myself on my knees before you . . . how can I go on? But I must — to kneel at your feet and press my lips in a kiss of reverence to the wonderful treasure that I knew must repose between your divine thighs . . . can you bring yourself to pardon so gross an intrusion on your perfection — imaginary though it was?'

'I see,' said Cecily in a dreamy voice, and she quivered a little to Monty's skilful manipulation of her little knot-hole, 'you are confessing that you wanted to bare my body and lick my pussy! Is that it?'

'Your *pussy*,' said Selwyn in a whisper of hushed reverence, 'ah, my dearest Cecily — how courageous you are to speak out so frankly! Tell me that you are not angry with me!'

'I respect your frank confession,' she replied, 'and to prove to you that I am not angry with you, I shall permit you to kiss my pussy. Your imagining shall come true — I shall stand by the window, for you to kneel at my feet and kiss me.'

Selwyn was trembling so much that Monty feared he might fall off the sofa. Cecily stood up, adjusting her negligee to cover her titties and legs, and walked to the window, and turned to stand with her back to it. Selwyn's face was purple with strong passion, and he stared at her with glazed eyes, much like a rabbit mesmerised by a stoat. When she held out her arms to him in welcome, his breath rasped in his throat, and Monty had to tap him on the shoulder to attract his attention.

'Go on, old fellow,' said Monty, 'Cecily is waiting for you — lucky dog that you are!'

Like a knight of Old throwing himself on his knees in homage before his Sovereign Lady and Queen of his Heart, Selwyn flew across the intervening space and knelt at Cecily's feet, gazing up into her face in blind devotion. She touched his cheek lightly and smiled graciously down at him.

'Dear Selwyn — I truly believe that I have been smitten by a unexpected affection for you that is not far removed from love itself,' she said softly. 'There is no other way I can explain my immodest conduct towards you.'

As if to prove the truth of her words, her hips moved just a little inside her silk negligee, and it fell open just enough to give her admirer a glimpse of the dark-brown curls that grew lightly over her pussy. When she saw his ardent gaze fixed on her most intimate delight, she smiled and accused him of trifling with her affections to bring her to this condition of indecency.

'No, it is I who am infatuated by you,' he murmured.

'Ah, how cruel are the sufferings we poor women endure at the hands of heartless men,' she sighed, making not the least move to close her negligee and hide her brown-haired pussy from his burning eyes, 'if only I could trust you as I trust Monty!'

'You can!' he replied fervently. 'My heart is yours, Cecily, and from this day on, yours alone!'

As if reassured by this declaration, Cecily unfastened her fragile pink silk garment and let it fall open. Selwyn cried in joy as he saw presented to his eager eyes a delicious pair of titties, large, round, and firm, with crimson buds set on milk-white skin. In dumb delight he stared at them, and from the rapt expression of his face it could be seen that he yearned with all his heart for the privilege of kissing those peerless globes. A stern little look crept over Cecily's beautiful face as she prepared to take advantage of his enchanted condition.

'You forget yourself, sir,' she rebuked him, 'you aspire too high already. Lower your eyes at once!'

Mumbling heartfelt apologies, Selwyn dropped his gaze – and found himself looking straight at her uncovered pussy. With a long moan of bliss, he swayed forward on his knees, to press a feverish face between her thighs. Cecily parted her feet on the carpet, opening her legs to let him have a full sight of her fleshy mound and its thatch of dark-brown curls. In a moment his tongue was at the pouting lips of her pussy, seeking out in delight her hidden nub and licking at it. The stimulus had a galvanic effect on her – her body trembled all over and she sighed, *Oh, Selwyn my dear – you will make me come off if you continue! But if it will make you happy to submit me to this shameful ordeal, then I willingly give myself up to the embrace of your mouth . . .*

Through all this bamboozling, Monty sat on the sofa watching the by-play between the two, with all the interest and relish of a theatre-goer in the Drury Lane stalls. Cecily, dear clever Cecily, was smiling at him over the top of Selwyn's head, and when he gave her a wink, she put out her tongue and waggled it at him, as if to convey that she was enjoying the sensations emanating from the rapid up-and-down motion of Selwyn's tongue in her pussy. Monty suddenly felt somewhat excluded from the proceedings, and decided to amuse himself.

He unbuttoned his trousers, pulled up his shirt-front and let his stiff length jut impudently out. Over Selwyn's fair-haired head, Cecily smiled at the sight this old acquaintance of hers now brought out of concealment to be presented to her sight. Her smile grew broader yet to see Monty's clasped hand gripping One-Eyed Jack tightly and jerking him up and down. Freed from the restraint of dark trousers, that ever-eager gentleman began to jump for joy in Monty's friendly clasp and thrust his purple and swollen head boldly upwards.

Monty leaned comfortably back on the sofa, breathing lightly and quickly through his open mouth, his limbs shaking a little to the blissful tremors that rippled through him from head to toe. Cecily was regarding his lascivious actions with much interest, he noted, and a thought came into his head.

'Have I ever recited Mr Southey's verses to you, Cecily?' he asked. 'His ballad of the cruel fair one?'

'Not to my recollection,' she sighed, her eyes half-closed as Selwyn continued his caresses. 'Why do you ask now?'

'They seem appropriate to the present circumstance,' Monty replied with a grin. 'Listen, my dear:

She showed a pair of titties ivory white,
A belly white as snow, a lily hand,
Enrapt, I watched her with my secret stand,
That tented out my trousers hard and tight;
Her taper fingers in another's hair
Held close his head, while he her pussy saw
With ardent gaze for that he must adore,

The soft-lipped treasure she for him laid bare.
Methought the toy he played with was her heart
(Ah, beauteous wretch whose pussy is her pride)
But my keen shaft which steadfast still she eyed
And would not let it pierce like Cupid's dart;
Shall I not then condemn this cruel hussy,
Who lets me see another kiss her pussy?'

'Oh Heavens — I'm coming off!' Cecily gasped.

She shook like a slender branch of a young tree in a gale, and kept her balance only by grasping Selwyn's shoulders to hold herself up on her feet. The enraptured expression on her lovely face advised Monty of the depth of her feelings for him, and at once his hand flew up and down One-Eyed Jack in a manner that allowed no further delay.

'Oh, Cecily!' he gasped, feeling that the dammed-up torrent of passion in his belly was about to burst through the barriers that held it back. One-Eyed Jack was straining himself upwards to an impossible size as he prepared to gush his hot flood.

'Oh, you dear lustful beast!' Cecily gasped out breathlessly as she stared transfixed at Monty's throbbing shaft. 'Who gave you permission to excite yourself? But let me see you fetch off, you beast!'

Selwyn, his tongue still busy with her pussy, took her words to apply to himself, and though his shaft was decently confined within his trousers, it was evidently in a condition of highest arousal. He groaned and shook, his shoulders heaved, his back arched — and he spent mightily inside his trousers and drenched his underclothes.

'Selwyn, how could you!' Cecily exclaimed in astonishment.

There was a greater surprise yet to come, for having attained the supreme point of ecstasy, Selwyn moaned and swayed and then fainted completely away. Under the staring eyes of Cecily and Monty, his wet and open mouth slid slowly down her bare thigh and then he fell sideways to the fine Turkey carpet, where he lay limp and still.

With a muttered oath, Monty thrust away his clamouring shaft and did up his trousers quickly, before rushing across the room to where Cecily knelt at Selwyn's side. She chafed his hands between hers and called his name anxiously, but he made no stir in response. Monty got his hands under his senseless friend's armpits, and with Cecily lifting by the ankles, between them the carried him to the sofa.

'This is perfectly absurd,' Monty complained, while Cecily loosened Selwyn's cravat, 'I have watched this fellow roger his sister twice in a row with great energy — yet now he spends at the touch of your pussy under his lips and faints dead away! What do you make of that, Cecily?'

'Why, that he has fallen deeply in love with me and that his nature is so sensitive that his first coming off with me was so profound an experience for him that his nerves proved to be incapable of sustaining the ecstasy,' she answered.

While Monty watched, she unbuttoned Selwyn's waistcoat and trousers and laid him bare, to inspect the long splashes of his creamy white essence that had spurted up a good hands-breadth above his belly button. Monty heard the tiny sigh she uttered when she caught her first sight of Selwyn's dolly-whacker, for though it had collapsed from its full length of eight inches at full stretch, it remained impressive of size.

'How very flattering he should spend so profusely when

he kissed my pussy,' Cecily murmured, her fingers straying lightly over Selwyn's shrinking shaft, as if to prolong its distension for as long as she could, 'I have the greatest affection for him already.'

'Then I shall leave him to recover in your capable hands,' said Monty with a grin. 'Treat him gently when he comes to and he will be your devoted slave for life.'

Leaving Selwyn to come out of his swoon by natural stages, he took Cecily in his arms to bestow a farewell kiss on her lips. She did not ring for her maid, not wanting the girl to see poor Selwyn lying unconscious on his back with his person completely exposed, and so she declared that she would see him downstairs and to the front door herself. But no sooner had he kissed her a second time in acknowledgement of her courtesy, than Monty's interrupted letch for her returned in full force. He quickly pulled Cecily's pink silk wrapper open to bare her body again, and handled her titties freely.

'Come into the bedroom with me, Monty,' she whispered, but he shook his head and said there was no time, for Selwyn would be awakening very soon, and Cecily must be at his side then.

'Then I shall relieve your nervous tension *so*,' she said, and as they stood close together by the sofa on which Selwyn lay in his deep swoon, she flipped open Monty's trouser buttons, and felt inside to pull out his stiffened shaft and massage it.

'No — kneel down for me, dear Cecily,' he said.

Without a moment's hesitation, she was on her knees on the carpet at his feet, her wrapper falling open to display all the treasures of her body. Monty reached down to seize her ample titties, and laid One-Eyed Jack between them.

'Is that what you're after, Monty?' she asked, with a grin, 'To roger my titties? And so you shall!'

He squeezed their fleshy abundance together round his shaft and thrust quickly inside the soft warm pouch they made. Cecily gazed up smiling at his flushed face, and pulled his trousers down his thighs so that she could put her hands under his shirt and grasp the cheeks of his backside.

'Does that feel nice?' she asked. 'Do you like my titties?'

'They're stunners!' he panted, squeezing them together hard to accommodate his long sliding thrusts.

Cecily glanced down at the shiny purple head that emerged and disappeared with regularity between the cleft of her big breasts.

'I do believe that One-Eyed Jack is at the point of having a seizure!' she said. 'How dark is his colour, and how angry his appearance!'

Monty moaned in bliss, his shaft slid hard and fast against Cecily's satin flesh, and his body shuddered to the gushing torrent that he released between her plump titties.

CHAPTER 5
Conjugal Secrets Revealed

Try as he might, Monty was quite unable to get out of
his head the question that had enslaved his imagination
— whether the rogering of your own sister differed in
any way from rogering any other woman? If it was in
some measure different, then in what lay this difference
and how did it feel? It had been useless to ask Selwyn,
for whilst he had experience enough of rogering his dear
sister, he had none of any other woman, and therefore
he could add nothing to the enquiry. After Cecily had
induced him to get astride her a time or two, Selwyn
would be able to form a useful opinion on the matter,
but that lay in the future.

By ten o'clock that night Selwyn had still not
returned from St John's Wood, and it seemed evident
to Monty that Cecily was training her new admirer
in the ways of love too intensively to let him leave
her that night. There would then be no chance of
questioning Selwyn before the next evening and this
being so, Monty went to bed. He took with him the
book that provided interesting insights into the
education of young ladies at Lady Bumslapper's
academy in Gloucestershire, but it lay unread on the

eiderdown while he puzzled over the question of brothers and sisters.

Commonsense and logical deduction informed him of the truth of several pertinent facts. To take the case of a brother and sister parted since earliest childhood — say, orphans brought up separately and ignorant of each other's existence. Suppose them to meet when they are grown up, strangers wholly unaware of the close family bond between them. They are attracted, let us say, to each other, and their kisses lead on to a feel of the girl's titties, and then of her pussy. One thing leads to another, as is the way of life, and the man has her drawers off soon enough and gives her a good rogering. Brother and sister have done the deed together without knowing of their kinship, and so to neither is it in any way special or different.

Or to take another instance, Monty addressed himself in the silent debating chamber of his mind — let us suppose a family in which an unmarried sister of the head of the household lives as a permanent member, and assists her brother's wife to manage the children. On a particular night, for reasons we need not particularise, the wife is away, and in the middle of the night the sister slips into the bed of her sleeping brother. He wakes to find an enticing female hand on his stiff shaft, and forgetting in his newly awakened state that his wife is away from home, he lifts the nightgown of the woman beside him and rogers her.

When he has gone back to sleep she returns to her own bed, and in the morning he finds himself alone and recalls that his wife is elsewhere. A few moment's thought convince him that his midnight poke was only a wet dream, delightful though it was at the time. While he was at it in the dark, nothing was strange to him, for he did not know it was his sister — he was aware only of a soft bare belly under his and a wet pussy holding his dolly-whacker.

Therefore, said Monty to himself, what we may be sure of is that the difference in rogering a sister lies entirely in the mind. It is the knowledge of the close blood relationship that provokes the extra libidinous delight, or else detracts from it, whichever way it may be. This leads on to the inescapable conclusion that if I roger Gwendolen Fanshawe, my emotions can never be the same as Selwyn's, when he rogers her, for she is his sister, not mine. It is possible that I shall be fearfully disappointed when I get One-Eyed Jack into her!

To turn his thoughts away from so dismal a prospect, he took up his book and read a page or two:

'Hear me now, Belinda,' said Her Ladyship, 'you have been entrusted by your papa to my complete charge and I shall demand absolute obedience. Make up your mind to it, you are to mark me well, for I exact the most meticulous submission from the young ladies of this Academy. On your first day under my care I shall teach you this lesson in a way you will not readily forget.'

Belinda's beautiful young face turned pale at the threat and she was scarce able to speak. But propriety demanded that she make her protestations known.

'Lady Bumslapper,' said she faintly, 'I cannot accept that it is correct or decent for me to be summoned from my bed in only my nightclothes at this later hour — to find myself rebuked by you in the presence of a gentleman.'

'The gentleman in question, who is seated upon the divan, is Sir Everard Knightley,' said Her Ladyship.

Sir Everard rose to his feet, a tall thin gentleman

wearing evening clothes, and bowed mockingly to the terrified girl.

'Enough of introductions!' exclaimed Her Ladyship. 'We have a lesson to teach and learn. Bend over the divan, Belinda, and draw your nightgown up to your hips. Hurry, girl — and spread your feet apart on the floor.'

Belinda flushed crimson in shame, but did not dare to disobey the instructions she had been given. She placed herself on the edge of the divan, her face down, and stretched out her legs behind her, her bent toes on the floor. Her hand was trembling mightily as she raised her nightgown level with her thighs.

'What ridiculous modesty!' Lady Bumslapper exclaimed. 'But it will do you no good, for your person is to be fully bare!' *While Belinda lay trembling in her refusal to expose herself more completely, Sir Everard laughed lewdly and reached under her nightgown. With a flick of his wrist he jerked the garment up to the small of her back, so that the entire lower portion of her tender young body lay bare.*

'Damme! But there's a sight to give a man a hard,' *he cried.* 'The girl has devilish fine thighs, and a superlative pair of creamy white cheeks to her backside!'

'Then you shall be the first to redden them, Everard,' *said Her Ladyship and, stepping up close to the shuddering girl, she put her hands on her back to hold her, and gave her lascivious companion the word to undertake the chastisement.*

With a hard hand, Sir Everard smacked Belinda's bare bottom until she wailed and struggled to escape. She could accomplish nothing, for the hands on her back pressed her firmly down on the divan. Belinda kicked out backwards, hoping that her foot might strike Sir Everard on some vulnerable part of his body, but he stood to the side of her, and Lady Bumslapper stood on the other side, where she could not be reached.

The repetition of the kicking motions raised Belinda's legs high in the air and spread them apart, so that without knowing it she was presenting to Sir Everard an opportunity to gaze at her uncovered parts.

'Damnation take me!' he exclaimed gleefully, 'I vow that's the prettiest pussy I've seen for many a day!'

Belinda sobbed with shame to know that a man, Baronet though he might be, was staring into the deep cleft between her thighs where lay her most intimate secret part. She tried at once to close her legs together, to conceal her brown-haired pussy from his lustful eyes, but to her mortification she felt one of Lady Bumslapper's hands inserted between her thighs. A faint shriek of dismay escaped her when pitiless fingers pulled open the soft lips of her pussy and explored within.

'Well done!' Sir Everard cried. 'Give her a good fingering, Hortense my dear, while I tan her backside! We'll see how soon between us we fetch her off!'

Monty closed the book with a sigh of annoyance and dropped it on the night table. His interest lay elsewhere that evening and the dastardly violation of poor Belinda's chaste parts by Sir Everard failed to hold his imagination. Gwendolen Fanshawe was in his thoughts and could not be dislodged by schoolgirl tales of woe. Without closing his eyes he could picture the beautiful Gwendolen as he had observed her secretly through the hole in the ceiling – lying on her back on her brother's bed, her frock off and her chemise turned well up to display her lace-trimmed white drawers.

By this time, acting without thinking of what he was doing, Monty had pulled his nightshirt up to his chest and clasped his hot and hard shaft in his hand. His legs spread themselves wide of their own volition and he jerked One-Eyed Jack briskly up and down, sighing at the pleasurable sensations the simple action provided him. He summoned up in his heated mind the fond memory of the slit of dear Gwendolen's drawers being opened to reveal a joy of a curly haired pussy, pouting between smooth-skinned white thighs.

A strenuous feat of imagination put himself in Selwyn's place on the bed with Gwendolen, so that it was he who bent over her to press a kiss on the plump lips of her charming pussy. His were the hands, not Selwyn's, that slid up the gleaming insides of her parted thighs, right up to the delicate skin nearest her bush of dark curls.

'Gwendolen, I must have you soon!' Monty gasped. 'Unless I may get this hairy monster of mine into your pussy, I shall go mad with longing!'

His hand rubbed up and down his straining shaft, his heart beating faster and stronger as he felt the moment coming closer and closer when his passions would be relieved in hard spasms of delight. A frenzy of sensation seized him then, and his legs kicked wildly as his essence came gushing out in long jets that sprayed the bed sheet above him.

'Gwen, Gwen, my dearest!' he gasped out to each wet throb of his shaft. 'I adore you — this is how I mean to come off in you, again and again!'

For fully fifteen seconds One-Eyed Jack continued to throb and spurt until he was fully satisfied, after which Monty gave a sigh of content and fell asleep, leaving the bedside lamp still burning.

He was already awake in the morning when Minnie brought his morning tea, and One-Eyed Jack was stiff as an iron bar, having been in that condition since before Monty woke. Nevertheless, he did not request Minnie to ease his tension with her hand, as in the past, for he had made up his mind to settle the puzzle that troubled him in the only practical way — by personal trial of what emotions were raised in a man's heart when he rogered his own sister.

Monty had four sisters and three brothers, he himself being the youngest of all of them. The others were all married and had families of their own, with the exception of Gustavus, who was an officer in the Royal Navy and was hardly ever to be seen in England. The sister of whom Monty was most fond was Grace, some four years older than himself, and the wife of a solicitor who lived at Putney. It was therefore to Putney that he went by the train, to present himself in mid-morning at the large house by Putney Heath where the Austins dwelled. Grace was pleased to see her dear brother, and regaled him in the back parlour with a glass of Madeira wine and a slice of seedcake.

Mr Austin was at his business in the High Street, and Grace's small daughter was being given an airing on the Heath by the nursemaid. The housemaid was busy upstairs cleaning, so Monty had a clear run at what he proposed, devilish difficult though it seemed to him to achieve. Sisters do not commonly let their brothers roger them, whatever Minnie claimed was usual in the hovels of the East End. Indeed, Selwyn and Gwendolen were the first pair of siblings Monty had ever known or heard of who pleasured each other in this way. Without doubt, the rarity of the aberration played some large part in Monty's obsession with Gwendolen.

But how to make a start with Grace, that was the question! After a while, Monty told his sister that his head ached, which was an untruth, but it aroused her sympathies. She made him lie on the sofa at full length while she fetched a large bottle of eau de cologne and a fine white linen handkerchief, and bathed his forehead. To accomplish this act of mercy she sat sideways on the sofa by his side, bringing herself into close proximity with him. Monty gazed through half-closed eyes at Grace's bosom hovering above him as she tended his brow, and wished he could see through the grey satin of her frock and through her chemise to her titties.

'Grace, my dear,' said he, 'I have a great secret to tell you and that is why I am here this morning. I have fallen in love with someone you have not yet met — Gwendolen Fanshawe. It is in my mind to propose marriage to her.'

Grace congratulated him warmly and leaned down to kiss him, and for a moment her soft breast rested lightly on the hand he held across his chest. He almost grasped that choice bubbie, but commonsense restrained him, and she sat up again, removing the temptation. She resumed the bathing of his brow with eau de cologne, whilst asking questions about the woman who had captured his heart. Monty was careful not to let it come out that Gwendolen already had a husband, for that would have exploded his plot. After a while he informed Grace that he had a serious question to ask, and begged her not to be offended.

All their other sisters and brothers, with the exception of Gus, were well blessed with children, three, four, five, six, and even seven for Lou, the oldest. In contrast, Grace had been married to Arthur for five years now and had only one child so far. What could be the secret of this freedom from continual pregnancy, Monty asked, surely not permanent abstinence from marital pleasures? Grace blushed and was reluctant to answer him, but he was persistent and eventually came to the truth of it. She and Arthur were followers of the Oneida way of conjugal duties, which brought tranquillity and sweet release from nervous tension without the risk of child-bearing.

'Lord!' Monty exclaimed. 'Do you mean that Arthur pulls out in the nick of time and fetches off over your thighs?'

'No, no!' said Grace, her eyes downcast in modesty at the thought.

'Then what?' he asked, baffled by her disclaimer. 'Are you telling me that you and Arthur satisfy each other by hand, and never join the parts together?'

With a becoming degree of bashfulness, Grace set forth the essentials of Oneida. The husband fondled his wife until he was appropriately stiff, said she, whereupon he mounted himself on her and penetrated her in the natural manner. Then both of the partners lay perfectly still, breathing deeply but in a steady and controlled rhythm. After about an hour of this, said Grace, the nervous tension dispelled of itself, the husband's natural organ lost its stiffness and became limp, and both partners experienced a feeling of gentle content.

Monty found it very difficult indeed to believe this could be true. Never yet had he got One-Eyed Jack into a pussy without fetching off soon after. But he had taken a slight advantage of Grace's bashfulness and averted gaze to slip his hand under her skirts and let it rest lightly just above her knee, only the thin material of her drawers between his fingers and the flesh of her thigh. She seemed not to notice it there, so involved in her explanation was she.

She was willing to explain again, when he insisted that he did not truly understand what she had described, and when she at last overcame her very natural embarrassment in referring to physical matters, she spoke more frankly. Although the male and female organs were joined together, she said, it was completely different from the ordinary common tiresome form of marital intercourse, and far superior to it, for it could be repeated at will, and did not exhaust the participants.

'Then this is what I shall teach my darling Gwendolen,' said Monty, who had no such intention, 'but first you must teach me, dearest Grace, or I shall get it wrong and spoil everything by spending.'

'Teach you? But how?' asked Grace, her fine dark eyebrows rising up her forehead.

'The best method of teaching is surely a demonstration,' said Monty.

She blushed fiery red and refused to contemplate so unnatural a proposal, but Monty used his charm and considerable powers of persuasion to convince her that, in her own words, there was no comparison at all between physical intercourse and the ethereal connection of Oneida. So it came about that while he remained on his back on the sofa, Grace sat over his hips and spread her wide skirts over him, so that nothing was to be seen. Beneath their covering folds, Monty unbuttoned his trousers and let his stiff shaft stand boldly out, then felt between Grace's thighs to pull open the slit of her drawers and feel her pussy.

He saw her cheeks blush crimson at the touch, and she stared fixedly at a painting on the wall of a wicker basket of oranges and apples. In another instant he brought his shaft up to the mark and pushed inside Grace's warm pussy. He was aroused to an extraordinary degree by the feel and the thought of being up his own sister, and it was with a struggle that he controlled his voice when he spoke to her.

'What next, Grace? Enlighten me, my dear.'

'Breathe slowly and deeply,' she said, looking down

at his face at last, 'take your time from me, and remain absolutely still — do not move a muscle, not even an eyelid!'

Easier said than done! Monty suppressed a sigh of delight at the feel of the soft and velvet folds of her pussy enfolding his hot shaft.

'Arthur is no fool,' he said. 'The sensation is very fine — and this you and he enjoy together every night, you say?'

'And twice on Sunday afternoons after church,' said Grace, her eyes sparkling at the pleasant thought. 'Now, Monty dear, I have gone further than is decent between brother and sister, to make you understand how best to manage your relations with your wife after you and Gwendolen are married. You must withdraw now and give me your word you will never mention what we have done to a living soul.'

'You have my word,' said Monty at once, making not the least attempt to withdraw from the warm haven that held One-Eyed Jack so snugly,' but unless I remain where I am lodged for a while, how can I believe that the tension fades away of itself, with no bodily spasm?'

'Very well, then,' said Grace, 'but you must lie very still.'

'Not a flicker will you get out of me,' he promised.

He watched as Grace closed her eyes and seemed to pass into a blissful trance, her face tranquil. He closed his own eyes and gave himself up to the thought of rogering Gwendolen. There was no need for him to stir himself — One-Eyed Jack did all that was required, by throbbing away gently but persistently inside Grace. She evidently was accustomed to a similar throbbing by her husband's shaft in the early stages of this strange marital rite, and she explained it to Monty.

'Do you now understand what I tried to make plain to you?' she asked, her cheeks a faint and becoming pink. 'The bodily sensations increase of themselves at first, to provide a degree of pleasure to the participants, and then they subside slowly until total calm and content is achieved — to the health and wellbeing of male and female alike.'

'Yes, I understand what you mean,' sighed Monty faintly.

After ten minutes inside Grace's pussy, his sensations were not decreasing at all — the reverse was the case, in fact. His shaft grew thicker and longer, and its throbbing became ever stronger. It could not last — Grace stared down in alarm at his flushed face and heard his rapid breathing — and understood that, far from his emotions fading away as she had promised, he was at the very brink of spending! At this supreme moment she jerked herself backwards away from him, and his leaping shaft was dragged willy-nilly out of her pussy, at the very instant his torrent of desire gushed out.

At the touch of his hot elixir soaking through her drawers to wet her belly, Grace's eyes opened wide in a stare of mingled amazement and outrage — and she herself came off silently! She clenched her fists and bit her teeth together, but otherwise her body hardly moved at all, as she fought to exercise control over herself. Then she was still and sagging forward, the expression on her face indecipherable.

'Grace, Grace!' Monty moaned, his belly still shaking with the force of his fetching off. He had partly answered his own question — physical connection with a sister had proved to be powerfully exciting.

Grace was not in a equal state of blissful reminiscence. She would have jumped off Monty and run out of the room, her face hidden in her hands, to lock herself in her bedroom and abandon herself to unnecessary shame and grief, but he took her by the waist and held her tightly, to keep her astride him.

'My dear girl,' he said, truly grateful to her.

'Oh Monty, what have you done, what have you done!' cried she. 'You've committed an unnatural act with your sister and we are both defiled by it! Why did you do it? Why?'

'Hush, Gracie, hush,' he soothed her, 'nothing of significance has happened, merely a trivial accident of nature while I am as yet unaccustomed to the Oneida way. Let me wipe you dry.' He took the handkerchief with which she had bathed his brow, shook out its folds scented with eau de cologne and carried it under her covering skirts, to wipe her belly gently. When she had recovered from her shock and realised that she had not been put at risk in any serious way her tense muscles softened and she sat still while Monty played with her wet pussy under the pretence of drying it for her. Under his fingertips it had a warm and inviting feel, and he longed to look at it, but knew that a request to do so might startle Grace and undo all that he had achieved so far.

His restraint paid him good dividends. Grace smiled when he told her that her pussy was now scented with eau de cologne, and she let herself be soothed to the point at which she felt underneath her spread skirts, where nothing could be seen, to take the handkerchief herself and use it to wipe his sticky shaft. The touch of her hand on One-Eyed Jack was galvanic! From his torpid, half-soft state, he leaped into hard-standing uprightness, with such vigour that Grace gave a little laugh.

'Monty, you are impossible,' she said, 'I am not

accustomed to the male part stiffening again so shortly after coming off. Are you always like this?'

'Always,' he assured her, making Jack twitch between her long fingers, as if in agreement.

'But how then do you resolve it?' she asked, a puzzled look on her face. 'Surely no woman has the stamina required to allow you a second connection with her so soon after the first?'

'Some have, I do assure you,' he answered.

'I am not one of them,' said she. 'Arthur has never made an approach to me in less than a hour after the first, nor would I ever wish him to.'

It was in Monty's mind that his brother-in-law's rogering of Grace did not truly satisfy her, and that the Oneida business was mere foolishness. The mere touch of his own shaft shooting out its essence had been enough to bring her off, without it even being inside her pussy. She had pretended that nothing was happening to her, from modesty maybe, but Monty had seen enough women in their climactic throes to be able to recognise Grace's condition at the moment of his spending.

What was also in his mind was that she felt all the better for having come off in the proper way for once. Her eyes were sparkling and there was a healthy touch of pink in her cheeks. Her hand was gliding up and down his stiff shaft in a way that gave rise to sensations of an extremely satisfactory nature, and he took her pleasuring of him as a sign of her gratitude.

'Naughty, naughty Monty,' she said, 'to want to do it again so soon. You must make do with the handkerchief as recipient of your second fetching off.'

'Dear sister!' he sighed blissfully.

CHAPTER 6
A Lesson in Self-Control

On the next day after his introduction to Mrs Cecily Massingham Selwyn returned from his employment at the Board of Education to his digs in Seymour Place a little after his usual time. He looked pale and fatigued when Monty, who had been waiting with his door open to the stairs for the past hour, dragged him into his sitting room and sat him in the best armchair.

'My dear chap,' said Monty, with a grin, 'you look well done up — though content. Let me pour you a stiff brandy to restore you while you give me a faithful account of what passed between you and Cecily yesterday.'

'Even now I can hardly bring myself to speak of that sublime experience,' said Selwyn, his voice shaking with emotion. 'You will recall that dearest Cecily was so understanding and tender of my fearful moral weakness that she permitted me to kneel at her feet and kiss in humble reverence between her legs.'

'You are a lucky dog,' said Monty, to encourage him into more confidences. 'This I saw, and told myself that you are one man in a million, to be allowed that familiarity.'

'She spoke to me,' Selwyn said dreamily, taking a long

sip of the brandy Monty had handed him,' she uttered words I never thought to hear from a beautiful woman, words that sent thrills of delight coursing right through me — *that she submitted to this shameful act if it made me happy*! Happy! The word is too puny to describe what I felt then. My emotions became so intense that I fainted away with joy. When I came to myself again, I was lying on the sofa and you were gone.'

'I thought it best,' said Monty. 'Cecily feared you might be agitated when you came to your senses again, and the fewer you found about you, the better. I'm sure that she took good care of you.'

'Yes,' Selwyn whispered, his pretty face flushing pink, 'she was an Angel of Mercy to me, though this I did not understand at first. You see, when I returned to a proper consciousness of my surroundings, I found that my buttons had been undone and my parts and belly lay bare, and were splashed with the cream of my spending. Cecily sat beside me, chafing my hand, and when I looked up at her in some embarrassment, she chided me. She told me that she now understood the cause of my moral weakness, and that if she and I were to remain good friends, I must let her help me to overcome it.'

'How noble a woman she is!' Monty exclaimed. 'So very kind and considerate towards those who have her affection! I really must offer you my congratulations, Selwyn, on your good fortune in finding a place in her heart in so short a time!'

'I am the happiest and the luckiest of men,' Selwyn agreed. 'Cecily has pledged her unswerving support in overcoming my moral weakness, now that she knows in what it consists. This I confessed in full to her, for she had mistaken it for a more common weakness at first.'

'To have a friend like Cecily!' said Monty. 'You and

I are amongst the blessed of this world. What do you mean?'

'Since we share her affections, you and I, I am emboldened to tell you all that passed between us,' said Selwyn. 'She took in her lily-white hand my limp and sticky part and spoke frankly to me. She said she believed that to have come off so easily in my trousers, and swooning away at the sensation, must indicate that I was a slave to the habit of self-abuse. I assured her it was not so, that never in my life had I brought myself off by the use of my hand, but she did not believe me. She insisted I must be taught a lesson in self-control, and ordered me to roll over and lie face down on the sofa.'

'Self-control!' exclaimed Monty. 'What a fearful thought! I give way instantly to every sexual temptation presented to me — and thereby derive a great deal of pleasure. Take my word for it, Selwyn, a pleasure put off is a pleasure lost. Although my affection for Cecily is by no means diminished by what you have said, I trust that she will fail in this disagreeable venture to teach you self-control.'

'No, no!' said Selwyn, his face pale with dismay at Monty's words. 'Cecily is right — because of my moral weakness my life has gone askew. If she can teach me to control my passions, it will be much better, I am convinced.'

'As you wish,' said Monty. 'What took place when you were on your belly on the sofa?'

'Cecily took down my trousers,' Selwyn replied. 'She had them down round my knees, and my underthings, to lay my posterior bare. A moment later she brought her slipper down across the cheeks, and the fierce pain made my body jerk as I cried out. *Bite your lip and be silent, sir*, she said, *I mean to teach you to keep your hands away from your shaft*. She leathered me ten or twelve times, and to my utter amazement my shaft grew to a tremendous size and stiffness. It was tightly pressed between my belly and the sofa cushions, and it throbbed so hotly to the blows of Cecily's slipper that I feared I would fetch off.'

'My word!' Monty interjected. 'I've never tried whipping — is it really so arousing?'

'I found it to be astonishingly so,' said Selwyn, red-faced with emotion. 'By great good fortune I was spared the further shame of fetching off on the cushions only because Cecily tired herself in chastising me. One more stroke would have finished me, but it was not delivered — she dropped into an armchair, declaring that she had exhausted herself for my moral benefit. *You are forbidden to play with your shaft from henceforth*, she said, *no one is to handle it when it is stiff but I — mark me well, or your backside will be beaten red-raw*!

'To show my gratitude for her efforts on my behalf, I crawled across the carpet to kneel at her bare feet and kiss them in adoration. It was if I was in Heaven itself when I glanced up — Cecily's wrap had become untied while she was so vigorously chastising me and it lay open, presenting the sight of the most delicious titties ever yet seen in the world. The skin was white as milk, tipped by full scarlet berries.

'I stared at those matchless delights of hers speechless with emotion, and she saw how my heart yearned for her. A smile of pure affection crossed her beautiful face and she rubbed the sole of her bare little foot against my rampant shaft. She said it was the biggest and strongest she had ever seen, and I very nearly spent over her foot.'

His words reminded Monty of an occasion when Cecily had held his shaft between the soft soles of her feet and rubbed slowly until she brought him off and splashed herself up to her knees. This was no time to tell that to Selwyn, who seemed almost to have undergone a religious experience with Cecily.

'The moment came,' Selwyn continued, 'when my nervous system could tolerate no more! I flung myself forward between dearest Cecily's thighs, forcing them to open widely! With a shriek of surprise, she fell back in her armchair, and in an instant I thrust my tongue between the pouting lips of her pussy! The touch caused her to cry, *Oh, Selwyn, you will make me come off, my dearest one*! My tongue licked at her pleasure bud, and in another minute her feet were waving in the air as she attained the supreme point of ecstasy and fainted away, just as I had myself earlier.'

'This is bamboozlement of the highest order,' thought Monty, for never yet had he known Cecily to faint when she came off, no matter how often the pleasure was repeated on the trot. He mentally raised his hat to her, for the skill with which she had played Selwyn.

'That is astonishing!' he said. 'Let me refill your glass to help you bear up while you continue. I see that when *you* roger a woman, evidently she feels the effect of it, my dear fellow! I commend your prowess!'

'What occurred next makes me ashamed of myself,' said Selwyn mournfully. 'I am a beast, and not fit to be the friend of such a noble and good-natured lady as Cecily. I needed then all the self-control she promised to instil in me but alas, I gave way to temptation. While she lay helpless in a swoon, I lifted her legs over my shoulders and plunged my raging shaft into her. At the shock, her senses revived, and she stared at me and sighed, *No more, no more! You will kill me with coming off, Selwyn*! But I was deaf to good sense and seized her lovely titties in my hands and violated her — I thrust furiously into her pussy, whether she would or not. The warm throbbing of that adorable pussy on my swollen shaft aroused me so fiercely that I gushed a stream of hot sap into her.'

'Well done!' exclaimed Monty, unable easily to reconcile the account of Selwyn rogering Cecily in a rage of lust with his opinion of him as an ineffective weakling.

'No, it was not well done!' Selwyn contradicted him. 'It was rape, not to put too fine a point on it. I used Cecily's body for my despicable pleasure without her consent. No sooner had my tallow been spilled than I pulled out and hid my blushing face against her belly in an agony of shame.'

'Did she rebuke you for making use of her so freely?' Monty enquired in surprise.

'She asked me to explain myself, and I could do no other than tell her of my abject weakness and how I had undermined my own moral nature in my youth. As you may imagine, she was shocked to hear of my depraved habit of feeling Gwendolen's titties day after day. I hung my head in shame and told her of my advance into wickedness, and Gwendolen with me, till we regularly undid buttons and raised skirts, to bare each other's privities and feel them.'

'And more than that as I recall you told me,' said Monty. 'You soon found how to bring each other off.'

'It's true — I cannot deny it,' said Selwyn in a low voice. 'You may imagine my humiliation when I related this precocious delinquency to Cecily. When I reached the point of telling her how a day came at last when I thrust my shaft up Gwendolen's pussy and fetched off in her belly, my shame was so great that I could hardly speak.'

'You are fortunate in that Cecily is a most

understanding and good-hearted person,' said Monty, who knew full well that there was no manifestation of human desire, be it never so curious or unlawful, that would surprise or dismay Mrs Massingham.

'She is an angel!' Selwyn declared again. 'She held my head on her soft belly and stroked my hair while she calmed me. The she gave me her solemn word that she would use all her power to break me of this habit of rogering Gwendolen. I was so glad to hear her words that I pressed kisses of gratitude to her belly, and then her thighs, which had parted, and soon I found myself kissing her pussy — wet still with the essence I had spent in it when she was helpless.'

The thought of Cecily permitting herself to be at the mercy of Selwyn — or any other man — seemed laughable to Monty, whose acquaintance of the lady was extensive. Nevertheless, he kept his face straight and nodded sympathetically.

'My confounded moral weakness gripped me again,' said Selwyn in a mournful tone of voice. 'From chaste kisses on that divine pussy I had violated in beastly fashion, I soon found myself pushing my tongue between the soft lips — and I had no strength to prevent myself licking her darling little bud yet again!

'*Ah take care, Selwyn,* she cried — *you may pay your resects with your tongue, but with no other part of your person.* In my gratitude for her kindness and forbearance, I continued to pay homage to that Heavenly part of her person, until she reached the very acme of delight. Judge my condition — I was on fire to plunge my shaft into her, but she pushed me away and spoke very calmly, informing me that this was the beginning of my lessons in self-control.'

'Good Lord!' said Monty. 'I don't believe I could bear

it if I had been kneeling between Cecily's legs then —
I'd have had no choice but to push One-Eyed Jack right
up her and roger her to a standstill! But what of you,
Selwyn — were you able to contain your emotions at so
exquisite a moment?'

'I thought I would have fainted with the effort,' said
he, a pallor on his cheeks that told of his ordeal. 'My
bared shaft was jerking up and down, and I would have
seized upon it, but Cecily ordered me to put my hands
behind my back and fix my gaze between her thighs. She
parted them to the limit, the lips of her darling pussy were
pulled open by the position, to show the pinkness of the
inside, and the wetness of her excitement! I begged her
to let me look away, for this was torture of the cruellest
kind, in my aroused condition. But she reproved me
sternly, saying that no lesson worth while was ever yet
learned without suffering.'

'Heavens above — this is agony so refined that it
surpasses imagining!' said Monty. 'I'm on tenterhooks!'

'You cannot form the least idea of my torment then,'
Selwyn told him. 'My shaft was standing longer and
thicker than ever before, and waving up and down
furiously. *Stop that at once* was Cecily's command and
when I confessed that I had no power to do so, she put
her dainty bare foot against it and held it still against my
belly. *Control yourself, sir!* said she, *keep gazing between
my thighs and learn that feelings of lust are not to be
indulged in at will, only when permitted*. The touch of
her foot on my shaft was sending waves of delicious
sensation rushed up my spine. I stared into her wet and
open pussy, and in another moment I would have fetched
off over her foot!'

'Delicious thought!' said Monty, his shaft trembling
within the prison of his trousers. 'I once was permitted

that honour — and I treasure the memory of seeing myself gushing between the delicate little soles of Cecily's feet!'

'She denied me that pleasure,' Selwyn confessed, red-faced and hot-eyed at the memory. 'She removed her darling foot from me, closed her legs, and instructed me to breathe deeply and slowly, until I became calmer. You cannot conceive of my mental and physical torment — every fibre of my being was yearning to come off — while Cecily held my gaze with hers and said again and again, *Control yourself, Selwyn!*'

Secretly, Monty could find no words of praise sufficient for Cecily's female skill in getting the upper hand over Selwyn. It was evidence, he thought, of her true devotion to himself, that she had performed with such diligence his request to attach Selwyn to herself. Aloud he enquired, in a manner appropriately sympathetic, what had ensued when Selwyn gained self-control.

'She caused me to lie on the sofa,' said Selwyn, 'and she sat beside me, speaking most kindly now that with her help I had at last gained a victory over my moral weakness. My trousers were still unbuttoned and open, and she held my shaft in her little hand and rolled back the skin to allow full view of the purple dome while she spoke. *Give me your solemn word*, she said, *that this monstrous proud and ill-disciplined fleshy implement of yours will never fetch off again, never, never, never, neither in my pussy, nor any other woman's pussy, nor in any woman's hand, mine or another's, nor in your own and, however fierce may be your lust, without you first seek my express permission. Swear it now!*'

'Gracious — I hope you refused!' Monty exclaimed, tongue in cheek, but Selwyn shook his head.

'How could I refuse my dearest Cecily anything?' he said, his eyes alight with the fire of devotion. 'I have no desire to roger any other woman now that I have found her — I gave her my word at once!'

'But what about Gwendolen?' asked Monty. 'When she visits you next, she will expect your loving attentions — what will you do?'

'I must disappoint her,' Selwyn told him. 'I have pledged myself. No drop of sap shall ever escape my shaft from this day forth except when I am with Cecily and have her consent to come off, either in or about her divine person!'

'A little more brandy,' said Monty, tipping the bottle, 'I am lost in admiration for your strength of purpose, and Cecily was surely touched to the heart by the warmth of your affection and allowed you a spasm or two of delight as your reward?'

'She spoke to me in the most loving manner,' Selwyn breathed, as if describing a momentous event in history, 'and while she told me how glad she was that we had become close friends in so short a time, she slowly fondled my shaft, until it stood like a flagpole. *O that is delicious, Cecily*, I cried, *but you will ruin my self-control and make me fetch off if you continue so*! She replied that I had her complete permission and rubbed at a brisker pace. My heart sang with joy to hear her words, whilst my shaft thrust and heaved in her dainty white fingers. A mere heartbeat before I came off mightily in her hand, she ceased her massage, and applied the most forcible pressure at the base of my shaft — and stopped me dead in my tracks!'

'By Jove!' Monty exclaimed. 'Had it been me to whom she did that, I fear I would have undergone a seizure on the spot! Did she then resume her stimulation?'

'When she saw by the shocked expression on my face that I was in no danger of fetching off, she recommenced her titillation — first a soft fondling, then a firm rubbing, until she again had me trembling on the brink of ecstasy. And again she balked me of the crisis at the last moment!'

'But the Spanish Inquisition could have inflicted no worse torture on a helpless victim!' said Monty. 'This is an aspect of Cecily's character of which I have been hitherto ignorant.'

'It was delicious, what she did to me,' murmured Selwyn, his face bright and his eyes aglow, 'ten times she used her hand on my quivering shaft to lead me up to within a breath of felicity — and each time she dashed my hope with a calculated pressure! I truly thought her purpose was to precipitate a heart attack and so put an end to me — and I was happy to die with my shaft in her hand. Then the eleventh time, when she had weakened me almost to swooning with her forcible lessons in self-control, she smiled sweetly on me as her fingers glided up and down my shaft, and said, *You may come off now, Selwyn*. At once my emission burst forth in hot gushes, wetting her hand, and soaking my shirt as high as my chest!'

'Capital!' said Monty, his mind elsewhere, as he carried out a feat of calculation. 'But to reckon from when I left you, and allowing your swoon to endure for somewhat longer than is usual, and your sweet torment at Cecily's hand to have lasted a half-hour, it would by then be five o'clock in the afternoon. But you had not returned here by the time I retired to bed. How were the several intervening hours passed, Selwyn?'

'Cecily had her maid bring up food and drink to refresh me — her kindness knows no limits! I, in the meantime, had adjusted my clothing to be decent again, and we sat together, Cecily and I, and ate and drank and talked merrily. After that pleasure, I was granted the greatest privilege of my life.'

'Namely?' Monty enquired, pouring more brandy.

'Darling Cecily invited me into her bedroom! O the joy of that shared moment! I thought I would die of purest bliss when she threw off her wrap and permitted me to see her in her naked beauty! Then she assisted me to remove my clothes, down to my shirt, and she asked me to lie on her bed! *Now, Selwyn*, said she, *you had me when I was helpless and at your mercy — I mean now to have you — what have you to say to that, sir?*

'Only that I adore you as no woman was ever adored before, I replied. *I mean to ride a St George on you*, she said, *but you are not to come off until I give you permission — otherwise I shall be angry with you — do you understand me?* I had scarce time to assure her I would obey her, before she was astride me. She squeezed my shaft in her hand and brought its head up to the mark, uttered a tuneful little laugh, and with a sharp jerk of her loins, thrust me deep into her warm pussy.

'I nearly came off at once, to feel soft flesh throbbing and gripping my enslaved shaft, but I compelled myself to remain still, and as calm as was possible. Cecily rode me slowly, and paused every few minutes, to draw out her own pleasure and to imprint on my whole being another lesson in self-control. Half an hour at least passed with my beloved in the saddle, before her sensations caused her to sigh and to shudder, and then she gasped in delight *O Selwyn — I cannot prevent myself coming off any longer! I must have you now, my dear!* So saying, she plunged very fast up and down my shaft, moaning as she fetched off and I moaned in joy beyond compare to feel the gushes of my essence pouring into her.'

'By Heaven — my shaft is as stiff as a broom handle!' said Monty. 'I must find an accommodating woman at once, or I shall expire of thwarted lust! It's me for Mrs Lee's house!'

'No need for that,' Selwyn assured him, 'Cecily expects both of us to call on her at nine this evening.'

Monty was surprised to be invited to St John's Wood at short notice, but Selwyn reported that Cecily's only appointment that evening was a stock-broking gentleman who dropped in for an hour on his way home from his place of business. By seven she would be at liberty, and by nine rested and refreshed. That being so, Monty took Selwyn to a chophouse in Welbeck Street, and they ate well, to build up their strength. At nine o'clock sharp, a hansom cab deposited the two of them outside Cecily's villa.

The maid took their hats, coats and sticks and said they were expected. She added that Mrs Massingham had been taken by a fit of the vapours earlier in the evening, and had retired to her bed to rest. If the gentlemen did not object to being received informally, they were to go up. Needless to say, neither Monty nor Selwyn had the least objection to being received in their dear Cecily's bedchamber, and the maid led them upstairs and announced them.

Cecily was propped up in bed against large soft pillows, her hair unpinned and loose about her white neck. She wore a little bed jacket of quilted pink satin, edged with white fur. Monty and Selwyn advanced to the bed, and took a seat on either side of it, each taking one of the hands Cecily held out to them. As they chatted, commiserating with her on her indisposition, she gently allowed her bed jacket to fall open, revealing that her breasts were only half-contained in her flimsy silk nightgown.

Monty took full advantage of her almost naked condition right away, by slipping a hand into the lace-trimmed front of her garment for a good feel of her titties. From there, he slid his hand down under the bedclothes, gliding down Cecily's warm and smooth belly, with only thin silk between his fingers and her flesh. The nightgown was drawn up about her thighs, he found, not stretched down to her ankles. He fumbled under it until he had a hand between her legs, and happily felt her hairy pussy.

His long middle finger slipped without fuss between the warm and moist lips and he tickled her button with delicate little movements that brought a charming flush to her cheeks and sent tremors of sensation through her belly. She parted her thighs a little wider in the bed, to afford his skilful finger an easier access to her person.

Monty saw that with her right hand she had undone the buttons of Selwyn's trousers and she was rubbing his shaft. In the same way, her other hand had found its way into his own trousers and was performing the same agreeable office for him. When both had reached a degree of stiffness that pleased her, she pulled them out of their gaping trousers, and Monty was slightly abashed. From his secret observation through the ceiling, he knew that Selwyn at full stretch had the advantage of him, being blessed with a good eight inches, but Cecily had the courtesy to make no comparisons, saying only that to bring her out of her vapours, she needed a sound rogering.

'By all means,' said Monty with a laugh of delight. 'Which of us will you have first, my dear?'

'You and Selwyn are both so hard-on that there is nothing to choose between you,' was her tactful reply.

'I shall have both shafts up me together — the two of you shall roger me at the same time.'

She threw aside the bedclothes to show her bare legs and her dark-curled pussy, Monty having pulled her nightgown up round her waist while he was fingering her. She parted her legs wide and stroked herself between them with both hands, smiling the while at the two men. Selwyn was at a loss — the thought that two friends might share a woman together had never entered his head. He glanced from Cecily's pussy up to Monty for guidance on what should be done next, and Monty laughed and dipped into his fob pocket for a golden sovereign.

'Call,' he said, flicking the coin high into the air with a jerk of his wrist.

'Heads,' said Selwyn, waiting until the last moment.

Monty caught the spinning coin on the back of his left hand and clapped his right over it.

'Heads, you say?' he cried. 'We shall see who has the first choice!'

He exposed the sovereign, to show the tails side uppermost, before slipping it back into his pocket safe out of sight. It was not a genuine sovereign at all, if the truth were told, but a trick double-sided coin he had purchased years ago. He had found it useful on many an occasion, for the majority of those asked to call would choose heads without thinking.

While Selwyn was recovering from the disappointment of losing the call, Monty had his clothes off and lay down on the bed on his back. Cecily sat up and slipped off her bed jacket and silk nightgown, and then, naked as Venus, she sat herself astride Monty's legs. He sighed to feel her take hold of his straining shaft and direct it into her slippery pussy. Her delicious wet warmth engulfed his stiff flesh, and she forced it up into her.

As soon as he was well accommodated, Cecily glanced over her bare white shoulder where Selwyn still held his place on the bed in open-mouthed contemplation of the coupling below him. To enlighten him as to what was required, she reached behind her and spread open the soft white cheeks of her backside with her slender hands.

'Selwyn!' she said. 'Why do you delay? I want to feel you up me too — come here and put it in!'

He obeyed her at once, removing his clothes quickly, before kneeling on the bed behind her. Although unfamiliar with this mode of congress, his sensual nature taught him by instinct how to go about it. He put his hands on the cheeks of Cecily's bottom and pulled them wide, pressed her little knot open with his thumbs and brought the tip of his stiff shaft up to it. A hard push, a cry from Cecily, and he had penetrated right into the tight passage!

'Deeper!' she moaned. 'Push deeper, Selwyn!'

On this occasion she did not ride a St George. She held still and let the men do the work — Monty underneath her was poking strongly upwards, and Selwyn behind her was matching Monty's rhythmic strokes with his own — and she throbbed in ecstatic sensation between them.

'Oh my Lord!' she gurgled, her tender body shaken violently by the double thrust of their desire. 'Do me hard! O my God, I can't stand it! I've come off twice already!'

Monty felt the floodgates burst open in his belly and he gave a throaty gasp as he flooded Cecily's clinging pussy. She too cried out in a soprano wail, instructing Selwyn to come off at once! Her hot and naked body convulsed in another climactic release, this time brought on by Monty's furious discharge into her. The squirming of her body undid Selwyn — he brought his hands up from her hips to clasp her bare titties, and he gave voice to a long-drawn moan as, in half a dozen quick spasms, he emptied his passion into her rearward opening.

'Oh Cecily, Cecily my dearest, I love you,' he gasped.

Monty grinned in satisfaction that his scheme was working out so well. In future Cecily would keep Selwyn too busy for him to have time to roger his sister. Monty had plans of his own for darling Gwendolen.

CHAPTER 7
Monty Reaches an Understanding with a Lady

Monty's plans for beautiful dark-haired Gwendolen were put into operation on the occasion of her next visit to London. By then he had talked very seriously to Selwyn, reminding him of his sworn oath to Cecily never to allow himself to fetch off with another woman but her, and offering to relieve him of the heavy burden of Gwendolen's carnal passions. At first, Selwyn could scarcely believe the offer was genuine, but when he was at last convinced that it was, he expressed his gratitude to Monty with words of everlasting respect and friendship.

For beautiful and desirable though Gwendolen was, Selwyn told Monty that he regarded himself as her hapless victim, shackled unwillingly to her by his own moral weakness — a destruction of character he had unwittingly brought about himself when he had first been tempted to feel her young titties. He had hoped, he said, that he would be free of her desires when she married Mr Elliot Fanshawe of Reading, a well-to-do gentleman of a kindly disposition.

Alas, this was not to be. A month after the wedding,

hardly a week after she had returned from honeymoon in the Highlands of Scotland, Gwendolen commenced her twice-weekly expeditions to London to visit the shops, she told her husband, but in actuality to engage in rogering her brother Selwyn. Worse yet was to follow, for after only a week or two she declared herself to be fatigued by the travelling and asked Selwyn to give up his digs and move to Reading to live with her and Mr Fanshawe. This he had steadfastly refused to do, being afraid that if he lived in the same house, Gwendolen would soon become careless and her husband would find out the truth.

Over a bottle of Madeira an arrangement was reached between Monty and Selwyn to the satisfaction of them both. Selwyn was to become a subscriber to Mrs Cecily Massingham's services and call upon her regularly to be taught how to overcome his moral weakness and learn self-control. Gwendolen's affections were to be transferred, without her prior knowledge, to Monty.

So it came about that when Gwendolen arrived for tea with her brother in his digs in Seymour Place, she discovered Monty with him, partaking of tea and cake and conversing as a friend. She several times glared at Selwyn behind Monty's back, willing him to get rid of this inconvenient visitor, so that nothing would impede their removal to the bedroom and a fine rogering on the bed before she left to catch her train. Selwyn pretended not to see, or to understand, her signals, and Monty continued to make cheerful conversation. Finally, at a wink from Monty, Selwyn stood up, consulted his pocket watch and announced that he had an urgent appointment.

He was well gone before Gwendolen had time to recover from her open-mouthed astonishment. Monty smiled at her in his most encouraging manner and told her that her brother had confessed, in agony of mind, his moral weakness, and that he, Monty, had agreed to help him overcome it. While Gwendolen was digesting that unwelcome news, Monty said that it was obvious to him that she had a deeply passionate nature that craved to be loved — he understood this very well, for he had a like nature himself.

Gwendolen stared at him icily, as if he had taken leave of his senses. Undaunted, he continued by telling her that he was here to offer himself humbly, an admirer only from a distance hitherto, who would deem it a proud honour if the beautiful Mrs Fanshawe could find it in her heart to look to him to assuage her needs.

'How dare you speak to me in this way!' she cried. 'I shall report this to my husband, who will thrash you in the street like a dog!'

With that, she leaped to her feet, clutching her gloves and reticule, to hasten away from an interview that was highly distressing to her refined nature. As she turned towards the sitting-room door, Monty threw himself violently to his knees on the carpet, and reached out to seize her. Gwendolen gasped aloud in horror to feel his hands on her hips, preventing her escape from his presence. She gasped even louder when he seized the hem of her skirt and raised it high behind, to uncover her legs in white stockings, and her lovely rounded thighs in white percale drawers with blue ribbons below the knees.

'Unhand me at once!' she cried, her face flushed scarlet as she glared back over her shoulder and down at him.

Monty was quite impervious to the demands of either reason or decency at that moment. His mouth hung open in panting delight whilst he observed how the fine material of her drawers clung into the deep and luscious crease between the cheeks of her backside. His shaft bounded rock-hard inside his trousers, and without hesitation, he parted the rearward slit of Gwendolen's pretty drawers and pressed his lips in an ardent kiss to the bare flesh of her right cheek. It was with keen gratification that he heard her long indrawn gasp of disbelief.

'Stop this unspeakable indecency!' she exclaimed hotly, and grasped at his hair to drag his mouth away from her exposed person. By then Monty had his head up under her skirts and both arms around her, and was stroking her soft belly. She struggled in his grasp to put an end to the vile and audacious advantage he was taking of her, but in the grip of his passion he had the strength of ten men. Gwendolen writhed and exclaimed to no real purpose, but he had her drawers wide open behind and was running his wet tongue up and down the cleft between the soft rounded cheeks he had so brutally uncovered.

'I shall scream and alert the neighbourhood to your infamy!' Gwendolen threatened.

It was too late for such warnings. Monty's stiff shaft leaped so wildly in his trousers that he ripped open his buttons and let it stick out nakedly. His clasping hand held it tightly, as he tried to still its uncontrolled jerking, but matters had already gone too far to draw back. He pulled Gwendolen to her knees on the carpet before him and, panting with lewd desire, thrust One-Eyed Jack bareheaded into the rearward slit of Gwendolen's drawers. She shrieked at the touch against her bare bottom and with five passes of his hand Monty came off and sent a raging flood up the crease between the fleshy cheeks of her rump.

At the sudden warm and wet emission, she uttered a long cry of dismay and fell forward, half-fainting in her ordeal, to lie with her upper body on the seat of an armchair. Her sadly abused body was twitching in spasms of horror, whilst Monty's manly elixir foamed against her soft flesh.

'You have defiled me, you cur!' she moaned, as Monty's last squirt pulsed up between her cheeks. 'My clothing is soaked all through and my person has been molested!'

'I adore you beyond reason,' Monty sighed in his delight. 'My dearest Gwendolen, you have no idea of how often I have woken up in the night to find myself ensnared in sweet dreams of you, and my nightshirt wet and sticky against my belly! I simply must have you, my dear, or it will be the end of me!'

She was most conveniently placed where she had fallen in her swoon, her bosom supported by the chair seat and her bottom toward Monty. Without waiting for a reply to his declaration of love, for such it was, he raised her skirts and petticoats over her rear and with a trembling hand pulled open her drawers to view the cheeks of her bottom, firm-fleshed and round. He stared in loving wonder at her hairy pussy, and was completely unable to resist the urge to finger it.

The warm essence he had spilled was trickling down from her bottom — he dabbled his fingertips in it and wet the lips of her pussy, before burrowing a couple of fingers inside it to stroke her nub gently. So intense was his desire for Gwendolen that his shaft remained long and hard, displaying not the least abatement from its full size, despite its having fetched off in her drawers.

'Forgive me, my dearest girl,' Monty sighed, his fingers well into her pussy, 'but the temptations of your naked person lies far beyond my enervated power of resistance, even if I wished to resist. Accept your Fate — I am going to roger you!'

'You are a cad, to treat a defenceless woman so!' she

cried. 'If you must, then be quick, the sooner to release me from this hideous ordeal!'

Monty brought his throbbing shaft up to her pussy and pushed, and sank in deep. The backs of her thighs pressed against his belly and he rogered away with a firm yet unhurried stroke, not wishing to dissipate the unforgettable pleasure of this moment too hastily. Gwendolen groaned, to feel her beautiful body used against her will for a man's delight.

'This is indecent beyond words,' she moaned. 'To be violated on hands and knees — like a female dog in the street! O, you shall pay for this, Monty Standish! My brother will horsewhip you on the steps of your Club — if there is any organisation so indiscriminating to accept you for a member! And my husband will have you thrown into prison and serving hard labour for the term of your natural life!'

'What nonsense,' Monty sighed, his engorged shaft gliding in and out of her wet pussy to his extraordinary delight. 'Selwyn knew when he left us alone together that it was my intention to poke you — he condones it completely, it being his opinion that you have forced him to roger you too often against his better judgment. Nor will you dare to say anything to Mr Fanshawe, for fear I shall inform him that you have been letting your brother roger you for years!'

'All is known! I am lost!' shrieked Gwendolen.

'Not at all,' Monty murmured, 'for I declare I adore you to distraction, dearest Gwendolen — my heart was given to you the first moment I laid eyes on you. I shall love you and cherish you and roger you forever! You may forget about Selwyn and the husband you deceive — here am I, your new lover!'

'No, never!' she cried.

'As to your other question,' Monty breathed, sensations of purest pleasure volleying through him to the slide of his shaft in her, 'why from behind? To roger a beautiful woman from in front and kiss her soft mouth and feel her heaving breasts all the while, is surely amongst the sweetest delights to which the human race may aspire. But by enjoying her from the rear, he brings her breasts and belly within reach of his roving hands — and the additional gratification of feeling her plump, warm bottom against his belly . . .'

He would have said more of the delights of rearward coition, but the spasms of joy coursing through his body grew too strong to permit further coherent speech, and he fell to sighing and panting as he thrust into her. Nor was Gwendolen unmoved by his words — she was a woman of strong sensual appetites and it was not long before her feelings overcame her outrage.

'Monty, you wicked, wicked man!' she cried. 'You are imposing your lustful will upon me — on a helpless female whose brother has taken advantage of her without respite, almost since childhood, and now the wife of an uncaring man who demeans her daily with his unwelcome lusts! Ah me, am I never to escape the vicious and cruel desires of men!'

During the whole of her mournful complaint, she was jibbing her bottom at Monty, to meet his strokes.

'Ah me . . .' he sighed in echo of her words, 'I love you . . .'

'Finish it, I beg you!' Gwendolen cried.

Monty was so fully possessed by his frantic desire to have her that he hardly knew what he was about. His steady thrusts became rapid jabs, then became a strong pounding against her, and finally a furious ramming into her. Ultimately, with a cry of triumph he reached the pinnacle of sensation and shot his hot sap into her pussy. She groaned and sobbed and shook under his weight, and whether with dismay or delight, he could not certainly tell, but the wet grasp of her pussy gave him reason to hope that she, too, had come off.

When their breathing had returned to its normal pace, he set her on the sofa and himself close to her, his softened shaft out of sight in his trousers. He held both her hands in his own while he spoke to her of his fond admiration for her, and his hopes that she would accept him as her dearest friend. She was at first most unwilling to speak of what had transpired, or to take heed of his expressions of deep affection. She no longer threatened him with reprisals for the violation of her person, and soon he came to understand why, when she asked him outright what Selwyn had told him of their frolicking together. For all her bluster when he had assaulted her person, she knew her Fate to lie in his hands, and wished to acquire his friendship.

'Selwyn had told me everything,' Monty replied, 'from when a keen interest in your titties led him to feel them, to when he first got his shaft into your belly. Though of that he was sparing in the details.'

'Then to show you that I trust you to keep my shameful secret I shall relate how that came about,' said Gwendolen, her face a pretty shade of pale pink.

'You may trust me with your life, as I trust you with mine,' Monty assured her, kissing her hands as he spoke.

'It happened like this,' said Gwendolen, giving him a forlorn smile, 'my brother Selwyn was confined to bed for a day or two with a sprained ankle from a fall, and I went to his room to keep him company for an hour one afternoon. I sat on the bed next to him and we exchanged words, but about what I have now no recollection, for my emotions became so stirred that nothing else made a lasting impression.

'While we were talking, I saw that his nightshirt was pulled up round his chest and I jumped to the conclusion that he had been seeking to pass the time by playing with himself. To find out whether or not he had fetched off, I slid my hand under the sheet and stroked his bare thigh. You must remember that by this stage in our familiarity we had been bringing each other off by hand for a month or more, several times a day, and I was thoroughly acquainted with the capabilities of his body.

'At my touch, Selwyn smiled at me and put his hands under his head on the pillow, and I put my finger to my lips to warn him to be quiet, for the servants were below. I tiptoed to the door and locked it, and went back to the bed, where I stood with my frock lifted and my drawers open at the front, to show Selwyn my pussy. The hair was growing well on it — thick and dark and shiny, and I was proud of it.

'Selwyn put his hand there and started to feel me, as he had many a time before, and I became aroused, I thought he would bring me off with his fingers, and I pulled back the sheets to see his shaft. He was naked below the chest, and his long shaft stood up hard — whereupon a new thought came into my head! He had a shaft between his legs and I had a opening between mine — what if the one were put into the other?'

'No sooner said than done! I held my skirts well up and sat astride him. Greatly daring, I sank down upon him, to push his shaft into me — with scarcely any discomfort at all when he burst into my maiden pussy! O Monty, I cannot describe to you the sensation of it as I started to roger him . . . I knew it was wrong to do this with a brother, and that made it all the more exciting.

'I began to have fantasies of what was going to happen when my brother fetched off inside me! My own dear brother Selwyn — fetching off in my pussy! The thought of it sent me wild with sensation and I came off myself — and two seconds later I felt the squirt of his hot sap. That was the first unlawful love we shared, he and I, but we have never ceased doing it to each other since that day — nor ever wanted to relinquish the sweet shame. There, I have told you everything now, Monty, all my darkest secrets. I am in your hands.'

'Yes,' Monty agreed simply.

He unbuttoned her long lilac jacket from throat to waist and ran his hand over her bosom through her blouse. In another moment he had the bow at her throat untied and the blouse open on her white chemise. He thrust his hands down the top of it to feel her bare titties.

'Consider this, Gwendolen my darling,' said he, 'there are no better hands for you to fall into. I shall love you and protect you and cosset you as no other man ever has, or ever will. You are mine, my dearest!'

'Oh Monty, can I truly believe your words?' she asked, her eyes misty with unshed tears of emotion.

She let her head fall against the high sofa-back, her lovely eyes half-closed. Monty knelt in silent homage at her feet and lifted her breasts right out of her chemise, baring those big white-skinned titties for his hands and lips to ravish. As his mouth flew from soft globe to globe, he sighed in bliss, whilst his tongue licked each in turn to the tip, where his lips took possession of each little rosebud and sucked at it.

Meanwhile, his hand was between Gwendolen's soft thighs, to force them apart and roam boldly over the smooth flesh till his fingers touched her silky haired pussy. He raised his head to kiss her mouth, whilst his fingers invaded her warm slit — and the feeling was evidently so delicious to her that she opened her thighs wider. He knew that he must have her again, for One-eyed Jack was more than half-hard, and twitching in fast little spasms at the sweet taste of Gwendolen's titties.

Indeed, so hard did One-Eyed Jack bound that he gained his liberty from the unbuttoned front of Monty's trousers and was sticking lewdly out towards dearest Gwendolen! This fierceness had been brought on by Monty's sudden memory that, not fifteen minutes ago, he had fetched off in Gwendolen's drawers, soaking them through, when she was on hands and knees on the carpet, and his shaft had rubbed bare-headed on the smooth skin of her bottom, until he had drenched it with his foaming flood.

With a shaking hand, Monty raised Gwendolen's skirt in front until he had a full view of her legs, encased in white silk stockings, and her rounded thighs in her white drawers. Through the forward slit he touched her handsome dark bush, then took her by the ankles to draw her feet wide apart. In mounting desire, he untied the string of her drawers and laid bare her curved belly and its delicious button. He pressed his mouth to it in hot and passionate kisses, then licked slowly down from her belly button to her dark curls.

He gazed in fascination at her uncovered pussy, fingering the soft fleshy lips, and hugged himself in secret congratulation at the recollection that he had already once plunged his shaft into this treasure and gushed his sap. An ecstatic proceeding he proposed to repeat in a very short time! He introduced two joined fingers gently into the delicious slit before him, found Gwendolen's sensual little button and tickled it. At once she sighed luxuriously, and the tempo of her breathing quickened.

Monty continued to play with her and soon her belly began to rise and fall, while her uncovered titties heaved and rolled in the agitation of her breathing. Her pussy had become very wet, and as the climax of sensation came ever nearer, she opened her beautiful dark eyes to look at Monty in loving affection, while her bottom slid forward along the sofa cushions, to bring her pussy closer to him.

Seeing his hard-on shaft jutting from his trousers, Gwendolen took a firm hold of it and brought it to the moist lips of her slit. In one more second she had the shiny unhooded head inside her and with a determined thrust, Monty slid into her right up to his hairy pompoms. He seized Gwendolen's bare breasts where they hung out from her chemise and rogered her furiously. She returned push for push, urging him on at his pleasant task.

'Dear Monty — what bliss!' she sighed. 'Push in deeper yet, I beg you! Push all of it inside me!'

'Oh Gwendolen!' he gasped. 'We are one — accept the tribute of my love, my dearest — I'm fetching off in your pussy!'

Gwendolen's round bottom heaved and squirmed on the sofa and she uttered exclamations of delight whilst she received the hot gush of his admiration, and she came off delicately and lay in Monty's arms, trembling and spent.

When they had recovered their tranquillity, Monty led her by her hand into Selwyn's bedroom, where she had been rogered more than once. In a daze of pleasurable emotion, he helped her out of her clothes, until she lay on the bed in only her chemise. He threw off all his own garments and lay stark naked beside her, kissing and feeling her. The chemise scarcely impeded him at all —

he reached under it to give his darling girl's bottom a thorough feel, then her belly and breasts, until he had made their buds firm and prominent again.

He rolled her on her side and slipped behind her, to lay his hard-on shaft in the cleft between her soft cheeks and slide it against the delicate skin there, while his restless hands were playing feverishly over her titties.

'Oh, my dear one, if only I had the words to tell you how much I love you!' he exclaimed, but Gwendolen's response was not what he expected — she jerked her body away from him!

'You are not to do that!' she exclaimed nervously. 'Be so kind as to keep your manly shaft away from my bottom. You may do anything else to me — even use my mouth — but I will not let you poke my bottom!'

'Heavens!' said Monty, startled by her vehemence. 'What can you be thinking of, my angel? I had no such thought in mind!'

In truth he had rogered Cecily Massingham's bottom enough times to be aware of what it was like, and Cecily seemed to find enjoyment in the proceeding.

'I am pleased to hear it,' said Gwendolen, calmer now for his assurance. 'The shameful truth is that my husband is addicted to that practice — three times a week he asks me to lift up my nightgown at the back and lie face down, while he makes use of my rearward entry. I find it aggravating that he ignores my womanly pussy and spends his strength elsewhere! It holds no pleasure for me, I give you my word, and I resent his lack of interest in satisfying me properly.'

Monty turned her round in his arms and kissed her face and felt her pussy until she was tranquil again.

'Mr Fanshawe is an inconsiderate husband,' he declared, 'but do not tremble, my dearest girl, my adoration will compensate for all the unsatisfactory state of his conjugal attentions.'

'Dear Monty — I believe you!' she replied tenderly.

'When were you first made aware of this tendency in your husband's nature?' he enquired, his hand between her legs to soothe her fears.

'On my honeymoon, before we had been man and wife for three days,' she said. 'The first night we were in Glen Pitlochry he displayed a man's normal desires — in short, he had me on my back with my nightgown round my waist and rogered me. I was no virgin, as you know, having surrendered my maidenhead to dear Selwyn years before but Elliot was not to know that. I made myself appear bashful and inexperienced, and he believed that his was the first male part to enter me.'

'He thinks so still?' Monty asked.

'He has never suspected otherwise. Nevertheless, on the next night he unmasked his true interest. Whilst I lay on my back in bed and awaited his entry into my pussy, he laughed and rolled me over face down and spread himself on my back. You can well imagine that I had no idea at all of what he intended to do to me. But I was not left in ignorance for long — I felt his hard shaft at my rear entrance and before I had time to complain of this unnatural conduct he pushed it right up me! He took his pleasure, kissed me goodnight, and went to sleep!'

'Lord!' Monty exclaimed. 'What a brute to treat a young girl like that! If that is his pleasure, he ought to have taken care to bring you to it by slow steps, and put himself out to ensure that you too were gratified to the point of coming off.'

'He cares nothing for me,' said Gwendolen, her musical voice trembling. 'My husband cares only for his own selfish pleasure. I have never asked why he prefers o use me in this unseemly way, and as a dutiful wife I submit to his desires, unnatural and unsatisfactory though they are!'

'My dearest Gwendolen, let me wipe away from your memory all such thoughts and fill your heart with happiness,' Monty said, his fingers wet with the moisture of her desire.

Without another word she spread her legs wide on the bed, and he sat up to lean over her and gaze in admiration at her pussy while he played with it. The curls that adorned the plump mound between her legs were wet, as were the lips. Monty's heart beat fiercely in his breast at the thought that he would in another instant be lodged inside his beloved.

He raised her chemise to her throat, baring her white belly and titties, and placed his belly on hers. With a hand between his legs he brought One-Eyed Jack up to the mark and pushed in, feeling Gwendolen tremble with passion as she accepted the full length and thickness. She threw her arms about him to hold him close to her bosom, kissed him hotly and squirmed underneath him to make him start poking her.

'Such heavenly bliss!' she cried in her joy, her belly all the time pushing upwards to meet his thrusts. 'Twice a week will never satisfy me, Monty — you must roger me more often, my dearest boy! Tell me that you are virile enough to sustain my desire! If only you could have me every day!'

Monty's fast-beating heart soared with love and desire when he heard these words from Gwendolen's sweet lips. But before he could give her the assurance she wanted, One-Eyed Jack bounded inside her wet pussy and spouted jets of thick essence, shaking Monty with rapture. He grasped her soft titties fiercely and held her tight while he spent inside her, and she moaned and dissolved in ecstasy.

It was only after his last drop had been deliver into her warm belly that he remembered the peepho in the ceiling! He wondered if Minnie was lying the floor above with a hand up her clothes to fing herself while she spied on him rogering Selwyn's siste The thought amused him, and also excited him, f One-Eyed Jack was still long and stiff. He decided give Minnie a run for her money if she was watchin and rolled over on his back to let his wet shaft sta upright.

'You see for yourself that I am able to satisfy yo desires, dearest Gwendolen,' he said, his fingers bu between her legs. 'I am eager to have you again now if you are ready for me.'

'Then have me! Or shall you rest while I do you?

He nodded, pleased that she had thought of what was about to suggest himself. Gwendolen stripped off h chemise and sat naked astride his belly, her white titti dangling above him. He put up his hands to feel the and whilst he rolled them in his palms, Gwendol reached between her thighs to hold his shaft upright a push it up inside her.

'How shall we arrange it so that we may enjoy ea other day after day?' he murmured. 'If I take the tra to Reading twice a week, is there somewhere we may me in private?'

'I shall find somewhere,' she said softly, 'somewhe secret where you can roger me as often as you wish

She rose and fell on him, the silken folds of her pus round his shaft sliding delightfully. He would very soo have fetched off, and she with him, but for her artf precautions in rogering him languorously and pausi

116

every few minutes, to prevent too impatient a response by his pulsating shaft.

After ten or fifteen minutes of this rapture, Gwendolen was unable to tolerate any more sensation and was compelled to seek a climactic finish to the delight. Almost swooning, she jolted up and down on him so fast that his emission gushed up into her and she sobbed for joy to feel it. Monty's wide-staring eyes were fixed on the ceiling, where he knew the peephole to be, close to the gaslight fixture. He hoped that Minnie was there, bringing herself off with her hand while she gazed down at his fine manly body and hard-on shaft, and spent on her fingers when she saw him fetch off in beautiful Gwendolen's belly.

CHAPTER 8
New and Interesting
Discoveries at Putney

Now he knew what it was like to have Gwendolen, Monty was more than ever interested to learn how that superb experience could be compared with having his own sister, so that he would be in the same position of vantage as Selwyn. Sad to recall, although Grace had shown herself to be not without all sympathy for his incestuous advances, he had not really rogered her when he went to call at her house in Putney He had almost succeeded — his shaft had been deep in her pussy, but she had pulled away when she guessed he was about to fetch off, and he had splashed his hot sap over her drawers.

Afterwards, when he had at last calmed her anxiety and fear, she had allowed herself to be persuaded to hold his new-risen shaft in her hand and play with it. It seemed that her interest in the fleshy advantage he had to offer had been heightened by the so-called accident of his emission in her drawers, for she had willingly manipulated it until she caused him to come off again, into the scented folds of a handkerchief. For Monty the enjoyment had been keen — so much so that he veritably believed that

119

to roger a sister must be a greater pleasure than a poke with another woman.

It might almost therefore be said that Monty set off by train for Putney in a spirit of scientific enquiry to try his luck once more with Grace. The short journey passed most pleasantly in reminiscences of rogering Gwendolen and feeling Grace — and his disappointment was great, as may well be imagined, when the housemaid who opened the door to him informed him that Mrs Austin was not at home. His further enquiry elicited the useful information that she was walking the baby on Putney Heath, the day being so warm and sunny, and he set off in pursuit.

Ten minutes stroll on the Heath were sufficient to find Grace pushing the high-wheeled perambulator. She was pleased to see her brother, and they strolled on together until they came to a convenient wooden bench set in an obscure corner under a tree. There they sat down to talk, and Monty made quite certain that the perambulator with its happily gurgling little passenger was placed as a screen in front of them.

The idea had become firmly fixed in Monty's mind that the way in which his brother-in-law rogered Grace without coming off or letting her do so, did not truly satisfy her, and that the so-called Oneida method was mere foolishness. By her account it took an hour of lying still under her husband with his shaft in her before her desire faded — probably from sheer boredom, in Monty's opinion. In contrast, it had taken no more than a touch or two of his own shaft to bring Grace off.

At the supreme moment, she had clenched her muscles tightly and pretended that nothing was happening to her — it seemed her modesty required her to deny that her brother had brought her off! But Monty had seen enough women in their climactic throes not to be deceived by Grace's display of stoicism, He had felt the wetness of her pussy and felt her tremors against him — and easily recognised her lapse into ecstasy.

Grace was in an excellent humour this fine morning. Her eyes were sparkling and there was a healthy touch of colour in her cheeks. Observing this, Monty put an arm round her waist kissed her until she was breathless, and enquired the reason for her satisfaction. She blushed slightly and then confessed that she had persuaded her husband to roger her hard and fast the night before — not just lie passively on her belly.

They had together both come off most satisfactorily — or a least Grace had found it so. Whether her husband was equally pleased, she did not ask, but it seemed logical to suppose that coming off was enjoyable for him. She would have liked a second bout before they slept but Arthur declined, insisting that to do it twice would be to surrender their worthier and higher instincts to animal sensuality. Nevertheless, it was obvious to Monty that his sister felt all the better for being rogered in the proper way for once, and he said so.

'It is a great source of satisfaction to me to hear that your dear Arthur has been persuaded to do his duty by you and give you that divine pleasure which is the right of every wife,' he said. 'Now, to show that we're the best of friends again, dear sister, and that there remain no uncharitable feelings between us for whatever trivial accident may have occurred when I saw you last time — I mean during our discussion of the method of marital relations you and Arthur employed until you were able to convince him that the old ways are still the best and most worth pursuing with enthusiasm — allow me to give your satisfied pussy a brotherly and affectionate squeeze . . .'

Without waiting for her answer, he bent down to slip his hand under her skirts and up between her legs, high above her knees, and between her thighs — and so at last into her thin drawers. She sat quietly while he stroked her and he, too preserved a joyful silence in his voluptuous amusement, fingering the warm and hairy lips between her legs.

'O Monty,' said she at last, 'it is wrong of me to allow you to do what you are doing, I know that all too well. Modesty and chastity — and duty — insist that my person is the property of my husband, and he alone. Yet I ask myself where lies the harm in so pleasant a caress from the hand of a cherished brother?'

'Not the slightest harm, dear Grace,' said he, 'which I shall prove by letting you fondle my shaft, if you wish to do so.'

'No, no — that would be going too far!' she breathed in her modesty, seemingly forgetting that she had brought him off when last he was in Putney. 'There is only one male part I may lawfully hold in my hand, as you well know — my husband's.'

'That selfsame shaft of his which last night was plunged into your pussy and poked you to ecstasy,' said Monty, fingering her delicately beneath her clothes. 'How sad that you were only once raised up to the summit of bliss!'

'If I'd had my way, it would have been half a dozen times at least,' said Grace, 'but Arthur restricted it to once, assuring me that any excess of sensual gratification was known to be injurious to the physical organism, not to mention the risk of enslaving the mind and soul to the habit, which he informed me would be pernicious. So once it was, and once only.'

'Dear me!' Monty said mildly. 'Were you able to sleep,

dear Grace, when your body still cried out for satisfaction?'

'Not for a long time,' she confessed. 'Arthur lay fast asleep beside me, but I was restless and unable to settle.'

'This insomnia brought on by undischarged desire is a fearful threat to the health,' Monty explained judiciously. 'Sensible people relieve themselves of it in a very simple way.'

'Surely you are not suggesting that I would ever satisfy my urges by hand!' Grace exclaimed in apparent indignation. 'That would be a most unladylike thing to do!'

'Of course you do,' said he, 'everybody does. The question is not *whether* you fingered yourself off last night when Arthur left you high and dry, but *how many times* you did it before you sank into a satisfied and refreshing sleep?'

Grace blushed scarlet and refused to answer his impertinent question. Nor did she avail herself of his kind offer to feel his shaft which was, it is needless to remark, in a condition of quivering stiffness. Nevertheless, his words affected her, and she sighed open-mouthed, and rested her bonneted head on his shoulder. She justified this to him — and to herself — by saying that she was somewhat fatigued from what Arthur had done to her the previous night. In this loving posture on the wooden bench, she was admirably well positioned for what Monty was doing to her under her full skirts.

'Rest, dear Grace,' he said softly, 'close your eyes and sink into a light slumber — I will watch over you.'

A glance about him revealed that there was no one in sight on the Heath and emboldened him to continue. No sooner were dear Grace's eyes shut than he raised her skirts up to the level of her waist, revealing white drawers with pale blue ribbons. He opened them and bared her pussy. This was his first glimpse of her female treasure — on his previous visit all had been covered by her voluminous skirts, so that even when he attained to the intimacy of being inside her, he was afforded no sight of her person, not even when he came off on her belly.

He feasted his eyes on Grace's pussy greedily — light brown curls grew not too thickly over her pale mound and the pink soft lips of her pussy. He parted the short curls and fingered Grace's warm lips in glee, till they opened as if by themselves and let his middle finger enter. He heard her sigh when he touched her tiny slippery button and rubbed it gently. Grace kept her eyes tight closed, though she was trembling all over before long.

'You must stop this now, Monty,' she murmured, 'or you will make me come off.'

'Dear Grace — how hot a nature must be yours if you fear to come off so quickly! I have scarcely touched you, and already your pussy is slippery wet and throbbing! I do not wonder that you are unsatisfied when Arthur abandons you after only once rogering you to a crisis of delight!'

He was not speaking the truth, for his hand had been up her clothes and his fingers stimulating her for five minutes.

'It is true,' Grace confessed, 'I am excessively hot-blooded and never content. On the first night of our honeymoon Arthur did me three times, and not even that was enough for me — I would have had him do me again, if his strength had not been exhausted. He has never risen to those heights since, alas.'

'You are and I are two of a kind,' said Monty, soothing her with his fingers on her secret nub. 'We need to come off again and again before we can rest easily. I have rogered a female friend of mine six times in an evening before my shaft would lie down and stay soft.'

'Six times!' Grace cried. 'How wonderful be to be poked six times! Monty — I do believe I'm coming off!' and she rubbed her wet pussy hard against his fingers.

'That's very nice, Grace,' he said, while she shuddered and moaned, 'your belly's quaking like jelly on a plate.'

When she'd finished and calmed down again, she was pleased to unbutton Monty's trousers and slip her ungloved little hand inside, under his shirt.

'Turn and turn about,' said she, giving him a shy smile. 'Who is the female friend you did six times, Monty — surely not the young lady you hope to marry?'

'Darling Gwendolen? No, I have not had the enjoyment of her beautiful body yet,' he lied. 'I was speaking of a young widow with whom I am acquainted in North London.'

During the conversation, Grace's hand was playing along the swollen length of Monty's shaft, exciting it to grow longer and harder still. Monty sighed in delight, telling himself that few more interesting ways of passing a Thursday morning had been devised than for a man to sit in the sunshine on Putney Heath while a pretty woman felt his shaft — and when the woman was no other than his own sister, then the experience was lascivious to the point of incredibility.

'You have a long and thick shaft,' Grace commented, her hand occupied out of sight in his trousers. 'Do you believe it has grown so because of the excessive use to which you put it? A man's muscles grow stronger and bigger with regular exercise — is this also true of his sexual organ?'

'I have always believed so,' Monty sighed, breathing faster and more irregularly as his passions were raised towards their zenith. He felt that at any moment now he was going to fetch off in an explosive manner.

'Monty, my dear — you are jerking so wildly!' said Grace, the swift movement of her fingers sending passionate thrills through him, 'are you about to come off?'

Monty cried out in a delirium of sensation, too far gone to give an answer to her question. His legs kicked spasmodically, his loins jerked, and the thick essence of virile love gushed in long jets up his belly inside his shirt. Grace uttered a gasp to feel the warm wetness flood over her fingers, and kept up the speed of her strokes until the emission was completed.

When Monty had recovered from his climax of delight and Grace had fastened his trouser buttons over his wet shirt and belly, she replaced her glove, got up from the bench and insisted that they return to her home, lest they be discovered by some casual passer-by. Reluctantly he agreed, and strolled beside her while she pushed the perambulator. Five minutes brought them to her home, where the baby was handed over to the nursemaid, tea was ordered from the housemaid, and Grace went upstairs. She said it was to take off her hat, but Monty was certain her purpose was to wash her hands and her person — for he guessed her to be nervous of having his sap on her skin.

After ten minutes absence she came to the parlour, where she found the tea had been served. Monty was drinking a cup of best Darjeeling, stretched out on the sofa, his trousers undone and gaping wide to let his stiff shaft stick out.

'This won't do, Monty,' said Grace with a slight frown, 'you must put it away, my dear, and let us have no more impropriety. I cannot think what came over me on the

Heath to permit you the familiarities not even my husband may claim in a public place.'

'But in all honesty, you cannot deny that you very thoroughly enjoyed it, Grace my dear,' said he.

'Then I am ashamed of myself,' she said, 'put it away, I beg you, or I shall feel compelled to leave the room.'

At that Monty tucked his rampant shaft under his sticky shirt and did up his buttons. Thus appeased, Grace sat beside him on the sofa and poured a cup of tea for herself.

'Your remark about a husband's claim on your person is true,' said Monty. 'The rights of a husband consist in raising up your nightgown in bed at night and having you on your back. This he may do every night if he wishes, and several times a night if his strength runs to it. Moreover, he has the right to take you upstairs on Sunday afternoons for an hour's lie-down, when only the outer garments are removed and the pair of you rest on top of the bedclothes, whereupon he gives you a good feel through the slit of your drawers and pulls up his shirt to lie on your belly and give you a good poking.'

'And what then?' Grace asked. 'What point is it you make?'

'Why, this point,' cried Monty, 'the rights of a woman's dear and loving brother are in all respects different from those of her husband. For him there is no marital bed to share with his sister, but in compensation for that, his is the right to take every opportunity that serves, indoors and outdoors, to stroke her titties and feel her pussy, as a sign and a token of his fraternal love for her.'

'What a fib!' Grace exclaimed, seeing where his words were leading. 'You shall not touch me again!'

'It is your duty to yourself and your nature — the hot

nature you share with me — to let yourself be satisfied as often as I am able to oblige you. How your eyes lit up when I mentioned I had rogered a female friend six times in an evening! Your own words lay bare your heart — you wished that you could be poked six times — deny it if you dare!'

'It's true,' she whispered, her eyes downcast and her cheeks a pretty pink in her confusion. 'I cannot deny it, Monty.'

'Then let me feel you again,' he said, taking her hand.

'But are you sure that a brother has this right?' she asked, 'and why, if I may be allowed to ask, why is your interest so strong in me, Monty, when you have female friends in London to accommodate your lustful desires?'

'Why you, my dearest girl? I hardly know that myself,' he admitted, 'but I have found it wisest all my life to listen to the urges of my nature and obey them. That way lies happiness, in my experience. Feel here, and you will know how strongly my nature impels me towards you.'

So saying, he thrust her hand down the top of his trousers, until she touched his virile shaft, stiff as a broom handle. At the touch of it, Grace laughed and said he was talking nonsense — but in spite of this objection, she seemed to be interested in One-Eyed Jack. She undid Monty's buttons with her free hand so that she could raise his sticky shirt-front and pull out his shaft. She held it between thumb and finger and stared at it.

'I fear you are a sensualist, Monty my dear,' said she. 'You allow yourself to be in this reprehensible condition all too often. Arthur has made it plain to me many a time that the proper state for the male organ is a modest slackness and smallness, not this feverish and demanding engorgement.'

'Not if a fellow is in bed with a pretty girl,' said Monty.

'Only husbands and wives have a right to be in bed together,' she reprimanded him.

'Very well then, if your wish is to be so loyal a help-mate to Arthur. But as you have confessed to me — when you and he lie in bed together, his shaft rarely stands up hard. Mine, as you have reason to know, is like a ramrod for the best part of the day and much of the night.'

'Arthur's way is to lie close to me, belly to belly, with our nightclothes raised and his organ clasped between my thighs,' said Grace. 'Together we experience a divine harmony many hold to be superior to the coarse act of coition.'

This seemed to Monty to be rather less than she had formerly told him took place between her and her husband.

'Whoever believes that anything is superior to poking is an idiot,' said Monty. 'Shafts were made to fit into pussies, and pussies were made to take shafts — the whole scheme of creation testifies to that.'

'The animal creation,' Grace agreed, 'but we are humans and not to be likened to beasts, nor follow their ways.'

'I've never heard that argued before,' said Monty, changing tack to come at the harbour another way, 'lie here by me while you explain it in more detail.'

He changed position to lie along the sofa, and pulled Grace to lie facing him. While she held forth on the moral nature of Mankind, he pulled up her skirts between them, to uncover her drawers to her waist, so that her pussy was close to his shaft in her hand. He felt between her legs for her hairy pussy, and soon had his fingers in her to titillate her slippery nub.

'In the Oneida method, which Arthur has studied,' said

Grace, her voice a trifle shaky, 'it is forbidden to approach with a hand the spouse's private parts.'

'Really?' Monty said. 'Why is that? How else are the parts to be joined together easily but with the guidance of hands?'

'The handling of the parts is conducive to lust,' said she, 'and it is for that reason that boys and girls are forbidden to touch their own private parts, as you very well know.'

'I seem to recall you admitted to me on the Heath that only last night after Arthur had fallen asleep you played with your own pussy until you came off a time or two,' Monty accused her.

'No . . . no . . . I said no such thing . . .' she breathed faintly.

Her distress of mind did not cause her to cease stroking his shaft, or require her to ask him to take his hand from between her thighs, and so they lay lewdly handling each other. As he expected, Grace's body was responding strongly to his handling, and a sensual experience longer and more intense in enjoyment, was well under way.

He made it last a good twenty minutes, for there was no need to hurry — his ambition was to subjugate her entirely to his will. She lay with her thighs wide apart, the slow teasing of his fingers in her pussy causing her to savour to the full the somnolent voluptuousness she had never known before. His shaft stood full size in her hand, jerking to its own rhythm of lust, while Grace held it fast and stroked it in a slow rhythm.

'You are to come off now, Grace,' Monty said at last, when he judged her ready for it. 'Squeeze your pussy on my fingers and let it happen.'

'Not yet,' she sighed, 'don't end this ecstasy yet!'

'Very well,' he murmured, 'a sister has rights over her

dear brother too — including the right to be raised up to heavenly sensation whenever she wishes it.'

He continued his slow manipulation, feeling her shaking and sighing against him, Eventually there came a time when her body could tolerate no more of the intense sensations he was giving her. She exclaimed, *Monty*! sharply, and thrust her belly hard against him. Her back arched and her nervous system collapsed in frantic delight — while One-Eyed Jack jumped furiously and spat hot essence into her clasping hand.

When they had recovered themselves a little, Monty gave her his handkerchief to dry her hands, and tucked away his dwindled shaft. Since both found it most comfortable to lie on the sofa instead of sitting up in a decent and respectable manner, they remained lying while they continued their discourse about human sensuality, and whether it should be sternly repressed, as her husband claimed, or continuously indulged, as Monty professed.

Needless to relate, no conclusion was reached between them, nor was any intended, and when at last Monty became bored with the conversation, he ended it by telling his sister that she was an extremely pretty woman. That was most gratifying to her natural female vanity, and she made not the least objection when his hands found their way up inside her clothes to feel her bare titties. Indeed, she responded to praise of her person by unbuttoning his trousers again and taking hold of his shaft — which lengthened fast the longer he played with her loose and soft titties. Their hands titillated each other, whilst they lay silent with voluptuous thoughts and sensations.

'Let me bring you off again,' said Monty.

'I can't, so soon!' she said, but he shifted his position on the sofa to bring his face over her thighs and bent to kiss her through the slit of her drawers, and bury his nose in the curls of her pussy.

'Oh Monty!' she exclaimed. 'I've never been kissed there!'

'Then you have no possible thought of what you have missed.'

He was certain now that he had found the key to his sister's lubricity. He licked with the tip of his tongue along her wet slit and her thighs opened wide, even though she at first cried out that he must stop doing that to her. Then she submitted and he put the end of his tongue on the wet little button that stood exposed in her open pussy and licked gently. This soon aroused a tremulous motion of her belly and thighs, which grew stronger and stronger still.

She sighed and moaned and cried out, she rubbed furiously at his shaft, strained her thighs wider apart yet and cried out to be brought off! Now she was Monty's to take! He had her on her back in a trice and his belly flat on hers — and with a shaft as stiff as a rod of iron, he pushed in between the loose wet lips of her pussy, until he was right up her.

Grace was almost delirious with pleasure, and the inside of her pussy was slippery, smooth, clinging and very warm. Monty rogered her slowly and delicately, intent on savouring the strange emotions that arose within his breast from this act of forbidden intercourse. He wished to know once and for all if to have his sister was at all different from having another woman, such as his dearest Gwendolen.

He was constrained to admit to himself that he was enjoying the experience very greatly, but he could not determine whether this was because he was wild with desire for Grace herself, or whether it was because the pleasurable act he was performing was prohibited on pain of penalty by Church and State. Hoping to clear up this question, he took care to control himself, and make the poke a long and delicious one.

Only by slow and measured stages did he let his sensations rise towards the peak, all the while taking every advantage he could of Grace's body — feeling her titties under her chemise and rubbing his belly on her warm belly. He felt her wet pussy grip him tightly and she moaned, 'You shouldn't be rogering me, Monty . . . you know you mustn't . . . stop it, you beast . . . make me come off, please!'

He paid little attention to her gasping words, but continued his rhythmic poking until he felt an exquisite convulsion inside his belly and knew the crucial moment had come at last.

'Oh Grace, my dearest girl,' he murmured as his desire raced up his shaft, 'I'm fetching off in you!

He shot his sticky essence up her in hard spurts, and she at once cried out and writhed under him, until her spasms of bliss had exhausted her and she lay quaking and twitching. When he was able to arrange his thoughts, he concluded that the sensations of rogering a sister were heavenly in the extreme — even more delicious than doing it to Gwendolen — or any other woman he had poked.

This seemed to him strange, for though he had all his life been fond of Grace, in beauty of face and figure she could not be compared with lovely Gwendolen, moreover, for ingenuity and sheer delicious lustfulness, neither woman could be compared to Cecily Massingham. And even Cecily could not quite touch the depths of lewdness with which Minnie the skivvy could make his shaft stand hard in an instant. It was all most confusing, this question of how much of ecstasy was in the shaft and how much in the mind.

To the Devil with that, said Monty to himself, what need here is there of elaborate reasoning and speculation? The plain fact of the matter is that to roger dear Grace delights me far beyond mere words. She, too, feels something of the same, for she almost swooned in pleasure when she came off now. Therefore the sensible thing to do is to roger her again as soon as she comes to herself. And then again. After all, she has never been done six times in a row before, and I did promise her!

CHAPTER 9
The Diversions of a Rainy Evening

On the day after his visit to Putney to settle the question of how pleasurable it is to roger a sister, Monty found himself in the unusual plight of being on his own and at home all evening. Selwyn, now a regular subscriber to Mrs Massingham's intimate circle of friends, had gone to St John's Wood to receive at her hands another lesson in overcoming his moral weakness. Monty's next time to call upon her was not until Sunday afternoon, and he gave consideration to strolling round to Mrs Lee's to see if lovely seventeen-year old Emmy was available for an hour or so − assuming that no noble Lord had got there first!

Against that must be laid the objection that the end of the quarter was close and Monty's purse would remain thin until the next regular payment came to him from his banker. This made him reluctant to lay out a couple of gold sovereigns for the use of the girl's commodity, no matter how pretty it was. Furthermore, it had come on to rain, which always put hansom cabs in great demand, and he had no intention of walking through the rain to Margaret Street and back afterwards.

He decided to pass a quiet evening at home, and read

another chapter of the book on educational methods for young ladies he had bought in Soho. He donned his crimson smoking-jacket with the frogged front, and made himself comfortable in his armchair with a cheroot clenched between his teeth. The account of Lady Bumslapper's Academy soon gripped his attention, and he read on for an hour before he felt the need for refreshment. He rang to have hot water brought up, to make a glass or two of toddy with a bottle of old Jamaica he had in the sideboard.

Minnie brought him a jug of hot water from the kitchen and stood grinning at him.

'Well, minx?' said he. 'What has amused you?'

'Something I saw not ten minutes ago,' she said.

'And what, pray, was that?'

'I was going down the stairs from my room and I heard a sort of gasping noise,' she said.'

'What sort of gasping do you mean?'

'Well,' said Minnie, grinning again, 'I was outside your door when I heard it. It was quite loud — it made me wonder if you were all right. I nearly knocked on your door to ask, but then I thought to myself — what if he's got a young lady in there and is poking her on the sofa? He won't thank me to interrupt him if that's what he's at. So to be safe, I had a quick look through the keyhole, just to make sure you were all right.'

'Well, well,' Monty said, grinning back at her from where he sat in the armchair. 'I begin to catch your drift, Minnie. Tell me what you saw — I won't mind.'

'I saw you sitting in your armchair, like you are now,' she told him, 'only you were in a great state of agitation. You had a book in your hand, and your trousers were unbuttoned all the way down. Your dolly-whacker was sticking out, hard and stiff as a broom handle, and you

136

were rubbing it for dear life. Your face was flushed red, and your eyes were starting from your head, the way you stared at the page of your book. I could see your lips were moving, as if you were reading in a whisper to yourself.'

'You saw all this in one quick look?' asked Monty in a tone of sarcasm that was lost on the girl.

'That's right,' she agreed, 'I only looked for a second, not wanting to disturb you.'

'Then you saw no more?'

'Oh yes,' she said, 'I saw your hand increasing the speed of its rubbing, and a creamy white spend spurted out of your shaft with such force that it landed on the carpet a yard or more in front of your feet. You lay back in you chair listless, with your eyes closed, and the book fell from your hand. So I knew you were all right and went away.'

'You're a wicked girl to watch a gentleman amusing himself in the privacy of his own rooms,' said Monty with a grin. 'Suppose I were to report you to Mrs Gifford for eavesdropping?'

'And let her know what you get up to on your own?' Minnie retorted, 'apart from poking me, that is.'

'Naturally, I deny it,' said he, grinning wider still, 'it is a figment of your salacious imagination, Minnie.'

'But you leave traces,' she replied, returning his grin, and she pointed down at the carpet. Monty glanced in the direction of her finger and saw the dark stain where he had spattered it.

'I was reading some very provocative scenes of disciplining a young lady in a boarding school,' he said, 'and I allowed the feverish excitement it aroused to carry me away, to the result that you observed.'

'What a lecherous gentleman you are, Mr Standish,' Minnie said, taking two steps nearer to him. 'Your backside ought to be properly tanned for reading books like that!'

'I might enjoy that, to judge by what I read,' he retorted. 'Listen to this, Minnie.'

She stood with folded arms while he read aloud to her the passage that had affected him so strongly:

. . . trembling with terror, Cynthia tapped at the door, and when she heard Lady Bumslapper's voice, she went into the room where Her Ladyship awaited her. Her face was so stern, and her cold blue eyes shone with such severity, that Cynthia threw herself to her knees and, with sobs and cries, entreated her to spare her youth and inexperience.

'Enough of your complaining,' said Her Ladyship briskly, 'you understand perfectly well that your misconduct has been so very abominable that Miss Harriet felt unable to deal adequately with it, and has sent you to me for chastisement. This happens too often, my girl — I have been too lenient and forbearing.'

'But I have been punished already,' Cynthia sighed miserably, 'Miss Harriet has beaten me so hard that I cannot sit down.'

'Former smackings have achieved nothing in improving your behaviour,' Her Ladyship replied. 'I know full well you've had your skirts up round your waist to have your backside beaten to a blazing red often enough — this time you are to be taught how I deal with young ladies who offend against the school rules.'

So saying, she seized the girl's wrists and tied them with a long sash to a ring fitted to the wall. Then with another sash she blindfolded her hapless victim, whose flowing tears soaked quickly through the soft muslin over her eyes. Poor Cynthia was helpless, her back pressed to the wall and her arms lifted high above her head.

'I never gag the mouths of the young ladies sent to me to be chastised,' Her Ladyship explained, *'I prefer to hear all their shrieks of mortification.'*

With remorseless hands she removed the veils of modesty that protected Cynthia's young body. She opened the girl's blouse, and pulled down her chemise to bare her tender titties — and, as if inspired by the sight, she pulled up her skirts and pinned them about her slender waist. Not satisfied by even that act of indecency, she proceeded to untie the tape of poor Cynthia's drawers, and let them fall down her legs to her feet.

The outraged girl emitted a forlorn shriek, to feel the other woman's lustful hands roaming freely over her bare titties — and then the suck of a hot mouth at their youthful tips of pale pink! Nor was this to be the full extent of the molestation — for with flushed face and panting breath, Her Ladyship sank to her knees and pressed hot kisses to Cynthia's quaking belly . . .

'Lord! Is that what goes on in posh schools?' exclaimed the skivvy, her plain face a bright pink.

'So this book assures us,' he answered, and put his free hand under the hem of Minnie's frock and up between her legs, until his fingers were in her drawers and on her warm pussy.

'What do you think of a young lady's titties being handled by another woman?' he enquired.

'I doubt if there's that much difference to the girl, whether it's a man or another woman who feels her,' was Minnie's reply — to Monty's great surprise, 'that's enough of your hanky-panky, Mr Standish — I've got my work to do and no time for this.'

'Ah, but there's always time for a nice feel,' said he in a most winning way. 'Think of this, dear Minnie — in fifteen or twenty years no one will want to feel you, or me. So take all that life offers while you may and never turn away a friend's helping hand.'

'The things you say!' she exclaimed. 'It's no secret what you'd be doing to yourself if I weren't here – your trousers would be gaping open again, I'll be bound, and you'd be playing with your dolly-whacker.'

Monty's breathing grew shorter and with a trembling hand, he opened his smoking-jacket and unbuttoned his trousers. Minnie moved to stand between his parted knees and leaned forward to pull up his shirt-front until she had bared his belly. The attitude of her body brought her titties close to his face, and only a layer or two of thin clothing shielded those soft young danglers from his eager mouth. In her hand his uncovered shaft gave a vigorous bound.

'Lord, how it jumps!' she exclaimed. 'You've gone and put yourself in a worse state than before when I saw you through the keyhole. It'll cost you two shillings for a helping hand!'

At his nod she massaged One-Eyed Jack with cunning, unaware that Monty's ambitions were ranging further than her offer. He raised her clothes in front and tucked them up round her waist, held in her apron strings. Through the slit of her drawers his fingers sought her pussy and teased shrewdly at her wet button, stirring her emotions to outpace his own. She began to gasp and sigh and press her cheek close to his, the passes of her hand on him quickening in proportion as her sensations grew – but she was no match for Monty in this game.

'I'm coming off!' she cried. 'I can't help myself!'

As her spasms began and her parted legs shook under her, Monty seized her with his free hand, and pulled her down to sit bow-legged across his thighs. His hand was down between their bodies, to take One-Eyed Jack from her hot grasp and guide him in through her drawers and into her pussy, for he was not very far from fetching off himself.

As events proved, Minnie had provoked his emotions much too strongly for his stratagem to be successful — at the moment he insinuated his throbbing shaft into her drawers, the familiar sensations started in his belly. The time to go further was not at his disposal — he gave a long sigh and his hand raced along his shaft as he came off on the girl's thin belly in a raging flood, his hot essence spurting over her pussy, not into it. She wriggled and heaved and kicked, but he held her firmly down across his lap until he had finished completely.

'You beast!' she cried when he released her and she at last rose to her feet. 'You've wet my drawers! Look at that!'

'Then you shall have two shillings and sixpence,' said Monty, pleased that he could have much the same entertainment in his digs as at Mrs Lee's, and at a fraction of the cost.

'That's all right, then,' said Minnie, smiling again, 'you're a gentleman, Mr Standish.'

'And you're a lickerish little minx,' he answered, determined to get his money's worth. 'I'll swear to it that you play with your pussy every night before you go to sleep — am I right?'

'What I do at night in my bed is no concern at all of yours, if you're not there,' she retorted.

'Then I may make it my concern,' he said, 'I shall creep up the attic stairs when the house is dark and everyone asleep, to get into your bed and roger you through the night. What do you say to that, miss?'

'I'm only a poor servant-girl and I can't be giving anything away for nothing to randy gentlemen,' said she. 'And besides, there are creaky boards in the attic stairs — Mr Courtney-Stoke would be sure to hear you and make a report to the landlady. I'd lose my position if she knew what I let you do to me.'

'I don't expect to have the use of your pussy for nothing,' said Monty. 'Haven't I always paid fair and square?'

'That you have,' she acknowledged.

'And as for Mr Courtney-Stoke, you need have no anxiety on that score, Minnie. He and I have become friends and he would never say a word to Mrs Gifford if he heard me on the stairs.'

'I saw you poking his sister,' Minnie said slyly. 'First you had her on her back and then she had you on your back. Where was Mr Courtney-Stoke while that was going on?'

'He'd gone out to keep an appointment, but he gave me the use of his bedroom,' said Monty.

'And the use of his sister,' Minnie added with a grin. 'Is he still doing her himself? Are you both having her now?'

'Mrs Fanshawe is mine now,' Monty explained. 'Her brother has made a new female acquaintance in North London.'

During this conversational exchange, Minnie had kept her seat across Monty's thighs, her clothes hitched up to show her white drawers and stockings. His trousers still gaped wide and his limp shaft lay in full view. He parted the slit of her drawers again to look at her brown-haired pussy and run his fingertips along the lips.

'Look at this plaything,' he said with a broad grin. 'You've the lewdest-looking pussy I've ever seen, Minnie — have I told you that before?'

'It's the same as every other,' she replied, not following his meaning at all. 'I know a rhyme about it — do you want me to say it?'

'Yes, do!' he cried, slipping two fingers into her wet slit.

Minnie paused to collect her thoughts and then recited:

'Pussy's a greedy unsatisfied glutton,
Girls are all ready to offer their mutton,
Finger them, roger them, do as you please,
Make them come off till you put them at ease;
Lick her and suck her and poke her galore,
A pussy's so greedy she'll soon pout for more.'

Monty laughed aloud while he fingered Minnie's most intimate portion and explained what he meant.

'Yours is by no means the same as every other,' he told her, 'nor are any two ever alike, take it from me, and I've seen a few, believe me. Some pussies have a maidenly look about them, even if they're been poked to a standstill not five minutes before.'

In this he was thinking of Miss Emmy at Mrs Lee's house, whose exquisite flower of female beauty he and Naunton Cox had rogered lavishly. Wet with the dew of Miss Emmy's desire, and brimming over with the creamy spend of the two men, the soft pink lips framed in nut-brown curls that nestled between white thighs had still preserved an unspoilt virginal appearance.

'Others have a plump and comfortable look about them,' Monty went on, his thoughts straying to his dearest sister Grace at Putney, 'and this may belie the truth, for sometimes a matronly aspect conceals the most sublime pleasure when a chap gets his shaft in.'

Whilst he held forth thus on the individual merits of female parts, Monty was watching his moist fingers sliding in and out of Minnie, to tease the sensitive little nub at the apex of the fleshy lips.

'Yours is a particularly interesting specimen,' said he, 'for as I said before, it has this astonishingly lewd look about it — how I cannot say, but no man could gaze on it without at once growing stiff and wanting to get into it.'

'Oh my!' Minnie sighed in delight under his touch, the cheeks of her bottom squirming on his lap. Faster and faster he rubbed and the girl's breath came in short gasps.

'Oh yes — make me come off . . . Oh my saints, yes!'

'Not so fast, hoyden,' Monty cried. 'You shall come off when I do myself!'

He gripped her waist between both hands and lifted her from his thighs, then set her down again a few inches closer to his belly — and in her aroused condition Minnie knew at once what was required of her. She grasped his stiff shaft as he set her down and steered its head into her wet pussy, and her descent to his lap pushed it home in her to the limit.

'Good girl!' said Monty. 'Now you may come off!'

With her hands on his shoulders, Minnie jerked and shuddered in a flurry of wriggling hips and quivering thighs, seeming to lose control of her limbs. Monty kept his hold on her waist to stop her from sliding off his shaft in her spasms of ecstasy. A moment or two later her writhings brought him off, too, and he sighed joyfully at the sensations of his essence shooting up in her pussy.

When she had quietened down, she grinned at him, her face red from her pleasurable efforts, and perspiration on her brow.

'Lord, Mr Standish,' she said, 'what with Mrs Gifford having me every night and you having me all day, I shall be a rag and fit for nothing before long!'

'What?' Monty exclaimed. 'Mrs Gifford has you at night? Is this true?'

'That slipped out as shouldn't,' said Minnie. 'Promise me you'll never repeat it to a living soul!'

'You may trust me completely,' said Monty. 'Your

secret is as safe with me as mine is with you — poking Mrs Fanshawe, I mean. But tell me the whole affair, Minnie — I find it not easy to believe that our respectable landlady has a taste for girls.'

The tale that Minnie related to him was astounding. The idea that women made love to women was familiar enough to him, this pleasant diversion being a theme in many of the books he bought in Greek Street. Nor was his acquaintance confined merely to literature, for he had actually seen it done a time or two in a house in Kings Cross he had gone to with Naunton Cox. Here it was a speciality of the house for the girls to bring each other off by hand, to provoke the men watching into taking them upstairs for a poke. But that Mrs Gifford, the quiet-mannered landlady of Seymour Place, should play the fingering game with her skivvy — that was the astonishing thing.

Minnie explained that her instructions were to take a cup of hot cocoa to Mrs Gifford at ten every night, when she had gone to bed. Minnie would wait at the bedside while her employer drank the cocoa, so that she could return the cup to the kitchen and wash it. The same routine was followed each night — Mrs Gifford would put down the empty cup and saucer and throw aside the bedclothes, to reveal herself with her nightgown up round her neck, and everything on show.

'She has a full bosom,' said Monty thoughtfully, as he tried to picture the scene to himself.

'Yes, she's got big titties,' agreed Minnie, 'but they flop about when her stays are off and they're bare.'

What took place next, she told Monty, was that Minnie would get down on her knees by the bed and suck Mrs Gifford's titties, sometimes for the longest time. When the landlady had had her fill of that, she pushed Minnie's head down her belly towards her thighs.

'What sort of pussy has she?' Monty asked.

'Big and fat,' said Minnie, 'and very hairy.'

'My word!' Monty exclaimed, and his shaft twitched as if it would grow long and stiff again.

Minnie would lick Mrs Gifford a few times, and then slide her fingers into her moist groove. Mrs Gifford's belly would quiver to the darts of sensation through it, and she would urge Minnie to 'do her like that, there's a good girl!' Minnie was clever at finger play, having practised this form of enjoyment since she was a child, alone and with others. She was soon able to bring the landlady to seventh heaven by her attentions.

'She comes off very noisy,' said Minnie. 'I wonder you don't hear her upstairs!'

'I am rarely in by ten o'clock,' Monty pointed out. 'But as I am this evening, I shall listen out for the cry. You cover her and leave her to sleep then, do you, after she has come off?'

'Bless you, no!' said Minnie. 'That's only the beginning. As soon as she's got her breath back she wants to have a go at me. She makes me take my drawers down and lie on the bed with my legs open while she plays with my pussy. Oh, she's a Devil when she starts — she tickles and touches and teases till she has me wriggling all over the bed on my back. Once won't do for her — she fetches me off never less than five times in a row before she's ready to be done herself again.'

'Still waters run deep!' said Monty. 'Who would ever have thought it of our respectable Mrs Gifford!'

By now his shaft was fully hard-on again and pressing itself against Minnie's belly, inside her open drawers. He stroked her thighs softly, urging her to continue her fascinating tale, and she told him how she was made to lie on the bed, face down, between Mrs Gifford's spread legs. She would open the wet pussy before her and touch her tongue to the slippery button within.

'How her pussy jerks up to meet my tongue!' she told Monty, 'and how she pushes her thighs wider apart yet! I give her a slow tonguing, the way she likes it, and I keep her waiting for her coming off till she squeals and rolls about and pulls her pussy wide open for me to lick. When I bring her off at last, she heaves her backside right up off the bed and sets up an almighty squealing — if you're listening tonight you'll hear it for sure! After that she tells me to kiss her goodnight and go to bed — and not forget to wash up the cup and saucer first!'

'By George!' Monty gasped. 'You've given me a hard-on stand with your tale that there's only one cure for!'

He pushed Minnie from his lap, leapt up and dragged her by the hand into his bedroom.

'Off with your clothes!' he cried, flinging aside his jacket and shirt and fumbling to remove his trousers. Minnie, her eyes shining lewdly, untied her apron strings and heaved her frock and her chemise over her head. Off came her drawers in a trice and she flung herself backward on Monty's bed clad only in her coarse black stockings.

Monty placed her on her back, with her bottom protruding over the edge of the bed, her thighs stretched wide open, and her legs resting on his shoulders. Seen close to and naked, Minnie could not be said to be a well-favoured girl. Her arms and legs were thin from insufficient to eat all her life, and although she was not yet eighteen, her titties already hung slackly from over-much handling. There was a slackness about the wet lips of her pussy that also spoke of constant usage, and the tufts of light brown hair under her arms exactly matched the hair with which her slit was sparsely furnished.

However, a man with a hard-on standing shaft has no

time to consider niceties of appearance, and Monty was indifferent to whether Minnie was plain or not – the important consideration was her willingness to lie on her back for him and let him make urgent use of her female commodity. She grinned up at him red-faced, and he drove his stiff shaft in between the hairy lips of her pussy.

From the position he had chosen for poking, standing and leaning over her, Monty had given himself a full view of their joined parts.

'Minnie!' he gasped, 'I'm going to watch myself roger you! What do you think of that?'

'My, it feels nice, your big fat dolly-whacker up me!' she sighed. 'I hope you don't think you're getting all this for half a crown, Mr Standish!'

'A first-class poke and you shall have five shillings!' said he, swinging his hips to drive his shaft in and out of her. The sight of his shining wet flesh slipping between the clinging lips affected him strongly, and very soon he was near the end of his course.

'What a magnificent sight, a hard shaft up a pussy!' Monty murmured, his legs shaking under him. 'I'm in you to the hilt, Minnie, and it won't be long now! Are you ready to come off?'

''Anytime!' she cried. 'Anytime at all!'

She moaned and sighed and bounced herself upward to meet his fierce thrusts and Monty heaved backward and forward with all his might, leaning right forward over her to drive deeper into her lean belly.

'It's all up inside me!' she cried, her eyes bulging at the sight. 'You'll burst me wide open!'

Monty grinned and fetched off copiously, filling her pussy to brimming with his hot flood.

CHAPTER 10
A Husband Deceived

When Selwyn informed Monty that he planned to pass the weekend with his sister and her husband at Reading and invited him to accompany him, Monty was delighted. They made an arrangement to meet on Friday at five o'clock at Paddington station. Selwyn proceeded there directly from his place of employment, while Monty took a cab from Seymour Place, bearing a hand-grip with a change or two of clothes, and Selwyn's luggage in addition.

The journey was passed pleasantly in talk and reminiscence of Cecily and Gwendolen, and from Reading station it was a twenty minute drive by hansom cab to the Fanshawe residence. It was a large house set in gardens of its own, the home of a man of substance, in Monty's estimation. He was eager to lay eyes on Gwendolen's husband, to learn something of the man whom he was cuckolding and so increase his own satisfaction in making good use of the man's wife.

Mr Fanshawe proved to be a man approaching forty, older than Monty had expected, a short and somewhat portly person whose brown hair was fast thinning. His manner was cordial and his welcome to Selwyn's friend seemed genuine enough. Over a lavish dinner they chatted inconsequentially and afterwards adjourned to the billiard room for a game or two. Selwyn appeared to be quite eager to play and, seizing an unlooked-for opportunity, Monty professed himself ignorant of the game. Instead of taking him on at once for a cash bet, as he had expected, Fanshawe dismissed him with a faintly insulting smile.

Seeing her husband and brother settling down to a session of billiards, Gwendolen proposed taking Monty to the conservatory for a game of two-handed whist and to this Mr Fanshawe gave ready assent. The conservatory adjoined the rear of the house with a view over lawns and a rose garden. It was lit by lamps, the gaslight not having been carried through from the house, and a golden glow suffused the many potted plants and shrubs. In these Monty had no interest and as soon as the door closed behind him he turned and took Gwendolen in his arms.

'My dearest, I must kiss you!' he murmured. 'All day long I have been yearning for an opportunity to hold you close to me and feel the trembling of your graceful body against mine!'

'And I, too, have been sick with longing for you,' she replied, her hands on his waist and her face up-turned to be kissed.

Monty's hands slid down her back until he was clasping the cheeks of her bottom through her clothes and pressing her belly hard against him. Her beautiful face coloured faintly when she became fully aware of the strength of his hard-on shaft trapped between them.

'Oh Monty!' she sighed, almost swooning from the intensity of her emotions, her eyes half-closed in bliss while he got his hand under her skirts at the back and raised them, to get into her drawers and treat himself to a good feel of her soft round cheeks. 'Oh, if only we dared!'

'With you, my dearest girl, I dare all!' he declared, his fingers probing between her legs from behind to touch the lips of her pussy.

Inside his trousers his shaft was throbbing furiously to call attention to its urgent needs. Gwendolen sighed to feel the motion against her belly, muffled though it was by layers of clothing, and Monty took her hand and pressed it lovingly against his trousers. At once she ripped open his buttons and delved deep inside, her fingers closing eagerly round his six inches of hard and jerking flesh.

'Monty — it is madness to think of doing anything here!' she said, with a short sigh. 'Suppose we are seen!'

'I am too deeply in love with you to behave prudently,' Monty answered, 'I've got to have you, Gwendolen or I shall come off in your hand!'

'Then so you shall, dearest!' she cried, her hand skimming up and down One-Eyed Jack in her anxiety to please, 'I shall stroke your darling shaft until it pours out its hot tribute for me!'

There was a new note in her voice, for Monty's hands had moved round under her clothes to feel her from the front, and already a knowing finger was in her moist pussy to tickle her button.

'Oh yes, yes!' she sighed, thrown into delight by this touch on her most sensitive portion. 'Bring me off, too!'

'I'm going to have you!' he sighed. 'Nothing less will ease the tension of my nerves.'

'No, that's out of the question!' she replied quickly. 'Not here and now, Monty, I beg you. Be satisfied with my hand until bedtime — I will come to your room as soon as Elliot is asleep, I promise you!'

'Yes, come to my room tonight,' he said, not believing such a meeting was possible, 'come as soon as you are able, and I will roger you to glory all the night!'

'I will be with you by eleven and stay for as long as you want me,' she murmured, her hand busy at his shaft to relieve him of his desire quickly.

In this intention she had mistaken her man — Monty was not at all persuaded to accept the pleasures of her dainty hand and trust that she could get away from her husband later to bestow upon him the supreme joy. The old saying advises that *A bird in the hand is worth two in the bush*, and although Monty's cock robin was in her hand, he wanted it in her bush. He thrust a hand into his trousers to remove his shaft from Gwendolen's manipulating hand, brought it out into the open, and guided it up between her legs.

Her pussy was open and ready for him, but with two fingers he stretched it wider still before pressing his swollen-headed and quivering shaft in to the quick. Gwendolen gasped at the sensation and threw her arms about him, resigning herself to being poked against the glass door of the conservatory.

'You are taking advantage of my loving nature to put me at risk if someone should come looking for us,' she whispered.

'I have the right!' he said, and to impress her he adapted the words he had used to cajole his sister Grace, or as near as he could recall them when he wanted to sample the pleasures of incest with her.

'It is the right of a lover to seize every opportunity that serves him, both indoors and outdoors, to stroke his darling's titties and feel her pussy, as a token of his undying love, and to roger her in whatever attitude is convenient, by day and by night. And it is the bounden duty of a beloved mistress to let her lover satisfy her, and himself, as often as the letch takes him. Surely you understand that, my angel-girl?'

'Oh yes, I understand fully!' Gwendolen murmured, and by then she no longer cared whether her husband found her being poked in the conservatory. Monty was pumping in and out strongly, and he had slipped his hands behind her to steady her by grasping the cheeks of her bottom. Gwendolen raised her mouth to his in a lasting kiss, and pushed against him to meet his thrusts.

'Oh bliss!' she sighed into his open mouth, and he echoed her words back into hers. Each time he jerked forward he felt his hardness slide into her, and each time he pulled back he felt the slither of her wet pussy along his throbbing shaft. He gasped in the delight of sharing the fierce palpitations of pleasure that surged through Gwendolen's body, giving rise to regular contractions of the velvet channel that held him in its loving grip.

She moaned into his mouth and begged him to bring her off — she who three minutes earlier had been fearful to let him sink his shaft into her in case they were discovered! Monty panted and poked harder, until she shook like a leaf in his grasp. A tiny scream escaped her lips and a long spasm shook her at the instant his triumphant desire gushed into her in thick jets. He held her tight while he flooded her darling pussy, she clinging to his shoulders with her fingernails in her excess of delight until she was spent and sank against him with a deep sigh of satisfaction.

They returned in due course to the billiard room, to find the game still in progress, Selwyn being as fanatic a player as his brother-in-law. At ten o'clock Mr Fanshawe drew the proceedings to a close and the party adjourned to the sitting room to partake of a light supper

— cold meat sandwiches with cocoa or tea. Goodnights were said and at ten-thirty all were in their rooms for the night. While Monty undressed for bed he wondered if Mr Fanshawe had brought the evening to a close early because he had a desire to poke his wife. 'At least he uses a different entrance to the one that received me in the conservatory,' our incorrigible hero thought.

He had brought with him in his luggage the book that had on more than one occasion affected him strongly by the very frank report it gave of stirring events at Lady Bumslapper's Boarding School for Young Ladies. Lying in bed with his night shirt tucked up to his middle and a hand on his twitching shaft, he read on:

. . . while Millicent was thus recounting with sighs and sobs to her dear friend Evangeline her sufferings and the outrage of her modesty at the hands of Miss Harriet, a hand was creeping furtively in between the sheets from the side of the bed. When Millicent least expected it, Evangeline's shameless little hand slipped under her chaste nightgown, and between her legs!

Before she could give utterance to the protest that rose at once within her bosom, the hand had hold of her pussy! Nor was that the total extent of these unwarranted depredations — for Evangeline inserted a skilful finger into the sensitive spot at the top of Millicent's hairy little slit!

Millicent trembled mightily and would have moaned, but her treacherous friend threw herself on her, and closed her mouth with a passionate kiss! The busy finger in her pussy tickled her hidden nub into an unwanted moistness of arousal, and tears coursed down Millicent's cheeks. How she had been abused and misused by Her Ladyship! And by Miss Harriet! And now by one she had trusted!

Try as she might to keep her thighs together, she felt them slide apart of their own will, as if inviting Evangeline to do whatever she chose to the maidenly body of her helpless victim. Spasms of shameful pleasure throbbed through Millicent's belly to the manipulation of Evangeline's finger, and in her heart was the humiliating knowledge that in another moment or two she would be brought off by the interfering hand between her legs!

It was too much for a gently bred and tenderly nurtured girl to bear! In the course of a single day she had been made to come off no less than eighteen times, by Miss Harriet and by Her Ladyship, singly and jointly! And now she must bear this undreamed-of renewal of the ravishment of her person by someone she had believed to be a true friend!

Evangeline had so aroused her that Millicent no longer knew what she did. Her groping little hands shook as if in a fever, as they found their way up under Evangeline's loose nightgown, to grasp at her unreliable friend's titties and feel them.

'Millicent, give them a good squeeze while I bring you off a time or two,' Evangeline murmured. 'Then you shall do me!'

So it was not to be once only! Evangeline was of a mind to repeat this shameful practice several times before leaving her alone! At the realisation of what lay in store for her at the hands of the other girl, Millicent felt her back rise from the bed beneath her, to push her belly and her wet pussy up hard to Evangeline's ministering hand. The overwhelming sensations of coming off throbbed through her, and although she squirmed and gasped in the throes of ecstasy, she cried out to her friend:

'Evangeline — traitress! You have undone me — I shall never speak to you again!'

Monty's shaft was throbbing mightily in his hand when, to his astonishment the door of his room opened silently and Gwendolen entered. She was wearing a long dressing gown, close round the throat and descending to her feet, its thin silk outlining the glorious fullness of her figure. With a finger to her lips to enjoin silence, she glided across the room and seated herself on the side of his bed. By then Monty had hurriedly concealed his book between the pillows. He would have taken Gwendolen in his arms and embraced her fondly, but she prevented him while she gave an account of her presence that amazed him.

After first warning him that they must speak very softly, she explained to him that her husband was a martyr to neuralgia. He had broken off the billiards game when he felt some twinges of his old complaint, for which it had for years been his habit to take tincture of laudanum, to still the pain. Tonight Gwendolen had made up an extra-strong dose for him, she said, that would keep him asleep until morning. Thus released from her conjugal obligations, she had hurried to be with the man she loved!

Whilst Gwendolen was explaining all this to him, it seemed to Monty that the scene from his book was being enacted for him, with himself as a principal player. For, as Gwendolen gave him an assurance that her husband would not miss her from his side in the marriage bed that night, her hand crept in between the sheets. Monty lay on his back in speechless delight while the hand slipped between his uncovered legs. In another instant it had hold of his engorged dolly-whacker and was sliding along the shaft in a slow and delicious manipulation.

'What's this?' said Gwendolen. 'So hard and big! And scarce two hours have passed since you raised my skirts and did me in the conservatory! How your darling shaft quivers in my hand — as if bidding me welcome to your bed! Oh Monty — what pleasure shall be ours this night!'

'My dearest girl!' Monty murmured, hardly able to speak.

'But why is your nightshirt round your waist?' Gwendolen enquired, her soft hand exploring further in the bed. 'Why were you lying here with your hard-on shaft uncovered? What were you doing, Monty? I insist on being told!'

'I was thinking of you, my dear one,' he said, 'and all the pleasure we had together in the conservatory! At that memory of delight, my shaft bounded and stood up! That is the effect your beauty has on me!'

'The dear sweet thing!' Gwendolen cooed, massaging it with affection. 'How I love to feel it jumping in my hand.! But what made you so stiff, lying here alone?'

'You had promised to be with me tonight and I knew you would keep your promise. I was resting quietly and waiting patiently for your arrival, so that I might roger you to glory and back.'

Gwendolen moved closer and let him put his arms about her and press hot kisses to her lips and cheeks. His wandering hands confirmed that her long silk dressing gown was her only garment — beneath it there was no nightgown, no chemise, no drawers, no stockings — nothing but her warm soft perfumed flesh. With a sigh of bliss, he pulled the darling girl down to lie beside him while he gave her bottom a good feel through the silk. Then, opening her frail night-attire, he gave her breasts a very thorough feel indeed, until their buds were firm.

'Oh, my dear one, if only I had the words to tell you how much I love you!' he exclaimed, rubbing his shaft against her bare thigh while his hands played feverishly over her titties.

'And I you!' she replied in a soft and tender voice, and took his leaping shaft in her hand to soothe it while he played with the plump and pouting pussy between her open legs. Soon the touch of his fingers told him that its fleece of curls was as wet as the lips of her slit and his heart beat furiously at the thought that he would be inside his beloved in an instant.

He pulled his nightshirt over his head and threw it to the floor, to be as naked as she. She sighed blissfully when he lay on her belly, and with a careful hand she brought his trembling shaft to the mark and held it while he pushed in. He felt her shiver in delight as she accepted the full length and girth and, before he could begin to roger her, she clasped her hands round his waist to hold him still on her while she asked him a question.

'Monty, my dearest – if you were my husband, how often would you do this to me?'

'Very often,' he replied at once, letting his shaft rest quietly in the warm clasp of her pussy, 'why do you ask?'

'It is impossible for me to know the truth of what goes on between husbands and wives,' she said. 'Mr Fanshawe must be considered an eccentric, and his three times a week may not be in any way representative of other husbands. Until that divine day I met you it was my custom to visit London twice weekly to let Selwyn assuage my unsatisfied desires. Before I was married to Mr Fanshawe, and Selwyn and I lived with our parents, we did it every day, two or three times. You will see from this that I am confused over a simple matter.'

'It will be a great privilege for me to enlighten you,' Monty sighed, his hands playing with her titties while he rogered her very slowly and lightly. 'From the ardent urges of your nature you cannot be unaware that healthy young persons revel in the delights of love very frequently. If you and I were married, my dearest Gwendolen, we would do it together twice every night, and another twice during the day.'

'Oh how delightful that sounds to me!' she cried, lifting her loins to push back at him to meet his strengthening thrusts. 'With all my heart I wish it could be so! Twice a night, and in the afternoon sitting astride your lap in an armchair, and lying on the sofa for you after dinner with my legs apart! With all that bliss, my dearest, could you find the strength to poke me in bed in the mornings before we rise, after the tea has been brought in?'

'A time of day I love for a quick poke,' said he, smiling at her most flattering enthusiasm, while his heart overflowed with love and lust. His boisterous shaft leapt joyfully inside its warm lodging and spouted jets of thick essence, shaking Monty with rapture. Gwendolen gasped and shuddered beneath him, and told him no man had ever been so adored as he was!

She stayed with him until past three in the morning, and in that time he had her on her back and rogered her no fewer than five times. It was as well, for all day Saturday passed without the slightest chance for him to be alone with her for a moment. He lived in hope that Mr Fanshawe would take another draught of his medicine at bedtime and sleep soundly enough for Gwendolen to slip away from her marriage bed and join him for a frolic — but, alas, midnight passed and there was no sign of her.

Monty was sure the worst had befallen his darling girl — her husband was claiming his conjugal rights! Surely nothing else would have kept her from her lover's side! Into Monty's mind came a frightful vision of Gwendolen made to lie face down on her bed, her nightgown up round her waist and her exquisitely round bottom bared, whilst her pot-bellied husband stood behind her, his nightshirt hitched up, to push his unwanted shaft up the dear creature's knot-hole!

To banish this atrocious vision, Monty dragged his own nightshirt up to his chest and clasped his stiff shaft in his hand. He jerked One-Eyed Jack up and down angrily, willing Fanshawe to desist, but the picture in his head would not go away and cease to trouble him. In his mind's eye he could see Fanshawe holding Gwendolen by the hips as he thrust in and out, she biting her lips, it seemed to Monty, in her humiliation.

Strangely, the vision in his heated mind served only to make Monty even more aroused than before and his shaft bounded in his clasping hand. *Fanshawe, you cad — I order you to cease and desist this instant*, Monty gasped out loud, hardly knowing what he did or said. *Stop it, you beast — I forbid you to come off in my dearest Gwendolen's bottom!* But his angry words were to no purpose, for they could have no influence on Mr Fanshawe's acts of conjugal connection, whatever they were that night.

In order to drive away with the power of his imagination the scene that haunted his heated brain, Monty pretended to himself that he was bodily in the room where Fanshawe was abusing his wife. He saw himself take hold of his hated rival to drag him off that smooth round bottom he was so cruelly misusing but, to his surprise, Fanshawe was the stronger and kept his position. By main force Monty rolled Gwendolen over on her side and flung himself on the bed beside her. In another instant, to her shrieks of joy, his shaft was deep in her welcoming pussy and he was rogering her with might and main. So, too, was Fanshawe, who had not been dislodged by this manoeuvre and the two men rogered her strongly, fore and aft, matching stroke for stroke. *Leave her, you bounder*. Monty said furiously over her shoulder to Fanshawe, but the latter grinned a vile grin and continued. In the heat of the moment Monty was unaware that his hand was racing up and down his shaft, until without a tremor of warning, One-Eyed Jack spurted his hot and sticky essence over Monty's belly.

On Sunday morning they all went to church together, Mr and Mrs Fanshawe, Selwyn and Monty. Gwendolen looked fetching in a new bonnet and a frock of darkest blue, and Monty felt that his temperature was rising by the hour in his frustration. Selwyn and he were due to catch the five-thirty train back to town, and there seemed no hope left that he could be alone with his beloved in the short time available. Monty's staff stood hot and throbbing in his trousers all through luncheon and tormented him with unsatisfied desire and secret thoughts of sliding through the slit of Gwendolen's drawers and into her dark-haired pussy.

Despair was in Monty's heart, but in all this he had reckoned without Gwendolen's equally hot desire for him. She, the dear charming creature, hot-natured and inventive as she was, found a way to slake his lust. In the front parlour Mr Fanshawe held forth to the assembled company on the criminal folly of taxing honest citizens to teach reading and writing to the children of the labouring classes and so giving them thoughts above their station in life. As a loyal employee of the Board of Education Selwyn argued strongly in favour of universal schooling, and the argument between the two of them swung back and forth while Monty and Gwendolen exchanged longing glances across the room.

By three o'clock, replete with a heavy lunch, Mr Fanshawe was dozing in his armchair but Selwyn was still in good voice and continued to press his case, whether he was heard or not. A nod of Gwendolen's head invited Monty to join her by the window, he nothing loth to quit Selwyn's vehement and radical nonsense and Mr Fanshawe's ignorantly dismissive half-snoring. At the open window Gwendolen and he stood side by side, close together, to gaze out into the well-kept garden. Moving cautiously so as not to disturb Selwyn or Mr Fanshawe, Monty caught Gwendolen's hand and pressed it lightly to the long hard bulge in his trousers. She smiled and glanced over her shoulder at her somnolent husband and her brother on the other of the room and then, greatly daring, she slowly undid every one of Monty's trouser buttons and pulled up his shirt and took out his hot and hard shaft. He sighed softly to feel the delicious sensations set stirring in him by the gentle rubbing of her hand.

'Gwendolen, my dearest, I adore you beyond life itself!' he whispered to her, gazing in admiration and delight at her face, so calm and so beautiful as she stared down to see the effect of her ministrations on One-Eyed Jack.

'And I adore you, my dearest boy,' she whispered back, her head close to his head, and the beat of her hand on his swollen shaft firmer and faster, 'I shall come to London on Tuesday — be ready for me by eleven in the morning and I wish to stay in bed with you all day long. How many times will you do me — five or six. More perhaps? It can never be enough, however often you do it to me!'

At these loving words, the turbulent desire that had hold of Monty tightened with an irresistible force. The muscles of his belly clenched and he swayed on shaking legs, almost falling, as the hot elixir of his passion gushed out in a raging flood. So furious was the strength of his fetching off that his cream flew out through the open window and fell down into the flower bed below, bedewing the red roses.

Perhaps without knowing it he gasped at this supreme moment for, when he recovered himself, Gwendolen whispered to him and he turned to look over his shoulder. Mr Fanshawe was asleep in his chair, his mouth open and his hands clasped over his pot belly, but Selwyn was staring at them. Monty winked at him, and Selwyn made a gesture with his head to indicate the two of them should leave the room for somewhere more secure. Monty tucked his shrinking shaft in his trousers and buttoned up, and went with Gwendolen to the dining room next door, tiptoeing silently past her sleeping husband.

In the dining room Monty took his darling girl in his arms to shower kisses on her beautiful face. Then with a gentle touch, he laid her backwards on the well-polished mahogany table top and pulled up her clothes until he had a superb view of her shapely legs in their black stockings. With her own fair hands she parted the slit of her drawers for him and he stared enraptured at the lusciously pouting lips of her pussy, rose-pink and gaping open slightly between her profusion of dark curls.

She parted her legs wider and he was down on his knees at once, to press his lips to her treasure. He kissed it hotly and licked at it feverishly, to the great delight of Gwendolen who sighed and squirmed with pleasure. Soon Monty could no longer contain his bursting desire and, getting up on his feet, he brought his hot shaft to the charge. Without a pause, he thrust it right in the gaping pussy and laid forward over her belly.

'My darling boy!' Gwendolen sighed, heaving up her bottom as if she would roger him from below! Monty responded to her with a strong poking, whereupon they commenced upon a most exciting struggle, his manly shaft working in and out fiercely.

'You are the most delightful dish ever served up to me at a dining table!' he cried, feeling how the wet lips of her pussy seemed to cling to his shaft each time of withdrawal, as if afraid to lose so delightful a friend.

'And I have never been so well satisfied at table!' his dear girl exclaimed, greatly daring in her passions. 'Feed me, Monty — feed me with rich cream, to sustain me until Tuesday!'

Their furious sensations could not endure long, for a limit has been set by Divine Providence to the degree of stimulation the human organism can tolerate. Their movements became faster and faster, shaft and pussy meeting in a embrace that brought on a wild and convulsive release. Gwendolen half-fainted away in her beloved's arms, and Monty was in no better condition than she, sobbing with love and gratification until his passion was spent. He lay still for a while on Gwendolen's belly, feeling the trickle of creamy moisture that escaped from her pussy and wondered if there was time to do her again before Fanshawe woke up.

CHAPTER 11
Mrs Gifford is Taken by Surprise

After Gwendolen had been to London on Tuesday to share Monty's bed from eleven o'clock in the morning until five o'clock that same day, during which length of six hours she was poked nine times and brought off by hand thrice more, it was a day before Monty's natural vitality restored itself and he was ready for a renewed frolicking. The account Minnie had given him of her nightly exercises with the landlady had remained vivid in his thoughts, and he decided to take a part in Mrs Gifford's revels.

Minnie was at first reluctant to assist him in this, fearing that she might be dismissed from her position. Monty gave her a feel and half-a-crown and explained to her that he would see that no action was taken against her whatever happened, and this assurance settled her doubts. Between them they arranged how it was to be done that evening — she would tip him the wink when she was ready to take in Mrs Gifford's cup of cocoa and he was to let five or six minutes pass before following her.

The remainder of the day passed slowly after that, and Monty went out to dinner to occupy the evening hours until the time was right for the adventure. He dined and drank extremely well, and was in a dare-anything mood when he returned to Seymour Place just before ten o'clock. In the privacy of his bedroom he undressed and put on a clean nightshirt, then his slippers and dressing gown and sat down to wait patiently on the sofa in his sitting room, until he should be summoned.

He had not long to wait. A tap sounded at his door, and then Minnie put her head round it and winked at him. He nodded and set his pocket watch on the sofa-arm to count off the minutes. The house was silent and dark as he crept cautiously down the stairs. In the hallway he paused to listen, but no sound came to his ear from the landlady's quarters. He put his hand on the door knob of her sitting room and turned, then pushed the door open a crack. With relief he saw that the light was turned out and she had gone to bed.

He crossed the room carefully, not wishing to announce his presence by bumping into furniture in the dark. The door of the bedroom was ajar, for Minnie had left it so for him, and from beyond there fell enough light to guide him safely through the dangers. He stood close to the doorjamb and peeped in, to see what Mrs Gifford and the skivvy were about.

Little Minnie was fully clothed still, though she had removed her long apron. She was assisting the landlady to undress, and playing the part of a lady's maid very acceptably. She removed Mrs Gifford's green bombazine frock, underskirt and petticoat, and shortly had her stripped to her chemise. Then Mrs Gifford seated herself on the bedside and drew up her chemise to her lap, displaying white drawers with frills round the legs. While Minnie went down on her knees to roll down the stockings and hang them over the brass bedpost, Mrs Gifford undid the knot of her hair and let it hang loose, shining and dark, over her shoulders.

Monty could see Minnie's hands were under the chemise, inside Mrs Gifford's drawers, and he guessed that the landlady's pussy was being treated to a good feel. In a short time Mrs Gifford's face began to flush, whereupon she stood up and allowed Minnie to remove her chemise and assist her into her long white nightgown. In the interval between the chemise being taken off and the nightgown being put on, the landlady stood revealed in the gaslight in no more than her drawers, her body bare down to the waist.

She was a buxom woman of about five and thirty, blessed with a fine pair of titties, somewhat slackened by the years, but luscious enough still to cause Monty's shaft to stiffen to the full and twitch impatiently. He observed Minnie kneel again and feel up underneath the long nightgown, to take down Mrs Gifford's drawers. It would have been the work of a second or two, but Minnie remained in that posture, as if in prayer, with her hands raised, for far longer than was needed to untie the bow of a pair of drawers and pull them down. By the sighs that escaped Mrs Gifford's lips and the manner in which she swayed on her feet it was evident that her pussy was being thoroughly felt once more.

When her drawers were finally removed she lay on her bed and drew her nightgown up to her belly button. Minnie was soon kneeling on the bed, fully dressed, her lean bottom in the air, her head between the wide-gaping legs of her mistress. For the benefit of Monty whom she knew to be watching, Minnie paused to gaze for some little time at Mrs Gifford's throbbing pussy and its bush of dark hair, so that he might take advantage of the situation to get a good look at it. Then she set her hand to it and plunged two fingers deep inside, causing the landlady to utter a little shriek of surprise and delight. She urged her servant to delay no longer, but to bring her off at once.

Minnie obediently bent her neck and brought her tongue to bear on the pussy she had titillated to a lustful impatience by the use of her fingers. Monty was in great agitation whilst he watched Mrs Gifford being licked so voluptuously. The sight was intensely arousing — Minnie's head down between the landlady's thighs and her wet tongue flickering at the exposed pussy! In a fever of impatience, Monty threw off his dressing gown to be ready when his moment came.

One-Eyed Jack was so big and hard that he was holding out the front of his nightshirt. Monty had no choice but to raise that to his waist, so that he could take hold of his quivering shaft to hold it still. He heard Mrs Gifford's gasping at the force of the fierce sensations she was enjoying beneath the darting caresses of Minnie's tongue. Her smooth bare legs kicked on the bed, announcing the supreme moment would speedily arrive.

Monty could hardly breath for his excitement. His body was ablaze with passion, and to cool himself he drew off his nightshirt and cast it to the floor. Delicious spasms racked him from top to toe, his clasped hand sliding up and down his shaft so gratifyingly that he knew he could not hold out much longer. Then Mrs Gifford gave a loud shriek and fell back on the bed, her belly heaving and her legs shaking to the throbbing of her climactic pleasure.

'I've come off, Minnie!' she gasped. 'It was lovely. — do me again!'

That was a signal for Monty to charge into action before he spent against the door. He held his jerking shaft in his hand while he sped to the bedside and pushed Minnie aside. She gave him a conspirator's grin, and yielded her place on the bed to him without demur. Monty, completely naked, his shaft as thick and hard as a rolling pin, leaned over the landlady's belly, staring down at her wet pussy with wolfish glee.

At this sudden and unexpected appearance, Mrs Gifford started upright in her bed. Her eyes were staring wildly and her mouth hung wide open in amazement and dismay to be caught out red-handed — and red-tongued! — in so intimate an embrace with the skivvy. Before there was any time for her to cry out in alarm, Monty took hold of her nightgown and hoisted it up over her slack titties. Mrs Gifford's body jerked, and it seemed as if her titties rolled towards his hands of their own accord.

She stared at Monty, struck speechless by the invasion of the privacy of her bed, whilst he handled the bulky softness of her titties with delight. He noted with pleasure that, although Minnie had brought her off not two minutes ago, the dark tip of each tittie stood up long and firm from its reddish-brown halo.

'Mr Standish — what can you be thinking of?' the landlady gasped, recovering the use of her voice at last. 'Do you mean to violate me in my own bed? Are you drunk?'

'Sober as a judge,' he assured her, with a singular lack of truth, 'and after what I've just seen done to you by Minnie my shaft's like an iron bar and I intend to roger you thoroughly.'

'What!' she cried. 'Do you think that you can burst into my private room and make casual use of my body? This is a foul outrage!'

Monty was fondling her with both hands, greedy for the feel of her soft warm flesh. He bent his neck and licked her buds one after the other and before she had time to renew her protests, he smiled up at her in his most winning way and made clear his point of view:

'Call it what you will, Hannah — I mean to have you!'

Whilst he had been occupied with Hannah Gifford's titties, Minnie had taken a seat on a padded chair in the corner of the bedroom. She was observing the proceedings on the bed with her customary irreverent amusement.

'Shall I run and get a policeman, Mrs Gifford?' she asked.

There was a pause while the landlady gave her consideration to the suggestion. At last she made up her mind.

'No! The shame of it would kill me, if it were known that I had been abused in my person by a man!' she said. 'Sit quiet, Minnie, and be ready to render aid when my fearful ordeal comes to an end!'

'Yes, Mrs Gifford,' said Minnie. 'Will he do you more than once, do you reckon?'

'Ah, Heaven protect me!' the landlady moaned, her plump legs wide open on either side of Monty, as he fondled her titties.

'You asked me what I was thinking of, Hannah my dear, to use you in this way,' said he. 'I shall tell you plainly — I am of the opinion that you are a hot-natured woman, who loves to be fetched off. Having no man to do it to you, who else can you employ for your gratification but Minnie? But if this became known amongst your neighbours here in Seymour Place, or by the parson and congregation of the church you attend so devoutly each Sunday, then you would never be able to hold up your head again for the infamy that would descend upon you. It is most fortunate that your secret has fallen into my hands and not those of a cad or a rotter, who might extort money from you for his silence.'

Hannah, blushing in the gaslight made no attempt to deny the truth of his words and only raised a note of pleading:

'Mr Standish — I am utterly at your mercy!' she exclaimed.

'You must call me Monty in bed,' said he jauntily. 'I mean to fill a void in your life, Hannah — the aching loneliness of an unmarried woman. And this I propose to do by filling the void between your legs.'

'Then you are a gentleman,' she said, 'and I trust myself to you without reserve.'

Monty set his mouth to her titties to tease them, whilst his hands felt up her legs, until he stroked her plump thighs.

'You seem to know your way about the female body,' said she, 'I've had my suspicions about you for a long time — I'd lay a pound to a penny that you've been taking advantage of Minnie. Speak the truth now!'

While she challenged him, her eyes were downcast, but it was not for reasons of modesty. She was staring at the stiff shaft that jutted boldly towards her, its unhooded head shiny purple in the gaslight. Monty thought the moment opportune to make a start with her and pushed her flat on the bed, dragging up her nightgown up over her head to bare all. She murmured a short protest at first, but her murmur turned to one of appreciation when he ran his hands over her plump belly, and her strong legs moved well apart to allow him free access.

'Mr Standish is a gentleman,' Minnie piped up from her chair in the corner, 'he wouldn't take advantage of a poor servant girl like me.'

'I've never known a young gentleman stay here yet who

didn't interfere with my servants,' Hannah retorted. 'Don't try to lie to me, girl — he's had his way with you more than once, I'll be bound! Watch out he doesn't give you a big belly!'

Minnie giggled, and Monty giggled, and then Hannah giggled too. Below her soft round belly, where the columns of her thighs joined, her fat and hairy pussy seemed to bestow a wink of welcome on Monty, as if to say: *Here's a grown-up pussy for you, not a young girl's tight little hole.* One-Eyed Jack jumped for joy when Monty parted the wet lips before him and burrowed a couple of fingers into Hannah to feel how slippy she was.

'Oh, Monty,' she murmured, 'put it up me, I beg you. I shall die of longing if you keep me waiting any longer.'

'There is no fear of that,' he answered. 'When I saw you on your back being fetched off by Minnie, the sight put me in such a state I very nearly came off in my hand and wet your carpet! I shall flood your pussy with my juices the instant I put my shaft into you!'

'Then do it!' she cried.

'Lord love us!' said Minnie to nobody in particular. 'One minute she's complaining about being raped and forced, and the next minute she's begging him to put it up her!'

With no more ado, Monty placed his twitching shaft to her wet pussy and pushed. He sank into her with the ease of a knife in a pound of best butter, until his bare belly was on hers. She sighed and wriggled her bottom under him, he laid hold of her titties and went at her briskly.

'Oh how delightful a feeling!' she cried, thrusting up her belly at him to meet his strokes. 'Roger me hard and fill me up to the brim — make my pussy overflow!'

The most intense emotions that the human organism

can bear possessed Monty at that moment. He plunged so forcefully into Hannah's hot slit that he reached the climax of voluptuousness very soon and flooded her with his spurting essence. She moaned and sighed and her belly shook under him to the spasms of her coming off.

'Lord, she does love it!' Monty heard Minnie exclaim. 'No sleep for any of us tonight, now she's got the feel of a shaft inside her! Ooooooh!'

He glanced round over his shoulder and saw that Minnie sat with her skirt pulled up in her lap and her hand between her open thighs to finger herself whilst she watched him roger the landlady. Her long moan had announced the moment of her coming off against her busy fingers.

'Well done, Minnie,' said he with an encouraging grin. 'Keep your pussy wet and ready, and we'll have you on the bed again before long.'

'What!' cried Hannah, pushing Monty off her naked body now that she was recovered a little from her culminating spasms. 'Do you think to give the orders here, in my bedroom, to my servant? Do you think that because you took me by surprise and ravished me, this confers on you the right to command me?'

'Hoity-toity!' he replied. 'I mean to start as I shall go on with you, Hannah. That you are by birth the owner of a pussy gives you no privileges other than those I allow you. Pussies are ten a penny, my dear, ten thousand women walk the London streets nightly offering the use of theirs for a few shillings. Privilege comes from the ownership of a male shaft like mine.'

He allowed her no time to complain further but thrust his hand between her thighs before she could clamp them together. He gripped the fleshy lips of her pussy between strong fingers, and pinched them together hard. Hannah gave a gasp of pain, but did not try to pull away from him.

'If I want Minnie to join us on the bed and suck my shaft or lick your pussy, then she shall do so,' he said.

'If this is your attitude toward me, you can go to your own rooms now,' Hannah warned him, her soft round belly squirming in discomfort at the tight grip of his fingers.

'My attitude is one of loving affection and unbridled lust, if you will let it be so,' he told her, 'as it was until you undertook to tell me what I must and must not do. You shall be either my dear female friend on whom I shall bestow continuous sensual delight, or you shall be a pussy I use when the mood takes me. You must choose now.

'I entreat you not to treat me with contempt, Monty,' she said softly. 'You cannot doubt that I wish to be your devoted female friend, with a pussy at your disposal whenever you want it. But leave Minnie where she is — we have no need of her. If you wish your shaft to be sucked, let me do it.'

'What do you say to that, Minnie?' Monty asked the skivvy in the corner chair. 'Do you wish to be made use of, mouth, pussy and the rest — or will you go to your bed and sleep?'

'I'll do whatever you tell me to, Mr Monty,' said the girl at once. 'I'd love to see you poke Mrs Gifford again — it gave me a real thrill to see somebody else besides me attending to her. And if you fancy me giving you a lick-off, just say the word.'

'You're a good girl, Minnie,' said Monty. 'Strip yourself off bare and come here and lie on the bed with us.'

'Ah, I see you mean to insult me!' said Hannah, displeased by his words and sulky of tone. She clapped her thighs together to make certain that Monty was in no doubt of her mood.

'Insult you?' said he, with a laugh. 'By no means! I mean not to insult you, but to roger you unconscious, as you will in a short time find out!'

'Where do you want me, Mr Monty?' asked Minnie, standing at the bedside naked.

Monty grinned at her obliging nature and reached out to touch the soft little pussy between her thin thighs and tickle it for a moment or two.

'Sit here on the bedside,' said he, 'and I will tell you what to do in a minute.

He turned to the landlady, lying in a silent sulk, seized her clamped thighs and wrenched them open. She brought her knees up to protect herself, but he was too strong for her and forced them wide apart so that her belly and hairy pussy lay readily exposed to his whims.

'Put three fingers up her pussy, Minnie, while I hold her,' he said. 'She may have gone dry while we've been talking, and I do so love a thoroughly wet pussy.'

Hannah protested at this new insult to her person, but could do nothing to prevent it. Monty watched in growing excitement to see Minnie's fingers inside Hannah's well-stretched lips, to tease at her pink nub.

'Stop it, Minnie!' Hannah commanded. 'Stop it this minute!'

'Why?' Minnie asked. 'You've made me do you like this two or three times a night since I've been working for you. Tonight was the same — you had me bring you off twice before Mr Monty burst in uninvited and gave you a good tousling. So why are you saying no to me now?'

'I will not be the plaything of a tenant and a servant-girl,' said Hannah with a sighing moan. 'Make her stop,

Monty — you are not a Turk and I am not your harem slave.'

'Scrumptious thought!' exclaimed Monty. 'I've got a book upstairs about a sultan in his harem — jolly exciting stuff, I can tell you. One night I'll bring it down and read it to you — we can try some of it out — what do you say to that?'

'You are a beast!' cried Hannah, 'Oh . . .!'

Minnie's sly fingers had done their work well and spasms of pure ecstasy seized Hannah and made her belly quake and rise as she came off. Immediately Monty was on her, thrusting his shaft into her twitching pussy while her throes still shook her body. To see her brought off had aroused him greatly and he lunged into her slippery split with verve.

'Go on — give her a good poking!' cried Minnie, her hand between his manly thighs to take hold of his pompoms and gently squeeze them.

Hannah sustained his strong lunging with an energy equal to his own, and returned his strokes with upheavals of her belly as eager as any man could wish for. With a cry of bliss, Monty gushed his ardent lust deep into her and she dissolved in joy to feel the sudden flow in her belly, and continued to come off even after Monty was finished and lay gasping on her.

'That's more like it,' said she faintly, when she could again speak, 'there is no need for Minnie to finger me off if you are going to roger me like that the rest of the night.'

This time Monty did not descend from the saddle. He lay on Hannah's belly, his shaft softening inside her but never being taken out. He played with her titties and told her of the deep delight she had given him. Meanwhile Minnie, seated beside him, fingered his knot-hole until his shaft grew strong again inside Hannah's pussy and he recommenced his rogering.

Monty prided himself on being a man of his word. He had told Hannah that he intended to roger her unconscious, and to prove that was more than empty words he remained ensconced on her soft belly between bouts while Minnie stimulated his interest by feeling his pompoms and between the cheeks of his bottom to make his shaft hard-on again. In this way, and by these means, in the space of half an hour he rogered Hannah three times more without ever dismounting, throwing her into noisy raptures at his performance.

After that feat, Monty lay on his back on the bed, his thighs wide apart to cool his pompoms, his limp dangler lolling wetly on his belly. Hannah also lay in languid contentment, her soft belly heaving gently and her legs open. From the plump lips of her hairy pussy a trickle of pearly essence escaped to run down to the bed sheet below as her well-filled belly brimmed over a little. Minnie lay trembling, her head resting on Monty's feet, for she had been so overcome by assisting him to roger Hannah that she had eased her nervous tension by hand at the same time and had come off as many times as had he and the landlady.

The first to recover from the soft fatigue that embraces all creatures in the sweet aftermath of love was Hannah. She raised herself on an elbow to gaze fondly at Monty's well-used shaft, showing her appreciation of its capability to thrill her by touching it fondly and tugging gently at it.

'If only it would stand up again!' said Monty, bestowing a friendly smile on her. 'I would poke you again gladly, Hannah — but I fear my bolt is shot for tonight!'

'Don't say that, my dear!' she cried. 'I want it again!'

Her ardent fingering had little effect, but before giving up as a hopeless task she told Minnie to see if she could achieve anything. With a grin, Minnie rolled on to her belly, took his shaft in her mouth and sucked strongly, all the while tickling his bung-hole with a finger pressed between the cheeks of his bottom. At last the limp little thing began to stir itself, whereupon Minnie tongued it lovingly until it stood straight again as a soldier at attention.

She raised her head to grin at Monty and her clasped hand slid up and down the swollen shaft, making it throb in amorous anticipation of the ecstasy to come.

'That's more like it,' said Hannah, keeping a close eye on the skivvy's progress, 'but stop now, girl — I don't want him finished off before he's properly begun.'

She pushed Minnie aside and took her place between Monty's legs, her hand about his shaft while she planted a brief kiss on the sticky purple head. She stared into his face with a look of deepest affection whilst her fingers circled his shaft and played up and down it until Monty was shaking and straining to fetch off.

'Ah, would you!' she exclaimed. 'I say you shall not! You shall not squirt your last few drops of sap wantonly over your belly, but into my pussy!'

So saying, she climbed over him, with her knees on either side. With shaking fingers she opened the wet lips of her pussy to display the slippery pink inside.

'Look at this,' she commanded him, 'see where your shaft is about to be plunged — in here, into my belly!'

She rubbed the engorged end of his shaft on her wet flesh, and Monty moaned in bliss to feel the sensations.

'You shall not go inside yet,' she said, 'not until you have rubbed my button a while to make me ready again.'

'Oh, Hannah,' Monty murmured, 'how delightful that

feels! I swear you will bring me off like that in another minute!'

'I will not let you cheat me by fetching off on my finger!' said she, seeing the near onset of his spasm.

She sat down hard on his shaft, driving it deep into herself.

'Minnie, squeeze my titties!' she ordered the watching girl, and at once Minnie squatted behind her over Monty's legs and slipped her arms about her. Monty watched with bulging eyes to see Hannah's big titties felt and rubbed, whilst Minnie's face stared at him over the landlady's shoulder.

No more than half a dozen jerks up and down by Hannah on his shaft were required to do the trick. Monty cried out as his hot essence spurted upwards and Hannah shrieked loudly and pumped him dry with her clinging pussy, while Minnie's fingers clenched in the flesh of her titties as if to screw them off. When it was over Monty lay under Hannah exhausted for the moment and she sat panting and perspiring on top of him.

Eventually she was helped to descend from her lofty perch by Minnie's arms round her to lie breathing slowly on her back. Minnie busied herself with her employer's comfort, wiping the perspiration from her belly and under her voluminous titties with a pair of drawers picked up from the floor, before wiping dry her sopping pussy. With the same pair of drawers she attended to Monty's shrunken shaft.

Completely content and worn out, Monty closed his eyes and felt himself sinking into a deep and refreshing sleep. The last thing he heard was Hannah's voice, speaking to Minnie:

'I've never before been poked as many times as tonight!' she said. 'Mr Standish is armed like a veritable

Goliath as to his person, and pussy-struck beyond words!
I mean to have him here night after night, until he rogers
me to death!'

'He'll wear your pussy out for you, that you can be
sure of,' the maid answered.

'I've got to have it again, Minnie,' said Hannah. 'Sit
here between my legs and bring me off with your fingers!'

CHAPTER 12
Selwyn Learns About the Female Nature

Two days after Monty's interesting evening in Hannah's bed Gwendolen visited London on her so-called shopping excursion. On this occasion she made no pretence of looking in shops — she took a cab straight from the railway station to Seymour Place and by eleven in the morning she and Monty were naked together in his bed. When she left, most reluctantly and with tears of sorrow at their parting, she had been as soundly done as any woman in the kingdom — five times by Monty's shaft, four times by his fingers, and three times by his tongue.

With sentimental agonies she confessed that she had not been able to find a suitable secret meeting-place in Reading for him to visit. He urged her to keep trying, for his desire for her gave him no rest by night or by day, he declared. Needless to relate, he said nothing of employing his energies on Cecily and Hannah Gifford, not to mention Minnie the skivvy.

Gwendolen kissed him in tearful farewell, vowing to him that the problem would be resolved, and sooner than he expected, for her love for him was too fierce to be denied, and *have* him she must, day after day and night after night. Monty played the sighing lover to perfection and when she had gone, went to bed again to sleep and rest until it was time for dinner.

The very next day, while he was at breakfast in his sitting room, Selwyn burst in waving in his hand a telegram that had just been delivered. It was from Gwendolen to her brother, and its message was brief but shocking – Mr Elliot Fanshawe had passed away in the night, and Selwyn's presence at Reading was urgently required to assist with the arrangements.

'You must be on the next train!' Monty cried, his emotions a mingling of satisfaction that Gwendolen was a widow and a free woman, and apprehension as to the manner of her husband's hasty demise. He suggested accompanying Selwyn to Reading, to comfort his grieving sister, but Selwyn thought that most improper and declared it to be a well-established social custom that a widow must needs abstain from sexual connection for some months.

Off he went, leaving a message to be delivered by hand to the Board of Education to account for his absence from his post for the next few days. He gave Monty his word to telegraph full details of the sad occurrence at Reading the instant he learnt the circumstances. He was as good as his word – in the early evening a telegram was delivered to Monty, and a perusal of it revealed that Mr Fanshawe had suffered heart failure.

The funeral was arranged for Friday, but both Selwyn and Mrs Fanshawe thought it wiser for Monty not to attend. Not that Monty had the least wish to be present – the information that so outwardly robust a person as Elliot Fanshawe had suffered heart failure had caused extreme vexation, for Monty was unable to put out of his mind the deduction that it was by using dear Gwendolen's lovely body for his vile pleasures that the

182

errant husband had overtaxed his heart and met his just desserts.

Nevertheless, jealous as he was, Monty would have liked the opportunity to see Gwendolen and get her alone long enough for a consoling poke or two. Since this was not to be, he set out to find diversions for the next days, awaiting Selwyn's return.

One afternoon he passed with Cecily, playing a lewd game of her devising, in which she dressed fully as a man, whilst he wore female clothing — stockings, drawers, chemise, and frock. By the time they had finished with each other, both declared themselves marvellously well satisfied. On two nights running Monty rogered the landlady in her bed, after Minnie had played her part in appeasing Mrs Gifford's appetite with fingers and lips. Two evenings were spent at Mrs Lee's with Miss Emmy, the first of the month having arrived and Monty's allowance duly paid.

Selwyn remained in Reading after the funeral and was not back at his digs until Sunday evening. As soon as Monty heard him on the stairs, he rushed out and dragged him into his own sitting room, agog to hear all that had passed. Selwyn assured him that Gwendolen was bearing up well and sent her fondest regards.

'No hitches with the arrangements?' Monty asked cautiously,' 'I mean, Mr Fanshawe's passing was a trifle sudden.'

'None at all,' said Selwyn, shaking his head, 'Dr Bowker, the family physician, knew of Elliot's habit of taking tincture of laudanum for his neuralgia and, so as not to distress Gwendolen in her grieving widowhood by causing public gossip, he wrote out a certificate to the effect that Elliot had died of heart failure. I thought that was very considerate of him.'

'Uncommonly considerate,' Monty agreed readily, 'and deuced convenient all round. Is he a young man or an older man?'

He had revised his previous thought that Mr Fanshawe harmed himself by too strenuous a session with Gwendolen's beautiful person, and now was secretly convinced that it was her session with himself that had induced her to mix a fatal dose for her inconvenient husband. Perhaps with the tacit connivance of the family physician.

'I can guess at your thought,' said Selwyn, 'but you do my dear sister a wrong. Never would she take part in deception of that nature! And your speculation that she would ever submit her person to Dr Bowker to gain an advantage — that is unworthy of you!'

'No such dreadful thought crossed my mind!' Monty assured him, although it had been precisely what he had deduced. 'You know I adore her beyond reason!'

'Gwendolen is innocent of all wrongdoing,' Selwyn declared, 'like Caesar's wife, she is above suspicion!'

'Certainly,' Monty agreed, seeing that nothing more need ever be said on the subject of Mr Fanshawe's demise. 'But you have a melancholy look about you, Selwyn. Buck up, old chap, all will be for the best and unless I am mistaken, your next rendezvous with dearest Cecily is tomorrow evening. That will restore your zest for life!'

'You must advise me, Monty,' said Selwyn, mightily agitated, 'something has happened which threatens to destroy all my new happiness with Cecily. I am in the most desperate of plights!'

'Lord!' said Monty. 'What a taking you are in, old fellow! Have a drop of malmsey wine with me and calm yourself. What can have happened to put you in this state?'

Selwyn took the glass of rich dark wine Monty poured for him and related with expressions of dismay the unfortunate incident that had unnerved him. It was at Reading, after the interment of Mr Fanshawe and after the many family mourners had at last glutted themselves on cold beef, pressed ham, cold mutton, eggs boiled hard and sliced, port wine, brandy and bottled beer, and departed. By then it was mid-afternoon and the poor distraught widow had retired with a headache to her room to rest. Selwyn too felt exhausted and went upstairs to lie on the bed until tea time.

'I thought to doze for an hour,' he told Monty, 'but into my mind unbidden came sweet thoughts of my dearest Cecily, and how sublime was our love when I was last at her villa. The curtains were drawn to darken the room to let me rest and this served only to intensify the pictures that formed in my mind. If only you knew how I delight in Cecily!'

'I never doubted your affection for the lady,' said Monty, 'but please go on — what happened to upset you?'

'To continue then, I lay on the bed lost in a sweet reverie of my darling, when of a sudden the bedroom door opened without a knock and in came Gwendolen. She had divested herself of her widow's weeds, and put on a long dressing gown of pale mauve with a lace collar. Her face was pale from the ordeal of the morning and she said she must speak to me, seating herself on the side of the bed. Now to spare myself all the trouble of undressing and then dressing again for tea, I had removed only jacket and waistcoat — and my footwear, of course, and lay with just the bedspread over me. What it was that Gwendolen wished to discuss I never found out, for without a word she dragged the bedspread right off me and in high dudgeon accused me of fetching off in my hand!'

'And had you?' asked Monty.

'No!' Selwyn declared. 'You know that I gave Cecily my word never to allow myself to come off except in her dear presence and with her spoken permission. Do you imagine I would break a vow made in the very peak of devotion?'

'Then Gwendolen was mistaken, and you were able to refute her accusation,' said Monty, a trace of cynicism in his tone.

'Why, no, not precisely,' Selwyn murmured, his cheeks a faint pink for shame, 'the thing was this — whilst I was thinking of Cecily and how I adore her to distraction, I happened to undo my trouser buttons and slip my hand under my shirt to hold my shaft. Not that I had any intention of making myself come off — you must believe me when I assure you that was very far from my mind. In fact, it was to discourage my shaft from twitching and jerking that I held it, to quieten its movements before worse could befall.'

'Quite so,' Monty cried cheerfully, 'I understand perfectly, my dear fellow — but I wager you had the devil of a job trying to persuade Gwendolen of the purity of your intentions.'

'She refused to believe me, whatever I said,' Selwyn replied mournfully. 'She dragged up my shirt and pulled out my shaft — and when she saw that it was stiff she upbraided me fiercely for neglecting a loving sister while pleasuring myself alone.'

'Then there was only one thing for it,' said Monty, 'out with your dolly-whacker and give her a good rogering!'

'Impossible!' Selwyn replied. 'I knew that Gwendolen would be angry with me if I told her I had taken an oath to another woman, and so I did my best to explain that I felt it would be unseemly for a widow to be poked by her brother when she had a lover — to wit, yourself, Monty. I said it would be a betrayal of you, for me to roger her.'

'Good thinking!' said Monty. 'Did that do the trick?'

'Not entirely,' Selwyn answered shame-faced. 'Gwendolen threw a leg over me and knelt upright over my chest, then seized me by the hair of my head and dragged me into a sitting position — it is exceedingly painful to be dragged by the hair, I assure you. Before I could guess what she was about, she had my face pressed against her belly. *Very well*, she cried in a voice that brooked no denial, *if you won't poke me, you shall do me with your tongue, Selwyn, for I mean to be satisfied before I leave this room!*'

'My word!' said Monty breathlessly. 'How did you escape from this compromising situation?'

Selwyn's face blushed scarlet and his eyes were downcast, not meeting Monty's bold stare of enquiry. 'To tell the truth,' said he, 'I was powerless to escape from Gwendolen's demands, try as I might. She rubbed the lips of her pussy against my mouth and repeated that she would not leave before I satisfied her. Thus held captive, I thought it best to do as she wished and so get rid of her quickly. There was no question of breaking my vow to Cecily, of course, either in deed or in word or in thought for, whilst I tongued Gwendolen's pussy, I firmly fixed my thoughts on my darling Cecily.'

'I say! That's devotion far beyond the call of duty, if you ask me,' Monty exclaimed. 'How did you keep your thoughts fixed on Cecily at such a moment?'

'I recalled the sublime moments when you took me to her villa to meet her,' Selwyn declared with pride in his voice, 'and how she stood by the window with her wrapper open to let me see her divine body, while I knelt at her feet and pressed my feverish face between her thighs. You remember the scene, I am sure, though you cannot hope to understand the feelings of love that flooded through me as I thrust my tongue into the pouting lips of her darling pussy.'

'I remember it well,' said Monty, pretending a solemnity he did not feel. 'The force of your emotions in some measure found an echo in my own heart, and I too, burned for Cecily.'

He was not speaking the complete truth, for whilst Selwyn had been lapping between Cecily's parted thighs, Monty had pulled out his stiff shaft and had played briskly with it to the amusement of Cecily, who had watched what he did over Selwyn's head.

'So much the better,' said Selwyn. 'Then you will know what was in my heart when, tonguing Gwendolen, I made myself believe that it was Cecily's pussy I was licking. This brought me great comfort, since I knew myself to be faithful to Cecily, even in this perilous plight.'

'Excellently well planned, my dear chap,' said Monty. 'What then? You brought Gwendolen off and she left you in peace?'

'Something of my devotion to Cecily must have transferred itself to the merely mechanical licking I was giving Gwendolen, for she came off almost at once, shrieking out, *Oh, I'm doing it, Selwyn!* I heard her words with much relief, thinking that she would return to her own room satisfied. But not a bit of it — I had thrown more fuel onto a blazing fire! Before the spasms of her pleasure had faded away, she threw me down on my back and sat herself on my shaft and began to roger me!'

'Hm,' Monty observed thoughtfully, 'but why was your shaft stiff enough for her to get it up her? Surely you did not become aroused by being compelled to tongue her pussy? Considering that Gwendolen was outraging your sworn devotion to Cecily, I would have expected your shaft to be small and soft in dismay.'

'It was because I had been thinking of Cecily whilst forced to satisfy Gwendolen that I was aroused,' Selwyn explained in haste, 'the thought of her alone suffices to bring me up hard.'

'Quite so,' said Monty, with a grin of disbelief, 'and so you had no choice after all but to resume your old game with your sister — is that the long and short of it?'

Selwyn nodded unhappily and asked for Monty's advice as a friend on how best he could explain this unfortunate lapse to Cecily when next he saw her.

'Least said, soonest mended,' said Monty. 'Only a fool tells a woman he desires to poke that he has recently poked another. Say nothing of it and no problem will arise.'

'But that is deceitful!' Selwyn exclaimed. 'I worship Cecily body and soul — she has a right to know of anything that bears on the loving affection between us.'

'You are being unbearably selfish,' Monty said, finding a way to tease poor innocent Selwyn. 'You only pretend this devotion to Cecily — your true devotion is to yourself, I fear.'

'What do you mean?' Selwyn gasped. 'It is a matter of honour and respect to confess my renewed moral weakness to her.'

'What stuff!' said Monty enjoying the game. 'Your wretched little conscience pricks you for conceding too easily when your sister wanted a poke. May I remind you that a gentleman would say nothing of her readily assuaged little urge. To unburden yourself of a peccadillo, you are prepared to blurt all out and make Cecily the most miserable woman alive. Shame on you, sir! Keep your counsel and let Cecily's happiness remain untainted by your moral weakness!'

'I stand rebuked,' Selwyn sighed, 'thank you, my dear fellow, for your eminently sensible advice. No word of what happened to me at Reading shall pass my lips when I am with Cecily. I am glad I have a true friend like you to preserve me from my own foolishness.'

He rose from his chair, dashed a tear of honest emotion from his eye, and shook hands warmly with Monty, who recharged their glasses with his excellent malmsey.

'When may I hope for the pleasure of seeing Gwendolen in town next?' he asked Selwyn. 'I yearn to see her, as you know. Does being in mourning preclude her from shopping trips?'

'I regret that is so,' Selwyn informed him. 'Six months must pass before she embarks on any visit outside her neighbourhood — and it will be a twelvemonth before she next shows herself in town, I believe.'

'Then I shall go to Reading tomorrow,' Monty declared. 'I am burning with desire for her — and she for me, I have no doubt.'

At that, Selwyn looked distinctly shifty, shuffled his feet on the carpet and glanced away from Monty.

'Out with it!' Monty cried, recognising the signs of evasion and deception. 'What are you concealing from me? Has Gwendolen found another love?'

'Lord no!' Selwyn murmured, shame-faced, 'but she let fall something that disturbed me greatly.'

'What was that? Tell me, before I go mad!' Monty exclaimed.

'It was after she had rogered me the third or fourth

time,' Selwyn answered in a whisper, 'she climbed off my violated body and lay down beside me to sleep, her arms about me . . .'

'Third or fourth time!' Monty cried in a voice of thunder. 'Once I could have forgiven, for my darling girl must needs be frustrated without my presence to satisfy her! But three or four times? This was an orgy! You have betrayed me, and you have abused our friendship!'

'For which I humbly beg your pardon,' said Selwyn miserably, 'but it was none of my doing — I swear it! Gwendolen was afire with lust and rode me until I was drained dry!'

'Well then, what was it she said after she was satisfied?' Monty asked, calming himself by breathing deep and slow.

'She said it had been lovely to be done properly again, and not to rely on her fingers to bring herself off,' Selwyn said in an embarrassed mutter. 'Naturally, I was appalled to think my dearest sister would contemplate abusing herself in so very disgraceful a manner. Even now, I cannot wholly believe it — I am of the opinion that she was speaking of what she had avoided by making use of my person, rather than of something she had ever done to herself. Don't you agree?'

His words had cheered Monty enormously. It relieved his mind to learn that his darling girl was fingering herself to quell her natural lusts in his absence. So long as she continued in that way of doing herself he had nothing to fear from a rival. As for Selwyn — she had rogered him because he chanced to be at hand when she had the letch. It meant nothing to her, and Monty entertained no hard feelings towards the supplier of the shaft that had rubbed Gwendolen's itch.

'Of course she brings herself off at bedtime,' he said,

'all women do it if they have no man nearby with a handy shaft.'

'You imply that Gwendolen strokes her pussy to fetch herself off?' Selwyn asked, his eyebrows raised. 'That is a calumny — I don't believe it. The female nature is far more ethereal than that of mere men — I refuse to believe any woman could bring herself to so degraded an act!'

'Help yourself to another glass of wine,' said Monty, 'and I shall return in a minute. There is much for you to learn about female nature, my boy.'

Leaving Selwyn perplexed Monty went down to the kitchen and found Minnie alone, ironing Mrs Gifford's lingerie. She grinned as he came in and winked at him, holding up a pair of white cotton drawers with rose-pink ribbons threaded though the leg-hems.

'All nice and warm from the iron,' she said. 'If Mrs Gifford put them on now, they'd warm her pussy for her! She'd want you up her a time or two, to calm her down!'

Monty grinned back and thrust his hand through the forward slit of the drawers, and then through the rearward slit, until his hand touched Minnie's titties. He fondled them through her clothes and said he was entertaining Mr Courtney-Stoke upstairs and there was a gold sovereign waiting for Minnie if she would join them for half an hour and perform certain actions by way of demonstration.

'Right!' said she, throwing down the drawers. 'Mrs Gifford's out for the evening and cook's gone to church. For a sovereign in my hand you can both do me, one after the other!'

On the way upstairs Monty explained that it was not precisely a question of doing her, but of acquainting Mr Courtney-Stoke with some facts of life of which he was ignorant. By the time they reached his rooms, Minnie understood perfectly well what was wanted of her, and she found the prospect highly amusing.

Monty ensconced her in one of his armchairs and asked her to demonstrate to Mr Courtney-Stoke and himself the matter they had discussed on the stair. Minnie grinned and lay back, parted her legs and picked up her skirts to reveal her drawers. In another moment she had opened them to show her lightly fledged pussy.

'Oh, Mr Courtney-Stoke, I do believe you are blushing,' she said, seeing Selwyn's cheeks turn red. 'Don't make out you've never seen a girl's crack before.'

'He's seen one lovely dark-haired pouting pussy that I know of,' said Monty with a knowing laugh, 'though I won't put a name to it! But you may believe me Minnie, he's been up it more times than you and I have had hot dinners.'

Minnie understood very well whose hairy delight was meant and, seeing Selwyn's blushes renewed, she pulled open the lips of her pussy and stroked inside with her middle finger. The two men stared in rapture at the finger that glided expertly over her uncovered nub.

'You've a most loving touch, the way you play with yourself, Minnie,' said Monty, 'how often do you do it?'

'Why, every night in bed before I go to sleep,' she answered. 'Just like everybody else.'

Selwyn gasped loudly to hear this item of information and his face turned crimson.

'Every night in bed,' Monty repeated for Selwyn's benefit.

'That's right,' she said softly, her thin belly starting to quiver to the tremors of pleasure she was sending through it.

'And you say that every girl does the same — and every

woman, too — she plays with her pussy before she falls asleep?'

'Right you are,' Minnie breathed, her thighs straining wider apart as the sensations of delight grew stronger in her belly.

'Well, I am sure that naughty girls like you rub your pussy off in bed, but surely you don't expect this gentleman and me to believe that ladies of breeding and refinement also handle themselves in this low way?' Monty objected, winking at her.

'Why ever not?' she retorted. 'A pussy's only made of flesh and blood — every one of them's got an itch that wants rubbing regular, and if there's no husband to ease it with his dolly-whacker, it gets done by hand, duchess or kitchen-maid.'

By this time Minnie was far advanced along the pathway that leads to climactic bliss. With the fingers of one hand she held wide the pink lips of her slit, and with the joined fingers of the other she caressed the slippery rose-pink bud that was exposed. She watched the two men through half-closed eyes, and they gaped open-mouthed and red-faced at what she was doing to herself.

'Oh, oh, oh!' she exclaimed suddenly, and her legs thrashed about as she brought herself off in quick spasms.

'By George!' said Monty, 'the little slut's given me a hard she'll have to take care of!'

With that, he threw himself to his knees between Minnie's open legs, and ripped his trouser buttons open with shaking and desperate hands. His shaft leapt out the moment his shirt-front was raised and, without a pause, he plunged six inches of hard gristle into her wet pussy and rogered away for dear life.

'My word!' Selwyn exclaimed, his eyes bulging from

his head, 'how can you do such a thing, Monty? What will Mrs Gifford say if she finds out you have taken advantage of her servant! She will tell you to leave the house at once!'

'Fiddlesticks!' Monty gasped 'Do you think this is the first time I've had Minnie? She's a dear girl, always willing to oblige for a shilling or two, and she enjoys a good poke!'

'No mistake about that!' Minnie gurgled, kicking up her legs either side of Monty as he plunged in and out. 'Give it to me hot and strong, sir!'

In six more strokes Monty reached the acme of sensation and squirted his lust into her quaking belly. She squealed joyfully and humped her belly under him, to extract the very last drop.

'There!' said he with a sigh of content. 'That was a first-rate poke.'

He raised himself from the floor and flopped down beside Minnie, who was lying with her legs spread and a foolish smile of satisfaction on her plain face.

'How about you, my dear chap,' Monty said to Selwyn. 'Is not your own shaft hard-on and ready to roger her? Indeed it is − I can see the bulge down your trouser-leg from here. Get it out and make use of this lovely wet pussy here at your disposal.'

'I cannot!' Selwyn groaned. 'I have given my word to a lady you know of, whose name I dare not mention in the presence of a third party. She alone may release my tension!'

Monty rested an arm over Minnie's thigh to slip his fingers between the lips of her pussy and stroke her bud slowly.

'We are men of the world, Selwyn,' said he. 'Ladies need to be cosseted and fussed over and flattered and rogered — but no man but a fool thinks that promises given with a standing shaft are meant to be kept. The lady you worship will be no worse for our private amusements so long as she never learns of them. Throw off this pious simpering attitude and make the most of what is offered to you.'

Whether it was the force of Monty's words that converted his primness, or the sight of Monty's fingers playing in Minnie's pussy, or her shrieks of bliss as she came off again, Selwyn rose from his chair and knelt between the girl's legs.

'Good man!' Monty encouraged him, taking his hand away from Minnie's thighs. 'Slip your shaft up her and give her a good poke!'

Blushing furiously, Selwyn undid his trousers and hoisted his shirt, to let his impressively large shaft appear.

'My stars!' Minnie exclaimed. 'Look at the size of that! I want it up me!'

'This is against my better judgment,' Selwyn sighed, pausing with his leaping shaft in his hand. 'You are urging me to do a deed I have promised not to do, save with one beloved person.'

'If I recall rightly,' said Monty, 'the promise you gave was not to fetch off in any other woman's pussy. Well then — there is no problem at all here to vex us. Give Minnie a feel of what she is dying for — push it up her. But take care not to fetch off, and then you will have kept your solemn word.'

'Dare I?' Selwyn murmured, as if to himself, staring all the while at Minnie's open wet slit.

'Go on, stick it up me,' Minnie urged him. 'I want to feel it in my belly.'

'It would be impolite to refuse a request so easily

granted,' Selwyn murmured. 'You shall have your wish, Minnie, if only for a moment or two.'

By an act of will Monty kept himself from grinning at this fine example of self-deception. He stared in fascination to see Selwyn set the head of his mighty shaft to the mark and slowly slide its eight-inch length into Minnie.

'Oh my!' said she, her eyes closing in rapture, 'I've never been so full up before!'

'You are a gentleman, Selwyn,' Monty exclaimed, suppressing his laughter, 'you have made the girl happy at no great effort. Stay in her a while and give her a memory to cherish forever.'

'That would be most unwise,' Selwyn gasped, his face becoming redder and redder. 'You are fully aware of my moral weakness — there is no telling to what depths of folly I might sink if I relaxed for one instant the self-control I have learnt from the dear friend you know of.'

'I am astonished at how far you have progressed in so short a time,' said Monty. 'The lady in question seems to have taught you most efficaciously to restrain your natural impulses. You have my congratulations. How long are you now able to contain yourself in this highly commendable way?'

'With my dear teacher I have endured the strongest sensations of sensuality for almost ten minutes before being compelled to surrender my essence,' said Selwyn, his body trembling.

All this time they were conversing, Minnie had been wriggling her bottom surreptitiously on the chair cushion, to transmit to the embedded shaft ripples of pleasure through the clinging flesh of her pussy. Of this Selwyn was unaware, being occupied with his conversation and with the thoughts of Cecily that were stirred by it. The spasm when it came was therefore surprising to him.

'Oh no!' he gasped. 'I will not!'

But he had no choice. His elixir was spurting freely, and in his delirium he rammed in and out of Minnie's pussy as if he would split her asunder.

'You're coming off!' she cried. 'It feels like a fountain inside me!'

CHAPTER 13
Grace Pays a Visit

Parted from his darling Gwendolen by the cruel necessities of the polite conventions, Monty had no recourse for his burning desire other than to summon up in his mind his fond memories of when last she was with him. It had been on her last visit to town, when she had come direct to Seymour Place by cab from the railway station and they had passed the whole day together in bed enjoying the sweets of love.

In this mood of gallant frustration that she was not now with him to repeat their joys, Monty wrote to her a letter in which he expressed his longings for her beautiful person, and he gave ardent promises of rapture without end when next they were with each other. A hot tear of love fell to the page whilst he wrote of his passion, and his hard-on shaft throbbed in his trousers.

The hour was a little after ten in the morning, Mrs Gifford had gone to the market to purchase green vegetables and taken Minnie with her to carry the shopping basket. There was nothing for it, Monty concluded as he sealed up his letter, but to take out One-Eyed Jack and ease his heavy burden of desire by hand. Yet even as his hand fell to his trouser buttons and his eager shaft bounded in anticipation, he heard a light tap at his sitting-room door and went to investigate, walking as stiffly and awkwardly as if he had a rolled umbrella under his shirt.

His visitor was, he was surprised to see, his sister Grace. She wore a new frock of chocolate brown with a green-braided jacket to match and a bonnet with artificial flowers. Monty kissed her on both cheeks and drew her into his cosy sitting room to a seat on the sofa. She removed her bonnet and gloves and began a lengthy explanation of needing to visit an Oxford Street store for something or other and, being so close to his dwelling, she had decided to drop in for a moment on her dear brother.

Monty waved away her explanations, took her hand and placed it over the bulge in his trousers.

'No excuses, Grace,' said he with a smile, 'tell me truly why you came here this morning.'

Her cheeks reddened a little at his very open approach, but she took her courage in both hands and spoke out.

'Some words you spoke to me when you were last at Putney have been running in my mind ever since,' said she, a tremor in her voice betraying her nervousness. 'You claimed that we had the same hot nature, you and I. You were pleased to inform me that it was my duty to this nature to let you satisfy me as often as possible. Do you deny your words?'

'Lord no!' Monty sighed, and his shaft jumped underneath her hand. 'That was the day I poked you six times before tea.'

'Yes,' Grace whispered, her eyes modestly downcast and her cheeks a pretty pink, 'and perhaps you may also recall that I enquired of you if a brother had any right to make use of his sister in so lustful a manner.'

'I say now what I said then,' Monty replied. 'Only by obeying the urges of our nature do we find happiness. Under your hand lies all the proof required to convince you of my right to poke you whenever I choose — a stiff shaft. Do you still doubt me?'

'No,' said Grace, a trifle hesitantly, but with sincerity in her tone, 'I have come here to tell you that I have given much thought to your claims and I accept them completely. It is my duty to submit myself to you in all things, for I am persuaded now that a brother must take precedence over a husband. You may satisfy me whenever you will, dearest Monty.'

With that, she undid his trouser buttons from top to bottom, pulled his shirt up to his belly and clasped his hot and hard shaft in her hand. With a grin of understanding, Monty spread his legs apart and she fingered One-Eyed Jack lovingly. Monty sighed with delight at the pleasurable sensations and he soon had her skirts and petticoats up over her knees, her legs apart and his hand in her drawers. His deft fingers played lightly over her curly-haired pussy and teased the soft lips, to coax them into opening themselves.

'How delicious a touch you have!' Monty gasped. 'For one who has never been allowed to handle her husband's shaft, you have learned the skill with commendable speed!'

'The skill is yours, dearest, in teaching me,' said Grace, a soft gleam of affection in her eyes.

While they were thus pleasantly engaged in provoking sensual pleasure by feeling each other's privities, Monty was nothing loth to explore his own emotions and motives. To this end, by a feat of imagination, he pretended to himself that the parted thighs and bush of brown curls that lay under his hand were not his sister's, but dearest Gwendolen's.

By dint of closing his eyes tight, he was able very nearly to deceive himself, and he found that his pleasure was greatly augmented by this flight of fantasy. It was not that he would have rather had Gwendolen to feel than Grace — that was not the point at all. It went without saying that because he loved his darling Gwendolen to distraction there was the most tremendous delight in feeling her pussy and then poking her. That aside, he had ascertained at Putney that it was also a source of very great delight to finger Grace and then roger her.

By the exercise of his imagination, it was as if he had both of his dear charmers to play with at the same time, and when he spoke he was not altogether sure to which lady his words were addressed — whether Gwendolen or Grace. Not that it made much difference, for words had ceased to be of any importance in the welter of emotion that swirled through him and through her.

In this delicious way and by these exciting means, Monty came to an understanding of what moved him. At Putney, on the sofa, he had shot his sticky essence up Grace's pussy and given her to experience spasms of true bliss until she collapsed under him of exhaustion. Lying in contentment on her belly, he had at that time drawn the conclusion that the sensations of rogering a sister were heavenly in the extreme — unquestionably far more delicious than with any other woman he had poked, including his darling Gwendolen!

This conclusion seemed to him strange. Fond as he was of his sister, she could not match Gwendolen in the beauty of her face and figure. Neither she nor Gwendolen could match Cecily for sheer delicious lustfulness, and none of the three could match thin-shanked Minnie in lewdness. Nor could any of the foursome — Grace, Gwendolen,

Cecily or Minnie — hold a candle to Hannah Gifford in her insatiable enthusiasm for sensuality.

What then was a chap to make of all this? Only this, Monty decided — that the most delightful woman in the world was the one he happened to be rogering at any given time, whether that was any one of his four darlings, or little Miss Emmy at Mrs Lee's poking academy, or even a buttered bun up against a wall behind Paddington station, The best pussy in the world was the one you were up at the time.

This abstruse point of philosophy settled at last, Monty gave himself up to the thrills running through him. Grace in all her willingness to please him rubbed her clasped hand up and down his straining shaft. His heart beat faster to feel the moment coming ever closer when his hot elixir would spurt from him in hard spasms of ecstasy. In the very nick of time he restrained Grace's hand by seizing her wrist.

'Dearest girl!' he gasped out, 'let us not waste this first precious emission — I mean to fetch off in your pussy, not in your hand — and you shall shriek in delight to feel me gushing into you!'

She sighed tremulously to hear his bold words and her pussy became wetter yet to his touch. To impress upon his dearest sister the strength and power of his manhood, Monty stood up, gathered her in his arms, and carried her into his bedroom. He deposited her on her back on the bed and sat beside her on the edge, leaning over to smile into her eyes, while his ever-busy hands felt up under her clothes. Grace tried to return his burning gaze, but some of her self-assurance had ebbed away now she found herself on a bed with her brother and her eyes closed in modesty when he put his fingers into her drawers to stroke her pussy again.

This did not content him for long, and Grace gave a nervous little laugh as he untied the string of her drawers and pulled them down her legs and cast them aside. She gasped when he took her hand and pressed it to his hard-swollen implement. She held it in the palm of her hand and it throbbed under her touch, until her eyes grew round at the wonder of it. She grasped the quivering length firmly again, as she had in the sitting room, and stroked it up and down.

Her clothes were turned up to her waist as she lay, her head on the pillow, so that Monty could lean over and press a kiss on her soft bare belly. Emboldened by the open affection he displayed, Grace opened her eyes and saw that his handsome face was flushed with powerful emotion, and that his eyes gleamed brightly while he stared at her uncovered pussy. Then in a sudden movement his face was between her naked thighs and his hot tongue lapped at her in a deliberate repetition of the sweet caress that had banished all her fears and doubts when at Putney he had first done this to her, to persuade her to let him roger her fully.

'Dearest Monty . . .' she whispered, her backside wriggling for joy on the bedspread.

His warm tongue penetrated her, licking and pulsating, until it found her hidden button. At that lewdest and most intimate of touches, Grace shrieked faintly and came off at once. Monty laughed to see how intensely he had moved her with so slight a caress and flung himself between her legs and over her belly. A moment later she felt his hard shaft thrust into her, prying her wet flesh open to reach deep into her belly.

'O, yes . . .' she moaned, and jerked her loins up and down in a frenzy of desire, working at his embedded shaft to make it gush out its elixir into her.

'Yes, Grace my dearest girl!' Monty gasped in response, and plunged up and down in short fast thrusts. Both felt the tides of lust rising ever higher, threatening to overflow the bounds and drown them in the sensations of pleasure. Grace pressed her mouth to Monty's in a frantic kiss, and his body jerked wildly to the sudden gush of his essence into her wet pussy.

'Monty, Monty!' she cried, to each throb of his shaft inside her. 'That's lovely, Monty — I can't stop coming off!'

For fully a minute she shuddered and moaned beneath him, even though One-Eyed Jack had long ceased to spurt, before she was satisfied and lay in a half-swooning limpness, sighing in deep satisfaction.

When she had sufficiently recovered herself to have the power of speech restored, she threw her arms about Monty and told him certain things which had come into her mind.

'Oh Monty — when at Putney I felt you kiss my pussy and tongue it, it was so very delightful that I knew nothing like it! To think I have reached the age of twenty-eight years and have been a wife for five years, and never until you did it to me last week had I any inkling that this exquisite pleasure existed and could be within my reach!'

From which Monty deduced that his sister's husband had been decidedly lax in his attentions to her. But then, according to Grace's account of her marital connections, only on the rarest of occasions did Arthur put his shaft up her.

'I must return the compliment,' Grace continued. 'Forgive me if I am clumsy at this, Monty, but this will be the first time I have tried to do it.'

As she was speaking, her ardent gaze was fixed on his

shaft, which lay limply in the gaping opening of his trousers. She took it in her hand, marvelling at its dwindled size and eager to restore it to its manly six-inch length. Whilst engaged in raising it to its former magnificence, she asked a question.

'Monty, my dear — when I first entered your sitting room this morning, your shaft was already stiff inside your trousers. Why was this — won't you tell me? Were you perhaps thinking about the person with whom you are in love, your dearest Gwendolen?'

'Clever girl,' murmured Monty, watching his shaft growing in Grace's hand. 'To be frank with you, as you deserve of me, my longing for Gwendolen was hot upon me. I was missing her dear presence and yearning to take her in my arms.'

'Ah, then there is no doubt left that you have had her,' said Grace, 'though you insisted to me that you have not yet had the enjoyment of her body. That I refuse to believe, in view of the evidence of your shaft being hard-on when you thought of her.'

'I cannot tell a lie,' said Monty, who told lies as often as it suited him to do so, 'I have visited her at Reading and she allowed me the inestimable privilege of rogering her! I dream every night of that divine experience! But cruel Fate keeps us apart — Gwendolen has suffered a bereavement in the family and cannot receive me at home, or travel to London.'

'My poor boy!' Grace murmured in sympathy, her hand sliding up and down his now hard-on shaft. 'You dream of her in bed, do you say? Then you must wake each morning with a sticky nightshirt, I fear. Let me comfort your dear lonely shaft!'

She brought her face down to it, and in another instant her tongue had darted out to touch the purple head which had grown shiny with passion. Monty sighed when she drew it well into her mouth, holding it with her lips whilst her tongue lapped at it briskly. To further Grace's sentimental education, he twisted himself about on the bed until his head was between her bared thighs and explained to her that this was the sixty-nine position.

Grace knew nothing of such refinements, of course, for Arthur had shown her but the one position for marital love, and that not often. Nevertheless, strange though it seemed to her at the beginning, she soon took to having her pussy licked while she sucked at Monty's shaft. Their spasm came together, he gushing his thick juice into her mouth, his tongue thrust deep into her to bring her off boldly.

Afterwards they at last undressed, Monty down to his shirt, Grace down to her chemise, and lay in each other's arms to rest a while from their delightful efforts and gather their strength to renew them. Monty raised with his sister the matter of her husband's shortcomings in the bedroom, and if it had always been so with him. For instance, during their long courtship and year-long engagement to be married, had Arthur made the least attempt to feel her titties or put a hand up her clothes?

'Never once,' said Grace sadly. 'On my bridal night I was a virgin, as is proper, but Arthur had not even tried to give my bosom a feel through my clothes. But for one incident that I myself precipitated, I would have judged him a neuter and with regret broken off the engagement.'

'Tell me of this incident,' Monty pleaded, his hand under her chemise to stroke her warm belly. 'What did you do to him?'

'Promise not to laugh at me,' said Grace. 'It was a somewhat shameful stratagem to find out if Arthur was at all susceptible to female charm. Soon after our engagement was announced, and I had enjoyed no more than a chaste kiss or two on the cheek from my new fiance, we were staying with his parents in Wimbledon. One sunny afternoon, when Mr and Mrs Austin had gone out in the carriage to visit friends . . .'

'You seized the Heaven-sent opportunity and invited Arthur to your room, where he found you lying on the bed clad only in a chemise and drawers!' Monty interrupted her.

'You're quite wrong,' said Grace. 'Arthur challenged me to a game of croquet on the lawn. I would happily have sat indoors and canoodled with him, but there we were, knocking silly balls about on the grass. A thought came into my mind, and at once I acted upon it! When my turn came next to play, I swung my mallet hard at the ball, and let it slip as if by accident from my hands. It flew through the air and stuck Arthur a blow, as I had intended, where his legs join.'

'By George!' Monty exclaimed. 'You hit him in the pompoms with a croquet mallet! But this would incapacitate him!'

''It did,' Grace agreed. 'By the aid of the gardener and cook we got him upstairs to his bed, where he lay moaning. I sent the gardener for the family doctor, and bade the cook bring me a bowl of warm water and some towels.'

'Great Heavens — surely you were not so audacious as to attend to his pompoms!' said Monty with a grin.

'He fussed and said how improper it was when I had the cook unbutton his trousers and pull them down his legs, but against my plea of medical emergency he had no defence and he was too much in discomfort to resist strongly. I wrung out a towel in warm water, turned up his shirt front and laid it over his . . . pompoms, as you call them. Arthur blushed scarlet to think I'd seen his shaft.'

'And the cook too,' said Monty.

'The impertinent creature was staring and grinning openly at this revelation of Arthur's person. Very soon it began to stand hard under the towel, which I removed to dip again in the warm water, so obtaining a full view of his endowment.'

'I would have given ten guineas to witness the discomfiture of Arthur Austin!' cried Monty. 'What then, dear Grace?'

'His shaft began to tremble after a time, and from this I was able to form the guess that his crisis was near. I sent the cook downstairs for more warm water and touched my hand to the wet towel over dear Arthur's twitching shaft, *to see that the water was not yet too cold* I told him. Then I slipped my hand under it for a moment, *to make sure that it did not lie heavily on his bruising*, I explained. Purely by accident my hand made contact with a length of hard and twitching flesh — I gasped — Arthur moaned — his legs shook! I felt a warm gushing over my hand and knew that he was coming off. This gave me an assurance that he would be properly capable of the act of love when we were married. As indeed he is, although he chooses to use this ability all too seldom.'

'My, my!' said Monty. 'I would not have thought you capable of so devious a scheme, dear Grace.'

'Now, I have confessed to you the full extent of my youthful transgressions, and in comparison with yours they are nothing,' she answered, her hand under his shirt to rub his shaft slowly, 'it is your turn to disclose the follies of your youth to me. Did you ever, during the years when we were growing up, ever take a fancy toward me?'

'Lord yes!' he exclaimed. 'Well I remember an afternoon when Mama had taken you out somewhere and Papa was dozing under his newspaper in the garden — I stole into your room and opened the wardrobe to feel your frocks and press them to my face to catch the faintest trace of the warm fragrance of your body. My shaft stood hard-on in my trousers and, greatly daring, I took from the laundry basket a chemise and a pair of drawers you had worn the previous day. I laid the chemise on your bed, and slipped the drawers into it, as if you were wearing both and lying on your back for me.'

Grace was blushing crimson to hear how her garments had been made use of, years before. She jerked fiercely at Monty's stiff shaft and squeezed it hard as if to crush it in her palm.

'I let down my trousers and rolled up my shirt, turned back the chemise and rested my bare belly on your drawers,' Monty continued in a voice that trembled with emotion, 'I slid my shaft into the slit of the drawers, pretending to myself that it was your virgin pussy I was penetrating.'

'Oh Monty — stroke it now!' Grace cried, 'Your words have set me on fire and I must come off!'

His fingers were in her wet pussy at once, to tease her warm and swollen bud while he completed for her the tale of his use of her undergarments long ago for his pleasure.

'I lay face down on the bed,' said he, 'sliding my shaft into the slit of your drawers so that it rubbed on the inside. I was in Heaven, my mind overflowing with pictures of you, my dearest Grace, lying beneath me to receive my rogering. Then in gushes of sheer bliss I shot my hot sap into your drawers with such feelings of delight as if I'd shot it up your maidenly pussy.'

'Oh, Monty!' Grace sighed, her legs shaking as her emotions grew ever stronger under the stimulus of his fingers fluttering inside her. 'To think you did me in your mind and I never knew of your interest in me!'

'It was more than in my mind,' said he, 'it was also in the drawers you had worn, for when I returned them to the laundry basket they were soaked through with my emission.'

'Oh, Monty . . .' Grace said again, her voice hardly audible now that she was on the brink of coming off, 'I'm glad it was nice for you . . .'

'So nice that I repeated it every time you were out and I had the chance to creep into your room, my dearest girl,' he told her. 'Over the years I rogered every pair of drawers you ever wore and left the white stains of my passion on them.'

'Oh!' she shrieked, coming off at last, and her belly bucked upwards against his busy hand.

When she was calm again, he rolled her onto her back and lay half over her while he kissed her face fondly, and asked if she too brought herself off with her fingers when she was a girl. She blushed and would not give him an answer, from which he was certain that she did. With a grin, he reached under the pillow her head lay on and brought out the book he had left there the night before. Undoubtedly Minnie had seen it when she made the bed that morning, and perhaps read a little of it.

'What is your bedtime reading?' asked Grace in all innocence of the existence of literature such as this.

'A story of schoolgirls,' said Monty with a laugh. 'I shall read a short passage of it to you, dear Grace, for it makes the point for me. Listen to this:

Jennifer flinched away from the stern look of authority on the coldly beautiful face of Miss Harriet, who stood glaring at a sheet of drawing paper she held in her hand.

'Explain this if you can!' Harriet cried, flinging the paper at the trembling girl. 'Is this your vile work? Answer me!'

It was one of the sketches Jennifer had made from life that morning outdoors. For her model she had taken the gardener's assistant, Dickie, a fair-haired lad. Her sketch depicted him in the vegetable garden, sitting on an upended wheelbarrow. Jennifer was talented with her pencil and it was a good likeness. The offence lay in that Dickie was shown with a hand thrust under his gardener's apron and a blissful smile on his face.

'Well?' Harriet demanded ruthlessly. 'Have you lost your tongue, Miss? Do you deny that this obscene sketch is your own work? Speak — I will have an answer.'

'The sketch is mine,' Jennifer admitted in a quavering voice, her pretty face flushing bright scarlet with shame.

'And what is this boy doing?' Harriet asked in an ice-cold voice. 'Why is his hand under his apron in that disgusting way? What is he doing to himself?'

'I don't know, Miss Harriet,' said the unhappy girl. 'When he sat like that for me to draw I thought that he was scratching himself. I could see his hand moving under the apron.'

'Do not play the innocent with me!' Harriet said harshly. 'I have been in charge of girls like you long enough to become acquainted with their tricks and schemes. Confess it now — you provoked Dickie to handle his private parts. Your sketch shows him at the very moment of sensual spasm, when he fetched off in his trousers!'

Jennifer thought she would faint away with shame. She stared at Miss Harriet, her pale lips moving but no words emerging.

212

'I thought as much!' said Miss Harriet, a cruel smile on her face. 'You are ashamed now that you have been caught out! And well you might be! Explain to me, if you can, how you came to be acquainted with the habit of self-gratification in boys?'

Jennifer burst into tears and hid her face in her hands.

'You understand the shocking gravity of your offence,' said Miss Harriet, 'and you well know the punishment for it. Bend over and raise your clothes behind.'

Terror stilled Jennifer's sobs, but she had no thought of not obeying the stern school mistress. She bent forward and with trembling hands lifted her frock.

'Untie the string of your drawers and drop them to your ankles,' was the next command of Miss Harriet. Jennifer did as she was told, so baring the soft round cheeks of her bottom for chastisement.

'Ten of the best!' cried the tormentor, and her flat whale-bone implement thrashed across Jennifer's tender cheeks making her scream for mercy.

When it was over, she ordered Jennifer to turn and face her, and get down on her knees. The chastened girl's face blushed as red as her bottom to observe that Miss Harriet had raised her own clothes to her waist, to expose her soft white drawers and stockings. With a firm hand she opened wide the slit and showed to the kneeling girl, without the least evidence of modesty or shame, her large and dark-haired pussy.

'It is my duty to make sure you understand properly what is involved in the act of self-gratification,' said Miss Harriet, her voice animated as her fingers prised open the soft lips of her own plump pussy. 'Of the habits of boys there is nothing to be said, but what young ladies do to themselves in private is of the greatest importance. Observe where I am touching with my finger, Jennifer,

213

this is the most sensitive spot of my person — are you aware of that?'

'I beg you, Miss Harriet, do not continue further!' Jennifer exclaimed, her face redder than ever.

'Do not be insolent!' said Miss Harriet, pulling open wider yet the lips of her pussy. 'Before our lesson is finished you will be thoroughly familiar with the many possibilities and the delights of sensuality. Put your tongue to the rosebud I have bared for you and let me feel you lick it.'

Monty broke off his reading, delighted to see Grace had gone a dark red in the face with her emotions. Her belly was quaking under her thin chemise, and her bosom rose and fell rapidly to her breathing. She implored him to lie on her and poke her hard to quell the storm of furious passion he had raised in her with his lewd book. He smiled at her in the most charming way, and told her that if things were that desperate with her, then she must relieve herself with her fingers.

'No!' she exclaimed, sounding as if she would swoon at the immodesty of his suggestion.

To encourage her, Monty slid off the bed, pulled her round on it until her legs dangled over the side towards him, then turned up her chemise above her titties. He stood between her knees, and pulled his shirt over his head, so that Grace imagined that he had relented and spread her legs wider to be mounted. With a chuckle, Monty took his stiff six inches in his clasping hand, and rubbed up and down in a brisk rhythm.

'Ah, you beast!' Grace moaned, her head rolling from side to side on the bed. 'To subject me to this indignity! But I have no power to restrain myself . . .'

Monty grinned down at her, his hand sliding up and down to see her pull open the wet lips of her pussy, to expose her firm nub and flick her fingers over it. In this manner they played with themselves, she staring at his straining shaft while he manipulated it, and he staring at her open pussy as she stroked it with nervous flicks.

'Monty — you beast — why didn't you make me do this before?' she gasped. 'In the past I've only done it alone, with feelings of shame — I had no idea that it would be so delicious to do it for you! The sensations are heavenly — now I know that I shall do it for you very often while you stand and watch me!'

'And I love to watch you playing with yourself while you see me playing with myself,' he responded eagerly, his hand moving all the faster as the crisis approached.

Only moments later, his creamy essence spurted out in a long curve over her, splashing on her pulsating belly and trickling down her sides in warm rivulets. Grace squealed in delight to watch the throbbing gushes, and feel the wetness on her skin, and with quick fingers rubbing in her slippery pussy she came off to a convulsive climax of lust.

CHAPTER 14
An Old Friend Reappears

By the first post on Thursday morning there arrived for Monty two letters, one of them with a Reading postmark and the other with a London mark. They were waiting for him on his breakfast table when he rose, propped against the toast rack. Naturally, it was the one from Reading that Monty's eager hand seized upon first, to have news at last of his beloved Gwendolen. It was contained in a thick square envelope, which he pressed a score of times to his lips in devotion, before using the butter knife to open it.

The letter in Gwendolen's firm, round and elegant handwriting was brief, but it stirred his deepest emotions.

My dearest boy,

A thousand, thousand thanks for your darling letter! You ask if I remember the joy and transport of being in your arms — ah, how it torments me by day and by night that I am prevented from enjoying that dear bliss! My charms, such as they are, are for you, darling Monty, and never can there be another since I have tasted with you the utmost delight that humankind may aspire to this side of Heaven! Only one other has ever penetrated to the innermost portion of my person — Selwyn — and of him you know all there is to know! As for my late husband Elliot, he never showed any interest in the treasure of mine that inspired your letter to me, but preferred a meaner route to his pleasure! I burn with impatience for the time when I shall be reunited with my dearest, and promise you faithfully that you shall not rise from the bed where we plight our troth until your manly shaft will no longer stand hard-on, and I lie prostrate and swooning before you from your mighty ravishing! May it be soon!

Your own loving Gwendolen

Secured to a bottom corner of the letter by a pin was a small dark-brown curl of hair. Monty caressed it with a fingertip, his heart pounding in his breast for joy that his darling girl had thought to send him this token of her love and affection — a curl clipped from her warm pussy! The thought flung him into so profound a reverie of love and devotion that his shaft stood thick and swollen and strong under his dressing gown, it being Monty's custom to postpone dressing until after his breakfast.

While he raised the letter to his lips and pressed a delicate kiss to Gwendolen's pussy curl, Monty slipped his other hand in his dressing gown and grasped his throbbing shaft through the thin material of his nightshirt. He sighed in joy when he felt how long and hard One-Eyed Jack had grown — and with every good reason, for Gwendolen in her letter was promising him hours of bliss when they met again! Ah, the ecstasy that would be his — lying on her bare belly, to fill her pretty pink slit to overflowing!

Sitting at the breakfast table, where the porridge was going cold under its cover, Monty crushed the letter to his lips and trembled through all his limbs with powerful emotion. One-Eyed Jack jumped in his hand, and Monty pulled his nightshirt up to his waist. His clasped hand gripped One-Eyed Jack tightly while he addressed him in terms of affection and optimism:

'Well may you stand hard and twitch,' said Monty, staring at the uncovered purple head of his shaft, 'for there are words of hope and encouragement for us from our darling Gwendolen — and more than words! Here is a silky little curl that grew on the pussy you love! What do you think of that, eh?'

One-Eyed Jack jumped for joy in Monty's grasp, demonstrating his approval very clearly. Monty's hand slid up and down the straining shaft, a vision of Gwendolen in his mind's eye — dear Gwendolen naked on a bed, lying on her back with her legs apart to make him welcome in that plump dark-haired pussy of hers.

'She misses you,' Monty sighed to his straining shaft, 'she longs to feel your solid six inches inside her. She yearns for your hot gush of love in her pussy! You may feel very proud of yourself that so beautiful a charmer as Gwendolen takes true delight in being rogered by you.'

Under the influence of Monty's affectionate fondling his hot shaft had grown to its fullest size and thickness and Monty smiled down at it in warm regard.

'Tell me what you feel for her,' he requested One-Eyed Jack. 'The same devotion as I do, I am sure, coupled with lust and a tireless desire to roger her.'

His enquiry was answered without delay. One-Eyed Jack bounded furiously and hurled a raging flood of passion into the air.

'Ah, yes!' Monty gasped, to the spurting of his shaft. 'You adore her and you display the manner of your adoration to me in the most unmistakable manner! So be it then — this is what you shall do to Gwendolen the instant she and I are reunited — I give you my word!'

During the time that One-Eyed Jack was calming himself after his demonstration of passion, Monty spoke to him in terms of warm comradeship, promising him most faithfully that he should soon enjoy all the delights of Gwendolen's beautiful body — not only her dark-haired pussy but also the bliss of fetching off up between her soft titties, and in her hot mouth, under her delicate armpits, and in various other delicious parts of her person. One-Eyed Jack heard this with great satisfaction, and after a twitch or two to show his appreciation, he curled up to dream sweetly of the delights in store until the moment came for him to unleash his strength yet again.

Only when his shaft had reverted to limpness and contentment did Monty think to open the second letter that lay on his table. He feared it might be a bill from his tailor or wine merchant, but it proved to be far more interesting than that. The envelope contained the briefest of notes — only two lines of writing — below which there stood for signature but a pair of initials.

Monty — I shall wait for you at three o'clock at Mrs Lee's and have much to tell. Keep my secret — tell no one of this!

NC

There could be no doubt who had sent this message — Naunton Cox, whom Monty thought to be taking refuge in Paris from the misfortunes that had befallen him for becoming interested in a Church of England vicar's wife on a train to town — a journey which had ended at Clapham Junction Station when he was caught in the very act of coming off in her hand. Evidently he had returned in secret to London. It would be a pleasure to see the dear fellow and hear of his adventures amongst the Frenchies.

The setting of the meeting place at Mrs Gladys Lee's in Margaret Street turned Monty's thoughts unerringly towards his favourite occupant of that house — namely, dear Miss Emmy, the seventeen-year-old with golden hair and lovely titties. So long did his reverie dwell upon her and how well he had rogered her at their last meeting, that Monty's shaft awoke again and stood hard-on, in spite of its recent tribute to darling Gwendolen.

It was Mrs Lee's very well-known custom to open her house to gentlemen visitors with guineas in their pocket at two o'clock each afternoon, thus affording to herself and the young women under her protection the whole of the morning to themselves. If any lecherous gentlemen required the use of a female commodity before lunch then he must look for it elsewhere and not in Margaret Street. In dire necessity he could take a hansom cab to Covent Garden market, where the flower girls made themselves available from four in the morning.

There was nothing refined about them, and who could expect it for the shilling or two they charged? Not that a man in urgent need is fussy, and the market girls would stand readily against a wall and raise their bedraggled skirts to bare a pussy for the accommodation of a paying guest. Nor were the men who went to Covent Garden for relief of their letch of good class, or so said Mrs Lee, whose considered opinion it was that a gentleman did not require female service before noon.

'I see,' said Monty, when she explained her views to him over a glass of brandy in her parlour, 'and to what do you attribute this, if I may enquire?'

'In society,' said Mrs Lee, 'a gentleman rises early and goes out to ride in the park. He has no time to take an interest in poking until later in the day.'

'But it is a well-known physiological fact,' Monty objected, 'that a gentleman wakes in the morning with a hard-on stand. It cannot be dismissed as of no significance, as you would appear to do. For the married there is no problem in this — he simply rolls on top of his dear wife as she lies sleeping beside him, and wakes her with a morning poke. The unmarried have no such useful recourse to hand — what are they to do?'

'You have answered your own question,' said Mrs Lee with a coarse chuckle, 'their remedy is readily to hand. They make use of their own five fingers, or summon a servant to perform the task for them.'

'Quite so,' said Monty, who had paid Minnie to bring relief to his stiffness on many a morning, 'a willing maidservant is a boon and a blessing.'

'And the ruination of my business!' Mrs Lee retorted. 'Maid servants are in general stupid and soon find themselves with a big belly and are turned out in the streets without a reference and in disgrace. The titled gentlemen who honour my house with their presence do not demean themselves to poke servant girls, that I can assure you of, Mr Standish.'

'But you said a moment ago that a servant is summoned to the bedside to unburden them of the morning stand!' said Monty.

'I meant their valet,' she replied. 'A gentleman's gentleman is trained in the art of slipping a hand into the bed to bring off his master with a delicate touch in the early morning, even before he is fully awake and ready for his tea. I fear you are not acquainted with the customs of the upper classes.'

'I confess that I am not,' said Monty, 'and to be truthful, I am surprised by what you have told me. Is this general, do you suppose, or is it the whim of one individual you know of?'

'I am given to understand that it is universally in vogue in good society,' Mrs Lee replied, 'and I have heard this from the lips of three lords, a marquis and a duke, who have honoured my girls. Naturally, the valet wears white cotton gloves when he performs this duty, in order that the aristocratic shaft is not in contact with common flesh.'

'Except when it rogers your girls,' Monty pointed out.

'That is different,' said Mrs Lee, 'for in the conjunction of shaft and pussy, there are no distinctions made of aristocratic and common. In the act itself all are considered to be of equal worth, as when our ancestor Adam rogered Eve, before divisions of class had arisen.'

'This is all most interesting,' said Monty, 'and I am your debtor for enlightening me as to the daily duties of valets in noble households. Now, if we may reach our usual arrangement about fee, I will take my leave and go upstairs to present my compliments to Miss Emmy.'

He had arrived at Mrs Lee's house not at three o'clock, as he had been bidden by Naunton Cox, but immediately the front door was opened to visitors, at two. His intention was to first pass a pleasant hour in poking Miss Emmy before Naunton arrived.

'That will not be possible, I regret to say,' Mrs Lee said to him with a shake of her head. 'The desirable Miss Emmy has gone to Limehouse today to attend her father's funeral. But there is a new girl since you were last here — a darling little creature named Miss Arabella. She is only sixteen, and of a beauty that has thrown Lord Granston into a perfect rapture — at the sight of her titties he shot his noble roe in his trousers and needed a large glass of brandy to revive him before he could continue with her!'

'Is she fair or dark?' Monty enquired.

'Her hair is as black as a raven's wing and her eyes as dark as a starless night,' said Mrs Lee in a fine poetic frenzy. 'An hour with her will bring you all the delight of half a day with any other of my girls.'

'His Lordship's accidental spillage is not a recommendation,' said Monty thoughtfully. 'He is surely one whose valet fetches him off before he stirs in the morning. Miss Arabella sounds to me like a chimney-sweep's wench from your description.'

'It is unworthy of you to dispraise the girl before you seen her,' Mrs Lee told him. 'I'll tell you what I'll do, since you are one of my regulars and a favourite of mine — instead of the five guineas I'd ask anyone else, you shall enjoy the dear girl for only three. I can't say fairer than that, can I?'

'Two guineas,' said Monty.

'You're a shrewd bargainer, Mr Standish,' said the old bawd, 'but I like you — very well, you shall have her for two!'

Monty handed over the money, and Mrs Lee escorted him up the stairs and knocked at the door of the front bedroom. Without waiting for a response, she turned the knob and nodded to Monty to go in.

'A gentleman to visit you, Arabella dear,' she called from the doorway. 'Be pleasant to him for he is a friend of mine, and a handsome young fellow.'

The door closed behind Monty who stared at the girl who lay on the bed. She wore only a chemise and drawers — no stockings or stays — and his heart lurched in delight at the sight of her. At Mrs Lee's voice she had turned on her side towards the door, disclosing to Monty's sight her smooth bare shoulders and, down the loose front of her chemise, the plump soft roundness of her titties.

Her long and softly waved hair was as black as Mrs Lee had promised, making Monty at once speculate whether the curls that grew between her legs were of the same raven hue. He introduced himself to the lovely girl whilst crossing the room to the bed, where he took a seat on the edge and gazed down at her in warm admiration. She gave him her hand to hold between both of his — a dainty little hand with a tender palm and slender fingers. He imagined those fingers curled about his shaft, which at once reared itself upright in his trousers and stood quivering.

'Dear Miss Arabella,' said he, 'you are even more lovely than Mrs Lee was capable of informing me. I beg you will enrol me on the list of your devoted admirers from this moment on.'

'How kind you are,' she murmured, her jet-black eyes glowing with affection, 'I hope you will come and see me often now that we have made each other's acquaintance.'

'You may rely on me,' he assured her, 'and I trust that you will admit me to your confidence in a matter that is giving me some little puzzlement.'

'And what might that be?'

'Why, it is this, my dear — are your nether curls as blackly beautiful as the hair that graces your pretty head?'

'You must judge of that for yourself,' said she, and slid her legs apart on the bed. Her delicate fingers drew open the slit of her cotton drawers, and there in full sight lay one of the prettiest playthings Monty had ever set eyes on. Framed between deliciously creamy white thighs, her thicket of curls was as black as the Ace of Spades! Monty breathed out in a long and ardent sigh of desire at the very sight of it, and pressed his hand to his trouser-front to hold his wildly shaking shaft still.

'Oh, not you too!' Miss Arabella exclaimed, her dainty hand resting on a thigh so that her fingertips just touched the pretty pink lips of her pussy. 'Have you come off already?'

'You need have no fear,' said Monty. 'I am no effete lord who shoots off his essence into his shirt-front before ever he gets it near a girl's pussy, let alone up it.'

'Are you quite sure of that?' she asked with a smile.

She sat up on the bed and opened Monty's trouser buttons with a skilled hand, pulled up his shirt and felt between her cool fingers the hardness of his shaft.

'How it leaps in my hand!' she cried, her fingers gliding up and down its length. Monty sighed in delight and put his hand into her drawers to play with her warm pussy and part the lips to find her proud little bud and tease it gently.

'And does it match up to your expectations?' she enquired.

'Oh, Arabella — I declare that you have the prettiest pussy I have seen for a very long time,' he murmured, his belly quaking to the spasms of delight her fingers on his shaft sent rushing through him.

'And you fully intend to roger it?' she asked with a smile.

'Yes . . .' he sighed, 'yes . . .' and at that very instant his sap gushed out of his leaping shaft under the ministrations of her busy hand. She laughed and drew out his pleasure to its limit then, when he spouted no more, released his sticky shaft and lay back on the bed again.

'I love a good rogering,' she taunted him. 'Why do you delay? Push your shaft up me and do me hard!'

'So that is your game, you minx!' said Monty, astonished by how easily and quickly she had brought him off. 'Two can play at that, my girl!'

His hand was in her drawers, his fingers thrust deep into her moist pussy, rubbing her pink nub until her back lifted off the bed and she moaned in climax. Before she recovered from that, a resumption of his stimulation caused her to gasp and throw her legs about, and in another minute he brought her off again. By then his shaft was standing hard-on once more and, even as she spread her legs wide to be fingered to yet another climactic spasm, Monty threw himself on her and pushed One-Eyed Jack deep into her slippery split.

'Ah, so you do mean to roger me after all!' she gasped. 'I had put you down as another lordling's son and heir who lacked the stamina for poking, and needed to be brought off by hand!'

'Then you mistook your man,' Monty grunted as he poked her fast and hard, his hands up under her chemise to grasp her soft titties and squeeze them. They rose and fell to the swift pace of her agitated breathing and she rolled her bottom from side to side beneath him whilst he ravaged her with sensations. She came off with a little shriek, her hot belly pressed so tightly to Monty's that the jet-black curls about her pussy were twined into the chestnut-brown curls round the base of his plunging shaft. Monty moaned in heavenly bliss and flooded her clinging pussy with long throbbing spurts.

After that, Arabella wanted him to stay with her and repeat their pleasures but Monty begged off, saying with truth that a friend was waiting for him at this very moment. She extracted a sincere promise from him that he would return to her soon and give her another taste of ecstasy. Monty adjusted his clothes decently, kissed her *farewell* and went downstairs. He found, as he fully expected, Naunton Cox in Mrs Lee's parlour, conversing with her while he finished her bottle of brandy.

They wrung each other's hand and slapped each other's back in the joy of their meeting. Monty suggested they should repair to the Cafe Royal to crack a bottle of Napoleon brandy by way of a celebration, but Naunton explained that he dare not be seen in a public place for the police had his description. Mrs Lee's alone seemed to him a safe haven.

'Then I'll leave you gentlemen to talk,' said Mrs Lee, rising to her feet. 'I'll send another bottle in for you.'

They thanked her for her kind hospitality, fully aware that they would be required to pay for it, and she left them alone.

'Lord above, Naunton — why are the police looking for you?' Monty asked. 'And why have you come back from Paris so soon?'

'You recall my telling you of that infernal bank manager who burst into the carriage and discovered me with Louise?' said Naunton. 'Thwarted of his prey at the time, when we both gave him the slip, the damned busybody wrote a nasty letter and sent it to my aged uncle at Effingham — the one whose heir I hope to be! In this letter the wretch blabbed all he had seen and gave it as his opinion that I am not a suitable person to inherit uncle's property and investments when the Grim Reaper pops down to Effingham! The frightful cheek of it! What a bounder this Bramley is, to go sneaking on a chap like that!'

'Great Scot!' Monty exclaimed. 'He should be horse-whipped! Is there anything I can do to help?'

'I've already revenged myself on him,' said Naunton, a savage grin on his handsome face. 'I crossed the

Channel yesterday and reached London by the boat train that set me down at Victoria station in the early evening. I concealed myself in the station buffet until eight o'clock, when I knew that Bramley the bank manager would out of his house in Clapham . . .'

'Wait!' said Monty, 'How could you know that? You have been in Paris since the ghastly day Bramley found you fetching off with the vicar's wife.'

'I am not without influence,' said Naunton, mysteriously. Then taking pity on Monty's bewilderment, he revealed that from Paris he had been in touch by letter-post with Minnie!

'She's a useful girl to know and she'll do anything for me,' said Naunton. 'Many is the poke I gave her when no other slit was available to me. Have you had her yourself, Monty?'

'As you say — she's handy in those otherwise lonely moments,' said Monty. 'Particularly in the early morning, when a fellow wakes up with a standing hard-on. But were you aware during your residence at Mrs Gifford's that Minnie's domestic duties include her bringing off the landlady by hand every night at bedtime?'

'No!' Naunton exclaimed. 'Who'd have thought it! You have truly astounded me. How did you get it out of Minnie? It must be her deepest secret?'

'I got it *out* of her at a time when I had it *in* her,' Monty answered, 'and to cure Hannah of her Sapphic tendencies, I went to her room at bedtime and had her enough times to assuage her curious urges and give her a rattling good night!'

'Damn me!' cried Naunton. 'You've been busy since I left! But to get back to my story, through Minnie I found out when my hated bank manager attends his Lodge Meetings. I made my way to his house and the servant showed me into the sitting room when I told her I was a colleague of her master. As I had intended, Mrs Bramley was alone, passing the time with embroidering. She went very pale when she recognised me but my tale was that I had come to apologise humbly to Mr Bramley, and I gave a fine appearance of being disappointed when she told me he would not return home before eleven, or even later.'

'You are a sly devil, Naunton,' said Monty, in admiration. 'I have no doubt your golden tongue was able to persuade her that nothing untoward was taking place in the railway carriage, and that she mistook what she saw that day.'

'Not at all!' his friend declared. 'The contrary, in fact. I explained that I was at the time head over heels in love with the lady she and Mr Bramley found with me when they entered the carriage at Clapham Junction but that family reasons prevented us from marrying. On the day in question I was escorting dear Louise to London to care for her paralysed mother and we knew that we should never see each other again. What Mrs Bramley and her husband had witnessed was the natural expression of a profound love Louise and I felt for each other.'

'By George — did she swallow it?' asked Monty.

'An interesting choice of words,' said Naunton with a grin, 'for as you will remember what Mrs Bramley — whose given name is Flora — had observed was dear Louise swallowing it! Take my word for it, Monty old sport, when a woman has had a good look at your shaft in a condition of full erection, she indulges in fantasies of it and is like to want to see it again. Flora had seen mine not only stiff but at the instant it was pulled out of Louise's mouth as I came off. No woman could forget that, or the trickles down Louise's face. As we sat talking

I could see Flora's agitation growing as she rehearsed the scene again and again in her mind's eye. I observed her covert glances down at my trousers and the trembling of her legs. In short, I need do nothing at all but sit there and let Flora see me and remember — and in remembering she became more and more excited.'

'But this is fiendish!' Monty exclaimed. 'You had her!'

'Simplicity itself,' Naunton agreed. 'At the right moment I whipped out my hard-on shaft in front of her and she uttered a long sigh. I left my chair to kneel at her feet and raise her skirts. Her legs opened like a pair of cabinet doors and I had her drawers gaping wide and my shaft up her in a flash.'

'You told me that Mr Bramley was middle-aged,' Monty reminded him. 'Was Flora not above the age of desirability also?'

'She is not yet forty,' said Naunton, 'and many a good tune is played on an old fiddle, my boy. I poked her sitting in her armchair to the best come off she'd ever had in her life, then laid her on the sofa and rogered her three more times. When the time came for me to go before Bramley returned, she implored me to visit her every day, in the afternoon when her husband is at the bank. Needless to say, I shall not do so, for my revenge is now complete.'

'But why are the police looking for you?' asked Monty.

'A small miscalculation on my part,' Naunton confessed. 'I pawned my gold watch in Paris and there being no clock in the Bramley parlour, I lost track of the passing of time. As I left by the front door, the bounder Bramley was coming in! A look passed between us on the doorstep and from my expression of triumph he guessed what I had been doing! He chased me for at least half a mile down the road, shouting vile imprecations and waving his walking stick at me in a threatening manner. But I am fleeter of foot, and made my escape.'

'And the police?' Monty asked.

'A news item in the morning newspaper reports a break-in at a house in Clapham last night, with the abuse of females and the theft of valuable property. The householder is named as Alfred Bramley, a bank official. I am certain that in his rage he lied to the police about my presence in his house and demanded my arrest on these monstrous charges. So I shall remain here until time for the evening boat train, then go by closed cab to the railway station to slip out of Old England yet again.'

'What about your uncle at Effingham?' Monty asked. 'Has he cut you off as a result of Bramley's sneaking ways?'

'Thank Heaven, no,' said Naunton in great relief. 'Uncle Bart was a goer in his day, it seems, and he wrote me a kind letter in Paris to congratulate me on pulling it off with a woman on a railway train — a feat he had more than once attempted, but had never achieved.'

'"Then there was no need to seduce Bramley's wife, since his evil plan had miscarried,' said Monty.

'Yes, there was,' Naunton retorted. 'I wanted my revenge and I had it. I have written to my uncle with the full facts, and I am sure he will be proud of his nephew when he reads that I have exacted vengeance on my persecutor. He enclosed a twenty-pound note with his first letter — I have every hope he will do the same again when he hears of my double achievement last night.'

'Double? What do you mean by that?'

'After I had shaken off Bramley, I rested for half an hour in a low drinking den in Vauxhall. It was there that I penned the letter you had from me this morning. Whilst

I refreshed myself with a glass or two of gin, a thought struck me with the force of a thunderbolt — if I had revenged myself so pleasantly on Bramley by poking his wife, then why not his daughter too?'

'Has he one?'

'Most certainly — a plump girl of sixteen. When Bramley took me by surprise in the railway carriage, his whole family trooped in behind him and caught me in the act of coming off. There was Flora and her three children — of whom the girl is the eldest, and two boys. With a renewed thirst for revenge in my heart, I waited for an hour and then returned to Bramley's home. It was silent and dark and locked up for the night, but I effected an entrance by means of a scullery window. Upstairs I prowled the dark passages and pressed my ear to doors, till I located the room shared by Bramley's sons, and the one next to it in which his daughter slept alone.'

'What a fearful risk you ran!' Monty exclaimed. 'If you ever are captured by the police you will be convicted of a serious crime and sent to Dartmoor prison to break stones.'

'I slid into Hermione's room — for that is her name — put on the gaslight at half-full and woke her with a kiss,' Naunton continued. 'She recognised me at once, and the same forces were at work in her as in her mother — she had seen my shaft at full stretch on the train, and the image remained in her imagination to excite her. Believe me, dear old chum, all it took was three or four minutes persuasive talk by me and her nightgown was up round her neck and I was sucking her titties.'

'You are a perfect devil!' said Monty, his eyes shining with amusement. 'She was a virgin, I make no doubt.'

'Quite so,' Naunton confirmed, 'but willing to be

relieved of her virginity by the shaft she had seen in action elsewhere. I bared it for her and she fondled it with such enthusiasm that I fetched off in her hand. After that nothing would satisfy her but to have it up her! She spread her chubby thighs wide for me and I lay on her fat belly. I brought my shaft to the mark and pressed it slightly between the lips of her pussy. Shudders of delight passed through Hermione's tubby body and with a dear little smile she whispered, *I know it may hurt, my darling, but I must have it up me.* She heaved up her bottom to meet me, and with no more ado, I gave a good hard push and broke through her maiden membrane. The dear girl winced but she made no outcry. I did her with caution that first time and she came off most voluptuously the instant she felt my gushing cream inside her. Before I crept out of the house in the light of dawn I had rogered her thrice more, and she had developed a strong liking for it.'

'Where did you go then?' Monty asked, from curiosity.

'As it happens,' said Naunton, 'I have for some long time now been acquainted with a young married woman at Battersea and I took myself by cab to her house. Her husband is employed by the Gas Light and Coke Company and departs for his place of work at half past six every morning. I lurked opposite until I saw him leave the house, then presented myself to Matilda. She was very pleased to see me after so long an absence abroad and she made me most welcome. After I had told her of my pursuers and given her a good poking in the manner she prefers, she allowed me to sleep until it was time to come here to meet you.'

'And what, pray, is the manner she prefers?' enquired Monty.

'Sitting on the kitchen table, stripped down to her

stockings and drawers,' Naunton explained, 'her legs clamped tight about my waist as I stand between her knees and do her slowly. I find it fatiguing to roger in the standing position, particularly at the third time of coming off, but in the circumstances, it was needful to keep Matilda sweet by falling in with her desire to be poked upright. Naturally, after I had restored my energies in sleep, before I left her I insisted on throwing her down on her back and doing her the proper way.'

'We have some hours until you leave for the railway station,' said Monty with a grin, 'I intended to suggest to you that good use could be made of them upstairs here with a newcomer to Mrs Lee's — a charming young creature by the name of Miss Arabella. Between us we could roger her royally — but I fear you have so exerted yourself with Mr Bramley's women-folk and your married friend Matilda that you have no strength left for poking.'

'You do me an injustice,' Naunton replied at once. 'My sleep, after I had done my duty by Matilda's hot pussy a time or two, refreshed me completely and I am ready for another bout. Your account of Mrs Gifford's tastes has whetted my appetite and I owe Minnie a guinea or two and a good poke for her assistance. Miss Arabella can wait for some other time — let us take a closed carriage to Seymour Place now and together give maid and mistress the rogering of their life until it is time for me to depart.'

'By all means,' said Monty, ready to oblige his old friend whatever he proposed.

'Mrs Gifford, as I recall, has a large pair of titties under her clothes,' said Naunton, 'Are they a good feel?'

'When her stays are removed, her titties are heavy though slack and pendulous,' Monty informed him, 'But they are warm and soft — ideal for wrapping round your shaft and fetching off between. We can take turns at doing that, while the other makes use of her pussy at the same time.'

'Capital!' cried Naunton.

CHAPTER 15
Lovers United in Bliss

In the week that followed Naunton Cox's clandestine journey to London to wreak vengeance on the person who was trying to ruin his life and prospects, Monty received yet another letter from his darling Gwendolen. This was of a strikingly different tone to the first, written not in the yearning of thwarted passion, but in confident hope and expectation. It was delivered in the midday post and the postmark showed that it had been sent that morning from South Kensington.

At the sight of his dearest girl's handwriting, Monty kissed the envelope and tore it open with a trembling hand. Within he found a missive that was brief and to the point:

My darling boy,
Our love has triumphed over all adversities! Come to me at the above address! Hasten!

Your own loving Gwendolen

The address at the head of the page was in Brompton Road. Monty put on his hat and hurried along Seymour Place to the cab rank, and was on his way within minutes of reading Gwendolen's note. His brain whirled in speculation — what could this address be at which she awaited him? The house of a friend, perhaps? Not that it mattered in the least — she was in town and would soon be in his arms! Yet it seemed to him strange that Selwyn had said nothing of friends in South Kensington, nor of a visit by his sister to London.

The house, when Monty was set down outside it, appeared very respectable and well-kept. He bounded up the steps and rang the doorbell with a light heart, his hat at a jaunty angle. A maid opened the door, a pleasant-faced woman of thirty, and enquired his name. When he told her, she stepped aside for him to enter, saying that Mrs Fanshawe was expecting him. She conducted him upstairs to the drawing room, announced him and withdrew. With a racing heart and outstretched hands, Monty stepped forward to where Gwendolen stood by the piano. From head to toe she was dressed in the deep black of mourning.

She ran to meet him and was in his arms in a trice, her lips to his in a burning kiss and her belly pressing hard against him. Monty's arms were about her in a loving embrace and while the kiss continued, his hands slid down her slender back until he was kneading the cheeks of her bottom through the silk crepe of her dress.

'Yes — take me!' she cried. 'I have dreamed of this moment night after night! Make my dream reality, my dearest Monty!'

With no thought for the time of day or fear of interruption, he pressed her down on the sofa and laid her on her back. She trembled and her beautiful face flushed pink, and she implored him to be swift and put her out of her sweet suffering. On his knees at her side, Monty turned up her skirts over stockings as black as jet to find to his astonishment that she was wearing thin black drawers!

This was by no means the first time Monty had rogered a young widow but never before had he seen black underclothes. He ran his hand over the fine material, feeling up between her legs, and Gwendolen smiled at him and asked did he not find her drawers stylish?

'They are utterly delightful,' he said, 'though I must admit it is what they conceal that gives them their *bon ton*!'

'They shall not conceal anything an instant longer than you choose,' said she. 'Take me however you will, my dearest!'

Monty's trembling hand had parted the slit of her drawers to bare her treasure for his attentions. The piquant contrast of jet-black crepe juxtaposed to her creamy white belly made him gasp loudly in admiration, and his hard-on shaft throbbed and leapt in his trousers. Then, with a hoarse cry of ardent desire, he bowed his head and pressed his mouth in a burning kiss to Gwendolen's pouting pussy.

'How many times I have dreamed of this blissful moment!' she exclaimed. 'How man nights I have lain awake in the torment of love, wet with passion!'

She reached down and jerked so hard at Monty's trousers, to open them and release his straining shaft, that all the buttons were torn loose and rolled under the sofa she lay on. One-Eyed Jack leapt out from under Monty's shirt at full stretch and eager for the fray. In a flash, Monty sprang to his feet, threw off his jacket and loosened the knot of his necktie, preparing himself for the pleasant exertions to come.

The moment that Gwendolen saw that he was ready for her — his straining shaft in his hand, its purple head bared for action — she spread wide her legs with deliberate slowness. The effect was extremely arousing — Monty stood motionless and hardly able to breathe as he watched

239

her black-drawered thighs moving apart on the cushions. The slit in the raven-hued crepe gaped open to the full, revealing to him her dark fleece, the delicate white hollows of her groins, and the fleshy groove of her pussy.

Monty groaned in delight and got on the sofa with her, on his knees between her thighs, his swollen shaft sticking out over her belly like a signpost showing the way to pleasure. He was running his clasped hand up and down it, aroused almost to the point of delirium by the pink-lipped pussy held wide open for him by the position of Gwendolen's legs.

'Put it in me before you fetch off over my drawers,' she said with a sigh of longing.

Monty obliged her at once, flinging himself onto her heaving belly and guiding himself into her with an eager hand. Even as he started to slide into her with a strong push and felt the warm wet cling of her pussy about his hot shaft, he knew that he had been away from his beloved too long. He was trembling on the very brink of coming off without even a single thrust! He shook passionately, transmitting to her his desperate condition, so that she smiled and said softly, *Love me, Monty, love me*!

Thus urged by his darling, Monty continued with his upward progress and pushed slowly into the depths of her warm wetness. The sensations were so prodigious that he fetched off at once, spouting his frantic desire into her.

'Oh yes — you are mine!' Gwendolen sighed as she felt his hot pulsations in her belly. 'Mine, mine, mine!'

She raised her legs and wound them about his waist to hold him fast, then moaned in ecstasy as his hard and gushing shaft reached her ultimate depths. He writhed on her, continuing to pour his youthful virility into her in fast spurts, while she lay squirming beneath him, uttering little cries of triumph.

'Yes, you are mine, Monty, mine!' she panted. 'You love me with all your heart and soul! I feel it in your coming off.

He thrilled to her words and emptied his tumultuous passion into her quivering belly. When at last he was calm once more, he lay beside her holding her in his arms, his lips pressed to her soft cheek, while he assured her of his undying devotion.

'When I felt your rapture gushing,' said she, 'the sensations aroused in me were so sublime that I understood for the first time the force of those lines of poetry by Mr Matthew Arnold in which he speaks of the awareness of life's flow.'

'The lines to which you refer do not spring readily to mind,' murmured Monty, his hand right up her clothes to feel her soft titties. 'Remind me, if you will be so good.'

'With all the pleasure in the world. This is what Mr Arnold said on the subject:

A bolt is shot back somewhere in our breast,
And a lost pulse of feeling stirs again.
A man becomes aware of his life's flow,
And hears its winding murmur, and he sees
The meadows where it glides, the sun, the breeze.'

'How true, how very true!' Monty sighed. 'And now I come think of it, there are some other lines by the same poet which have always struck me most forcibly.'

'Recite them to me, I beg you,' said Gwendolen, and her small warm hand clasped his limp shaft.

Monty collected his thoughts for a moment, then launched into the little-quoted lines of strong sentiment:

'A life time of wet dreams my strength to drain
I gladly would endure and not complain,
To gain possession of my darling's charms
And pass an hour of bliss in her soft arms;
My trembling hand to feel her snow-white breast
While tongue and lips make free with all the rest!
I hear her lusting sobs, her eager sighs,
To feel my hard-on shaft between her thighs,
My hairy pompoms dangling down below,
And swinging in between those cheeks of snow,
As in her slit I thrust with might and main,
And feel her heaving belly quake and strain,
Until my passion gushes hot and fast,
And she comes off, and tranquil lies at last.'

'Yes!' Gwendolen cried. 'The yearning of the lover is well expressed in these lines, and the satisfaction that comes from a good rogering!'

'To Monty's surprise, she freed herself from his embrace, rose from the sofa and went to the grand piano, smoothing down her clothes before she sat at the keyboard and raised the lid to play. He sat up and put his feet on the floor as the strains of *Come into the garden, Maud* sounded through the room. A moment later he stood at his darling's side, his hand on her shoulder and his limp shaft dangling loose from his open trousers, while he raised his pleasant tenor voice in song to her melody:

'All night have the roses heard
The flute, violin, bassoon;
All night has the casement jessamine stirred
To the dancers dancing in tune;
Till a silence fell with the waking bird,
And a hush with the setting moon.'

Whilst he sang he watched Gwendolen's nimble fingers over the ivory keys and wished they were playing on his shaft, which at the suggestion twitched a little in sleepy approval. Gwendolen seemed almost to read his thoughts, and paused a moment or two in her playing to turn her head and bestow a tender little kiss on One-Eyed Jack as he swung close to her.

Monty warbled the next stanza as the piano resumed its music:

> *'Queen rose of the rosebud garden of girls,*
> *Come hither, the dances are done,*
> *In gloss of satin and glimmer of pearls,*
> *Queen lily and rose in one;*
> *Shine out, little head, sunning over with curls,*
> *To the flowers, and be their sun!'*

He saw Gwendolen's bosom heaving with emotion under her black mourning garb and, stirred by the thought of her white titties beneath that sombre crepe silk, he serenaded her with a stanza not sung round the piano in mixed company:

> *'Sweet rose with the rosebud hid twixt your thighs,*
> *Come with me, lie down by the stream,*
> *For feeling and licking and hot lustful sighs,*
> *And all the long thrills of love's dream;*
> *Be wet, little pussy, be open, my prize,*
> *While I fill you brimful with my cream!'*

'Oh!' Gwendolen exclaimed. 'Are they the words of dear Lord Tennyson?'

Her hand took an affectionate hold on Monty's strengthening shaft and tugged him round to stand with his back to the piano. She stood up and raised her clothes in front to reveal to him again her thin black drawers.

'Then in the immortal words of our revered Poet Laureate, my pussy is wet and open for you, my darling,' cried she, parting wide the slit of her drawers to show him that she spoke only the truth. Monty stared down open-mouthed, to see her fingers stretching open her dark-curled slit, and he sighed in deep joy when with a dainty hand she took hold of One-Eyed Jack, now at his full six-inch length again, and slipped his swollen purple head inside her.

'Gwendolen — how delicious that you want to be rogered again so soon!' Monty sighed in delight.

His arms were round her waist and his hands laid flat on the plump cheeks of her bottom to squeeze them through her dress. Gwendolen pushed slowly forward against him and, looking down, he observed how his shaft stretched her pussy wide open as it slid in. She placed her small hands on his shoulders and leaned forward to kiss his mouth while she pressed her belly to him. Her hot kiss and the movements of her loins set Monty's blood racing faster in his veins.

'You are mine, my dearest one,' he babbled, feeling his shaft jerking furiously of its own accord inside her, 'every darling sweet part of you — your darling face, your darling eyes and mouth, your darling soft titties, your darling warm belly and thighs, your darling pussy . . .'

'No, Monty,' said she, with a soft, loving smile. 'It is you who are mine. I told you that — you cannot have forgotten.'

'What difference is there?' he sighed. 'I am yours, you are mine, my darling girl . . .'

With the loving smile still on her beautiful face, Gwendolen started to roger *him* with thrusts of her belly against his, as she pressed close.

'The difference is nothing you need trouble yourself with, my dearest,' she said, her voice becoming tremulous as the thrills running through her grew stronger. 'Let me concern myself with the subtleties of such matters — all you need do is to remain in readiness to roger me whenever I tell you, day or night!'

At her confident words, Monty felt the sap begin to surge up his shaft and in another second it would fill her pussy with a delirium of sensation! He grappled her to him with hands that clenched on her bottom and thrust up in her to the very limit. Then, with a long gasping moan of heavenly enjoyment, he gushed his copious flood into her belly.

'More, more, more!' Gwendolen cried.

At this he realised that she had not yet achieved her moments of ecstasy and was waiting for him to carry her up to a climax of bliss. His shaft had ceased to spurt but she maintained her vigorous thrusts against him until the moment came, and with a long moan she shuddered and thrust her tongue into his mouth. When at last her tremors of delight were over, she sank limply down from his arms until she sat on the piano-seat.

Monty sat beside her, and raised her clothes to her waist yet again to pull open the wet slit of her drawers. With pride in his beating heart he saw the traces of his passion — his white essence trickling down the insides of her soft thighs from the loose lips of her pussy.

'Gwendolen, my dearest girl,' he whispered in her ear, whilst he stroked her slippery thighs with languid fingers, 'I hardly know whether to say that I rogered you then, or you rogered me, for in the joys of our coming off it seemed to me that we were united as one flesh. Did it seem like that to you, my angel?'

'Dear sweet Monty — do not speak so foolishly,' she

replied, 'I rogered you, my dear, and made you come off very nicely.'

'Not so,' he returned fondly, 'for I brought *you* off.'

By way of answer Gwendolen stood up, holding her clothes up about her waist, turned herself round to face him and sat down astride his thighs. She took his soft and sticky shaft in her fingers and rubbed the head slowly up and down the soft moist lips between her black-clad thighs.

'We will have no misunderstanding between us as to which of us is going to roger the other from now on, my dearest,' said she. 'Since there appears to be some question in your mind as to what precisely occurred when we were standing up together, I shall enlighten you now we are sitting down.'

Although he had only just fetched off, the sustained sight of Gwendolen's jet-black silk drawers, coupled with her soft, slow rubbing of One-Eyed Jack against her wet pussy, aroused Monty almost at once. No sooner was his shaft at full stretch again than Gwendolen raised herself from his lap, held it to the mark and sank down on it, impaling herself neatly.

'Now, my precious boy,' said she, 'I am going to roger you — so do not pretend otherwise after you have come off.'

With that, she threw her arms about his neck drew his face to hers, and kissed him and sucked his tongue whilst riding up and down on his embedded shaft. Immediately Monty's head began to swim as if he were drunk on the best brandy, and he clasped Gwendolen by her slender waist and abandoned himself utterly to the blissful sensations that rolled through him like a tide of the mighty ocean.

She, too, was enjoying the most divine thrills, he was aware — and from her broken gasps and the little spasms that shook her body, Monty knew that his darling was about to come off! His heart pounded for joy in his breast and he sighed his passion into her open mouth. His eager hands were under her clothes and inside her black drawers, stroking her warm thighs and belly in divine rapture. Her rise and fall on his shaft became brisker as her excitement gathered strength towards a crisis, forcing his penetrating shaft deeper and harder into her.

The bliss became too overpowering to bear! Monty gasped out in broken little words his eternal love for her and gushed his passion into her massaging pussy.

'I've brought you off!' she cried. 'Admit that you've been soundly rogered, Monty!'

'Yes . . .' he sighed, as his love and desire spurted into her, 'yes, my darling girl, you have rogered me . . . I admit it with pride and delight . . .'

On hearing his words, Gwendolen at once attained the peak of sensation. With One-Eyed Jack right up inside her she shook to the throes of her own coming off, uttering cries and moans and shuddering continuously in ecstasy. When at length her pleasure was completed she sat half-swooning against Monty, her head on his shoulder, her body shaken from time to time by little tremors.

'I must rest a little,' she whispered. 'Help me to the sofa.'

To demonstrate to his beloved that his manly strength was at her disposal in all possible ways, Monty rose to his feet with her in his arms and carried her across the room. He stretched her out at full length on the sofa, and would have pulled down her clothes to cover her endearing young charms — but she with a sweet smile asked him to remove her drawers.

With shaking hands he did as his darling bade him, and on her soft white belly and dark-haired mound he planted a score or more of kisses. She instructed him to remove her frock and by raising her bottom and then her shoulders, aided him in getting it off. Like her drawers, her thin chemise was of finest black silk, completing her mourning attire.

Was this all for the sake of a husband for whom she felt no love and no respect? Monty pondered the question while he slid her black stockings down her white legs, so rendering her completely naked. This for a husband who shot his elixir in the wrong orifice and cheated her of her conjugal pleasures? The thought was absurd — the purpose of this beautiful black finery was to sensually arouse the beholder, namely himself.

'Put your back to me for a moment,' said Gwendolen.

She sat up on the sofa, her full round titties swinging to her movement. Monty bowed his head to press a kiss to the pink bud of each, then obeyed her, wondering at her intentions. Then he knew — he felt his wrists drawn together behind his back and bound with one of her stockings. Even while his mind ran wildly on this new development, Gwendolen put her black drawers about his face and tied them behind his neck, covering his mouth and nose but allowing him his sense of sight.

He turned towards her and she lay on her back once more, her legs slightly parted to show her plump and pink-lipped pussy to best advantage. Above his jet-black gag Monty gazed at her with eyes filled with devotion. The scent of her warm flesh lingered on the thin silk, mingled with the Lily-of-the-Valley perfume she had dabbed on her drawers. Monty's head swam with giddiness and desire as his limp shaft grew long and thick yet again to this stimulus.

'Now do you doubt that you are mine?' she asked with a smile that sent a thrill of ecstasy through him.

Her hand played with his shaft, coaxing it skilfully to ever greater size and strength.

'Everything is mine now,' she told him. 'Poor Elliot left me a great deal of money and property, I have discovered. I never knew he had so much, for we lived modestly. The house down at Reading is mine and I have decided to let it out to rent. This house we are now in is mine for as long as I wish, for I have taken a lease. I mean to live in London now, not in Reading.'

Monty's brown eyes were misty with emotion as Gwendolen held his hard-on shaft and stroked it with tender fingers.

'Best of all,' said she, 'you are mine, and I shall roger you by day and by night, my dear. You will give up your rooms and move here to live with me, before bedtime tonight.'

Monty nodded his agreement and his shaft nodded in her hand, as if also agreeing. Gwendolen raised her knees a little and invited Monty to mount her. He did so awkwardly, lacking the use of his hands and arms. She guided his standing shaft to her moist split and he pushed it in.

'Oh!' she exclaimed, as he thrust home to the hilt. 'Bliss, pure bliss, my dear! How I adore this rogering!'

With an arm round his neck, she kissed his mouth through the black silk of the drawers that gagged him.

'Oh!' she exclaimed as he thrust home to the very hilt. 'Oh, Monty dearest boy, what a superb shaft you have!'

Even while she spoke, he felt her slender legs closing over his back like a steel man-trap, thereby increasing his state of helplessness. She began to move herself beneath him, thrusting her hot loins up at him with fast and nervous little strokes, in effect sliding herself along his embedded shaft and back. At once he responded, as would any virile young man, but Gwendolen clamped her legs tighter round his middle and her arms around his back.

She held him with his belly tight to hers.

'Be still, Monty!' she exclaimed sharply.

There was little else he could do now, held fast as he was by her, except to lie still while she had her way with him from below. On top of her he might be but there was no doubt at all in his mind that he was the one being rogered, not his dearest Gwendolen. It did not matter — the outcome would be the same as if he were the active partner and she were the one being poked.

Monty's passions rose in a throbbing crescendo towards their eventual summit, and he stared down tenderly at the face under his. Gwendolen's dark brown eyes were set in a stare, her mouth was open in a victorious smile. It was obvious that she derived an unnatural and yet thrilling pleasure from compelling him to submit to her in this way. Her pussy thrust up and down beneath him, the velvet flesh rubbing along his wet and jerking shaft with a hot remorseless desire. Her climactic moments were tardy to arrive, but when at last they did, their intensity was such as to fling her into throbs of bliss.

Spasms of joy flitted across her beautiful face, while her arms squeezed him so tightly to her that the breath was forced from him. Her back arched off the sofa to ram Monty's shaft in her to the uttermost depths, and the sensation was so thrilling that he fetched off instantly. He could feel her pussy sucking at his shaft, draining it of every drop of his essence.

'You are mine, Monty!' she moaned, 'mine to have and hold!'

The Delights of Women

PUBLISHER'S NOTE

Although this novel was first published anonymously in the late 1870s, the initials A.McK.H. on the title page make it possible to identify its author as Alexander McKendrie Hammond. He was a highly respected barrister of the Middle Temple, and a friend of Henry Spencer Ashbee, compiler of the best-known catalogue of Victorian erotica.

It is by means of Ashbee's lists that Hammond was identified, several of his novels being therein mentioned. On the present work Ashbee's comment was:

'The substance of the story before us is of an idle young man's search for sensual pleasure, which leads him into licentious episodes among the highest and the lowest. It is needless to add that the foundation for these curious episodes lies in the author's own experience of every kind of debauchery.'

CHAPTER 1
A Young Gentleman About Town

Very little by way of apology will be required for putting into print the following narrative for the instruction, and perhaps also the edification, of the reading public. It concerns itself with the adventures of a young gentleman of birth and breeding and the recorder of these events is assured that every genuine student of human nature will derive much of interest therefrom.

The subject of these memoirs was one of the many handsome and well-to-do young men to be encountered about London in the year 1877. The Hon. Randolph Joynes, for so was he named and styled, was a tall and slender gentleman of twenty-five years, fair-haired and elegant of manner and of attire. In addition to all the usual advantages of birth, kindly Nature had endowed him with an unusual warmth of constitution that made him unable to resist the attractions of the female sex, in all their most seductive variety. Never a day did he allow to pass without partaking of the divine frenzy of the sensual spasm that unites the fleshly male and female parts in throbbing ecstasy.

One fine evening in May, soon after dinner, Randolph left the house in Cavendish Square where he resided with his parents, he being the youngest son of the Earl of Broadwater, and the only child remaining at home. The intention he had announced earlier of popping into his club for a game of billiards with friends, or a hand of cards, was false. Needless to say, he had no such mundane intention, for this was his almost nightly excuse to leave the house. He took a hansom cab to St James's and after he had paid off the driver, he turned his back on Boodles Club and sauntered towards Haymarket to choose a young whore.

Randolph was still in the unmarried state, from which it must necessarily follow that the women with whom he shared so freely his natural exuberance were well beneath his station and rank. It would have been unimaginable for any young gentlewoman to allow access to her physical charms to one to whom she was not joined in the bonds of lawful matrimony. The conventions demand that a well-bred female is brought up in the knowledge that she is to maintain her young pussy unfingered and unbroached, her hymen intact, her titties virginally unhandled.

By dint of this strict restraint placed on the warmer aspects of her nature, a carefully brought-up female is enabled, on her wedding night, to reap the reward of virtue. She lies fearful on her back, half-dreading and half-longing for what is to come next, with nightgown drawn up about her waist and her bare legs well parted. In this sacrificial attitude, she offers her *all*, as ladies are pleased to call it, to a panting new husband. He, well-experienced in rogering by his sorties to females who set a cash price on the use of their cunny, now forces his way into his bride's tight little pussy, the first man ever to tread her pathway to pleasure, and relieves her of her young maidenhead in a gush of the hot essence of manhood.

In Randolph's view, marriage set too high a value on

2

female flesh. In his short life to date, he had taken his pleasure in hundreds of pussies, and hoped to attain the impressive figure of 10,000 before his rogering days were ended. In few words, since he had no intention of terminating his pleasant bachelor mode of life by taking a wife, Randolph had recourse daily to maidservants and girls of the streets, whose useful commodities were on offer for a few shillings in most parts of London.

Respectable society frowns upon men who slake their lusts on the compliant bodies of harlots, strumpets, demireps, Cyprians, and other beauties of the night. To that Randolph paid no heed — his hot masculine nature was such that it required constant lascivious gratification, capricious perversions, secret sexual aberrations and shameful fancies. Why this should be so, he did not know, nor much care. He held to the view that men and women have a right to make full and regular use of their bodies in any manner they chose.

He dismissed out of hand all attempt to theorise why some men took a young wife and made faithful and legal use of her cunny night after night, except for when she had been made too big-bellied to accept him, and by way of contrast, why other men, himself pre-eminently, lusted after change and diversity. It made no odds — no experience in life could ever compare with the glorious sensation of a hard-thrusting shaft fetching off inside a wet and throbbing pussy, whether the same one all the time or a different one every time. Each to their own taste, as the old woman said when she kissed the cow, or as it is more elegantly put in the language of scholars, *de gustibus non est disputandum*.

Young and pretty females were wont to congregate in a number of well-known places about the West End, both indoors and out. Most especially regarded as useful meeting points for lustful young men desiring the use of a cunny were the Argyll Rooms and Cremorne Gardens in Chelsea, and many a time had Randolph taken his way to either the one or the other. That notwithstanding, a fine evening seemed to require a stroll in the open air, and to that purpose the Haymarket, off Piccadilly, was a fine spot for the observation and selection of available doxies.

In his black tail-coat and white tie, a shiny top hat on his head at a rakish angle, and a silver-knobbed stick in his hand, Randolph was a fine sight. As he made his way uphill along Haymarket, past the theatre, towards Piccadilly, little groups of unescorted young women chatting together on the pavement separated. Each hopeful young trull displayed herself to best advantage in order to attract his attention. Randolph strolled on in good humour, smiling and touching the silver knob of his cane to his topper in salutation to the wenches he recognised — the many who had rented their pussies out to him in the past.

As he walked along, he twirled his opera stick dashingly, but with his left hand. His other hand was thrust nonchalantly into his trouser pocket, and through the thin material of the lining his fingertips caressed that part of his person he addressed by various names, in accordance with the whimsy of his mood.

At this moment he had in his mind bestowed on his up-rearing shaft the appellation of *Mr Percival Proud*, that being a useful description of the admirable firmness to which he had fingered it. A smile flitted across Randolph's face as he strummed on Mr Proud with a delicate touch, and was rewarded with tiny tremors of delight in return.

One girl who was bidding for his attention he remembered in particular as exceptionally talented — a tall thin girl in a green cloak and a straw bonnet. She had brought him off three or four times when he had her, though he was damned if he could remember her name. Here she came smiling towards him, and he smiled back pleasantly and nodded, half of a mind to take her and fill her slit with his spending.

Not only her hot slit, but her mouth too, for as he recalled the detail of their encounter a fortnight or more past, she had conducted him to an accommodation house in Orange Street, where he had paid five shillings for the use of a bedroom. No sooner had he removed his trousers than she was on her knees, her arm round his hip to reach his pompoms from behind, whilst with her other hand she held his fast-hardening shaft and drew the soft skin up and down before placing the purple head to her lips.

There was no time to say her nay, and precious little wish to do so, after she had taken almost half of his straining shaft into her mouth and sucked at it. On principle, Randolph gave no consent or approval to any course of action he had not himself initiated, and to have a thirty-shilling trull take charge of his person was, to say the least of it, a piece of impudence that in other circumstances he would have resented and stopped. Yet the girl had a way of using her mouth on his leaping part that almost reconciled him to her insolence.

Instead of drawing away, he twined a hand in her hair to hold her at his mercy, whilst he moved swiftly backward and forward, rogering the girl in her mouth. Now the tables were turned, and she would have pulled back if she could, but he gave no quarter and kept at it until his shaft jumped and throbbed and spurted its stream of sticky sap down her throat.

Afterwards, while she was red-faced and gasping,

Randolph put his hands under her armpits and threw her bodily on the bed. In a trice he had turned her skirts up above her waist and had three fingers up her pussy, ravishing it by main force till she shrieked out and came off. By then Mr Percival Proud was stiff once more, and without a pause, Randolph rammed him deep into the squirming girl and rogered her soundly.

The memory of the satisfactions of that evening very nearly persuaded him to hire her again, and make her repeat the entire process as before. But the urge for novelty was strong in him, a fresh bit of meat to whet his appetite, another pair of soft titties to feel, a different pussy to finger and come off in.

That being so, he shook his head at the advancing girl, still smiling at her, and said, *Another night, my dear*. She fell back crestfallen into the shadows, while Randolph walked on slowly. He shrugged his shoulders — the doxy's disappointment was none of his concern. His masculine pride and vanity informed him it was very probable that the girl would prefer to be poked by a handsome young gentleman like himself than some pot-bellied old businessman. But that was not the point. Randolph was the buyer and she was the seller. The laws of economics held sway here — he was in a buyer's market and his decision was not to shop at her stall that evening.

A girl who stood alone in a doorway caught his eye, and he halted in front of her for a better look. She wore no hat and her hair was yellow, drawn back loosely in a bun. Her face was round and her expression sulky. Randolph tipped his hat to her and bid her *Good evening*, allowing her time to assess his fine features and the quality of his clothes. Evidently she was much impressed by both, for though she gave no hint of a smile, she informed him that she charged two pounds for a short time, during which satisfaction was guaranteed.

'You set a high price on your cunny,' Randolph informed her. 'I've only once paid that much for a girl along here. Thirty shillings would buy you for a short time, if I were disposed to haggle. But low and demeaning usages of that sort are for the mercantile classes, not for a gentleman. To show my magnanimity of mind, I shall ask you this — what will you do for three pounds?'

Her face unsmiling, but with a sudden gleam in her eye, the girl replied that for three pounds he could roger her lying, standing and sitting, front and back, up, down, and however else he chose.

'I admire spirit in a girl, damned if I don't!' exclaimed Randolph, reaching out to touch her titties through her frock. 'What do they call you?'

'Polly,' said she, opening her shawl to permit his hands to roam over her body.

The feel of warm flesh through her frock and chemise aroused in him a burning and unquenchable fire of lustfulness, with the immediate result that Mr Percival Proud, already stiff as a rod of iron, began to quiver inside his trousers. He stepped closer to the girl, and she pushed her belly at him, as in invitation. Their legs were close together, and his shaft pressed against her thigh. He moved his hips in a slow circular motion, to rub Percival on her and rouse blissful sensations.

She let him excite himself on her leg, then her hand touched the front of his trousers, and her fingertips traced through the costly cloth the length and thickness of Mr Percival Proud.

'You've a cockstand like a broom handle,' said she, 'I'm sure you've heard the rhyme —

7

*"My titties and my cunny
Are yours to use for money,"
A girl said to a gent along the Strand,
"I've no cash with me," he cried,
But a cockstand she espied,
And felt it in his breeches with her hand.*

*He said "All right. I'm willing,
But only for five shilling,"
His piteous state would melt a breast of snow;
But the farthing-grudging gent,
While she held his cockstand, spent
And in his breeches freely shot his roe!"*

Randolph chuckled, and the girl said slyly:

'That's enough feeling me for now. Any more and you'll come off up your shirt-front and diddle me out of earning my money.'

'If I do,' said he, his knees trembling a little under him at the force of the sensations coursing upwards through his entire body from his excited shaft, 'then you shall have half a crown for your trouble, and I will move along in search of another.'

'Give me five shillings and I'll put my hand down the front of your trousers and bring you right off standing here,' said she pertly. 'But why should a fine gentleman like you be satisfied with fetching off in your underclothes, when you could do it up my cunny?'

'It's your far-from-virginal little cunny I mean to make use of for my poking business,' said he, taking a step back from the girl, with reluctance, but to relieve the pleasant pressure on Mr Percival, lest that over-zealous gentleman wasted his riches in linen rather than in warm female flesh.

'If it's a young virgin you want for your pleasure,' said the girl, 'you must go and see Mrs Williams in Drury Lane. For fifty pounds she'll find you a girl who's never been done before — but my understanding is that such things are for weary old men with drooping rods, not for upstanding young gentlemen like yourself. My pussy's been poked plenty of times, I won't say it hasn't. You won't hear me crying out when your prick slides up it, howsoever long and thick it is.'

'Damme if you're not the most honest-sounding little trull I ever did talk to!' Randolph exclaimed. 'You'll be a fine poke, if I'm not mistaken.'

'Try me and see,' the girl offered, sliding a hand between his thighs to feel his dangling pompoms. 'Will you really give me three pounds?'

'Willingly,' he answered, 'but on the conditions you set out — I am to have your full consent to do you however I like, and as many times as I choose. Is it agreed?'

'There's nothing you can think of I haven't had done to me,' she told him. 'You can use me as you wish for your three pounds. Come on, there's a place just round the corner we can go to.'

As Randolph expected, she led him into Jermyn Street, where a great many upper rooms over shops were let out to young whores to ply their trade. He had been in a dozen or more of these convenient rooms, and in some of them several times. The one to which Polly conducted him was above a dressmaker's shop, and not one he had seen before, so far as he could remember. Not that there was much to identify it or recall it from memory — when Polly turned up the gaslight the sole furnishings of the room were a wooden chair and a wide bed with an old patchwork quilt and a mahogany headboard in need of polishing.

Randolph gave the girl her three sovereigns, hung his top hat on a peg on the back of the door and sat on the chair.

'Remove your clothes, my dear,' he instructed her, 'show me your titties first. How old are you?'

'Seventeen,' she told him, her expression remaining as sulky as ever while she unbuttoned the bodice of her dark brown dress and pulled it over her head.

Randolph observed that she wore a white cotton petticoat tied round her waist and descending to her ankles, with a flounce of cheap lace round the hem. That came off to reveal a knee-length chemise, also of white cotton, tied over the shoulders with bows of coloured ribbon. She came closer to where Randolph sat and stared at him in silent petulance while she took off her chemise and threw it with her other clothes over the footboard of the bed.

Long and intimate contact with girls of the street had taught Randolph that these handy little creatures hardly ever removed all their clothing, even for a good rogering. He felt sure that Polly's clients were content to have her remove only her outer clothing, and make use of her pussy through the long slit of her drawers. In the yellow gaslight her flesh was pale of hue, and her titties, bared for his inspection, were neither large nor small, but of a middle size. For all her youth, they were a little slack already from the daily handling they received, but Randolph's hard-on shaft bounded at the sight of them.

'There's something you like about me,' said Polly, noting the sharp movement within his trousers. 'Let's have it out − I want to see this mighty shaft that's going to do me upside down and sideways!'

She sank to her knees, a small insinuating smile on her face at last, and she pushed his legs apart. Her hand darted between them, and Randolph emitted a gasp as she ripped wide open his trouser buttons. Mr Percival Proud was so swollen and frantic that he leaped out of his own accord, at which yellow-haired Polly chortled and administered a few deft manipulations of her hand. In this part of his body, as throughout, Randolph had been well endowed by Providence, and the throbbing shaft held in Polly's hand was long, thick and well-shaped, with a loose fleshy hood that slid back to reveal a head as plump and shiny purple as a large plum.

The pleasing aspect of Randolph's person in the form of his male organ was lost on the wench — to her it was no more than another man-tap, through which desire could be drained away, to earn her money. She had seen bigger, and she had seen smaller, and had accommodated all sizes and shapes in her slit.

'Half a dozen pulls and you'll be finished,' she commented, sliding her clasping hand briskly up and down the hard shaft, 'you'll shoot your tallow in my hand — do you always come off so easily, or do you fancy me that much?'

'You're an inquisitive little trollop,' said Randolph. 'What is it to you whether I come off slow or fast? You'll be paid the same, either way. And if it's not my way to plunge straight into a pussy and shoot off in the twinkling of an eye, of what concern can that be to you? You've contracted your person to me, and I shall make such use of it as pleases me best.'

'I do love a masterful man, who knows his mind,' Polly said with complete insincerity. 'Tell me your fancy for tonight and it's yours — shall I bring you off in my hand?'

Randolph grinned at her compliance and reached out to seize her soft titties, and lay Percival Proud between them.

'That's what you're after, is it?' she asked, sounding very

uninterested. 'You've a mind to roger my bubbies — and so you shall! No man's done them for ages — they're almost virgins.'

He squeezed the warm fleshiness together round his throbbing shaft and thrust strongly inside the soft pocket he had made. Polly knelt with her head on one side and grinned quizzically up at him. Her hands felt inside his gaping flies to take hold of his hairy pompoms and roll them between her fingers.

'I've been done between my titties, up my cunny, in my mouth, up my armpit, between my thighs, on my belly, in at the back door — there's no way of telling how a gentleman will fancy to come off,' said she. 'Some girls object, but I'm always ready to oblige a generous gentleman, howsoever his fancy takes him.'

Randolph panted as he squeezed her soft titties together to accommodate his long fast thrusts. Polly stared downward at the shiny purple head of Mr Percival Proud, popping out and then disappearing again between the cleft of her pale flesh.

'You've started to fetch off!' she exclaimed. 'Look there — the little eye's wide open!'

Randolph moaned in bliss, his swollen shaft slid fast against the girl's hot flesh, and his whole body shook to the release of a gushing torrent between her titties. She grinned briefly to see it and feel the wetness on her skin, evidently of a mind to believe he would require little more of her now beyond perhaps a slow poke lying on her back on the bed. In this she grossly underestimated Randolph's interest and stamina.

When he was again in possession of his faculties, he told her to remove her drawers and let him see the rest of her body, to judge whether her lower half could raise his shaft

12

to a hard-on stand as efficiently as her titties had done. She stood up and complied with his wish, posturing for his delectation with her arms akimbo, hands on her hips and her stockinged feet well apart.

Randolph nodded in approval as he noted the pleasing points of her person. Her belly he deemed good — it was round and just slightly curved, with a button deep-sunk in the soft flesh. Her bush was profuse, yellowish rather than brown, and but a shade darker than the hair of her head. Her thighs had a round female plumpness, and he could well understand how a gentleman might take the notion of fetching off between them, well up above her stocking-tops.

In the meantime, while he was assessing her for his pleasure, Polly was appraising him. Mr Proud had been relieved of all his pride and lay limp in the wide opening of Randolph's evening trousers. Young as she was, Polly had more experience of the ways of men than any married lady of seven-and-thirty. Most usually her fee was bartered down to a pound by the men who wanted a use of her cunny, their desire being no more than to have her on her back with her drawers down for a few minutes and slide in and out of her split until they spent and were done for.

Sometimes an officer of the Foot Guard from nearby St James's Palace would seek her out and have her a couple of times on the trot before he was satisfied.

Only one customer had ever rogered her more than twice at a session — and he didn't want her on her back at all. He had her on the bed, but on her hands and knees, and did her from behind — like a pair of mongrel dogs at it in the street. But he was a jolly sort of man, and he'd paid the full two pounds she asked him for.

There was, Polly dimly recognised, something about the cheeks of a bare female behind that made men letch and want to unload their cargo. What it was, she couldn't think. She had seen more than enough men's backsides and found nothing interesting about them at all. Except once a fat gentleman had paid her to spank his bare bum with her hand, and that had entertained her.

As if to prove her point, Randolph reached out towards her to fondle her bare bottom and give the cheeks a good squeeze. He put his face against her belly, and she felt the touch of his wet tongue thrust into her belly-button. He drew her down to sit on his lap and lean against him, her head on his shoulder. Her right titty lay loosely against the starched white front of his dress shirt, and while his attention was distracted by handling her titties, her sly fingers imperceptibly delved into the pockets of his evening waistcoat. Gentlemen frequently kept golden sovereigns there, she knew.

There were two or three small coins in Randolph's pocket, but being naked she had nowhere to put them for the moment, and let them be, until a better opportunity served. When he'd finished with her pussy she could easily slip them inside, but that lay in the future — under her bare bottom she could feel his shaft hardening, and guessed he would want to broach her very soon.

Indeed, the long wet trickle of his first spending descended between her titties to her belly, and the sight caused Randolph to breathe faster and rub his finger over her reddish-brown teats, until he had made them stand up firm.

'What are you going to do with me now?' she asked curiously.

Before he replied to her question, Randolph dropped his hand down between her bare thighs, and tickled the pouting lips of her pussy. Before long, despite her lack of interest in him as anything other than a paymaster, he had made the soft and hairy slit gape apart, and had a fingertip inside to find her secret button and tease it.

'Open your legs wider,' he instructed her, and she obliged by spreading them very wide apart. His fingers probed deep inside and rubbed her button until he had made her pussy wet.

'This is the source of women's pleasure and satisfaction,' he said, as he fingered her deftly. 'Talk to me a little before I have you again, Polly. I will not ask how many men roger you in the course of a day, for that is unimportant — but what arouses my interest is this — how often during the space of a day does the female orgasm overtake you?'

'What do you mean?' she asked, not knowing or understanding the word he had employed.

Randolph smiled to himself and continued to manipulate with a fingertip her slippery button.

'I mean the sensual spasm,' he explained. 'How frequently do you yield to it? Or to put the matter as simply as is possible without coarseness, how many times a day do you come off?'

'Why do you want to know that?' she sighed, her bare thighs beginning to tremble as his finger raised her passions towards their natural culmination.

'I am a student of sensual matters,' said he. 'In the course of my research and investigation I have formulated a theory of female sexuality which is astonishing and runs clean counter to all accepted opinion. Your views will be most useful, Polly.'

'Oh my Lord — I'm near to coming off!' she gasped in a weak voice, spreading her legs even wider. The pull of her muscles opened her cunny as if it were a book — the type of salacious book Randolph bought now and then for his amusement in a little shop he knew of in Greek Street, Soho.

Polly was by then shaking and sighing, her belly was heaving and her titties flopping. The one thing she desired most in the world at that moment was to be brought off. Her entire body and soul demanded the satisfaction of a long deep hard spasm, as her gentleman client had called it. Seeing the plight to which he had reduced her, Randolph deliberately slowed down his deft manipulation of her button, to extend her sensations up to the limit her nervous system could endure, and undermine her will.

'How many times a day do you come off, Polly?' he asked her, 'I want the truth now!'

'Not many!' she gasped. 'Bring me off!'

'As soon as you tell me what I want to know, not before.'

'Once, maybe. Twice if I'm lucky,' she panted out. 'Most men don't make me — they push it up me and shoot off as if they'd sneezed. Sometimes I'm with a man of middle years who takes his time about it and brings me off without meaning to. But mostly I have to fetch myself off with my fingers before I get up in the morning.'

'Good girl,' said Randolph, quite fascinated by what she said. 'The answer is once, then. You shall come off now.'

He joined three fingers together inside her pussy and flicked the tips expertly over her button. She gasped continuously and wriggled the soft bare cheeks of her bottom in his lap, rubbing her warm flesh on stiff Mr Percival Proud trapped beneath her.

'Don't stop now!' cried she. 'I'm fetching off!'

Randolph maintained his brisk manipulation of her wet parts, until in another moment she shrieked and her body jerked wildly to the spasms of her delight. The sight and sound of it aroused Randolph to a perfect frenzy of lust, and while she was still shaking and sobbing in her joy, he rose to his feet with her in his arms and sat her on the side of the bed. She fell on to her back, her stockinged legs dangling loosely down over the side, and he was at once between her parted knees, his stiff shaft at the mark.

'You'll kill me!' she whispered, her dark blue eyes staring at the long thick shaft aimed at her belly like a sporting gun in the hand of an expert huntsman, cocked and ready to fire.

Randolph gazed in delight at her yellow-haired pussy — open and wet from his attentions, and as lascivious a sight as he could remember laying eyes on. The hairy mound seemed to thrust forward from between her thighs, the pink-fleshed lips pouted clear of her bush, ready to engulf his shaft when he brought it close enough. He stroked quickly up and down the insides of her pale thighs, then slid three fingers into her.

'Do me,' she begged, 'bring me off again!'

In an instant Randolph was poised over her, his hard-on shaft between her thighs, its swollen head butting at the voluptuous lips of her cunny. She slipped an eager hand between their bellies to grasp Percival Proud and steer him into the haven he sought. With a long push Randolph sank his length into her, and she bucked her belly up at him in a lively rhythm.

'Excellent!' he panted, jabbing into her with short hard strokes that raised his sensations swiftly towards the oncoming of the sexual spasm, 'you are to come off when I do, and not before — do you understand me, girl? Wait for my sap to spring and then come off — not a second before, or a second later!'

CHAPTER 2
Continuing Diversions with a Doxy

In the room above a shop in Jermyn Street, to where he had been brought for the purpose of lustful pleasure, Randolph was close to the point of consummation of his sexual frenzy within Polly Bates's wet commodity. She lay on her back, naked but for white stockings, on the side of the bed, her legs hanging down toward the floor, and Randolph stood between her knees, ready to leap upon her as a ravening wild beast on its trembling prey.

He stared greedily at her yellow-haired pussy — open and wet from the diligence of his earlier attentions, and as lascivious a sight as he could remember laying eyes on. The soft and hairy mound seemed to thrust out forward from between her thighs, the pink-fleshed lips pouted clear of her bush, avid to engulf his shaft when he brought it closer, and swallow it down into the wench's hot belly.

The contrast between their appearances he had purposefully engineered aroused Randolph immoderately. He remained fully and elegantly clothed, in white tie and black tails, starched shirt and shiny, patent leather shoes, thus demonstrating his superior station over that of the girl stripped naked for his pleasure. He almost sobbed in his

19

joyful lust as he threw himself on her and penetrated her with a hard push of Mr Percival Proud.

In his hands he grasped her slack titties, using them freely for his delectation, whilst he assaulted her belly with short sharp jabs that made her body jerk on the bed and caused her to pant to catch her breath. No more than a minute after lodging his throbbing shaft within her, he spent copiously, and short though the poking had been, she too gasped and came off.

'There, you've had me on my back at last,' said she, grinning up at him slyly from her flushed face, 'I thought you'd want me that way before you'd finished. Whatever antics foreigners and Frenchmen may get up to, to lie down belly to belly is the most natural way to poke.'

'Damn this lying on beds,' Randolph answered, feeling his wet and softening shaft slide out of her, 'that's only for married milksops rogering their simpering wives in the dark twice a week, to get children. Come with me.'

He rose, took her by the wrist and pulled her to her feet, to lead her back to the chair on which he had first toyed with her bodily assets. He sat down, fully clothed, his limp wet shaft hanging out of his open trousers, that being his whim, and took Polly on his lap again. She lay against him easily and meekly, awaiting his further pleasure.

When he made no move to do more than stroke her bare belly with his palm, it came into her mind that this might be a good moment to abstract the coins from his waistcoat pocket and secrete them in her pussy until she was alone. To distract him from what she purposed, she asked what was the theory he had mentioned, when he asked her about coming off.

'You shall be the first female to hear the present outcome of my researches,' he said. 'Hitherto only a few close chums have been advised of my findings, over a bottle or two of port after dinner. Not all of them are yet convinced of its truth, since I have established facts that go against all accepted opinion. As you shall hear now. It is universally believed amongst the educated classes that lust is a wholly masculine attribute, and never experienced by females, whether ladies or common women.'

'Whatever gave you that idea?' Polly asked in surprise.

'It is the general belief, not mine in particular,' said he. 'The reason given for this one-sided circumstance is that the female constitution is too frail and unstable to sustain the physical force of the sexual spasm without grave injury.'

Polly looked at him sideways and said nothing, her fingers in his waistcoat pocket.

'Nevertheless, between husbands and wives who have sufficient confidence in each other to exchange views most often remaining a deep and inviolate secret,' he went on, 'it is known by those interested in sexual matters that an admission is occasionally made that, in the conjugal act the female sometimes experiences a slight paroxysm of sensation which can only be described as a type of coming off.'

'What's the conjugal act?' asked Polly.

'Rogering between married people. But to continue, the slight spasms which some wives confess to experiencing in the act are discouraged by medical men, and it is strongly recommended that married women avoid these emotions, save when they occur wholly by the chance of a husband being over-vigorous. And even then, this female paroxysm must not be allowed to take place with any regularity, but only on infrequent occasions, lest the female's health be seriously impaired.'

'Then I'm safe enough,' said Polly, 'since once a day is

the most I ever seem to be brought off, and usually by accident.'

'By no means,' Randolph advised her. 'The celebrated Dr Acton will tell you, should you care to consult him, that your life is in imminent peril. He believes more than one or two spasms a year to be injurious to the female constitution, and should a woman, married or single, be so ill-advised as to permit sexual excitement to get a hold on her, it must necessarily terminate in nymphomania, which is a form of insanity, and brings about physical decline and early death.'

'This Dr Acton — has he ever poked a woman?' Polly asked.

'Of that I have no knowledge, but he has written books on the topic, and his views are very widely respected. Nevertheless, having been with not a few girls myself since attaining the age of puberty, my own observation is that females come off almost as easily as men, enjoy it as much, and are eager to repeat the pleasure. This, as I say, represents a complete reversal of all medical and religious opinion at the present time, and has been of great interest to me.'

'Poking is always interesting to a man,' said Polly, 'but for women it's usually a question of spreading her legs to keep a husband quiet, or of doing it to make a living, like me.'

'That is the way of things,' Randolph told her, 'men poke and women are poked. My present area of research is into how often the female can repeat the spasm without the total collapse of her physical constitution.'

'You mean, can she be poked to death?' Polly asked. 'I've not heard of it, and I know plenty of girls on the game.'

'And I've poked plenty of them,' Randolph informed her, 'from which I have ascertained that a normal healthy young woman like yourself is capable of coming off as many times within twenty-four hours as a man of the same age.'

Polly had no interest in his nonsense. She had succeeded in extracting the coins from his pocket and had them folded in the palm of her hand. By then the discourse on females in sexual spasm had aroused Randolph's lust once again, and he required her to turn round on his lap, to sit astride his thighs, facing away from him. His arms were about her waist, his hand thrust down between her parted thighs, tickling at the wet lips of her pussy with a bent middle finger.

'I see you like it awkward,' she commented, 'lying down on a bed's for married couples and too dull for you, you say.'

'Keep a civil tongue in your head,' he answered. 'You agreed to as often and however I chose. Lift your backside.'

She leaned forward and raised her bottom, to present to him an unimpeded view of her hairy slit from the rear. He dabbled a finger inside it, making her slippery again, then took her by the hips and pulled her down on his upright shaft, spitting her on it. She sighed to feel his long hard gristle slide up in her depths, and whether her sigh expressed the anticipation of pleasure or resignation to a tedious performance, only she knew — and she sighed again when Randolph reached round her to take hold of her slack titties and grip them tight, while he rogered her from behind and beneath.

'You have the privilege of entertaining Mr Percival Proud in your cunny,' he told her, 'I trust that you appreciate the very considerable honour bestowed on you in having a gentleman come off up your slit.'

'Proud is right,' she sighed, shaken by his vigorous thrusts.

'And with good reason,' he said, his voice tremulous as

his sensations grew delicious beyond compare. He was pinching her russet teats between thumb and forefinger and rolling them hard as he neared the climax.

'Now, Polly!' he exclaimed. 'I have used you better than any girl of the streets has a claim to be, and I have brought you off as diligently as if you were myself. Now you shall feel the force of my flood inside you!'

His words stopped, and he cried out incoherently when his sap squirted up into her. She, to her amazement, succumbed to the manipulation of her titties by his fingers, and came off again. Afterwards she leaned back limply against his shirt front, her head back on his shoulder, whilst he slumped trembling in the chair, his chest heaving and his mouth open in shallow breaths.

Five or six minutes passed with no change in their position, then a tap on the door aroused both.

'Who the devil's that?' Randolph demanded. 'If the bawd who keeps this fusty place thinks to hustle me out before I've done with you, I'll lay my walking cane across her behind!'

Polly rose from his lap and slipped her chemise over her head before going to the door. She did not open it, but stood close while she asked who was there. Randolph heard another female voice reply, and Polly turned to look at him and explain.

'It's only a friend of mine,' she said, 'she hasn't come to disturb us. But she's got a bad cold and will catch her death if she hangs round in the streets waiting for men.'

Randolph glared at the young doxy as if he would murder her. 'What the devil does she want here, then?' he asked coldly. 'Send her away at once and get your backside on my lap again.'

Polly was rummaging through her discarded clothes,

anxious to hide from him the coins taken from his pocket.

'She's earned no money today and she wants a few shillings to buy a bottle of grog to help her sleep and throw off her bad cold, that's all. I'll lend her enough, and she'll be gone.'

'How old is she, and what's her name?' he enquired.

'She's about my age, though she can't be certain. And she's called Meg.'

Randolph left his chair and strode to the door, flung it open and stared at the girl standing outside. She would have been thought pretty, save for her reddened and dripping nose and her pale cheeks, the signs of her feverishness. She wore a black bonnet tied with ribbons under her chin, and was wrapped close in a long cloak. She was surprised to see Randolph at the door, where she had expected her friend Polly, and then as her eyes fell and she caught sight of his limp shaft dangling out of his trousers, she smiled and sniffed.

'Sorry to disturb you, sir, when you're occupied with Poll,' said she, her voice hoarse.

'It's money you want, is it?' he said, a lewd thought coming into his head at the sight of her. 'You shall have a pound from me if you will step inside and amuse me for twenty minutes.'

Even as he spoke, he wondered why it was that after rogering a thousand women, another pussy was irresistible to him. Was it simply because it was new to him, an unknown plunge into sexual adventure? This friend of Polly's was not much different from the little trollop whose parts he had made use of already this evening, and meant to use again. Her pussy would be similar to Polly's, though with curls of a slightly different hue.

The feel of her wet love-flesh round Mr Percival Proud

would be much the same as if he were inside Polly, that he knew, and the delight it gave would not be at all different from that he had felt already tonight. Yet, although the owner of this new pussy was an ordinary-looking wench, the unseen female charm in between her legs was exercising its silent spell over him. He felt that he must have her, he must gaze upon her bare pussy, finger it, poke it, and squirt his hot sap into it.

'For your pound you shall have whatever you can get from me in twenty minutes,' said Meg, 'though I think it won't be all that much, seeing the state of your dangler. I reckon Polly's taken it right down, and it won't do much more tonight.'

'That's for me to decide,' said Randolph.

He took her by the wrist and pulled her into the room, then led her to the bed, where Polly sat naked with crossed legs, to await the outcome of the conversation at the door.

'One thing, though,' said Meg, pulling off her bonnet to show a wealth of mid-brown hair, 'I won't take my clothes off for you tonight, like Poll, for with this cold in my head, there's no telling what might happen.'

'As you wish,' Randolph conceded, 'but you shall take down your drawers, at least. Polly — relieve your friend of them!'

He seated himself on the chair to watch, whilst Meg took off her warm cloak, and Polly slipped off the bed and sank down to her bare knees before her friend. She lifted her skirts and her petticoats, smiling slyly at Randolph whilst she uncovered for his avid gaze Meg's knee-length white drawers with frills.

'Show me her cunny,' he ordered.

Obediently, she held Meg's clothes up with one hand, and with the other she opened the slit in her drawers to reveal a thatch of mouse-brown hair.

'Give it a feel for me,' he said, 'tell me what it's like.'

He saw Polly's hand slip inside her friend's drawers, and by the way it moved, he knew that the new girl's pussy was being treated to a good fingering. In a short time Meg grinned, and her face began to flush, though that might have been caused by her head cold as much as by what was being done to her.

'Well?' Randolph asked. 'Do you mean to bring her off before informing me what she feels like?'

'She has a soft warm cunny,' said Polly, 'ready to take in a shaft at all hours of the day or night, and unburden it of its splash of tallow. Will you poke it?'

'In a while,' said he, 'sit yourself on the side of the bed, Meg, and be comfortable while your drawers are removed.'

She did as he bid her, sitting with her clothes up about her hips, and Polly, kneeling before her, untied the string of her drawers and took them down. Meg's thighs parted, giving him an open view of her brown bush.

'A pretty sight!' he exclaimed. 'Lie back now and take your ease while I survey your pussy and reach a conclusion as to how it shall be best used.'

Meg lay on her back, affording him a fine sight of her mound and the long lips under the brown curls. Mr Percival Proud, so long asleep, twitched and began to grow longer and thicker. The whim seized upon Randolph to recite for the benefit of his two doxies some lines by Mr Leigh Hunt, the celebrated poet:

A female thing that bears a well-known name,
But is in truth a warm and tender spot,
It sets always my mind and heart aflame,
And just to catch a glimpse will make me hot.

27

It is the sweetest thing this world can show,
Therefore my praises ring out loud and long,
It sets my blood to rage and fervent glow,
And brings my aching shaft up firm and strong.

When pussy is uncovered, take my tip,
To be ignored or shunned it will not stand,
But throbbing must be kissed by tongue and lip,
And to its spasm caressed by loving hand.

He heard Polly chuckle at the poet's words, and saw how she wiggled her bare bottom at him, her wet and hairy pussy visible below the crack of her cheeks.

'Delay no further, Polly,' he instructed her, 'bring the minx off at once.'

With perfect obedience, Polly bowed her head and brought her tongue to bear on the pussy she had stimulated by the use of her hand. Randolph experienced a deep and delightful agitation to see Meg being licked in this voluptuous manner. The girls formed a spectacle he had rarely witnessed before, but which he vowed to arrange again as often as he might, he found it to be so intensely arousing – Polly's head down between her friend's bared thighs and her wet tongue flicking in her exposed slit!

Mr Percival Proud had grown so hard and long that he stood up from Randolph's gaping trousers to halfway up his waistcoat. To clasp him in a trembling hand was the only practical course of action, and to slide his fingers up and down, to enhance those sensations of bliss that Mr Percival emanated by the regularity of his involuntary throb.

'No more, Poll!' he heard Meg moaning. 'Don't bring me off, for I'm not well enough for it. Leave me alone now . . .'

But Polly had her orders, and seemed to be taking enjoyment and pride in her work. Soon Meg was panting at the force of the sensual thrills inflicted on her by the darting caresses of her friend's tongue. Her stockinged legs kicked up from the floor, signifying that the culminating point of her bodily paroxysm would speedily arrive.

Randolph could hardly breath for his excitement. He was all on fire with a delicious lustfulness at the action before him. His encircling hand slid up and down his shaft so gratifyingly that he knew he would not be able much longer to restrain his fetching off. In the nick of time, Meg gave a loud squeal and kicked her legs high in the air as she surrendered to the spasm and fell into a climactic convulsion.

'I've come off, Polly, you bitch!' she gasped, 'I told you not to make me!'

Her physical climax prompted Randolph to take a more active part before he spent in his own hand. He held his jerking shaft tightly whilst he sped to the bedside and pushed Polly to the side. She gave him a conspirator's grin, and yielded her place on the bed to him without demur. Randolph's shaft was as thick and hard as a rolling pin. He set a hand flat on the bed to support himself, then leaned over the prostrate girl and stared down at her wet pussy with a ravening glee.

Meg stared back up at him, her eyes red-rimmed and her nose a-drip from her head cold. Her mouth hung open in amazement and dismay, to find herself brought off so casually by her friend's tongue and now at the mercy of a man with a shaft standing up like a broom handle. She looked speechlessly at Randolph, maybe thinking to herself that this was a damned hard way to earn a pound. Polly was giggling, either at her friend's discomfiture, or at the sight of Randolph in evening clothes seized by an access of hot lust, holding his bared shaft in his hand.

His feverish eyes were fixed on the brown-haired pussy below him, and in his mind ran the thought that here was another soft female slit to plunge his shaft into and enjoy to the full — a slit he had never before seen or unloaded his lewdness into. Mr Percival jumped for joy when Randolph brought his shiny purple head to the wet lips before him, and burrowed him slowly in.

'Ah, so wet and soft!' Randolph gasped. 'So slippy she is!'

And well he might say so, for Polly's tongue had liberally wet Meg's parts, within and without, so that Mr Proud slipped in without let or hindrance, until Randolph's muff and Meg's touched and intertwined. At once he commenced a long and busy course of sliding in and out, using the entire length of his shaft, from head to root.

'Be quick about it,' Meg implored him, moving her legs as far apart as they would go, 'I can't stand much more — I don't feel at all well and I'm hot and sweating with fever.'

'That be damned for a tale,' Randolph grunted, 'you're here to be poked, my girl, and poked you shall be, hard and wide!'

He still resented her impertinence in interrupting him whilst in the throes of his earlier encounter with Polly, for some paltry excuse of wanting a few shillings. That a street slut dared to burst in upon a gentleman at his lustful devotions! It was lucky for her that he had taken a fancy to rogering her while yet she stood at the door, otherwise he would have sent her packing penniless, to die of pneumonia in the street, if so she chose. And even after taking his money, the wretched trull had made it a condition that she would not take her clothes off for his pleasure.

Revenge was sweet, and his time for it was here — she

was pinned to the bed beneath him, her legs spread, and his hard-on shaft deep inside her. Whether she felt well or ill, of what concern was that to him? Seeing her on her back being fetched off by Polly had thrown him into a state of frenzy, and he was going to use her to the limit. If she died underneath him, then so be it — he would walk away and leave her on the bed, thighs parted and clothes up round her waist, for the peelers to find. But not before he had shot his angry load into her pussy!

'No more, sir, please!' she cried. 'I can't put up with it! Poke Polly if you must, or let me bring you off with my hand . . .'

'Lord!' said Polly, at Randolph's side. She had taken a seat on the bed, to observe the poking from close up. 'I've known the time when she's had a dozen men roger her between lunch and suppertime — yet now she's complaining about her first poke of the day!'

'Her pussy is so hot!' Randolph gasped, tupping away. 'It is the fever of her cold, I believe! Oh, how delightful a feeling it is! In another few seconds I shall fill her up to the brim and her pussy will overflow!

The strongest and most intense thrills the human organism can ever bear possessed Randolph at that moment. With sighing and moaning, he rammed so forcefully into Meg's slit that he came to the very pinnacle of voluptuousness, and flooded her with spurting essence. She shrieked aloud, though for what reason none could tell, and her belly shook under him to the jerking of his coming off.

When his revenge was complete, he rose from her with a smirk of triumph and resumed his seat on the chair, telling her to remain as she was until he gave her leave to depart. In truth, she was trembling and half-swooning from the ordeal she had but now undergone, and lay lethargic, legs apart and clothes still up to her belly-button. Randolph pulled his chair round to face the bed, and nearer to it, in order to survey with wondering eye the pussy he had just used so vigorously. The lips lay wet and slack, the curls plastered down to the flesh.

How strange a thing it is, Randolph pondered silently whilst he stared between Meg's thighs, how strange that even when I have rogered so many, I pine always for every young pussy that has not yet felt the force of my shaft! They say that there are ten thousand whores in London — I want to poke every one of them under the age of twenty-five and after that every pretty married woman in the Capital, and then every unmarried girl, gentle and common alike, above the age of sixteen!

'Can I go now, sir?' Meg asked weakly, raising her head from the bed to cast a pleading look in his direction.

Randolph picked up his shiny black walking cane and held it out at arm's length until with the silver knob he could gently prod her wet pussy. At the touch of the cold metal, she closed her thighs, but the stick lay between them, the knob bumping on her with little pushes, as if a monstrous long and thin shaft tried to get into her.

'Go?' said Randolph. 'Yes, you may go, for I've had all that I wanted of you, a poke up your cunny. Off you go, girl, for I fear you will be neither use nor ornament while I roger Polly again. Take your drawers and go this minute!'

She rose somewhat weakly from the bed and stood with her feet apart while she wiped between her legs with her chemise.

'Go,' Randolph repeated, 'off with you!'

Without a word, Meg snatched up her drawers from where Polly had dropped them on the floor, and fled from the room, carrying them in her hand. The door had scarce closed behind her before Randolph told Polly to sit on his lap again. From her place on the bed she came naked to him, and took up the position that he required. They sat thus for three or four minutes whilst he ran his palms over her titties and toyed with them, she naked and he dressed.

'I hope you've found out all you wanted for your theory about girls coming off,' said Polly. 'What would your Dr Acton say if he'd been sitting here on this chair and watching for the last hour? Would he tell us we shall be dead before morning?'

'I do believe he would,' said Randolph, 'for he holds that we ought to employ our vital energies in building up the physical frame, and in educational activities of the mind. He thinks it most injurious to allow sexual impressions or fancies to affect either mind or body. In men this is mighty difficult to achieve to a high degree, as he himself allows, for the nervous system has a tendency to produce erections of the male organ without the need for external stimulus.'

'We all know the ways to bring down a standing shaft,' Polly remarked, 'but what does he say about women?'

'The woman of a well-regulated life and well-ordered thoughts is not susceptible to casual sexual excitation, Dr Acton says. Had he been present tonight to observe our frolic, his censure would alight on me for indulging my lusts so freely on you and on Meg, but his greatest strictures would have fallen upon you, in that you have allowed your desires to be inflamed again and again, to the detriment of body and soul.'

'If ever I meet this Dr Acton of yours, I'll offer him a free poke and see if he turns me down,' said she with a lewd laugh. 'More than likely he'll have me on my back and his shaft up me before I can draw breath! Is he old or young?'

'I hardly know,' said Randolph, 'but I take him for a man of mature years — about sixty, perhaps.'

'Then he's past it, and so are you for now,' she said to him, with her artful smile. 'You'll learn no more about female lust tonight, but if you'd like to try again tomorrow with me, for the same price, I'm game. Set a time and I'll be waiting.'

'Ha!' he snorted, displeased that she, a common girl of the streets, should think herself capable of besting him. 'Do you suppose that because Percival's head lies low it will not rise again — is that what you think, slut?'

'Not tonight, it won't stand again,' she said slyly, 'take it from me, you haven't a poke left in you.'

To prove the truth of her words, she took his soft shaft in her hand and tugged at it, letting her titties lie against his shirt front and her cheek against his. Randolph sat calm and still, summoning up his last reserves of strength. Before long, blissful tremors ran through his belly and he felt his shaft begin to rise once more to its proud length and girth.

'No, it can't be true!' Polly gasped, realising too late now that she had put him in a mind to roger her pussy again.

Randolph reached down between them, to press his fingers into the opening of her hairy cunny and rub her button with slow and steady strokes. He had no true desire, but he was impelled by the assertiveness of his nature into making a demonstration of his superiority over any female.

'I mean to poke you once more,' he said. 'You shall tremble to the push of my hard-on length, and remember ever after how you were poked to a frazzle on this evening by a man with an iron cockstand.'

He made her change position, to sit astride his thighs, pussy open and accessible to him. She lifted her backside a little, whilst he held his hard-on shaft at the best angle, so that it was driven up into her when she sank down again on him.

'Place your hands on my shoulders and do nothing more,' said he, 'for I mean to roger you, not allow you to roger me.'

She obeyed, and lay motionless on him in her languor, her arms hooked over his shoulders, and her legs dangling outside his, making no effort to assist him further. He drew in a long deep breath, then initiated a feeble rogering of her. It came as no surprise to either that the action was long and slow, and although Polly wanted no more of Percival Proud's attentions to her pussy, she was compelled at last, against her will though it was, to experience certain pleasant sensations from his sliding over her sensitive button.

'You mean to poke me to death,' she sighed, 'I see that now, too late! And according to your Dr Acton, you will drop dead when you shoot your last drop of juice into me . . . well, why not? It beats dying of cold and hunger.'

She lay still and let him have his way with her, content to know that the gentleman had paid her a week's keep for the use of her slit for a couple of hours. That was apart from the coins she filched out of his pocket, and which were now safely concealed inside her rear entrance. They'd be no worse for that, after a scrub with soap and water.

Eventually, she felt his shaft grow harder still and stronger inside her, and knew he was nearing the end of his journey. Not that she expected him to die of rogering — that was her joke to please him — but he'd be wrung out like a dish rag by the time he'd fetched off one more time. In another twenty strokes he sighed and moaned, then within her wet pussy his shaft jerked fiercely and he spouted his last few drops into her.

Polly shrieked at the ecstatic pleasure that tore unexpected through her, so intense as to be almost painful. It made her twitch and squirm against Randolph's belly, spiked as she was on his throbbing length. His jerking faded to a faint trembling and she guessed that he was faint in the aftermath of his long rogering. She let herself collapse upon him and sink down into oblivion.

CHAPTER 3
Improprieties of a Mayfair Society Hostess

After leaving the premises in Jermyn Street in which he had so greatly indulged himself in illicit sexual pleasure with Polly and her sniffly-nosed friend, Meg, Randolph strolled up toward Piccadilly in search of a cab. In truth, he had to admit with a wry smile that his knees were somewhat shaky underneath him, an outcome not to be wondered at after so extended a bout with the two doxies, and spending so often in a short time. That apart, a feeling of general contentment suffused his being.

The theatres had come out, and Haymarket and Piccadilly were crowded with people. The common sort would return to their home by public omnibus, but the better people were looking for cabs, and that would reduce Randolph's chance of finding one to take him to Cavendish Square and his bed. The roadway was equally as crowded as the pavement, for a variety of hansom cabs, private carriages and other conveyances were jostling past each other, to the imprecations of coachmen, the rattle of hooves and the creak of springs.

He heard his name called, and turned, to see a four-wheeler at the kerb, halted there for a moment by the great throng of vehicles. The nearside window was down and a top-hatted head thrust out.

'Lorimer!' said Randolph, recognising by the street lights the luxuriant mutton-chop whiskers of a good friend. 'Have you room for me, for I am damnably tired of walking?'

'Jump in, my dear chap,' said Lorimer Mawby, and swung open the door for Randolph to get in, 'what have you been up to this evening? Were you at the club?'

'I've been . . . nothing in particular,' he answered, sinking into the vacant seat. He had been on the very edge of replying that the had been hard at it since dinnertime rogering a brace of young trollops and in the nick of time he had noted the presence of a lady in the vehicle. Lorimer introduced him to her, and to the man who sat beside her. She was Miss Dorothy Harker, and the other was her brother, Devlin Harker, a distant cousin of Lorimer's. They dwelt in the wilds of Warwickshire, it seemed, and were making a stay of some weeks in London.

The party of them had been to the opera at Covent Garden, to hear the celebrated Adelina Patti sing. In the interval, said Lorimer, he had visited the box of Mrs Alice Hamilton, taking his cousins with him, to pay his respects, for he was of that lady's acquaintance. She had invited him and his party to join her and other friends for refreshment at her house after the end of the performance.

'By Jove!' Randolph exclaimed 'I envy you your acquaintance with a society hostess of such renown. How did you come to know her, if I may ask?'

At that Lorimer laughed oddly and suggested he should go with them to Mrs Hamilton's house, where he was sure to be welcome. Then speaking in an undertone so that Miss Harker did not hear, he declared that Randolph would be of damned little use to Mrs Hamilton, since by his pallor it was evident that he had been on the poke all evening.

'But you're not bad-looking, and she might well take a fancy to you,' he added with a chuckle. 'She's a devoted admirer of chaps our age, Randolph, just as long as they are strong-backed and vigorous.'

'Is that the way of it?' Randolph asked.

'Take my word for it,' said Lorimer, keeping his voice down lest any hint of impropriety should reach and disturb the young lady sitting opposite him, 'she drained me completely dry on a Wednesday afternoon last year, between luncheon and tea time, when I paid a social call on her, expecting nothing beyond a cup of tea and perhaps a quick feel of her bubbies, if I were lucky. While we were chatting I took the liberty of touching her knee lightly, and damme if Alice didn't push me down flat on my back on a sofa and straddle me, with her clothes up round her waist. Imagine my surprise and confusion!'

'She's a lady I could easily become fond of,' said Randolph. 'What then, Lorimer?'

'What indeed! She had my shaft stiff as an iron bar and well up her without so much as a by-your-leave, and rogered me twice before she let me sit up! Now I like a nice poke as much as the next man, but she was too confounded strenuous about it for me. Since then I've remained friendly with her, but at arm's length — a week or two of her would drain a chap for ever and finish him off for life! After she'd done with him, he'd never be able to get another stand or poke a woman again. So beware, my dear fellow, if she offers to lie down for you.'

No possible words of Lorimer's could be better calculated to arouse Randolph's interest in the well-known Mrs Hamilton than this reference to an affair of the heart started and called off in the space of a single afternoon. To dignify so curtailed and scant a friendship as *of the heart* was to do Lorimer too much honour, Randolph decided. What had been commenced was an affair *of the parts*, and had no more significance than an hour or two with a paid whore.

As for Lorimer backing away from Mrs Hamilton's enthusiasm, in all probability the situation was reversed — more likely she had cooled off after finding him to be an unsatisfactory bed-partner. That was the way of it, in Randolph's view, for he had never heard of Lorimer accomplishing any noteworthy feat as a cocksman. On the occasion or two in the past they had together sought recreation in a house of ill-fame, by the time Randolph poked his trollop to a standstill, Lorimer had long since done with his and was gone. From which the only deduction to be made was that twice was Lorimer's limit.

Mrs Hamilton's house was in South Street, Mayfair, and there were several carriages at the door when Lorimer Mawby's party arrived. For as long as Randolph could remember there had been gossip about the lady, some of it unflattering if any truth in it was to be discerned. Her first husband when she was a girl had been a fashionable captain of the Horse Guard, who died and left her a widow at twenty.

The manner of his dying was unusual and unfortunate — he had been shot to death in a highly unlawful duel in Hyde Park early one morning. The cause of the fatal meeting was said by those in the know to be his wife's honour, which no doubt meant that the Captain had surprised her in bed with another man between her legs. Randolph thought it extraordinary that a man should take the risk of being shot at with a pistol to decide who had the use of a particular woman's commodity. In these modern times only the French went in for highflown nonsense of that sort. Be that as it might, the lively young widow had shortly after remarried — and to the gentleman who was said by rumour to have shot her first husband to death under the trees by Park Lane.

This was Mr Moncrief Hamilton, a wealthy connection of a most distinguished family, and for a time it appeared that illicit love had triumphed. The newly-weds honeymooned abroad in Italy, and then were seen everywhere about fashionable London, seeming marvellously devoted to each other. Lady Antrey informed her close friends that she had been astounded and shocked to near-swooning by seeing the Hamiltons in a box at the theatre one evening, he with his hand thrust up his wife's clothes, and this in the second act of the great Shakespeare's *Macbeth*!

As for Mrs Hamilton's hand, Lady Antrey refused outright to particularise its position, though to her very closest friends she confided that Mr Hamilton's trouser buttons were undone and his person was exposed and erect. From that they must draw what conclusion they could as to the whereabouts of Mrs Hamilton's hand, for to say more would be indecent in the extreme.

Yet love-birds do not always continue to bill and coo on the perch together. Less than a year of wedded bliss with Alice was in the event as much as Mr Hamilton could sustain. He had gone abroad, and there he remained, leaving her in possession of the house in Mayfair and an adequate income.

Perhaps Mr Hamilton had been another like Lorimer, unable to roger the lady into submission, thought Randolph, as he handed Miss Harker out of the four-wheeler and to the open front door. A footman showed them up to the drawing room, where twenty or so people stood in conversation, sipping at iced champagne. All the guests but three were men, Randolph noted.

In addition to Miss Harker, whom he now saw by the gaslight to be a very pretty girl, there was a yellow-haired Frenchwoman in pink, her dress cut so low that her titties were near to bare. She evidently was the mistress of the man who stood next to her and who smiled foolishly at her conversation. Randolph eyed her with interest, drained though he was, and thought that she'd be a damned fine poke, if a fellow got a chance with her. Everyone said that Frenchwomen were highly skilled in the art of taking a man's shaft in their mouth and that was a national accomplishment he would be interested to pursue further, should opportunity arise.

The third female guest in the drawing room was a plump white-skinned girl of sixteen or seventeen at most, who looked quite lost. No doubt she was someone's sister, who had been with him at the opera, when he was honoured with an invitation by Mrs Hamilton. The little innocent could have no thought that the men in the room, her brother included, were much like swarming male bees round a queen, Mrs Hamilton, each vying to be the one who got his shaft into her.

That notwithstanding, the girl had promise, in Randolph's view — for no female escaped his assessment of her usefulness on her back. Little Miss Sixteen was possessed of a plump and warm succulence, like a ripe peach ready to burst in the mouth. At another time, and in another place, he would be most pleased to relieve her of her maidenhead, if sweet words and kisses could persuade her to allow a hand in her drawers.

It was some time before Lorimer could break through the crush about their hostess to present Randolph. He, nothing loth, used the respite to down a glass or two of iced French champagne, to raise his spirits and put spring into his step.

He wished that it might also put lead into his pencil, but that was to hope for too much after his long indulgence with Polly and Meg in Jermyn Street.

Mrs Hamilton, he observed, was a well-fleshed lady of middle height, almost thirty years of age, and of a markedly healthy appearance. She was sturdy of form, almost buxom, as the common parlance has it, full-breasted and short-necked, with a great profusion of thick and shiny black hair dressed upwards and set with small pearls. Her face was open and pleasant rather than pretty, her eyes large and lively, her jaw firm and resolute.

In short, a woman designed by Nature for daily and vigorous rogering, Randolph concluded. In his imagination he strove to see through her fashionably low-cut evening gown, in order to envisage the broad warm belly which Lorimer had been shown one afternoon, and the soft pussy into which that ineffectual young man had been awarded the privilege of fetching off.

Hers would be a pussy of weight and substance, Randolph was utterly certain, adorned by a thicket of jet black hair, with plump pink lips a man could kiss until they parted to reveal a well-developed pleasure-button for his tongue to caress. Even to think in this way made poor, worn out, shrivelled Mr Percival twitch faintly in Randolph's trousers, but no more than that. He could be compared with a bare-fist fighter in the fortieth round of a boxing match, who had been knocked down one time too many, and could not rise to his feet again, however loud the crowd roared for him.

Mrs Hamilton had a throaty chuckle and an ease of conversation, he found when at last he was introduced and allowed to take her hand for a moment and press it. As they talked together, he was aware that her eyes were on him boldly, weighing him up, and he stood straight and smiled for her. How it came about, he had no conception, but she was skilled in the social graces and from being one of a group of young men around her, he found himself alone with her by the drawing-room windows, where stood a grand piano, and they were leafing through pages of music, her hand touching his arm lightly.

To his delight and chagrin, she was asking, without the least indication of false bashfulness, if perhaps he might stay on a moment or two after the other guests had gone, to give her his views on the relative merits of something or other to do with music. Randolph had precious little taste for music, apart from the sentimental ditties and the low catches of music hall and public house, but he was aware that music was not the topic she wished to discuss in private with him.

'Dear Mrs Hamilton,' he said, a touch of sorrow in his voice, 'nothing would, I assure you, give me greater pleasure than to declare my views to you, in particular on organ music, where I consider myself to be something of a connoisseur.'

'Organ music!' said she, her dark eyes alight with interest. 'And an expert — delectable thought! Who are your favourite composers, Mr Joynes?'

'Why, Bach and Handel are supreme for organ performances, in my experience,' he replied, with a smile.

'You say that with a degree of warmth that hints at more than you make plain — acquaint me with your meaning, if you please.'

'I shall be happy to oblige you,' he said, bowing slightly at the double-meaning. 'For I am sure that with you on your *back*, and my *handle* at the ready, together we could enjoy an organ recital of some virtuosity.'

'You have a naughty wit, I see. I feel that I must learn

more of your qualities before you leave, much more!'

'The problem is,' said he, sounding most rueful, which indeed he was, 'I must in confidence confess that earlier this evening I dined with the widow of an old friend, a clergyman of Ebury Street, who was taken by the apoplexy not a month ago.'

The lie was absolutely necessary — to admit he had paid a pair of young whores to let him have the use of their cunnies would result, he feared, in his dismissal from Mrs Hamilton's side instantly. His ruse worked, and she heard his story with her eyes on him and a look of amusement on her face.

'I felt it my duty to do all I could to console the lady's loneliness,' he went on. 'After a good dinner and a bottle of port wine, one thing followed on from another, as often it does on occasions of this type . . .'

'Say no more,' exclaimed Mrs Hamilton in disappointment. 'How very provoking! The trigger was pulled and the shot fired, now the pistol is uncocked.'

'The question was not merely one of a shot being fired,' said Randolph, 'a veritable fusillade was shot off, a *feu de joie*, as the French have it, until the ammunition locker was empty. I am grieved beyond reason at this particular, for I feel that you and I, were you to permit it, could become fast friends.'

'We shall see,' she answered, tapping his wrist with her fan, 'call on me tomorrow at five.'

With that, she was gone. Not half a minute later Randolph saw her in conversation with another man, one with a neatly trimmed red beard, her hand resting lightly on his sleeve as, no doubt, she enquired of him if he were minded to stay behind after the rest departed, to explain something or other to her.

With a shrug of his broad shoulders, Randolph made himself acquainted with one or two of the other guests, including the Frenchwoman in pink, Madame Du Rocqueville, she called herself, and she had a lascivious and rolling eye. Her almost uncovered titties were a delight to behold from close at hand, until her protector took her by the arm and led her away from Randolph's attentions.

He would have transferred his interest to the pretty Miss Harker, but Lorimer seemed unusually attached to her, keeping a conversation going uninterrupted. That being so, Randolph made his way to the plump young girl in white muslin, who seemed to have been deserted, and she was overwhelmed by the attentions of so elegant a gentleman.

Flattered by the girl's response and to prove that, even if he were drained dry of sap, he retained his charm for the fair sex, Randolph led young Adelia, for that was her name, into a corner of the drawing room where the long brocade curtains made a useful place of concealment. He praised her looks and figure, and she, being unused to the deceit of flattery, made no move to stop him when he touched her face, and then her neck. She stared up at him in surprise when his hand sank lower, but gave no sign of distress while he treated himself to a good feel of her plump titties down the front of her evening frock.

A line or two of verse he had read in a volume of Mr Thomas Hood came into his mind, apropos of what he was doing to her, and he recited them softly to Adelia:

> *When she was twelve, I slipped my hand*
> *Up in her dress behind,*
> *And stroked her bum, you understand,*
> *Much as I felt inclined.*

She giggled and she squirmed about,
But liked my daring rudeness;
She dragged my trouser buttons out,
Returning all my lewdness.

At his words, Adelia herself giggled, and he would have gone on a little further and treated himself to a feel of her maiden cunny. Before he could do so, her brother came across the room in haste, with a suspicious look in his eye, whereupon Randolph desisted and went home to his bed and sleep.

Punctually at five o'clock the next afternoon he presented himself at the front door of Mrs Hamilton's house and gave his name to a footman who opened it. He was shown straightway into a ground-floor room furnished as a library, and asked to wait. Some minutes passed before a smiling lady's maid appeared, to conduct him to Mrs Hamilton upstairs, in a pretty sitting room looking out over a small formal garden.

She shook hands and said she was glad to see him, and hoped that he had recovered his powers of discourse. He gave her his assurance that his natural abilities were fully restored, and a pleased smile spread over her face. Before there was time for the conversation to progress to an elaboration of the topic of sensuality that was in both their minds, the maid and a footman together brought in tea. Mrs Hamilton did the honours with the silver teapot and handed Randolph a cup.

Seeing that some conversation was required of him to preserve the social decencies for ten minutes, he enquired of his fair hostess if she were acquainted with the theories of Dr William Acton on the regulation of the sensual impulse.

'Acton?' said she, 'I've met Lord Acton a time or two — is this one related? And how on earth does he propose to regulate the strongest force in human nature?'

'The strongest force in masculine nature, you intend,' said Randolph, setting out to chaff her a little, 'but not in female nature. Dr Acton's opinion is that women are not much troubled with sensual feelings of any kind. However, if in exceptional circumstances such emotions become aroused, then they are very moderate, compared with those of the male, he believes.'

'What!' Mrs Hamilton exclaimed. 'The fellow is a fool! I've yet to meet the man who could match my own nature for strength of sensual impulse. Do you regard me as abnormal for that?'

'Not I,' said Randolph, smiling at her indignation, 'but the learned Dr Acton says in his book that frequent indulgence in sexual excitement by women leads inevitably to nymphomania, and early decline.'

'Pish!' said she.

'With that sentiment I agree,' said Randolph, 'for to my way of thinking, Acton is mistaken. In my own family there exists a useful example to the contrary — an aunt, a widowed sister of my father's — a lady above forty years of age, with an adequate income of her own. She some years ago ran off to France with a drayman half her own age whom she encountered in Cheapside. She lives there happy still, having pensioned off her flagging drayman and exchanged him for an even younger Frenchman.'

'I like the sound of this aunt,' said Mrs Hamilton. 'Long may she live and be rogered! They say that Frenchmen are skilled in bringing ladies off by the use of their tongue, although I have not found one yet who was any good at it.'

At the open use of words that few ladies had heard of

and, if they did, they would blush scarlet bright and cover their ears, Randolph decided that the barriers were down. He leaned forward in his chair and placed a hand lightly on Mrs Hamilton's knee, smiling knowingly at her the while. This was what Lorimer said he had done, to start off her lewdness. Would she try to throw him on his back, as she had Lorimer, and bestride him?

'There's a surprise waiting for you,' said she, and before he could ask what it might be, she rose from her chair and stood before him, her hands on his shoulders in a manner encouraging to his ardent nature. She was that day dressed in a blouse of white silk and a black satin skirt, her full round bubbies and her broad hips filling out her garments in a manner suggestive of delights to come.

Randolph reached underneath her long skirt, smiling to feel her stocking under his fingers, then up her leg, as high as her knee. Above the knee lay the ribbon that served as garter and when he slipped his hand higher yet, his fingers lighted upon bare warm flesh.

'Oh!' he exclaimed, his mind reeling at this impossible and yet incontrovertible fact.

'Yes,' said she with a smile on her face, 'your senses do not deceive you, Randolph — I am wearing no drawers. Feel a little higher up my thigh, and assure yourself it is so.'

His hand lay flat between her fleshy thighs, and he sighed to feel it caught and pressed by them.

'How very delightful!' he said. 'And how truly surprising — do you often go without underwear, dear Alice?'

It was quite out of the question to continue to address her as Mrs Hamilton now that his palm was squeezed between her legs within an inch or two of her pussy.

'After luncheon was finished I went to my bedroom and removed my drawers, to be ready for your assault,' she replied. He wished to raise his hand higher and touch her pussy, but the clasp of her thighs held his hand immobile.

'Don't you believe me?' she asked, seeing his expression of mingled astonishment and delight. 'Then I'll show you.'

All pretence discarded, she raised a leg and rested her foot on the seat of his chair, then hitched up her skirts and lacy petticoats as high as her hips, to display her bare thighs. Between their soft creamy-skinned fullness was set a pouting black-haired pussy. Randolph stared, his breath catching in his throat, while Alice ran her fingers over her uncovered cunny and drew the lips apart. Contemplating that soft pink and hairy delight, he felt very near to fetching off in his trousers, for it seemed almost to have a life of its own, not waiting passive to be rogered, but palpating with vitality and appetite.

'Damme, but I must pay my respects!' he cried, and clasped Alice by the hips, to ease her back a step or two, so he could slide off his chair and down to his knees. She stood with her legs apart and her clothes held up high, while he pressed his lips feverishly to the nether mouth that invited his hot kisses.

Her bare thigh touched his ear in a casual caress that made his shaft leap boldly under his shirt. He dropped his hand down between his legs, to press the lively organ close to his belly and stifle its jerking, lest its friskiness brought him off prematurely.

Alice's voice reached him through his sensual confusion.

'I like your manners, Randolph — we shall become good friends if you continue to please me, as you have begun.'

He knew precisely what she intended by her words, and what she required of him as a gesture of goodwill, if he expected to be allowed to poke her in due course.

'Allow me to demonstrate to you that an Englishman can

beat a Frenchie hands down,' said Randolph. 'Damn all foreigners — our ways are better than theirs, on that you may rely!'

'Show me!' she cried, a tremor in her voice.

Obediently he thrust out his tongue and brought it to bear on her impatient pussy. Very quickly he attained a great agitation of mind, whilst he licked her voluptuously, and he soon became intensely aroused.

'Ah, that does feel very nice!' Alice exclaimed. 'No doubt but you've kissed a cunny or two before, Randolph! I'm glad of it — I do so hate the fumblings of beginners.'

Her hand rested on his head to encourage his administrations, and her smooth thigh pressed against his cheek. Before long he heard her gasping at the force of the sensual sensations she was enjoying, and he redoubled the flickering of his wet tongue in her. Down below in his trousers Mr Percival Proud had become so big and hard that Randolph had no choice but to force a hand down inside his waistband and take hold of his quivering shaft, to control its furious leaping.

He heard Alice panting loudly under the darting caresses of his tongue, and he knew that her supreme moment would not long be delayed. He himself could hardly draw breath for his raging excitation. His body was ablaze with passionate lust, delicious spasms racked him from top to toe. Under his shirt his firmly clasped hand slid up and down his shaft, and he knew he could not endure much longer. Then Alice gave a shriek and jibbed her belly at him, her legs shaking to the throb of her climactic pleasure.

'You've brought me off, Randolph!' she gasped out. 'It feels wonderful! Don't let me stop!'

Nor did he — his busy tongue impelled her through a long and intense paroxysm of pleasure, until she breathed out in a long sigh and stood with her hands resting heavily on his shoulders, to support her trembling frame. Her clothes slid down over his head, and concealed him in intimate darkness, whilst her warm thighs clasped his face between them in repose. It was too much for Randolph's nervous system to tolerate longer. He moaned in delight, his hand rubbed faster, and an instant later he spent copiously in his trousers, his open mouth pressed to Alice's darling pussy.

CHAPTER 4
Some Doubt Cast on a Medical Man's Theory

Upstairs in Mrs Hamilton's pretty little sitting room, Randolph knelt before her, with his head thrust up her skirts and his hot mouth pressed against her hairy pussy. Homage had been paid to her charms, and an emotion of pleasant lassitude suffused his limbs. Against his belly, his shirt was sticking warmly, by the copiousness of his fetching off.

'Darling boy,' he heard Alice say, 'that was extraordinarily pleasing — you may come out now.'

She raised her skirts and petticoats to uncover his head, and for yet a moment he gazed in admiration at the fullness of her creamy-skinned thighs and the pouting black-haired pussy that was set between them. She could hardly deny him the use of it now that he had pleasured her in the French fashion with his tongue. Her dark eyes stared down at him, shining with approval and respect for his skill — and with perhaps a glint of greedy anticipation of what he would do to her next.

Whilst she stood with her hands on his shoulders, leaning her weight a little on him, and in some measure recovering herself, Randolph took the opportunity to find the placket of her skirt and undo it. He untied the strings of her petticoats, so that all fell down to the floor. Without commenting on what he had done, she stepped out of her skirts, and he rose to his feet to unpin the carved jet brooch that closed her blouse at the neck, and unbutton it all the way down.

'I've a mighty desire to be rogered by a hard-on shaft,' said she, 'are you able to oblige me so soon, Randolph?'

'Without a doubt,' he replied, 'for my desire matches yours.'

'Will you have me on the sofa?' she enquired.

Before answering her question, he lifted her chemise with an eager hand, and assured himself again that Alice was wearing no drawers. He slid a bent middle finger between the wet pink lips of her pussy, and tickled her.

'Damn all this talk of lying down,' said he, attending to her black-haired pussy's delight with a skill that brought a smile to her face, 'that's for ninnies and mollycoddles. I'll have you on your back only when I've had you so many times my legs won't bear me up any longer.'

He rose to his feet and gazed quickly round the sitting room, making his choice.

'Put your hands on the chair arm and bend over,' said he.

Without any word of objection, Alice tucked her lace-trimmed chemise up about her waist, placed her hands on the padded arm of the nearest chair. She leaned well forward from the waist, supporting herself with straight arms, displaying to him her bare bottom, full and round-cheeked, white-skinned and soft as down-filled pillows. Randolph stood behind her and clapped his hands to her lower cheeks, to squeeze and stroke to his heart's content. Then with firm fingers he parted her magnificent orbs and with a deft finger tickled her knot-hole.

'There's more to be said for this standing up to it than I at first thought!' Alice opined. 'You may kiss my bottom, my own dearest man.'

From a woman of lower rank, the same words would have been an insult beyond bearing, but from the lips of Alice Hamilton they constituted an open invitation to sensual pleasure beyond the ordinary. Randolph went down on his knees behind her, to do her homage, his mind in a frenzy of delight. He kissed her rotund backside and nipped the soft flesh between his teeth, causing her to squirm and cry out in pleasure.

'Roger me!' she pleaded. 'I am on fire for it!'

He stood up and tore open his buttons — and out there sprang Mr Percival Proud, quivering in his eagerness to show off his mettle. His hands grasping Alice's hips to steady her, Randolph pressed Percival's uncovered purple head into the hot and wet slit that awaited him. The bliss of that moment was beyond all belief, as his shaft sank by slow inches into Alice's slippery cunny. It gripped him closely, though there was nothing of the virginal about it, nor had been for many a year, but it fitted him well. He made a deduction that regular daily penetration and use had accustomed Alice's pussy to accommodate and welcome any dimension of male shaft.

'Do me harder!' she cried out, as he began to roger briskly. 'Ravish me to death, Randolph!'

He thrust in to the very hilt, his belly up hard against the cheeks of her bottom, and poked her with short and savage tups that brought whimpers of joy from her. Together in harmony of mind and body, they drew near to the sensual climax, Randolph's hands feeling up underneath Alice's loose shift, to grasp hold of her plump titties and roll them in his palms. She shrieked in rapture, and jerked her bottom back against his loins at the moment he spilled his essence into her hot and clinging pussy.

So thrilling were the sensations of that moment that in his exultation Randolph thought he would never stop fetching off in her! His stiffly swollen shaft throbbed and bounded while it discharged into the palpitating pussy that clung about it as if it would never again release it. Alice's cries of *more, more* rang shrilly about the room, whilst the ecstatic shaking of her body rattled on the floor the legs of the chair she leaned on.

However intense the pleasure, it can last but seconds. Soon the sharp thrill grew less, faded in both of them, then ebbed away to mere memory. Alice was left trembling over the chair, and Randolph close up but motionless behind her, his softening shaft sliding from her wet parts. They smiled at each other in approbation, then sat down on the sofa, side by side, to regain their equanimity a little before going further with their play.

'Are you now convinced that your Dr Acton is ignorant of the strength of sexual feeling in women?' Alice asked, rubbing her titties where Randolph had sunk fiercely grasping fingers into their soft flesh.

'Why, no — quite the reverse!' he said with a sly smile, 'Dr Acton predicts a raging nymphomania as the fate of any female who allows herself to indulge in repeated sexual gratification. My observation is that he is correct, for I never met a finer example of nymphomania in a woman than now — for which I am appropriately grateful. Be warned, dear Alice, for I mean to take every advantage of this sexual madness of yours.'

'If this is madness, then it is most enjoyable,' she replied. 'You have my fullest permission to take every advantage of me that you can, whatever the hour of day or night.'

There was good reason why Mrs Hamilton's servants had strict orders never to enter any room where she entertained a visitor unless she rang the bell. Leader of society though she was, and a frequent dinner guest of the highest in the land, here in her own house in the full light of day she sat on a sofa clad only in a thin shift and stockings, and the shift drawn up about her waist to expose her plump white thighs most indecently, to say nothing of the black-haired delight between them — on which Randolph had laid a comforting hand.

He too was in no condition befitting a gentleman calling upon an acquaintance at tea time. His grey trousers gaped open from waistband to seam, revealing his shaft — limp, yet thick and powerful of appearance even in repose.

'Explain this to me,' said Alice, 'why is it that, according to your foolish Dr Acton, men are able to sustain the sexual paroxysm repeatedly without ill effect, but women must refrain on peril of moral and physical decline. Does this not seem to you grossly unfair?'

'What the devil has fairness to do with it?' Randolph asked. 'Physical circumstances are as they are for an excellent reason — Nature intended it so. Mr Charles Darwin explained all about that in his book. There are the strong and the weak, the rich and the poor, the English and foreigners, the rulers and the ruled, the clever and the slow, men and women — how else could it be in a rational scheme of things? Nature gives to men a long thick shaft, and to women a soft slit, so that the one may be plunged into the other, for the release of the male essence, for his pleasure and gratification. How can anyone take exception to so very sensible an arrangement?'

'That be jiggered for a tale,' said Mrs Hamilton, lapsing

in the heat of disagreement into coarseness of expression better suited to a drab in a public house.

She rose from the sofa and collected up her clothes from the floor where they had been thrown.

'Come with me, Randolph,' she ordered, 'and we'll change this foolish notion of yours for the better.'

He followed her from the small sitting room into an adjoining dressing room beyond which, he guessed, lay her bedroom.

'Off with your clothes, and be quick about it,' said she with an ambiguous smile.

In short order Randolph was stripped down to his long under-drawers and socks, all else bare and exposed. Now it was that he received his first inkling of the far reaches of depravity to which Alice Hamilton's imagination extended, and her abiding lust for strong sensation. But only by degrees did this dawn upon him — at first he watched with some amusement whilst Alice donned his discarded clothes.

'My word!' she exclaimed when she pulled his shirt over her head. 'How wet and sticky you have made your shirt front with your spending, Randolph — I trust that you have enough left in you to continue?'

'Have no fear on that score,' he assured her, 'I have ample and to spare, to satisfy you, Alice.'

'A bold boast! Well, we shall see.'

His trousers were too long for her legs, and the sleeves of his shirt too long for her arms, as also were the sleeves of his frock-coat, but she turned them back to fit as well as she could make them.

'Now,' said she, attired in male clothing, 'since you have so kindly explained to me how very dangerous is the sexual spasm to the female constitution, though it is not so to the male, I have decided to change sex for a few hours and make myself out a young gentleman. By this contrivance no ill effect shall come to me from repeated rogering.'

Randolph laughed and seated himself on a chair by the window.

'Until further notice,' said his volatile companion, 'I am Mr Charles Hamilton, and so you must address me. I am at home from school for the hols. I suppose you must be my Mama's lover, as I find you here in her dressing room.'

When she moved within his reach, Randolph slipped a bare arm about her waist and pulled her down on his lap.

'No, no, you must not touch me, sir!' she exclaimed at once, 'I have been warned about the sort of men who desire to take advantage of young gentleman like me . . .'

'Do not be alarmed, young sir,' Randolph, putting on a manner meant to soothe and allay misgivings, 'you may entrust yourself to my honour, without reservation.'

'Not so!' she replied. 'For your bearing indicates that you have wicked and unnatural designs on my person! Fie, sir, for shame! I am sure you have a cockstand, you horrid man.'

During this complaint, Randolph's hand had slowly and almost imperceptibly, unbuttoned her trousers, and insinuated itself most stealthily inside, to touch the flesh of her inner thighs, and stroke there with a touch as soft as a child.

'But this is monstrous!' said she. 'How dare you touch me!'

Randolph's fingers were at her hairy cunny, hardly moving at all, but the sensation was so very thrilling to her and to him alike that only an effort of will held Alice back from pushing her split against his hand, and a similar effort restrained him from sliding his middle finger into her wetness.

'You are a wicked man, to finger an innocent young gentleman, and an Etonian to boot, in this shameful manner!' Alice said shrilly, her face flushed bright pink with emotion.

'You mistake my intention, I do positively assert,' Randolph replied suavely. 'As one with more experience than yourself in the intimacies of the sensual emotions, I mean only to examine your parts, in hope to establish that there has been no manual misuse or premature manipulation.'

'You insult me, sir,' said she, breathing more quickly to the gentle stimulation of his hand. 'I vow I have no idea of what you can mean by these words.'

'Do not attempt to deceive me,' Randolph retorted, 'if you were as innocent as you claim, you would not have let me put my hand in your trousers. I suspect the truth of it is that like all young gentleman of sixteen or thereabouts you have fallen into the forbidden habit of self-abuse, and make sport with your shaft continually.'

Whilst he was speaking, the tip of Randolph's finger grazed delicately along the wet lips of Alice's pussy, and her body shook with tremors of bliss within the arm that held her.

'Please, sir,' she said faltering, 'I humbly beg you not to inform anyone that you have discovered my secret shame, or I shall be beaten on the bare bottom. I don't make myself fetch off too often, you may believe me, hardly ever more than twice or thrice a day.'

'A likely story!' Randolph retorted. 'You will not bamboozle me with your untruths — the prevalence of precocious sexual excitation in adolescent males has been carefully studied by expert medical men, and the symptoms described. The celebrated Dr Acton goes so far as to declare that early incontinence and self-abuse are undoubtedly the most vicious of all courses.'

Still playing her role of young gentleman, shaken though she was by the thrilling sensations caused by the regular movement of Randolph's fingers, tiny thrills that made her pussy pout in eagerness for more, Alice raised her voice in protest.

'No, you are not to do this to me,'she said. 'It is infamous to handle a young gentleman's private parts in this way! I beg you to desist before you cause me to come off.'

'The bringing on of the sensual spasm by manual titillation is to be avoided,' said Randolph, 'for Dr Acton has explained in detail how it leads inevitably to an unmanly condition of undeveloped muscles, a pale complexion, and a soft skin. If the evil habit is persisted in, it brings on degeneration of body and intellect. The misguided youth who indulges himself may end up a lifelong invalid, or even a drivelling idiot, if the case is an extreme one.'

Alice was rubbing her pussy against his fingers. The lips had parted to allow him to feel the slipperiness within, and by it to appreciate the warm invitation it was extending to him.

'From this melancholy circumstance,' Randolph continued, 'we may note that wanton self-gratification by young males is equally as pernicious as a deliberate indulgence by females in the spasm of sexual excitation, and for both sexes the habit must eventually lead to the same mournful fate.'

'Then you must advise me,' Alice gasped, her hot breath on his neck, 'how is a young person like myself to throw off this habit and escape the perils attendant on persistent stimulation of the sexual organ?'

'I shall instruct you in the means of avoiding solitary abuse and its outcome,' said Randolph, 'only be patient and trust to me, however odd you think my course of action.'

He undid the buttons of her braces and pulled down her loose trousers round her knees, she lifting her bottom a little from his lap to assist him. Mr Percival Proud had been at the stand and poking upright out of the slit of Randolph's underdrawers for long enough. His abundant spend in Randolph's clothes, when Alice had been licked off to the spasm, had not at all impaired his capacity, and he vibrated gently, begging to be plunged into a hot and wet slit.

Randolph slipped a hand under Alice's thigh to adjust her position relative to his own, so that her legs were well apart and his shaft stood up hard-on between them.

'What a beauty,' Alice sighed, gazing down at its length and thickness, 'how handsome a fellow he is, with his thick shaft and engorged head. I vow that if he were mine I would take him in hand and bring him off ten times a day!'

'You must cease from such talk,' said Randolph sternly, 'in a minute or two you will understand how perverse impulses of that nature may be banished.'

With eager fingers he parted the plump lips beneath her curls of shiny black, and tickled her exposed button till she uttered little squeals of joy. Then, she seated sideways on his lap, he manoeuvred Mr Percival Proud's swollen head between the swollen lips of her cunny, and placed her hand over their joined parts. Without a pause, she seized upon his lewd intention, and jerked Mr Proud quickly up and down, making the soft head rub over her button.

'Why yes!' she panted. 'This is an excellent way to prevent a lapse into self-stimulation. By manipulating your parts to the sexual climax, I ensure my own pleasure, without the shame of having fingered myself for even a moment! Nor do I submit to being rogered as a woman, which too leads to debilitation, you have asserted. Your contrivance to avoid these dangers is well thought out — I am most obliged to you.'

'And I to you,' Randolph exclaimed, greatly enjoying the rub of Mr Percival's tender head on her slippery flesh, 'for I too am engaged in neither rogering nor digital manipulation of the parts, yet I shall surely fetch off in another minute!'

'You are most welcome,' sighed Alice, her hand sliding faster over their contingent and throbbing organs of delight.

'Oh!' said Randolph. 'Oh, my dearest Alice!'

Even as he spoke, his belly heaved strongly to the deep inner surge of his sap. An instant later it was expelled from his convulsing shaft in a creamy torrent, that spurted high over Alice's secret button, then out from between her parted pussy lips, and halfway up the front of the shirt she wore, causing her to emit sharp cries of delight as she too came off.

They rested content for a time, hardly speaking in the soft languor that eased their limbs, relaxed their minds, and calmed their emotions. But not for very long, both being uncommonly greedy of sensual pleasure. It was Alice, her fingers stroking along his limp and wet shaft, who commenced the conversation.

'In your examination of the doctrines of Dr Acton,' said she, 'have you established beyond doubt in which class of society he conducted the researches on which his views are based? I mean, he would at the expense of a few shillings have free access to the private parts of as many adolescent girls of the labouring classes as he wished. But to observe the condition of the same parts in young ladies of the upper classes would be impossible, even for a doctor, in any numbers that were meaningful.'

'There is some truth in what you say,' Randolph said, struck by the logic of her argument. 'I cannot answer your question at present. I shall tomorrow or the next day refer to his books to ascertain if the extent of his researches into the well-being of young ladies' pussies is made plain.'

'My deduction is this,' said Alice, 'your Acton's strictures on indulgence in sexual excitement applies only to the lower classes, who are not so healthily bred, or fed, as we are. For persons like ourselves, there is no risk attached to constant rogering, of that I am convinced, for we have the appetite to it, and the leisure for it, and comfortable homes in which we may take as much pleasure as we choose.'

So saying, she rose from his lap and held out her hand to him — and led him through a door into the next room, which was, as he had already deduced, her bedchamber. Whilst he removed his underdrawers and socks, his only garments, Alice threw off the frock coat and trousers she wore, and the wet-fronted shirt. At that, she stood naked and unashamed before him, her plump round titties and belly exposed to his ardent gaze.

'Since it seems you have an aversion to poking a woman on her back, I shall respect your preferences,' she said. 'Lie down.'

Randolph mounted the matrimonial bed and lay with his legs spread wide, whilst Mr Percival Proud performed his usual trick of growing twice as long and twice as thick as when at rest. Alice seated herself naked on the bed beside him, her shining eyes attracted unerringly to the stiff and strong-looking shaft that pointed upward toward her face.

She stroked Randolph's bare belly with one hand, whilst

with the other she took hold of Mr Percival and gave that gentleman a hand massage that made him quiver and jerk in expectation of more to come. Seeing how susceptible he was, she bent over him, her tongue flicked out and teased the purple head, which soon began to ooze tiny droplets of love juice. Randolph smiled and reached out to play with her soft dangling titties, whilst her little tongue flicked out to tease Mr Proud, before she sucked the shaft in between her lips.

She sucked vigorously at Randolph's throbbing muscle, until on the bedcover his bottom was squirming in blissful sensation, at which she transferred the seat of her attentions, lest she should inadvertently bring him off before she was prepared. She ran her tongue up and down his belly, brushing her soft cheek against his trembling shaft. Her hands moved over his body, to pluck at his flat teats and tear gasps of joy from his lips.

'I mean to have you again, Randolph,' she announced, 'three or four times, before I send you away. Conserve your strength, and let me arrange things to my own liking.'

At that, she slid herself on top of him, her mouth searching eagerly for his lips, and kissed him passionately, her bare thighs moving on his until their hairy muffs rubbed together. A hand felt between their hot bellies — her hand, shaking with emotion — and steered his straining shaft to the opening of her slippery-wet pussy. Then with a strong push, worthy of a man, she moved her hips forward, and cried out in delight to feel Mr Percival's swollen head forced deep into her.

'How many times can you fetch off before your shaft lies limp and useless?' she demanded of him. 'Four, five?'

'You must find that out for yourself!' he gasped.

'Then I shall roger you until you can no more,' she said

most firmly. 'I will send you home a nervous wreck in a cab, before dinner.'

Her plump belly plunged on his, rubbing her love-button up and down his embedded shaft, to bring on her own pleasurable thrills. Randolph moaned and rolled his head from side to side, as the climax of sensation came ever closer.

'Acton's warnings are for shopgirls and working-men's wives, not for people like you and me!' Alice panted. 'Rogering's the healthiest exercise in the world — I've known that since the very first time I came off as a girl!'

Randolph was unable to make any coherent reply to her daring statement, for sensation overwhelmed him just then and he shot spurt after spurt of hot essence up into her pussy. Her eyes opened wide as she felt him spend, and together they jerked and bounced in their paroxysm, each biting at the soft flesh of the other's shoulder. They both shrieked in their excitement, until all was done and they sank back, sated for the moment.

CHAPTER 5
A Halt is Called, or Nearly So

In the days that followed his introduction to the enthusiastic Mrs Hamilton, Randolph acquired by intimate acquaintance with her desires some small knowledge of her character, and of the reach of perversity she was wont to enjoy with never a qualm or second thought. Had she been born a male, this would have been of no account at all, and certainly not a reproach — merely the sign of a good fellow, who enjoyed rogering in its many forms and variations.

In a woman, no such easy verdict could be given. Perhaps, to stretch a point, this degree of lubricity was acceptable in a young whore, seeking to gain her livelihood. Even then, such a trollop would have the sense to await her client's lead, before plunging into the wilder forms of sensual pleasure. Men are men — and are by no means pleased if their male right to choose the sport is undermined by female pushfulness.

More to the point yet, when found in a gentlewoman of style, these characteristics of demanding constant rogering were not wholly admirable. To speak frankly, Alice Hamilton's insatiable need for a shaft inside her was becoming tedious to Randolph. He had known her for a little less than a fortnight, in which period he had rogered her 32 times, if his reckoning was right, brought her off in the French way by the use of his tongue 17 times more, and fingered her cunny to climactic spasm another dozen times, in round figures.

In addition to fetching-off in her pussy 32 times in the 12½ days, he had shot his roe between her titties 4 times, besides in her mouth 7 times, and in her rear entrance twice more, she having an occasional fancy for the Turkish style of love, and between her thighs once, by accident. He said nothing of the times he had come off in his trousers, manipulated by her busy fingers in hansom cabs and carriages, in the theatre and once at dinner in the Cafe Royal, under cover of the tablecloth.

The fact had to be admitted that the superb and haughty Alice Hamilton, in the world's eyes so refined, so fastidious, and so lady-like, was in private the most lascivious of harlots. Even Randolph, experienced as he was in the ways of women, high and low, was astonished and almost daunted by the intensity of her passions and the never-ending requirement to be brought off.

Whenever she was alone with a likely young man, some devil of lechery seemed to take possession of the lady. Propriety and common decency meant nothing to her at such times — she ceased to restrain her sexual propensities and gave fullest vent to them. Like Eve herself in the Garden of Eden, Alice had tasted the forbidden fruit, and was determined to gorge herself on it to total repletion, let the consequences be what they might.

These displeasing thoughts passed through Randolph's mind one morning when he awoke in his own bed after an evening out with Alice that had drained him of every drop and fatigued him to the point where he had fallen asleep in the cab conveying him at midnight to his home in Cavendish Square.

He could see very well that, far from being Alice's lover, he was only the recipient of her lust and the handy instrument for her sensual satisfaction. He had heard tell of great ladies who used their footmen in this manner, summoning them to their side in idle moments, to pull open the buttons of their breeches and lift out the fleshy shaft, without so much as a word addressed to the menial who owned it.

Indeed, Randolph recalled reading more than one account of an exploitation of their servants by ladies of title and quality. These domestic secrets were not published in *The Times* or any respectable periodical, of course, but in books published most confidentially. They could be purchased from only a very few booksellers in the Strand and elsewhere in town, by gentlemen trusted by the vendors. One such that Randolph had bought for a couple of guineas recently, and perused with great attention, concerned a youngish countess, who dwelt in Belgrave Square.

It was made apparent by the relater of this curious account that her husband was somewhat older in years, and incapable of supplying her need more than once a day. From this particular there arose in the lady an untoward attention to the servants, the male ones, that is to say.

On an evening when, after dinner, the Earl of Caterham had departed to his Club, the Countess rang the bell in her drawing room for a servant. The scene Randolph had read still remained clear in his mind.

The Countess was seated on a chair by the fireplace, having cast aside a novel by Mr George Meredith as much too dull for her mood. Her summons on the bell pull was answered by Henry, the handsomest of the four liveried footmen kept by the family. He inclined his head and waited for his instructions from Her Ladyship, but she with a little gesture of her soft white hand made him stand closer.

A strange expression passed over the footman's face when the slender fingers of the Countess tugged open all his breeches' buttons and reached delicately within to find his thick though quiescent shaft. His eyes stared down respectfully at her face, which was as calm and gentle as a child's — no man, or woman either, unless a witness to the lewd movement of the Countess's hand inside her servant's breeches would dream that she whose face showed such tranquillity to the world could be capable of so grossly improper an act!

Not so Henry, for he had been fingered by the consort of his employer many a time before. He stood straight-backed and still while she pulled into view his lady's plaything, now long and stiff. The Countess was left-handed, and in her right she held the balloon glass from which she had been sipping her after-dinner brandy. She held the glass close to the uncovered head of Henry's shaft while her other hand moved on his hot flesh, which continued to expand under her manipulation.

Soon it could grow no more, but bucked in her hand, for the footman was almost fetched off. He expected she would collect his gushing cream in her brandy glass, and braced himself on sturdy legs for the spasm that he felt to be imminent. Why Her Ladyship was bringing him off did not concern him at all — his duty was to wait upon her, and if her whim was to play with his shaft, then so be it. It relieved him of the need to perform the same office for himself when he went to bed, for he had no access to the female servants.

The mood of the Countess changed when she saw Henry's great shaft leaping in the premonitory spasms of coming off. At once she relinquished the grasp of her slender fingers, and left him shaking, while she turned up the skirt of her evening gown and her petticoats, to uncover fully her lacy drawers. Henry stood quivering in a frenzy of sexual excitation, his massive out-thrust shaft nodding up and down.

Her Ladyship parted the slit of her white drawers to bare her brown-haired aristocratic pussy. She was watching Henry's eyes bulge from his head, and his mouth, which hung open.

'Ha!' said she. 'I'm sure you'd finger me if I let you, but you are to remember your place and keep control of your emotion — indeed, now I come to think of it, it's highly insolent for you to have sensual emotions when you look at me!'

Henry was staring desperately at the pink lips of her cunny, afraid that he was about to fetch off involuntarily, over Her Ladyship's drawers! No doubt she'd punish him if he subjected her to so gross an insult — stop his wages for half a year, or even perhaps dismiss him. She noted on his face his feeling of alarm, and at once took the opportunity to remind him of his lowly station in life — for his own good, naturally.

'Stare you may, till you turn black in the face,' said she, 'I possess the prettiest pussy you'll ever see. I've been told by more than one admirer how very pretty it is. But how could you possibly tell, in your position? The only ones you've had to do with are the common slits between housemaid's legs.'

'Yes, milady,' he gasped, scarce able to speak.

'You've a good big shaft, Henry,' she told him, her face as tranquil as if she were conversing with a vicar on good works and charity. 'Far too well-grown for a servant's need or use — it should stand between the thighs of a gentleman of breeding, who knows how to satisfy a lady with it.'

Henry said nothing more, only ravished with his eyes the soft and hairy pussy exposed to his view by the immodest Countess. He could hardly believe his ears when she ordered him to kneel down and put his shaft up her.

'Are you deaf?' she cried, when he hesitated, quite unable to trust himself to such luck. 'Do as you're told!'

Her graceful white fingers reached for the lips of her pussy to part them, while the footman sank to his knees between her legs. She moved them wide apart, abandoning her cunny to him, but turning her head to the side, lest he forget himself and try to kiss her mouth. She uttered a little sob of joy to feel his long thick shaft penetrate her deeply, then began to gasp to the thrust of his heavy body rogering her fast and hard.

The ecstatic spasm overtook her well before he came off. She cried out in bliss, her uncovered legs kicking in the air, her hands tugging at the hair above the footman's ears, to pull him closer to her. He groaned aloud, then his body heaved in great convulsions, while he spurted his creamy liquid into her.

The moment that her tremors of pleasure faded, she pushed at his shoulders with both hands, to indicate he should dismount. He scrambled to his feet, his shaft still hard and standing up, though slippery and spent.

'Thank you, Henry. You may go now,' said Her Ladyship.

A like position was his own, Randolph saw — Alice had turned him into a lackey, to bring her off whenever she felt the urge. Confound the woman, it was intolerable — good though the poking was. Randolph was no flunkey and would not permit himself to be used in so slighting a manner, not for all the poking in the Kingdom. Last night, for example, after they returned to her house in Mayfair after attending a performance of Mr Gilbert's and Mr Sullivan's operetta *Trial by Jury*, Alice had removed her clothes completely in her bedroom — keeping not even a chemise to preserve her modesty, and on her hands and knees had invited him to play stallion to her mare.

Naturally, he had obliged her, for the sight of bare lips and black curls was quite irresistible. Being in a generous mood, he obliged her twice without getting down, but that proved to be insufficient. She looked over her bare shoulder at him, her eyes glowing with lewd intention, and recited some lines which he recognised as forming part of *Don Leon*, a work by Lord Byron in favour of unnatural pleasure:

> *Oh, lovely woman, by her Maker's hand*
> *For man's delight and solace wisely planned.*
> *Thankless is she who Nature's bounty mocks,*
> *Nor gives Love entrance, whereso'er he knocks.*

Her meaning was plain enough to him — that she wished him to seek admittance at another, and less conventional, entrance. So with scarcely a pause to recover himself, Randolph placed his trembling hands on the full round orbs of her bottom and parted them. No warm saliva or other artificial aid was needed to ease the insertion of Mr Percival into where she would have him next lodged, for he was wet with the slipperiness of spending, and the dew of Alice's arousal. Randolph thrust him strongly into her back door, and pleasured her in the Levantine style.

So much for the past. Randolph's pride was bruised and broken beneath Alice Hamilton's despotic sway, for he was reduced to a slave, and less than a slave — a living dildo to gratify her in any manner she chose. He would have no more of it — he meant to put a complete stop to his mortification.

There being little if any hope that Alice's nature could be changed to conform with his preference, the single course of action open to him was the drastic one of not seeing her again.

This was the decision he had taken by the time an undermaid brought his morning tea to his bedside. Her name was Lizzie, a girl of seventeen or eighteen years, of pleasant aspect and fair-haired, not long in service at Cavendish Square. Without being fully aware of what he was doing, Randolph had been stroking his shaft in a consolatory manner during his train of thought concerning Alice and with the result that Mr Percival stood stiff as an iron bar.

'I have made a resolution,' Randolph told the maid, at which she stared at him puzzled.

'What might that be, sir?' she enquired.

He sat up in bed, arranging the pillows at his back to prop him in a comfortable position, the bedclothes about his waist.

'My resolve is to have no more truck with female tyrants, but to allow my nature full scope and resource for its expression,' said he, smiling at the girl.

'I'm sure you know best, sir,' she said, not understanding.

She set the tea tray down by the bedside, whereupon Randolph seized her wrist and dragged her hand under the bedclothes, and down his belly, to where Mr Percival reared stiffly hard-on. After one brief pass of her palm over the rearing shaft, Lizzie struggled to disengage her hand from his grasp, and looked most awfully abashed.

'Oh sir, what are you doing?' she cried, her eyes downcast.

'Damme, Lizzie, don't be so innocent,' said Randolph. 'I want your hand here, on my instrument of pleasure. Feel how hard and strong it is to the touch. Grasp it in your hand — it throbs with desire to be brought off.'

74

The girl's face was scarlet to the roots of her hair, but as if mesmerised by his words, she ceased from trying to pull away and let him rub her passive hand over his fleshy shaft.

'Why is your nightshirt up round your waist?' she asked, 'I think you must have being doing something very wicked, to make yourself as big and hard as this.'

'I had a strange dream,' he answered untruthfully, 'and when I awoke I was in this condition.'

That caught her attention and held it, for like all her kind she was prodigiously credulous and interested in tea leaves and other omens and the interpretation of dreams.

'What did you dream?' she asked, and made no resistance when Randolph pulled her down to sit beside him on the bed.

'In my dream I was alone in the morning room, and I rang the bell, but no one came. After a little time I went downstairs to the kitchen, to enquire further, and you were there alone, none of the other servants to be found. You stood at the sink, your sleeves turned back to your elbows, and you were washing a pair of drawers.'

He watched her face blush fiery red again at the mention of her underwear, and continued to make up his story.

'I asked you what you were doing, Lizzie, and you explained that my father's valet had caught hold of you on the stairs and touched you up, so that you came off. You were rinsing through your drawers to remove any sign of your spasm.'

'Good Lord!' she gasped. 'I swear he's hardly ever tried to touch me, sir. And then only up above the waist! I'd never let him do what you say to me, never!'

'Then you admit that John has felt your titties? Where did this take place — in the kitchen?'

'In the pantry,' she confessed, her voice trembling to her confusion and dismay at being questioned closely, 'he asked me to make him a cold beef sandwich, cook being in her room lying down, and he followed me in while I was spreading butter on bread for him, and put his arms round me and interfered with me.'

'I expect you thoroughly enjoyed it,' said Randolph, 'and I'm sure that you had his trousers undone in a jiffy and stiffened his shaft. Did you bring him off, standing up together?'

Crimson from hairline to throat, Lizzie insisted that she'd done no such thing, but had eluded the valet's grasp.

'Strange,' Randolph said musingly, 'for in my dream you made no effort to elude my grasp, when I pinned you against the sink and had a feel of your titties from behind. I vow my shaft was every bit as thick and hard as it is now — have you ever held a better one?'

The better to respond to his query, Lizzie clasped her hand around Mr Proud, who bounded nervously as her touch aroused in him lively sensations of pleasure. Randolph took advantage of the maid's perplexity by slipping a hand underneath her clothes and upward to where her black woollen stockings were gartered. She had neither the wit nor adroitness to prevent his fingers entering the slit of her drawers, until he had possession of her cunny. Nor was that the limit of his unwelcome attentions, for he inserted a skilful finger into the sensitive spot at the top of her hairy little pussy!

Lizzie trembled mightily and would have moaned, but Randolph ordered her to be silent. His active finger in her pussy tickled her hidden button into the moistness of arousal, causing Lizzie to blush yet again, to feel her person being abused and, worse, her emotions responding.

'You've had your fun, sir,' she stammered, 'let me go now.'

'Not I!' said he. 'For I have a great letch to do what I did to you in my dream, when you stood at the sink, your drawers in your hands, and I pressed close behind you. I raised your skirt behind and made you bend over while I pushed my shaft up your cunny, and did you until I spent.'

'Let me go, and I'll do anything else you wish,' she implored him, 'but not that.'

'Then use your hand to relieve me of my raging lust, Lizzie. I'm sure you know well enough how to.'

She took his words as a promise, started to rub firmly up and down the jerking shaft she held under the bedclothes. Randolph spread his thighs and leaned back at ease against his pillows, breathing faster to the raising of his lust. In his considered view, servant-girls were put on this earth for the use of the gentry, and it was an indication that all was well with the world that she was at work to pleasure him and he awaiting the moment of his fetching off in gentlemanly style.

'I can feel my shaft shaking like a leaf,' he gasped to the thrills coursing through his belly to the fast movement of her fingers, 'in another minute you'll have a sticky handful!'

Lizzie felt his loins rising up from the mattress, to push his throbbing shaft hard into her ministering hand. Then the sensations of fetching off coursed through him, and he writhed and squirmed to the gush of his thick white essence.

When no more squirted into her hand, she drew his nightshirt down to his knees and stood up from the bed, wiping her hand on her long white apron.

'Will there be anything else, sir?' she asked.

'That's all for now, Lizzie,' he replied.

He thought she would depart, but at the door she turned and came back to stand at his bedside, and stare down at him with a thoughtful expression on her face.

'Excuse me if I'm speaking out of turn, sir,' she said, 'but

I thought that you being a sporty sort of gentleman, you might want to see a contest that's being held tomorrow, in a public house not far from here.'

'A contest, Lizzie? Do you mean a prizefight?'

'In a manner of speaking, sir, you might call it that, for there is a prize for the one that beats the rest. But he's not allowed to use his fists.'

'What then? What manner of contest is it?'

'A poking match, sir. I'm sure you know what that is.'

'I've heard of such bouts but never seen one,' said Randolph in sudden interest.

Though he had only a moment or two ago finished fetching off, he looked at the maid with a rekindled interest. Yet again he wondered what it was in his Nature that drew him to unfamiliar pussies, as a steel bar is drawn to magnet. After his long stint with Alice Hamilton the previous evening, he had woken indifferent to women and poking, pussy and the use thereof. The prospect of fingering Lizzie's, a new one to him, had proved to be more than he could resist. Though it differed in no way from a thousand he had felt before, he had found the experience comforting, and he was pleased that she had made him spend.

Now, even before the wetness of his spending had dried on Mr Percival, the girl was arousing his raging curiosity again with talk of a poking contest. The name itself was enough to ensure his fervent interest — if he had been invited to dine with the Queen at Buckingham Palace that evening he would have refused for the sake of attending the lewd entertainment that Lizzie had mentioned.

'Will you go?' she asked. 'Several gentlemen will be there, by all accounts.'

'Damme, I wouldn't miss it for the world!' said he. 'Tell

me the name of the public house where it is to be held and I'll see you right, my girl.'

'The Ratcatcher's Arms in Marylebone,' she informed him. 'You will find it in Norton Street. Tip the landlord the wink and say Mrs Laycock asked you to drop by.'

'How do you come to be in possession of this information? An honest girl like you?'

'If you promise not to tell, sir, the coachman next door let on to me, when we met by chance on my afternoon off.'

Randolph took note that a coachman's rough fingers had parted the pussy-lips he had himself played with only a few minutes ago. Perhaps more than that even. Lizzie might have allowed the fellow's low-class shaft to penetrate her slit. And the valet — he was sure that sly one had done more to the girl than fumble with her titties in the pantry.

No doubt, Randolph's feverish imagination suggested to him, other servants have handled Lizzie's titties and fingered her pussy. In his experience of housemaids, those that were made use of by the master of the house got a taste for being poked, which they then indulged with their fellow menials in off-duty hours. A warm young pussy was too damned good for coachmen and lackies — it was for his disposal, and roger it he would!

Without a second thought, Randolph threw aside the bedclothes and swung his legs over the side of the bed, where he sat with his nightshirt pulled up about his waist, to show off Mr Proud to the best advantage.

He took the startled girl's hand, to pull her down beside him on the bed. He darted his hand up her clothes once again.

'Open your thighs, Lizzie,' he instructed her, 'Damme if you haven't given me another mighty cockstand. There's nothing for it this time but to have you.'

'No, you will hurt me!' she said.

'What!' cried he, his fingertip busy with her fleshy little button, for he had forced an entrance between the lips below. 'Do you take me for a fool, to pass yourself off as a virgin to me? I've spent in more girl's cunnies than you've had cooked meals — there's little or nothing I don't know about girls of your class, I'd wager of ten pounds you lost your maidenhead to some low class ragamuffin boy a long time ago.'

'Sir, you must not say such a wicked thing!' Lizzie gasped. 'And you shall not take away my honour.'

'What the devil have housemaids to do with honour?' Randolph exclaimed scornfully. 'Open your legs, girl, for I like better than anything else the touch of pussy flesh under my hand.'

'You will ruin me!' she exclaimed, scarlet of face.

'Fiddlesticks! Do not presume against good sense,' Randolph retorted. 'My shaft will not be the first up you, not by a long chalk. Would that it were — I'd gladly give you five sovereigns in gold if your cunny was virgin, and my sap the first to flood it. But my finger informs me that your maidenhead went years ago, and therefore you must be satisfied with a present of 10 shillings, when I've poked you.'

'No, none of that!' she said hastily, her hand clutching at his stiff shaft, to push it away from herself. 'I won't let you do that to me.'

'Then you'll be the loser,' he replied, 'for if you won't let me, I'll get one of the other maids to come in, and she shall have the money.'

'Lord! Have the other servants let you poke them, sir?' she asked, looking curiously into his face.

'For 10 shillings a time I've had everyone of them, with only the exception of the housekeeper,' said he, 'and she is too fat for my taste, and besides, she must be near forty years old, and I have a letch for young girls.'

He could see that she was hesitating at this information, and guessed she might be at the point of surrendering herself to him. He directed her attention to Mr Percival Proud.

'See the frisky fellow in your hand,' he said, 'he shows his pleasure by bobbing up and down. Rub him a little for me.'

'Seems to me he's been rubbed enough for one day,' she said, her former coyness beginning to be lost in wonder at Randolph's rapid recovery to full size. All this while his deft finger had been busy in her pussy, to good effect, for the wetness of her arousal imparted itself to his touch, and he judged her ripe for broaching. He put both hands on her shoulders to press her down on the bed, then turned up her clothes to her waist. She began to breathe more rapidly, and her uncovered legs shook.

'A girl like you with no education is unlikely to have heard the verses by Lord Macauley, the celebrated author and poet,' said Randolph, 'but they are apt to the moment:

> *Drawers and shirt both off together,*
> *Naked is our sweet embrace,*
> *Nothing is concealed by either,*
> *All as naked as your face!*
>
> *See, my eager wandering hands*
> *Fondle cunny, belly, tit,*
> *And my upright manhood stands*
> *To pierce your wet and open slit!*

'Oh sir, do you really mean to do me?' she murmured timidly.

Her eyes were fixed in apprehension on his face, as he leaned over her. Without deigning to reply, Randolph threw himself on top of her, his nightshirt about his waist to uncover his parts and behind. In an instant his hot belly was on hers, her thighs forced to spread wide by his own thighs between. With expert hand he slid the head of his straining shaft into the open slit of her drawers, and up against the hairy lips of her pussy. A strong push of his loins rammed Mr Percival right up her.

'Oh my Lord!' she moaned. 'It's too big for me – you'll tear me apart!'

She resigned herself to being rogered and ended her complaint when he began to slide in and out. Not that she made any move to assist him in the Rites of Love, for her sensuality was not engaged, and the first tremors of pleasure he had aroused by his finger vanished when his shaft entered her. She lay still, staring at the ceiling, while he had his way. Soon the short strokes were reached, and Randolph started to fetch off.

He had no reason to consider the housemaid's feelings, for she was to be paid for the use of her commodity, over and above her natural duty to make herself available to her betters. Randolph enjoyed himself fully, groaning and panting, while he inundated her cunny with spurting floods of hot lust. Then, his career on horseback finished, he dismounted from the saddle and rolled on his back to draw deep breaths of satisfaction.

He watched Lizzie get up from the bed and dry herself between the legs with her chemise. He told her to take 10 shillings from the tallboy, where the previous night he had deposited the contents of his pockets, whilst undressing for bed.

CHAPTER 6
A Sporting Contest in Deplorable Taste

When Randolph stepped down from a hansom cab at the corner of Norton Street, he saw it to be a collection of shabby buildings of the sort put up by a speculative builder half a century ago and now let out in rooms and in apartments. These were not the foul-smelling slums to be seen in the East End of London, but the dwellers in Norton Street were not likely to be the cream of society. Bankrupted shopkeepers, Randolph guessed, pimps and counterfeiters, small gentry down on their luck.

The Ratcatcher's Arms stood on the far corner, and he made his way at a genteel stroll over the broken and uneven pavement towards it, swinging his silver-knobbed stick, and whistling a jolly music hall catch. Gentlemen in full evening fig of topper and tails were a rare sight in this street. A five-shilling whore pressed forward from the shadows, and slunk back again at the curt shake of his head. Two ragamuffin lads who played bat and ball against the wall stared as he passed, and touched their peaked caps respectfully. Randolph felt in his pocket and threw a penny coin at them.

Inside the public house there was a great deal of noise and tobacco smoke, but only a few workmen. Behind a long counter of beer-stained wood, a bruiser with only one eye stared curiously at Randolph and asked his pleasure.

'A glass of your best brandy,' said he. 'Mrs Laycock informed me that there was entertainment to be had here, though I see no sign of it.'

The other filled a large glass with amber-coloured liquor and set it before Randolph, asking for four pence. Then with a nod of his head he indicated a fat man in shirtleeves standing by a door in the rear of the taproom.

'See Hankey if you're a friend of Mrs Laycock's,' he said.

Hankey proved to be the landlord of these dubious premises, and on seeing a gentleman approach him with the password, he grinned to show broken teeth and stood aside to let Randolph pass through the door.

'Up the stairs, sir,' said he, 'you'll find plenty of company there already. The match is just about to start — you're in the nick of time. That'll be a guinea, and well worth it, for the cunnies are in for a hard time tonight.'

Randolph paid his entrance money and passed through the door. Up a flight of unwept stairs lay a large room, where twenty or more well-dressed men stood in conversation. In the centre of the plank floor half a dozen straw-stuffed mattresses had been laid down side by side, forming a rough arena of sorts for the athletic contest shortly to take place.

By the wall was a long bench, on which sat five young women, gin glasses in their hands and blankets wrapped about them. The contestants, thought Randolph, eyeing them with keen interest, stripped and ready for action under their blanket, no doubt. He contemplated them while deciding which he would choose to poke, if given a free choice.

Before he had settled the issue between the two middle women, the landlord came upstairs, bowed to the company and took up a position in the centre of the room by the mattresses.

'My lords and gentlemen!' he bawled in a loud voice. 'Your silence, if you please! You are bid welcome to the celebrated Ratcatcher's Arms, Josiah Hankey at your service.'

That got him a round of applause from the crowd, which with a clumsy bow he acknowledged before continuing his announcement.

'Now, since I see you are all sporting gents here,' said he, 'and impatient for the first bout of the evening, with no more ado I shall call forward the first contestant to get us off to a good start. The contest is for a purse of two guineas, and here is a favourite of yours and mine, Miss Dolly Burkitt. The sweet little lady is barely twenty years of age, but she is endowed with the strength of Hercules.'

At his words a hardy young woman rose from the wooden bench and advanced to the centre of the arena, where she threw aside the blanket that served her as cloak, and stood revealed to the noisy crowd. Her yellowish hair was cut short as any man's, and she wore nothing whatsoever but a pair of white drawers, tied firmly about her waist and stretching to below her knees.

The crowd fell silent in awe to see her take up the classical pose of athletes, leaning forward on bent knees, with one fist raised to her forehead. The biceps of her arms were well grown and developed, and when she turned so that all around the room might inspect her broad bare back, the muscles there rippled in fine style, and stood out strongly.

'She has not much by way of titties,' Randolph commented to the man standing next to him, a gentleman of middle years with a face reddened by the constant and liberal imbibing of brandy and port wine and other delicious liquors.

Indeed, Miss Dolly's titties were set high on her chest, but they were ungrown and flattish, offering a man little to fondle and even less to take hold of.

'What you say is true,' Randolph's neighbour agreed, 'but for all that, she'll not prove an easy filly to mount and ride, you mark my words. There's a wild gleam in her eye, and a flare of the nostrils that bodes ill to the unwary. I'd want four strong fellows to take an arm and a leg each and hold her down, before I'd go near her with my shaft at the ready.'

The landlord resumed his laudatory introduction of the woman, a hard grin on his face.

'Miss Dolly will take on any male adversary in a poking bout, offering the pleasure of her cunny to whoever can pin her down and get into it. No punching or kicking, no biting or gouging is allowed, and we give no guarantee against broken bones or other accidental injuries.'

The woman in the drawers raised her arms high in the air and paraded herself around the arena, letting all see as much of her body as was bare. About the ring voices were raised by top-hatted gentlemen, making offers of a guinea or thirty shillings for the pleasure of rogering her without having to fight her to secure the prize. She stared at them scornfully, and declared that she set a higher price than that on the use of her cunny.

'We have a volunteer to go into the ring against the lovely Miss Dolly,' announced the landlord in his hoarse voice, 'your applause if you please for this young hero who will take on our Amazon, Mr Will Hocking, a market porter of this parish.'

The newcomer who pushed through the crowd to gain the arena where the mattresses waited was no sudden volunteer, Randolph guessed. The bouts and opponents had been arranged ahead of the match, as a sporting spectacle, and there could be little doubt that the female contenders would be available to be rogered for a price at the conclusion of the athletics.

Will the market porter was bare-legged and unclothed to his shirt, the male labouring classes having no thought of wearing underdrawers or socks. He was a strongly built young fellow of perhaps five-and-twenty, and Miss Dolly acknowledged his entry into the arena with a vigorous nod of her head. By way of reply he lifted up the front of his shirt and, as if threatening her, showed her his hard-on upright shaft. The crowd roared their appreciation, and he grinned foolishly and took it in his hand.

'Of average size,' said Randolph's neighbour, who had by now introduced himself as Hartley Bingham, MP, 'but he's a sturdy rogue and may just get the better of her.'

In the sight of all, Will was running his clasped hand up and down his shaft, stimulating it to grow stronger and harder. The expression on Miss Dolly's face as she observed her opponent's antics was one of derision.

'Call that a shaft?' she said loudly, for the whole room to hear. 'I've seen bigger on twelve-year-old boys pissing against a brick wall!'

'Is that right?' Will retorted. 'Well, take a good look at it, bitch, because it'll be up you before long, and you'll sing a different tune then!'

'Take your places,' the landlord ordered, gesturing the two together in the centre of the mattresses, 'no rounds, no breaks or rests. The bout ends when Miss Dolly is well and truly poked or when Will abandons his attack on her virtue.'

'I'll wager five guineas that fellow doesn't best her,' said Hartley Bingham to Randolph. 'Will you take it?'

Randolph stared thoughtfully at the contestants, now circling each other slowly on the mattresses, arms outstretched to make a sudden snatch at the other when the moment came.

'They're well matched, and no mistake,' said he, 'but surely the advantage must always lie with the male, for so Nature has decreed. I'll take your bet, Bingham. Five guineas says that he pokes her.'

Even as he spoke, Dolly feinted swiftly, then seized Will's wrist in a twisting grip that forced him to bend over sharply. She turned her hip into him and threw him down on the mattress, following him down smartly, to lock his head between her thighs and hold him helpless. He squirmed furiously, but she had him pinned firm, until his hands found her hips. Then like a shot, his hand was in through the slit of her drawers, and he crowed in triumph to have possession of her pussy.

Dolly released her leg hold and twisted away, rising to one knee above him, but he gripped her round the waist and thrust his head up under her. She let out a loud cry, and the cheering spectators saw that he had his face between her thighs and his tongue at her pussy. To break his hold, she reached far out to seize hold of his hard shaft, and run her hand rapidly up and down its length.

Whilst she was thus occupied in attempting to relieve him of his urge by manual abuse, Will had without her knowledge undone the string of her drawers. With a heave of his back, he rose to his knees, and dragged her undergarments down her legs. Long and loud and fervent were the plaudits of the crowd to gain at last a sight of the mouse-brown curls that adorned her cunny. Dolly struggled to rise to her feet and escape from her danger, but her movements were hampered by the drawers Will had pulled down about her ankles.

She was badly off her balance, crouching with one leg folded beneath her and the other stretched out, so that her heel only touched the mattress. She would have fallen over backwards but for her hold around Will's neck, and he, seizing his glorious opportunity, pushed his outthrust middle finger up her pussy. She screeched, and the crowd shouted their encouragement to Will as, in plain sight for their benefit, he slid his digit in and out of his struggling opponent.

'Damned if I didn't get it wrong!' exclaimed Hartley Bingham in dismay. 'He's got her now!'

It was no more than the truth. Before Dolly could devise a means of escaping the finger that was invading her pussy, Will threw her on her back and himself on top of her. Her legs waved in the air above him, and she shouted out, *No, no!* But he had a clear advantage of position now, and with a heave of his hips and a sharp push, he was into her, and tupping fast.

Dolly had missed her chance by trying to hold her opponent by his shaft too soon. If instead she had grasped him around the body and thrown him on his back, she could have pinned him with her legs while she used her hand to drain him of his juices and win the bout. As matters stood, it was she on her back, and his shaft well into her — and in another ten or a dozen strokes he cried out in victory and squirted his essence into her. At once she ceased to resist and lay still, recognising defeat.

The landlord parted them and helped Dolly to her feet. Will had already jumped up, to raise his arms and wave them in the winner's gesture. He lifted his shirt front and made a tour of the arena, proving his win by letting the spectators observe that his shaft was wet and sticky with his spending, and waning shorter and softer. He was cheered to the echo for his success and essayed a comic bow and scrape.

After that came Dolly, led round by the hand of the landlord, so that all might see her slippery pussy, and know that she had been truly poked and defeated, and had not tricked her opponent to bring him off between her legs or on her belly. She too was cheered, though derisively, the loudest acclamation saved for Will, when the landlord handed him his prize money.

Randolph too extended his hand, for Bingham to count out the five guineas in his palm.

'Better luck next time,' said Randolph, privately wishing him no such thing, for he saw a golden chance here to part his new acquaintance from as much money as he had with him, 'will you take a glass of brandy with me?'

'Why, gladly,' said the other, 'after which I shall look to win back my money, with interest.'

Randolph gave the order to a potman making the rounds of the crowd, and asked Bingham if he had witnessed a contest of this sort before, or was it his first time, as in his own case? The genial Member of Parliament freely avowed that he had seen many a titanic struggle between young men and women for the use of a pussy, or otherwise, according to the outcome of the bout. Most especially in public houses south of the Thames, he apprised an interested Randolph, in the area generally known to the local inhabitants as the Elephant and Castle.

Whilst they drank their brandy and awaited the next contest, he told Randolph of one bout especially he had seen, a year or two past. The opponents were so close-matched, said he, in each particular of height and size and weight, and possessed of such physical strength and endurance, that the bout had gone on for nigh half an hour! By then every stitch of clothing had been torn from both contestants, and they were wrestling stark naked down on the mattress, their bodies glistening with sweat.

Eventually, he said, the bout had ended in a win for the

man, but only because the woman had become bored with the struggle, and though she was by no means fatigued, she desisted from all further resistance. She turned on to her back, spread her legs wide, and let her panting opponent's shaft stab into her and roger her, till he spent and claimed the victory.

'I wish I had seen that bout,' said Randolph, 'it sounds to be most stirring.'

'It stirred me, I must confess,' said Bingham, 'for my shaft was at such a stand that I could do no other than give the girl a couple of sovereigns to let me stick it up her and add my sap to her brother's.'

'What?' Randolph exclaimed. 'Her brother?'

'So she told me, the opponent so much like her was indeed her brother, who rogers her regularly, she claims, at contests for money, and at home for pleasure.'

'My lords and gentlemen!' the landlord called. 'Your kind attention, if you please. The next contender of the evening for your entertainment, and for a purse of two guineas, is none other than the ever-popular Miss Phoebe High. Your applause, please.'

The woman who rose from the wooden bench by the wall and came to the centre of the room was hardly older than the first had been — Randolph put her at twenty-one or twenty-two — but she was in all other respects very different. She was, not to conceal the truth of it, excessively stout.

Her huge lax titties hung almost to her belly-button, which itself was nearly lost in a belly round as a beer barrel. She troubled with neither blanket about her shoulders nor drawers, so that her great columns of thighs were plain to see, and her massive behind was like a regimental drum.

The hair on her head was a light brown in colour, and tied in a short pigtail by a red ribbon. The hair between her thighs was very sparse, and did nothing at all to cover the long thick lips of her cunny. She stood solidly in the middle of the arena with her arms raised high, proudly showing off her naked body to all who wished to inspect it.

'Ah,' said Hartley Bingham, 'I'd love to give her a rogering. Just imagine to yourself the sensations of lying on that great fat belly and getting your shaft up her! And those titties — by George, I'd dearly love to get them into my hands and stuff one into my mouth!'

'I make no doubt you will be able to do that later on,' said Randolph. 'My own taste is for thinner wenches. But to our bet, sir — do you fancy Miss Phoebe to win or to lose?'

'To lose,' said Bingham, regarding her backside with his head tilted to one side, 'she cannot possibly have strength enough to move that heavy body about nimbly. When her opponent has her on the floor, she will be unable to rise, and she will be poked in no time.'

'I fear you may be right,' Randolph agreed, 'but what of it? Betting is all a matter of luck. The same stakes as before, but to give me some faint chance of success, will you set a time in which she must be rogered?'

'Your request is a reasonable one,' Bingham conceded. 'I bet five guineas she's done soundly within five minutes — does that satisfy you?'

'Accepted,' said Randolph.

In another noisy burst of information, the landlord told his patrons that the volunteer to take on Miss Phoebe was Ned Aker, a soldier of the Queen who had been discharged after service in the Ashanti War. Ned bounded into the arena in lively style, a burly man of two or three-and-twenty, with a back marked by old scars from a field punishment flogging for misconduct.

He stared at the expanse of Miss Phoebe's nakedness and

said loudly, *If that's the way of it, naked as savages, so be it*, and he peeled off his shirt, to stand in his nudity, as she did. In an instant exclamations of surprise rose from the spectators, who saw now that Ned's shaft hung limp between his thighs. Miss Phoebe pointed at it with an extended forefinger and mocked him.

'Pooh!' she cried. 'Do you think you'll ever get that weak little dangler into me? Say your prayers, Ned Aker, for you're a goner, my lad!'

'Don't count your chickens till they're hatched,' he retorted to her scorn. 'It'll stand up hard enough when I've got you on your back and your legs open. I've poked black women in Africa bigger than you, and they haven't forgotten me yet!'

'Stand ready,' the landlord ordered. 'Get set — fight!'

He moved well back out of the way as Ned took two short steps and hurled himself bodily at his opponent. His scheme evidently matched Bingham's assessment of the position — that as soon as Miss Phoebe was on her back, her bulk would render her helpless as an overturned turtle on a beach. To this end, his shoulder struck against her breastbone, between her fat titties, whilst he pushed at her wide hips to up-end her.

However, in this Ned had taken on more than he knew. Phoebe grunted hard as she received his charge, and stood fast on the firmly planted pillars of her legs. Before he could recover from his thwarted assault, she had his head clamped under her arm, and being shorter than he by half a foot, it was necessary for him to bend over forward. She held him thus trapped whilst she reached over his bent back and delivered a smart smack or two on the cheeks of his bottom. At this he howled and wiggled more than ever, to break loose from her hold.

Only when she had humiliated him enough did she release

his head from under her arm, and let him stagger away. He was game, whatever the odds, and after a second or two of deep breathing to recover himself, he dashed at her once more. He came in low this time, running his head at her fat belly, his hands groping for her meaty titties, to get a firm hold on her. She gasped to the escape of her breath from the impact of his head, but even so, Ned was unable to turn her off her feet.

He would have retreated to try again, but she had her hand on the nape of his neck and forced his head down lower, and lower yet, until his face was pressed to her pussy.

'By Jove!' said Randolph, 'She's going to make him lick her, I do believe!'

He was wrong in that. Phoebe got Ned's neck between her great thighs and squeezed until he fell onto his knees, held fast in a trap he could not open. She stood laughing, her hands juggled under her titties, to bounce them up and down for the delight of the crowd, who roared their encouragement.

'There's not a man here who can get into my cunny free,' she boasted, 'but if any gentleman offers me a couple of pounds, he shall have his will of it.'

'A bargain!' cried Hartley Bingham, MP, 'I'll pay you that, Miss Phoebe, as soon as you're at liberty, whether or not this fellow has you first.'

His was not the only voice raised to accept her offer, but he was the first. Phoebe smiled and waved her hand, from where she stood on the mattresses, with Ned's neck squeezed between her legs.

'What do you think?' Randolph asked. 'A drawn bout, I fancy, for he cannot overturn her, but she is too ungainly and slow to best him. Shall we cancel our bet?'

'Not a bit of it!' said Bingham, his face flushed red with

the thought that he might be rogering the stout Miss Phoebe ere long. 'Let the bet stand — never let it be said of me that I am not a sportsman!'

'But you've bet against her,' said Randolph, 'you've bet that she will lose the bout.'

'I regret to say that I am still of that opinion,' said his companion, his lips pursed, 'for she will sooner or later have to release him from Chancery, whereupon he will try again, till he in the end succeeds in getting her off her feet. On her back she will be easy meat.'

Even as he spoke, Miss Phoebe shuffled her bare feet apart to open her legs, and took a step back. Ned had evidently reached the identical conclusion to the sporting Member of Parliament, for, without rising from his knees, he seized Phoebe's ankles and tugged, whilst he butted his head into her belly. Her pudgy arms waved, but her balance was lost, and she sat down hard on her well-padded backside.

A roar arose from the spectators as Ned launched himself at her, rolling her flat on her back, with himself on top.

'I knew it!' Bingham exclaimed. 'She's as good as rogered!'

He spoke too soon, for Phoebe was an experienced contestant at poking matches. She used one arm and one leg to push hard on the mattress and roll herself over, bouncing Ned off her belly. Before he could get clear, she completed her turn and lay on top of him, pressing the breath out of his lungs by her weight of flesh.

Her movements were ponderous and slow, but Ned was not in the position to counter them, for he lay gasping on his back, half-dead from being overlaid. Phoebe sat astride his belly, facing his feet, her bulk pinning him immovably to the floor.

'Yes, Miss Phoebe!' Hartley Bingham called out to

encourage her. 'You have him now! Finish him and come to me to be poked, my Amazonian queen!'

She grinned at him from her sweating face, and her thumb and forefinger closed round Ned's soft shaft and jerked it briskly to shake some life into it. He squirmed and swore beneath her, furious at being bested. His fingers were at her bottom, hoping to get at her pussy and torment it until she released him, but she was too heavy for him to slide a hand under her, nor were his arms long enough to reach over her thighs and reach to her slit from that direction.

Meantime, her vigorous stimulation had brought his shaft up hard. Her hand clasped round it, and she rubbed swiftly along its length. Ned sustained his resistance to the very end, his legs thrashing on the mattress as he attempted to unseat her — but to no avail. She had beaten him fair and square, and she let out a wail of defeat as the creamy liquor of his defeat spurted high, almost up to her grinning face.

The crowd roared its approbation of her success and several gentlemen threw florins and half-crowns into the arena, to add to the prize money. Hankey the landlord took hold of her wrists and heaved strenuously, to help her rise from Ned and gain her feet. He led her round the edge of the crowd, showing her pussy unbroached and inviolate, before giving her her prize.

'Get a move on, damn your eyes!' Bingham called out to him. 'I'm standing here with a hard-on shaft like a rolling pin! If I can't poke Miss Phoebe soon, I'll come off in my trousers!'

The gentlemen spectators laughed at him for that, Hankey took the hint and pushed Phoebe towards him, before leading Ned on a tour of the arena, displaying his dwindled part. Bingham seized Phoebe by one hand and one titty, so eager was he to get into her. She grinned and led him through a door into the rear part of the public house, where,

Randolph presumed, a bed or two was available for the use of the contestants and the clients who wanted them.

Bingham had been too hot for Phoebe's pussy to remember that he owed Randolph another five guineas for his lost bet. Randolph nearly went after him, then thought better of it — it would be damnably poor taste to interrupt a chap while he was unloading his lust into a willing whore. Nor was he required to wait long for his money — the landlord was announcing the next bout, when the MP returned with a contented smile on his face.

He resumed his place alongside Randolph and removed his topper to wipe the perspiration from his brow.

'Was she up to scratch?' asked Randolph.

'A damned good two sovereigns worth,' said the other, 'I had so violent a letch for Phoebe's body that I came off twice in her for the price of one. Here is the five guineas I owe you. What say you to this match — will you bet on it?'

On the mattresses Miss Sal Roper was in contest with Lemmy Bly for her virtue — if she yet possessed any remnant of that elusive quality. She was a strongly built woman of nineteen or twenty, of a dark complexion and hair, with loose titties and sturdy hams. Her opponent was younger — not more than seventeen or eighteen at most, and his rolled-up shirt sleeves displayed impressive biceps.

'By his broken nose and thick ear he is an apprentice bare-fist boxer,' said Randolph, studying the man and woman locked together in a wrestler's hold, their bosoms pressed together, their fingers interlaced, as they fought for mastery, pushing and panting.

'What of that?' said Bingham. 'Punching is barred. His skill at boxing gives him no advantage. And the woman looks capable of heaving sacks of coal. She'll be no easy lay for him.'

At that moment the struggling contestants lost their footing on the mattresses and fell together. To Randolph's surprise, it was Sal who was the quickest witted — she was on Lemmy's back in a flash, her legs wound about his waist, an arm round his neck to pinion him. He flailed his arms about, but could secure no grip on her.

'Commonsense instructs me that a strong male must always have the advantage over a strong female,' said Randolph. 'The stiff shaft is mightier than the female slit, for Nature designed it in the shape of a weapon to stab between women's legs and wreak its lustful will. Men are constructed to ravish women, and not vice versa. Lemmy will overcome her and spend in her cunny — oh damnation, look at that! She's got a hold on his shaft!'

Sal had her opponent on his side, his face pressed hard into the mattress, his legs trapped in the grip of her encircling thighs, and her hand over his waist to flip up his shirt out of the way and massage his stiff shaft with rapid movements.

'She's got him!' said Bingham, grinning broadly. 'Where is your commonsense now, Mr Joynes?'

'You asked me to lay a bet,' said Randolph, 'and so I will — I'll wager 10 guineas that Sal wins.'

'But the flag's up and the runners are over halfway round the course!' Bingham protested.

'I took you to be a sportsman, sir,' said Randolph, 'not a confounded bookmaker.'

'Very well,' the MP grumbled, 'no one shall say I turned down a bet because I feared the odds. I'll take your wager.'

Randolph stared at the locked combatants, waiting eagerly for the moment when Lemmy's sap spurted out and Bingham's money was his. He reckoned without Lemmy's experience of the boxing ring as training for poking contests. How it happened was hard to say, for Lemmy moved very quickly when he chose to — but a gasp arose from the crowd as he, from being underdog, shook off the woman on his back, rolled her over with his bare foot in her belly, seized her by the hair, and dragged her up on her hands and knees, with himself behind her.

At once he brought his throbbing shaft up to the slit of her drawers and pushed into her pussy. She shrieked to feel him go in, then his belly was pressed to the backs of her thighs and he rogered her with a masterful stroke. She panted and groaned, to feel her sturdy body so used against her will, whilst Lemmy grinned and slowed down, now the tables were completely turned. The wondering spectators observed his engorged shaft gliding in and out of Sal's pussy, and raised a cheer for him.

'I've got you now, my girl!' he crowed, tupping at her. 'And for a thirty-shilling whore you're not a bad poke.'

Sal moaned and swore and tried to shake him off, but he held her head back by her hair and rammed against the round cheeks of her behind.

'You'll have the lot up you in another second,' he boasted, 'like a bitch in the street. Do you like being done backwards, Sal, or are you only comfortable on your back? Not that I give a tinker's damn what you want — you'll get what I give you!'

No doubt if he had the time to spare he would have said more about the pleasures of rearward rogering, but a sudden tremor passed visibly through his body, and with a loud cry of triumph he shot his sap into her pussy. Or nearly so, for at the first spurt of hot tallow, Sal made a supreme effort and pulled away, collapsing to her belly on the mattress. Lemmy howled in rage whilst his cream gushed over her fat bum.

'Devil take it!' Randolph exclaimed. 'Did he poke her or

did he not? I say yes, for he got his shaft into her, at least.'

'But can he be said to have rogered her when he is coming off over her backside?' Hartley Bingham countered. 'He's dribbling on her cheeks still. We must wait for the referee's decision to settle our bet.'

'Which must be in my favour,' said Randolph spiritedly, 'for had she been a virgin, he went far enough into her to take her maidenhead — will you concede that?'

'Women like Sal can't even remember having a maidenhead,' the MP replied with a shake of his head. 'But if she had — what of that? I define the act of poking as requiring an insertion and an emission in the pussy. Otherwise a man could claim he rogers twenty times a night, when in truth all he does is push his shaft into a pussy twenty separate times at ten-minute intervals and wait for it to go slack, but fetch off only on the last time.'

'There is some truth in your argument, I must allow,' said Randolph. 'But what of *coitus interruptus*, as medical men name it, when a man pulls out at the moment of spending, not to put the girl in the family way, and comes off on her belly? Surely you will agree that he has rogered her, though he has not spent inside her pussy.'

'These are complicated matters,' said Bingham. 'What do you say of the man who thrusts his shaft up a woman's rearward hole and spends there? Has he rogered her, even though he has come off in her body? Yet she may remain a virgin, however often he may do her in this way.'

'Complicated indeed,' said Randolph. 'It may be that a great specialist in rogering, such as the celebrated Dr William Acton himself, may be required to settle the finer points of the bout — but as he is not likely to lend us the benefit of his wisdom, let us agree to leave it to Hankey to decide.'

CHAPTER 7
Solace in
Mrs Jeffries' Household

Randolph's emotions were heated to a lustful glow by the poking bouts he witnessed at The Ratcatcher's Arms, yet he found that he had no great letch for any of the female contestants. All of them seemed to him too muscular, too sweaty, too coarse, or too damned something or other, for a gentleman of his taste and refinement. Accordingly, after the final match of the evening, he went straight by hansom cab to Chelsea.

There were many houses he knew where abatement of his passion could be pleasantly arranged, and all closer to hand than that he chose. However, by way of repulsion from the brawny women he had seen wrestling down on the floor to keep common shafts out of their cunnies, he had taken a fancy to having a ladylike and tender creature. He felt certain that Mrs Mary Jeffries, whose house in Church Street, Chelsea, catered to royalty and titled persons, would be well able to provide for his needs.

Money was no object, for he had ten guineas he had won in bets from Hartley Bingham, the affable Member of Parliament for some dismal Midlands manufacturing town. He would have had more, but after much consideration the landlord had declared the contest between Sal Roper and Lemmy drawn. All bets were called off, to the anguish of Randolph and those others who had wagered that Lemmy would roger the wench, and to the delight of that portion of the crowd that had fancied Sal to beat him.

Mrs Jeffries was a genteel sort of woman, for a bawd, above fifty years of age and neatly dressed in shiny black satin. It was said that she had been housekeeper to Lord Mountrosset for many years, and more than that to him, and that when he died he left her money enough to set up her place of business in a pleasant Chelsea street. She sent out printed cards, it was rumoured, to His Lordship's wide acquaintance, informing them where she was to be found, and the particular services her house offered.

Be that as it may, she greeted Randolph with a warm regard, though some weeks had passed since last he was there. Her way was to offer gentlemen a glass of wine in her sitting room, not to hurry them, and when she had ascertained to her satisfaction by discreet conversation the thrust of their desire, she would send for whichever of her fair throng she judged most suited to the alleviation of their letch.

Randolph drank a glass of port wine with her, and the matter of the drawn bout being still on his mind, he explained to her the circumstances and asked for her expert opinion. Had Lemmy well and truly rogered the wench, or had Sal brought off a feat of deception in the final moment, and kept herself unpoked?

Mrs Jeffries had no doubt at all.

'If he had it up her, then he poked her,' she declared, 'that is the rule of the house here.'

'Whether he comes off or no?' asked Randolph, to elucidate.

'Coming off has nothing whatsoever to do with it,' insisted Mrs Jeffries, 'for some gentlemen produce so little essence as not to be noticed, and some arrive too far gone in drink to be able to come off at all — and lucky to get it hard-on enough to put it in. But once in, the contract is complete.'

'Your approach is refreshing in its simplicity,' Randolph was compelled to reply. 'I declare you are a veritable Solomon, my dear Mrs Jeffries — I would you were with me earlier tonight in the public house, for then I would be twenty guineas better off.'

While they thus conversed politely, the woman summed Randolph up and sent the parlourmaid to ask Miss Jane to come down and take a glass of wine with a gentleman visitor of distinction.

'Miss Jane,' said Randolph thoughtfully, 'I do not believe I have had the pleasure of making her acquaintance before. Is she a newcomer to the house?'

'Tolerably so,' Mrs Jeffries replied, 'for she has been here but six weeks or two months, not a day longer. I take care to choose who she shall meet, for as you will see, she is a young woman of rare charm and beauty, and not to be pawed about and poked by persons of questionable breeding and background. In short, Mr Joynes, she is in reserve for gentlemen like yourself who truly appreciate the bloom of youth on a snowy bosom, milk-white thighs and other charms too superior to be spoken of in general conversation.'

'Damme, but the girl sounds a paragon!' Randolph exclaimed.

'You will be delighted by her, and you may have her all night and poke her thrice or more, to your heart's content,' said the smiling bawd.

'What fee do you ask for this young Venus?'

'Ten guineas,' said she, 'and worth every penny of it, I have been assured by several peers of the realm and a bishop.'

Randolph thought it damned steep, and would have said so, but he guessed the wench must be exceptional to command so elevated a price. He would take a close look at her, the size and shape of her titties, the state of her teeth, the colour of her hair, and the fullness of her backside, before deciding whether she was worth a poke or two by him, at that price. He had questions to ask of Mrs Jeffries, but the parlour door opened to admit the young charmer herself, and he rose politely to shake hands. She was eighteen or nineteen years of age, he saw, her tresses raven black and her large eyes so dark brown as to be almost jet. She wore a simple white gown, cut square on the bosom to reveal the upper slopes of plump titties, the skin white and smooth.

At Mrs Jeffries's invitation Miss Jane seated herself and took a glass of port with them. She had a soft voice, without a trace of lower-class accent that Randolph could detect, and her manner was affectionate without being forward or pert. In all, she could have been mistaken for a young lady by those not in the know.

Randolph decided that he must have her and conveyed this to his hostess. She smiled with toothy graciousness, and asked for the price to be paid to her. The transaction completed, and the golden guineas safe in Mrs Jeffries's clutch, Miss Jane rose and extended a hand toward Randolph, inviting him to accompany her to her room above, that she might make his better acquaintance.

It was a well-furnished bedroom to which she conducted

him, equipped with a four-poster bed with green plush curtains tied back, and a green counterpane. There was a fire burning in the fireplace, and over the mantle a large gilt mirror on the wall. There was a sofa and two chairs, and a cheval glass which could be placed to reflect the antics on the bed, for those who liked to watch themselves poking.

Miss Jane smiled at Randolph and drew her long white dress up over her head and removed it, to reveal that she was completely naked but for pink stockings. Her titties were a fine sight — plump and full, each one more than a man's handful. Randolph stared at them in fascination, and she took his hands and laid them on her fleshy bounties, for him to feel.

Her hand moved over his trousers outside, to gauge the length and girth of his shaft as it rose upright in salutation to her naked beauty. He told her he was dying to have her, and with a laugh of pleasure she lay on the bed for him. His heart pounded like a drum at the sight of her parted legs, whilst he hastily took off his clothes.

What a sight for a man with an iron stand is a lovely young girl wearing no drawers! Miss Jane's soft, lovely, bare thighs were spread for Randolph, to display in full view the choicest flower of female beauty, the delightful plaything that nestled between her creamy white thighs! He could scarce restrain the murmur of approval that rose to his lips when he saw her thick bush of dark brown silky curls, and the soft lips of her pussy.

'I see now why Mrs Mary lets you out by the night,' said he, 'for you are so desirable, my dear, that no man would quit your side after only one poke!'

Miss Jane's jet-black eyes opened widely to gaze at him, and a fond smile spread over her lovely face. Her hand crept down her belly, until her slender fingers lingered at her pussy.

'Is it this what so attracts you?' she asked him, her words sending thrills of delight up his spine.

At the instant Randolph threw himself naked beside her on the bed, his mouth pressed to her bare belly in a kiss, she drew open her pussy a little way to display the delicate pink inner lips and the button standing proud at the soft threshold of her depths.

'I must have a feel of it!' Randolph exclaimed.

He could hardly speak for the intensity of the emotions this delicious girl had aroused in him, but he succeeded somehow to tell her how beautiful and tender a morsel was her pussy, and his intention to fill it brimful with his creamy spending. Then words failed as he set eager fingers to her youthful blossom in a long caress that seemed to draw the soul out of his body and send it adventuring in glory into her warm split ahead of his questing hand.

He heard the softest of sighs then, and happily he flicked between her parted pink pussy lips in their soft and dark brown nest, teasing at her little button until she made sweet sounds and moans of delight.

'You'll bring me off,' sighed she, her looks languid and her thighs ashiver.

'Very like,' he commented, with a wolfish grin. 'Do you know the lines by Mr Walter Savage Landor, the poet? They might have been written with foreknowledge of this very moment:

There on a downy bed they fondly lay
Teasing each other's parts in amorous play,
Till Nature seizing on their luscious game,
To fiery lust did both of them inflame.

106

He lay upon her in love's hot embrace,
And pressed his shaft deep in her yielding place,
They pant, they throb, their fierce convulsions start,
As through their limbs sensations quickly dart.

They thrust, they push, they tremble to their letch,
Then taste the truest joy, and gasping fetch,
Her wanton belly heaving up to his,
And as his juices spurt, she swoons in bliss.

Miss Jane had by now Randolph's stiff shaft in her hand and stroked it whilst she was pleasured. She sighed tiny breathless words of bliss whilst his fingers ravaged her with the divinest sensations. She rolled her bottom on the green counterpane, and her ample titties rose and fell vigorously to her heavy gasps.

There could be but one way of it now. Her loins twitched in a rapid motion and her whole body shook convulsively, from crown to heel. A shriek of joy escaped her and she came off, rubbing her wet pussy against Randolph's fingers. At that he could bear no more — with an exclamation of urgent need he hurled himself on Miss Jane. A single hard push took him deep into her pussy, his shaft buried in her up to the hilt.

Miss Jane cried out again to feel herself so deeply plumbed, for she was still fetching off from the ministrations of his fingers. Whilst he rogered her hard and fast, she continued to come off, crying out in her bliss without stop, her mouth hard on his and her tongue thrust in deep in the enthusiasm of her lust to be done.

Her wet pussy seemed to suck at Randolph's throbbing shaft in its avid thirst for his essence, and incoherent exclamations of delight too deep for words escaped from him. No man, be he ever so strong, no human organism, male or female, could long bear a blissfulness so devastating, and sensations so immense! A moan fled from Randolph's mouth into the girl's clinging mouth as he felt his sap surging in great spasms into her pulsating pussy.

There ensued a period of languorous contentment, the two of them lying side by side, her hand lightly holding his dwindling shaft and his hand between her warm thighs. Soon his interest returned, and in pursuit of his everlasting curiosity about the sensual nature of females, he asked Miss Jane to confide in him the circumstance of her first coming-off, if she recalled that event clearly enough.

'Remember — how can I ever forget it!' cried she. 'For I was a young girl, orphaned by the sad death of my doting parents in a railway train collision near Stoke Poges. In this sad plight I was taken into the service of Lord and Lady Grantonby, as an undermaid. I was, without wishing to sound in the least vain, a pretty child, and soon noticed in the household. There seemed never a day to pass but a footman or a groom did not try to get me into a corner alone and slide his hand up my clothes to feel my pussy.'

'Servants' morals are a disgrace,' said Randolph. 'It ought to be clearly understood that maids are to remain virgins till the master of the house, or the sons, avail themselves of it. I find it damnable that so many young maidenheads are thrown away and wasted on low-class scullions and boot-boys!'

'Then you will be pleased to hear that I eluded all attempts on my virtue by the male servants,' said Miss Jane, tugging his shaft to see if it was ready to stand hard-on again, 'but only to find myself pursued by Lord Grantonby himself. He is a short gentleman, of thirty-five or forty years of age, and almost bald before his time. He caught me one evening at bedtime, busy with my duties upstairs, and had his hand on my pussy before I could say him nay.'

'It was your clear duty to say yes to him,' Randolph told her with a slight frown. 'Young female servants are supposed to be used by gentlemen. Your person was his to do as he chose with.'

'Whether it was or not,' said Miss Jane, 'I had no intention of letting him poke me. I slipped out of his grasp and escaped along the passage, His Lordship in pursuit. At the bend of the stairs I concealed myself behind a half-open door to the sewing room. At once an arm encircled my waist from behind and I near screamed out.'

'Did he throw you down across a bed to have his will of you, or was he too hot to wait, and had you on the stair?' Randolph asked, his curiosity greatly aroused.

'Neither, for it was not His Lordship,' she replied. 'A soft female voice whispered close to my ear, *There is no need to be afraid, Jane. It is I, Lady Grantonby, and I shall save you from being ravished by my husband.*

As you may imagine, I was greatly relieved at that, and stood silent, waiting for instructions. *We must not try to move from here yet*, said Her Ladyship, *for I can hear him grumbling up and down the passage as he searches for you. We must wait a little until he gives up and retires to his room.*'

'This is very strange,' said Randolph, turning to face Jane, so that he could play with her ample titties, 'why should Lady Grantonby care whether His Lordship poked his servants or not? Is she a jealous woman by nature?'

'The same question was in my own mind then,' said Miss Jane, 'and it was soon answered, though in a way I did not expect. We stood silent together, Her Ladyship and me, she pressing close to my back, and her arm tight round my waist.

Then of a sudden she was handling my titties through my dress, and sighing loud. I was near to crying out in my astonishment, but to be heard by His Lordship and dragged off to his bedroom was not to be borne at any price, and so I smothered my cry and controlled myself.'

'By George!' said Randolph, 'Her Ladyship's appetite is for young girls, is it?'

'So I found,' Miss Jane confirmed, 'for her other hand slid under my dress and explored between my thighs. I squirmed about a little at the unusual touch, and felt my bottom rub against Her Ladyship's thighs. *Little minx*, she whispered, *do that again*. An instant later her fingers were at my pussy and it was as if a bolt of lightning flashed through my body to feel her dainty hand open my soft split. She laid her middle finger along the slit between the lips and pressed gently inside to tickle my little button.'

The effect of Jane's story was to bring Randolph's shaft up hard-on in her clasping hand, whilst he to emulate her former employer, laid a finger between her parted cunny lips.

'What happened then you may well guess,' said Jane, 'for Her Ladyship's delicate touch on my button undid me almost at once, and a dozen tiny caresses sufficed to bring me off with ease.'

With a long moan, Randolph rolled Jane over face down on the bed, raised her hips and pushed his hard shaft into her pussy from behind, lying over her back, his hands clasping her plump titties. As when Jane had stood leaning back against the Lady Grantonby, so now he came off in less than a dozen strokes, and gushed his hot elixir into her.

'My word, that was quick!' said she, when he released her to turn over and face him again. 'It appears that the adventures of my girlhood have a strong attraction for you.

Though nothing much out of the way took place, merely the rub of fingers in a pussy to the point of coming off. Would you have been so hot to roger me if it had been the footman handling me?'

'Why no — that would have been shameful,' Randolph told her firmly. 'But what of Her Ladyship after? Was her kindness to you repeated?'

'Hardly ten minutes passed before she wished to make me the recipient of another charitable act,' said Jane with a smile, 'for as soon as we were sure His Lordship had gone to his room to sulk, she made me go with her to her own bedchamber. It was winter and there was a comfortable blaze in the fireplace, and a brocaded armchair pulled close to it. Her Ladyship sat at her ease and pulled me on to her lap. *You're a fine well-grown girl*, said she, her hand undoing my clothes to make bare my titties and play with them.

'I stared down at what she was doing to me, half coming off in the bliss of being caressed by this aristocratic lady. She bent her long slender neck to worry at my titties with her lips and tongue, and I could feel her hand under my clothes probing ever deeper into my hot little slit. Her face was flushed red with emotion and I knew I could, with impunity, touch her body then. I slipped a hand down the front of her low-cut evening gown and devoted myself to playing with her titties and the little hard teats that crowned them. I wondered if I could bring her off by stimulating her titties only, perhaps at the same moment that she fetched me off.'

Randolph's shaft was at the stand again, and twitching within Jane's loose grasp.

'And were you successful?' he gasped.

'Almost — for soon Her Ladyship began to wriggle her

bottom on the chair and heave her belly up and down in nervous rhythm. *You saucy little baggage!* she sighed. *I gave you no permission to touch me — and I'm half coming off already. You must pay for your impertinence!* With that she rubbed my secret button fast until my body shuddered and my pussy wept tears of sheer joy — in short, she caused me to dissolve in the spasms of coming-off yet again. I pinched her teats hard in my fingers and she too called out, *Ah, yes!* in the sweetness of the paroxysm.'

It was perhaps the simple and sincere way in which Jane told her story of girlish lust, or perhaps the cool and gentle touch of her hand on Randolph's swollen shaft, or perhaps it was some combination of the intellectual and the physical stimulation — for as she described the event of Lady Grantonby's coming off, he gave a long sigh, his body shook, and spurts of his creamy liquor flew from his leaping shaft into her palm.

'Good Lord!' said Jane in amused surprise. 'How easily you come off! Will you rest a little now?'

'Needs must,' Randolph answered her, surprised himself by his fast and full response. 'Turn over with your back to me, Jane.'

She obliged him by putting her ivory-skinned back to him and drawing up her knees, so that he could lie against her like two spoons, her bottom against his belly and loins, his arms about her and his hands cupping her titties.

'I think I may take forty winks to restore my strength before I roger you again,' he murmured. 'Lull me to sleep, my dear, with a continuation of your truly charming tale of Lady Grantonby's seduction of her little undermaid.'

'If it will please you,' said Jane, wriggling about the soft cheeks of her bottom in Randolph's lap to settle herself. 'When Her Ladyship had somewhat recovered from the sweet fatigue of coming off she asked me to help her to undress, not wanting to send for her personal maid and interrupt our games. I was glad of the chance to see what fine garments a great lady wore, and assisted her to remove her stylish evening gown, to marvel then at the delicacy of her underskirts and petticoat, and at the wealth of fine lace on her chemise.'

'I know what underclothes ladies wear,' said Randolph, 'for I have undressed more of them than you. Get to the point.'

'As you wish,' Jane agreed in perfect good humour. 'Suffice it to say that before long Her Ladyship was seated on the side of her bed in her fine batiste nightgown, and I knelt at her feet to roll down her stockings for her. The skin of her legs was so very smooth and fine that I was unable to refrain from running my fingers up and down, from ankle to knee, until seeing that she was flattered rather than annoyed by this piece of presumption, I became greatly daring and caressed lightly above the knees also.'

'And higher still, I hope,' Randolph said with a yawn, 'when did you get to her cunny?'

'As soon as Her Ladyship encouraged my boldness by opening up her thighs,' Jane replied. 'My searching hand found her pussy — and her face began to blush a pretty pink at the touch of my fingers on the moist lips. Soon after that, before I could bring her off, she lay on the bed and asked me to pull her nightgown up to her neck.'

'Ah, she showed herself to you naked,' said Randolph with a sigh of pleasure, 'and you were still fully clothed, I take it. Is she a pretty woman, Lady Grantonby? For I cannot recall ever meeting her in society.'

'A well-made lady,' Jane replied, 'with an excellent pair of titties for her age, which is approaching thirty years, I think. She is flat-bellied and somewhat broad across the hips, which may sound a trifle ungainly, but I can assure you that when she lies on her back she is as arousing as any woman on earth, for she seems to be made especially for the sensual act.'

'But does Lord Grantonby think so?' Randolph enquired.

'Why no, His Lordship is averse to sinking his aristocratic shaft in any female over twenty, being so inclined by Nature.'

'Continue,' Randolph urged.

'Her Ladyship had me kneel on her bed, my head down between her parted thighs, to lick her curly haired cunny. I ministered to her button with my tongue, till soon enough it throbbed most voluptuously and became slippery wet with the honey dew of high excitement of love. *Ah, Jane*, she gasped faintly, *I've never been tongued so delicately before — how delicious are the sensations you offer me! I'm sure you will fetch me off in a minute . . .*'

Randolph's ever-eager shaft had grown hard again, and to keep it still while he heard the remainder of Jane's account of her night of seduction, he slipped it between her closed thighs. He was tempted to insert it into her wet pussy, offered temptingly to him by her position, but refrained. He was well aware that he would come off in seconds if once he broached her, and for a while he wished to retain the flow of his sap to hear her out.

'The very idea of bringing off Her Ladyship aroused me to the peak of frenzy,' said Jane, squeezing Randolph's shaft between her soft thighs. 'I had done it once by stimulating her teats, but that was almost by chance. Now she had given herself to me completely, and lay on her back fully exposed to me. She moaned and sighed to the flick of my tongue on her button, and bounded upward to push her open pussy at me. I had wrought her up to a state of lustful impatience, and I delighted in the sound of her gasping at the tremors that darted through her beneath my urgent caress. And then! Ah, never shall I forget that moment — Her Ladyship's smooth bare legs kicked upwards on either side of me, advising the supreme moment was at hand.'

Randolph's sleepiness had vanished, as morning mist before a rising sun, and he was again ablaze with passion. His shaft was of itself jerking in the gentle clasp of Jane's thighs, and he knew he would not long hold out.

'Yes, yes!' he gasped. 'She came off — tell me of it!'

'She came off hard,' Jane agreed with a little laugh at his impatience. 'She uttered a loud shriek and heaved up her belly, gripped my head between her thighs and shook to the convulsions of her climactic pleasure.'

'And so must I!' Randolph exclaimed. 'On your back, quick!'

'What an impetuous gentleman you are, to be sure!' said Jane in a tone of understanding and acceptance. 'I know some lines that Lady Grantonby taught me before I left her service to make my fortune. She said they were written by the celebrated poetess Mrs Felicia Hemans:

Oh come, beloved, lay your body down
Upon your darling's naked belly white,
And rapture shall our dear embraces crown,
As stroking pussy brings us true delight!

Such spasms of desire I have for you,
Who lead me down the blissful ways of love,
I welcome everything you mean to do,
When I am underneath, and you above!

Smiling lustfully, Jane moved swiftly to place herself on her back for him, and even as he got his belly on hers, she used her dainty white fingers to open the pouting lips of her love-split. With a shaking hand he guided the head of his throbbing shaft to the entrance to Paradise and lodged it within.

He took a deep breath and pushed straight — and in the same instant Jane pushed up to meet him. In a long and delicious slide his shaft was embedded as deep in her wet cunny as a man could ever desire. He rogered in and out, enjoying to the full the sensual pressure of her tightly clasping pussy.

'Great Heaven, the sensation!' cried Jane, her ardour as his own in intensity.

Randolph rammed hard and furious until he felt the floodgates yield within his belly. He uttered a triumphant cry to the feel of a torrent of hot sap racing from his tight pompoms up his jerking shaft.

He was thinking to himself, in as much as any man is capable of rational thought at the moment of fetching off, that what it was that most delighted him and raised his pleasure to unknown summits, was to roger a pliant young female like Miss Jane, not a demanding virago like Alice Hamilton. His pleasure was to use and ravish a female, not to be used by one. From this it was a small step to renew his resolve to be the master always.

'Ah, ah!' he cried, and spent his lust in Jane's pussy.

CHAPTER 8
The Keeping of a Resolution

The resolution Randolph had renewed when he was ensconced in Miss Jane's person was not put to the test during the next day, for after his night in her bed, he lacked his customary energy to pursue young females for the use of their pussies. In his mind was a warning passage he had read in Dr Acton's celebrated book, *The Functions and Disorders of the Reproductive Organs*. On a memorable occasion advice was sought of the learned doctor by a colleague suffering from a general debility, an inaptitude for work, disinclination for sexual intercourse, and a most ominous dimming of his eyesight.

In answer to Dr Acton's questioning, the sufferer admitted to connection with his wife *several* times a week, ever since their marriage seven years ago, and often *more than once a night*. The doctor at once informed him that this excess accounted for his troubles. Though he had been a hearty, healthy man at the time of his marriage, he had by over-indulgence in the conjugal act brought himself to this sorry pass!

Randolph bore it in mind that the sufferer was a middle-class sort of person, and therefore by Nature unable to sustain equal performance with a member of the titled classes, such as he was himself. Nevertheless, after poking Miss Jane six times during the course of a night, he felt it prudent to rest, till all his normal ebullience was restored. Therefore he passed much of the day quietly at his club in St James, where he dozed all morning in an armchair over the newspapers, and then after a sustaining luncheon, played a hand or two of cards.

On the following morning he awoke in his own bed in Cavendish Square, feeling much refreshed and ready for any friskiness, so long as it ended in rogering. When the undermaid brought in his morning tea, he was already up and out of bed, and standing at the window in his long dressing-gown, watching female servants at work washing the steps of houses all round the square.

'Put the tray down, Lizzie,' said he, turning from the sights that had held his interest. 'I have not seen you since I went to the poking-match, to tell you that it was a fine spectacle.'

The girl blushed faintly, her eyes looking down at the floor. Randolph smiled to see the effect he had on her, and determined to pursue it further, to assert himself as master of the girl's cunny, if he chose to make use of it. He undid the front of his frogged dressing-gown and let it fall open.

'See here, Lizzie,' said he, drawing up his nightshirt front to bare his shaft to her.

It was in a condition of readiness, standing hard-on, as the result of his contemplation through the window of a wench down on hands and knees scrubbing the steps of Number 14 next door. Young though she was, she had a good fat behind, the cheeks presented roundly through her dress because of her position on the steps. He had amused himself by imagining how it might be to come up behind the skivvy and poke her from the rear.

Fair-haired Lizzie gasped and put a hand to her mouth to see his shaft so boldly displayed. He was, whether or no the wench appreciated the fact, well endowed in the matter of his sexual part. He had not given the nickname of Mr Percival Proud to it without good reason.

This thick and long shaft pointed strongly upward toward her face, attracted her glance, whatever her confusion and dismay.

'If you were a pretty little trollop, such as hawks her wares in the West End,' said Randolph, smiling to see the scarlet of Lizzie's cheeks, 'and for a sovereign or two you had conducted me to a convenient room, then at the sight of my shaft standing forth uncovered like this, you would by now have knelt and put your arms about my loins . . .'

He paused momentarily to savour Lizzie's loud gasp of dread, then continued:

'Your tongue would flick out to tease the head of my hard-on shaft, till it oozed tiny droplets of love juice. Whereupon I would take your head between my hands and pull your face toward me, and you would draw a good half of my shaft into your mouth.

'Sir, sir — stop it!' Lizzie gasped, seemingly rooted to the spot in her agony of mind.

'No little trull who stops when she has a man's shaft in her mouth, before she brings him off, is worth a light!' said he. 'Nor would I allow you to pull way from me. I would hold your head firmly whilst you sucked at my throbbing muscle. And then what bliss — my elixir would start to gush forth, bringing on those ecstatic sensations which melt the soul in bliss.'

'Can I go now, sir?' Lizzie asked in desperation.

'Go? What the devil do you mean?'

She gulped and turned to leave the room without permission, at which Randolph strode smartly across the carpet, to reach out and seize hold of her by the nape of her neck. He whirled her about and pushed her towards the bed, until her legs were against the side of it. She squirmed in his grasp and begged to be released, but Randolph was enjoying the scene greatly.

'Don't be a ninny, girl,' said he, 'I've had you before, and mean to have you again. Why this show of resistance, when there is no cause for alarm? You were no virgin the first time I poked you, and who shall miss another slice off a cut loaf?'

'Don't, sir,' Lizzie pleaded.

Randolph was overjoyed at her reluctance and the opportunity it provided him to deploy his strength and mastery to poke her. He told her to climb up on the side of the bed on her hands and knees, with her bottom towards him. The tone of dominance that she detected in his voice evidently carried some weight, for no further protest escaped her lips as she did what he required of her. She placed herself on her knees, her face crimson with the shame of it, and he turned her dress and petticoats up over her back, to reveal her drawers.

It was the work of a moment to pry open with avid fingers the rearward slit of her undergarment. He stood in contemplation of the pale cheeks of Lizzie's backside sticking out towards him, and her brown-curled split. She stared over her shoulder, her expression troubled and yet also puzzled, that he merely looked at her secret parts, and made no move to touch them.

He for his part was rapt in thought, standing naked, for he had by then removed his dressing-gown and nightshirt. His hand slid along his stiff shaft, teasing Mr Percival to his maximum dimension, as a prelude to sinking him in the wench's slit. The moment was delightful to him — he had a female at the mercy of his hard-on shaft, and she was his to poke or not to poke, in whichever hole he pleased.

Lizzie summoned up the courage to enquire if he meant to do her like that, on her knees, or whether she should lie on her back for him. She asked without interest, and in resignation, to get it over with as soon as could be.

Randolph ignored her question, and stared at her bottom and parts to his full content. By then Mr Percival was leaping hard in his manipulating hand, and he bounded faster when Randolph put his other hand to Lizzie's hairy slit, to spread apart the lips and finger the button till he had made it slippy.

Lizzie was by then shivering and sighing, and Randolph came to understand that he had aroused her so that she wanted to be done. He found her attitude impudent in the extreme, and became annoyed with the girl for her presumption.

'Damme!' he exclaimed. 'I'm not here for your benefit! If I choose to finger your slit, it is for my pleasure, not yours! How dare you allow yourself to get into this condition!'

'I'm sorry, sir,' Lizzie gasped, 'I never meant to, but there was no way I can stop myself when you touch me.'

'You are a little trollop, and you let your cunny be felt by every manservant in the house!' Randolph accused her. 'A dozen times a day you're fingered and poked, I'm sure of it!'

'No, sir, I really don't,' she stammered, not knowing what he wanted of her, whether to scold her or have her.

'Lying will not serve you,' said he, his fingers probing into her wet pussy to add to her confusion. 'Tell me the truth now — when was the last time this common slit of yours was poked and spent in? Last night, I'll be bound.'

'Oh no, sir! The last time was when you did me, I swear.'

'Then who last fingered you?' Randolph demanded. 'Out with it, my girl — which of the servants was it?'

'If you please, sir,' said she haltingly, 'it was James, the second footman, who tried to interfere with me yesterday in the afternoon, when all the family were out of the house and most of the servants too. He caught me in the still-room, and had me seated on the table and his hand up my clothes so suddenly that I had no time to complain.'

'The filthy beast!' Randolph exclaimed. 'What did he do?'

'He wanted to do *me*,' Lizzie confessed, 'for he had my skirts up to my waist and his hand in my drawers to feel my parts. Two fingers together he pressed into my slit, groping for the most sensitive spot of all which, when he found, he rubbed, for all my protestations and struggling.'

'How dare the fellow make free of what belongs by right to his betters!' said Randolph. 'Did he have the effrontery to bring you off?'

'No, sir, I swear he didn't, for he was too eager to get into my pussy. Out came his shaft, as stiff as a poker, and he held it in his hand and stroked it while he boasted that he would have it up me to the limit. Now I, to put him down, said that I had never before seen so miserably small a shaft on a grown man — and he was mortified and jerked at it to bring it up longer and harder before pushing it in me.'

'Was it more than usually small?'

Lizzie blushed furiously and declared that she had seen very few male parts and had not the experience to judge.

'Well, was it smaller than mine?' Randolph demanded.

'Oh yes, a good deal shorter! I've never seen another as big as yours,' said the girl, though whether she spoke the truth or whether she spoke to please the young master, there was no way to be certain.

'It felt small inside you?' asked Randolph.

'He never got it inside me — I've told you that already, sir. What with rubbing at it to make it swell up bigger, James went further than he intended, and with a sudden cry, he spent and his sap flew out over my thigh, and wet my drawers through.'

'Where?' Randolph gasped, his arms about the girl to fumble at the fronts of her thighs, 'show me where he wet you. Was it here, close up to your pussy, or lower on your thigh, nearer to your knee?'

'It was about where your fingers are now,' said Lizzie.

'So near!' said Randolph, whose fingers were in her groin, 'An inch higher and the foul beast would have fetched off right over your pussy! Did he leave you then?'

'He swore at me, saying I had made him spill his tallow on my leg instead of in my cunny, but he let me go, for his bolt was shot and he could do no more.'

'Common people are not endowed with the natural strength and virility of the upper classes,' Randolph informed her loftily. 'I can come off twice in a row, as you have experienced, but an ordinary person is limited to once by a beneficent Deity.'

His fingers were toying with Lizzie's rearward-facing cunny the whole time he spoke, and she was squirming to sensations of pleasure that he had forbidden to her, and which she attempted to conceal.

'Why is there this difference between master and man, sir?' she asked, a trifle breathlessly. 'What is the reason?'

'Poking is the supreme pleasure in life,' Randolph told her, 'and Nature encourages persons of title and quality to indulge freely. This abundance of pleasure is denied to the labouring classes, who would neglect their work otherwise, to the great detriment of the Nation and the production of its wealth. Among the lower classes, the sole purpose of poking is reproduction of the species, to perpetuate the supply of labour required by titled families as servants, and by the business classes for their manufactories, and by landed gentry for agricultural work and as beaters for shooting parties. Now do you understand?'

'Yes, you have made it plain for me. Thank you, sir.'

'For the reasons I have adduced,' Randolph continued, 'it is given to males of the lower classes to come off but once within a period of several hours. This curtails the duration of their poking, so that their time is available for more useful tasks.'

Even as he spoke, the unanswered question entered Randolph's head — what was the period of hours required for a labourer to recover the power to roger? There was no doubt in his mind as to the truth of his statement, for commonsense required that no common persons should enjoy poking in the same way the upper classes did. Sexual intercourse was, to put it simply, far too damned good for servants and labourers!

The sense of self-satisfaction that pervaded his being at the conclusion of this train of thought so elated Randolph that, at a stroke, he put Sir Percival Proud's velvet-purple head to the female slit confronting him, and pushed him strongly in. Lizzie uttered a slight moan, to feel herself thus invaded, and then braced herself on hands and knees to receive the assault.

Randolph gripped her tight at the hips, to steady her for his thrusting.

'Lizzie — I hope that you appreciate the considerable honour bestowed upon you by having a gentleman's shaft up your pussy — and the even greater honour of his essence deposited in it!'

He waited on no reply while he slid Sir Percival in fast and rhythmic shoves into her. Her head turned, and she stared over her shoulder at him, her eyes pleading with him not to come off in her, lest he put her in the family way, to lose her position and be turned out into the streets, big-bellied and penniless. Her very helplessness added to Randolph's enjoyment, adding to his awareness of being the master, to use females as he willed.

'By God — I'm fetching off!' he cried, his sensations beyond compare delicious.

In another instant his belly heaved and he squirted his juice into her slit, and slumped over her back in trembling bliss, a condition which extended itself to several minutes. All through his spasms of delight Lizzie bore his weight on her back, and his belly against her bottom. She never moved, nor complained, but remained still and solid on her hands and knees, careful to do nothing to detract in any way from Randolph's pleasure, lest he become angry with her.

After luncheon, Randolph strolled forth to take the air, well contented with himself for the way he had asserted his mastery that morning. It was a pleasant day, the sun warm but not hot, and the rain clouds of the previous day passed over and gone, and in black frock coat and shiny top hat, he was elegant and perfectly comfortable. From Cavendish Square he walked south by Regent Street, pausing to purchase a small white flower for his buttonhole from a fat woman in a shawl on the corner. At Beak Street he turned into that district known as Soho, and before he had gone above a hundred steps along the narrow street, there were whores plucking at his sleeve and offering him the freedom of their persons for a guinea.

It was not in search of cunny that he had come to Soho, and he declined all that was offered, and sauntered on. He went by the church, where he caught a glimpse of a gentleman, to judge by his clothes, and a street woman, pressed hard against each other in the church porch. A religious poke, thought he with a smile, with the benefit of the Church, if not of the clergy.

In the next street, through a ground floor window of a house, he sighted a pair of bare titties, and a thick-bodied woman who wore nothing but her blue drawers, beckoning to him to come to the door. He halted for a moment, tempted in spite of himself, but the titties, although large and round, looked well-handled, and the woman was above thirty and had a foreign appearance. After a moment or two, he shook his head and walked on.

He was making for Greek Street, and the premises of Mr Avery, a bookseller of note. The volumes displayed in his dusty window and on the shelves inside the shop were unexceptional — sermons by celebrated preachers, bound up together, books of verse by esteemed poets such as Lord Tennyson and Mrs Elizabeth Barrett Browning, three volume novels by Mr Thackeray and other damned long-winded writers.

No doubt Mr Avery sold a book or two to innocent passers-by now and then, but to rely on lawful sales of wholesome and uplifting publications would have driven him into bankruptcy in double-quick time. The truth of it was that, for gentlemen he knew and in whom he could place his trust, Avery brought out from his back room books of particular interest. In the strict definition of law, these special books were reckoned lewd and obscene, dealing as they did frankly with sexual matters likely to catch the interest of gentlemen.

Nor was Randolph disappointed on this visit. After assuring himself that there was no constable to be seen outside in the street, Avery handed him a handsomely bound volume, which had on the title page an engraving of a naked man and woman in the act of coition together, standing under a palm tree. This, the bookseller told Randolph, was a learned and yet amusing work, a tome that dealt with unusual aspects of the act of generation. The author was a well-travelled gentleman, it appeared, who had an eye for oddity.

Randolph studied the engraving, noting that the man's organ must be at least a foot long, for the top part was thrust into his female partner's cunny, and he was shown in the very throes of fetching off, an expression of foolish delight on his face, yet he stood far enough away from the woman for their bellies not to touch. Such anomalies were known in the East, Randolph knew from previous reading, and a male organ of twelve and a half inches from root to head, in full erection, was thought to be the world's largest. He turned to the Table of Contents, which testified to many strange and little-known facts the author had noticed:

— *Colloquial names given to the male organ (various)*
— *Emergence of the sexual impulse in English females*
— *Earliest growth of hair on the female parts*
— *Copulation with Bombay women rendered difficult by an excessive development of the clitoris*
— *Heaviest female breasts by weight and race*
— *Signs of virginity from Antiquity to the present day*
— *Luxuriance of hair on the private parts of women*
— *Sodomy committed in three ways in Portugal*
— *Erections at the age of three in Bulgarian infants*

Without reading further down the Table, Randolph determined to make an assessment of the thoroughness or otherwise of the author's researches, and took at random a subject, turning to the page indicated. There with much quickening of his interest he read:

Madame Regnier was tall and thin, with expressive eyes and a sensuous appearance. She was a brunette, hairy as to her parts, had a long clitoris, a vigorous anus, slight bosom, passionate temperament, and cruel desires. She gave herself to every vice, offering her body to women as well as to men, whom she preferred to make use of her rear orifice. From which it may be seen as a characteristic of extremely erotic women that they have an abundance of hair on their sexual parts. It has been noted also they have a brilliant gleam of the eyes, and thick red lips.

It was the custom of Madame Regnier to lead her lovers to an alcove whose walls she had ordered to be covered with mirrors. There she repeated a thousand times all the different positions of love, so that the other party could see any part of her body and the most appealing postures for sexual congress . . .

There was much more, and the interesting statement that the volume was embellished with seventeen engravings, executed under the direction of the author, from his own sketches. Randolph told the bookseller that he would take it, and enquired whether he had in stock any new novel, romance or treatise dealing with a long-standing concern of his — namely, the strict and proper education of young ladies at boarding schools?

Avery smiled and put into his hand a book entitled *Selina Simcott, or The Tribulations of Virtue,* saying it had come in a day or two day before, being printed in Antwerp, and excellent value at three pounds.

Randolph opened the book at random and read:

Selina jumped in bed with her, and Susy nestled up close to her bosom, as if to keep warm, but in truth to feel the size of her titties. She passed her hand over these delicious globes a score of times, then asked Selina to open her nightdress, that she might lay her face against them. Thinking only to please, and without taint of sensuality in her motives, Selina let her bedfellow do as she wished, and soon Susy's inquisitive hands were wandering in a searching manner about her person, handling her soft plump titties, her round belly and bottom, her touches seeming to set her blood on fire and rouse every voluptuous emotion . . .

'Damme, Avery,' said Randolph, with a smirk, 'you've hit just the thing for my taste. How does it continue − let me read down to the end of the page.'

Judge of Selina's indescribable horror when the door was flung open and there stood Miss Rodwell with a candle in her hand to light the scene, and a swishy cane in the other. With a fierce jerk she pulled away the bedclothes, revealing Selina on her back, with her nightdress about her waist, and Susy's hand between her rosy thighs, her finger at the very slit of Venus.

'Upon my word,' exclaimed Miss Rodwell, 'I find you debauching a maidservant, Selina! Have you no shame, miss?'

Randolph's eye fell to the bottom of the page, to know what was the outcome of the schoolmistress's discovery. Nor

was he disappointed, for he saw that Miss Rodwell, forcing
a reluctant Susy to assist her, tied Selina's hands to the
bedpost, and her ankles to a heavy chest which stood handy
at the end of the bed so that she was well stretched-out.

*'Your bare posterior shall pay for your lubricity,' said Miss
Rodwell, nor would she listen to Selina's plea for forgiveness
or in any way abate her wrath. She cut her bare bottom five
or six times, each blow leaving a long thin red line and
bringing to the soft cheeks a peach-like bloom and glow.*

*Tears of shame and mortification welled from Selina's
eyes, but her loudest outcry was wrung from her when Miss
Rodwell put aside her cane and thrust her hand between her
victim's legs.*

*'How far had matters progressed between you and this
wretched maidservant?' she demanded. 'Had you
succumbed to the sensual paroxysm? Ah, there is a moisture
here between the lips that ought not to be present. It betrays
your condition of arousal before I so fortunately interrupted
your antics!'*

*'Ah no, no, Miss Rodwell — do not handle me in so
indecent a way, I implore you,' cried Selina, her plump
bottom wriggling about as she sought to escape the fingers
that probed into her virgin pussy.*

*'It is my duty to find out if you have been brought off,
as it is commonly called. Lie still, girl!' said her tormentor,
stimulating her secret button with a busy fingertip, with
more zeal than her avowed investigation warranted. The
outcome could not be long in doubt — the sensual spasm
seized on the pinioned girl, and with a long moan she came
off.*

*'What!' Miss Rodwell exclaimed. 'You dare allow
yourself to do that in my presence? Hand me my cane, Susy,*

I must thrash her behind until she repents and promises to reform her ways!'

'No, Miss!' cried Susy, 'for you will only arouse her again, and make her fetch off a second time!'

'Keep your insolent remarks to yourself,' Miss Rodwell said, 'her bottom shall suffer the cane until she has learned in pain and humiliation her lesson, and can come off no more when I put my hand between her thighs.'

Avery wrapped the two books carefully, to conceal from prying eyes their titles, and Randolph paid him and left the shop. He had gone only a short distance, his thoughts engrossed in what he had read, before he was accosted by a young girl. She said nothing, but stared knowingly at the long bulge in his clothing where Percival Proud stood hard and stiff from the misfortunes of Miss Selina Simcott.

'I wish I could spare the time,' said Randolph, 'but I am in somewhat of a hurry.'

'Won't take but a minute, the state you're in,' she answered pertly. 'In here.'

As if in a dream, he followed her into a narrow entry between two houses. The street was but a few steps away, where draymen passed with their loads, and pedestrians were walking by. That notwithstanding, the girl put her hand under Randolph's elegant frock coat and opened his trouser buttons all the way down. She pulled his shirt up out of the way, to take his hot and hard shaft in her hand.

'Two shillings, and I'll put him to rest for you,' said she.

'Done,' Randolph accepted.

'Not yet, but you will be in a minute,' she said with a grin. He leaned his back against the wall behind him and spread his feet apart a little. The girl jerked Percival Proud briskly up and down, making Randolph sigh at the pleasant feelings the simple action provided.

'Stand close,' he said, 'let me feel your cunny.'

She hitched up her threadbare brown skirt to let him slide a hand into her drawers and finger her between the legs. By the use of imagination he summoned up the memory of how he had that morning imposed his will on the under-maid Lizzie's pussy, shown to him as she knelt on his bed, quavering in her fright.

'What's your name, girl?' he asked the wielder of his shaft.

'Peg,' said she. 'You've a good-sized thing on you, sir. It's been up plenty of girls' cunnies, I'll be bound.'

Mr Percival was twitching in delight at the way he was being handled, and also from the lewd pleasure Randolph gained from feeling the girl's sparsely fledged pussy. He pressed a finger into it and rubbed her tiny button.

'Do you poke, Peg?' he asked.

'How much would you give me?' she said.

'Another day,' he sighed, 'I'm almost coming off already.'

'That you are,' Peg agreed, 'your hairy monster's jumping in my hand like a chicken with its neck wrung!'

Her hand rubbed at his straining shaft strongly, and Randolph felt his heart beating faster as the moment came closer for his passions to be relieved in wet spasms of delight. A fine frenzy of sensation seized upon him then, and his knees turned shaky under him, as his essence gushed in long jets up his belly, and soaked his shirt.

'Now I've done you!' the girl exclaimed.

CHAPTER 9
A Young Lady
Is Shamelessly Abused

After the young trollop in Greek Street had completed, wholly to Randolph's satisfaction, the process of inducing Mr Percival Proud to throb and spurt, she released her sticky hold to grin and ask for her money. Randolph put his clothes to rights, then paid her the two shillings he had agreed, bestowing a word or two of commendation for her skill in handling a gentleman's part so agreeably, after which he strolled on into Shaftesbury Avenue, thinking to find a cab.

To his surprise he was hailed by a dulcet female voice as he crossed the pavement and, turning, he saw leaving a milliner's shop none other than pretty Miss Dorothy Harker, accompanied by her brother Devlin. Randolph raised his top hat and returned the greeting. She looked deuced pretty, he thought, in a short jacket that buttoned tightly over her bosom, making her titties prominent. Her hat had small flowers sewn on it, and under her arm she carried a rolled umbrella with a round ebony knob for a handle. After the usual exchange of trivial remarks required on social occasions, Miss Harker declared that she veritably believed that Randolph had neglected her brother and herself.

'We have been in London for two weeks or more,' said

she, 'in which time you have never once visited to pay your respects. Do you find our company tedious, Mr Joynes?'

'Lord no,' he replied, 'but my time has been so taken up with family matters that I have neglected all my friends. I shall do my best to make amends by calling on you tomorrow, before noon, if you will be so good as to inform me where you are staying.'

'There is no need to wait until tomorrow,' said the sprightly Miss Harker, 'for you can accompany us to our lodgings now and take tea with us, mayn't he, Devlin?'

'Of course he may, but I've just remembered that I am to meet Lorimer at his club at four. Do you mind seeing my sister safe home, Mr Joynes, while I dash off?'

'With the greatest of pleasure,' said Randolph, offering his arm politely to Miss Harker.

It seemed to him that Devlin Harker had the look of a man who is intent on searching out a pussy to make use of, and not one going to meet another man in a boring club.

'Walk down Haymarket,' he advised, 'and through Jermyn Street towards Lorimer's club. There are fine wares displayed for sale along there, and you may well see something you like. I shall enjoy a cup of tea meanwhile with Miss Harker.'

In the hansom cab that bore them towards Paddington Green, where the Harkers had taken an apartment for their stay, she prattled happily of the many things she and her brother had seen in London, and of the excellent shops and the clothes she had bought. Randolph smiled encouragingly the whole time, even though his thoughts were on quite another topic.

He was pondering, in deep amusement, what this pretty nineteen-year-old virgin from Warwickshire might say if he were suddenly to inform her that, not ten minutes ago, he had been fetched off by the hand of a little trull in a Soho alley? Or what if he seized Dorothy Harker's hand now and thrust it down the front of his trousers, to make her feel the wetness of his spasm on his shirt, and his shaft lying limp between his thighs?

This sweet-smelling, smooth-skinned, soft-spoken young lady had never seen a male sexual organ in her life, of that he was certain. No thought ever entered her head that men she spoke to were eager to put their hard-on shafts up into the secret slit between her legs, and shoot their sap into it. Surely she would die of shame outright, if that were suggested to her face!

By dint of stretching his faculty of imagination, Randolph envisaged, under Miss Harker's snuff-coloured satin dress, legs encased in thin white drawers, ivory-skinned thighs and a dark-haired plump pussy nestling between. Mr Percival Proud approved wholeheartedly of the fantastical vision, and rose in readiness to his full height, inside Randolph's trousers.

Whatever strictures Dr William Acton might place on the over-frequent repetition of the sensual paroxysm and its harmful effect on the human organism, Randolph had formed a great letch to finger the maiden pussy of this untouched young gentlewoman, and gush his elixir into it. He knew perfectly well that there was not the least chance she would let him do so, or even speak of it, and that knowledge brought his emotions to the boil. His whole being yearned to roger Miss Dorothy Harker.

The pleasure would reside wholly in the physical conquest and the knowledge of being the first to spend in her, he knew, for often there was precious little more than the bare satisfaction of fetching off to be had with English gentlewomen, married or single. This Randolph had learned from his own experience, and it accounted for his predilection for whores. Quite the most beautiful woman he had ever rogered, disgraceful though it may be thought to admit it, was his sister-in-law, Lady Turringby, the wife of his eldest brother, who would inherit the earldom.

Randolph stayed often enough at his brother's country home in Surrey, and on one occasion had paid an unexpected visit during the hour when the household was dressing for dinner on lovely Gertrude in her room. She turned pale to see him there, though he had flirted with her for two days before this, and she had accepted his suit, though discreetly. Now the moment for action was at hand, she seemed to draw back, looking timid, and would have wished him to leave her.

This was not to be — as soon as the door was shut behind him, Randolph caught her in his arms and gave her a lengthy kiss of the most passionate nature. At this her reserve melted, and she clung to him, one arm clasped about his waist, the other around his neck, her dainty fingers playing in his curly hair. There was little time to spare on the delicacies of courtship with a married woman, and Randolph squeezed her titties through the lace-edged *robe-de-chambre* she wore.

'You do not love me,' she said, gazing deep into his eyes, 'I fear all you want of me is to make use of my person for you coarse pleasure. How banal that seems to me, how unworthy!'

She spoke the truth, of course, but that had little enough to with the matter. Without troubling to answer her, Randolph drew her tongue into his mouth, hugging her close in his arms, until she was breathless and ready for anything.

'I was hasty,' she murmured, her eyes searching his face, 'I see now that perhaps you do love me a little . . .'

Before she could go further into foolishness, Randolph slid a hand into her robe below the sash and felt quickly upwards between her thighs, to find the opening of her drawers and slip inside, to touch her soft skin.

'Ah now!' said she. 'Is that love, Randolph?'

'The fiercest, most passionate kind!' he declared.

His fingers were twining in the fine curly locks that covered her pussy. She continued to hold her legs together, especially when his fingertips stroked her moist lips. Eventually there came a relaxation of her muscles, as pleasant sensations manifested themselves within her, and he was able to press his finger into her pussy and tease her secret bud.

After some moments of this pleasant manipulation, he took her to the bedside and laid her on it. He got between her legs, fully dressed as he was, ripped open his trousers and brought Mr Percival Proud up to the mark. With one thrust he introduced that twitching gentleman into Gertrude's cunny, and rogered her with short hard strokes. Beneath him, her eyes were wide open to stare into his face, and she was so beautiful to look at that Randolph almost forgot what he was about. She did nothing to stir his blood, but lay passive on her back, her legs apart, allowing him to do what he wanted to her, almost as if her soul was elsewhere and only her body at his disposal.

'Do you like to be rogered, Gertrude?' he asked, panting.

She made no reply, but blushed fearfully at the suggestion, for all the world as if she were a young virgin with a shaft in her for the first time, and not the twenty-nine-year-old mother of three small children.

'Randolph — do not despise me!' she sighed.

Her words meant nothing to him. He rogered her strongly, and soon his creamy fluid came rushing out in thick jets, gushing up her pussy, and he squirmed in the bliss of fetching-off. But Gertrude, thus flooded, lay still, breathing perhaps a little more quickly but otherwise unaffected.

Since that time Randolph had made use of her commodity often but never once had he had the success of bringing her off, not by the use of his shaft, of his fingers, or of his tongue. It was because Gertrude was such a stunner in looks and figure that he was drawn to her and wanted to poke her each and every time he could, but her beauty was as nothing, he learned, for by Nature she was unreceptive, and he could as easily have been poking a dressmaker's dummy.

Nor was Gertrude the only woman of his acquaintance who was disappointing when her drawers were down. He had made trial of enough married gentlewomen to find that out. For some reason he could not understand, it was as Dr William Acton claimed — that as a general rule, a well-born, gently nurtured, virtuous woman desired little or no sexual gratification. She submitted to her husband or her lover only to please him and, except for the fear of losing him, she would far rather be relieved from his attentions.

Ladies like Alice Hamilton, who delighted in being poked by night and day, were all too few and far between, Randolph knew. It was in his thoughts that he had been hasty in breaking off with her, for she had given him some damned fine poking. Yet it had irked him that she wished to play the man's part and take the lead; it offended his manhood to be used for her pleasure, and he set his face against a return to her bed.

In the meantime, there was Dorothy Harker to think about, and if there was any chance of getting his hard-on shaft into her. If he did, it was extremely unlikely that he would be ever able to make her come off, English gentlewomen being too ashamed of their bodily functions, it appeared, to permit themselves to be gratified by poking. Yet it would be amusing to try.

The apartment Harker and his sister had taken for their stay in London had a large drawing room that overlooked the Green. Dorothy took off her bonnet and rang for tea, which was brought in by a maid with a bosom so well-developed that Randolph could scarce take his eye off her whilst she remained in the room.

Miss Harker poured him a cup and offered him a slice of fruit cake, and they chatted through the institution of afternoon tea until the social conventions had been sufficiently respected, in Randolph's opinion. A delicate and soft glow on Dorothy's face suggested to him that she was at her ease and well-disposed to him. Not that she would be receptive to his sexual advances, of that he was pretty sure, but at least he might make some little progress before she cried a halt.

They were seated side by side on a sofa, and he reached out boldly to take her hand in his own. At once her pretty face was suffused with the pink blush of modesty.

'Fie, Mr Joynes!' she exclaimed, trying to free herself from his grasp. 'What on earth can you be thinking of, to take this liberty!'

'Calm your distress, my dear Miss Harker,' said he, 'there is something of vast importance that I must ask you — and I hope you trust me sufficiently to take my question in good faith and answer it truthfully.'

'You must leave at once,' she told him firmly, 'release my hand that I may ring for the maid to show you out.'

'Do not be so hasty,' he said, 'the matter holds the greatest importance for you, and for me also.'

So saying, he slid a hand lightly over the full bodice of her dress, feeling the swell of her bosom. Had she been

139

dressed for the evening, with gown cut low, he would have slipped his hand down the front to clasp a titty and press it warmly. But in her high-necked walking-out dress, he could do no more than handle her titties through the satin.

'Dearest Dorothy,' said he, 'are you familiar with the lines written by Mr Leigh Hunt, the celebrated poet?'

> *Stolen sweets are always sweeter,*
> *Stolen kisses much completer,*
> *Sly feels of titties never pall,*
> *But stolen pokes the best of all.*

He saw Dorothy's mouth open to reprove him severely, and to prevent her outcry, he moved closer to her along the sofa and pressed a kiss to her lips.

'Unhand me!' she cried in alarm, jerking her head back from his to deny the touch of his mouth. 'This is a monstrous abuse of hospitality! Know, sir, that your friend Mr Lorimer Mawby has made me a proposal of marriage. I am to give him his answer at the weekend.'

'Dorothy – you must listen to me for one moment, and then I will release you,' said Randolph, smiling at her protest. 'Tell me truthfully now – have you allowed Lorimer, under the guise of a promise of marriage, to roger you? I have every faith in your maidenly virtue, and do not believe you have let him, even if he begged on his knees for it.'

She stared at him speechless, and he was very pleased by the strong effect his words had on her.

'Put aside this futile coyness,' said he, 'speak out freely – has Lorimer not put his hand under your clothes, and up between your legs, to feel your pussy, at least?'

'Oh!' she gasped, almost swooning from the excess of her

emotions, her eyes half-closed, while Randolph treated himself to a good feel of her big soft bubbies.

She would had risen to her feet, to escape from his insults, but Randolph threw himself to his knees before her and thrust both hands up her skirts. She cried out in horror, to feel his hands on her thighs, and attempted to press her clothes down on her knees, to prevent him from turning her hem up to her lap to uncover her knees and her stockinged legs.

'Stop this at once!' she cried, her face flushed scarlet as she stared down at him.

Randolph had not the least concern for decency or modesty just at that moment for, as the proverb informs us, *A standing shaft knows no pang of conscience.* His eyes glowed and his mouth was open in delight to observe how provocatively the fine material of Dorothy's drawers clung to her well-rounded thighs. Mr Proud bounded iron-hard inside his trousers, and without a moment of hesitation, Randolph tried to force his hand between her thighs to get at the opening of her drawers.

She pressed her legs tightly together to thwart him, and it was with the liveliest gratification that he heard her gasp of disbelief and dismay.

'For shame, sir!' she cried out. 'You must desist from this unspeakable indecency!'

Alas for outraged modesty, Randolph was by far the stronger, and his hand forced its way between her thighs, until he could slide forward on his knees and wedge her legs apart by placing his body between them. She struggled all the more then, to halt the vile advantage he was taking of her person, but in the grip of lust he was remorseless.

'You seem not to be a lover of poetry,' said he, panting with lust, 'but there are a few descriptive lines by the celebrated Mr Thomas Moore which bear exactly on our situation:

There is not in this wide world a valley more sweet
Than the vale where the thighs of a naked girl meet,
Oh, the last ray of feeling and life must depart,
Ere the love for that valley shall fade from my heart.

Miss Harker was in no mood for poetry at that time, not even if it were from the pen of the Poet Laureate himself.

'I shall scream to summon the servants unless you cease this infamous conduct!' she warned him. 'A constable shall be sent for and you given in charge!'

'I shall say that you spread your legs and asked me to feel you, but drew back when I begged to roger you,' he replied, to counter her threat.

It was in any case too late for warnings and consequences. His fleshy shaft was leaping so wildly in trousers that without a second thought he ripped open his buttons and let it stick out nakedly. He gripped it laxly between thumb and forefinger, stroking it suggestively to attract Dorothy's attention to its condition of readiness to devirginise her. At the sight of his thick and strenuously jerking implement, she uttered a long cry of dismay and collapsed against the sofa-back in a deep swoon.

Randolph stared at her with fierce delight, thinking how very fresh and pretty she was. Her eyes were closed and her cheeks pale, and she looked calm and pure. Her mouth was a little open to show her small white teeth, her breathing so light as to be almost imperceptible, hardly stirring her bosom. He panted in lewd desire, whilst he parted the slit of her drawers to bare her plump pussy, with its profusion of silky brown curls.

He did not hesitate, but pressed the tip of his middle finger to the soft lips and opened them, to gaze at the delicate pink of the interior, and her unbroken little maidenhead. His blood raced in his veins and he felt for a moment that he too might swoon, though in sheer bliss, at the sight of Dorothy's girlish pussy, so utterly at his mercy.

He slid forward on his knees, forcing her legs ever wider, to where he was close enough to present the swollen purple head of Mr Percival Proud to the lips of her cunny. One long straight push would take him into her, and his would be the first shaft ever to penetrate that beauteous pussy! One bold shove was all it would take to give him possession of her innermost charms! A dozen or twenty short stabs and his essence would gush up her deflowered slit, and the deed would be done!

Even on the very brink of his victory, something caused him to pause, though he could scarce breathe for the raging sensual emotions that had him in an inescapable grip. If Dorothy were of no more account than a common girl picked up and paid for along the streets of the East End, or out in the suburbs of Hampstead or Balham, he would have no qualm. More than once he had bought the use of a young virgin from her family and rogered her with merciless thrusts, her cries and sobs adding to his delight. It was beyond question that the daughters of the labouring classes had no higher destiny than to be poked by the gentry.

That notwithstanding, the uncomfortable fact was that Dorothy Harker was not a daughter of common people, but of a well-to-do land-owning family in Warwickshire. If she were deprived of her maidenhood outside marriage, there would be a devil of a fuss. In agony of mind, unable to go forward or back, Randolph stared at the sweet young pussy before him, while his trembling hand slid up and down the length of his throbbing shaft.

The sexual impulse was overpowering and would not be denied. With a moan of mingled joy and sorrow, Randolph fetched off to the wild jerking of his hand, and spurted his creamy sap on the soft white belly that lay bare above Dorothy's virgin cunny.

'Oh, oh!' he moaned, 'how blissful the sensations — but how mortifying that my essence is *on* her, and not *in* her!'

He sank back to sit on his folded legs, Mr Proud still in his hand, and stared in deep fascination at the white trickle down Dorothy's belly, into the silky curls that adorned her *motte*. A dissatisfaction possessed him, for there came into his mind the disgraceful story Lizzie had told him, of the attempt by James, the second footman, to interfere with her.

The damned fellow had pulled out his shaft, as bold as brass, and shown it to the under-maid bragging that she would shortly have it up her. He had stroked it to make it bigger, whilst at the same time he fingered the girl's slit — which was not his to use for his pleasure, he being only a servant in the house. Some such consideration must have entered his head, for he had brought himself off by hand and squirted his sap on to Lizzie's thigh. She believed it was by accident, but Randolph guessed at another reason — James had done it deliberately, to relieve his emotions without trespassing further on what was reserved to his betters.

Where now was the difference? For Randolph too had allowed his will to action to become *sicklied over with the pale cast of thought* as the Bard of Stratford put it, so that *enterprises of great pith and moment, with this regard their current turn awry, and lose the name of action.* He had behaved like a lackey in diverting his divine lust from its natural receptacle and letting it dissipate itself in a cowardly gesture. Meanwhile, the swooning girl lay pale and still, mercifully unaware of the great danger that threatened her.

'Damned if I'll be fobbed off like a flunkey!' cried Randolph in his anger and mortification.

Reckless of what might befall, he jumped to his feet, seized Dorothy by the hips, and turned her over to lie face down, her bosom supported on the sofa and her knees on the floor. Only an instant was required to turn up her skirt and petticoats to her waist and reveal her round bottom, clad only in thin drawers of fine white linen. Randolph flung himself down on his knees near this provocative vista of young female charm, and in a trice he had her drawers wide open behind, and was running his fingers up and down the charming cleft between the soft cheeks he had so brutally uncovered.

Although he had spent less than five minutes before, Percival Proud was standing to attention once more, eager to assert his mastery over the senseless girl who lay before him. Nor was he to be denied his raging desire — Randolph took him in hand and steered him bare-headed into the rearward slit of Dorothy's drawers. He bounded like a stag when he touched the smooth skin of her bare bottom. Then he was at the mark, and after taking a deep breath, Randolph pushed slowly forward into the puckered little pink knot-hole between his victim's nether cheeks.

He sighed to feel felt the tight sheath of forbidden flesh on his shaft, for it contracted in nervous spasms that imparted a succession of delicious sensations to the male organ it held so fast. He passed his hands under Dorothy's thighs, to finger her sweet little pussy while he poked her backside with short sharp digs. Delightful sensations flooded through him, emanating not only from the sliding pressure on Mr Percival's embedded head, but equally from the savage pleasure Randolph took from his act of perverse domination of the girl.

'Here's a new conundrum to ask the chaps at the club,' said he in panting glee as he worked at his shameful task, '*How can a girl be rogered and spent in, yet remain a virgin?* That will baffle a noddle or two!'

The rapid thrusts of his shaft and the feel of Dorothy's warm pussy under his fingers combined to rouse him to the very peak of pleasure in double time. He began to gasp in time with his strokes, and rub his belly against her backside as his emotions became intensified to near-delirium.

'Oh, Dorothy — I'm spending in your knot-hole!' he cried.

She heard him not at all, lying as if lifeless all the time he wreaked his will on her defenceless person. But he spoke the simple truth — his body was racked with ecstatic feeling, sighs were torn from his lips, and then he shuddered mightily whilst he discharged his sap into her ravished bottom.

He lay trembling on her back, his limbs relaxed in the sweet lethargy of satisfied lust. He was satisfied that he could not be accused now of acting like a timorous lackey, fearful of the consequences of his own desire. He was a gentleman who insisted on taking whatever he wanted, from young lady or slut alike. A faint groan beneath him brought him to his senses. At once he leaped to his feet, thrusting Mr Percival into his trousers, to fasten up his buttons, before lifting Dorothy in his arms, and placing her fully on the sofa, her head propped up on a cushion and her clothes decently arranged.

Her eyelids were fluttering, and he noted a slight

movement of her fingers. She was regaining her senses, and he did not wish to be there when she became aware of the ravaged condition of her knot-hole. He rang the bell urgently for the maid.

Bella of the big bosom came into the room and gasped with her hand to her mouth to see Dorothy stretched out on the sofa at full length, with her feet a little apart still.

'Oh sir, what has happened?' she asked, her eyes darting in curiosity from Miss Harker to Randolph and back again.

'Your mistress has fainted away,' he told her, 'I have placed her on the sofa, so that she may recover.'

'So I see, sir,' said Bella, her tone implying more than her words, whilst her gaze rested in turn on every smallest detail of the young lady's clothing, looking for signs of disturbance.

'Bring the *sal volatile* and assist her,' said Randolph. 'She must be kept quiet and rest for an hour or two — it is better if I leave, not to be in the way.'

'I'm sure you're right, sir,' said Bella.

She looked as if she might, excepting for the gravity of the circumstances, have smiled a little at the unusual scene that lay before her — the young lady flat on her back and bereft of her senses, the young gentleman flushed of face and with his frock coat only half-buttoned. It needed no very extraordinary powers of intellect to make out what had happened here on the drawing-room sofa.

She stared at Randolph with such knowing eyes that he dipped into his waistcoat pocket and found a gold sovereign.

'That's for your trouble,' said he, and he pressed it into her hand and folded her fingers over it, smiling at her.

'Leave everything to me, sir,' she said. 'I'll take good care of Miss Harker. Look — her eyes are starting to open.'

Randolph reached out to give Bella's enormous titties a quick squeeze through her clothes, then skipped out of the room. He collected his topper in the hall, and left in prudent haste.

CHAPTER 10
A Gentleman Goes Shopping for Ladies' Apparel

When Randolph walked out at midday, he proposed to take lunch at his cub and enjoy a day amongst men friends, away from all female influences and interests. The train of his thought while he strolled down the length of Regent Street was complex — for him, at least, for he preferred a simple approach to life and to rogering. His adventure with Dorothy Harker had been, it ought to be said, outside his past range of sensual experience, and puzzling, even to himself.

He was strolling past the Cafe Royal, looking the devil of a swell in his nipped-in frock coat, his top hat and shiny patent leather boots, when he became aware that his thinking had taken him on further — in his imagination he had reached Shaftesbury Avenue, and the shop where he had by chance met Dorothy and her brother Devlin, on the fateful day when he violated her bottom.

As he remembered, it was a milliner's shop Dorothy had been leaving when he passed, looking for a cab to take him home with his newly-purchased books, after he had been brought-off by a young trollop in an alley. The reason he recalled the shop was because he had dreamed of having

Dorothy against the window of it, leaning forward with her hands on the glass, her clothes up over her bottom, and he standing close to roger her.

Randolph was not a man much given to philosophising, or even to an examination of his motives, particularly not those having to do with poking girls. To his way of thinking, the pleasure of the poke was reason enough to do it, and no further debate was necessary, nor even desirable. That said, there were times when his curiosity was aroused beyond the ordinary — and this was just such a time.

He had dreamed of poking Dorothy Harker — all well and good. But why outside that particular shop? Why had he not dreamed of poking her in a hansom cab on the way to Paddington Green? Or in the privacy of her own lodgings? Randolph did not much believe in random events — there had of necessity, he argued to himself, to be a sufficient reason for his sleeping choice of location. In brief, there was something about the shop itself which had caused him to select it for his dream-poke.

Needless to say, the matter could not be left unresolved like that. Lunch could wait, while he walked round to Shaftesbury Avenue to look at the shop and see if anything occurred to him. Surely more must be involved than merely the name of the street — a thoroughfare for shafting in!

On the occasion of meeting Dorothy coming out of the shop, he had given it scant attention. The first discovery of interest he made now that he regarded it closely was that it was not, as he had assumed, a milliner's shop at all, selling only hats and gloves and ribbons, but an establishment that provided ladies with those items of underwear in general described as *lingerie*.

That was enough to set lewd speculations stirring in his mind for the most interesting item of lingerie was female drawers — a garment on which Randolph could never think without going yet further and summoning up visions of those choice parts of young ladies which were contained in drawers, and the uses to which these delightful parts could be put. Evidently he had noted the shop's true character when first he saw Dorothy Harker emerging it, and in his dream mind had spun a fantasy of rogering.

When he pushed the door open to enter, a little bell set on a spring tinkled merrily, bringing a smile of welcome to the lips of a young lady standing behind the long counter. She wore a white blouse with a high neck, and a dark skirt, the business-like severity of the ensemble mitigated by the merest touch of lace beneath her chin and at her thin wrists.

'Good day to you, miss,' said Randolph politely, tipping his hat to her, for though she was only an employee, and therefore rated not much higher than a servant, she was well-turned out, pretty, and eminently pokable, given the right circumstances.

She returned his greeting pleasantly and asked how she could be of assistance.

'I am the Hon Randolph Joynes,' said he grandly, 'and my pater is the Earl of Broadwater. A female friend of mine was in your premises a couple of days ago, in the afternoon. The young lady's name is Miss Dorothy Harker, and she was wearing a short blue jacket and a hat with small pink flowers around the brim. Under the jacket she had a high-necked walking-out dress in a lighter shade of blue. And I think she may have been carrying a rolled umbrella, though I cannot swear to it. Do you perchance remember the lady?'

Why he was asking this question, Randolph was not sure, but he wished to engage the pretty shop assistant in conversation and to make enquiries of a customer seemed as good a way as any he could invent. Nor was his sudden

151

interest to be wondered at, the shop girl was a ravishing brunette, twenty-two or twenty-three years of age, erect of carriage, gracefully shaped, with a full bosom and a wasp waist, an engagingly pert smile on her pretty face. There was neither engagement ring nor wedding band on her finger, but she was a girl who knew herself to be attractive to men, and who treated every man as a possible admirer.

'So many young ladies come into the shop to buy,' she said, 'that it is hard to recall one in particular. Of course, if we delivered her purchases, her address will be recorded. What was her name, did you say?'

'Harker,' he answered, 'with an address in Paddington Green. If I may enquire, what is *your* name, my dear? I have told you mine, and it seems awkward not to complete the introduction.'

'My name is Maria Peabody,' said the shop girl, with a smile that struck Randolph as pleasingly coquettish. 'If you will wait for one moment, sir, I will consult the sales ledger.'

She departed through a door behind the counter into a room at the back of the shop, leaving Randolph to look about him. Very little of what the shop sold could be put on display, owing to the intimate nature of the garments, but he looked at morning wraps and neck scarves and imagined the rest.

Miss Peabody returned quite soon, to confirm that Miss Harker had made a purchase, and it had been delivered to her the same day at an address in Paddington. Finding the transaction in her ledger had jogged Miss Peabody's memory, and she said she could recall Miss Harker clearly.

'What did she buy?' Randolph asked idly.

'I am sorry, Mr Joynes, but I am not at liberty to discuss a customer's purchases,' said Maria.

'Not even to a very close and trusted friend of hers?'

Maria's dark eyebrows rose slightly up her smooth-skinned and ivory forehead in amusement, and she said:

'If you are as close a friend of the young lady's as you say, then you may already have seen her purchases for yourself — or if not, then that pleasure may be yours shortly.'

Randolph grinned at her across the counter.

'Drawers, was it?' he asked, with his accustomed boldness to females. 'Your finest drawers for her soft thighs and delicious belly. With a hand-stitched slit for a hand to enter and have a feel of her pussy?'

'Oh sir!' Maria exclaimed, suppressing her laughter. 'What a thing to say! I ought to ask you to leave at once, but I hate prudery, so I shall let you remain, if you will give your word not to make any more immodest remarks.'

'You have my word,' he agreed at once. 'Now, Maria, my dear, I wish to see a pair of drawers similar to those bought by Miss Harker for herself.'

'Is it your intention to buy them?' she enquired. 'Or is it only a gentleman's interest that prompts this request? Mr Wyck would not wish me to pass time showing goods unless you mean to purchase something.'

'This Mr Wyck — is he the owner of the shop? Where is he?'

'He is the proprietor,' she confirmed, 'and he is today about his regular weekly visit to Spitalfields in East London, where many of the garments we stock are sewn.'

'Really?' said Randolph. 'I rather thought these charming little garments to clothe young ladies' delicious naughtiness were brought from Paris. Nevertheless, show me a pair of these drawers made by London seamstresses.'

'How can I do that?' Maria protested. 'Suppose that garments of so confidential a nature were to be spread out here on the counter for your examination, and in walked another customer, most probably a lady — how would that look? You must see that it is out of the question, though I would oblige if I could.'

'But of course you can, my dear,' said Randolph, 'turn the key in the door and the shop is closed for the lunch hour. Then we can go into the stock room at the back and you can show me in complete privacy what I wish to see.'

His choice of words made Maria look at him closely. When she still hesitated, he plunged on boldly, having nothing to lose.

'Look here, Maria, you can trust me. Are you Wyck's mistress? For I have been told that employers normally take advantage of the girls who work for them. Does he treat you well? Does he provide for your welfare? Does he pay you a proper wage?'

'What a cheek!' Maria exclaimed. 'You walk in here from the street and ask questions like that! How do I know you're what you say you are? For all I know you could be a coal-heaver in stolen clothes!'

Randolph drew out his card case and pressed into her hand his handsomely engraved calling card, showing his name and status. He removed his black silk top hat and honoured the girl with a little bow, smiling at her the while, letting his good looks and easy manner impress her.

'Well,' said she at last, 'it is highly irregular, but seeing that you are a gentleman of standing, and have the intention of making a purchase, I shall depart from my strict instructions and let you into the back room to inspect our merchandise.'

She was perfectly correct to call him a gentleman of standing — Mr Percival Proud was standing hard-on in his grey trousers and had been for some time. Furthermore, the prospect of being alone with the pretty young shop assistant in the back room was cheering enough to make him twitch mightily, as if it were then a foregone conclusion that he would soon be into her pussy. As the common saying has it, but with more truth than elegance, a standing shaft is ever an optimist.

Unaware of these considerations, or as unaware as a charming young girl who is no maiden can ever be when a gentleman shows his partiality towards her person, Maria gestured with a graceful hand that Randolph should walk round the open end of the counter, but before he did so, she went to the street door and locked it and bolted it top and bottom.

Randolph followed her into the back room, which was larger than he had supposed. It was fitted with shelves stacked with cardboard boxes along two sides, but under a window there stood an oblong writing desk littered with bills and lists and other commercial papers. The view from the window was into a small paved yard, where empty boxes lay higgledy-piggledy.

Randolph turned the straight-backed chair out from the desk and sat himself on it, crossing his legs and settling himself comfortably, while he was waited on. Maria took down a long box from a shelf, removed the top and held out for his inspection a pair of female drawers of finest white cambric, with pink rose bud ribbons threaded through the ends of the legs.

'Very pretty,' said Randolph, nodding in approval, 'are these what Miss Harker bought when she was here?'

'Three pairs,' said Maria, with approval in her tone.

'Are they the style you wear yourself?' he asked.

'At four shillings and sixpence a pair!' she cried, a tinge

of blush pink on her pretty cheeks, 'you must think my wages of Mr Wyck exceptional!'

'What!' said Randolph in pretended outrage. 'Do you mean to say the damned skinflint doesn't furnish a charming and sweet-natured young person like you with the best his shop has to offer? The man must be wholly deficient in decency and common goodwill! How can his pride as a shopkeeper, if such a thing can be in so low a calling as commerce, allow him, with a clear conscience, to slip his hand into your drawers for a feel of your pussy in the knowledge that your darling bum is encased in an inferior garment?'

'You go too far, Mr Joynes!' she reproved him.

'No, damn it all, let us speak frankly to each other. To me it is very apparent that this Wyck indulges himself in fullest use of your pussy, but hasn't the decency to dress you or pay you as you deserve. If I owned a shop — which I never would, it being beneath my station in life to engage myself in trade — I would say to you: *Maria — you are to pick whatever you choose from the stock, for the pleasure I have in rogering you is made all the keener by first undressing you and releasing your soft and delightful body from the prettiest undergarments that we stock!*'

'Heavens above! I think you must be a poet!' said Maria.

'Alas, not myself, though I have a great liking for poetry and number a poet or two amongst my acquaintance,' he replied. 'I have more than once got drunk with Mr Rossetti, who is also a painter of pictures, besides being a poet. Shall I recite a line or two of his for you?

> *Fain would I feel my darling's dainty leg.*
> *Which is as white and hairless as an egg,*
> *Fain would I kiss her titties' rose-red tips,*
> *And feel the curls upon her pussy lips.*

It continues for several verses in this vein, but I shall stop there until we know each other better, Maria, for the poet then becomes exceedingly personal in his address to his beloved, and what he wishes to do to her.'

'Lord!' said she. 'I am surprised there is much more for him to say. Now, sir, I have shown you what gentlemen are not shown ordinarily of our stock — do you mean to buy this pair?'

'I mean to buy half-a-dozen pairs,' he replied, in a briskly cheerful tone.

'Your intentions towards the young lady are not hard to guess at,' Maria commented with a half-smile. 'Six pairs of finest cambric drawers comes to . . . let me see . . . one pound and seven shillings. Do you wish them to be delivered to the same address as before in Paddington, or will you take them with you?'

'Neither, my dear,' said Randolph, 'for I mean them as a gift for *you*. But there is a small condition attached.'

The shopgirl's pretty face blushed a delicate pink at that.

'I am not entirely an innocent, Mr Joynes,' said she, 'and I am perfectly well aware of what you would be at. I must decline your gift, for I have an arrangement with my employer, Mr Wyck, and I cannot contemplate an act of disloyalty towards him.'

'What tomfoolery!' cried Randolph. 'What loyalty can there be to a tradesman who deals with you meanly? I have formed a high opinion of you, Maria, and it irks me to see you ill-used by your employer. How many times in a week does he roger you?'

'You have no right to ask such a question!' she retorted.

'My concern for your welfare gives me every right,' he said 'Wyck is a man in his middle years, I dare say, like almost all shopkeepers I have ever seen, and is from a pretty

157

common sort of family. He is surely married and has six or seven children. I put his capacity for poking, even with a girl as delicious as you, at not above twice a week. Is my supposition correct?'

'I cannot divulge information about my employer,' said Maria, now blushing furiously.

'No need, for it has not the least importance. Your agitation confirms all that I said. But to revert to more interesting and immediate matters — you have refused my gift before hearing the condition attached to it. Are you not curious, Maria?'

'I am quite sure I can guess what condition an upper-class gentlemen like you would attach to a gift of undergarments.'

'You have a nicely lascivious fancy,' Randolph told her, with warm approval in his voice, 'but you run ahead too fast. I only want to see you wearing a pair of these very superior drawers, no more than that, and the half-dozen become yours.'

Maria found it difficult to believe that he would settle for that, and make her a gift costing as much as she earned a week from her employment with the absent Mr Wyck. Randolph took care to give her assurances — that she should stand out of his reach to display herself to him, and that he would remain seated on the chair the whole time. In return, she would allow him to see her with her skirt raised for as long as he wished.

That settled, she removed herself to the far end of the room and turned her back to him while she bent over to raise up her long black skirt, drop the drawers she was wearing and replace them with the expensive new pair. When all was to her liking, she turned herself to face Randolph, who sat at ease to enjoy the spectacle.

'Now, Miss Maria, if you are quite ready,' said he,

gesturing with a hand to indicate she should lift her skirt.

With only the faintest hint of a blush, she stooped to grasp the hem of her skirt and raise it slowly. Randolph stared with eager eyes, as if watching the curtain going up at the theatre. Maria wore plain black stockings, and the slow lifting of her skirt revealed that, above well-polished but not new footwear she had trim ankles and well-rounded calves. A little below the knee, her stockings disappeared up inside the fine white cambric drawers, where the rosebud pink ribbons were threaded through the legs.

'How utterly delightful,' said Randolph to encourage her, 'a pair of legs that would grace the greatest ballerina!'

Maria seemed to preen herself a little at the compliment, and slowly she raised her skirt higher yet. Now came into view her thighs, and concealed inside the thin white drawers though they were, their round fullness could not be hid. She stood so that they were pressed close together, and Randolph sighed happily to imagine himself slipping a hand between them and feeling her warm flesh through the linen.

'Oh Maria,' said he, 'you are even lovelier than I could guess — how very tragic that so much youthful female charm should be thrown away on a miserable shopkeeper! Why do you let him, my dear, when you could advance yourself so much higher?'

'Could I?' she asked coolly. 'How would I set about that?'

'Why, I am certain there must be scores of gentlemen about London — perhaps even hundreds — who would take you out of this dreary shop and keep you in style, if you consented to it.'

'The gentlemen I have met so far have been interested only in giving me a couple of guineas if I will let them have me for a short time,' she answered. 'I find such offers insulting to my good name, for I am not a street girl of the sort who stand on the corner by Piccadilly and sell themselves to any who ask.'

'Certainly not!' Randolph exclaimed, feeling the throb of Mr Percival Proud in his trousers. 'But continue, if you please, for I have not yet seen all of my gift to you.'

Maria poked out her pink tongue at him, and lifted her skirt up to her wasp waist, revealing the drawers fully. He stared in open admiration at the provocative curve of her belly under the fine material, and at the place where her thighs met.

'There — that's what you want to see, isn't it?' she cried.

Randolph could not speak for the intensity of his emotions. His gaze was fixed on the closed slit in the drawers, the long opening into paradise, the place of concealment of the tender morsel that could give such rapture to a man. Maria saw that he was strongly affected, and perhaps in a condition of mind that could be prevailed on to her own advantage, always bearing in mind that she would do nothing against Mr Wyck's interests.

'Of what does a gentleman think when he sees a female in her drawers, posing for him in secret?' she asked with a smile.

'He thinks of this, and its satisfaction,' Randolph answered, bold as brass now that his power of speech had returned to him.

So saying, with nimble fingers he undid his coat and then his waistcoat, leaned back in the chair, stretched out his legs to their full length, opened his trousers wide and pulled up his shirt. Maria stared astonished to see him extricate from out of his gaping trousers his shaft, and finger it without the least sign of embarrassment.

While she stared at it, and he at her face, he took firm

hold of his shaft and stroked it up to its full height, so that it stood stiffly.

'See how very hard-on he has grown,' Randolph exhorted her, speaking in all seriousness, but smiling, 'not a minute's rest will he allow me now until he has discharged his desire.'

'A trouble-maker, is he?' Maria asked softly, mesmerised by the frank display of a hard male organ.

'No, he's a pleasure-maker!' said Randolph, and staring hard at where Maria's white drawers covered her pussy, he began to rub up and down his cockstand firmly.

'Stop,' Maria cried out, 'this won't do at all. Stop, please, Mr Joynes, or I shall lower my skirt.'

'We made a bargain,' he replied, 'you are to stand there for as long as I require, with your clothes up.'

His fingers moved faster on his straining shaft, the movement sending such thrills through him that he sighed aloud, whilst his legs twitched.

'This is not what I agreed to,' Maria complained, though not in earnest, seeing advantages to herself in Randolph's lack of self-control at the mere sight of her drawers. 'No gentleman exposes his person and abuses himself before a helpless female, only low drunks outside public houses on Saturday night.'

'Drunk or sober,' said Randolph, 'a cockstand brooks no delay or denial — it insists on spending.'

'Be careful, or you'll soil your shirt front,' Maria warned in a solicitous tone. 'Here, make use of these!'

With those words she let go of her raised skirt with one hand to pull from the box in which they rested another pair of the expensive drawers, and throw them fluttering across the space between herself and him, to land in Randolph's lap.

'Maria — you are a perfect angel!' he exclaimed, seizing on the intimate garment and draping it over his jerking shaft.

A frenzy seized on him at once, his hand slid up and down rapidly, then he cried out as the sexual spasm took him in its unbreakable grasp. His body was jerking to the spurting of his essence, which soaked at once through the fine cambric of the drawers, to make a dark wet stain that spread quickly.

'My word,' said Maria, when he had finished spending and sat tranquil again, 'I never thought to see a gentleman do that to himself! Mr Wyck would rather die than abuse himself in the presence of a female.'

'Wyck is a prudish clod,' said Randolph. 'All his class are. I doubt if he even knows how to poke properly. Does he bring you off when he rogers you?'

'I shall answer no questions about my employer,' she said at once. 'Are you on the slack now you have spent?'

'Almost,' he replied, removing the drawers to display his wet and softening shaft. 'How very pleasurable it was – I am much indebted to you for your help, Maria. Tell me something – if a rich gentleman came into the shop and asked your advice on what gift he should send to a female friend who had conducted him up to the very peak of bliss, what would you say to him?'

Maria let her clothes slide down her legs to conceal all but the toes of her shoes. Randolph made no complementary move – he lolled on his chair, trousers agape, his soft shaft lying limp in full view.

'What I would advise such a gentleman is this,' said Maria in a thoughtful tone of voice, but with a cheeky smile, 'he should send his female friend a complete set of undergarments. By that I mean several pairs of fine stockings, two or three chemises with lace edging, a petticoat or two with flounces on – and as many pairs of our best drawers as he thought suitable.'

'Capital advice,' Randolph returned.

'But only for a free-spending gentleman,' she added, 'for the cost of all that would run to ten pounds or even more, which few would want to expend on undergarments, however close the friendship.'

'I am a very free-spending gentleman,' Randolph informed her with a smile, 'for I spend in the pussy of any pretty girl who takes my fancy. But that apart, you must break out of this confined way of thinking. To a common person like your employer the thought of buying a girl ten pounds worth of underwear may bring on an apoplexy, but to a man about town it is hardly more than an amusing gesture. You, dear Maria, shall have all that you mentioned, and at my expense, in return for a small favour.'

'If you wish to spend freely here, then it must be in money,' she retorted, 'for nothing else will be accepted.'

'Gad, if you were my female friend I'd treat you with respect and affection and give you everything you desired,' he replied, pleased by her ready wit to turn his joke back on himself.

'You must not try to subvert my loyalty to Mr Wyck by bribery and seduction,' she said, her tone slightly rueful. 'He has my word that no other male shall be allowed to take advantage of me whilst I remain in his employ. Do not tempt me, Mr Joynes.'

'By Jove, you are a pearl amongst women!' Randolph exclaimed in delight. 'Never have I come across such loyalty in a female — would the object of it were more worthy of you! But have no fear, dear girl, for I will not insult your integrity by trying to roger you, much though I would enjoy it. The favour I ask in return for the vast deal of underwear you mentioned does not require you to let me poke you.'

'Then what is it?' she asked him, somewhat surprised.

'Only this — hold up your clothes again and let me kiss your darling pussy. There — that is no betrayal of your loyalty to Wyck, is it?'

'You wish to kiss me *between my legs*?' she asked, hardly able to believe what she heard.

This was something no man had ever yet done to her, and it seemed to her very strange, and almost unnatural. Neither Wyck nor the man before him who had her maidenhead ever tried more than a straight poke — a moment or two fingering her pussy till it was wet, then his hard-on shaft up her and a fast poke to a spend. Nevertheless, Maria Peabody was a young woman able to learn fast, and if a titled gentleman had an urge to kiss her pussy, then it must be perfectly all right.

'Just that?' she asked. 'A kiss? You give me your word you would not try to force me?'

'A warm kiss of affection and respect,' said he, 'no more.'

Privately, Maria thought it almost too good to be true, but she had seen Randolph come off, and basing her estimate of all men on Mr Wyck's limited capabilities, she thought it safe to accept Randolph's offer. She gave him permission and raised her skirt waist-high once more.

Randolph knelt at her feet, opened the hand-stitched slit of her drawers, and pressed his lips to the soft and yielding pink cunny that was the heart of her female nature. He heard above his head the softest of sounds then, a half-stifled sigh that was almost a gasp, and he guessed he was the first man to kiss her cunny. He guessed further, in view of her ready response to it, that she had a hot nature, which she concealed.

He clasped her bottom in both hands whilst his tongue flicked up and down between delicious parted pink lips in the nut-brown little nest of her curls. The sighs he elicited were louder now and even more emotional, and after some hesitation she placed her hands on his shoulders to support herself.

'Surely you've kissed me enough now!' he heard her gasp out, but he ignored her words and continued to ravish her with his wet tongue, pervading her with sensations so divine that she swayed on legs that had become weak.

'Oh, this is so improper!' she sighed, 'and yet so nice . . .'

There could be only one way of it then — Maria's belly began to jib forward in rapid little thrusts to press her open pussy against his mouth, and she shook convulsively from head to toe. A shriek escaped her lips and she came off briskly and would have fallen helpless to the floor but for Randolph's arms about her, supporting her staunchly whilst he squeezed the cheeks of her plump bottom, and rubbed a fingertip over the puckered little knot between them.

'Oh my dear lord!' she exclaimed, when she was able to speak again. 'Now you've done it! You promised not to take advantage of me if I let you kiss me.'

'Nor have I,' he retorted pleasantly, 'for I have not rogered you, my dear, nor fingered your pussy — your bond of loyalty to your miserable employer is unbroken.'

'But you brought me off!' she protested.

'What of that?' he asked. 'I'm sure you come off on many an occasion without the benefit of Wyck's shaft up you. When you play with yourself in bed, for example, and when you wash your darling little pussy and dry it. That you fetched off because I kissed you is neither here nor there — it cannot be construed a breach of your trust.'

'I suppose you're right,' said she, relief in her voice, 'but all the same, if you were given half a chance, you would be up me like a shot — admit it now!'

'I freely admit it,' he said, 'but until you of your own

free will invite me to roger you, I shall restrain the force of my natural desire for your beautiful person.'

'Perhaps I am a fool,' she said, 'but I trust you.'

'Excellent!' he cried. 'Now we have agreed that I shall not attempt to get my shaft into your pussy, that delight being the sole prerogative of the undeserving Wyck, nothing stops us from giving each other pleasure in other possible ways. The logic of that must surely be acceptable to you, my dear. I am aware that the eminent Dr Acton disagrees with me on this point, but it is my considered opinion that two pokes a week from a decrepit and decaying shopkeeper cannot be enough to satisfy a warm-natured young female like you. Does he poke you here behind the shop, after hours?'

'I have said I will not answer questions about Mr Wyck,' said Maria firmly.

'Then I'm right, and he must do it to you on this desk, there being no other convenient place here in your stockroom. But as the desk is not large enough for you to lie on, he must sit you on the edge and stand between your legs to poke you.'

There was a trace of pink on Maria's cheeks that informed him he had arrived at the truth of the matter. He took her hand and led her to the desk, sat her on the edge and raised her skirt to her lap.

'A sad waste,' said he with a sigh, 'poking in a back room. A pretty girl should be delicately and lovingly and frequently rogered in a four-poster bed, on a swansdown-stuffed mattress, between sheets of purest linen, wearing a nightgown of silk, pulled up above her titties for her love to lie on her belly.'

'What are you doing!' she exclaimed. 'Remember your promise not to touch my pussy!'

'Nor shall I,' he said reassuringly, his hands busy with the buttons of her blouse, 'I gave my word not to put either shaft or fingers into your pussy, but there is no reason in the world not to have a feel of your bare titties.'

In a trice he had her blouse open, her chemise pulled down, and her warm and plump titties bare for his hands to fondle. In this she gave him no argument, for she enjoyed having them felt and Mr Wyck rarely obliged her in this, being in too much of a hurry to get his shaft up her. She put her hands on Randolph's hips whilst he stroked and squeezed and touched her. Soon her teats were standing stiff, and she was sighing a little. As if by chance, her hands moved from their resting place and found the gaping entrance of Randolph's trousers.

'Oh, you are stiff again!' she exclaimed, staring curiously into his handsome face.

'How could I not be,' he said, 'with so delectable a pair of titties in my hands?'

In a little while Maria's slender body was trembling from the force of the sensations he roused by his skilled handling of her, and he too began to shake gently — for she held in a warm palm his hairy pompoms, and her other hand was clasped about his cockstand and slid up and down it with affection and lust.

'As long as you make no attempt to get this furious thing up my pussy, Mr Wyck is not being deprived of his rights,' gasped she, making a pious attempt to salvage her sense of duty as she was fast approaching the culmination of her pleasure.

Randolph made no reply, for he was past rational expression. Mr Percival Proud had swelled himself up to his thickest girth and his maximum length, and was hard as a broom handle. Maria's pussy was wet and open, and her hips were making little thrusts as she sat on the edge of the desk, as if inviting a shaft to plunge into it.

It amused Randolph to keep his word, and instead of sliding his hard-on shaft straight into her and coming off before she could push him off, which would have been the most sensible and natural course of action for a gentleman to take, he kept his hands away from her cunny and continued his stimulation of her titties. It took him some time to bring her off thus, but eventually the pleasurable sensations became more than her frame could withstand.

She cried out and came off furiously, and the sliding of her hand on Randolph's jerking shaft carried him up to the peak of bliss. He moaned joyfully to feel the fast surge of his sap up the length of his pulsating shaft, and in nervous and urgent spasms he gushed his creamy essence over her bared pussy.

CHAPTER 11
A Messenger is Given
an Unexpected Answer

At half past ten o'clock in the morning Randolph left Cavendish Square with the intention of calling on his tailor to place an order for a *suit of clothes*, as the new style for gentlemen had been named. This consisted of a short jacket and trousers made of the same material, instead of a black frock coat and sombre grey trousers. It seemed dashing, even audacious, to depart so far from tradition, but Randolph liked to think of himself as a bold spirit, eager for novelty.

On the corner of the Square, where Wigmore Street ran, he saw standing on the pavement in an attitude of watchfulness a woman he recognised from a distance and approaching more nearly he saw that he had been correct, for it was none other than Miss Dorothy Harker's maid — Bella of the huge titties.

When he drew level with her, he naturally did not raise his hat to a mere servant, but stared at her. Her eyes dropped to a suitable abased position, and she addressed him humbly:

'Mr Joynes — excuse me, sir, for the liberty of speaking to you in the street, but I have been entrusted with an important message by a young lady whose name I need not mention.'

'The devil you have!' Randolph exclaimed, astonished by this act of insolence on the part, not only of the maid, but also of her mistress in sending her to accost him in a public place.

'The young lady is in the gravest of conditions, sir — I beg you to listen to what she has sent me to say. It will take but a few minutes.'

Randolph paid no attention to what Bella said. It was only to be expected, though devilish irksome, that Miss Harker desired to have some words of reproach delivered to him. He had, truth to tell, been daily expecting to receive a tearful letter of remonstrance from her. That would have been irksome enough, but to send a maidservant was past the limits of all decent behaviour!

Nevertheless, it had to be admitted that Bella sported as big a pair of titties as Randolph had ever seen on a young woman in his life. Concealed though they were under the cloak of greenish-grey wool she wore, they looked devilish inviting to the hands.

'I cannot be seen talking to you in the street,' said he, cutting off her words. 'What on earth would people think! But I am a reasonable man, and I will give you five minutes of my time to deliver your mistress's message. Do you know where Holywell Street lies?'

'No, sir, for I am a stranger to London, being here with Miss Harker for the first time in my life.'

'It runs off the Strand,' Randolph informed her. 'I have most important business to conduct at this moment, but afterwards I will go there, at great inconvenience, I may say, to hear you in private. In Holywell Street you will find Black's Temperance Coffee House. Ask for me there at twelve noon.'

Without waiting for a response, he walked on, swinging

his silver-knobbed stick in jaunty fashion, sure that Bella would be there to meet him, when he had completed his business with his tailor. In this his assumption was correct — he found her standing outside the coffee house when he got there. Hardly pausing, he instructed her to wait for ten minutes and then to go inside and ask for him of the waiter.

Rooms to accommodate couples desiring an hour or two's privacy were to be found in every part of London. Some were in lodging-houses, where half a dozen lettings a day produced a superior profit to the owner than to have a regular tenant. The easiest to find, and the least costly, were the many coffee houses that showed a sign in the window saying *Beds*. The respectable world at large took this to mean that bona-fide travellers unable to afford the price of a hotel room could be accommodated cheaply for the night, but the true significance of the sign was that a room might be had for rogering at any time of day.

The waiter's name was Will, an elderly man with a fringe of white hair. A few words sufficed, five shillings changed hands for the room, and another shilling for Will himself, then Randolph was directed upstairs. A glance about showed him that the room was adequate to his requirements, being clean furnished with a large bed. Randolph seated himself on a cane-bottomed chair, his top hat pushed to the back of his head, his hands resting one above the other on the silver knob of his stick.

Soon there came a tap at the door, and Bella entered. Black had only two rooms to rent out, and the other was unoccupied so early on in the day, so she had needed little guidance to find Randolph. She closed the door, and at his order bolted it, then stood in before him in a respectful posture, hands folded, eyes downcast.

'Well?' he demanded, eyeing her natural abundance greedily.

'First, sir, I am to return this to you,' said she, fetching out from under her loose cloak a wrapped parcel Randolph knew — it was the books he had bought from Avery and, in his hurry to quit the Harker apartment, he quite forgot them and left them behind in the drawing room. He had missed the parcel before he reached home, but could think of no easy way of retrieving his precious bundle.

'I'm obliged to Miss Harker for the return of my property. Is there more, or was that your whole errand?' he said, hoping to embarrass Bella further.

'No, sir, there is more.'

'I trust that your mistress has made a full recovery from her fainting spell.'

The tone of his enquiry was casual in the extreme, though his eyes never once left the impressive rotundities beneath Bella's clothing. He had determined that she would not leave the room before he had viewed them bare and felt them very thoroughly.

'She keeps her bed, sir, feeling weak and unsettled, and out of sorts. Mr Devlin wanted to send for a doctor to attend her, but she refuses that. What ails her is distress of mind, sir, and uncertainty.'

'I'm sorry to hear it,' said Randolph off-handedly, 'but what has it to do with me?'

'I think you know that, sir,' Bella answered, her voice firm.

'Do I? What do you mean?'

'After you left the house, I assisted Miss Dorothy up to her room, and put her to bed, to rest. There was a wetness about her undergarments that betrayed what had been done to the poor young lady, while she lay helpless in a swoon.'

'Damme! Do you accuse me of taking advantage of her?' cried Randolph, in a fine show of virtuous outrage.

Secretly he was wondering if, when Bella's dress was taken off, her massive titties would hang down low and slack to her belly-button, or were they still young and firm enough to stay in place, with only a provocative dangle.

'It's not my place to make accusations, sir,' Bella replied, unabashed, 'but the signs were clear that a gentleman had spent on her belly, for her drawers were soaked through.'

'Oho!' said Randolph with a grin. 'It appears to me that you know more than you ought about these matters, for an unmarried woman. How old are you, Bella?'

'Twenty-six years of age,' said she.

'And you have experience of men coming off in your drawers?'

'That's as may be, sir,' she replied impertinently, 'but what is troubling Miss Harker is that she thinks she was ravished by you while she lay fainting. She fears she is a maiden no longer and in her ruined condition may not wed Mr Mawby, who has asked her to become his wife.'

'And do you believe that I ravished her, Bella?'

'No, sir,' said she, looking him in the eye, 'that is, not in the usual way of ravishing, so to say. I bathed Miss Dorothy's parts in warm water before I put her to bed, and examined them closely. Her curls were wet with a man's spending, and stuck to her skin, so at first I thought the ravisher had pulled out in time to avoid putting her in the family way. I feared the worst but a closer inspection showed me that she is a maiden still, as the world reckons these things.'

'Then there is no more to say,' cried Randolph.

'Ah, but there is, sir, for virgin she may be, but untouched she is not. To be frank and open with you at the risk of giving offence, Miss Dorothy has been unnaturally used in her rearward passage. She, poor innocent, has yet formed no suspicion of her plight, being concerned entirely with the honour of her other opening remaining intact. She knows that something unlawful was done to her, for a gentleman's amusement, but not what.'

'Then there is no reason to tell her,' Randolph suggested. 'A disclosure of something unfamiliar to her way of thought might only distress her to the point of upsetting the balance of her mind and casting her into a fit of the vapours. My advice is to leave well alone — what harm can there be to her from a bung-holing, if what you suspect is true.'

'If only it were that simple!' said Bella. 'But Miss Dorothy is certain in her mind that you interfered with her in some way and that she is, as a result, unworthy to marry Mr Mawby. She will answer him no when he comes on Saturday for her response to his proposal of marriage, as she will answer no in future to any other gentleman who seeks her hand. She feels that she is consigned to lifelong spinsterhood by what you have done to her, and is greatly agitated.'

'This is ridiculous!' Randolph exclaimed. 'Her pussy is pure as the driven snow, for aught I did to it! A feel, perhaps, no more than that. Neither finger nor shaft did I put into it.'

'Yes, sir, I truly believe that,' said Bella, 'but it is not the point. The trouble lies in Miss Dorothy's mind, not between her legs. What can be done about it, sir?'

'Damned if I know!' he replied. 'Will she tell anyone of her misgivings, do you suppose?'

'Not at first, sir, for she is too ashamed to confide in any but me. But with the passing of time, and her continuing misery of mind, her family will take note, and she will be pressed by her mother or her father to speak out. When she does, I greatly fear that you will be called to reckoning, Mr Joynes. It is no light matter to ravage a young lady's backside while she lies swooning on her own sofa. In fact, sir, should it be brought to the notice of a magistrate, then I have been told that to have unnatural connection with either woman or man is held a fearful crime, and punished by long years in prison, with hard labour.'

'But why should there be any question of magistrates, Bella? The dishonour of being named in open court as victim would be too great for Miss Harker to bear, I am convinced.'

'I hope that you're right, sir,' said Bella, pursing her lips tightly and shaking her head, 'but it must be remembered that the young lady's own father is a Justice of the Peace out where we live in Warwickshire.'

'Damnation take it!' Randolph cried. 'Here's a fine kettle of fish! What's best to do, I wonder, bearing in mind that the well-being and good name of Miss Harker are the main concern in this. Sit down, Bella, and give me the benefit of your advice.'

There being only one chair in the room, and he sitting on it, Bella seated herself on the edge of the bed, removing her cloak at last, as he had hoped. She wore the usual maid's plain black dress, without the usual white apron, since she was out of the house. Her great bosom swelled out the bodice of the dress and set Mr Percival Proud to twitching lightly.

'Whilst we discuss how to promote Miss Harker's happiness, it is in your hands to do me a considerable favour,' said Randolph with an encouraging smile.

In truth, he was not overly concerned at the hidden threat of Mr Harker Senior, Justice of the Peace, learning that his dear daughter had been briskly bung-holed. At any threat from that quarter, Randolph was ready to skip across the

Channel to Paris and enjoy himself there for a year or two. Indignation cannot last forever, and his madcap escapade with Miss Harker would be forgotten in an eighteen-month at most. On the other hand, he wished to keep Bella beside him for a while yet, to implement his lewd designs on her, and so he pretended to take seriously Miss Dorothy's predicament.

When Bella asked him what the favour might be that he wanted of her, he told her that he had an unquenchable desire to view her titties. If she would bare herself to the waist to give him sight of them, she would find him particularly grateful. Bella blushed a little at his words, but only for form's sake, before she unbuttoned her bodice all the way down from neck to waist, and slipped her arms out of the sleeves.

'Ah!' he sighed in blissful anticipation, his shaft swaying under his shirt like a metronome beating time.

Bella smiled at him, a meaningless smile, though that he did not notice in his eagerness to see her bubbies. His eyes shone lustfully to see her slide the ribbons of her chemise off her shoulders and pull it down, exposing her bare titties to him.

'By Jove!' Randolph said emotionally. 'What whoppers!'

Bella was thin of form, her arms and shoulders very slender and fragile of appearance. This emphasised the contrast with the fullness of her titties, which were the size of fully grown pumpkins, vast globes of soft white flesh, looking for all the world like over-ripe fruit depending from a bough.

Seen thus in all their fleshy glory, Randolph confessed that never had he laid eyes on a more letch-provoking pair. This he told to her, and she smiled at him with her knowing eyes, and asked if looking was enough for him.

It was obvious to Randolph that she recalled his generosity of the preceding day, when he had put a golden sovereign in her hand — and she undoubtedly expected more where that came from. *Why not*? thought he to himself, for he had never in his life grudged full payment to any girl or woman who made him an offer of her bodily charms. Smiling, he asked Bella to come and kneel between his legs — *and to bring her titties with her*!

She knew what he was after, for he was by no means the first gentleman who had sought the same thing from her. She left the bed to come forward and kneel on the floor, as he had asked. His legs were spread wide apart, his trouser buttons undone, his hard-on shaft sticking out and up for Bella to clasp in her hand.

'Good Heavens — then this is the monstrous thing that forced an entry into poor Miss Dorothy's bottom!' she exclaimed. 'How long and thick it is! How pitiful she must have seemed, while you were at your wicked task!'

Her skilful hand sliding firmly up and down Mr Percival was like to have brought that quivering gentleman off, but she refrained from inducing the sensual spasm too soon.

'There is something I do not understand,' said she, gazing up into Randolph's face. 'You spent on Miss Dorothy's belly, for her drawers and chemise were wet through. Yet you also spent in her bottom, for when I washed it, your sap came trickling out. You were alone with her for only twenty minutes or so — how can it be possible that you fetched off twice in so short a time?'

'Why, when my rogering mood takes me and I have a pretty girl at the end of my shaft, I can come off in her cunny, or on her belly, or any other part of her, five or six times in a row,' said he boastfully. 'Your mistress was not the only female to be the recipient of my cream yesterday — there were two more.'

He did not tell her that one was a servant like herself, and the other a young trollop in Soho, but left her to assume that he had rogered three gentlewomen.

'My word! To spend so often, and still have a shaft standing up stiff again the next day!' Bella sighed.

She pressed herself close in between his open legs, and laid his leaping shaft between her massive soft titties, stroking it with her hand and making her globes close upon it, until he was able to slide it between them. That, she knew well, was what he wanted for that was what every gentleman who had laid bare her bubbies had wanted — to roger them.

'There now, he's in a warm and cosy place,' she said, 'is it to his liking, or would he rather be in me elsewhere?'

'For now he's happy with his billet,' Randolph sighed, as he tupped up and down against her smooth skin, 'later on he will try out other parts of you, my dear, to see which he prefers.'

The sight and feel in his hands, and about his shaft, of her huge titties made him as eager as if he had not had a poke for a week or more. To see Mr Percival rubbing himself in between those cushions of soft flesh brought on blissful sensations and soon overcame him. He cried out in rapture to the spasms that shook his body so furiously that his topper fell from his head and rolled on the floor behind him. *Ah! Ah!* he went, emitting a profuse flow into the warm hiding-place between her titties.

'Well!' Bella commented brightly. 'What a lot he has given, after spending with three ladies yesterday — and twice with at least one of them! If the truth has been told, that is.'

Her words instigated in Randolph a determination to show this sceptical maidservant that she was in the presence of a virility she had never encountered among men of her own class. The last drop was scarcely out of his twitching shaft than he rose from the chair, dragged Bella upright and took her quickly across to the bed.

'Lie down,' he commanded, 'on your back.'

'Oh, sir, surely you must rest for a while,' said she pertly, 'for your shaft will be soft and useless in a minute, and needs time to regain its stiffness before you can think of repeating your spending.'

'Nonsense,' said Randolph with a sneer, 'I need no rest.'

He gave her no opportunity to delay or disobey him, being resolved to demonstrate his male superiority. With a hand that shook a little from his recent exertion, he pushed her down to sit on the bedside, and then to lie on her back with her legs hanging over the edge. Her vast titties rolled slackly towards her armpits, spreading themselves widely apart, as if forming a mattress on which his weight should rest while he did her.

He raised her skirt in front until he had a full view of her legs, encased in cheap black stockings, and her slender thighs in her white drawers. Through the forward slit he touched her sparse dark bush, then pushed her knees wide apart. In mounting desire, he untied the string of her drawers and laid bare her white-skinned belly, and pressed his mouth to it in hot kisses. He gazed in fascination at her bare pussy, fingering the warm fleshy lips with one hand, whilst with the other he massaged Mr Percival strongly, to restore his hardness.

'Oh, sir!' Bella murmured. 'You're standing hard again!'

'Did you dare doubt my word?' he cried.

He brought the hard-on shaft jutting from his trousers close to the moist lips of her slit. With a sharp jerk of his loins he pushed Mr Percival Proud's shiny unhooded head inside, and then with determined thrusts, slid into her right to the limit. As his curls lay tight to hers, he threw himself forward on to her belly and seized her bare breasts where they hung slackly on her chest, whilst he rogered her furiously. After three or four strokes, she returned push for push, to urge him on.

'Oh what bliss!' she sighed. 'It's as stiff as a cast-iron poker in me – you're a marvel, sir!'

Her thin-cheeked bottom heaved and squirmed on the bed, the while she uttered exclamations of pleasure. At another time, he would have taken deep offence at a servant expressing enjoyment in so open and disrespectful a way, but his present intention was to impress on Bella his utter mastery, and her cries were tributes to his achievement in that respect.

Her cries grew shriller as he reached the short strokes, then turned to open-mouthed gasping when she received the hot gush of his lust. She made no effort to hide it, but came off loudly and with gusto, then lay trembling and spent beneath him.

She thought he was finished with her then, having fetched off twice, but he had other plans, and refused to let her depart. To her protestation that Miss Dorothy was awaiting, in agony of mind, her return with news, he said brutally that she must wait longer, and that another hour or two wouldn't hurt her. He made Bella strip naked and sit up on the bed for him to look at, for he was greatly taken by the piquancy of her monumentally large titties on her thin frame, and wished to study her further.

To render himself more comfortable, he removed his clothing and sat beside her in only his shirt, whilst he handled her big bubbies, lifting them on his palms and rolling them, fascinated by their fleshiness. Bella let him do as he pleased, for in her mind she was sure that she had caught him with her titties, and stood to profit considerably.

'Do you know what is in the parcel you returned to me?' he asked her, his shaft beginning to stir again between his legs.

'No, sir, but from the weight of it, books, I would say.'

'Your inference is correct,' said he, reaching for the parcel which lay close to hand on the bed, where he had cast it aside earlier.

'Have you been taught to read?' he enquired.

'Why yes, sir,' Bella answered, 'for although my father could not afford the twopence a day to send me with my brother to the village school, they taught me free at Sunday School, so that I can read the Scriptures.'

Randolph opened the parcel, and selected the volume entitled *Selina Simcott, or The Tribulations of Virtue* and handed it to Bella.

'This is a tale of girls at school,' he explained, 'though it is not a Sunday school but a boarding-school, where games are played with pussies. Open the book at random and read aloud to me, while I stroke your titties.'

'I've heard about books like this,' said she, grinning, 'but I never expected to see one.'

She let the book fall open where it would, smoothed down the page and began to read, somewhat hesitatingly, but with a note of interest in her voice that more than compensated for a lack of fluency:

'Come closer, girl,' said Miss Rodwell.

Selina moved toward the high-backed chair on which the schoolmistress was seated. At once Miss Rodwell reached out to pass an arm about Selina's waist and hold her fast, whilst with her other hand she opened the startled girl's long dressing-gown and raised her nightdress up to her waist, laying bar the expanse of her thighs and belly. Before Selina could collect herself to utter a respectful protest, Miss Rodwell's hand was playing freely between her thighs and over her sweet and soft-haired pussy.

'Without the word of a lie,' Miss Rodwell declared, 'you have the prettiest cunny in the school, and the smoothest, whitest pair of thighs. You may believe my words — there is not a girl in the school, from Juniors to Sixth Form and Prefects, that I haven't inspected in person, and handled thoroughly.'

All the while she was running her hand across Selina's naked flesh, in the most shameless manner, causing the mortified girl to blush scarlet.

'Oh!' she cried out then, to feel Miss Rodwell pressing with a gentle middle finger on the junction of her thighs.

'Good gracious!' exclaimed Bella, looking up from the book at Randolph, her face a fiery red, 'This schoolmarm is a beast who handles the girls for her own pleasure, under pretence of correcting them!'

'Indeed she does,' Randolph agreed, his tongue flickering over his lips to wet them, 'read on, my dear, for there can be little doubt now that Selina will be made to undergo the final ordeal of being brought off in Miss Rodwell's hand.'

Miss Rodwell's finger fluttered and lingered, seeking out the maiden slit within the mossy bower of Selina's silky curls. It found what it sought so insistently, and began caressing and teasing.

'Oh, Miss Rodwell,' murmured Selina, 'I beg you, for the love of all that is wholesome and precious, do not make me undergo this shameful ordeal!'

She spoke in vain, for the older woman's fingertip slid up to that sensitive spot at the top of her slit, where sensation is the greatest. Selina twitched and squealed, but Miss Rodwell held her firm while she spurred her agitation to fever pitch.

'Shameful ordeal, do you say?' she exclaimed. 'You did not think it shameful to get into the maidservant's bed the other night and allow her to feel you! Why is it shameful now — am I less worthy than a servant to play with your pussy?'

'No, Miss Rodwell, that is not what I meant!' gasped Selina in her confusion. 'I did not know what Susy was doing, when she put her hand between my thighs, I swear it!'

'But you knew soon enough when you came off at her touch, you wicked girl! Do you think I'm a fool, to believe that you were innocent of why pussies are felt?'

'Oh, sir,' Bella gasped, 'do you believe that she really let the maid bring her off — or is this another contrivance of the teacher's to finger her?'

'A contrivance, of course,' Randolph replied at once. 'Selina will be brought off shortly, as also will you!'

Whilst Miss Rodwell spoke thus unfeelingly, she rubbed with her immodest finger at Selina's button and the lewd movement grew ever faster and faster. The victim's breath came in short gasps, interspersed with incoherent words that she had little or no knowledge of uttering:

'Oh no, Miss Rodwell . . . oh Heavens . . . I am near to coming off . . . stop . . . do not make me do that . . . too late, too late!'

Her hips jerked and her uncovered thighs quivered. For some seconds she seemed quite to lose control of her limbs, and but for Miss Rodwell's supporting arm about her waist it is certain she would have collapsed in a heap on the floor.

To hear Bella reading affected Randolph greatly, His colour became heightened, as also did his fleshy shaft, which bounded hard-on between his thighs, uncovered by his shirt, which he had drawn up to his belly-button. His hand had crept down from Bella's enormous titties, over her smooth belly, and between her parted thighs. In the same way that the lascivious schoolmistress manipulated Selina's parts, so he addressed himself to Bella's, delighting to feel the slippery wetness he caused to descend over her secret button.

'Oh, what a wicked girl it is to fetch off so quickly,' Miss Rodwell exclaimed. 'The feel of your tender pussy has undone me and I must have you again, little Selina.' So saying, she pulled the half-fainting girl down on to her lap and thrust her tongue into her mouth. She opened the front of Selina's nightdress, to handle her smooth soft titties and tickle their rose-pink teats.

'Tonight you shall sleep in my bed, Selina,' said she, 'and by morning we shall have brought each other off a dozen or more times and sleep through tomorrow morning in the languor of love satisfied.'

Randolph's fingers had done their work well, and spasms of an ecstasy beyond the ordinary seized Bella, making her belly rise as she came off. Randolph gave her no opportunity to enjoy her paroxysm in peace — he was on her immediately, thrusting up his shaft into her twitching pussy, while her throes yet shook her. He was greatly aroused by the sight of her coming off, and he lunged in and out of her slippery cunny zestfully.

184

'You're killing me!' cried Bella, her belly writhing beneath him, yet sustaining his hard tupping with an enthusiasm that equalled to his own.

'Die then!' cried he. 'Yield up your life to the stabbing of my shaft in you!'

Needless to say, she did not die, but returned his thrusts in good measure, with upheavals of her belly and slidings of her wet pussy on his shaft, showing herself to be as lively as any gentleman could hope for. With a cry of bliss, Randolph gushed his ardent lust deep into her, and she too dissolved in joy to feel the sudden surge in her belly.

Bella Gurney, it must be said, for all her lasciviousness of spirit, was a well-trained servant who had her mistress's good at heart. She waited for Randolph to recover himself, lying at her side, his head cushioned on her bare titties, before coming back to the reason for her presence with him in Black's Coffee House.

'What am I to tell Miss Dorothy?' she enquired, her tone now respectful again since her sensual throes had faded. 'She is in a pitiable state of mind, sir, and unless she can be calmed by good news of some sort, I fear she may sink into a decline.'

'Tell her?' said Randolph lazily. 'You may tell her I am not unsympathetic to the inconvenience in which she finds herself. But you must add that I have no immediate solution to offer for the relief of her predicament, as she alone sees it, except to guarantee that, for aught I have done, she is a virgin intact. If she feels herself unable to rely on the word of a gentleman, then she may consult her medical adviser, who will inspect her parts and confirm what I have said.'

'Then you do not offer to make amends, sir?'

'What the devil do you mean, *amends*? Does Miss Harker

think I have some sort of duty towards her to offer her marriage — is that what she hints at?'

'I won't go so far as to say an offer of marriage on your part would make her happy, if you'll excuse the liberty,' said Bella, 'for happiness will remain a stranger to her for many a year to come, I believe. But a proposal from you would set her mind wonderfully at rest, when she declines Mr Mawby.'

'Marry a chit of a girl on account of a quick bung-holing?' Randolph expostulated. 'I've never heard such confounded nonsense in my life! Let her marry Mawby and be done with it. He's not a hot-blooded man — the use of her cunny twice a week will content him, and he'll have no interest in other orifices, even if she becomes inquisitive as to their use.'

'That she can no longer in good conscience do, sir. She holds Mr Mawby too honourable a gentleman to deceive by fobbing him off with part-worn goods. She looks to you to help her out of her difficulty.'

'Damnation take it all!' Randolph exclaimed. 'If any more is needful, then you may tell Miss Harker that I will think about the matter further, when opportunity serves, and may reach some useful resolution in a few days. If so, then I shall send word for you to meet me here and hear the outcome.'

'Very good, sir,' said Bella, 'on behalf of Miss Dorothy, may I say that's very kind-hearted of you. If you've finished with me for now, sir, I will dress myself and return in haste to Paddington Green, to convey your message to my mistress.'

'Not so fast,' said he, catching her between the legs with a clasping hand to keep her on the bed with him, 'you have other warm openings I have not yet made use of, Bella, and it would be a pity to let them go to waste. A guinea a hole — that's the price I'm giving today. You've earned two guineas and you've two more orifices yet untouched. What do you say?'

'At that rate of pay you can use me as you like,' said she.

'Capital! Roll over, girl, and brace yourself!'

CHAPTER 12
Some Slight Feelings of Guilt are Purged

After Randolph had his full four guineas worth of Bella's orifices it might be thought that he would sleep like a top that night, and wake up next day with a zest for life and a hearty appetite for breakfast. On the other hand, the followers of Dr William Acton would no doubt insist that he fell into a comatose state of senselessness, brought on by reckless over-indulgence in the sexual spasm, and lay twitching and moaning all night long in a clammy sweat, tormented by incoherent dreams of dark despair.

In the event, neither opinion held any truth. When Randolph retired to his bed that night, he fell asleep at once, as well might be expected after his lustful exertions, but he was made restless by dreams throughout the night, and woke several times in dismay.

Nevertheless, though he dreamed, he was not troubled by the nightmares that Dr Acton believes to be the lot of a gentleman who has rogered four times in the course of a single day, whose nervous system is thereby exhausted and like to collapse into invalidism. Randolph's dreams were odd and puzzling visions, but not frightening, and Miss Dorothy Harker played a leading, if ill-defined, part in them.

At one moment he thought he stood at the foot of a staircase, down which she came towards him, a candlestick in her hand to light the way. He hoped she meant to lead him upstairs to her bed, for he had a letch to poke her, but she halted when she reached the lowest stair. She stared at him mournfully, asking why he had ravished her bottom, for no decent person would have her to wife now that her person had been defiled.

Later in the night, when Randolph's dreaming returned, he and Dorothy were looking into the window of the milliner's shop in Shaftesbury Avenue where he had met her. For no reason he knew, she undid the tight buttons of her short jacket and opened it wide, to show him she wore no blouse underneath, and above the waistband of her skirt, she was stark naked.

Randolph stared at her titties, and though she would not let him feel them, she turned to place her hands flat on the glass and lean forward a little. He tipped his hat in salute, before raising her clothes behind to her waist and parting the rear slit of her drawers. He slipped his hard-on shaft into her, but whether he rogered her pussy or her knot-hole, he could not say in his dreaming state, nor did it matter.

Towards dawn he woke again, gripped by a vision of Dorothy down on her knees before Lorimer Mawby. She was fully dressed, but he had removed his trousers and she held his stiff shaft in her hand and toyed with it. Randolph wished to call out to her, to advise her not to continue, but he was unable to speak, and in another moment she had taken Lorimer's shaft into her mouth.

When he finally awoke, roused by Lizzie with his morning tea, his mood was unsettled and uneasy. His powers of concentration were in abeyance, for he could not turn his thoughts away from Dorothy. He had himself accused her of allowing Lorimer to put his hand up her clothes and feel her pussy, but it was only to put her out of countenance, and he had not believed it for even an instant. Yet in his dream she was sucking Lorimer's shaft to bring him off!

It was damnably confusing and made him irritable and lacking in his normal confidence. Lizzie handed him his cup of tea and stood at the bedside while he drank it, humbly waiting for him to pull her down on the bed and roger her. Yet with so much on his mind, Randolph had no heart to fumble with a servant girl, and he sent her packing.

He passed the morning in solitude at his club, over brandies and soda and the newspapers, having no desire to converse with anyone. After a frugal lunch, his mind was made up — he needed to seek advice over his confusion of mind. Naturally, it would have been the act of a complete cad to risk exposing the good name of a lady by consulting any of his old chums at the club. After much agitated thought, he made up his mind to seek advice of a person whose knowledge of sexual matters was unrivalled — namely, Mrs Mary Jeffries.

Soon after two o'clock in the afternoon he took a cab to her house in Chelsea. She thought at first he'd come to further his acquaintance with Miss Jane, who had slept through the morning and was well-rested and available to receive visitors. Randolph explained that it was advice he sought, which made Mrs Jeffries frown, until he made it clear he was prepared to pay cash for the benefit of her counsel. That being understood, she took him to her private parlour, sent for a bottle of brandy and asked how she could be of service.

Randolph stared at her in thought for a moment, uncertain how much he might prudently reveal to her. She had a respectable look about her, seated opposite him in her genteel black satin, almost like a kindly aunt, but her knowledge of fornication and its attendant problems must surely be without equal, she being the kept woman of an eccentric peer of the realm for ten or more years, and procuress to the gentry for another ten after that.

'Dear kind Mrs Jeffries — I am sure that you will understand my predicament very well,' said Randolph, settling himself into an armchair. 'Any consolation you are able to give me at a most difficult time will be very gratefully received by me.'

He went on to relate to her, mentioning no names, something of his unusual interlude with a certain young lady of quality, after she had swooned on her sofa. He did not tell all — some vestige of an unfamiliar sense of embarrassment acted on him to curb his tongue. Mrs Jeffries listened with a look of interest on her face. When he fell silent, she offered some comfort:

'I can't say I'm surprised that a hot-blooded gentleman like yourself found it hard to resist the temptation of exploring a little, when you were alone with a beautiful girl and she quite senseless on her back,' said Mrs Jeffries, her voice warm and sympathetic. 'How far did you go with her — did you have a feel of her titties?'

'I did,' he answered, 'but only through her clothes. They were divinely full and firm, satiny globes that my soul yearned to lay bare and kiss.'

'Hmm! No harm done so far!' said Mrs Jeffries. 'Did you put your hand up the young lady's clothes?'

'Yes,' said he, a little more able to discuss the matter now that he had made a start on his confession. 'And more — I felt her thighs, so smooth and firm to the touch!'

'Ah, I understand now,' exclaimed Mrs Jeffries. 'You had

her clothes up round her waist and your hand in her drawers.'

'My hand lay between her thighs and I fingered her warm and silky-tufted mound,' he answered proudly.

'Silky-tufted, eh? You've a dash of the poet about you, Mr Joynes,' said she. 'That's an excellent thing in a gentleman of your years. Older gentlemen lose all fine power of discernment and see a cunny as no more than a handy place to shove into and unburden their carnal lust, not caring whether it has hair like silk over it or coarse carroty bristles, or is as bare as the palm of your hand.'

'Can you keep a confidence, Mrs Jeffries?' he asked. 'When I parted the slit of the lady's drawers and looked at her pussy, gracefully adorned with a profusion of silky brown curls, the delicate pink lips and the virginal bloom that lay over all, it seemed to me then that never in my life had I seen so lovely a female organ. I have seen hundreds, large and small, dark, fair and ginger, and poked them! Yet this dear lady's pretty little toy caused me to experience an exceptional intensity of emotion — indeed, my blood raced in my veins and I was dizzy from sheer lustful joy.'

'Well!' said Mrs Jeffries softly, beginning to understand a little of what ailed Randolph. 'You had a good feel between the young lady's legs. And why not? Did she go wet and slippy when you interfered with her?'

'A little,' he replied. 'I played with her delicious cunny — oh, if only I had words to describe how perfectly formed are the lips, how delightful to touch! I thought I was about to come off in my trousers.'

'You have a very warm nature,' Mrs Jeffries said, 'and that is a source of much enjoyment to any gentleman. So she became a little wet, you say, from your handling?'

'Her heavenly little pussy became slippery with a sweet dew of love, and I was desperate to thrust my shaft up it.'

'You poked her? Is that what troubles you?'

'No, I refrained,' said he, 'though Heaven alone knows where I found the strength to contain myself at that moment.'

He made no mention of the fact that he'd rubbed at his shaft until he fetched off on Dorothy's belly, for that was the act of a timorous underling, not of a gentleman.

'Then if you did no such thing,' said Mrs Jeffries, sounding puzzled, 'why are you now concerned? I'm sure a little gentle tampering with a swooning young lady's privates is nothing to be troubled about. You held back and behaved very properly, far more so than many another would have in your position, in that you respected the young lady's virginity.'

'I did something I have not yet told you,' Randolph admitted with a touch of reluctance now he had reached the crucial point of his confession.

'Whatever can that be?' she cried. 'Are you telling me that you took advantage of her after all — that you did *not* refrain from plucking her bloom? Are you saying that you poked her?'

'Mrs Jeffries, please try to understand,' he said, hardly able to get the words out, 'the beauty of her face and form so aroused my passions that I had no choice at all but to do as I did. When I felt her sweet moisture on my fingers, it was quite impossible to hold back — I had to make her mine! I turned her over on the sofa, bared the cheeks of her darling bottom, and did the forbidden deed.'

'What? You back-buttoned her?' exclaimed Mrs Jeffries.

'Yes,' he said simply, 'I ravished her bum, since which time I have been uneasy. What shall I do?'

'Does she know what was done? When she recovered from her swoon, did she feel the effect of your ravishment?'

'She is aware that something was done to her lower parts, but not what,' he said, 'for she is wholly innocent and without any thought that a bung-hole may be used for copulation.'

'Then you must leave her in fortunate ignorance. The memory will fade and she will resume her life as if nothing happened, mark my words. But as for you — the difficulty sticks in your mind and must be dislodged. An hour or two's rogering upstairs with Miss Jane will bring you back to your normal self.'

'I think not,' said Randolph morosely, 'for yesterday I poked a girl four times, and even that was not sufficient to drive away the sombre thoughts that disturb me. In fact, it served only to make them stronger and more abiding, so that they intruded into my sleep in curious dreams.'

'What I can discern here is a feeling of guilt,' Mrs Jeffries pronounced. 'You wish now you hadn't bung-holed the lady, nice as it was at the time. Am I right?'

'Guilt?' he exclaimed. 'Damn it all, guilt is for the lower classes, not for persons like myself! I've never felt any sort of guilt in my life, and certainly not over poking women, not even when a near relation was involved. You are incorrect.'

'Pardon my error, Mr Joynes,' said she hastily. 'Guilt is not for the ruling classes — who should understand that better than I, who for many a year was the close companion of a noble lord, now sadly deceased. His Lordship with complete equanimity did such things as would cause a common person to sob with remorse and pray for forgiveness. You are of the same aristocratic turn of mind as he, and could roger a virgin in a church without the least pang of moral discomfort. This is a valuable and useful quality to have and makes for a contented life.'

'Thank you,' said Randolph, mollified by what she had said, 'guilt is a cheap emotion which plays no part in my being. Yet for some reason I fail to understand, I am troubled with qualms of some sort and cannot rid myself of them.'

'As you say, they are mere qualms, of no importance at all to you,' said Mrs Jeffries, sounding most understanding. 'It is my opinion that they can be quickly made to vanish, with the right treatment applied.'

'Then what do you suggest?' he enquired.

'You've come to the right place for advice,' said the smiling bawd. 'In your mind you half believe that there is something to set right, though not the trivial matter of button-holing your female acquaintance. The best and quickest way to put at peace these odd emotions is to have your backside properly tanned. If you laugh at my suggestion, I shall not be offended at all, but you may believe me, Mr Joynes, when I say I've seen it dozens of times — gentlemen like yourself arriving here burdened with heavy and oppressive feelings and after a sound thrashing, off they go relieved and contented.'

'Damme, but I think you may be right!' he exclaimed. 'A good whipping, such as I've not had since leaving school! Capital — the very thing to ease my mind! Can you arrange it at once?'

In Mrs Jeffries's house anything could be provided at shortest notice to visitors with enough gold sovereigns in their pocket. The housemaid was sent for — a sturdy young woman named Martha — and orders given to prepare the whipping room at once and ask Miss Emily to present herself there, ready to employ her skill with the instruments of punishment.

'Emily?' Randolph asked. 'I do not remember her. Is she new to the house, Mrs Jeffries?'

'Why no, sir, she has been in my service these three years or more. You have not met her yet during your visits here, for the reason that you have not required to be chastised, that being Emily's especial talent to satisfy gentlemen by.'

'Is she young?'

'You'll take to her,' Mrs Jeffries assured him. 'She is a fine example of female flesh, not yet thirty years of age, strong as she needs must be for her particular work. You will see her shortly for yourself, but until then, I can tell you that she has a pair of titties on her big enough to put your face between — if she would let you. As to her cunny, I shall say nothing, for if she likes the look of you, she may just give you a glimpse when she toils at punishing you.'

'Does she not poke, then?' Randolph asked, surprised.

'Not often. I see you are astonished at that, to find one in my house who does not lie all day on her back. Yet Emily earns her keep by the use of her strong right arm, and for the rest I let her do as she pleases. A few gentlemen make request for her services outside the whipping-room, and are content to pay very highly for the pleasure.'

'What sort of gentlemen are they?' Randolph asked curiously.

'Why, the sort who like to be roughly treated for pleasure by a female, who enjoy being abused and mistreated. The sort who like to lie underneath in rogering, and have Emily's weight lie above them to thump them into the mattress with her belly and thighs till they fetch off and are satisfied.'

On another occasion Randolph would have been so taken by what Mrs Jeffries told him that he would have asked questions about this strange-sounding form of poking, so very far removed from his own pleasure in domineering and browbeating a helpless girl and vanquishing her with his manly shaft. But his spirits were low and he said nothing, but waited for the whipping room to be made ready to receive him.

In less than ten minutes Martha returned to tell Mrs Jeffries that all was prepared, and that Miss Emily was in there and at the gentleman's disposal. On hearing this, Randolph glanced at the mistress of the house in a condition of mind akin to sudden panic, though he would never admit such a thing, not even to himself. Fortunately, Mrs Jeffries was too wise in the ways of men not to interpret his look correctly and immediately she spoke to reassure him:

'Come with me now, Mr Joynes, and we will put all to rights for you. I shall remain with you, to supervise the proceedings, so that you do not feel yourself put into strange hands for the treatment. Trust me now — all shall be done properly and wholly to your satisfaction.'

Randolph thanked her and followed her from her parlour into a room on the top floor of the house, at the back. Though large, it was sparsely furnished, containing no more than a couple of straight-backed wooden chairs and — there near one end, upright and fixed firmly to the bees-waxed wooden floor, the *whipping frame*! Randolph stared at it as if fascinated, having not seen such a piece of equipment before. It was a frame of heavy wood, the posts joined across at top and bottom, so that no amount of heaving or writhing would shake it, and the four corners were provided with black leather straps to pinion wrists and ankles. Close by this fearful apparatus stood a raven-haired woman, dark-eyed and strongly built. Mrs Jeffries presented her to Randolph as Miss Emily, and as he acknowledged her with a slight nod, she smiled cruelly at him. As to her attire, she was clad in only a short chemise ending halfway down to her knees and she wore neither stockings nor drawers, a particular which went some way to reconcile Randolph to the ordeal which faced him.

The plain linen chemise was thin enough for him to note that Emily had good-sized titties inside it, and a fat round belly. Even while he was observing her, and she standing still to let him, the maid performed a valet's part in assisting him out of his frock coat and his waistcoat, his silk cravat and his tall stiff collar. Mrs Jeffries meanwhile took a seat on one of the chairs, set back some little way from the whipping frame, yet close enough for all that went on to be seen and directed.

The maid was down on her knees now in front of Randolph, to take off his elastic-sided boots and his black silk socks. She was a heavily made woman of about the same age as Miss Emily, he observed, with the trace of an impertinent grin permanently about her broad face. Had she been his servant, he would have disciplined her severely to bring her to a proper appreciation of her place in life. At that moment, she undid his braces and buttons and pulled his trousers down his legs — her incipient grin blossoming forth into a hearty smile.

Randolph scowled down at her, thinking it insolent beyond any acceptable bounds for a lowly female servant to wear any facial expression at all when waiting on a gentleman, even if she was staring at close quarters at his dangling shaft. The moment his feet were clear of his trousers, he stepped away from the woman and turned to face Mrs Jeffries and saw that Emily was at her side, bending down to bring her ear close to her employer and catch her whisper.

The leaning posture drew up Emily's short chemise at the rear and afforded Randolph a good view of much of her sturdy thighs. He pondered a moment on the bountiful curve of her bottom, and wondered what it would be like to be rolled on and brutalised by her. The memory came into his mind of the poking bouts that he had seen at The Ratcatcher's Arms in Marylebone, and it occurred to him Emily would make an amusing contestant — and one who was hard to beat and poke by the look of her!

Mrs Jeffries stared at him and told him that his shirt must be removed before he was strapped into the whipping frame, so that he was naked for the kiss of the lash.

'Damned if I like the look of the thing,' said he. 'It's more like a flogging post for criminals in prison than anything else — and that does not please me.'

'There is something in what you say,' Mrs Jeffries agreed, at once, for to her way of thinking, gentlemen with cash to spend were invariably correct, however improbable their opinions.

'It is a pity we no longer have the secret of the celebrated Mrs Berkley's chastisement frame,' she continued. 'It was her own invention, fifty years ago, and in great demand by gentlemen who visited her house in Charlotte Street.'

'Who was she?' Randolph enquired.

'Why, sir, Theresa Berkley was the queen of the profession in her day,' cried Mrs Jeffries. 'Noblemen and the gentry were her patrons and, it is reported, royalty also, for King George IV when he was yet Prince of Wales went to her house, besides the Duke of Queensberry, and many another.'

'She procured by Royal appointment, eh?' said he. 'Did she put the Royal coat of arms on the wall outside her door too?'

'She was a very discreet woman,' said Mrs Jeffries, 'and

she could hold her tongue about her visitors, including bishops and even a great lady or two whose taste ran that way. This I know from the lord in whose service I was, he being a client of hers at one period in his life.'

'This invention of hers, what was it like?' Randolph asked.

'It was reported to be in shape not unlike the human form, to accommodate the victim in comfort. But alas, when Mrs Berkley died, the frame was lost and never seen again. Her property and her fortune, which was considerable, passed to her only brother — a religious person who had been a missionary among the black savages of Australia. But he was too ashamed of his celebrated sister to accept, and in default everything went to her medical adviser. He took the cash and sold off the property, and it is believed that the frame was bought for a large sum of money by the keeper of a Paris brothel.'

'Confound all Frogs!' said Randolph, patriotically.

'They make good whores,' said Mrs Jeffries, 'hardworking and ingenious in poking. I employ them gladly when they apply here. But to conclude my story, my dear kind lord once told me that at Theresa Berkley's a gentleman could have himself whipped or birched, scourged, fustigated, caned, thrashed with stinging nettles, or whatever took his fancy, till he was fully spent and wrung out.'

'It sounds devilish painful to me,' said Randolph doubtfully.

'Lord love you, sir, each to his taste, and I see that yours is not that of gentlemen who find bliss only through agony. You are in a different way of things, as we have agreed, for you do not seek pleasure here today, but the removal of certain qualms that stick in your mind. That being so, it is my proposal that you be chastised on your bottom with a cane, as when you were a schoolboy. Does that meet with your approval?'

'Excellent,' Randolph agreed, 'so long as I need not be hung in that evil-looking frame of yours.'

'No, sir, you shall be horsed on Martha's back, while you are chastised. Prepare yourself, Martha.'

'Yes, madam,' said the sturdy maid at once.

She bestowed on Randolph the benefit of her impertinent smile and said she was sure he would have no objection if she removed her dress, in case of accident. He did not take her meaning, and before he had time to ask what the Devil she meant, she had unbuttoned and unhooked herself and had her plain black servant garb off and across a chair with his own clothes. She stood in only chemise and drawers, her fat titties dangling inside and a wisp of brown hair visible through the slit of her drawers.

'Now, Mr Joynes, if you are quite ready,' said Mrs Jeffries.

Martha placed herself in front of him, her broad back turned towards him, her plump backside within an inch of his person.

'Put your hands on my shoulders, if you please, sir,' said she, glancing backwards at him.

Speechless now that the moment was at hand, Randolph obeyed, resting his hands on her shoulders. At once she reached up and back to take hold of his wrists and pull his arms over her, and down, her back now pressed hard against him. She bent forward sharply, lifting him right off his feet, and he hung helplessly on her back in the traditional posture of being horsed.

She was strong of grip, and her hold on his wrists was not to be broken. She had thrust his hands down the loose front of her chemise, to take hold of her plump titties, but he was prey to such emotions of fearful apprehension that the feel of her warm flesh went unnoticed in his clasping hands. He gasped to feel Emily's hands on him, tucking up his shirt tail to uncover his bottom and make it ready for the caning to come.

This touch of her hands on his rearward cheeks, to which she gave some moments of manual attention, smoothing her palms over them, pinching the flesh between forefinger and thumb, parting the cheeks to press her fingers into the crease between, had an effect on Mr Percival Proud, that forlorn and forgotten friend hanging down between Randolph's legs. He woke up from his long sleep, shook himself, and raised his head.

'Is the gentleman ready yet?' Mrs Jeffries enquired.

'Almost,' said Emily, her fingers busy between the cheeks of Randolph's bottom in a way that made him squirm against Martha.

Then Emily pressed her belly against his bottom, both arms round his waist, so that he was squeezed between two big female bodies as if in a human sandwich, they the bread slices and he the meat in the middle. It was a peculiar feeling, and one that he found very agreeable. Emily slid her hands between him and Martha, and took hold of stiff and twitching Mr Percival. She held his pompoms in one cupped palm, and ran her fingers up and down the hard-on shaft, handling it with contempt — and yet the touch excited Randolph beyond words.

Finally, she arranged his cockstand neatly against Martha's well-filled chemise, where it was trapped and held firm. Then at last she stood back and picked up the long cane that leaned upright against a chair. Randolph turned his head to stare hard at her, and his heart leaped to see her stern face and sombre dark eyes regarding him with an expression of disdain. Her full titties and belly filled out her thin chemise in a provocative manner that caused Mr Percival to jerk furiously.

'I hope all is to your liking, now you find yourself prepared for your punishment,' said Mrs Jeffries from where she sat down the room. 'Miss Emily will wield the cane very briskly, you may take my word for it.'

'I hardly know what to think,' replied Randolph, his voice shaking to the intensity of his emotions, his hands squeezing Martha's big bare titties and rolling them about in her chemise so that she grinned and grunted.

'You are about to find out, not by any words of mine, but by virtue of suffering pain, that some things ought not to be done — and if they are, then they are to be forgotten quickly. Have you understood me?'

'I take your meaning,' he answered, 'and it is to be hoped an outcome as satisfactory as you promise will result — though by keeping me waiting you add to my suspense.'

Truth to tell, now that Mr Percival was at hard-on stand once more, Randolph was no longer certain that he wished to proceed with being caned. A good poke or two with Miss Jane was surely a better remedy for his low spirits. He considered asking to be released, but decided that was the act of a coward, and set his face against it.

'Begin, Emily!' said Mrs Jeffries.

Randolph, his head turned to the side, watched Emily raise her arm high above her head, so that her heavy breasts rolled and slid under her chemise, and a tuft of jet-black hair showed in her armpit. A moment later she brought the cane down across his behind, making him jerk to the cut, whilst the fierce pain made him cry out, *Oh no, no*! Again she caned him, the rod whistling through the air as it descended, to end in a loud crack across his flesh. In desperation he tried to kick backwards and pull his wrists free, but Martha held him firmly. Miss Emily struck again, making his bottom feel as if it were wrapped in a sheet of fire. In his suffering he was unaware how his shaft was swollen to tremendous size and stiffness, for it was trapped tightly between him and Martha's back, squeezed between his belly and her chemise, on which it rubbed to the writhing of his body as once more the cane cut savagely through the air and cracked across his tormented backside.

Excruciating though the pain was, Randolph could not help but notice that Emily's short chemise was now hitched up around her waist, to permit her legs to move freely as she swung the cane. He saw her full round snow-white belly, inset with the tiniest of buttons, and below, her cunny, almost hairless and with lips no larger than those of a young girl not yet poked. Yet Emily could be no virgin, living in this house. Was her pleasure to come off with other women, Randolph wondered — with the lovely Miss Jane, perhaps?

'Oh!' he exclaimed. 'Your little pussy is adorable, Emily — I want to roger you!'

'Be silent, sir, and take your punishment like a gentleman,' Mrs Jeffries said. 'You will thank me for driving out of your mind the unwelcome memory of interfering with a young lady when she lay in a faint and at your mercy! Ah, how shameful — not a proper ravishing in her cunny, even, but a furtive approach by the back door! Lay on hard, Emily, turn his backside scarlet.'

'Yes, Mrs Jeffries,' Emily answered, 'and it is my intention after I've reddened his bottom to give his shaft a good beating to teach it to mend its ways.'

'Capital idea!' said Mrs Jeffries. 'How many's he had — six of the best? That will do his bum for the time being — punish his offending part!'

Emily ceased to cane him and, to Randolph's horror, she slid a hand between him and Martha to take hold of Mr Proud and tug hard at him, as if to stretch further his already impressive length.

'Yes, half a dozen cuts across this will reduce his conceit,' Emily agreed. 'The cheek of it — to say he wants to put this up me and fetch off! Am I to continue, Mrs Jeffries?'

'You cannot mean to beat me there,' Randolph cried. 'You may thrash my backside all you will, for it might perhaps be argued that I have deserved no better — but do not inflict pain upon me there! It could maim me for life! Spare me this agony, and you shall be well rewarded, I promise you!'

'Maim, is it?' cried she, still handling him roughly. 'Some gentlemen who come here to appreciate my services like nothing better than to be bound to the frame and whipped on their shaft until it turns blue and red, being bruised and battered until they faint clean away.'

'Ah no, no!' Randolph moaned.

He need not have feared, for he was in the hands of experts, the trio of females attending to him being highly experienced and skilled in ministering to the whims of gentlemen. Out from Randolph's caned bottom there had spread a hot glow to embrace his loins and raise Mr Percival to his extremity of erection.

Randolph's fingers were firmly clenched on the soft flesh of Martha's titties, and the rubbing of Emily's hand did the rest. A bolt of sensation passed through his body, as if he had been struck by a pistol shot and, with a shriek of unexpected bliss, he squibbed his hot sap on to the back of Martha's chemise so forcefully as to soak it almost up to her shoulder-blades.

When at last he lay calm, she stood upright and lowered

him to his feet, and Miss Emily passed a strong right arm about his waist to support him. He took advantage of the moment to reach under her chemise and have a feel of her maidenly looking cunny — and she did not prevent him, but stood with her feet apart to facilitate his groping.

Randolph, apart from the sting of his backside, was in high spirits. He sensed that whatever had ailed him had been set to right by the caning, that the slate was wiped clean, and there was nothing to trouble himself about further. In his elation he handed Mrs Jeffries a five pound Bank of England note, and announced an intention of poking the perspiring Miss Emily a time or two.

She at once delivered a smart smack of her hand on his bare backside and told him he was much mistaken, but that she would roger *him* to a standstill, if he so desired. Whereupon Randolph recalled the sporting match he had attended in Marylebone and offered to wrestle her the best of three pokes, and to that she agreed.

CHAPTER 13
A Most
Disconcerting Discovery

Randolph allowed the weekend to pass before getting word
to the maid Bella that she was to meet him again at Black's
Temperance Coffee House, there being a matter of some
importance he wished to acquaint her with. She arrived
promptly at half past two of the afternoon, eager for any
least shred of comfort she could convey back to Miss
Harker.

It is unnecessary to say that, having some experience now
of the Hon Randolph Joynes' way with females, Bella came
to the meeting in the expectation that she would be rogered.
In this assumption she was correct — she had been in the
upstairs room with him not even five minutes before he had
her dress and drawers off, and she flat on her back on the
bed, thighs apart and chemise up above her titties.

To demonstrate his authority over her, and to experience
that high feeling of total domination he so much enjoyed,
Randolph divested himself of none of his garments — not
even his black silk topper, which remained clamped on his
head during the entire operation! His frock coat stayed
buttoned, only the flaps parted in front, and if he could have
devised a way to do her without opening his trousers, he

would, but that was beyond the wit of any man, and gaping wide they were to allow out his stiff shaft and plunge it into her pussy.

Once installed in her, he rogered her long and artfully, slow in thrusting yet deep and piercing, for he had a mind to poke her to the point of hysteria and prolong the duration of his pleasures that day. In this manner, Bella was driven almost out of her senses by the luxurious feelings that emanated from her well-filled cunny and spread throughout her body. She became lost in transports of ecstasy long before Randolph was ready to spend, and when at last his essence gushed into her, she gasped very loud and fell into paroxysms of bliss that almost caused her to lose consciousness.

After he had dismounted he sat upright on the side of the bed and gazed down at her thoughtfully, his sticky shaft back in his trousers and his topper a trifle askew on his head. Bella lay motionless, her legs spread wide and her heart filled with contentment. He smiled to see how her frame was shaken by an occasional tremor from the still-trembling strings of joy that had been plucked to sound out the melody that had enraptured her senses.

He was well pleased with what he had done to her, knowing she would be more amenable to his suggestions now that he had by means of his manly shaft carried her up to the very heights.

His conclusion proved true, for when Bella regained the power of speech, she turned on her side to stare at him in wonder and speak most flatteringly:

'Lord above, sir, I've never been done like that before,' she said. 'It's a pity you can't do it to Miss Dorothy, for I swear she would forget her troubles in an instant, if you brought her off as you have me.'

'There is much in what you say,' Randolph agreed, 'for in my own experience a good poke cures most of the concerns that ail humankind, and we aristocrats are very expert at it, as you may suppose. Is Miss Harker still dejected, then?'

'She is, for on Saturday Mr Mawby arrived by appointment for an answer to his proposal of marriage. She refused him, as she told me she would, and as I informed you when we met before.'

'How refused him? Briskly? Sadly? Indifferently?'

'Not without tears and sighs, sir, for she has an affection for Mr Mawby that is a neighbour to Love itself. He was first distressed, and sought to know why he was refused, enquiring if she thought him not good enough for her. But there was little enough Miss Dorothy could tell him of the reason why she felt herself unworthy of him, and he became angry and demanded to be told if there was someone else. I heard voices raised in the drawing room and was in fear for my poor mistress, but then Mr Mawby left in a huff, banging the door behind him.'

'Were you able to bring any comfort to her mind?' Randolph asked. 'Did you offer solace?'

'Comfort? What comfort could there be for one in her piteous condition? I do not understand what you mean, sir.'

'Then I shall explain myself, Bella,' said he, his hand lying on her uncovered titties, to feel them and toy with them whilst he spoke.

'When you came here before,' he continued, 'to acquaint me of the details of Miss Harkers misgivings, something you said lodged in my mind. I pondered for the next day or two what it might signify and finally, I reached a conclusion of interest.'

'What do you mean, sir?' Bella asked.

'In telling me of your actions when Miss Harker recovered at last from her swoon, you said that you conducted her into her bedroom and there bathed her parts in warm water. Is that so?'

'What of it? She was still half-swooning and unable to do anything for herself, and you had spent freely on her. I feared that if even a drop of the prolific juice trickled inside her, a calamitous result might make itself apparent in nine months time. Some gratitude must be due for saving you from paternity, sir. Or is that an impudent suggestion?'

'Not in the least,' he said cheerfully, 'and I shall remember your solicitude. But — be frank now, Bella — is it not an act of extraordinary intimacy for a servant to bathe her mistress's private parts, even in an urgent situation?'

The maid made no answer, and he squeezed her nearside titty whilst he spun the thread of his argument.

'To perform so intimate a function without hesitation, or any afterthought of embarrassment, implies to me that it was not at all the first time you had done it, Bella. I strongly suspect that you bathe Miss Dorothy's pussy for her regularly as part of your duties — am I not right?'

'What of it?' said Bella, giving away nothing.

'Well, my dear, I have seen Miss Dorothy's pussy, as you well know, and it is quite the prettiest little thing I have seen in many a year. In my opinion, Bella, in bathing it, you would not be able to resist touching it, and stroking it, and tickling it to make it pout. Do you deny taking these pleasures?'

'My word!' she exclaimed. 'However did you guess?'

'You gave yourself away, for when you read aloud to me of the tribulations of Selina at the hands of Miss Rodwell, there was a bright blush on your cheeks that showed the pleasure you took in hearing of a young girl's cunny being played with by another female intent on fetching her off.'

Bella smiled up at him and laid her hand flat over her own exposed cunny, and teased the wet lips a little with her middle finger as if in fond reminiscence of former bliss.

'Seeing the effect the book had on you, sir, when I read from it, I suppose you are curious to know more about Miss Dorothy's bedtime preparations.'

Randolph signified his enthusiasm to be better informed, and Bella launched into the story of her duties to Miss Harker.

'As you are aware, sir, I am no housemaid, but lady's maid to Miss Dorothy, and have been for three years now, since she passed sixteen and was thought old enough to have her own maid. At night it is my duty to undress her for bed, to help her out of dress and underskirts and drawers, until I have stripped her to chemise and stockings. To enable me to remove her stockings, she seats herself on the side of her bed, whilst I kneel down and reach under her chemise to roll down her stockings.'

'Ah, what a jolly scene!' Randolph sighed, aware of Percival stretching himself inside his closed trousers, and growing hard and thick. 'You feel her pussy — am I right?'

'She loves me to do so, sir, and has since she was a girl. My hands are out of sight up under her chemise, her legs are apart to let my hand between, and I treat her to a good feel, outside and in, and then with a fingertip on her secret button until her beautiful face begins to flush.'

'Do you bring her off fully?' Randolph asked.

'Oh yes, sir, I tickle her button until her back arches and she emits a long sigh and comes off. I let her recover while I remove her stockings, whereupon she stands up for her chemise to be taken off — and for a moment or two I see her lovely body as naked as day! Then I slip her nightgown over her head and she gets into bed, a contented smile on her face, and is asleep before I have cleared away her clothes and left the room.'

'And how often do you do this, Bella?'

'Every night.'

'Well, well,' said he, 'it seems that the innocent young Miss Dorothy Harker knows more about the joys of coming off than any unmarried gentlewoman of her age ought! Why then should she be upset to the extent you claim she is at being interfered with a little by me? There is something here out of place.'

Bella had two fingers within the soft lips of her pussy and was stroking slowly and with evident enjoyment.

'Miss Dorothy knows nothing at all about poking,' she said, a smile crossing her face at the thought. 'She believes that what I do to her — which she also does to herself most days, for I have observed her — is just something which ladies do to amuse themselves. She has not been instructed yet that her pussy is not only for playing with by hand, hers or mine, but is formed to be poked by a gentleman's hardon shaft. Nor does her mama intend to tell her, until the evening before her wedding day. I fear that is put off, for she sent Mr Mawby away.'

'When do you bathe her cunny?' Randolph asked, being not at all interested in Lorimer Mawby and his disappointments. 'In the morning, I presume.'

'That's right, sir,' said Bella, a little breathless from the tremors of pleasure rippling through her uncovered belly from the movement of her finger in her open cunny.

'Tell me about it,' said Randolph, equally breathless, for Mr Percival was standing very firm and jumping about, so eager was he to get inside the wet split the maid was fingering.

'Miss Dorothy rises at nine o'clock,' said Bella, 'when the housemaid brings the hot water for her to wash in. I help her out of her nightgown and put down a towel on the rug in front of the washstand. She wakes in a sunny mood every day, and she smiles and chatters to me while she stands on the towel and I wash over her face and neck and under her arms with a soft facecloth.'

'Ah, I'd give a hundred pounds for one day of your duties,' said Randolph with a long sigh. 'Tell me you wash her lovely titties.'

'Of course I do — and a prettier pair you'll never lay eyes on — should you ever be so fortunate to see hers! I wash over them with my palm, very softly and gently, and her tiny pink teats stand proudly up beneath my touch.'

'By George!' he moaned 'I'll come off in another second if you continue like this! Tell me more, Bella, more!'

Mr Proud stood untouched by human hand inside Randolph's dark grey trousers, but bounding like a stag in full rut. The time was not far away when his hood would roll back to bare his head and he would discharge his creamy fluid in spurts of bliss.

'I bring a chair close to the washstand and on the seat put another towel,' said Bella, her words punctuated with sighs as she too approached the zenith of enjoyment. 'Miss Dorothy sits on this, her legs apart, and I place a bowl of clean warm water between her feet. Then I wash her pussy, using only my fingers, until it is perfectly sweet and pure, and she gasps and shakes and comes off.'

'Every morning?' Randolph asked hoarsely.

He was astonished that Bella without the least sign of shame was bringing herself off by hand in plain view. Paid-for doxies would do it on request, of course, but to see a maidservant do it to herself unasked was new to Randolph's

215

experience. It was extremely arousing, and for that reason he enjoyed watching her — though in some part of his mind there was a nagging suspicion that Bella was stroking her pussy because she liked to be *seen* bringing herself off. And if she was merely using him for her own pleasure that would be unbelievably insolent and he would take punitive measures. He pushed the thought away, not wanting to spoil his own enjoyment.

'I give her a thrill every morning, and some mornings twice,' Bella whispered, her eyes closed and her hand moving fast on her own cunny. 'Often there are days when, after she is calm again, she insists that I have not done my duty diligently enough and orders me to wash her pussy better, and I bring her off a second time.'

With that, Bella moaned, her loins jerked hard upwards and she fetched off to her own fingers. Randolph watched her squirm and heave, enrapt by what he saw, feeling his own spasm about to overwhelm him. Was it possible that a man could come off and shoot his roe with no stimulation at all of his shaft, only the power of imagination at work in his mind? He had never heard of it happening, except of course in dreams, an involuntary joy severely condemned by Dr Acton.

Whether possible or not, he was not to discover that day, for no sooner had Bella's throes of passion faded, than she rolled over towards where he sat on the bedside, opened his frock coat with busy fingers and ripped apart his trouser buttons. His shirt was still bundled up round his belly, from when he had poked her before, and Mr Percival leaped out like a Jack-in-the-Box.

Without a pause, she brought her mouth to bear on the jerking shaft, drawing it in over her wet tongue and licking it fast. A sensation of extreme voluptuousness enveloped

Randolph — rarely had he been so aroused as now, to observe the maid's head down between his thighs and her tongue flickering at the head of his throbbing shaft. Almost at once he felt the supreme moment arriving — the most delicious spasms racked him, shaking him from head to foot like a sapling caught in a strong gale.

'I'm coming off, Bella!' he gasped, and his cream gushed out of his shaft and into her sucking mouth.

The afternoon passed very pleasantly, for he had her on her back and rogered her twice more before they parted. He told her how he wished her to prepare Miss Dorothy's mind for a meeting with him the next day, when he would endeavour to resolve her moral difficulties. Bella listened with care and attention, for she was wholly won over to him and entertained secret hopes he would marry Miss Dorothy, so that she and her mistress had the benefit of his poking on a daily basis.

Thus encouraged by what she saw as in her own interest, Bella did her work well. When Randolph presented himself at three the next afternoon at the Harkers' apartment in Paddington Green, he was shown up to the drawing room at once, where Miss Harker received him. Her face was pale of hue and her eyes downcast, her manner somewhat distant, but undoubtedly she wanted to hear whatever Randolph had to say to her. Tea was brought in and a cup poured for him, though he noted that she kept the tea table between her chair and his.

He spoke to her cheerfully and in a spirit of friendship and admiration for her many qualities, by degrees turning round the conversation to the particulars of her plight — or what it was she perceived as her plight. Knowing now that she was very well acquainted with the pleasures of the sexual spasm, even if only when induced by her maid's nimble fingers, he edged towards the topic never to be spoken of in polite society — the harmonious bodily relation between loving husbands and wives, and how this felicitous state of matrimony was accomplished.

'Of all that I am aware,' said Dorothy faintly, 'for in these past few days I have made it my business to find out what it is men want of women, and how they go about it.'

From this Randolph understood that Bella had obeyed him fully and had made some explanation to her innocent mistress of the mechanics of rogering, perhaps even making all clear by means of her finger playing, however inadequately, the penetrating role of the hard-on male shaft.

'Even now I know,' Dorothy continued, 'I confess to finding it next to impossible to believe a lady will allow a gentleman, even if he is her dearly beloved husband, to insert his fleshy organ of generation into any part of her person and discharge his vital fluid. Yet I needs must accept that this is what an All-Wise Deity has ordained, however distasteful it may seem, for the continuance of the human race.

'There's more to it than getting heirs,' said Randolph. 'That would require doing it no more than two or three times a year, to bring on pregnancy. You may not be aware, Miss Dorothy, that young married couples perform the marital act nightly, not just once but several times, and often by day also.'

'What you say is monstrous!' she cried out. 'It cannot be true. Why on earth should any modest wife permit her body to be abused so vilely, however much respect and love she may have?'

'Why, for the pleasure of it,' he replied. 'Perhaps you find it difficult to understand this, for you are a virtuous young lady who has never experienced the sensations of a hard-on male shaft inside her private parts.'

At that, Dorothy blushed crimson to the ears, and for a moment Randolph thought he had offended her past retrieval. Be that as it may, she did not rise and leave the room, but stayed to hear what he would say next.

'You have no experience,' said he, knowing that she had enjoyed years of it in Bella's hands, 'but you may believe me, the pleasure ladies find in coming off is intense and they wish to repeat it as often as their husbands can manage the affair.'

'Can this be true?' she asked thoughtfully, and he saw that he had scored a point.

'I give you my solemn assurance that it is,' said he. 'Surely it is obvious to all that the female body was formed to receive within itself the all-important male organ, not once or twice a year, but constantly. There are many medical cases on record of females being deprived of that bliss for which there is not in this world any substitute, and falling into melancholia.'

'I would rather have supposed the opposite,' Dorothy informed him. 'This so-called pleasure you talk of is surely reserved to gentlemen. It seems to me that ladies would be driven into deep and unbearable distress of mind by husbands enforcing marital rights on their hapless body with a frequency that destroys all dignity and trust.'

'Dear Miss Dorothy,' said Randolph, 'believe me, when you are a wife yourself, and lie abed at night by the side of a loving husband, you will come to an appreciation of the exact truth of my assertion. The sensations of the sexual spasm are common to men and women alike, as is the strong and wholesome desire for carnal pleasure. These divinely implanted instincts were never intended to be borne without relief — and the proper management of this relief lies within the union of the sexual parts. Has no hint, howsoever distant, ever imparted to you in sleep, when the mind ranges freely, the bliss to be found in intercourse?'

As he was well aware, Dorothy's custom was to experience the divine sensation night and morning, ministered to by her maid. Yet her face turned paler yet at his words, and she stammered:

'Shameful! What you suggest is shameful, Mr Joynes.'

Her agitation was great, and Randolph wondered whether she might be about to swoon. If she did, then he proposed to take full advantage of her, front and rear.

'Great Heavens!' he cried. 'That you should stigmatise the wondrous works of Nature as shameful! But you cannot be held responsible for this opinion, for it has been taught to you by others, who ought to know better. How infamous and hypocritical is the society in which we live, that allows the fresh beauty and youth of young ladies to be blasted by a withholding of the simple facts of Nature which would so much ease their minds!'

Common girls, he could have told her, suffered from no such ignorance, for by the time they were twelve years old they had been shown by their playmates in the alleys and courtyards the uses to which their hairless little cunnies could be put. Unhappily, they were soon in the family way thereby. Their problem lay in too much knowledge at too early an age, not in too little, as was the case with gentlewomen like Miss Dorothy Harker.

By the time the tea things were cleared away, Randolph felt that he was making great strides. Dorothy was listening avidly to his words, and she seemed to trust him — at least as far as not flinching when he crossed the room to seat himself at her side.

'Mr Joynes,' she said, somewhat timorously, 'will you tell me something truthfully? You speak with such easy familiarity of the union of the sexes that I cannot help but think that, even though you are a bachelor, you have tasted these pleasures. To be blunt, it seems to me that you must have experienced carnal connexion with at least one female. Is this so?'

Randolph acknowledged that it was, whereupon she pressed him with questions to know what females they were, and why they had allowed him ingress to their bodies.

'Dorothy, Dorothy,' he exclaimed, 'there is so much I could tell you, if I wished. But believe me, my dear, a single ounce of example is worth a half-ton of talk. Trust me, for I will do you no harm, I swear.'

With that he pressed her gently back on the sofa, and with a delicate hand, raised her clothes. Dorothy stared at him with eyes bulging with apprehension while he uncovered her drawers, and she kept her legs close together. He made no move towards the forward slit of her drawers and her hidden pussy, but tried to reassure her with soothing words.

'Do not be alarmed, dear Dorothy, I mean you no insult, only an explanation. Remain calm, while I reveal to you every secret that has been kept from you for so long.'

It was his intention to demonstrate to her what a gentleman's organ looked like, and say some words as to how it fitted into the female aperture. To this end, he pulled open the buttons of his trousers and brought out his fleshy shaft to show her. Then his face turned a fiery red with the humiliation of realising that he had no cockstand! Mr Percival Proud belied his name — for he was hanging his head in shame, without the least hint of stiffness in him, and he was shrunk to his smallest size.

Never in his life had Randolph found himself to be

unequal to sensual activity. He stared down in amazement at his limp part, wondering why this had come about. There was nothing he could think of to account for this feebleness. He had slept well, he had abstained from poking Lizzie when she woke him, he had made a hearty breakfast on porridge with cream, a brace of Scottish kippers and a pair of mutton chops.

He had no inconvenient feelings about having taken advantage of her when she lay in a swoon, for a sound caning had rid him of that nonsense. What the Devil could be amiss? Here at hand sat a young lady he found most provocative because of her youth and innocence, a choice example of female flesh! He had the strongest letch for her, to repeat in her cunny what he had done a few days before in her back door. That notwithstanding, his shaft lay meek and useless between his fingers.

'My God, what must you think of me!' he exclaimed in dread, hardly able to look Dorothy in the face, sure that she despised him for his unmanly weakness, 'I don't know what is the matter with me!'

Dorothy's words showed that she had not the least idea that anything was in the least wrong: 'Oh,' said she pleasantly, 'how small and tender is your . . . I hardly know what to call it . . . this part of your person. In my ignorance I imagined it to be enormously thick and hard, far too big to go into my modest opening, that being what I have been given to understand gentlemen do to females. I was afraid it would hurt me dreadfully, and perhaps even split my poor little thing wide open. Now I see it, there is nothing fearful about it at all. Rather the reverse, for I find it endearingly small and soft, and I would not be in the least afraid to hold it in my hand and dandle it.'

'Do so,' he begged her, hoping that the touch of her dainty

hand would stir Mr Percival into life and make him stand hard.

She stretched out her delicate white hand and took his shaft on her palm, raising it up to inspect in detail the first male organ she had ever been allowed to view. What she saw evidently pleased her, for very soon her other hand crept slowly forward until, with a fingertip, she could tickle Mr Percival Proud's head, for all the world as if he were a kitten to be petted and cuddled tenderly.

For reasons of her own, he understood, Dorothy had decided to entrust her honour to him, and allow him to roger her. Perhaps she thought that he then would feel obliged to ask her to marry him. Her reasoning was of no importance, only the physical fact of her surrender to him. In his mind he envisioned it complete — how his eager fingers would part the slit of her drawers and stroke her pretty pussy.

He longed to see that fleshy jewel of hers once more, to kiss the delicate pink lips of it, and press a gentle finger inside to seek out her tiny button, so sensitive to the manipulations of her maid, and tickle it until she near-fainted with excess of joy. Then he would lay her on her back, her firmly rounded thighs spread wide apart in a state of delightful anticipation, the globes of her titties heaving beneath her clothes.

He saw in his mind's eye how he would bring up his throbbing shaft to the charge and present the swollen head to the lips of her darling pussy. And then *Farewell* to her maidenhead, for with strong pushes he would force it into her, opening her out as he entered and penetrated her. She would tremble beneath him and stifle her little cries of pain, then with her tender cunny clasping Mr Percival like a velvet glove on a finger, he would roger her gently until he fetched off and flooded her with the warm balm of his spending.

The bliss of it would be ineffable! Moments like that came but rarely and were to be savoured. Randolph stared down into his lap, praying silently that Dorothy's soft touch and toying would infuse his shaft with vigour and cause it to grow strong and mighty. Nothing availed – it remained as lifeless as ever, a small limp stub of flesh that lay still on Dorothy's hand. He was utterly mortified and brought to an end the humiliating examination, tucking his childishly soft dangle swiftly into his trousers and taking his leave of Miss Dorothy.

Outside in the street he walked at random, not knowing where he was going, nor caring. The world had turned upside down and he had no thought but one – his dreadful incapacity! Nothing else held the least significance, compared to that. Into the travail of his mind came a recollection of the fearful ending a few years before of Captain Edward Sellon of the Indian Army who came home to write his memoirs.

To judge by what he wrote of his early life, Sellon went the pace with Indian women, finding that their smoothly bare-shaven cunnies aroused him to constant heights of lustfulness. Nor did he neglect the European ladies he met abroad, whose hairy slits were equally stimulating. On his return to England, he carried on in the course he had set himself – incessant poking by day and night, wife, servants, mistresses, whores.

So much so that, while still youngish in years, the gallant Captain found himself no longer capable to perform the sensual act, his shaft being too over-used and done to death to rise to any occasion again, as Randolph found himself now to be. The conclusion was fearful – Sellon despaired and shot himself to death in a hotel in Piccadilly.

'No!' Randolph exclaimed aloud to no one as he walked

along. 'Not that! There are doctors who specialise in the disorders of gentlemen. I shall consult the best of them, and I make no doubt that a course of treatment, rest and good food, will soon put me back in the way of rogering.'

Then he remembered what the most celebrated expert of all had said on this very subject, Dr William Acton:

'. . . *the morally purblind man indulges himself in the trivial pleasures of sexual indulgence, thinking nothing of the heavy penalties attached. He is unaware that, if the sexual desires are stimulated frequently, it will require a greater power of will to master them than falls to the lot of most men, and he will be a prisoner to the harmful habits of his own making. How foolish and short-sighted, to be insensible of the inescapable truth that an awful risk attends on frequent sexual intercourse — and not take heed that self-indulgence, long pursued, leads ultimately to insanity and self-destruction . . .*'

'I am lost,' Randolph groaned, 'consigned to perdition, cut off from the acme of all human felicity, never more to know the wondrous sensations of fetching off in a warm pussy!'

CHAPTER 14
An Opinion is Offered by a Titled Lady

In his sad confusion of mind, Randolph walked for a long time, following the pavement and making no deliberate choice of which way he turned but letting blind Chance direct his feet. It was only when he was called to by an angry voice that he came to an awareness of his whereabouts. He stood in New Bond Street and the voice that had called to him was that of Lorimer Mawby.

Randolph looked at his friend in some surprise, for the truth was that Lorimer's luxuriant mutton-chop whiskers bristled with rage and his eyes seemed to flash fire. He was accompanied by an elegant lady dressed all in bottle-green satin but he made no attempt to effect an introduction. Indeed, he took a step forward away from his charming companion, to confront Randolph.

'Lorimer, what the deuce is the matter?' Randolph asked, for he could think of no reason why the other should harbour hard feelings toward him.

'The matter? I'll tell you what the damn matter is!' cried Lorimer. 'The matter is that you are a low bounder, a scoundrel who deserves horse-whipping!'

'What on earth do you mean? What can I have possibly

done to offend you? I haven't laid eyes on you for ages.'

Lorimer seemed to swell up inside his smartly waisted frock coat, till Randolph thought the buttons would burst.

'You have tampered with the affections of a young lady whom I had reason to believe would accept my proposal of marriage! That's what you've done to offend me, you cur!'

'I have done nothing to interfere with your plan to marry Miss Harker,' Randolph insisted feebly, quite unwilling to accept the responsibility thrust upon him.

'You lie!' Lorimer bellowed, his face dark red with emotion. 'How you have achieved your evil end, and for what purpose you have ruined my prospects, I do not know! Nor do I care to, for it is certain that both means and motive are unspeakably vile. You are a cad and I shall have you blackballed at the Club and thrown out!'

'Now look here,' said Randolph, his dejection swept aside by this tirade of abuse, and his own temper rising fast, 'if Miss Harker doesn't want you, that's not my doing. I've seen her but twice since you introduced me, and that by chance. For what it may be worth, I have made no overtures of marriage to her, nor have I spoken slightingly to her of you. Are you sure it wasn't some action of your own that set her against you?'

'What the Devil do you mean, sir!' Lorimer said in a squawk. 'I have behaved with perfect propriety towards her!'

'So you say,' Randolph struck back verbally at his assailant, 'but why should I believe you, I who have seen you fumbling up skirts and squeezing female backsides? You are not entirely a paragon of purity and respectfulness, are you?'

'Damn you! That was with whores and well you know

it! With Miss Harker I have been the very model of etiquette!'

'What!' Randolph exclaimed, letting the grievance he had for his own incapacity deflect on to his friend. 'Did you believe you were with a whore when you rogered Mrs Hamilton on her own sofa? Or when you had Miss Violet Burkington-Hutchins in the conservatory at her coming-out ball?'

'You are no gentleman, sir, to mention the names of ladies in this offensive manner,' said Lorimer, his voice half-strangled with rage.

'You accuse me of God-knows-what in the street and then cry foul play when I remind you of your own misdeeds?' Randolph at once countered. 'I am sorry for your disappointed hopes, yet if they were dashed because you forgot yourself, there is none but yourself to blame.'

'Forget myself! Damn your eyes, Joynes, it is you who forget yourself. My manners have been exemplary towards Miss Harker.'

'Evidently not, if you have been turned way. Did you have a cockstand in your trousers while you wooed the lady, which gave her gentle nature cause for alarm? Or did you chance your luck and put a hand up her clothes for a feel of her pussy?'

At these outrageous suggestions, Lorimer became so incensed that he began to gobble like a Christmas turkey and shake his fist at Randolph.

'Ah, I see I have touched on the sensitive spot,' the latter crowed, enjoying the spectacle of his erstwhile friend reduced to fuming rage.

'You utter blackguard!' Lorimer screeched, scarce able to speak. 'I'll pay you out for that!'

Then, unable to contain himself longer and fearful he

would engage in fisticuffs there in the street like a common drayman, Lorimer turned on his heel and strode away across the road, and was almost run down by a four-wheeler passing by. Randolph eyed his retreating back with glee, and tipped his hat mockingly.

In the heat of his anger, Lorimer had stalked off without any thought for his fair companion, who stood pretending not to hear the altercation. Randolph looked at her properly at last and saw she was a lady of quality, dressed in the very height of fashion and *bon ton*, as the Froggies call style. She wore a thin summer coat of silk, with elegant leg-of-mutton sleeves, and a short train she held off the ground with one gloved and graceful hand. He put her age at between thirty and forty years, near to the latter rather than the former, although she was slender of form and face.

'Forgive me for addressing you without an introduction,' said Randolph, raising his topper, 'but Mawby went dashing off like a mad creature before doing the honours. May I present myself — I am the Hon Randolph Joynes. Please allow me to be of some assistance to you, for it would be unthinkable to leave a lady unescorted in a public place.'

'You are very kind, Mr Joynes,' said she, smiling politely at him. 'I am Lady Fotherington, and I am exceedingly vexed with Lorimer for abandoning me in the street. As to the uncommon way of our introducing ourselves without a third person present to conform to the niceties, perhaps it will help to know that you and I have friends in common, quite apart from Mr Mawby.'

'I am glad of it,' said he, wondering who these friends might be and what was the nature of her friendship with Lorimer.

'I cannot stand here in the street one moment longer,' said Lady Fotherington, 'for strangers are beginning to talk!

Pray be so good as to summon a hansom cab, Mr Joynes.'

That was soon done and when he handed her into it she requested him to escort her to her home, for she had hardly ever been out alone and needed a gentleman's superior knowledge to cope with the petty business of travel and shops. The unexpected row with Lorimer had bucked Randolph up a bit, and he sprang lightly into the hansom with the lady, who informed him that she lived in Belgrave Square.

He passed on the address to the cab driver up above, and the number. The cabbie cracked his whip, and the horse set out at a smart trot towards Piccadilly. Lady Fotherington then showed she had an ulterior motive in asking Randolph to accompany her, for she referred to his quarrel with Lorimer Mawby which polite manners required that she had not listened to — though it was very obvious she had.

'It is fearfully vulgar, I know,' she said, 'to overhear the conversation of others, but you and your friend were shouting so very loudly that I could not help but catch a word or two. I did not know that Mr Mawby had a sentimental interest in a lady and had proposed marriage to her.'

'Why yes, Miss Dorothy Harker, from Warwickshire,' Randolph confirmed.

'A young lady of fortune, do you know?'

'I believe I heard it said that she will have seven thousand pounds a year from her father when she marries,' said Randolph with complete disregard for the truth, but to land Lorimer deeper in trouble. The conclusion he had reached was that Lorimer was poking Lady Fotherington on the side while he courted Dorothy, and neither knew of the other's existence.

'He has not been open with me,' said Her Ladyship,

frowning, 'but no matter now, for I shall cut him dead in future.'

'After his extraordinary behaviour today, so shall I,' said Randolph. 'You cannot imagine my astonishment to be attacked by one I thought a good friend.'

'He holds you responsible for the collapse of his prospects with Miss Harker. Your denial was forthright, Mr Joynes, yet if I look at him and then look at you, I cannot help myself from wondering if there is not some grain of truth in the charge — or is that too fanciful?'

Randolph turned sideways on the cab seat they shared to look at her more closely. There was a smile on her long aristocratic face that betokened more than amusement.

'You accused him of having a *cockstand* in his trousers in the young lady's presence,' she continued, her smile broadening.

At her ready use of a word not thought to be known to ladies, he gasped, then recovered himself and gave as good as he got.

'You're very free of expression, for a lady of title,' said he, 'I also asked Lorimer if he'd put a hand up Miss Harker's clothes for a feel of her pussy, and he did not deny it.'

'Nor did he confirm it,' Lady Fotherington replied. 'And as for my openness of expression, why should I not have the same latitude as a gentleman? It requires two to poke, one to part her legs and one to push his shaft in. Then since both sexes do it, I see no reason why both cannot talk about it.'

'Damned if you'll not be wanting equal rights next!' said he with a hand on the lady's knee. 'What then — will you insist on lying on top every time, to prove you're as good as any man?'

'I shall do whatever gives me most pleasure,' she replied, 'I always have and I mean to go on in the same course. Now, this business of feeling Miss Harker — in my opinion it is much more likely to have been *your* hand on her pussy.'

'None but the lowest bounder would name a lady whose pussy he had felt,' Randolph cried. 'Tell me if you will, dear lady, who are the friends we have in common, for I am mighty curious.'

'As it happens, Miss Violet Burkington-Hutchins is a niece of mine and I was interested to hear you say that Mr Mawby poked her at her coming-out. I knew that you had, for she told me of a handsome young fellow named Randolph Joynes who rogered her when she was still in the schoolroom, before her debut into society. You had her virginity, I believe. She still speaks of you fondly, though she is married this twelve-month past to Lord Henry Chevening and six or seven months gone in the family way.'

'Damme! How a chap's sins do find him out!' Randolph said cheerfully, much taken by the lascivious way in which his new acquaintance spoke.

'More particularly, though,' she went on, 'Alice Hamilton is a dear friend of mine, and from her I have heard much about you — not all of it to your credit.'

'Surely she can have no complaint against me?' he said, 'for I rendered her sterling service in the days of our friendship.'

'Quite so,' Lady Fotherington agreed, 'she awards you high marks for rogering. Her grievance against you is that you left her after too short a time and did not return to continue your pleasant games together. But she is a woman of the world, not a stay-at-home, and she has replaced you with two or three Guards officers who rotate their attendance on her as if doing military duty.'

The hansom stopped outside her imposing town house and as he hoped, she invited Randolph to come inside to continue their conversation over a glass of champagne, the hour being past six o'clock. A footman in blue livery opened the door with a deep bow to Her Ladyship, and took Randolph's top hat and stick.

She led him up a curving marble staircase, two flights, into a cosy sitting room he took to be her private retreat. A lady's maid bustled in before he was even seated, and was sent away to instruct someone named Ronan to bring a bottle of Veuve Cliquot at once.

Divested of her summer coat, Lady Fotherington showed herself to be in the simplest of silk dresses, cut somewhat after the French Empire style close to her form, to display her shapely hips, and very high-waisted, to throw into prominence titties of only modest size. Thinking it best there should be no sudden and unwelcome surprises if their acquaintance were to develop into any loser acquaintance, he enquired as to the whereabouts of Lord Fotherington.

'Abroad,' she told him, 'in Baden-Baden, to take the waters for his liverishness. Or so he said when he left, though I rather suppose that he has gone to roger a German Baroness or two.'

Ronan proved to be another footman, who brought in a bottle of bubbly and glasses and poured it for them. When he was gone again Randolph raised his glass to the lady and drank to her. She suggested that he quit his chair and sit alongside her on the sofa, which he willingly did.

In the cab, he had put a hand on her knee, and she had let him do so without reproof. He did so again now, the instincts of his entire adult lifetime driving him on to make trial of the lady, even though he was wholly unsure whether he would be able to achieve anything. Mr Percival lay limp in his hiding-place, and appeared to be in deepest slumber, even when Randolph turned up Lady Fotherington's skirts over her knees.

His hands began to wander gently over the uncovered treasures and she moved her legs with artful thoughtlessness to provide a view of a charming portion of her person — two smooth bare thighs! The very thought that a lady of the upper classes went out into the streets of London wearing no drawers blazed like a fire in Randolph's mind. How deliciously audacious of her, how truly aristocratic, to hold in contempt the polite and petty conventions of lesser mortals!

If only he had known this of her when they rode together in the cab from Bond Street, he would have given her a feel on the journey!

At last his gliding fingers reached the join of her legs and touched the centre of delight, her warm hairy pussy. It seemed to throb and palpitate in his hand, like a living creature. At the touch of his fingers on her dearest part, she hitched high her skirts and opened wide her legs, until Randolph could see the entire length of her fine slender thighs and the fringe of dark-brown hair that covered her cunny.

'Dear Lady Fotherington — what can the world offer lovelier than a warm cunny waiting to be poked,' cried Randolph.

'To be poked? Fie, sir,' said she. 'Nothing has been said about poking — I have given you no permission to do so. But you may play with my cunny, and whilst you do so you may call me Henrietta.'

Truth to tell, Randolph was relieved to hear her words, there being as yet no flicker of life from his shaft. He tickled her cunny lips expertly, and pressed a finger between them to find her button and tease it.

'You do that with a noticeable loving care,' said Henrietta, 'I take it that you enjoy playing with cunnies as much as doing them — is that so?'

Before he could reply, she was up off her bottom and kneeling on the sofa, her legs astride his knees and her dress held round her hips. The furry join of her thighs was no more than a handbreadth from Randolph's face, and he stared in warm admiration at her bared belly and dark bush.

Ah, the bitter irony of that moment, the sad mockery of Fate, that Henrietta was revealing to him the lovely secret charms of her soft little belly in which the button was sunk deep and a long lipped cunny almost hid from sight in dark-brown curls. All this was wasted on Randolph, for his shaft made no response, not even a twitch. His mind was filled with lust, but his loins were feeble and neuter.

Almost driven to distraction by his plight, he leaned forward to open Henrietta's split with trembling fingers and plunge his tongue into her.

'Ah yes,' sighed she at once, 'Alice Hamilton told me you had a way with your tongue that threw her into a perfect delirium of sensation. Bring me off, Randolph.'

He clasped the bare cheeks of her bottom in his hands to hold her close while he licked her button speedily. Her loins jerked back and forth, and in moments she gasped that she was coming off. Randolph gripped her tightly, to support her throughout a long and voluptuous climax of bliss.

When she was calm once more, though her limbs still shook to tiny after-spasms, she sat herself across his lap and dragged open his trousers to take out Mr Percival — and found him limp and small in her hand.

'What!' she cried out. 'You dare to insult me? I permit you access to my person and you have no cockstand? What are you — a eunuch? Or are you a damned Molly, preferring boys' bottoms to a juicy cunny?'

'God damn it to black perdition!' Randolph groaned. The caning of his bare backside had obviously not cured him of his lingering emotions of uneasiness about Dorothy's bottom and his unauthorised use of it. Shamefaced and stammering, he explained as best he knew how the dreadful misfortune that had befallen him only that day — after years of diligent poking. Lady Fotherington was not won round, for she was a lady who desired action and had no time for excuses.

'Confound you,' said she, annoyed by his condition, 'you've done me out of my pleasure! Lorimer would have managed one or two pokes, if you hadn't chased him away.'

'Believe me,' said Randolph miserably, 'you cannot be half as put out about my incapacity as I am. Yesterday afternoon I passed in rogering until my partner was half-dead with the exhaustion of coming off time after time — and today, yours is the second cunny I have felt and prepared for a poke, only to find myself in this wretched state.'

'Why?' Lady Fotherington demanded. 'Were you so wrung out yesterday that you have nothing left today — is that it?'

'No, it is more complex than that. Unless I mislead myself, I am paying in some way for taking advantage of Miss Harker when she lay in a swoon.'

'You claim that your conscience is preventing your shaft from doing its duty? Pish — what utter nonsense from a man of your reputation! Have you never before taken advantage of a young girl — what of Violet Burkington-

Hutchins? She was barely sixteen with not the least notion of what a male shaft could do to her, when you had her.'

'The truth is this, something held me back from taking young Miss Harker's maidenhead when she lay in my power and instead I ravished her bottom. Since then, it is as if a powerful spell has been laid on my mind, rendering me uneasy.'

'That be jiggered for a tale!' said Lady Fotherington, with more heat than propriety. 'I refuse to be cheated of my due without making my feelings known. Get down and kiss my ladylike backside, for that is all you are good for.'

So saying, she stood up and turned her back to him, raising her clothes to bare her small-cheeked aristocratic rump.

'At once!' she commanded briskly, as if he were a flunkey in her household, 'Do not keep me waiting in this, as well!'

His face scarlet with shame, Randolph slipped from the sofa to his knees behind her, grasped her thighs and kissed the twin cheeks of her bottom in submission.

'At least you know your place,' Lady Fotherington commented over her shoulder to him. 'Again, till I tell you to stop.'

He kissed her again, many times, then parted the cheeks and licked up the crease between them.

'I'll be damned, but you've got a letch for bung-holes!' Her Ladyship cried. 'You'll not roger mine, for I have no taste for backstairs poking. You shall pleasure me as before.'

She lowered herself gracefully on the sofa, sitting with her legs splayed wide and her summer dress up round her waist, the long lips of her pussy pulled slightly open by the posture to display the dewy moisture that gleamed inside. Randolph turned, still on his knees, and slid closer to stroke her bare belly.

'Still no cockstand?' she enquired, hoity-toity. 'How vexing for you. I can't be kept waiting, for I must come off again. If your shaft's no good, then use your tongue once more.'

Humiliated to be spoken to in this off-hand manner, Randolph slid his hands up her ivory-skinned thighs, which lay as fully open as a book to be read. He stared in disappointment at the soft pink lips that gleamed through her dark-haired thatch, and his fingers moved inexorably towards them to satisfy her and then leave, to hide his shame.

Henrietta Fotherington's pussy was neither tight virginal, nor yet loose and flabby, but somewhere nicely between – much used and ready, well adjusted to its purpose of engulfing stiff shafts and receiving the tribute of their gushing desire. Just the sort of pussy Randolph adored to poke if circumstances had been normal. Alas, they were not.

The tip of his middle finger titillated those enchanting lips to part them wider yet, and Henrietta awarded him a brief smile of encouragement. He bent forward, his face pressing between her naked thighs, and she spread her legs further to give him room in which to work. His mouth took possession of her pussy, causing a little cry of pleasure to spring from her as his tongue entered and rolled over her secret button.

For Lady Fotherington these were moments of bliss and triumph – she had a handsome young gentleman down on his knees before her, licking her cunny to bring her to the sexual spasm. After which she would rest for five minutes and then order him to do it again. Yet for Randolph these same moments were an ordeal – his once-proud shaft had betrayed him into an unmanly weakness, and in his debilitated condition he could do nothing more to this willing beauty than bring her off by use of his tongue!

Whether to hate her for using him as if he were a servant, or to admire her for allowing him to make such use of her person as he could, he was in doubt to decide. He wanted to vindicate his manhood by poking her, more than anything he ever wanted before in his life, yet Percival hung too soft and small even to thumb into a cunny.

Or did he? The stimulation of Henrietta's pussy seemed to be having some sort of mild effect — or was this the delusion of a mind tottering on the edge of complete breakdown? To settle the matter one way or the other, he put a hand down between his legs, opened his buttons and released his member. A tremor of hope passed through his mind, to find it somewhat engorged, though by no means stiff.

Her Ladyship lay back on the sofa, legs sprawling immodestly wide, her soul soaring up into the Celestial Sphere, lifted by the intensity of blissful emotion Randolph's tongue imparted. She neither knew nor cared what he did to himself, so long as he continued to tongue her towards the sensual paroxysm that she lived for.

Randolph's clasped hand slid up and down his part, to bring it to life, to make it go hard enough to plunge into the cunny he was licking. Perhaps because nothing else occupied his mind other than the process of bringing off Henrietta, his frantic efforts were rewarded with some measure of success. Mr Percival grew thicker and longer in his hand, and gratifyingly hard-on.

Henrietta was sobbing in joy as she fast approached the apex of felicity. For Randolph also, a crucial moment was close at hand. His tongue flicked furiously in the wet cunny before him and all his limbs shook from tremors that racked him from head to toe. His clasped hand gripped his shaft tightly, sliding up and down in quickstep rhythm.

At this moment there occurred the miracle he had prayed for. Mr Percival Proud leaped in his hand, whilst the pent-up desire in Randolph's belly swelled into an uncontrollable explosion. He thrust his tongue deep into Henrietta and heard her faint cry of bliss, at the instant that Mr Percival spurted the creamy fluid of virility in gushes, soaking the sofa cushion between Henrietta's parted thighs.

'Ah yes, yes, yes,' Randolph gasped into her hot palpitating pussy with each throb of his shaft, his soul relieved beyond measure that he had been able at last to come off and satisfy his tormented mind that his powers were undamaged.

When Henrietta became quiet, he pulled slowly away from her, to sit back on his heels. His sexual ejaculation had sprayed an inside thigh and she feeling the trickle on her flesh, reached down to rub her fingers in the warm slipperiness.

'Well!' she exclaimed. 'You did something after all!'

'Henrietta, you have put right whatever the Devil it was that ailed me,' Randolph said. 'I am more grateful than you can ever imagine — and if a good rogering is still to your liking, you shall have it.'

'Let me see this Lazarus raised from the tomb!' she cried.

She took him by the hand and drew him up to sit beside her on the sofa, then clasped Mr Percival in her soft hand and rolled him up and down.

'He isn't stiff enough yet,' said she, 'he's only half hard-on, after spending in the air. But if you are truly restored we shall not wait long for, according to Alice Hamilton, you've poked her four or five times in a row with scarce a pause for breath between. That's why I hoped for great things from you when I invited you here.'

'You shall not be disappointed, I swear it,' said Randolph, a degree of conviction he did not feel in his voice, being as yet uncertain as to his degree of manly strength.

'Properly spoken like a gallant gentleman!' said she. 'Lie on your back along the sofa, Randolph, so that I may render you every assistance in making a good recovery.'

Under her guidance, he stretched himself out on the sofa at full length, and Henrietta opened wide his waistcoat and tucked his shirt up to bare his belly and thighs — and his half-hard shaft, which she rubbed briskly. It was not long before she had induced that condition of useful stiffness she craved, and she requested Randolph to remain as he was, on his back, Percival straining upwards anxiously, whilst she sat over his hips, her knees either side of his waist, and spread her skirts over him.

Beneath the covering folds of her dress, her hand found his shaft and guided the head to her pussy, then impaled herself on it. Randolph heaved a long sigh of delight to feel the soft and velvet folds of her wet split enfolding him.

'Dear Lady Fotherington,' he said, 'my darling Henrietta, you are a saint direct from paradise to have brought on this happy transformation of my condition. When I entered this room with you, my shaft lay cold and lifeless and I veritably believed my joy in existence to be gone forever. Yet now the miracle has been worked and I feel the bodily spasm fast approaching, even though I have been lodged within your sweet cunny for so short a time! You have saved my sanity and I am in your debt.'

'Then you must pay your debt,' said she. 'Do not insult me by coming off the moment you are in me, as my husband used to in the days when I spread my legs for him. Instant discharge may satisfy a man, but it does nothing to gratify a woman's needs.'

'Have no fear!' he replied. 'Now I have regained control of myself, you shall have a full measure of sensation before the paroxysm overtakes you.'

He watched the smile of concentration on Henrietta's long and aristocratic face whilst she rode up and down on his embedded shaft, giving herself delicious tremors of bliss.

'How adorable you are!' he exclaimed. 'Mr Dobson's sublime lines express the situation admirably — you may know them:

> *Angelic creature, fashioned in such wise,*
> *With love-wan eyelids and love-wanton eyes,*
> *Unveil thy titties, show those wondrous toys,*
> *All naked to my hands, my lips. Our joys*
> *Shall endless be, I hear thy love-sick sighs*
> *And sink my shaft between thy rounded thighs,*
> *While on thy mouth I dote in loving kiss,*
> *And roger thee to soul-disturbing bliss!*

'Oh, how very romantic that is!' Henrietta cried. 'You shall put those lines on paper for me before you leave, so I may learn them by heart.'

Under the stimulation of her wet cunny sliding up and down on his shaft, it had grown thicker and longer, and throbbed in joy and gratitude for the pleasure it was receiving. Henrietta was staring down at his face, assessing the strength of his emotion and his nearness to the physical convulsion.

If at that moment a servant had entered the room, footman or maid, nothing of a sensual nature would have betrayed itself to inquisitive eyes, though Her Ladyship and her visitor were both only heartbeats away from the sexual spasm. True, his position lying on the sofa was very strange and hers, seated on his body, stranger still. But highly improper though their posture undoubtedly was, nothing of the truth was revealed, her skirts covering all — the intimate embrace of stiff shaft by wet cunny and the friction of wet flesh on wet flesh.

Lady Fotherington's face was flushed a bright pink and her breathing was rapid, for she like Randolph was at the brink of fetching off. She bounced on his shaft with frantic vigour, making the hard-used sofa creak beneath them, and Randolph felt the floodgates open in his belly and his essence surge free. The shudder through his body communicated itself to Henrietta, who at this supreme moment thrust her loins hard down on him to force his leaping shaft deep into her belly, and at the very instant his torrent of desire gushed out.

At the spurt of his hot elixir within her cunny, her eyes opened wide in a stare of ecstatic sensation. She bit her teeth together, clenched her fists and beat them against Randolph's covered belly, driving the breath out of him as he bucked under her and spent mightily.

When Randolph was finished he lay still and gazed up at her flushed face, trusting that his performance had been sufficient to improve matters between them. Henrietta sagged forward, for the moment satiated, and smiled down at him.

'That was a damned fine poke,' said Her Ladyship.

CHAPTER 15
The Path of True Love Never Did Run Smooth

Refreshed in spirit by the gratifications of his before-dinner escapade with Henrietta Fotherington, Randolph went to bed that night a happy man. Whatever malign influence had lain heavily upon him, he now believed it had been lifted, for his shaft had stood hard-on as readily as always and performed its pleasant duty with frantic enthusiasm.

Sometime during the night he woke in his bedroom in Cavendish Square in an exuberant state of mind, for he had dreamed about Dorothy Harker. In that dream he stood in her room to observe her morning toilet when she rose from bed. It was as Bella had described — darling Dorothy sat on a towel spread over a chair, a bowl of warm water on the floor between her feet, her night gown up round her waist. The maid knelt at her side to wash her lovely young pussy with teasing fingers.

When Bella told this to Randolph, she said that she brought off Dorothy every time she washed her, and sometimes twice or more. In the dream it happened otherwise — Dorothy glanced up from watching the maid's deft fingers stroking her soft young pussy and caught sight of Randolph standing with his back to the door. At once she smiled at him, and instructed Bella to stop what she did and dry her.

Bella looked at Randolph, disapproval on her face, but she obeyed her mistress and patted her pussy dry with the towel. Then Dorothy rose from the chair, her nightgown held up with one hand about her waist to expose all her belly and thighs, and she hurried on bare feet across the room to where Randolph stood. As is the curious way of it in dreams, where the normal considerations of the material world are suspended, he seemed to be wearing no trousers, only a frock coat and top hat.

Dorothy's dainty hands unbuttoned his coat and moved over his body, sending him into raptures of delight. She took firm hold of his hard-on shaft whilst she kissed him passionately, her bare thighs rubbing on his.

'You shall have me, my dearest,' she murmured.

Her hand brought his full-risen shaft to the entrance of her maidenly pussy and held it there, throbbing intensely. Randolph did nothing — she herself pushed her belly forward and sighed a long moan when she felt the swollen head pressed inside her.

It was a curious sort of poke — Dorothy's belly was squeezed against his, his strong shaft all the way up inside her. He did not tup her, nor she move on him, but they stood locked in that silent embrace, and he knew that the climax of sensation would be reached and his creamy flood would pump itself into her in two more seconds.

Instead, he woke up to find himself alone in bed, his shaft standing up like an iron bar in his nightshirt and throbbing powerfully. In his jubilation he clasped it in his hand whilst he spoke aloud into the dark, his words a hymn of praise to the female parts he loved the best:

'May God bless every pretty young pussy in the world!'

cried he. 'Bless every delicious one for the power it has to bring a man's shaft up hard-on in a trice! Bless each sweet warm pussy for the delight and sensations of bliss it can give to a man! Parsons and politicians may say what they like, but pussy is the source of all human happiness! How fortunate the man who finds one he can love between the soft swelling thighs of a lovely and amenable young female, who is as keen on poking as he! In the union of their parts lies the highest felicity that mankind may achieve! When they share a bed together, their joyful rogering is a foretaste of the divine happiness we are told shall be our portion in the Hereafter! Pish, let Heaven go hang — give me a lovely young pussy to poke every time!'

Whilst thus celebrating in words the pleasures of the sensual act, Randolph pulled his nightshirt up to his chest slid his legs wide apart. With the affection due to an old and valued friend, he rolled Mr Percival Proud up and down, whilst in his fervid imagination he thought he spied a vision of dear Dorothy as he had seen her on her sofa, her dress pulled up, the slit of her drawers open, to reveal her curly-haired pussy between smooth-skinned white thighs.

In sad reality this was the moment he had made the fearful discovery that his shaft was unready — but alone now in his bed Mr Percival was hard and thick, and bounding in his hand.

'Oh Dorothy, I shall have you!' Randolph gasped. I shall get this shaft of mine into your pussy, and flood you with my cream for the very first time! I'll bring you off, I swear it!'

His hand slid up and down his quivering shaft until the frenzy of sensation seized him. His legs jerked wildly and his essence came gushing out in rapid jets that soaked the sheets above him.

'Dottie, my dearest Dottie!' he gasped out to each wet throb of his shaft. 'This is how I shall poke you, again and again!'

Mr Percival, freed from whatever mental fetters had bound him, bucked and reared and spurted to full satisfaction, after which Randolph gave a sigh of content and fell asleep. He had no more dreams that night, but when Lizzie brought his morning tea his shaft was stiff once more.

He told her to leave the tea and sit on the bed beside him, and to pull up her clothes so that he might have a feel of her pussy. She had become extremely submissive since he had started on this course of handling her in the mornings and poking her, and obeyed him without a word. It was scarcely necessary to ask before she had thrown aside the bedclothes and pulled up his nightshirt to bare Mr Percival, pointing stiffly upwards.

'Take my shaft in your hand,' Randolph commanded, 'and play with him – you know what is required.'

Lizzie blushed bright pink, but all the same she clasped his hard and heavy shaft in the palm of her hand and bounced it up and down very pleasantly. Randolph lay at his ease, his eyes closed, indulging himself in a shameful fantasy.

'My darling Dorothy,' he murmured, not caring if the maid heard him or not, 'how nicely you handle my shaft! I dreamed I rogered you, my dear, and woke up in this state you find me in. The soft touch of your hand throws me into ecstasies of delight unequalled before!'

Whatever thoughts Lizzie may have had at hearing herself thus addressed as *Dorothy* she said nothing, but continued to rub firmly at the straining shaft she held, whilst, meanwhile, her thighs were spread to let Randolph's hand fumble at her pussy.

'How you raise my passions!' he sighed. 'But a moment yet and you will cause me to fetch off, Dorothy!'

Truth to tell, the make-believe that he was being manipulated by Miss Harker and not the under-maid, sent tremors of bliss through Randolph that made him gasp and pant, and his belly to twitch wildly. His nervous system had reached the limit of its toleration and was about to discharge his emotions in a spasm of climactic sensation. His fingers gripped Lizzie's bare pussy with cruel strength and thick white essence gushed like a tall fountain from his upright shaft.

When he became tranquil and Lizzie had wiped his belly dry, she ventured to ask timidly whether it had been to his liking.

'Very competent, Lizzie,' said he, 'you've a useful hand on a man's shaft now I've taught you.'

She flushed red at his arrogant tone, but when he ordered her to lie on the bed beside him and raise her dress to her waist, she did so without protest. Randolph propped himself up on his elbow and with inquisitive fingers pulled open her drawers. He felt her pussy to see if it had become moist with longing, but could detect nothing.

To be truthful, having been pleasured by, in his imagination, sweet and virginal Miss Dorothy Harker, he had little appetite for Lizzie's easily available cunny just then. Yet his natural urge to domineer would not let him send her away before he had again demonstrated his mastery over her.

'Put your fingers to your cunny and fetch yourself off,' was his order to her.

Lizzie's face blushed brick-red at the words, and her sense of outrage was great enough to refuse to obey him in this. He, not to be denied, took her wrist and forced her arm down, until her work-roughened hand lay across her belly.

'No, for shame!' she cried.

Randolph pushed her hand lower, till it was between her legs. Still she said him *nay* even when he moved her fingers over her bush and pressed them against her cunny.

'Do it for me!' he said masterfully, 'I insist!'

'Please don't make me, sir,' she pleaded. 'Poke me if you want, but don't humiliate me by asking me to do that.'

'The damned insolence of it!' said Randolph, enjoying to the full this show of resistance to be broken down. 'Do as I tell you, girl, or it will be the worse for you!'

Intimidated by his vague threat, her cheeks afire with shame and her eyes tight shut, Lizzie let her fingers trail over her pussy lips.

'Faster,' Randolph commanded. 'Faster, girl — open it and stick your finger inside! Do not pretend to me that you've not done it to yourself before — I'm sure you do it nightly.'

'Oh no, sir, no!' she exclaimed sincerely. 'How can you say such a thing!'

Whether she did it nightly, or weekly, was of no importance. She knew how to go about it, and there being no other way but to obey Randolph, she set herself to comply with his wishes.

His greedy eyes devoured her pussy. The sight of it drew him irresistibly to her, just as if it were a strong magnet and the hard shaft under his nightshirt a bar of iron to move towards it under the pull of its attraction.

'I am so ashamed, sir,' Lizzie whispered, 'to do this with you watching . . . it's not right.'

'Don't be a little ninny, girl,' he said forcefully, 'how can it be shameful for you to handle your own property and for me to observe it? Lascivious enjoyment resides not only in poking but in every amusing game the human mind can devise for the employment of shaft and pussy. If then it is permissible to handle each other's parts when a man and a female are together, then it cannot be shameful to handle their own privates by way of diversion when they rest between pokes.'

'I'm sure it must be wrong,' Lizzie protested.

'Fiddlesticks! There can be no objection to indulgence in these innocent sensual amusements, save the false prejudices of canting humbugs, whether of the cloth or the medical profession — for I have proved in my own person that even the greatest of them is mistaken — Dr William Acton's strictures on the heavy consequences of frequent indulgence in the sexual spasm are so much nonsense! I can do it again and again — and always will.'

Lizzie only sighed, not understanding of what it was he spoke so eloquently.

'Stop that miserable noise,' said Randolph. 'Pull the lips of your cunny open wider and let me see the button.'

Although the under-maid sighed and complained without cease at this gross abuse of her modesty, she continued to play with her pussy as ordered until she had progressed far along the pathway that leads to climactic bliss. Then her plaints ended at last, and she held wide the pink lips of her slit with one hand and with the joined fingers of the other rubbed at the slippery rose-pink bud that was exposed.

Randolph observed that she would shortly come off, and bring his fun to an early conclusion.

'Stop now!' he said. 'Move your fingers away from your pussy at once — at once, I say!'

Lizzie's eyes opened and she gaped open-mouthed and red-faced at him, not fully comprehending what he was at with her.

'You've given me a stand that needs to be taken care of,' he said. 'Leave your pussy alone, you slut, and take a hold of my shaft and give it a good feel.'

What he intended was to inflict the suffering of frustration on Lizzie, by causing her to stop when she was almost at the peak of her sensation. That was real mastery — to halt her when she was within moments of bringing herself off! He would have her stroke his new-risen shaft until he too was on the verge of spending, then disappoint her hopes of being rogered by putting her on her back and ravaging her rear entrance — for it was in his mind that he would feel easier about Dorothy if he took the pains to accustom himself to backstairs ingress.

In this he had reckoned without the vital force of Nature, if only the Nature of a downtrodden servant-girl. Lizzie was much too close to her culminating moment to be able to obey, even if she would, his cruel command. Her fingers rubbed furiously in her wet split, and her heels drummed on the bed.

'Oh, oh, oh!' she exclaimed, her back rising in an arch as she brought herself off in quick spasms.

'Damn you for a trollop!' Randolph gasped, astonished to see her coming off against his order. 'You've cheated me!'

Lizzie gave no sign that she heard his words or was aware of his anger. As for depriving Randolph of anything at all that was rightfully his, she was too far gone in sensual delight to hide anything from his sight. Her legs strained wide apart, her narrow loins bucked, and her hand flickered up and down at her wet pussy.

Randolph was undone by this display of female gratification — with a low moan of despair he threw himself between Lizzie's legs, his hand rubbing and pulling at his stiff shaft. His belly rested on hers and without a pause, he plunged six inches of hard gristle deep into her pussy, an rogered away for dear life.

'Oh sir, sir!' Lizzie gasped, her eyes bulging in her head, to feel herself being poked so fiercely. 'You'll kill me!'

'Yes,' he moaned back, 'I'll damned well kill you stone dead with poking, you slut! Shut up and keep coming off!'

Lizzie gurgled and gasped, kicking up her legs either side of him as he plunged in and out. In six more strokes he attained the very acme of sensation and spurted his hot lust deep into her quaking belly. She squealed and humped her body under him, while he spent in her to the very last drop.

After a sustaining breakfast of kedgeree and kippers, toast and best Oxford marmalade, Randolph took a turn about Cavendish Square, to settle his thoughts. He was in an exceptionally fine mood as he strolled round by the railings, even going so far as to throw a penny piece to an urchin in a peaked cap who was at work sweeping clean the road crossing.

The significance of his dream was clear — his heart was set on Miss Dorothy Harker. She came to him in visions of the night and asked him to have her, she stroked his belly and his stiff shaft and slipped it into her sweet little pussy. A fantasy of the night it may have been, but when he had tested the truth or otherwise of his nocturnal longing by having his shaft stroked in broad daylight by the under-maid, a veritable paroxysm of joy had been the outcome.

In this way, as he sauntered around the Square, tipping his hat to those other residents whom he encountered, Randolph at last persuaded himself that he was deeply in love with Dorothy. This conclusion was a bit of a facer for him, given as he was to playing the field and scattering his largesse with careless abandon. It threatened a change in his mode of daily life.

There had never been any doubt in Randolph's mind, not since he had first experienced the sensual spasm, that to be in love implied and required getting his shaft up the girl's pussy. Otherwise, it was merely sentimental rot. Therefore it followed that he must poke Dorothy Harker, soon and often. In spite of her apparent willingness to let him do so on the last occasion they had met, with curious results, he was tolerably certain that the moment he declared his undying love for her, she would close her legs tightly together and wait for a proper proposal of marriage.

'Confound it!' he said aloud, and hit the iron railings of the Square with his walking stick. 'If marriage is the price to be paid for rogering Dorothy at will, then so be it! I shall take a cab to Paddington after lunch and throw myself as her devoted suitor at her darling feet! She's of a decent family with land-holdings, and the pater will approve my choice.'

His mind made up, he returned home to change into his newest grey frock coat, and set off for his club, to lunch lightly and put the finishing touches to the elegant little speech he meant to deliver on his knees to his beloved. His liveliest hope was that, when Dorothy had accepted his proposal and given him her promise of betrothal, she would graciously allow him to set the seal on their agreement by giving her a jolly good poke.

Over lunch he chatted to a couple of his chums at the club — Billy Toothe-Tarkington, who knew something about proposing to a girl, he having been engaged to be married to the beautiful Miss Ella Blenkinsop for a twelvemonth or more; and Gussy Cranborough, who was in love with Charlotte, youngest daughter of Lord Fitchnewton, but could make no progress at all with his suit because the girl's father opposed it, thinking him of too restricted prospects.

After a bottle or two of wine, Gussy's advice was practical and useful. Win the lady's heart by taking her a large bouquet of red roses, he said, and some little trinket of a present to show her how thoughtful you are towards her. This had succeeded admirably with Charlotte, who worshipped him, but had no effect on her tyrannical pater. Billy had no advice to offer, but only smiled mysteriously when he spoke in the vaguest of terms about the bliss of being engaged to be married. From that Randolph deduced that he was rogering Miss Blenkinsop regularly.

Thus primed, he walked along Piccadilly after lunch to where he knew there to be a flower-seller on the corner with Regent Street, and there purchased for a couple of shillings every red rose the flower girl had to offer. For another shilling or two he could have had the girl as well, up against the wall in the mews, but his heart was set on Dorothy. To complete the advice he had been given, he strolled on into Shaftesbury Avenue, to the shop where Maria Peabody was employed.

His intention was to buy some small gift to take with him to Dorothy — a pair of gloves, perhaps, or a pretty fan, it being unseemly to take anything more personal. After they were truly engaged, he would make her secret presents of drawers, to have the pleasure of assisting her into them before rogering her on the sofa. Those were pleasures for the future, not for this important day of proposal.

When he entered the shop he was somewhat taken aback to find the proprietor present and behind the counter, though there was no good reason for surprise, for commonsense said that Mr Wyck would be more in than out. It was seeing him standing alongside pretty Maria that displeased Randolph. Mr Wyck was, as Randolph had thought, a man in his middle years, stout of body, with whiskers down his cheeks and a bald patch on the front of his head. He wore a vulgar turned-down collar and a tightly buttoned jacket, under which a paunch showed.

Maria concealed her embarrassment very well, and brought out fans and gloves to show Randolph while her employer looked on benignly and held forth on the high quality of the merchandise. If only the unwanted proprietor had been absent, Randolph would have slipped into the back room with Maria for a quick feel of her pussy, even though his mind was set on Dorothy. With a wink and a grin he conveyed this to Maria, and she blushed faintly.

Notwithstanding, it was disagreeable to contemplate that Wyck could at any time take Mara into the stock room and do as he pleased with her. The wretched shopkeeper had short and stubby fingers, Randolph noted — those fingers would toy with Maria's pussy later that day, after closing time. And horror of horrors — Wyck's wick would force itself into her and come off in that pretty slit Randolph had seen but been denied.

How monstrous it was, how infuriating! There stood the stout and cloddish shopkeeper, an ingratiating smile on his greedy face, and here stood, almost within arm's length of him, a most lovely and lascivious young female — a female Randolph had the most sudden urgent letch to poke, though it would postpone for a little while his visit to Dorothy.

Yet there was nothing to be done about it. The vile tradesman was in the saddle, so to speak, and there was no way to unseat him without bringing about Maria's dismissal. In the end, with gritted teeth behind his apparent indifference, Randolph bought a painted fan, had it wrapped, and left the shop in a far worse mood than when he entered it. He found a hansom cab to take him t Paddington Green, and sat fuming and calling down curse on the heads of shopkeepers who take advantage of pretty female employees and vent their low lust on their tender bodies. That activity should be reserved solely for gentlemen!

At the house in Paddington Green he plied the knocker briskly and the door was opened by Bella. She stared at him and at the bouquet of roses he carried, the strangest expression on her face. Randolph smiled at her and reached out to give a friendly squeeze to her vast round titties, but she drew back and told him that she could not let him enter.

'That be damned!' cried he, impatient of delays, and pushed past her into the entrance hall, and straight up the stairs to the apartment rented by the Harkers. Bella came scurrying after him, insisting that he was not to disturb Miss Dorothy, and in her haste forgetting her position and almost taking hold of his coat tails. As things were, he was nippier on his pins than she was, and gained the landing well ahead of her.

Not taking the time to tap at the sitting-room door, for fear Bella would overtake him and engage in insolent wrangling, he set his hand to the knob, turned it and pushed open the door. The scene that confronted him halted him dead in his tracks in the doorway. Lorimer Mawby was rogering Dorothy on the sofa!

The bodice of her dress was open to bare her plump titties, and the skirt was up round her waist to uncover her drawers — the very ones purchased from Wyck's shop, Randolph recognised. She had one stockinged leg stretched out along the sofa, and the other hanging over the edge, her foot on the floor — the posture requiring her legs to be widely apart.

The slit of her fine cambric drawers was also pulled apart by her position, the bare pink lips of her cunny and her neat tuft of curls on show to her companion. Lorimer had taken off his frock coat and his trousers were unbuttoned for his stiff shaft to stand forth in readiness — a shaft which, Randolph saw with distaste, was the equal of his own in length and thickness.

Neither of the lovers heard the sitting-room door open, being too engrossed in their sensual pleasures. Even as Randolph's eyes bulged astounded from his head, Lorimer treated himself to a feel of Dorothy's pussy, making her tremble and sigh. Then he kissed the fingers that had been privileged to touch her maiden charm and slipped them into her.

'This is so very indecent, Lorimer, my dearest,' Randolph caught her murmur, 'yet I would not have it otherwise . . .'

The blood drummed in Randolph's temples until he thought he would fall down in a swoon, to see Lorimer present the head of his shaft to the mark and sink it into Dorothy with a sharp push. She cried out a little, at losing her maidenhead, but her arms were about Lorimer, hugging him to her.

'Lorimer, Lorimer,' she gasped, as he thrust sturdily in and out of her pussy, and then, sooner than would be expected, her crisis of sensation arrived to the stab of his hard-on shaft.

'My darling!' Lorimer exclaimed, his voice choked by fierce emotions at the first throb of his spending. 'You are mine now, my dearest Dorothy, all mine!'

Randolph stood with a black scowl on his face to see darling Dorothy's stockinged legs kicking up in the air, and Lorimer's trousered bottom driving to and fro between her spread thighs as he spurted his desire into her.

To find himself forestalled in courtship of Dorothy by that fool of a Lorimer Mawby was more than could be borne! Randolph threw his bouquet of roses furiously across the sitting room, hoping he might score a hit on Lorimer's bouncing backside. The flowers fell short, landing harmlessly on the carpet, while the lovers continued to sigh and squirm in bliss, all unaware that they were observed.

Randolph turned on his heel and strode away, casting a look of detestation at the cowering Bella, and leaving the sitting-room door wide open.

of dear Alex Power : do not know.'

'Why might she be?' asked Randolph. 'A bored who todays you among girls to bring down your cocktand?'

CHAPTER 16
A Convenient
Arrangement is Reached

Consumed by anger and jealousy at having seen Dorothy Harker being rogered by another man, Randolph flounced out of the house and hailed the first cab that passed by. Before long, he was back at his club in St James, where he found that Billy Toothe-Tarkington had left, but Gussy Cranborough was well into his second bottle of port wine.

Randolph joined him, sent for another bottle, and drank fast, being soon in a mood to confide in Gussy the failure that had been inflicted on him by a young woman he cherished, and the awful humiliation he had experienced to see her bestowing her priceless maidenhead on another. Unrequited love, said he, was the very devil, and he wondered how Gussy bore with fortitude Lord Fitchnewton's ban on an engagement to his daughter.

'It takes it out of a chap, keeping a stiff upper lip all the time,' said Gussy, who was by now a trifle glassy-eyed from the quantity of vintage Cockburn he had drunk since lunch. 'How I would bear up under the strain without the solace of dear Mrs Potter, I do not know.'

'Who might she be?' asked Randolph. 'A bawd who keeps you in young girls to bring down your cockstand?'

Gussy denied it indignantly, and claimed never to indulge his lust with doxies out of respect for Charlotte, the woman he loved and whom one day he hoped to make his wife, perhaps when Lord Fitchnewton was dead and gone and his eldest son, Hampton, succeeded to the title. Mrs Mavis Potter was, he explained, a dear and sympathetic female friend who lived in a villa he had rented for her by Wandsworth Common.

'By George, Gussy — you keep a woman for poking!' Randolph cried. 'Tell me about her — what class of person is she? Where did you meet her? Is she a good poke?'

Augustus Cranborough was far enough gone in his cups to have no objection to acquainting his good friend Randolph with some of the details of the case. He had met Mrs Potter on top of a horse-bus by Green Park, said he, on a rainy evening when there was not a cab to be had. She was a handsome well-fleshed woman of eight and twenty, in a dark coat and hat, with a fur wrapped round her neck. She was sheltering from the rain under her open umbrella and, there being no other place available, Gussy took a seat beside her on the bench.

He had left or lost his own umbrella somewhere that day, and sat exposed to the downpour as the bus rattled along, until the tender-hearted female next to him took pity and said he might share hers. Deeply grateful, he edged close to her and thought it no more than polite to introduce himself. She returned the favour, and they looked at each other with mutual liking. One thing followed from another, as the saying is, and instead of returning to their own homes, they found themselves becoming better acquainted in a rented room in Pimlico.

'By the Lord Harry!' cried Gussy. 'It was a damn fine poke, that first time with Mavis! There was a good fire burning in the grate, and we sat warm and snug, she on my lap, while I had a good feel of her titties. She has a good pair on her — not over-large, but nicely shaped and soft to handle. There we were together, chatting away, and she kissing my cheek now and then whilst I put a hand up her clothes. Her thighs moved apart to open the way to me, and we fell silent and joined our mouths in a long kiss when I fingered her cunny.'

'You've a talent for story-telling,' said Randolph, who was enthralled by his friend's frank account. 'What did her cunny feel like, Gussy?'

'There's no way to describe it — it was soft and hairy, with warm lips that parted easily to my touch. Damn it, Randolph, no words can capture the feel of a female article. We sat as if we were mesmerised, Mavis in the lascivious enjoyment of having her cunny fingered, I in the feeling of it. What more can I say of the moment?'

'Did she remain passive throughout?'

'Not she! When I'd made her cunny wet and slippery with my fingers, she exclaimed, *Let's have your trousers undone and see what you've got to offer me*, and an instant later she had out my shaft and dandled it between her fingers.'

'A sensible female who knows what she wants from a man,' was Randolph's comment. 'What then?'

'Before much time had passed we made our way across the room to the bed,' said Gussy. 'She took off her dress and drawers to lie on her back, the front of her chemise turned up to bare her thighs and belly. She has a great thick bush of reddish curls between her legs — a sight for sore eyes, believe me! I lay beside her and fluttered my fingers in her wet cunny, while she handled me until I was halfway coming off. *Oh, I must have you, Mavis!* I cried out, and at once she spread her legs wide for me. My frock coat was off and my trousers — I pulled my shirt up and laid my bare belly on hers.'

'A fine and comfortable poke,' said Randolph, 'no haste, no fuss — I prefer that myself, sometimes. At other times I would rather show off my mastery of the female slit. But go on, do.'

'What more is there to say?' asked Gussy. 'My aching shaft found the way easily enough into her cunny and I gripped hard the cheeks of her behind whilst I poked and she jerked her belly up to meet my thrusts. *That's marvellous*, Mavis cried, *I haven't had a poke for a week*! Her words threw me at once into a perfect frenzy of poking, my belly beating on hers in a rapid tattoo that stirred overpowering sensations in both of us. Her fingernails clawed down my flesh from shoulder-blades to rump, and I fetched off like the firing of a cannon.'

'Evidently it was a first-rate poke, for you continued your association with her,' said Randolph pensively. 'Why so, when so many pretty willing young females can be had for a sovereign or two anywhere in the West End?'

'I paid Mavis nothing for the poke,' said Gussy hotly, 'both of us did it for the pure pleasure of it. I arranged to see her again the next night, and then again the next, and after a week or so I came to realise that Mavis was filling an urgent need in my life.'

'Certainly,' said Randolph, 'the urgent need we all feel for a daily poke. What interests me most is why you continue so long with the same female.'

'I was — and I am — deeply in love with my darling Charlotte Fitchnewton,' said Gussy. 'I cannot look at another woman, so intense is the flame of my love and desire for Charlotte. The obduracy of her pater prevents the consummation of our love — I have for the past twelvemonth had no other consolation than my own hand on my shaft whilst I gaze fondly on a photograph of my dearest girl.'

'A twelvemonth without rogering – Good God!' Randolph cried, 'Fitchnewton should be made to sit with a bare bum on his own coronet, for putting you to such torment!'

'I have on more than one occasion, in deep distress, picked a young whore from the ranks along Haymarket and gone with her to her room,' said Gussy, 'only to find that, be she as pretty as a picture and hot for it as a bitch in season, my shaft refuses to stand, for in my mind I can think only of Charlotte watching me and I can do nothing.'

'Damme!' said Randolph. 'A pretty pickle to be in!'

'But you see,' said Gussy, 'with Mavis it is otherwise. When I first felt her pussy, no reproachful vision of dear Charlotte interposed between us. Then as now, when I lie upon her belly and roger her, I have no concern but the poke itself. Oh happy circumstance that I may fetch off without the least regret in Mavis's throbbing cunny! Do you wonder that I have continued with a woman who alone of her sex can afford me a fragment or two of pleasure to mitigate the pain of my separation from Charlotte?'

'All is clear to me now, Gussy. I find your arrangement to be admirable. How long is it since you installed her in lodgings at Wandsworth?'

'Nothing so mean as lodgings,' Gussy replied at once, 'I have rented a villa there, for which I pay a rent of twenty-five pounds a year. For the past five months or so, I have been there four times a week and rogered my fill.'

'It appears to me that what you have there are the conjugal pleasures without the inconvenience of marriage,' said Randolph in a thoughtful tone.

He remained at the club in conversation with Gussy until after six o'clock, then set out at an easy pace on foot, by way of St James's Square. His noddle was abuzz with lewd thought and speculation on the incessantly interesting topic of females and that most necessary item between their legs.

In retrospect, his escapade with Dorothy Harker had led him to nothing but trouble and unease, from the time he had found by chance an opportunity to knot-hole her, to this afternoon he had called to propose marriage to her, only to find her being poked on the sofa by another man!

Indeed, the very thought that he had been about to propose so serious a course as marriage to any woman at all, and thereby ruin his life of pleasure — the very memory made his blood run cold. As a wife, Dorothy would be a good poke for a half-year or so, young and frisky and apt for bedtime games — but motherhood and young children would put a stop to that, he suspected.

Her face would lose its youthful bloom under the endless care of parenthood, her titties would drop, her belly sag . . . how sad it was, how very sad, and yet that was Nature's great scheme of things for the female sex. He could recall some lines on it by Mr William Wordsworth:

When years ago, I Lucy loved
and she was but thrice five,
With eyes that flashed in amorous glow,
The prettiest girl alive!

Her lovely titties, round and fresh,
My shaft stood when I felt;
Her darling pussy, warm and soft,
Beneath its silky pelt!

> *But see her now — with children eight,*
> *Her bubbies swoll'n and coarse;*
> *Her burly shapeless dumpy frame,*
> *Hind-quarters like a horse!*

'No, the Devil take young virgins,' said Randolph to himself, 'for all such are a man-trap baited with honey, and the unwary enter this sweet trap between maiden's thighs, lured into it by a standing shaft. Unless they spend quick and pull out and run for their life, they perish in the embrace, perish by stages of boredom and sameness, perish slowly and most miserably when the first fine careless rapture of rogering turns at last stale and unexciting.'

Dr William Acton, whose doctrines Randolph held to be more or less true, although he despised the doctor's penny-pinching morality, had summed up the tragic lot of the married in a few well-chosen words:

As soon as the married female conceives, during the nine months that follow she experiences no sexual excitement, and therefore the consequence is that sexual desire in the husband is greatly diminished and the act of copulation takes place but rarely. After the birth, while she is suckling a child, the call made on her vital forces by the organs secreting milk annihilate all sexual emotions. As it is proved that a reciprocity of desire is necessary to a large extent to excite the male, we need feel no surprise to observe that, in the sanctity of married life, excessive indulgence is very rare, for the sensual feelings in the man become by degrees calmed down and extinguished.

That be damned for a Fate, thought Randolph, for if a

man has no letch for poking, he is well advanced towards old age and the tomb, though he be but thirty.

On the other hand, he had little regard, now he thought about it with care and logic, for titled ladies and all other society figures, pretty or not, such as Alice Hamilton and her friend, Lady Fotherington. These females and their ilk were fine for an evening's poking, but because of their elevated position in life they thought themselves able to demand at any time of day they chose an instant cockstand and a fast servicing.

They gave no heed to whether their companion of the moment had a letch to roger them or not. Their own female wishes were paramount, and this was a reversal of the proper roles of male and female. It was a gentleman's right to say when he wished to roger a woman, not the other way about.

Indeed, Alice Hamilton had all but worn him out with her keen relish for constant poking, so that he had given her up before long. Henrietta Fotherington had easier manners and conducted herself in a less Harpy-like manner in the bedroom, yet she too wanted her pound of flesh — or more precisely, her six inches of hard flesh, over and over, until it ceased to be interesting for a gentleman of quality.

Besides, confound it all, Henrietta was no longer young. She was not far off forty and, to Randolph, a gap of fifteen years between their ages put her in almost the same generation as his revered Mama. A gentleman of breeding made no impolite reference to a lady's age, whether he poked her or not, but it was impossible not to be aware that Henrietta Fotherington's titties were starting to droop and there were wrinkles appearing across her belly.

What then remained, if neither young gentlewomen or letching society ladies would meet the case? London was full of pretty young doxies, of course, costing only a few pounds for the best of them. Yet since he had passed his sixteenth birthday he had poked so many young whores that he was tired of their ways and wanted a change.

He enjoyed their skill in bringing a chap off, and the total willingness they exhibited to let a client do with them and to them whatever strange thing his fancy prompted. At a mere word a doxy picked up in Cremorne Gardens, or elsewhere, would get down on her knees and take a shaft into her mouth — and use her tongue on it until a chap spent fully.

Never in a lifetime would Miss Dorothy Harker be persuaded to lick a hard-on shaft, not even when she became Mrs Lorimer Mawby and the shaft was her lawful husband's, Randolph was sure about that. Nor would she ever permit Lorimer to make use of other orifices after they were wed — Randolph could take pride in having had the one and only use of her knot-hole.

Fortunately, of that she was still unaware, and would remain so forever, unless her maid Bella took it upon herself one day to reveal what had been done when Dorothy lay in a faint on the sofa. Then what of it? As Lorimer's wife, she would shy away from the least hint of scandal and keep her secret close. Poor Lorimer was welcome to her as wife, and to whatever he could get from her in the way of poking.

Meanwhile, what was to be done to satisfy Randolph's need for a sentimental attachment to a female as devoted to rogering as he was himself? A year before he had been head over heels in love with chestnut-haired Mrs Theodora Danty whose husband was away from their home in Camden Town very often, and for weeks at a time, attending to his employment of overseeing the laying of new permanent ways for the London and North Eastern Railway Company.

Being a full-blooded woman of five and twenty, Theodora

Danty had early succumbed to Randolph's dashing good looks and they indulged themselves very frequently in sensual delight. An age of blissfulness was compressed into less than a year, and never in their lives would he or she forget the delicious transports caused by the stiff insertion of his shaft into her pussy, time after time. However often they repeated their amatory exercises they were both thrown into voluptuous paroxysms at the stirring up of their Nature by his ravishing instrument and by the ready way in which Theodora received his assault, and returned it.

So lively and so repeated were the delicious enjoyments that together they participated in, that Theodora was brought into the family way, and to resolve her predicament she went north to lodge with her husband, declaring to him that she was alone too much. After a week or two of lawful rogering with him, she returned to London well able when the time came to persuade her spouse that the babe in her belly was his doing.

For another month or so, Randolph tried to revive the lively joy of their earlier days, but knowing her pussy to have been used by Mr Danty at his lodgings in Sunderland had lessened his appetite for it, though it was still freely at his disposal. When Theodora was four months gone, Randolph broke off with her altogether, declaring that she must lead a calmer life now that motherhood loomed near.

It disappointed her to lose him but she saw the good sense of his advice, and accepted by way of a parting gift a hundred guineas, with which to provide a layette when her child was born, and to be an endowment for its future. His child proved to be a girl, Theodora sent to inform him, when the happy event took place.

Even now, long afterwards, Randolph thought of dear Theodora with rueful lust, and as he continued his stroll from his club towards Haymarket, his shaft rose with his trousers in loving memory of the many days and nights of luxurious rogering he had of her. *Ah, Percival*, said he in his secret thoughts, *you were well provided for in those days, with a wet pussy awaiting your pleasure whenever you chose!*

In King Charles Street he overtook and passed by a man of his own age — not a gentleman, but a person poorly dressed in what must be described as a threadbare brown jacket and a billycock hat. The hat was brushed and the man's boots clean, from which Randolph deduced that he was a lowly but respectable employee in some nearby commercial enterprise, making his way home. A copying clerk, or something similar, paid thirty shillings a week.

Such creatures had not the easy access to soft young pussies that Randolph enjoyed, nor was there any reason why they should have. Even a two shilling poke in the dark standing against a wall was more than they could afford from their wages, and the first pussy they ever got their shaft into was on their wedding night. Their wives fell pregnant regularly, but that was the only pussy available, and they must get what pleasure from it they could.

In passing the fellow, who moved to the kerb to allow passage to his better, Randolph stared curiously into his face. He had a worried look about him, but that meant little — the working classes normally looked worried. How wide the abyss set between himself and this clerk of a man, Randolph thought — suppose he tapped the fellow on the shoulder and astonished him with the information that in the space of the last four weeks, the Hon Randolph Joynes had rogered no less than nine different females — maidservants, whores, society ladies? To say nothing of the time he had bung-holed a young gentlewoman in a fainting fit.

It was tempting to bowl an inferior over, but on reflection Randolph decided against the prank. Envy of the upper classes was a dangerous emotion in these days of Chartism and insolent workers demanding social reforms. Let the clerk go to his hovel and his squalling brats and console himself with his dismal wife if he could, happy in his ignorance that Randolph intended to make voluptuous use of a young cunny that evening, even if he had to pay a couple of guineas for it.

By the time Randolph reached the Haymarket and turned towards Piccadilly, he had lost the desire to choose a young doxy from the score or more waiting there for customers. Instead, he had come to the conclusion that he ought to take Gussy Cranborough as his example and provide himself with a fresh young female of middling class and education for a regular poke. A woman with no great prospects of marriage or advancement, was the ticket, a woman who would be honoured by a friendship with the son of an earl and give good value in return.

Not a whore, of course — it would be folly to become involved beyond a quick paid-for poke with a street woman. They lied and cheated when they could, they were unreliable and untrustworthy — in short, they were qualified for nothing more than a poke in a hired room. Nor did he want a servant, for having rogered the entire female staff of his Cavendish Square home, Lizzie being only the last of them, he could not bear their ingratiating way and their total ignorance of anything beyond cleaning, brushing and serving.

What he wanted, he saw clearly, was a young woman who had not lost all modesty, though she had had a lover before, a female with some refinement of manner, though not one of his own class hoping to be his equal. A pretty young female of the middling class, clean, cheerful, amusing, hot-blooded for a poke at any time. And who matched this description better than the shop girl in Shaftesbury Avenue — Maria Peabody?

It wanted ten minutes to seven o'clock when he stood outside Wyck's shop and, gazing through the window, he saw Maria alone, putting articles away in their boxes and tidying up prior to closing. Wyck might be in the back room, reckoning up the day's takings and waiting for Maria to close up and join him, to give her a poke before he departed for the bosom of his family.

Faint heart ne'er won fair lady, said Randolph aloud, though he could not recall which poet had penned the immortal line. He pushed open the shop door, setting the little bell to tinkling, and raised his hat to Maria. He asked softly, with a glance at the door behind the counter, if she was alone, and she told him that Mr Wyck had already left for the evening. Her manner was distinctly cold towards Randolph.

When he sought to find the reason for this, it soon became apparent that she had taken umbrage earlier, when he had called in with a bouquet of roses in his hand to buy a gift for a female friend, for thus she shrewdly assessed the situation.

'If you pass your afternoons with close female friends whose undergarments seem to be of such interest to you,' said Maria huffily, 'there is no reason for you to come here afterwards, for I have nothing for you, and seek nothing from you.'

'How your eyes flash when you are angry!' cried Randolph, in raptures at her heightened beauty. 'Before you send me away, hear me out, Maria! This afternoon I have felt no titties nor fingered any pussy.'

He spoke with perfect truth, though his failure to achieve a poke with Dorothy was by chance, not intent.

'Then who did you call upon?' Maria enquired, suspiciously.

'The flowers you saw and the fan I purchased here were for no female friend,' said he firmly, 'but for my Aunt Tabitha, from whom I have prospects. Today is her eighty-sixth birthday, and I called at her house in Hampstead village, to present my good wishes and compliments.'

'Is this true?' asked Maria.

'On my honour,' he replied, placing a hand on his heart.

'Then you are forgiven,' said she, smiling at him. 'Have you returned to make another purchase? Something of more interest to you than a fan?'

'I am here to make a certain proposal to you, Maria, one that I most sincerely hope you will give your diligent consideration before responding to it. But we cannot discuss it here where we may be overlooked by passers-by glancing in through the window. Close the shop, lock the door for the night, and let us adjourn to the back room, so that I may fully lay out my proposal.'

'It seems to me this proposal of yours may be concerned with the display or removal of undergarments not normally shown to a gentleman customer,' said she with a bewitching smile.

'There is an element of truth in what you say,' he told her, 'but what I wish to suggest to you is much more comprehensive.'

'Will you give me your word that it will in no way affect the loyalty and duty I owe to my employer, Mr Wyck?' she asked.

'You may trust me absolutely, Maria.'

With that assurance, she pulled down the blinds over the

door and the window of the shop, turned the key twice in the lock, then accompanied Randolph into the stock room. He gazed coldly for a moment at the desk, wondering if Wyck had poked Maria on it since last he was here. The irritating question passed and he handed Maria to the chair, taking his position close by, one cheek of his bottom resting nonchalantly on the fateful desk.

'I will not disguise from you, dear Maria, that in the short time we have been acquainted with each other, I have formed a high regard for you. This, coupled with affection and respect, emboldens me to hope you may accede to a plan of action I have devised that would enable me to offer you a far better mode of life than is at present your lot.'

'You mean to tempt me away from my duty,' said she, frowning slightly, 'that is unworthy of you after your promise not to!'

'By no means!' Randolph cried. 'For what I wish to propose to you is that you leave the employment of this mean-spirited shopkeeper and free yourself from his despicable abuse of your beautiful person.'

'What!' she exclaimed. 'Give Mr Wyck notice of leaving his employ? But how shall I live without my wage?'

Randolph took her trembling hand in his and pressed it gently while he explained that it would give him the very greatest of joy to acquire for her the lease of a villa in the pleasant suburb of St John's Wood, and to pay a wage to a maid to clean and cook for her. In addition to all that, he would put thirty gold sovereigns into Maria's hand on the first of each month, for her clothes and food and outings.

'Great Scott!' she exclaimed, amazed by the sums of money she was being offered in cash and in kind. 'I can scarcely believe it! How often would I receive you there?'

'Very often,' he said, 'for I have a warm nature and delight in giving it constant expression with a sympathetic female.'

Seeing that she was sorely tempted by his munificent offer in return for the use of her cunny, Randolph hastened to convince her fully of the advantages.

'First thing tomorrow morning,' he said, 'you must tell Wyck you are leaving his employment, being unable to tolerate for a day more his contemptible desire to take advantage of you. At half past nine o'clock, I will be outside in a hansom cab, to take you away from this awful place where innocence and female modesty are abused, and carry you to St John's Wood, to inspect unoccupied villas. You shall choose the one you please, and we will go at once to make the arrangement. Before the day is out, furnishings shall be ordered and delivered and you, dearest girl, shall be installed in your own household. What do you say to that, Maria?'

'Oh yes,' she cried, 'I accept!'

'Excellent!' Randolph said, very pleased by her enthusiasm. In her own establishment, she would be a damned lively rogering partner, he was convinced.

As if to seal the bargain, Maria rose from the chair and put her arms about his neck, to press her soft warm mouth to his in a tender kiss. He returned it willingly and holding her hips, he turned her round and himself with her, until her back was to the desk.

'Prove to me that you are mine, my dearest girl,' he said.

Without a moment of hesitation, she reached down to haul up her skirt and part her legs. Randolph eased her down until she lay on her back on the writing desk, her head hanging down over the far end and her legs off the end nearest him. He turned up her dress and petticoats to her waist, and took down the white cambric drawers he had paid for, to expose her nut-brown nest of curls and the delicious pink lips of her pussy.

How ravishing a sight she was to his gaze, this pretty Maria of the brunette locks and the wasp waist! How enticing a cunny laid bare for him to pierce! He grasped her ankles and raised her legs to the perpendicular, then parted them a little, until her pussy jutted out from between, as if pouting pertly at him.

Though her head hung over the far edge of the desk, he could see the sweet smile on her lovely face as she awaited the plunge of Mr Percival Proud into her cunny.

'Oh Maria, you make my shaft stand like a cast-iron rod,' said he, and gazing fondly down at her charms, he recited some lines penned by the celebrated poet Mr Samuel Taylor Coleridge:

> *I gazed upon a lovely maid,*
> *Whose smile was warm and sunny,*
> *She'd full red lips and golden hair,*
> *A plump and open cunny.*

> *I laid her down upon a bed,*
> *To assuage my fiery lust,*
> *And brought her off, and me beside,*
> *With many a pleasing thrust!*

'How very charming are the lines!' said Maria. 'You may put in your stiff part and bring me off as soon as you like!'

On hearing that, Randolph stood close in to her bottom, and as if knowing his wish without the need to be told, Maria took hold of his hard-on shaft and slipped the head between the soft lips of her split.

'My darling!' cried he, and with a strong heave of his hips, he speared her as deep as he could go.

'Ah,' she sighed, 'you have more than I'm used to!' Randolph was not surprised to hear that his shaft was thicker and longer than a shopkeeper's, for that was the proper order of things. Wyck might have four flabby inches or so to slip up a girl and come off in a tepid dribble, but Maria was now about to learn that a titled gentleman's shaft was massive, noble and profuse in its spending.

He felt the warmth of her bottom against him, and held high her legs, close to his chest, while his belly touched against the backs of her thighs. She wore grey stockings, gartered with black watered-silk ribbons above the knee, and while he slid in and out of her pussy, he opened and closed her legs like a pair of dressmaker's scissors, by means of working her ankles. The lewd movement revealed and hid by turns her dear little split, in which he was preparing to unleash his hot lust.

'Maria – darling girl! What a marvellous pussy you have!' exclaimed he, an almost insane excitement gripping him whilst he closely observed how he was using her.

'I'm sure it's very ordinary, really,' she sighed modestly.

'No, it's a gem amongst pussies,' he insisted breathlessly, as he tupped into it with long sliding strokes, 'I don't think I ever liked one better!'

'Then do it as you will,' Maria moaned softly, 'for I am sure I have much to learn from you, and I shall be a willing pupil.'

Randolph's boisterous shaft leapt joyfully inside its lodging as he came to the short strokes and increased his pace. Only an instant later he fetched off in spurts of thick essence which shook him in rapturous spasm. Underneath him, Maria shuddered and gasped and jibbed her belly up to meet his out-pouring. The blissful throes diminishing at last, Randolph concluded that he had made a useful choice, and that Maria Peabody would do well for him for a year or two.

Lustful Liaisons

Erotic adventures in the capital city of love!

Anonymous

PARIS 1912 – a city alive with the pursuit of pleasure, from the promenade of the Folies Bergère to the high-class brothels of the Left Bank. Everywhere business is booming in the oldest trade of all – the trade of love!

But now there is a new and flourishing activity to absorb the efforts of go-ahead men-about-town: the business of manufacturing motor cars. Men like Robert and Bertrand Laforge are pioneers in this field but their new automobile has a design defect that can only be rectified by some cunning industrial espionage. Which is where the new trade marries with the old, for the most reliable way of discovering information is to enlist the help of a lovely and compliant woman. A woman, for example, like the voluptuous Nellie Lebérigot whose soft creamy flesh and generous nature are guaranteed to uncover a man's most closely guarded secrets...

FICTION/EROTICA   0 7472 3710 7

More Erotic Fiction from Headline:

EROS IN THE FAR EAST

Anonymous

Recuperating from a dampening experience at the hands of one of London's most demanding ladies, the ever-dauntless Andy resolves to titil.ate his palate with foreign pleasures: namely a return passage to Siam. After a riotously libidinous ocean crossing, he finds himself in southern Africa, sampling a warm welcome from its delightfully unabashed natives.

Meanwhile, herself escaping an unsavoury encounter in the English lakes, his lovely cousin Sophia sets sail for Panama and thence to the intriguing islands of Hawaii – and a series of bizarrely erotic tribal initiations which challenge the limits of even her sensuous imagination!

After a string of energetically abandoned frolics, Andy and Sophia fetch up in the stately city of Singapore, a city which holds all the dangerously piquant pleasures of the mysterious East, and an adventure more outrageous than any our plucky pair have yet encountered. . .

Follow Andy and Sophia's other erotic exploits:
EROS IN THE COUNTRY   EROS IN TOWN
EROS IN THE NEW WORLD   EROS ON THE GRAND TOUR

FICTION/EROTICA   0 7472 3449 3

A selection of Erotica
from Headline

FONDLE ALL OVER	Nadia Adamant	£4.99	☐
LUST ON THE LOOSE	Noel Amos	£4.99	☐
GROUPIES	Johnny Angelo	£4.99	☐
PASSION IN PARADISE	Anonymous	£4.99	☐
THE ULTIMATE EROS COLLECTION	Anonymous	£6.99	☐
EXPOSED	Felice Ash	£4.99	☐
SIN AND MRS SAXON	Lesley Asquith	£4.99	☐
HIGH JINKS HALL	Erica Boleyn	£4.99	☐
TWO WEEKS IN MAY	Maria Caprio	£4.99	☐
THE PHALLUS OF OSIRIS	Valentina Cilescu	£4.99	☐
NUDE RISING	Faye Rossignol	£4.99	☐
AMOUR AMOUR	Marie-Claire Villefranche	£4.99	☐

All Headline books are available at your local bookshop or newsagent, or can be ordered direct from the publisher. Just tick the titles you want and fill in the form below. Prices and availability subject to change without notice.

Headline Book Publishing PLC, Cash Sales Department, Bookpoint, 39 Milton Park, Abingdon, OXON, OX14 4TD, UK. If you have a credit card you may order by telephone - 0235 831700.

Please enclose a cheque or postal order made payable to Bookpoint Ltd to the value of the cover price and allow the following for postage and packing:
UK & BFPO: £1.00 for the first book, 50p for the second book and 30p for each additional book ordered up to a maximum charge of £3.00.
OVERSEAS & EIRE: £2.00 for the first book, £1.00 for the second book and 50p for each additional book.

Name ....

Address ....

....

....

If you would prefer to pay by credit card, please complete:
Please debit my Visa/Access/Diner's Card/American Express (delete as applicable) card no:

Signature .... Expiry Date ....